of love & life

ISBN 978-1-780-20027-9

www.readersdigest.co.uk

Published in the United Kingdom by Vivat Direct Limited (t/a Reader's Digest),
157 Edgware Road, London W2 2HR

Three novels selected and condensed
by Reader's Digest

The Reader's Digest Association Inc., London

CONTENTS

Chapter One

Drop Scones

8 oz self-raising flour.

1 oz caster sugar. Can be licked off spoon.

1 egg. Budget for four eggs if working with under-sevens.

½ pint full cream milk. 10 oz for recipe, plus one glass to be
taken with results.

Pinch of salt. This is a small amount of salt, Issy. Tinier than
your little finger. Not too much! Not! Oh. That's too much.
Never mind.

Put the dry ingredients into a bowl and stir well.

Make a well in the centre—a well, that's like a place you get water.
Like Jack and Jill. Yes. Drop in the egg. Yes, and milk.

Whisk everything together thoroughly. The batter should have a
creamy consistency. Add a little more milk if necessary. Preheat and
butter a heavy-based pan. Grampa will pick up the pan. Do not try to
lift the pan. Good. Now let the mix drip off a spoon. Don't rush it. A few
splatters on the side of the pan is fine. Now let Grampa flip them, but
you can hold the handle . . . yup, that's it. Hurrah!

Serve with the remainder of the milk, butter, jam, cream and whatever else is in the fridge, and a large kiss on the top of the head for
being a clever girl.

Issy Randall refolded the piece of paper and smiled.

'Are you absolutely sure about this?' she said to the figure in the easy
chair. 'This is the recipe?' The old man nodded vehemently. He held up

one finger, which Issy recognised immediately as his cue for a lecture.

'Well, the thing is,' Grampa Joe began, 'baking is . . .'

'Life,' filled in Issy patiently. She'd heard the speech many times before. Her grandfather had started sweeping up in the family bakery at the age of twelve; eventually, he had taken over the business and run three large bakeries in Manchester. Baking was all he knew.

'It is life. Bread is the staff of life, our most basic food.'

'And very un-Atkins,' said Issy, smoothing her cord skirt down over her hips and sighing. It was one thing for her grandfather to say that. He had spent his whole life skinny as a rake, thanks to a full-time diet of extremely hard physical work that started with lighting the furnace at 5 a.m. It was quite another when baking was your hobby, your passion—but to pay the bills you were sitting down in an office all day. It was hard to show restraint when trying out . . . She drifted off, thinking about the new pineapple cream recipe she'd tried that morning. The trick was to leave enough of the pith in to give the flavour bite, but not so much that it turned into a smoothie. She needed to give it another shot. Issy ran her hands over her cloudy black hair. It went well with her green eyes but created absolute havoc if it rained.

'So when you describe what you're making, you must describe life. Do you see? It's not just recipes . . . Are you listening to me?'

'Yes, Gramps!'

They both turned to look out of the window of the nursing home in north London. Issy had installed Joe there when it became clear he was getting too absent-minded to live on his own. Issy had hated moving him down south after he'd spent his life in the north, but she needed him close enough to visit. Joe had grumbled of course, but he was going to grumble anyway, moving out of his home to anywhere that wouldn't let him rise at 5 a.m. and start pounding bread dough. So he might as well be grumpy close by, where she could keep an eye on him. After all, it wasn't as if anyone else was around to do it.

As he so often did, Grampa Joe read her mind.

'Have you heard from . . . your mother recently?' he said. Issy nodded, noting as ever how hard he found it to say his own daughter's name. Marian had never felt at home as a baker's daughter. And Issy's grandmother had died so young, she hadn't had long enough to provide a steadying influence. With Gramps working all the time, Marian had rebelled before she could even spell the word; hanging out with older boys and bad crowds from her teens, getting pregnant early to a travelling man who had given Issy her black hair and strong eyebrows and nothing else. Too much of a questing spirit to be tied down, Marian had often left her only child behind while she went off in search of herself.

Issy had spent most of her childhood in the bakery, watching Gramps as he beat the dough or delicately shaped the lightest, most mouth-melting filigree cakes and pies. Although he trained bakers for each of his shops, he still liked to get his own hands white with flour, one of the reasons Randall's were once the most popular bakers in Manchester. Issy had spent countless hours doing her homework by the great Cable Street ovens, absorbing through her pores the time and skill and care of a great baker; much more conventional than her mother, she adored her grampa and felt safe and cosy in the kitchens, even though she knew, of course, that she was different from her classmates, who went home to little houses with mums and dads and dogs and siblings.

Now, at thirty-one, Issy had just about forgiven her troubled, untethered mother. She didn't care about the sports days and school outings—everyone knew her grandfather, who never missed one—and she was popular enough, rarely without a cast-off box of scones or French cakes to bring to school occasions, while her birthday-party spreads were the stuff of local legend. Issy never felt short of love in the cosy flat above the bakery. Even Marian, who on her flying visits would strictly admonish Issy not to trust men and always follow her rainbow, was a loving parent. Nevertheless, sometimes, when she saw happy families larking in the park, Issy felt a desire at the pit of her stomach so strong it felt like a physical gnawing for the traditional, the safe.

It was no surprise to anyone who knew the family that Issy Randall grew up to be the most conventional girl imaginable. Good A levels, good college and now a good job with a commercial property company in the City. But deep down she had a passion for kitchen comforts—for cream horns, balanced with the perfect weight of caterer's cream and light, flaky pastry, set off by the crunchiest diamond crystals of clear sugar; for a perfectly piped butter icing on top of the highest, lightest, floatiest lemon cupcake. Issy loved all of those things. Hence her project with Gramps: to get as many of his recipes down on paper as possible, before, although neither of them ever referred to it, or in case, he started to forget them.

'I got an email from Mum,' said Issy. 'She's in Florida. She's met a man called Brick. Really. Brick. That's his name.'

'At least it's a man this time,' sniffed her grandfather.

Issy gave him a look. 'Anyway, she sounds happy. Says she loves it over there. Said I should send you over for some sun.'

Issy and Gramps looked at one another and burst out laughing. Joe got tired out crossing the room.

'Yes,' said Gramps, 'I'll just go catch the next plane to Florida!'

Issy tucked the sheet of paper away in her handbag and stood up.

'I have to go,' she said. 'Keep doing the recipes. But you can keep them quite, you know, normal if you like.'

'Normal.'

She kissed him on the forehead. 'See you next week.'

Issy got off the bus. It was freezing, with dirty ice on the ground left over from a short day's snowfall just after New Year. Still, as ever, Issy felt pleased to be getting off at the Stoke Newington Municipal Offices, the rather grand edifice at the end of her street. Home, Stoke Newington, the bohemian district that she'd stumbled upon when she moved south.

The smell of hookahs from the little Turkish cafés on Stamford Road mingled with the incense sticks from the pound shops, jostling next to expensive baby boutiques that sold children's designer Wellingtons and wooden toys, perused by shoppers with headscarves or Hasidic ringlets and young mothers with buggies. Issy loved it all. She adored the sweet Jamaican bread; the honey baklava sitting out by the cash registers in the grocers; little Indian sweets or dusty slabs of Turkish delight. She liked the jumble of buildings: from a handsome square of pretty houses to blocks of flats and red-brick conversions. Albion Road was lined with odd shops, fried-chicken joints, cab firms and large grey houses. It was neither commercial nor residential but lay somewhere in between.

The grey houses were stately, Victorian and potentially expensive. Some remained grotty subdivided flats with bicycles and wheelie bins cluttering up the front gardens. Some, though, had been reconverted into houses and gentrified, with reclaimed oak front doors, topiary trees on the steps and expensive curtains. She loved the area's mix of shabby and new, traditional, rough-and-ready and smart-and-alternative, with the towers of the City on the horizon and crowded pavements . . . All types of people lived in Stokey. And it was more affordable than Islington. Issy had lived here for four years since she moved out of south London. The only downside had been moving out of range of the tube.

Just behind the bus-stop was a little close. It was lined with tiny shops, older places that had been left behind by the Victorian development. Once upon a time they would have been stables; they were quirky and oddly shaped. There was an ironmonger's with ancient brushes round the door and old-fashioned toasters for sale at inflated prices; a telephone/wifi/internet office, and a newsagent that faced onto the road.

Right at the very end of the row, tucked into the corner, was a building that looked like an afterthought. It was pointed at one end, where a triangular corner of glass stuck out towards the road, widening into a bench, with a door coming out onto a small cobbled courtyard with a tree in it. It looked quite out of place, a tiny haven in the middle of a village square; something absolutely out of time—like, Issy had once reflected, an illustration by Beatrix Potter. All it needed were bottle-glass windows.

Issy turned off towards the flat. Home. She had bought at the very height of the property boom. For someone who worked in the business, it hadn't been very astute. This was before she began dating her boyfriend, Graeme, who she'd met at work, otherwise, as he had said several times, he would certainly have advised her against it.

Even then, she wasn't sure she'd have listened to him. After hunting through every property in her price range and hating all of them, she'd been on the point of giving up when she got to Carmelite Avenue and she'd loved it straight away. It was the top two storeys of one of the area's stately grey houses, with its own side entrance up a flight of stairs, so really it felt more like a little house than an apartment. One floor was almost entirely an open-plan kitchen/dining room/sitting room. Issy had made it cosy, with huge faded grey velvet sofas, a long wooden table with benches and her beloved kitchen. The units were going cheap in the sales, almost certainly because they were a very strong shade of pink. Issy had never thought of herself as a pink type of person. This, however, was such an endearingly full-on pink. It was a kitchen that just wanted to be loved.

She had added black-and-white-chequered lino and implements and some guests were surprised to find that they actually quite liked the pink kitchen and they certainly liked what came out of it. Even Grampa Joe had liked it on one of his carefully choreographed visits, and had nodded approvingly at the gas hob (for caramelising) and the electric oven (for even heat distribution). Issy and the sugar-sweet pink kitchen seemed made for one another.

In it she felt properly at home. Now she bustled around, gathering her vanilla sugar, her finest French *pâtissier's* flour that she bought from the tiny *alimentaire* in Smithfield and her narrow silver sieve, and selecting which of her wooden spoons she would use to whip her sponge into shape. She cracked eggs perfectly two at a time into her large blue-and-white-striped ceramic mixing bowl without even glancing, and used her eye to measure out the exact amount of creamy, snowy Guernsey butter.

The cupcakes were in the oven and she was on her third batch of icing when her flatmate pushed open the door. Helena never arrived subtly anywhere. She wasn't fat, just tall, and extremely generously proportioned in true fifties style, with large creamy breasts, a tiny waist and a wide bottom and thighs, crowned by a towering mass of Pre-Raphaelite hair. She would have been considered a beauty in any period of history other than the early twenty-first century, but not now when the only acceptable shape for a beautiful woman was that of a hungry six-year-old. As it was, she was constantly trying to lose weight.

'I have had a *terrible day*,' she announced dramatically.

'I'm on it,' said Issy hurriedly.

Helena looked at the two dozen perfect cakes emerging from the oven. 'Who are you cooking for, the Red Army? Give me one.'

'They're too hot.'

'Give me one!'

Issy started squeezing on the icing with an expert flick of the wrist. She should wait till the cakes had cooled enough not to melt the buttercream, but she could tell Helena wasn't capable of waiting that long.

'So what happened?' she asked, when Helena was comfortably ensconced on the chaise longue (she'd brought her own chaise longue when she moved in) with a vast vat of tea and two cupcakes on her favourite polka-dot plate. Issy was pleased with the cakes; they were as light and fluffy as air, with a delicate sense of oranges and cream; delicious, and they wouldn't spoil your dinner. She realised she'd forgotten to get in anything for dinner. Well, they *were* dinner then.

'I got punched,' sniffed Helena.

Issy sat up. 'Again?'

Helena was a ward manager and practically ran the busy A&E department at Hemel Park. Her staff adored her, as did the many junior doctors she had guided through their first anxious months; as did her patients. When they weren't off their heads and throwing punches, naturally.

Even though she made more money and didn't have to work ridiculous shifts, Issy, in her safe corporate job, sometimes envied Helena. How lovely to work at something you loved and knew you were great at, even if it was for a pittance and you occasionally got punched.

'He thought I was a fire engine, apparently. Anyway, how's Mr Randall?' asked Helena. She adored Issy's granddad, who admired Helena as a damn fine woman. She had also cast her formidable professional eye over every nursing home in the district, an act for which Issy felt she would be forever in her debt.

'He's good!' said Issy.

Helena nodded.

'Have you taken Graeme in to see him yet?'

Issy bit her lip. Helena knew she hadn't.

'Not yet,' she said. 'I will though, he's just been so busy.'

'Mmm,' said Helena. She popped another cake in her mouth. 'You know, these are divine. You really could be a professional. Are you *sure* they don't contain one of my five a day?'

'Definite.'

Helena sighed. 'Oh well. We all need something to aspire to. Quick! Telly on! It's a Simon Cowell day. I want to see him be cruel to someone.'

'You need a *nice* man,' said Issy, picking up the remote control.

So do you, thought Helena, but she kept it to herself.

There are pretty horrid days to go back to work and then there's today, Issy thought, peering out along the length of the queue to see if the bendy bus was starting to trundle round the corner of Stoke Newington Road.

Yep, the first Monday after New Year had to be up there with rotten blooming days really. The wind was raw against her face as she hugged her large tin of cupcakes. She glanced at the faces next to her—the same faces she stood next to in rain, snow, wind and the occasional sunny spell.

'Hi there,' she said to Linda, the middle-aged lady who worked in John Lewis. 'Happy New Year.'

'Happy New Year!' said Linda. 'Made any resolutions?'

'Oh, the usual,' said Issy. 'Lose a bit of weight . . .'

'Oh, you don't need to do that,' said Linda. 'There's nothing wrong with your weight! You look lovely. Take a picture now and look back on it in ten years if you don't believe me. You won't believe how good you looked.' She couldn't resist glancing briefly at the tin Issy was carrying.

Issy sighed. 'These are for the office.'

'Of course they are,' said Linda. The other people in the bus queue were coming forward now, making enquiring faces and asking Issy how her holiday had gone. She groaned.

'OK, you gannets.' She opened the tin. Wind-chilled faces cracked into smiles; iPod buds were removed from ears as they cheerfully descended on the cakes. Issy had, as usual, made twice as many as she thought she might need so she could feed the office and the bus queue too.

'These are amazing,' said a man through a mouthful of crumbs. 'You know, you could do this for a living.'

'With you lot I feel like I do sometimes,' said Issy, but blushing with pleasure as everyone clustered around. 'Happy New Year, everybody.'

The entire bus queue started to chat and perk up. Linda, of course, was doing nothing but worry about her daughter Leanne's wedding. Leanne was a chiropodist, the first person in Linda's family to go to college, and she was marrying an industrial chemist. Linda was organising the entire thing. She had no idea how difficult it was for Issy, having to listen to a mother who wanted nothing more than to put in corsetry eyelets for her twenty-six-year-old's wedding to a wonderful man.

Issy glanced behind her into Pear Tree Court. The oddly shaped shop with the grilles tightly down looked like a grumpy sleeping man in the drear grey light of a January London morning. Over the last four years various people had tried to turn it into a business of one kind or another, but they had all failed. Perhaps the area wasn't up and coming enough, perhaps it was the proximity of the ironmonger's, but the little children's clothes shop had not lasted long, nor had the gift shop, and nor had the yoga shop, for which the entire frontage had been painted a supposedly soothing pink and a tinkling Buddha fountain placed outside.

Issy, while far too intimidated ever to set foot inside, had thought it might do rather well, considering the high numbers of local trendies and yummy mummies; but it had turned out not to be, and once again there was a 'For rent/enquiries' board in yellow and black, clashing horribly with the pink.

'That's a shame,' said Linda, seeing her looking at the closed-down shop. Issy *hmm*ed in response. Seeing the yoga shop every day—and the lithe, ponytail-swinging honey-coloured girls who worked there—had just reminded her that, now she was over thirty, it wasn't quite as easy to stay a size twelve as it used to be, especially when you had Issy's grand passion. It wasn't as if she could ever have been a skinny minny. When she came home from school, Gramps, although he must have been tired from a full day's work already, would beckon her into the big kitchens. The other bakers would stand out of her way and smile at the little girl when Gramps announced, 'Now your education truly begins.' She had nodded, a round-eyed quiet child, prone to blushing and self-consciousness.

'We shall start with drop scones. Now, here is the secret to the drop scone,' he said seriously, after he had made Issy wash her hands and patiently scooped up the four eggshells that had fallen on the floor. 'It's in the burner. Not too hot. A hot burner kills pancakes. Gently now.'

He held on to her, up on the brown kitchen stool that wobbled slightly, her small face poised in concentration as she let the mixture drip gently off the wooden spoon and into the pan.

'And patiently now,' he said. 'You can't rush these things.'

Joe had poured all his energies into his beloved granddaughter, teaching her the techniques and tricks of baking. It was his fault, thought Issy. She would definitely bake less this year, lose a couple of pounds.

Still no sign of the bus. As Issy looked round the corner, glancing quickly at her watch, she felt a raindrop hit her cheek. Then another. There was no shelter at the bus-stop, unless you counted three centimetres of guttering from the newsagents behind them. Eventually the bus arrived and she squeezed on, turning her thoughts to her boyfriend Graeme.

Graeme was the best-looking person at Issy's firm. He was tall, honed from the gym, with piercing blue eyes and black hair. Issy had already been working there for three years, and his arrival had caused a stir with everyone. He was definitely cut out for property development; he had an authoritative, fast-moving style and a manner that always said if you didn't snap up what he was selling, you were going to miss out.

At first Issy had regarded him as out of her league. She'd had plenty of nice, kind boyfriends, and one or two arseholes, but for one reason or another nothing had ever worked out. Issy didn't feel she was in the last-chance saloon just yet, but she also knew, in the back of her mind, that she would like to find someone nice and settle down. She wanted a family. And Graeme clearly wasn't the settling-down type; she'd seen him pulling away from the office in his little sports car with gorgeous-looking skinny girls with long blonde hair—never the same one, although they all looked the same—so she put him out of her mind.

That was what made it such a surprise to both of them when they were sent on a training day to the company's head offices in Rotterdam one week. Trapped indoors by the howling rain, their Dutch hosts having retired earlier than expected, they had found themselves together in the hotel bar, getting on far better than they'd have expected. Graeme had set about seducing her partly for something to do, but had been surprised to find in her a softness and a sweetness that he really rather liked. She wasn't pushy and sharp-angled like those other girls, and she didn't spend her entire time complaining about the calories in food and retouching her make-up. He had rather surprised himself by going against one of his golden rules and calling her after they got back. Issy had been both sur-prised and flattered, and had gone round to his open-plan minimalist flat in Notting Hill and made him an outstanding bruschetta. They had both enjoyed the experience very much. That was eight months ago.

It had been exciting. And gradually Issy had started to wonder if maybe, just maybe, he was the man for her. He liked to talk to her about work and she liked the novelty factor of making dinner for him and them sharing a meal, and a bed.

Helena had not failed to point out that, in the months since they'd got together, not only had he never stayed over at the flat but he often asked Issy to leave before morning so he could get a proper night's sleep; that they went to restaurants but she had never met his friends, or his mother; that he had never come with her to see Gramps; that he'd never even called her his girlfriend. And that while it might be nice for Graeme to play house on a casual basis with some girl from the office, Issy, at thirty-one, might be looking for a little bit more.

Issy tended to stick her fingers in her ears at this point. The thing was, well, yes, she could break it off—although there was hardly a line of eligible suitors, and certainly none as hot as Graeme in view. Or, perhaps, she could make his life so pleasant and lovely that he would see how awful things would be without her and propose. Helena thought this plan very over-optimistic and did not keep this thought to herself.

'Well, we can't really go public, because of the office,' Issy had said.

'What, even after all this time? And you think they don't already know?' Helena had countered. 'Are they all idiots?'

'It's a property developer's,' Issy said.

'OK,' said Helena, 'they're all idiots. But I still don't see why you can't stay over at his house once in a while.'

'Because he doesn't want us walking into the office together,' Issy had said, as if it was the most natural thing in the world. It wasn't as if eight months was terribly long. There was plenty of time for them to decide when to take it to the next level. It just wasn't the right time at the moment, that was all.

Helena had sniffed in a characteristically Helena way.

Issy smiled to herself. Graeme's days were full of jockeying for position and being the Billy Big Bollocks. Property development was a profession that encouraged that sort of behaviour. That was why sometimes Graeme could appear a little . . . aggressive. It was a façade he had to keep up at work. Underneath it all she knew, from their many late-night chats, from his moods and occasional outbursts, that he was a vulnerable man; sensitive to the aggression in the workplace; worried, deep down, about his status. That was why Issy was so much more confident of her relationship with Graeme than her friends were. She saw the soft side of him. He confided to her his worries, his hopes and dreams and fears. And that was why it was serious, no matter where she woke up in the morning.

The rain was heavier when Issy got off the bus and turned into the street near Farringdon Road that housed the offices of Kalinga Deniki Property Management, or KD as it was known. It was a sharp chunk of modern glass, six storeys high, that looked out of place among the lower-set red-brick flats and offices. Issy stumbled through the puddles, completely soaked by the time she arrived at KD. She ducked into the ladies' loos on the ground floor, which were usually empty. A few blasts of the hand dryer were all she could muster for her hair. She looked at herself and sighed. Her hair looked like she'd knitted it. The cold wind had put some colour in her cheeks—Issy hated her propensity for blushing at everything, but this wasn't too bad—and her green eyes, fringed with lots of black mascara, were fine, but the hair was undoubtedly a disaster. She scrabbled around in her bag for a clip or hairband but came up empty-handed except for a red elastic band. It didn't quite go with her floral print dress and tight black cardie, worn with thick black tights and black boots, but it would have to do.

Slightly late, she hopped into the lift up to the second floor, which was accounts and admin. The salesmen and the developers had the floor above, but the atrium was made of solid glass, which meant it was always easy to see who was around and about. At her desk she nodded to her workmates, then realised with a start that she was late for the 9.30 meeting she was meant to be minuting; the meeting where Graeme would talk about the results of the board meeting to staff lower down the chain. Cursing under her breath, she grabbed her laptop and ran for the stairs.

In the meeting room, the senior sales team were already seated round the glass table, trading banter with one another. They glanced up uninterest-edly when she walked in, muttering apologies. Graeme looked furious.

Issy smiled and sat down without grabbing a coffee, even though she desperately wanted one. She sat next to Callie Mehta, the only senior woman at Kalinga Deniki. She was director of Human Resources and looked, as ever, immaculately groomed and unperturbed.

'Right,' said Graeme, clearing his throat. 'Now we're all finally here, I think we can start.'

Issy felt her face beam red. She didn't expect Graeme to give her any special favours at work, of course she didn't, but she didn't want him thinking he could pick on her either. Fortunately, nobody else noticed.

'As you know, it's been a bad year here . . . we've been hit hard in the US and the Middle East. The rest of Europe is holding up, as is the Far East, but even so . . .'

Graeme had everyone's attention now. 'It doesn't look like we can continue as we are. There are going to have to be . . . cutbacks.'

Beside Issy, Callie Mehta nodded. She must have known already, thought Issy, with a sudden beat of alarm inside her. And if she knew, that meant 'cutbacks' would be staff cutbacks. Redundancies.

Issy felt a coldness grip at her heart. It wouldn't be her, would it?

'This will be strictly confidential. I don't want these minutes circulated,' said Graeme, looking at her pointedly. 'But I think it's fair to say they are looking for a staff reduction of round about five per cent.'

Panicking, Issy did the figures in her head. If they had 200 staff, that was ten redundancies. It didn't sound like a lot, but where did you trim the fat? She realised Graeme was still talking.

'. . . but I think we can show them we can do better than that, aim for seven, even eight per cent. Show Rotterdam that KD UK is a twenty-first-century lean, mean business machine.'

But if it was her . . . how would she pay the mortgage? How would she live? What would she do? Issy suddenly thought she was going to cry.

'Are you getting this down, Issy?' Graeme snapped at her, as Callie started discussing packages and exit strategies. She looked up at him, almost unaware of where she was. Suddenly she realised he was looking back at her like she was a total stranger.

Chapter Two

ISSY HADN'T HAD ENOUGH cakes left over from the bus queue for the office the day before and anyway she would have felt hypocritical handing them out in a jaunty fashion after what she'd heard in the meeting. However, the entire team had gathered round, demanding a treat after the break, and were horrified.

'You are why Ah come to work,' François, the young ad designer, had said. 'You bake like aha, the *pâtissiers* of Toulon. *C'est vrai.*'

Issy had blushed bright red at the compliment, and later searched among the recipes her grandfather posted to her for something new to try. And although she felt slightly sneaky doing it, she was at least wearing her smartest, most businesslike navy dress with the swingy hem and a neat jacket. Just to look like a professional.

It wasn't raining quite so hard today, but a chill wind still cut through the bus queue. Linda, concerned about Issy's anxious expression, found

herself babbling about how haberdashery had never been so busy—
something to do with everyone taking on a huge dose of austerity and
starting to knit their own jumpers—but she could tell Issy was barely
listening. She was staring at a sleek blonde woman being shown the outside
of the little shop by a man she vaguely recognised as one of the many
local estate agents she'd met when she bought her flat.

The woman was talking loudly and Issy edged a little closer to hear
what she was saying. Her professional curiosity was piqued.

'This area doesn't know what it needs!' the woman was saying. She
had a loud, carrying voice. 'There's too much fried chicken and not
enough organic produce. I don't consider myself to be a mere foodie,' she
continued, 'I consider myself to be more of a prophet, yah? Spreading the
message. That wholegrain, raw cooking is the only way forward.'

Raw cooking? thought Issy.

'Now, I thought we'd put the cooker over here.' The woman was pointing
through the window into the far corner. 'We'll hardly be using it.'

'Oh, yes, that would be perfect,' said the estate agent.

No it wouldn't, thought Issy instantly. You'd want it near the window
for good venting, and so people could get a look at what you were doing
and you could keep an eye on the shop. That far corner was a terrible
place for the oven, you'd have your back to everything the entire time.
No, if you wanted to cook for people, you needed to do it somewhere you
could be seen, to welcome people in cheerfully with a smile, and . . .

Lost in her reverie, she barely noticed the bus arriving, just as the lady
said, 'Now, talking about money, Desmond . . .'

How much money? wondered Issy idly, climbing in the back door of
the bus, as Linda wittered on about cross-stitch.

As she entered the administration floor, clicking her entry pass to go
through the wide glass doors, she sensed a strange quietness in the air.
Tess, the receptionist, had said a quick hello, but hadn't engaged her
beyond that. Ever since she'd started seeing Graeme, Issy had stayed away
from office nights out, just in case she had a couple of glasses of wine too
many and accidentally spilled the beans. She didn't think anyone suspected anything. Sometimes she wasn't sure they'd actually believe it.
Graeme was so handsome and such a go-getter.

And there he was, standing at the far end of the open-plan office, just in front of the conference room, with a serious look on his face, clearly the cause of the silence over the twenty-eight desks.

'I'm sorry about this,' Graeme said, when everyone was in. He had thought about his approach for a long time. He wanted to show his bosses he could make the tough choices, and he wanted his staff to see that he could be straight with them.

'You don't need me to tell you what things are like,' said Graeme. 'You're seeing it yourselves; in accounts, in sales, in turnover. You guys deal with the bread and butter; the nuts and bolts, the figures and projections. You know the harsh realities of business life. Which means that, although what I have to say is difficult, I know you'll understand and you won't think it's unfair.'

You could have heard a pin drop in the office. Issy swallowed loudly.

'There isn't a nice way to do this,' said Graeme. 'You'll all get an email in the next half-hour to let you know if you're staying or going. And then we're going to be as generous to you and as reasonable as we possibly can. I'll see those of you who aren't going to be staying with us in the boardroom at eleven.' He glanced at his Montblanc watch. 'Again, I'm sorry.'

He retreated into the boardroom. Through the slatted venetian blinds, Issy could see him, his handsome head bent towards his laptop.

Instantly there was a flurry of panicky noise. Everyone at their computers, pressing the refresh button on their email programmes once a second; all muttering to themselves. Issy told herself not to panic, but it was too late. She must breathe. Breathe. Two nights ago she and Graeme had been under his navy-blue Ralph Lauren duvet, safe and comfortable in a world of their own. Nothing was going to happen. Nothing.

Issy relaxed. Just as she did so, she heard a ping.

Dear Miss Issy Randall

    We are sorry to inform you that due to a downturn in economic progress and with no improvement in our forecasts for the growth of commercial property uptake in the City of London this year, the directors of Kalinga Deniki CP are making redundant the post of Office Manager Grade 4 London Office, with immediate effect. Please go to Conference Room C at 11 a.m. to discuss your ongoing options with your line manager Graeme Denton.

    Yours sincerely

    Jaap Van de Bier, Human Resources, Kalinga Deniki

Issy was frozen. She just stared at the screen. It wasn't just the job—well it was, of course; to lose your job was the most upsetting, depressing thing ever. But to know that Graeme . . . to realise that he had had sex with her, let her cook him dinner, all the time knowing . . . that this was going to happen. What was he thinking? What was he *thinking*?

Without pausing to think Issy jumped out of her seat and approached the boardroom. Fuck waiting till eleven o'clock. She wanted to know about this *now*. She almost knocked on the door but instead boldly walked straight in. Graeme glanced up at her, not entirely surprised.

'Issy. I'm so sorry.'

'*You're* sorry? You're blooming sorry! Why didn't you tell me?'

He looked surprised.

'Well, of course I couldn't tell you. Company confidentiality.'

Issy was stricken that he didn't even trust her that much. 'But I could have had some warning; some time to prepare myself a bit.'

'But it wouldn't have been fair for you to have that advantage,' said Graeme. 'Everyone else would have liked the same.'

'But it's *not* the same,' shouted Issy. 'For them it's just a job. For me it's a job *and* it's not getting to hear it from you.'

She became aware of a large group of people behind her, listening in through the open door. She turned round furiously.

'Yes. That's right. Me and Graeme have been having a secret affair. That we've been keeping from the office.'

There were some murmurs but not, Issy noticed in her heightened emotional state, the surprised gasps she'd been expecting.

'Well, yes, everyone know that,' said François.

Issy stared at him. 'What do you mean, everyone?'

The rest of the office looked slightly sheepish.

Issy turned back to Graeme. 'Did you know that *everyone* knew?'

To her horror, Graeme was also looking sheepish.

'Well, you know, I still don't think it's good for morale to have people flaunting personal relationships at work.'

'You knew?'

'It's my job to know what my staff are talking about,' said Graeme primly. 'I wouldn't be doing my job if I didn't.'

Issy gazed at him, speechless. If everyone knew, why all the creeping around and the secrecy? 'But . . . but . . .'

'Issy, would you like to sit down so we can start the meeting?'

Issy became aware of other devastated-looking people inching their way into the boardroom; suddenly Issy hated the firm, Graeme, her colleagues, property management and the whole damn capitalist system. She turned on her heel and stormed straight out of the office.

Issy needed a friendly ear, and pronto. And Helena was only ten minutes away. She wouldn't mind.

Helena was stitching up a young man's head, none too gently.

'I thought you did stitches with glue nowadays,' said Issy, once she'd stopped snivelling.

'We do,' said Helena grimly, pulling the needle tight, 'except when some people *sniff* glue then think they can fly over barbed-wire fences. Then they don't get any glue.'

'I just can't believe it, Len,' said Issy. 'I can't believe that bastard would let me walk into work knowing all the time that, one, he was going to fire me, and two, everyone knew we were going out together.'

'Mmm,' said Helena noncommittally. 'Well, you're better off out of it all. You know you're always saying you don't like . . . being a medical student,' she added quickly for the patient's benefit.

'You can only be better off out of it,' said Issy, 'if you have somewhere to be better off in. Whereas I'm looking at the most depressed job market for twenty years and . . . I'm single again, Len! At thirty-one!'

'Thirty-one is *not old*,' asserted Helena firmly.

'Come on. If you were eighteen you'd think it was old.'

'It's really old,' said the young man. 'And I'm twenty.'

'And you won't live to see thirty-one if you don't stop your ridiculous habits,' said Helena firmly. 'So you keep out of it.'

'I'd do you both though,' he said. 'So you don't look over the hill yet.'

Helena and Issy looked at each other.

'See?' said Helena. 'Things could be worse.'

'Well, it's nice to know I've still got something to fall back on.'

'And as for you,' said Helena, finishing up his wound with an expertly applied pad and bandage, 'if you don't give up that stuff, you won't be able to get it up for anyone. Do you understand?'

For the first time, the young man looked frightened. He swallowed. 'It's time for me to get off the stuff anyway.'

Helena handed him the card of the local cessation project.

'Len, I'd better go.'

Helena looked up sympathetically. 'You sure?'

Issy nodded. 'I know I stormed out, but I need to go and . . . well, at least find out about my redundancy payment and stuff.'

Helena gave her a hug. 'It's going to be fine, you know. Fine.'

Walking back into the office again was nearly unbearable. Issy felt so nervous and ashamed. She went straight to Human Resources. She didn't think she could face talking to Graeme again. She checked her phone for the ninth time. No texts. No messages, nothing.

'Hello, Issy,' said Callie Mehta. 'I'm very sorry. This is the worst part of my job.'

'Yeah, and mine,' said Issy stiffly.

Callie lifted out a file. 'We've worked out a package that's as generous as we can be . . . Also, as it's the beginning of the year, we thought rather than working out your notice, if you like you can take your full holiday entitlement and we'll continue paying for that.'

Issy had to admit that seemed quite generous.

'And here . . . if you like, and it's completely up to you, we're funding resettlement courses.'

'Resettlement courses? That sounds a bit sinister.'

'It's a training course, to help you figure out . . . where next.'

'To the dole queue in this climate,' said Issy tightly.

'Issy,' said Callie, kindly but quite firmly. 'Can I just tell you . . . in my career I've been made redundant three times. It is upsetting but, I promise, it's not the end of the world. Something always comes up for the good people. And you're one of the good people.'

'That's why I'm out of a job,' said Issy.

Callie frowned slightly and put her finger on her forehead.

'Issy, I'm going to tell you this . . . it may not be welcome, but I hope you don't mind, just in case it helps. You're obviously bright, you've got a degree, you're pleasant to the people you work with . . .'

Issy wondered where this was going.

'Why are you just an office administrator? I mean, you have talents and skills but I just don't see where they've been used with you running around chasing up expenses and timesheets.'

Issy shrugged uncomfortably.

'It's not too late in life to change direction, you know. I'm sure you think it is, but,' Callie checked the paper in front of her, 'thirty-one is nothing. And if you end up doing the same job for someone else . . . I think you'll probably be as dissatisfied there as you have been here. And don't tell me that's not true, please. I've worked in HR a long time. Redundancy is the right choice for you now. Because you're still young enough to do what you want. But it may be your last chance. Do you understand what I'm saying?'

Issy felt her face burn up. All she could do was nod, at the risk of breaking down completely. Even her ears felt hot. Callie pushed the piece of paper across the desk. Issy picked it up and looked at it. Nearly £20,000. That was life-changing money. Surely.

'Please don't spend it all on lipstick and shoes,' said Callie, obviously trying to lighten the mood.

'Can I spend a little bit?' said Issy, appreciating the gesture, and Callie's frankness; she felt there was kindness in it.

'A little bit,' said Callie. 'Yes.' And they shook hands.

Thank goodness Helena worked shifts, which meant she was often at home in the mornings. Issy wasn't sure afterwards how she'd have coped if she'd had to face those first couple of weeks alone. To begin with, there was some sort of novelty value in not having to set an alarm, but it soon wore off and she would lie awake, fretting, into the night about what she was going to do with her life now.

Helena and Gramps were encouraging, telling her that something would turn up, but it didn't feel like that to Issy. She felt untethered, rootless. It took her all day to get to the newsagent's to buy a paper and some Smarties to make a Smartie cake. It wasn't good. She didn't want to do anything: leave the house, play Scrabble with Gramps. And no Graeme of course. That stung too, horribly. Issy was realising she had had more invested in this relationship than she'd ever let herself think.

Helena hated to see her friend sad—apart from anything else, it meant she didn't have her best mate to go out and have a laugh with—but she understood Issy had to grieve for what she had lost. It was tough in the flat though; all through the miserable days of January and February, it was horrible coming home to a dark, unheated house, with Issy cloistered in her bedroom, refusing to change out of her pyjamas. The flat had always been such a haven, mostly because Issy made it comforting and warm and always with something to nibble or taste. After some harrowing days at work, all Helena wanted was to curl up on the sofa with a cup of tea and a slice of one of Issy's experiments so they could have a good gossip. She missed it. So it was with selfish motives in mind too that she decided it couldn't go on, and that Issy needed a stern dose of tough love.

Dressed in a plum velvet top that made her look, she felt, pleasingly gothic, she marched into the sitting room. Issy was sitting in the gloomy light, eating dry cereal out of a bowl in her pig pyjamas.

'Darling. You have to get out of the flat.'

'This is my flat though.'

'I mean it. You have to do something.'

Issy stuck out her bottom lip. 'I don't see why.'

Helena glanced at the pink-striped see-through plastic bag beside Issy, filled with Smarties.

'Have you been *out*? Did you go to the corner shop?'

Issy shrugged, embarrassed.

'You went to the corner shop in your pyjamas?'

'Hmm.'

'But what if you'd bumped into John Cusack, hmm? What if John Cusack had been standing right there, thinking, I'm sick of all these Hollywood actresses, why can't I find a real girl with real home values? Who can bake? Someone like her, only not wearing her pyjamas, because obviously that makes her a *crazy person*.'

Issy swallowed. 'Behave like you might meet John Cusack at any minute' was a prevailing mantra of Helena's, which was why she never went out without her hair and make-up done absolutely perfectly, dressed in her best. Issy knew better than to dispute it.

Helena looked at her. 'Graeme hasn't called, I take it?'

Of course, they both knew he hadn't. It wasn't just about the job. But for Issy, it hurt so much to own up to the truth. How could she have been so stupid? All that time, when she thought she was so professional, thinking she was keeping her private life so separate, when in fact everyone was sniggering because she was shagging the boss—and worse, it obviously wasn't even a serious relationship. There didn't seem to be the least point in getting out of her pyjamas.

'So, what? Your life is over now because your boss no longer requires personal services?'

'It wasn't like that,' said Issy quietly. It hadn't been, had it? She tried to think of some moments of tenderness; some sweetness or kindness he'd done for her. Annoyingly, in eight months, all that came to mind was him telling her not to come over one night, he was tired from work, or getting her to help him file his management reports—she'd been so pleased, she recalled, to be able to take some of the strain off him; exactly, she thought, why she'd make him a perfect wife. What an idiot.

'Well, whatever it was like,' said Helena, 'it's been weeks and frankly you've done enough wallowing in your pit. It's time to get out and claim the world again.'

'I'm not sure the world wants me,' said Issy.

'Well, that is total bullshit and you know it,' said Helena. 'Do you want me to start again on my Poor Souls list?'

Helena's Poor Souls list was a record of terrible cases she saw in A&E—the neglected, the abandoned; the children who had never been loved, the youngsters who had never heard a kind word in their lives. It was unbearable to hear, and Helena only ever used it as an argument winner in really desperate cases. It was a cruel trick to play now.

'No!' said Issy. 'No. Please don't.'

'I'm warning you,' said Helena. 'You count your blessings or else. And while you're doing that, go and do that redundancy course they promised to send you on. At least it'll get you out of bed before noon.'

'I only sleep late because I can't sleep at night.'

'Because you sleep all day.'

'No. Because I'm depressed.'

'You're not depressed. You're slightly sad. Depressed is when you're a new arrival in this country and someone confiscated your passport and forced you into prostitution, and—'

'Stop it, please. I'll go, OK? I'll go! I'll go!'

Four days, a haircut and some ironing later, Issy stood at her regular bus-stop, feeling like an imposter. Linda was interested to see her.

'Did you go on a nice long holiday? Ooh, how lovely to get away in the winter, it is dreadful.'

'No,' said Issy sadly. 'I got made redundant.'

'Oh,' said Linda. 'Oh dear. I am very sorry to hear that, dear. Still, you young folk; you'll find something else in five minutes, won't you?'

'I hope so,' said Issy. 'I hope so.'

Her attention was distracted by someone behind her. She glanced round. It was the tall blonde lady again, at the deserted pink shop. She was trailing along behind the same slightly defeated-looking estate agent.

'I'm just not sure the feng shui is going to work, Des,' she was saying. 'And when you're trying to give people a holistic body experience, it's really, really important, do you understand?'

No it's not, thought Issy mutinously, it's important that you put your oven in the right damn place so you can run the rest of the shop. She thought of Grampa Joe. She *must* get up to visit him, she really must. It was unforgivable having this time off and not making the effort.

She inched over so she could hear what the woman was saying.

'And twelve hundred a month is far too much.'

The woman was wearing tight leather trousers. Her stomach was flat. Her face was a peculiar mix of very smooth skin and wrinkly bits, presumably where the Botox was wearing off.

'Everything organic!' she trilled. 'People don't want nasty chemicals in their bodies!'

Apart from their foreheads, thought Issy. She wondered why she had taken such a dislike to this woman. Why should she care that the woman was going to have a silly raw juice café in her little shop? She meant, Issy corrected herself, *the* little shop. The little hidden shop, in the little secret square that never seemed as loved and cared for as it should be. Of course, she knew, knew completely that having a shop that was hard to find and tucked away was far from ideal.

Something struck her. She was used to working in commercial property where space went for fifty or sixty pounds a square foot. She eyed up the shop. Plus there was a basement, the sign said, which doubled the space straight away. Issy did some quick calculations in her head. That made it about fourteen pounds a square foot. OK, obviously this was in a London suburb, and not entirely a posh one at that. But still, £1,200 a month— say £1,100 if the woman was right and could negotiate a discount, which in this market she should be able to. If she could take out a six-month lease on that to do . . . well, to bake, maybe.

Issy closed her eyes as the bus came round the corner. That was ridiculous. There were millions of things involved in working with food, not just taking on a rent. It was completely impossible, and stupid, and she didn't even want to work in a café.

The redundancy course, although it wasn't called that, was held in a nondescript building off Oxford Street. There were about a dozen people in the room, from the bullish and sulky-looking, who gave the impression they'd been sent on this course as a kind of detention, to the utterly terrified. She half smiled at everyone. Nobody made a friendly face back.

A woman in her mid-fifties, with a tired, impatient face, arrived on the button of 9.30, launching into her spiel so briskly that it rapidly became clear that the only people overworked in the current climate were redundancy resettlement trainers.

'Now, starting your positive *new life*,' she announced, 'the first thing you must do is treat job-hunting as a job in itself. You have to make your CV stand out from the two million CVs circulating at any one time.'

The trainer spread her lips in what Issy supposed was meant to be a smile. 'And that's not an exaggeration. That is the approximate number of CVs being submitted for available vacancies at any given time.'

'Well, I'm feeling empowered already,' muttered the girl sitting next to Issy. Issy glanced at her. She was glamorous and perhaps slightly over-dressed—with jet-black ringlets, bright red lipstick and a fuchsia mohair jumper that totally failed to conceal massive bosoms underneath.

The trainer ploughed on. 'So, you need to stand out. Some people like to use raised fonts, or even write their CVs in rhyme to give them that edge.'

Issy raised her hand. 'Can I just say that I've been hiring staff for years and I hated gimmicky CVs, I always threw them in the bin. Whereas if I got one with no spelling mistakes, I'd interview them immediately.'

The trainer had gone pink and tight-lipped.

At lunchtime Issy and the ringleted girl fled. 'That was the most hideous thing ever,' said the girl, whose name was Pearl. 'It was actually worse than getting the boot.'

Issy smiled gratefully. 'I know.' She looked around. 'Where are you going for lunch? I was thinking Patisserie Valerie.'

Patisserie Valerie was a long-established fancy-cakes-and-tea chain, which was always crowded and always a delight. They had a new vanilla icing she'd heard about that she was anxious to try. The girl looked a bit uncomfortable and Issy immediately remembered how pricey it was.

'My treat,' she added quickly. 'My redundancy payment is not bad, thank goodness.'

Pearl smiled. 'OK!' she said.

Ensconced in a tiny wooden booth, they swapped horror stories. Pearl had been the receptionist at a building firm where things had got gradually worse and worse. She hadn't even been paid for the last two months and, as she was raising a baby single-handed, things were getting desperate.

'I thought this might help,' she said. 'My Restart sent me here. But it's just rubbish, isn't it?'

Issy nodded. 'I think so. But at least we got cake.'

Chapter Three

Issy was about to spend the day marching cold into estate agencies and asking for work. She was starting near the flat. If she could find a job within walking distance, so much the better. The door to Joe Golden Estates pinged as Issy went in, her heart in her mouth. She reminded herself she was a calm professional, with experience in the property trade. There was only one man in the office, the same distracted-looking balding chap who had been showing that woman around the shop.

'Hello!' said Issy, too surprised to remember why she was there. 'Aren't you renting Pear Tree Court?'

The man peered up at her with a wary look in his eyes.

'Trying to,' he said gruffly. 'Bit of a bloody nightmare.'

'Why?'

'Doesn't matter,' he said, suddenly remembering where he was and switching into salesman mode. 'It's a fabulous property, so much character and loads of potential.'

'Hasn't every business that's gone in there failed miserably?'

'Well, that's because they're not approaching it the right way.'

I will make friends with him *then* ask him for a job, Issy told herself. I will ask him for a job . . . shortly. Soon. In a bit.

But what actually came out of Issy's mouth was, 'I couldn't take a look at it, could I?'

Des, of Joe Golden Estates, was tired of the market, tired of being on his own in an empty office, tired of endless to-ing and fro-ing with this stupid Pear Tree Court property as one person after another thought they could make a go of it, when, pretty as it was, it remained a commercial property that didn't actually face a road. People got dreams in their heads that were nothing to do with business. This looked like another one.

For the first time in what felt like weeks, Issy sensed a tiny flame of curiosity spark inside her. As Des somewhat reluctantly opened up the heavy door with three different keys, she could see at once that while there were all sorts of problems with it (no road frontage being only the most glaringly obvious), 4 Pear Tree Court had a lot of plus points too.

The large glass window faced west, which would let plenty of sunlight into the shop in the afternoon, making it a nice place to come and linger over coffee and a cake when business typically was quieter. Issy tried not to let her imagination run away with itself. Although the alley had rubbish in it, it also had cobbles; and, although it was as unhealthy, stunted and metropolitan a specimen as one could hope to find anywhere, there was a real live tree next to the ironmonger's. Once you were inside the court, the noise from the traffic seemed to fade away; it was as if you were stepping back to a quieter, gentler time. The little row of shops was higgledy-piggledy and jammed together and number 4, with its low wooden doorway, odd angles and ancient fireplace, was the sweetest of them all.

'Things busy in your line of work these days?' she asked nonchalantly. Des looked down, stifling a yawn.

'Hmm,' he said. 'In fact, I've just taken an offer on this place, so if you wanted it you'd have to be quick.'

Issy narrowed her eyes.

'Why are you showing it to me if someone else has already offered on it?'

Des cringed. 'Well, you know. I'm not sure if it'll go through.'

Issy thought about the blonde woman. She'd seemed very sure of herself.

'And what were you thinking of doing with it?' asked Des.

She looked around. She could visualise the whole thing—little mismatched tables and chairs; a bookshelf where people could bring books to exchange; the lovely low-slung glass catering desk where she could array her cupcakes in different flavours and pretty pastels, making sure there were cake stands in the windows to tempt people in off the road. Making up gift presentation boxes for parties . . .

Issy realised through her reverie that Des was waiting for an answer.

'Oh, I was thinking a little café,' she said, feeling her ever-present blush rising to the surface 'A kind of bakery place.' Des's face fell.

'Oh,' he said. 'Actually the other bidder wants to open a café too.'

Issy thought back to the blonde woman. Hers would be nothing like that! she thought indignantly. Hers would be warm and inviting, and cosy and indulgent and somewhere to come and enjoy yourself, not somewhere to come and feel like you were atoning for bad behaviour. Hers would be a lovely focal point for the community.

'I'll take it!' she said suddenly. The agent looked at her in surprise.

'Don't you want to know how much it is?' he asked.

'Oh, yes, of course,' said Issy, suddenly totally flustered. What on earth was she thinking? She wasn't qualified to run a business. All she could do was bake cakes and that would never be enough, surely. Although how, a little voice inside her said, how will you know unless you try? And wouldn't you like to be your own boss? And have your lovely, cleaned-up, gorgeous local café in this perfect spot? And have people come from far and wide to taste your cupcakes and sit and relax for half an hour, read the paper, buy a gift, enjoy a little bit of peace and quiet? Wouldn't that be a nice thing to do every day: sweeten people's lives, give them a smile, feed them? Now she had this once-in-a-lifetime cash; this once-in-a-lifetime opportunity?

'Sorry, sorry,' she said, confused. 'I'm jumping way ahead of the gun. Can I just have a brochure?'

The following Saturday, Issy made good use of the slow bus up to Gramps's nursing home; she worked on some calculations and schedules in her newly purchased notebook and felt a little rising bubble of excitement. No. She mustn't. It was a daft idea. What would make her different from everyone else who had gone into that space and failed miserably?

The Oaks was an austere, former stately home and Helena had recommended it as the best of its kind. Taking Issy up, the plump young nurse called Keavie seemed a little distracted. 'What's up?' asked Issy.

'You should know,' she said, 'he's not having one of his better days.'

Issy's heart sank. To hear those words was chilling. Steeling herself, she popped her head round the door.

Joe was propped up in bed. Never a fat man, his weight, she noticed, had fallen away even further; his skin was beginning to sink and drop off his bones. He had kept his hair, though it looked now like fine white fluff.

'Hi, Gramps,' she said, kissing him fondly. 'Thanks for the recipes.' She perched at the end of the bed. 'I love getting them.'

Issy looked at her grampa. He'd had a funny turn before, just after he'd moved, and they'd put him on some new medication. He'd seemed to zone out a lot, but the staff had assured her that he could hear her talking, and that it probably helped. '*Anyway*,' she found herself saying now— almost as if trying it out just to see what it sounded like—'I'm thinking of opening a little café. People like little cafés these days. They're getting sick of the same old chains. Well, that's what I read in a Sunday magazine.

'My friends aren't actually being very helpful. Helena keeps telling me to think about VAT. I think she's trying to be those scary guys off the telly that make fun of your business ideas, because she always says it in a really growly voice, like she's a total millionaire mogul and I'm just some idiot, not fit to run a business. But all sorts of people run businesses, don't they, Gramps? Look at you, you did it for years.'

She sighed.

'So obviously I remembered to ask you all the intelligent questions about it while you were still in a fit position to answer them. Gramps, *why* didn't I ask you about running a business? Please help me.'

Nothing. Issy sighed again.

She remembered coming home from school and making a strawberry tart, pastry as light as air and the glaze as fine and sweet as fairies' breath. Gramps had sat down in silence with a fork and not uttered a word as he savoured every bite, slowly, and she stood, hands clasped over the front of her apron. When he had finished, he had put down his fork carefully, reverently. Then he had looked at her.

'You, love,' he had said, deliberately. 'You are a born baker.'

Issy's heart was aflame with her grandfather's praise, rarely bestowed.

Suddenly, her grampa sat up. Issy flinched as his watery blue eyes struggled to focus. She crossed her fingers that he would recognise her.

'Marian?' he said at first. Then his face cleared like the sun coming out. 'Issy? Is that my Issy?'

Issy's heart lifted with relief. 'Yes!' she said. 'Yes, it's me.'

'Did you bring me some cake?' He leaned over confidentially. 'This hotel is all right but it has no cake.'

Issy peered into her bag. 'Of course! Look, I made Battenburg.'

Joe smiled. 'So what's with you, my darling?' He looked around. 'I'm here on holiday but it hasn't been terribly warm. It's not very warm.'

'No,' said Issy. It was boiling in the room. 'I know. And you're not on holiday. You live here now.'

Gramps looked around for a long time. Finally, she realised it was sinking in, and his face seemed to fall. She reached over and patted his hand and he took it and changed the subject briskly.

'Well? What have you been doing?'

'I've been thinking about opening a bakery.'

Her grandfather's face broke open into a wide grin. 'Of *course* you are, Isabel!' he said. 'I just can't believe it took you all this time!'

Issy smiled. 'Well, I've been very busy.'

'I suppose,' said her grampa. 'Well. I am pleased. I am very pleased. And I can help you. I should send you some recipes.'

'You do that already,' said Issy. 'I'm using them.'

'Good,' said her grandfather. 'Make sure you follow them properly.'

'I'll do my best.'

'I'll come down and help out. Oh yes. I'm fine. Totally fine. Don't worry about me.'

Issy wished she could say the same about herself. She kissed her gramps goodbye.

'You always perk him up,' said Keavie, walking her out of the door.

Issy smiled. 'Thank you,' she said. 'Thank you for looking after him.'

'That's our job,' said Keavie, with the simplicity of someone who knew her vocation in life. Issy envied her.

Emboldened, Issy marched back into her flat. She went into the cosy sitting room to find Helena.

'I've made a decision,' Issy announced.

Helena raised her eyebrows. 'Go on then.'

'I think I should go for the café. My gramps thinks it's a great idea.'

Helena smiled. 'Well, I could have told you that.' She did think it was a good idea—she had no doubt about Issy's ability to bake the most delicious cakes, or the skills she'd bring to working with members of the public. She worried a little more about Issy handling the responsibility of her own business, and the paperwork, seeing as she'd rather watch *World's Goriest Operations* than open her own Visa bill. Still, anything at the moment was better than moping.

'Just for six months,' said Issy. 'If it fails, I won't be bankrupt.'

'Of course you won't fail! You'll be brill! Let's open some wine. What are you going to call it, by the way?'

'I don't know. I thought maybe Grampa Joe's.'

'That makes it sound like a hot-dog stand.'

'Hmm. The Stoke Newington Bakery?'

'There is one of those. It's that little place on Church Street.'

'Oh.'

'You're selling cupcakes, aren't you?'

'Definitely,' said Issy, her eyes shining.

'Well, why don't you just call it the Cupcake Café? Then people can say, "Oh, you know, that place with all the cupcakes," and they'll say, "I can't remember what it's called," and someone else will say, "It's the Cupcake Café" and everyone will say, "Oh, yes, let's meet there."'

Issy thought about it. It was simple, a bit obvious, but it felt right.

Des was trying to cope with what was supposedly colic but mostly meant baby Jamie arching his back and screaming to get away from him. His wife and his mother-in-law had gone to the spa for some 'me' time when Issy rang, and at first he found it a little hard to concentrate. Oh yes, the impulsive one who was just wandering past. He hadn't really expected to hear from her again; he'd thought she was just killing time.

'Oh right. Only that other woman's made me a firm offer.'

Issy felt an instant letdown. Oh no, surely not. She had a vision of her dream being dashed before it had even begun.

'I've got a few other places I can show you . . .'

'No!' said Issy. 'It has to be that one! It has to be there!'

'Well,' said Des, 'she did offer less than what the landlord was asking.'

'I'll make an offer too,' pleaded Issy. 'And I'll be a very good tenant.'

Des jiggled Jamie up and down in front of the window. The baby laughed, and warmed Des's mood.

'OK,' he said. 'Let me talk to Mr Barstow.'

By the time Issy headed out to meet Mr Barstow, the landlord of Pear Tree Court, Helena had given her a quick pep talk. She would convince him with her level of organisation and research. Or fell him with her secret-weapon Grampa cakes. They met in Des's office. Des had had a shocking night with Jamie and felt like death in a cup.

The blonde woman was there, looking incredibly sleek and expensive in £200 jeans, spiky heels and a ludicrously soft-looking leather jacket. Issy narrowed her eyes. This woman didn't need to earn a living. She probably spent more than Issy's old salary on highlights alone.

'Caroline Hanford,' she said without smiling, extending a hand. 'I don't know why we're having this meeting, I put my offer in first.'

'And we've had a counter-offer,' said Des, pouring repulsive sticky black coffee from a push-button machine into three cups, the first of which he gulped down like medicine. 'And Mr Barstow wanted us all to meet to discuss the offers in more detail.'

A short, bald man marched into the room and grunted at Des.

'This is Mr Barstow,' said Des unnecessarily.

Caroline let forth a very toothy grin, impatient for this to be over. 'Hello,' she said. 'Can I call you Max?'

Mr Barstow grunted, which didn't seem to indicate an answer one way or the other. Issy didn't think he looked like a Max at all.

'I'm here to offer you the best deal I can,' said Caroline. 'Thanks so much for agreeing to see me.'

Hang on, Issy wanted to say. Don't you mean to say 'see *us*'? Issy knew if Helena were there she would make some remark about this being business and tell her to get tough. Instead she just said, 'Hello,' then felt cross with herself for not being more assertive. She clasped her favourite cake tin—decorated with a Union Jack—to her side.

Mr Barstow looked at both of them.

'I've got thirty-five properties in this city,' he said in a strong London accent. 'Bloody none of them have given me as much trouble as this one. It's been one damn lady thing after another.'

Issy was taken aback by his bluntness, but Caroline looked totally unfazed. 'Thirty-five?' she cooed. 'Wow, you are successful.'

'So I don't just care about the money,' said Mr Barstow. 'I care about bloody not having someone move out without warning leaving the back rent unpaid every bloody five minutes, do you understand?'

Both women nodded. Issy fingered her notes. She'd done research into what made a nice café and how a good bakery could add value to surrounding houses, and hopefully how many cakes they'd sell every day (admittedly, she'd plucked this figure out of thin air, but pasted into a spreadsheet it looked quite good. This way of working had been reasonably successful in property management so she couldn't imagine things were much different in baking). But before she could speak, Caroline opened up a tiny silver laptop that Issy hadn't even noticed.

'I've prepared this presentation,' she began. It was relentless. There were screeds of it. Caroline had gone in, out and round the houses. She had categorised the postcodes, designed the website and sourced organic carrots being grown on an allotment on Hackney Marshes.

Mr Barstow watched the entire presentation in silence.

'Now, have you any questions?' she said after twenty minutes.

Issy's insides had begun to shrink. A few days' Googling was definitely not up to scratch here. In fact, she couldn't give a presentation after that one, so immaculately researched and explained. She would look like a total idiot. Mr Barstow looked Caroline up and down. He still hadn't removed the sunglasses he'd been wearing when he came in, even though it was only February. 'So, what you're saying is, you're going to stand there all day, in an alleyway 300 metres from Stoke Newington High Street, and try to push beetroot juice.'

Caroline was unperturbed.

'I believe my extensive in-depth customer-based analysis . . .'

'What about you?' said Mr Barstow, pointing at Issy.

'Uh . . .' There was a long pause. Des raised his eyebrows. Caroline smirked nastily. She didn't know, though, thought Issy suddenly. They didn't know about her secret weapon.

'Um,' said Issy. 'I make cakes.'

Mr Barstow grunted. 'Oh yeah? Got any?'

Issy had been hoping for this. She opened the tin. As well as iced lemon cake, which few could resist trying, she'd gone for a selection of cupcakes to show her range: white chocolate and fresh cloudberry; cinnamon and orange peel, which tasted more Christmassy than Christmas cake; and a sweet, fresh, irresistible spring vanilla, decorated with tiny roses. She'd brought four of each.

As she'd known he would, Mr Barstow stuck a fat hairy hand in the box and took a piece of the lemon cake, as well as a vanilla cupcake.

Before anyone else dared move, he took a bite out of each of them. Issy held her breath as he chewed, slowly and deliberately, his eyes closed as if he were a top wine taster at work. Finally, he swallowed.

'All right,' he said, pointing straight at her. 'You. Don't muck it up, love.'

Then he picked up his briefcase, turned round and left the office.

Issy arrived home with a bottle of champagne. Helena, who got back after her shift weary, suddenly perked up. 'You got it!'

'It was Gramps's cakes,' said Issy with feeling.

'To Gramps,' said Helena, raising her glass. 'And to you! And the success of the Cupcake Café!'

The two friends clinked glasses and hugged. Suddenly, Issy's phone rang. She stared at the number. Helena caught her expression—half terror, half longing—and wanted to stop her from answering the phone. She had known immediately who it would be. But it was too late.

'Graeme?' said Issy huskily.

'Babes, where have you been?' said Graeme, as if they'd last chatted about two hours ago and he'd been looking for her in a shopping centre.

It had taken more from Graeme to make this phone call than Issy could know. At first he'd told himself that things would have come to an end anyway; he wasn't ready to settle down, it wasn't like they were serious.

But then, gradually, as the weeks had gone on and he hadn't heard from her, he'd felt an unfamiliar emotion. He missed her. Missed her gentleness, and her genuine interest in him and what he was doing; missed her cooking, obviously . . . there was something about being with Issy that was just so easy-going. She didn't give him hassle, didn't nag his ear off or want to spend his money. He liked her. It was that simple.

Although normally he didn't like to look back in his life, Graeme decided to give her a call. What had happened at the office . . . it was just business, wasn't it? She'd probably have another job by now anyway. He'd written her an amazing reference, a bit more than her admin skills deserved, and Cal Mehta had too. By the time he picked up the phone, Graeme had managed to convince himself that it would all be cool.

Issy, deliberately not looking at her flatmate, got up and left the room. It took her a long time to speak—so long, in fact, that Graeme had to say, 'Hello? Hello? Are you still there?'

Over the last few weeks she had lain tossing and turning in bed; the shame and the pain of losing her job would then be overtaken by the misery and frustration of losing Graeme. It was unbearable. Awful. She hated him. He had used her like some kind of stupid office perk.

But he hadn't, she heard herself say. There had been something there. There had. Something real. He had told her things . . .

But had he just been saying those things to any willing ear? Was it useful having a professional confidante who would also cook for you and sleep with you? Just handy on his way up the career ladder? And, really, why would someone so handsome and successful be interested in her?

And now the café coming along—that had seemed providential; perfect really. Something good and concrete she could pour her energies into; a new door into a new life. A way to start afresh.

'You still there?'

She panicked. Should she play it cool, pretend she'd hardly been thinking about him—when she had, compulsively? For the first few days she'd been sure he'd ring to say he'd made a terrible mistake and that he loved her and please could she come back. Then those days had turned into a month; she had a new course now and there was no going back . . .

'Hello?' she said finally, her voice coming out like a strangled whisper.

'Can you talk?' said Graeme. This riled her for some reason. What on earth did he think she was doing?

'Not really,' she said. 'I'm in bed with George Clooney and he's just gone off to open a fresh bottle of champagne to top up the jacuzzi.'

Graeme laughed. 'Oh, Issy, I have missed you.'

Issy felt, out of nowhere, a sob hit her throat and desperately tried to gulp it back down. He hadn't missed her! Because if he'd thought about her at all, he'd have realised the one single solitary time she needed him more than anything or anyone in the world had been after she'd lost her job. After he had decided that she should lose her job. And he hadn't given a shit.

'No, you haven't,' she managed. ''Course you bloody haven't.'

Graeme sighed. 'I didn't think you'd be like this.'

Issy bit down on her lip. 'As opposed to what—grateful?'

'Yes, well, you know. Maybe a bit. Grateful to be given the opportunity to go out and do a bit more with your life. You know you're capable, Issy. And anyway, how could I have contacted you before? It would have been completely inappropriate, you must understand that.'

Issy didn't say anything. She didn't want him to think he was sounding reasonable.

'Look,' he said honestly. 'I've been thinking about you a lot.'

'Have you really? When you just dumped my job and then dumped me?'

'I didn't dump you!' said Graeme, sounding exasperated. 'Your job disappeared. Everyone's job was at risk! And I was trying to protect you from the fact that you and I had a personal relationship, then you went and shouted about it all over the office! That was really embarrassing, Issy.'

'They all knew about it anyway,' said Issy sulkily.

'That's not the point.'

'So why are you calling me now then?' she asked.

Graeme's voice went soft. 'Well, I just wanted to see how you were. What, you think I'm a complete bastard?'

Was it possible? Issy wondered. Was it possible that she had got it wrong? After all, she had stormed out of the boardroom, shouting. Maybe she wasn't the only injured party here. Maybe he'd been as shocked and upset as she was. Maybe it had taken quite a lot of guts for him to make this phone call. Maybe he was still—you know—the one.

'Well . . .' she said. Just at that moment, Helena marched into her room without knocking. She was carrying a hastily erected sign, scrawled on the back of a council tax reminder. In big black letters was written 'NO!'

Helena punched her fists in the air like they were at a demonstration, mouthing, 'No! No! No!' very ferociously in her direction. Issy tried to wave her away, but she just advanced even more. Helena was reaching out a hand to grab the phone.

'Shoo!' said Issy. 'Shoo! I'm fine. But we do need to talk. So would you mind pissing off for five minutes and giving us some privacy?'

She stared hard at Helena until she retreated back to the sitting room.

'Sorry about that,' Issy said finally to Graeme.

'Are we fine? We're fine,' he said, sounding relieved. 'Oh good. That's great.' There was a pause. 'Want to come over?'

'You're not going,' said Helena, standing in the doorway with her arms folded. 'You're not.'

'It was a misunderstanding,' said Issy. 'He's been feeling terrible too.'

'So terrible he lost his phone for weeks and weeks,' said Helena. 'Issy, please. You're making a clean break.'

'But Helena,' said Issy, fired up. She had necked the glass of champagne as soon as she'd come off the phone. He had called! He had called!

'He's . . . I mean . . . I mean, I really think Graeme might be the one.'

'No. He's the boss you had a crush on and you're nearly thirty-two and in a panic.'

'That . . . that's not it,' said Issy, trying to get her point over. 'It's not. You're not there, Helena.'

'No, I'm not,' said Helena. 'I'm back here, nursing you through tearful nights or mopping you up when he's let you walk home in the rain again, or accompanying you to parties as your plus one because he doesn't want to be seen out and about with you.'

'That was because of the office,' said Issy. 'I'm sure it'll be different now.'

Helena gave her one of her looks.

'Well,' said Issy defiantly, 'I'm at least going to find out.'

'I'm so glad he didn't even have to leave the comfort of his own living room,' said Helena to the empty space after Issy had gone.

Chapter Four

GRAEME HAD A BOTTLE of champagne open too. His flat was, as ever, spotless and minimalist, a huge contrast to Issy's colourful, overloaded home. It was quiet and calm. Robin Thicke was playing on the expensive sound system, which Issy thought might be overdoing it a bit. On the other hand, she was wearing her best soft woollen grey dress and heels.

'Hey,' he said, as he opened the door. He was wearing a fresh white shirt, unbuttoned at the collar, with very dark stubble on his fine jaw. He looked tired, a little stressed—and utterly, utterly handsome and gorgeous. Issy couldn't help it. Her insides leapt for joy.

'Hey,' she said.

'Thanks . . . thanks so much for coming over.'

She looked nice, Graeme was thinking.

Issy knew she should have played it cool, planned for a lunch in a few days' time, given herself breathing space. But she wasn't cool. She knew that. He knew that. There was no point beating about the bush any longer. Either he was in or he wasn't, and she didn't have months of pussyfooting about to figure out which.

He kissed her lightly on the cheek, and she smelled Fahrenheit, her favourite aftershave. He was wearing it for her.

She accepted a glass and sat down, perching on his imitation Le Corbusier black leather chair. It was like the first time she'd ever been back here; the mixture of fear and excitement; of being alone in this sleek apartment with this sensual, attractive man she fancied so much she could barely think straight.

'I have missed you, you know,' said Graeme, looking directly at her from under his straight black brows. 'I think . . . maybe I took you for granted.'

'You took me for granted,' said Issy. 'No maybe about it.'

'OK, OK,' said Graeme. He put his hand on her arm. 'I'm sorry, OK?'

Issy shrugged. 'Whatever.'

'Issy, don't say "whatever", you're not twelve. If you're cross with me and want to say something, just come out with it.'

Issy pouted a little. 'I'm cross with you.'

'And I'm sorry. It's this job, you know that.'

He tailed off. Issy realised suddenly that this was it, this was her moment to say, to ask: *What am I to you? Truly? Where are we going? Because if this is back on, it needs to be serious. It really does. Because I am running out of time and I want to be with you.* She knew she was unlikely to see Graeme in such a vulnerable state again. This was the time to put down the new ground rules of their relationship; to make him say it.

They sat in silence. Issy felt the familiar blush steal over her face. Why was she such a coward? Why was she scared to ask him?

Graeme crossed the living room. Before Issy got the chance to open her mouth, he was right there in front of her, his eyes, his beautiful blue eyes focused right on her.

'Look at you,' he said gruffly. 'You're blushing. It's adorable.'

As usual, having her blushing pointed out only made it worse. Issy opened her mouth to say something, but as she did so Graeme made a shushing motion, then moved forward very very slowly and kissed her full and hard on the lips, the way that had been haunting her dreams.

First reluctantly, then fully, Issy surrendered to the kiss. She'd forgotten just how good it felt; how good he felt; how good he smelled. Unable to help herself, she let out a sigh.

'I have missed you,' breathed Graeme. And for the moment, Issy realised, that was going to have to be enough.

It wasn't until the next morning, after an extraordinary night, when Graeme was getting ready that he thought to ask her what she was doing.

At first Issy was oddly reluctant to tell him. She didn't want him to laugh at her. She was enjoying feeling happily tired, her muscles liquid and relaxed, luxuriating in his big bed. She was doing something she rarely got to do: staying all night. It was bliss. She would get up and saunter down to Notting Hill High Street, have coffee . . . Suddenly she could see the positives of being out and about on a weekday, it made her feel like she was bunking off.

But then she remembered with a start: she couldn't bunk off. Not any more. She had stuff to do. She'd signed up to the lease and with the lease came a shop, and responsibility, and work and . . . She sat bolt upright in a fit of panic. She had an appointment with a small business adviser; she had to examine the property—*her café!*—she had to figure out what work was absolutely essential and what could wait till they were up and running; buy an oven, think about staffing. Last night, starting with the champagne and ending with the most incredible sex with the man currently gelling his hair in the en suite mirror—that had been a celebration. Today, she was self-employed. It was starting.

'Ooh,' she said. 'I have to rush. I have to go.'

Graeme looked perturbed but amused.

'Why? Urgent pedicure appointment?'

'No, actually.' And she told him.

'You're what?' He was halfway through knotting a natty blue tie. 'We're five minutes out of recession and you're opening a small business?'

'It's the best time,' said Issy. 'Rents are cheap, opportunities are out there.'

'Hang on, hang on,' said Graeme. Issy was half pleased at surprising him and half cross at his evident scepticism. 'What type of business?'

Issy stared at him. 'Cupcakes, of course.'

'Cupcakes? You're going to make an entire business out of cakes?'

'People like them.'

Graeme frowned. 'Those sugary things? But you don't know anything about running a business.'

'Well, who does when they start?'

'Almost everyone in catering, for starters. They've all worked in other bakeries for years. Otherwise you're sunk. Why didn't you go and work in a bakery if you wanted to bake? At least you'd have seen if it suited you.'

'Well, a shop came up that I think is just right, and—'

'In Stoke Newington?' snorted Graeme. 'They saw you coming.'

'Fine,' said Issy. 'Be like that. I have an appointment anyway with a small business adviser.'

'Well, I hope he's cleared his schedule,' said Graeme.

Issy stared at him. 'What?'

'I can't believe you're throwing away KD's incredibly generous redundancy package on something so ridiculous. Why didn't you ask me?'

'Because you didn't bother to ring me, remember?'

'Oh, Issy. Come on. I'll ask around. I'm sure there's a secretarial job going at Foxtons commercial. I'm sure we can find something for you.'

'I don't want "something",' said Issy mutinously. 'I want this.'

Graeme threw up his hands.

'But it's ridiculous. You don't know anything about business.'

'You don't know anything about me,' said Issy, which she realised made her sound dramatic and stupid, but she didn't care. 'I have to go.' She tottered out of the door, berating herself, once again, for being such an idiot.

Issy rushed home, shaking. The flat was silent, but not empty. She could sense Helena around somewhere; feel her disapproval wafting in her direction. Well, she didn't have time for that now. She had a meeting at the bank, had to sound clever and professional, even though she'd been up half the night.

Now, what to wear? She pulled open her wardrobe, looking at the array of work suits she'd accumulated. The grey pinstripe? Graeme had always liked it, he thought it looked like sexy secretary. But she didn't like to dress to emphasise her figure. Helena on the other hand had turned it into an art.

She pulled a white shirt closer. Shirts never seemed to fit properly. Sensing someone behind her, she turned round. It was Helena, holding two cups of tea.

'Don't knock,' said Issy. 'It's only my flat.'

'Do you want tea?' said Helena, ignoring her.

'No,' said Issy. 'I want you to stop wandering into my room uninvited.'

'Well, sounds like last night was romantic.'

Issy sighed. It was hard to stay angry at Helena for long. 'It was fine,' said Issy, taking the tea. 'Fine. I don't want to see him again anyway. I know I've said that before. But this time I mean it.'

'Fine.'

Helena looked at her. 'Are you going to wear that for your meeting?'

'I have a business now. I have to look the part.'

'But that's not your part. You're a baker now.' Helena reached into her cupboard and pulled out a lightly sprigged dress and a pastel cardigan. 'Here, try these on.'

'You don't think it's a bit . . . twee?'

'Darling, you're running a cupcake bakery. I think you have to make your peace with twee. And anyway, no, I don't. I think it looks pretty and approachable and it suits you.'

Actually, thought Issy, glancing in the mirror, in the new outfit, she did look nicer—younger and fresher. It made her smile.

'There you go,' said Helena. 'Now you look the part.'

Issy was nervous going to the bank, extremely so. It felt a bit like having to go in and explain away her overdraft, just as she had done in college.

'Um, hi,' she almost whispered. 'Can I speak to Mr . . .' she checked her notes, 'Mr Tyler.'

The young girl behind the desk smiled distractedly and leaned forward into her telephone, buzzing her through. Being on the other side of the security barrier was a little disconcerting; open-plan desks were scattered around, with people peering at computer screens. Issy glanced about her.

She didn't see anyone who looked like a Mr Tyler, so she sat down nervously, picking up and replacing a magazine about the bank, too anxious to read anything. Hoping she wouldn't have too long to wait.

Austin Tyler sat in the head teacher's office. It was exactly the same room he used to sit in, kicking his scuffed shoes against the chair when he was getting told off for running through the bushes or fighting with Duncan MacGuire. There was a new headmistress—quite a young woman, who said, 'Call me Kirsty,' when he'd much rather call her Miss Dubose, and perched on the front of her desk instead of sitting imperiously behind it like Mr Stroan used to do. Austin glanced sideways at Darny and sighed. Darny was staring at the floor crossly. At ten years old, Darny was smart, determined and absolutely convinced that anyone ever telling him what to do was in severe breach of his human rights.

'What is it this time?' asked Austin. He was going to be late for work again, he knew it. He ran a hand through the thick, unruly reddish-brown hair that was flopping over his forehead.

'Well,' started the headmistress, 'obviously we're all aware of Darny's special circumstances.'

Austin raised his eyebrows and turned to Darny, whose hair was more auburn than Austin's but stuck up at the front in a very similar fashion, and whose eyes were also grey.

'Yes, but Darny's special circumstances were six years ago, weren't they, Darny? You can't keep on using it as an excuse. Especially not for . . .'

'Using bows and arrows on the Reception class.'

Everyone at the school knew the tragic story. Six years ago, when Austin had been a postgraduate student in marine biology at Leeds, his parents and his baby brother (the result of a silver wedding celebration that had given them all the shock of their lives) were involved in a car accident. The four-year-old had been fine, but the front of the car had been completely crushed.

Knocked sideways by grief, Austin had immediately given up his studies, come home, fought off well-meaning aunties and social services, taken a mundane job in a bank and was raising his baby brother as well as he could. Now thirty-one, Austin had such a strong bond with Darny that although many women had tried to get in between them, no one had quite managed it.

'So would you say . . .' said Kirsty, 'that Darny is getting enough of a feminine influence at home?'

'Well, he has about nine million well-meaning female relations,' Austin said. 'But no one more permanent, no.'

Kirsty raised her eyebrows in what was meant to be a flirtatious manner, but which Austin immediately took to be disapproval.

'We do all right, Darny and I,' he insisted. Darny, although still staring at the floor, reached out a hand and squeezed Austin's tightly.

'I didn't mean to . . . I just meant, Mr Tyler . . . Austin. We can't have violence at this school. We really can't.'

'But we want to stay at this school,' said Austin. 'We grew up here! This is our area! We don't want to have to move and go to another school.'

Austin tried not to feel a bit panicked as he felt Darny's skinny fingers grip his long ones, but holding on to their parents' home, and his old school, and the area they'd always lived in, around Stoke Newington—well, it had felt so important to give their lives a sense of continuity. Staying here meant they were within a community of friends and neighbours who made sure they never went without a hot meal if they needed one, or a sleepover for Darny if Austin had to work late. He loved the area passionately.

Kirsty moved to calm him. 'No one is saying anything about moving schools. We're just saying . . . no more bows and arrows.'

'No more bows and arrows,' repeated Darny.

'And?' said Austin.

'And, sorry,' said Darny, finally looking up. 'Do I have to go and say sorry to the Reception kids?'

'Yes, please,' said Austin. Kirsty smiled at him gratefully.

Janet, Austin's assistant, met him at the door of the bank.

'You're late,' she said, handing him his coffee.

'I know, I know, I'm sorry.'

'Darny trouble again?'

Austin winced.

'Don't worry,' she said, patting him on the shoulder and picking some lint off it at the same time. 'They all go through the same phases.'

'With bows and arrows?'

Janet smiled. 'Consider yourself lucky. Mine went for firecrackers.'

Feeling slightly cheered by this, Austin glanced at his notes: someone looking for a café loan. He turned the corner into a small waiting area.

'Hello,' he said, smiling at the nervous-looking woman with the pink cheeks and tied-back, unruly black hair sitting fiddling with a magazine. 'Are you my ten o'clock?'

Issy jumped up, then, inadvertently, let her gaze stray to the large clock on the far wall.

'I know,' said Austin. 'I'm so sorry . . . Would you like to follow me?'

The meeting room was basically just a glass box set in the middle of the open-plan office. It felt peculiar, as if they were two fish in a tank.

'Sorry. I'm . . . hi, I'm Austin Tyler.'

'Isabel Randall.' Issy shook his hand, which was large and dry. His hair seemed a little messy for a banker, she noticed. But he had a pleasant, slightly distracted smile, and thick-fringed grey eyes—maybe she should put him on her list for Helena. She was swearing off men for good after last night. Focus! She wished she'd had more than three hours' sleep.

Austin fumbled about for a pen, noting his client seemed a little stressed. When he'd left Leeds, he hadn't been sure he'd make a natural banker. It was as far from examining coral as he could imagine, but the best thing he could find at short notice; the bank let him take on his parents' mortgage too. However, since joining, he'd worked his way up steadily; it turned out he had excellent instincts about sound prospects and good investments, and as his clients came to know him, they trusted him completely.

'Now then,' he said, having retrieved a pen from his pocket and blown the tissue fluff off it. 'What can we do for you?'

He glanced at the file and realised to his utter horror that this was a different café altogether. He pulled off his glasses. This was obviously going to be one of those days.

'Why don't you just start from the beginning,' he improvised.

Issy gave him a shrewd look. She'd spotted what had happened immediately. 'Don't you have the file?'

'I always like to hear it from the client. Paints me a picture.'

Issy's lips twitched. 'Really?'

'Really,' said Austin firmly, leaning forward and clasping his large hands in front of the folder. And while Issy caught the look of a shared joke in his eyes, she felt a spark of excitement at being able to tell her story properly. Either way, she was about to find out if her dream had the faintest possibility of becoming a reality.

Issy told him the story—missing out the sleeping-with-her-boss bits, and reshaping it more as a lifelong ambition, with lots of hard financial analysis backing it up. The more she told the story, she realised, the more real and plausible it sounded, like a creative visualisation. She felt she was making it come true.

'I brought you some cake,' she added as she finished.

'Sorry, I can't take that. Could be seen as . . .'

'Me bribing you with cake?' asked Issy in surprise.

'Well, yes, cake, tools, wine, whatever, really.'

'Gosh. I really hadn't thought of it like that.'

'What, you didn't bring me cakes to bribe me?'

'Well, yes, obviously I did, now you mention it.'

They smiled at one another. Austin rubbed his unruly hair. 'Pear Tree Court . . . isn't that the tiny tucked-away place off the Albion Road?'

Issy nodded fervently. 'You know it!'

'Well, yes . . .' said Austin, who knew every inch of the area intimately. 'But . . . it's not exactly a commercial area, is it?'

'There are shops there,' said Issy.

'I mean, I'm not sure it's . . . show me your figures again?'

Austin studied them with some care. The rent was certainly affordable, and when it came to the baking, the raw ingredients weren't expensive. Staff would be easy to find, if Issy was going to do all the cooking. But even so, the profit margins were painful, borderline minimal. For a very long slog.

He squinted at it again and looked back at Issy. It would all be down to her. If she would put the hours in, devote her entire life to cakes and nothing but, then it was just . . . just about possible. Maybe.

'Here's the thing,' he said. And, his second appointment forgotten, he took Issy so thoroughly through every single step of the way to run a business—from national insurance to health and safety, food inspections, banking, marketing, stocking, margins, portion control—that she felt as if she'd spent a year in business school. As he spoke, occasionally taking off his glasses to emphasise a point, Issy could feel her nebulous dreams take real, meaningful shape in his hands; he seemed to be moulding the foundations of her castle in the air. Step by step he explained to her exactly what she and she alone would be responsible for; what she'd have to do for as long as she wanted to make a living.

After fifty-five minutes, Austin sat back. He had gone above and beyond to help her and show her the pitfalls and possibilities. He kind of felt he owed it to her after turning up so late and with the wrong file. And also, although at first she'd seemed a little aggressive, once they'd started to talk she'd seemed nice—and she looked so sweet, in her pretty flowered frock—and he wanted her to be very clear about what she would be getting herself into. He was fond of the area she was talking about; he'd grown up near Pear Tree Court, and had often hidden there, under the tree, reading a book when that shop was derelict. It was a lovely spot. A little café—being able to sit out with a cup of coffee and a slice of something delicious—didn't seem that bad an idea to him. But in the end it would come down to her.

'So,' he said, finishing with a flourish. 'What do you think? If the bank was to support you, would you be up to it?'

Issy sat back with a thoughtful look in her eye. This was it. A full commitment—if she got the backing from the bank—for life, if everything went well. She would never be able to come home from work, forget all about it. She remembered Gramps, eating, sleeping, thinking of nothing but the bakeries. That had been his life. Would it be hers?

But then, if it was a success . . . maybe she could find other people to help her run it . . . open another one. All of that was possible too, she knew. She could end up with more freedom. A way to live her life by her own rules, to her own schedule, taking no one's minutes.

'Miss Randall?' Austin was pleased she was thinking about it. It meant she'd been listening to him. Too often he had wise guys in here who thought they had all the answers, who didn't listen and tried to talk over the top of him. They rarely lasted.

'Thanks for giving it to me straight,' she said.

'Have I scared the life out of you?' said Austin, apologetically.

'No. No, you haven't. And if the bank will help me out . . . well, I'd like to bank with you.'

Austin raised his eyebrows.

'OK. Well, OK. Good.' He ferreted in his briefcase for the forms she needed to fill out and instead came up with an apple and a catapult.

'You look like Dennis the Menace,' said Issy, giggling. She made a mental note to knock him off Helena's list—he wasn't wearing a wedding ring but he clearly had kids.

'Ah yes, we use this on defaulters,' he said. He buzzed the intercom on his desk. 'Janet, would you mind bringing in a set of business account application forms?'

Austin took his finger off the intercom. 'Janet will help you with the forms. Then just leave them at reception. I think my eleven o'clock is here.'

'Your eleven o'clock has been here for half an hour,' said Janet, appearing at the door with a sheaf of forms. She looked at Austin as if he were a naughty schoolboy. 'I'll tell him you're just ready.' She swept out.

Issy stood up. 'Thanks.'

'Good luck,' said Austin, standing up too, taking off his glasses and holding out his hand. Issy shook it. 'If you need anything else, here's my card. And here, would you like a bank pen?'

'You keep it,' said Issy. 'I wouldn't want anyone to think you were trying to bribe me.'

Although the weather was still cold and grey, at least it wasn't raining. While Issy knew she had plenty of things to get started on, she also had an awful lot to think about. As she came into Pear Tree Court and saw the sign up in the window—*Rented*—her heart leapt. She sat down, in the cold, on the little bench under the tree. Even in the chill weather, she felt a great sense of peace steal over her. The sun was only just showing its face. It touched a tiny piece of spring onto her winter-pallid face and she closed her eyes in bliss. Winter would come to an end; it would. And here, she would have a little haven in the very epicentre of one of the world's busiest cities. Could she make it her own?

When Des arrived to hand over the keys, he found Issy sitting on the bench, looking dreamy and far away. Uh-oh, he thought, worriedly. That wasn't really a good look for the putative owner of a business. That was more the look of someone who had a head full of castles in the air.

'Hey, hello,' he said, standing directly in her tiny shaft of sunshine. 'Sorry I'm late. My wife was supposed to . . . Uh, well, never mind.'

Issy squinted up at him. 'Hi! Sorry, it's just such a relaxing spot. I had a bit of a late night . . .' She let her voice tail off, remembering. Then she jumped up, trying to recover her professional demeanour. 'So, let's see what we're dealing with, shall we?'

Thick dust lay on an old countertop; the window was smeared with grime. The last inhabitants might have had spiritual yogic peace, but their housekeeping left a little to be desired. Shelves had been left, which would be completely useless to the new enterprise, while more useful things—a sink upstairs, plenty of plug points—were completely missing.

Issy felt her heart beat faster. Was this crazy? The fireplace was lovely, so beautiful, but she couldn't put tables and chairs in front of it if it was lit. She was 100 per cent sure the fire officer wouldn't let her light it. That Austin chap had been definitive on the subject of not to cross a fire officer. It seemed to be up there with crossing a US immigration officer.

'There's plenty to do,' said Des jovially. 'But I know it's going to be fine.'

'Do you?' said Issy, taking snaps on her digital camera. What had seemed so easy to visualise before—a nice fresh paint on the walls; sparkling windows to let the light in; beautiful pastel cakes temptingly set out on cake stands—suddenly was a lot harder to see in this dusty, dingy space.

'And downstairs of course,' said Des.

Tentatively she followed Desmond down the narrow, rickety staircase illuminated by a bare bulb. There was a toilet halfway down, then at the bottom a huge space opening out, with clear venting and plenty of room for the industrial oven she now knew she'd need. There were standpipes for plumbing and a good spot for a desk for paperwork. One poky window at the back looked out onto the basement of the next building along; the light wasn't great, but it would have to do. It would get warm down here too, warm enough to heat the shop.

'Isn't it wonderful!' she exclaimed, turning to Des with her eyes shining.

Des squinted. It looked like a mucky old cellar to him, but who was he to judge? 'Yeah,' he said. 'Now, I just have a few things here for you to sign . . . You must be signing a lot of stuff.'

'Yes,' said Issy, who had come away with files full from the bank, and was waiting for her trading licence to come through. The shop already had permission for café usage; it was just getting it to be her café that would be the problem, although Austin had said if her application was successful he'd be happy to look over the paperwork.

When they stumbled back upstairs, the weak afternoon sun had come round to the front of the building and was sending a watery stream of yellow through smeared glass and motes of dust, and lighting up the fireplace. Yes, it was mucky, Issy thought, revived. Yes, it needed work doing. But she could do it. She would show Graeme, who would be so proud of her, and she would bring Gramps down on opening day—she wasn't quite sure how she'd manage that, but she'd figure something out—and she'd totally impress Helena and all their friends and bring a whole new clientele to the street and get written up in *Metro* and the *Evening Standard* as a hidden gem, and people would come and have coffee, and a delicious cake, and be perked up by the lovely little courtyard and the beautiful shop and . . .

Des spotted the woman's face dropping into reverie again.

'OK!' he said, slightly desperately. 'Shall we get on? Or I can leave you here if you like, it is yours now.'

Issy smiled. 'Oh no, I have lots to do and sort out. I'll leave with you.'

He smiled back at her happily.

'How many kilos of coffee are you planning through here anyway?' he asked casually as Issy got to grips with the locks.

'What?' said Issy.

Des grimaced. He'd expected her to at least be au fait with the most basic levels of coffee-shop jargon. The brief moment of hopefulness he'd felt at her excitement with the cellar evaporated. He was going to be showing this place again in three months.

'Never mind,' said Des, getting out his car keys.

'Well, you'll pop in for a cup when we're open, won't you?'

Des thought of his slashed bonus. 'Oh yes,' he said. 'If I can.'

Chapter Five

IT HAD NOT BEEN as easy to deal with the admin as Issy had hoped. It was, in fact, a big long chore of filling out the same details over and over again. She had hygiene courses to attend, buying trips to make and all of this before she had sorted out the fixtures and fittings. She had received quotes for the catering oven she wanted and it would have swallowed up her entire budget for everything. So she started looking at second-hand, but even that seemed perilously expensive. And the look she had envisaged for the shop—to include reclaimed-looking tables and chairs, in pale colours of cream and eau de nil—was proving pricey too. And she still hadn't heard from the bank. Why did everything take so long? She couldn't hire anyone till she had a business account, but it felt like they wanted to wait until she had a business before they would give her an account. It was very frustrating. And that was before you even got to the baking.

Helena knocked on the door. 'How are you doing?'

'Oh, Helena. I can't believe I've done this on a whim. I need help.' She looked imploringly at her friend.

'Well, don't look at me, I'm just off a twelve-hour shift,' said Helena. 'And apart from stocking your first-aid cupboard and teaching you the Heimlich manoeuvre again, I'm not sure what I can do for you.'

'No,' said Issy, sighing. 'And my mate Zac said he'd design the menus for me, but that's it.'

'Well, that's a start,' said Helena comfortingly. 'A first-aid box, a menu and some yummy cakes. The rest is just cleaning up.'

'I feel so alone,' said Issy, who was missing Graeme more than she could admit. The shock of going from seeing him every day to never seeing him at all was one thing. To have a reconciliation, and then to have it all snatched away again . . . that was hard to process.

Helena sat down.

'But you're going to have to get staff, aren't you? I mean, you're going to have to pay people sooner or later. Maybe if you recruit someone now they could help you with all this stuff as well as the shop when it's open. Do you know anyone?'

Issy thought suddenly of the bright, cheery woman she'd met on the redundancy course. 'You know,' she said, scrolling down her phone where she and Pearl had politely swapped numbers, never really expecting to use them, 'there might just be something in this networking thing after all. I think she's got catering experience.'

She started to push the number as Helena held up her hand.

'Aren't you forgetting something?'

Issy glanced nervously at the piles of forms.

'Shouldn't you wait for the bank to give you the go-ahead—and the overdraft facility?'

Suddenly, Issy felt she couldn't wait until morning. She had been filling in forms and talking to government inspectors for three days; she needed to know. The bank was being horribly slow. She took out the card of Mr Austin Tyler and dialled the mobile number. OK, so it was after seven, but bankers worked late hours, didn't they?

Austin was considering letting Darny go without washing his hair for the ninth night in a row when his phone rang. He retrieved it, granting Darny a temporary victory as he stood up in the bath and started parading up and down it like a soldier, kicking bubbles as he went.

'Hello?'

Issy heard a strangulated yell from Darny as Austin attempted to make him sit down again. 'Sorry, is this a bad time?'

'Um, just in the bath.'

'Oh, sorry . . .'

'No, not me . . . Darny!'

'*Soldiers do not sit down to your authority!*' came clearly over the earpiece.

'Ah. You're bathing a soldier,' said Issy kindly. She hadn't thought the child would be so old; Austin seemed about her age. Which wasn't, she reminded herself, that young any more. 'Well, that *is* an important duty.'

'Darny, *sit down*! . . . Sorry about this, but who is it?'

'Oh, sorry,' said Issy, embarrassed. 'It's Isabel Randall. From the Cupcake Café.'

She could hear Austin struggle to remember her. It was excruciating.

'Oh yes,' he said finally. 'Uh. Yes. How can I help you?'

'This is clearly a bad time, I'm so sorry,' said Issy.

Normally Austin would have liked to point out sarcastically that yes, 7.30 on a school night was quite a bad time for all sorts of business enquiries, but there was something in Issy's voice—she was, he could tell, genuinely sorry; she wasn't just being polite but still trying to demand his attention. He groped around for his glasses, which were steamed up.

'OK, soldier, at ease,' he said to Darny, handing the boy a camouflage-coloured sponge and escaping out of the bathroom.

'Right, what's up?' he said to Issy as cheerfully as he could manage.

'Have you got lots of kids?' said Issy, genuinely curious.

'Oh no,' said Austin. 'Uh, Darny's my little brother. My . . . uh, well, we lost our parents, and there's a big age gap, so, um, it's just me looking after him. Boys together, you know! We get along pretty well.'

Issy immediately wished she hadn't asked. Austin sounded jaunty enough rolling off his spiel but, of course, she couldn't begin to contemplate the depths of agony beneath the words.

'Sorry,' said Issy. 'I didn't mean to pry.'

'Not at all,' said Austin. 'Perfectly normal question. Sorry the answer is a bit odd. I used just to say yes, he was my little boy . . .'

Austin didn't know why he was telling her this. It was strange, but there was something warm and friendly about her tone.

'But then I'd get lots of people saying he was so like me, and where was his mum and so on, so it just got more complicated in the end.'

'Maybe you should print it on your business cards,' said Issy, then bit her tongue in case that was in bad taste.

'Oh, I should,' said Austin, smiling. 'Definitely. Austin Tyler, dad-stroke-brother. Stroke animal wrangler.'

Issy found herself smiling down the phone. 'I'm sure the bank would be fine with that.' There was a silence.

'So, anyway,' she said, getting hold of herself, 'I know we have to wait for the official letter and everything, but I've got the keys now and I'm really anxious to start hiring staff and I'm sure it's totally confidential and you're not allowed to tell me so I'll have interrupted your bath time for nothing, so . . .'

'Are you going to apologise again?' said Austin, amused.

'Uh . . . well, yes, I was.'

'Come on! What kind of a hard-headed businesswoman are you?'

Issy smiled. For a banker, he was almost flirtatious.

'OK,' she said. 'Could you possibly give me a heads-up as to whether the bank is going to take my account?'

Of course, he knew he wasn't supposed to and it wasn't officially rubber-stamped yet. But she'd caught him at a vulnerable moment, and he could already hear a lot of noise coming from the other side of the door. And he could never resist a nice-sounding girl.

'Well,' he said. 'I'm absolutely not supposed to tell you this. But seeing as you asked very nicely, I can say that yes, I have recommended that we open an account for your business with our business.'

Issy jumped up and down and clapped her hands.

'The board just have to take my recommendation.'

Issy calmed down. 'Oh. Will they do that?'

'Do you doubt me?'

She smiled down the phone. 'No.'

'Good. Congratulations, Miss Randall. It appears you're in business.'

Issy hung up after thanking Austin a million times, and danced around the room, emboldened once more. Austin hung up and looked slightly quizzically at the phone. Was he imagining things, or had he just quite enjoyed taking a business call? That wasn't like him at all.

Pearl was sitting under the blankets with Louis. It was freezing outside. Their last combined electricity/gas bill had been absolutely dreadful, so they were huddling together in front of a plug-in fire. Louis had a temperature. He was mildly asthmatic and seemed prey to absolutely every bug that came along. In cheerier moments she suspected it was because he hugged everyone and caught whatever they had. At other times she wondered, deep down, if he ate enough of the right foods, was outdoors in enough fresh air and greenery to build the proper immunities, or if he just spent too long inside, breathing stale air. She'd told her mum not to smoke indoors, and she did her best, but when it was as cold as today, it felt cruel to make her stand on the stoop, exposed to the passing gangs of teenage boys who would shout and holler at anyone standing alone and looking even remotely vulnerable.

Her phone rang with a number she didn't recognise. Pulling Louis's sweaty brow to her and giving him a swift kiss, she answered it.

'Hello?' she said, as cheerily as she could manage.

'Uh, hello,' came a timid voice on the other end of the phone. 'I don't know if you remember me . . .'

'Patisserie Valerie!' said Pearl, pleased. 'Of course I remember you. And that course was so awful, did you go back?'

'I didn't,' said Issy, happy to hear Pearl so glad to hear from her. 'In fact, though, the course did work. Because it inspired me to go and do something quite different and actually network. So, uh, this is me. Networking.'

There was a long pause.

'Pearl,' said Issy, 'this may sound like a stupid question. It's just an on-the-off-chance kind of a thing. But I'm slightly up to my neck in it and I just wondered if you knew the answer to a question. Do you know how many kilos of coffee a coffee shop should be getting through in a week?'

Not only did Pearl know the answer to this but, having being trained by a major coffee chain as a barista (she'd had to give it up though; she couldn't find childcare to cover the antisocial hours), she knew how to tell whether coffee was overripe or burnt, what beans worked best at different times of day, how long you could store coffee and how, *and* she had her food hygiene certificate. The more she talked—and she could certainly talk—the more excited Issy became. They agreed to meet up the next day.

Issy was getting up just as Helena was coming in from night shift. 'Hey,' she said, noticing Issy grinding fresh beans for coffee. 'You're perking up!'

'Want one?' said Issy. 'I am go go go today.'

'No, thanks. I have enough problems sleeping off night shift as it is.'

'Well, try and catch up. I think I've found a man for your list.'

Helena raised her eyebrows.

'He's called Austin. He's got reddish-brown hair, works in a bank and—'

'Stop right there,' said Helena. 'Two gingers? It's a calamity waiting to happen.' She smiled at her flatmate. 'It's good to see you on form again.'

'I got the loan *and* I'm going to meet a potential member of staff.'

'Well, that is just great,' said Helena. 'Pretend you're always this upbeat.'

Issy kissed her and left the flat.

Across town, Pearl McGregor turned over in the bed. Something—someone—was kicking her. Hard.

'*Who* is that elephant in my bed?'

It wasn't really a bed, it was a mattress on the floor. She had a fold-out sofa for their little two-room flat—her mother had the bedroom—but it was just too uncomfortable so they'd got an old mattress and propped it up against the wall during the day. Pearl had tried to smarten it up by sewing a patchwork bedspread and some cushions. Louis was meant to sleep in with her mum, but he always gravitated towards her in the night and woke her up bright and early.

'Coco Pops, Mummy!' came a tiny voice from deep under the duvet.

'Who said that?' Pearl pretended to search the bed. 'I thought I heard a voice, but there can't be anyone in *my* bed.'

There were stifled giggles from down by her feet.

'Nope, no one is in *my* bed.'

Louis went silent till all she could hear was his excited breathing.

'OK, good. I will go back to sleep and forget about all those elephants.'

'*Noooo! Mummy!* Is me. Want Coco Pops!'

Louis flung himself into her arms and Pearl buried her face in his neck, sucking in the warm sleepy smell of him. There were a lot of drawbacks to single motherhood, but the alarm clock wasn't one of them.

With the curtains open (also one of Pearl's needlework creations), Louis propped up by the breakfast bar and her mother enjoying a cup of tea in bed, Pearl looked down at her notebook. It was today! She was going to see that scatty girl. Something about a coffee shop! She rushed to turn the shower on, just as Louis put his hands up round her neck.

'*Cuddles!*' he shouted joyously, as he launched himself at her again. Pearl hugged him back.

'You are *so* damn cute,' she said.

'*TV on*,' said Louis happily.

'No way,' said Pearl. '*We* have things to do today.'

It was a bright, frosty Friday morning when Pearl and Issy met outside the Cupcake Café. Pearl was holding Louis by the hand.

Louis was an exquisite-looking child: roly-poly and caramel-coloured, with wide, sparkling eyes and a ready grin. He sat down with two racing cars under the spindly tree.

Issy, having left the house in such a positive mood, suddenly felt a bit nervous; this was almost like a blind date. If this worked out, they would be spending eight, nine, ten hours a day together. Was it a huge mistake to be planning a business relationship with someone she'd only met once before? Or should she follow her gut instinct?

Her doubts, though, began to fade as she showed Pearl the shop, and took in her obvious excitement. Pearl could see what Issy saw in it; could envisage it finished. She even insisted on going down into the cellar. Why do you want to go down there? Issy had asked and Pearl had pointed out that before they agreed to do anything they might as well check that she could actually fit into the narrow stairway and Issy said of course she could, she wasn't that big, and Pearl had snorted good-naturedly.

The more Pearl saw, the more she liked it. It had character, this place. And Issy's pear cake had been frankly amazing; lighter than air and lingering. If the venue scrubbed up right—and here in north London, where there were enough people who didn't see anything wrong with paying over two pounds for a cup of coffee, she couldn't see why it wouldn't work—she'd love to work here. Issy seemed nice—a bit naïve in the ways of business, obviously, but everyone had to start somewhere—and a warm, cosy, scented café with friendly, hungry people and reasonable hours would be a lot nicer than most of the places she'd worked.

But there was one problem. She loved him to bits but he was, undeniably, a problem. 'What opening hours were you thinking of?' she asked.

'To begin with, seven thirty till four thirty?' said Issy.

'How many days a week?' said Pearl.

'Uh, I thought see how it goes. If it works well, I'd like it to be only five,' said Issy. 'But including Saturdays to begin with.'

'And how many staff are you going to have?'

Issy blinked. 'Uh, well, I was thinking maybe just us to begin with.'

'I mean, if one of us is sick or on holiday, or on a break, or . . .'

Issy felt a bit prickled. Pearl hadn't even started yet and already she was talking about time off.

'Well, yes, I thought we could work that out as we go.'

Pearl frowned. She was sad; this was by far the best, the most interesting opportunity that had come along for ages. It would be exciting trying to get a little fledgling business off the ground; she could almost certainly make herself useful here and there was nothing involved in the job that she hadn't done before. Louis was running up to the cellar steps, checking the dark depths with delighted terror and hopping back to his mother.

Issy was looking at her, troubled. When she'd thought of Pearl it had seemed like the answer to all her problems. But here was the woman now, not jumping at what Issy had assumed would be a fantastic opportunity for her. She swallowed hard. Pearl didn't even have a job. Why was she quibbling about this one?

'I . . . I'm so sorry, Issy,' said Pearl. 'I don't think I can.'

'Why not?' said Issy, sounding emotional without meaning to.

Pearl indicated Louis, who was trying to catch dust motes between his fingers. 'I can't leave him alone with my mother every single morning. It's not fair on her or me or Louis. We live in Lewisham, it's a long way away.'

'Oh,' Issy said. She glanced at Louis, who was making tracks in the dust with his cars. 'Oh, but couldn't you bring him in? He's no trouble. Just a couple of days a week or something?'

Pearl's heart leapt. Around here—playing safely out in the courtyard . . . warm and safe and not in front of the TV . . . Well, no. It was stupid.

'I think health and safety might have something to say about that,' she said, smiling to show Issy how sorry she was.

'No, but . . . we wouldn't tell them!' said Issy.

'Do you think that's the way to start a business?' said Pearl. 'Lying to health and safety? And don't even get me started on—'

'Fire officers. Yes, so I heard,' said Issy. 'Terrifying hell fiends.' She glanced at the shop. 'I mean, the ovens will be downstairs . . . more out of the way. I've decided just to keep the coffee machine up here.'

'With superheated steam,' said Pearl sweetly.

Issy smiled. 'Oh, Pearl, I could really do with you.'

At that moment there was a commotion outside the shop. Two men in dirty overalls had wandered up and were finishing off cigarettes and giving them enquiring glances.

'Oh shit, the builders are early,' said Issy. She was quite nervous about this; she had no room in her budget to employ an architect or bring in a professional shopfitter, so she had to trust that she could explain what she wanted sufficiently clearly. She hadn't been entirely convinced of her ability to do so when she'd called a firm in a whirl of positive activity the day before. Pearl raised her eyebrows.

'Don't go,' pleaded Issy. 'Let's have another chat anyway, afterwards.'

Pearl folded her arms and stood back as Issy opened the door to the builders. She caught them eyeing her up in a not entirely encouraging way as they introduced themselves as Phil and Andreas. Phil did most of the talking as Issy took them through, trying to explain what she was after—all the old shelving units stripped out, the whole place rewired, the counter moved and opened up, fridges and display cabinets put in, but not to touch the windows or the fireplace; shelving and a storage fridge for downstairs too. As she listed it, it seemed like an awful lot. It was a lot of money to put into something before it had even opened.

Phil looked around and sucked his teeth.

'Hmm,' he said. 'They're a nightmare, these old buildings. Ain't it listed?'

'No!' said Issy, delighted to be asked a question she could actually answer. 'Well, I mean, yes, the outside is, grade II, but the interior is all right as long as we don't pull down any walls or put anything up or brick up the fireplace, as if we would.'

'Well, your problem here is we'll have to thread the wiring through the walls, then there'll be a lot of replastering to do, and that's before you even look at the flooring.'

'What's wrong with the flooring?' There were simple wooden boards on the floor, and Issy had been planning just to clean them up.

'Nah, you can't do that, see,' said Phil. Issy didn't see at all. She started to feel embarrassed and uncomfortable.

Phil was proposing something complicated about lifting the skirting and putting in heating and wiring underneath then basically rebuilding the walls from the bottom up. Issy was looking at him helplessly, feeling out of her depth and nodding slightly. Phil took out a camera and a notepad and started to jot down measurements, until Pearl, standing in the shadows, couldn't take it for one more single second.

'Excuse me,' she said. Everyone turned to look at her quizzically. 'You're a good builder, right?' she said to Phil, who looked slightly wounded.

'I can do anything,' he said proudly. 'Jack of all trades, me.'

'That's great,' said Pearl. 'We're glad to have you aboard. But I'm afraid we can only pay you for the work that Miss Randall mentioned before. No floorboards, no skirting, no plastering. Just get the units in, get this place squared up—you know what I mean—and you'll get paid straight away, no messing. Do one iota more of stuff you aren't asked for, or overcharge us—and you're the fifth quote we've had in—and I'm sorry, but there simply won't be the money to pay you. Do you know what I mean?'

Pearl fixed Phil with a beady eye. He smiled nervously, then cleared his throat. 'Absolutely. Totally. Not a problem.'

He turned back to Issy, who was speechless but happy.

'We'll sort this place out for you, love.'

You were brilliant,' said Issy, as they headed up towards the bus-stop, each with one of Louis's hands in theirs. He was swinging as he went, insisting on more with a count of '*One-two-free!*'

'Don't be daft,' said Pearl. 'You've just got to ask for what you want, he wasn't going to bite you. He's in a selling job too.'

'I know,' said Issy. 'The time for being timid really isn't now, is it?'

'Not if you want to make it,' said Pearl thoughtfully. Issy looked back at the building. She'd just agreed to put a sizeable chunk of all the money she'd ever had in her entire life, and possibly more money than she'd ever see again, into this thing. Pearl was right. She was beginning to suspect that Pearl might be right about a lot of things.

They reached the bus-stop. Issy turned to Pearl.

'OK,' she said. 'I am going to ask for what I want. I want you to come and work for me. We'll figure Louis out between us. He'll be going to nursery soon anyway, won't he?'

Pearl nodded.

'Well, couldn't he go to a nursery near the shop? There's loads in Stokey. Come up and sit in the shop while we get opened up and the cakes go in, then pop him up to nursery and come back. He won't be far, and you can spend your lunch hour with him. What do you reckon?'

'Hmm,' said Pearl. There was a long pause. 'Well, let's give it a shot.' And the two women very formally shook hands.

Over the following weeks, Phil and Andreas did a lovely job. Several days of hands-and-knees scrubbing by Issy and Pearl, aided occasionally by a grumbling Helena, had sorted out the cellar, while the builders had hammered and drilled and sung along to Cheryl Cole songs on the radio and utterly transformed the place. Whereas before a bare bulb had swung from the ceiling, now there were gently inset halogen lights that made everything gleam softly. Tables and chairs in off-white shades had a gentle patina that made them look old (even though, as they had assured the crusty fire officer, they weren't, and they were painted with flame-retardant paint); the wooden floor was polished to a high shine, and the display cases were of sparkling glass to show off the cakes, with cake stands ready to go on each table. The coffee machine, a second-hand Rancilio Classe 6, which everyone assured them was absolutely the best on the market, fizzed happily away in a corner. (Alas, it was a curious shade of orange, but not everything had to tastefully match.) Issy had lined the mantel over the fireplace with books for people to read and smart wooden poles would hold the day's newspapers.

The crockery they had bought in a huge job lot in the IKEA sale, a collection of duck egg, teal and eau de nil bowls, espresso cups and plates that were so cheap they could afford to lose a few here and there to small hands or sticky fingers; and downstairs in the storeroom were industrial bags of flour and huge catering tubs of butter, all ready for the mixer.

They decided to have a proper opening party, to test everything out and say thank you to everyone who'd helped so much so far.

Everywhere was spotless; inspected, ticked off, registered and ready for action. They were set to open at 7.30 the following morning; Issy hadn't scheduled any marketing or promotion just yet. This was to be a 'soft' launch, a quiet week or so for them to find their feet and get into the rhythm of how the café would work. Issy kept repeating this to herself so she wouldn't panic too much if nobody turned up at all.

The local state nursery, Little Teds, had found a place for Louis, which was amazing (Pearl had perhaps told a very small lie on the form vis-à-vis Louis's home address—4 Pear Tree Court—but needs must). The nursery didn't open till 8.30, so he would have to come and have his breakfast in the café. Issy hoped he'd be happy with a few wooden toys she'd stashed behind the counter to distract customers' children.

And tonight, she was having a proper little party, a celebration to say thank you to everyone: to Pearl, for teaching her how to make coffee (she was still slightly afraid of the hissing steam pipe, but was learning); to Phil and Andreas, who'd done such a sterling job in the end; Des the estate agent and Mr Barstow the landlord; Helena, who'd chivvied delivery men; Austin, who'd patiently explained profit margins, portion control, tax accounts and depreciation to her, then explained them again when her eyes had glazed over, then explained them one more time just to check; Mrs Prescott, a slightly scary-looking local woman who did accounts for small businesses and was clearly not someone to be trifled with. She and Austin had looked each other up and down with some understanding.

'What do you think?' Issy had asked Austin nervously afterwards.

'Terrified the life out of me,' said Austin.

'Good,' said Issy. 'What about Helena?' She indicated the rather magnificent redhead who was laying into the builders one last time.

'Very . . . stately,' said Austin politely, thinking that actually, with her cheeks all red from the ovens, and her soft black hair dishevelled and loosening itself from where it had been tied back, and her black-fringed eyes, and her apron tied round her shapely form, the one he liked looking at was Issy herself. His professional client, he reminded himself sharply.

Issy glanced around nervously. Spring had been such a long time in coming, but now colour was seeping back into the world and, on this late March evening, soft light was filtering through the plate-glass window, illuminating in shafts the gentle colours and restful tones of the café. Zac, her old friend and a freelance graphic designer, had painstakingly picked out 'The Cupcake Café' in white, swirly, lower-case letters on the grey-brown frontage and it looked beautiful; pretty, but still understated.

Sometimes, when she woke too early in the morning, Issy wondered if they weren't being a bit too understated. Then she remembered the look on people's faces when they ate the Bakewell tart her grandfather had taught her to make and bit her lip. Would good ingredients and free-range eggs and good coffee be enough? Would they cover their rent and the power bills? Would she ever make a living wage? Could she ever stop worrying?

She phoned the nursing home again. Were they ready?

At his desk at Kalinga Deniki, Graeme was puzzled. This wasn't really what he'd expected at all, but he hadn't heard once from Issy. Presumably her business hadn't failed yet. Or maybe it had, and she couldn't bear to break it to him. Well, she would, she would.

Anyway, he had to concentrate. Work was still down, and he needed a really big project to impress the bosses back in the Netherlands. Something cool and cutting edge that would attract high-net-worth buyers just like himself. He gazed at his map of London, bristling with pins to mark his current developments. His eye idly traced up from Farringdon to the Old Street roundabout, up through Islington and on to Albion Road, diverting into the tiny, barely legible Pear Tree Court. He could take a look at it.

Issy smoothed down her new dress, which had little sprigged flowers on it. What she'd started off feeling was terribly twee had suddenly come into vogue, and everyone was wearing floral prints with tight waists and little skirts sticking out. She felt slightly better knowing she was on trend, and after all, what was she doing but baking cupcakes? The florals felt right somehow, like their dainty little aprons and the faded Union Jack pillows, Scotchgarded to death of course, that she'd bought to go on the new grey sofa they'd put along the far end of the shop; the sofa was a lovely thing, as hardwearing as they came but as soft and old and homey-looking as a sofa could be. Issy was delighted with it.

So that was the back wall, with the sofa underneath a large station clock. On the right was the fireplace, with books above, and then several small tables for two, with mismatched pale grey chairs set at companionable angles. The tables themselves were square. The room opened up as you walked towards the counter—obviously once it had been two rooms and the outline of the dividing wall remained. Near the counter the tables weren't so close together, so you could get a buggy in and people could (hopefully) queue, although it was still quite cramped. Cosy, that's what she meant, cosy. There was one long table near that room's fireplace, for larger groups, with a large, faded pink armchair at its head.

The counter was curved, shining and spotless, with a polished marble top and cake trays stacked high, ready to be filled the following morning. The small-paned windows on this side of the shop were balanced out by the huge floor-to-ceiling windows of the sofa section, which meant that when it got sunny, they'd be flooded with light. The coffee machine behind the counter, next to the door to the cellar, bubbled and hissed rather erratically, and the smell of fresh cakes filled the air.

Issy moved through the shop, saying hello to everyone. Austin's secretary Janet was there too. 'I never get to really see what the bank is doing,' she confided to Issy. 'It's so lovely to see something real happening.'

'Thank you,' said Issy, genuinely gratified, and went on filling people's glasses, keeping an eye on the door. Sure enough, at six o'clock, when the last rays of sun were hitting the close, a car backed up, illegally, into the close and a wheelchair-friendly door pinged open at the back. Keavie jumped down from the front seat to attend to it and out came Grampa Joe.

Issy and Helena rushed to open the door, but Gramps indicated that he didn't want to come in just yet. Instead, he halted the chair in front of the shop. Issy worried about the cold getting to his chest, then watched Keavie tuck him in with a warm tartan blanket that had obviously been ready in the car. He stared at the shop frontage for a long time, his blue eyes turning a little watery in the cold. Well, Issy thought it was the cold.

'What do you think, Gramps?' she said, going out and kneeling down to take his hand. He stared at the delicately painted frontage; in at the softly lit, cosy-looking interior, where you could see the counter with beautiful, ornate cake stands loaded with delicacies and the coffee machine steaming happily; up at the old-fashioned script above the door. He turned his face to his granddaughter.

'It's . . . it's . . . I wish your grandmother were here to see it.'

Issy grabbed his hand tight. 'Come in and have a cake.'

'I would love to,' he said. 'And send some nice ladies to talk to me. Keavie's all right, but she's a bit plump.'

'Oi!' shouted Keavie, not in the least bit insulted, and already with a cupcake in her hand and a steaming latte.

'Of course, I'm waiting for you, my dear,' he said to Helena, who had bestowed a kiss on his cheek as he was wheeled inside. Issy put his chair next to the gas fire that looked real in the original tiled fireplace.

'Well, well, well,' said Gramps, gazing around him. 'Well, well, well. Issy, this French cake needs a pinch of salt.'

Issy stared at him in affectionate irritation.

'*I know!* We forgot to get salt in this morning. Why aren't you working here? There's nothing wrong with you.'

Austin glanced around for Darny to make sure he wasn't creating mischief somewhere. To his surprise, he found his brother sitting outside with a fat little two-year-old, teaching him how to toss stones. The two-year-old, unsurprisingly, was terrible at it, but seemed to be having a great time.

There was just one important last piece of the puzzle, hot off the press, that they were still waiting for. Work had picked up, so he was running a little late with it, but any moment now he would—

Zac burst through the door with two large boxes in his hands.

'They're here!'

There was a flurry as everyone bustled to look. Issy tore through the plastic wrappings. From out of the fresh, sharp, inky-scented box, slowly, reverently, Issy withdrew her first menu. It was in the same soft pastels, with eau de nil and white predominating, as the exterior. Zac had designed an exquisite tracery of pear-tree blossom running up one side. The menu was made of stiff card—easily replaceable, easily changeable, without having that horrid shiny plastic laminate to wipe off spills. The lettering looked hand-printed and friendly, and was easy to read.

Issy looked at Zac, eyes brimming. 'Thank you so much.'

'Don't be stupid,' he said. 'You've done all this. It's helped me loads, anyway. I've used it as a calling card and got more commissions already.'

And then Helena proposed a toast to the Cupcake Café and everyone clinked glasses and Issy made a speech in which she said she would try to pay back the bank first (Austin raised his glass at that) before they had a proper celebration, but she thanked everyone for coming now, and everyone applauded. Gramps was deep in conversation with various people, until Keavie took him back to the nursing home.

Issy glanced outside. There was a shadow at the opening of the close. It looked like . . . no, it couldn't be. Her eyesight was playing tricks under the street lights. It was just someone passing who looked a little like Graeme, that was all.

Graeme was surprised to see the shop full of people—it must be, he realised, a party, and was amazed at how stung he felt, that Issy would have a party and not invite him. And he was amazed again at how finished and professional the café looked. It was pretty and inviting, with its warm pools of light projecting out over the cobbles of the courtyard. He glanced around at the other buildings; it was hard to tell if they were occupied.

Suddenly, from inside the café, a peal of laughter rang out. He recognised it at once as Issy's and felt his fists tighten in his pockets. She had no right to sound so happy and carefree. Why hadn't she listened to him? This was sure to be a failure. How dare she not come back to ask him what he thought? He stared up at the bricks of Pear Tree Court. Then he turned on his heels and walked back to his sports car.

Chapter Six

'ONE-TWO-FREE!' shouted Louis. And, ceremoniously, Issy turned the quaint 'Open/Closed' sign to 'Open'. Zac had made that too; he'd thought of everything. She had a stack of his business cards by the till in case anyone asked her who'd done her wonderful graphic design.

Pearl and Issy looked at each other.

'Here goes nothing,' said Pearl, and they took their places, expectantly, behind the counter. The entire place was spick and span, the day's produce lined up in the shining display cases, piled high on the stands. The air was scented with coffee and vanilla. The sun was starting a slow spring creep round the huge plate-glass window where it would illuminate each table in turn, starting with the big sofa on the end.

Issy couldn't keep still. She kept checking her oven, her storage shelves: the huge bags of flour all lined up so neatly, with the boxes of baking soda; baking powder, sugar, then row upon row of flavourings; fresh lemons in a box and the massive fridge filled with cream and big pots of creamy English butter—only the best. Issy's store cupboard made her feel secure and orderly. It gave her a huge sense of satisfaction just to look at everything.

'Are you always like this or are you making a special effort?' said Pearl. Issy was bouncing on the spot on her toes.

'A bit of both?' said Issy, cautiously. Sometimes she wasn't quite sure how to take her member of staff.

At 7.45 a labourer put his head round the door.

'Do you do teas?'

Pearl smiled. 'We certainly do! And our cakes are half-price all week.'

The labourer came in cautiously, wiping his feet ostentatiously on the new Union Jack doormat Issy had bought.

'This is a bit posh, innit?' he said. 'How much is the tea then?'

'One pound forty,' said Pearl.

The labourer bit his lip. 'Yeah?' he said. 'Wow.'

'We've got all sorts,' added Issy helpfully. 'And you're welcome to try a few cake samples.'

The labourer patted his belly regretfully. 'Nah, the missus will kill me.'

Pearl made the tea—she had noticed that Issy was over excited and liable to spill things—and without asking added milk and two sugars and handed it over with a smile, sealing the top of the paper container and adding a holder; it was very hot.

'Ta, love,' said the man.

'You sure you don't want to try some cake?' said Issy, a tad over-eagerly. The labourer glanced around awkwardly.

'It's all right, I'm sweet enough, love.' He laughed nervously, then paid and retreated. Pearl rang up the till triumphantly.

'Our first customer!' she announced.

Issy smiled. 'I think I scared him off though.' She looked thoughtful. 'What if he's right? What if we are too posh for round here?'

'Well, I'm not,' said Pearl, wiping up a tiny drop of spilt milk. 'And nobody wants cake at seven thirty in the morning anyway.'

'I do,' said Issy. 'Everyone will. People eat muffins. Muffins are just an American way of saying, "I eat cake for breakfast."'

Pearl looked at her for a second. 'Well, that explains a lot.'

For the next hour, curious locals wandered by, wondering who was the latest person to take on the blighted site in Pear Tree Court. Some rudely walked up to the windows, pressed their noses against them, stared hard then wandered off again.

'Well, that's not very nice,' said Issy.

'Issy,' said Pearl, who'd had a hard enough morning getting up at a quarter to six, then settling Louis in his new nursery. 'It's not your house. They're not judging you.'

'How can you say that?' said Issy, glancing around the empty shop. 'It's my heart and soul! They are totally judging me!'

At two minutes to nine, a dark little man with an old-fashioned hat pulled down over his forehead marched past the shopfront. Almost completely past, he stopped suddenly and turned forty-five degrees, staring straight in. He regarded them ominously for several moments, then turned and continued on. Seconds later they heard the rattle of metal shutters opening.

'It's the ironmonger!' hissed Issy excitedly. She'd tried to meet her new neighbour before, but the rickety little pots and pans shop that adjoined them to the right seemed to keep very odd hours and she'd never managed to catch anyone in before. 'I shall take him a cup of coffee and make friends with him.'

'I'd be wary,' said Pearl. 'You don't even know why those other businesses shut down. Maybe he poisoned them all.'

Issy stared at her. 'Well, maybe I'll give it a couple of days.'

At eleven, a tired, worn-down-looking woman came in with a tired, worn-down-looking child. Although both women fussed over the little girl, she didn't respond, mutely taking the proffered cake sample after shooting a look at her mother, who flapped a hand resignedly.

'May I have a small black coffee, please?' said the woman, who took it but turned down the cake samples (Issy was beginning to get paranoid) and counted out the change. She sat herself and the child on the grey sofa and sipped her coffee slowly as the child sat playing with her fingers, very, very quietly. With just the four of them in the space, Pearl and Issy soon found it difficult to talk normally.

'I'm going to put some music on,' said Issy. But when she put the new Corinne Bailey Rae disc in her old CD player, now officially donated to the Cupcake Café, and pressed play, the woman immediately got up and left, as if the music was going to cost her extra. She didn't say goodbye, or thank you, and neither did the little girl. Issy glanced at Pearl.

'This is day one,' said Pearl. 'And I'm telling you, I do not want to have to nanny you through this, OK? You are a hardheaded businesswoman and that is the end of it.'

But Pearl's encouragement got more hollow with every quiet day that passed. Feeling horribly weary, and with Pearl having her day off, Issy was in the shop doing accounts. She had two customers, which was better than none, she supposed. First of all the woman had come in again with the small child, which had slightly cheered Issy up; obviously she hadn't been so horrified she'd rushed away, never to darken their doors again. But once again the mother had retrieved her small cup of black coffee and perched herself in the corner of the sofa with her silent child. Issy had smiled nicely and asked her how she was, but the woman's answer, 'Fine,' with a slightly hunted expression, had put her off asking any further questions.

Issy had leafed through all the Saturday papers—she was becoming exceptionally well informed about the world—when the welcome sound of the little bell they'd installed above the door rang out prettily. She looked up and smiled in recognition.

'Hello, Des!' said Issy eagerly, before registering, one, that Des was probably going to expect a free cup of coffee (which she supposed, grudgingly, he did deserve), and secondly that he was carrying a baby who was screeching his head off.

'Well, hello, little . . .' She looked at Des for guidance.

'Boy . . . it's Jamie.'

'Oh, little Jamie. How sweet. Welcome!'

Jamie took in a great gulp of breath, filling his lungs. Des spotted the warning signs. 'Uh, can I have a latte, please.'

He got his wallet out firmly. He wasn't going to accept a free coffee; the noise pollution was already bad enough.

'And a cake,' prompted Issy.

'Uh, no . . .'

'You're having a cake,' said Issy, 'and that's the end of it.'

At that, the little girl at the end of the sofa raised her sad-looking face.

Issy smiled at her. 'Excuse me?' she shouted to the girl's mother, over the noise of Jamie's huge wail. 'Would your little girl like a cake? Free of charge, we're newly open.'

The woman looked up from her magazine, suspicious immediately.

'Um, no, it's all right, no, thank you,' she said, her Eastern European accent suddenly strongly marked; Issy hadn't noticed it before.

'It's OK!' hollered Issy. 'Just this once.'

The little girl, who was wearing a cheap and slightly grubby pink top that looked too thin for the weather, ran up to the counter, her eyes wide. The mother watched her, her eyes slightly less guarded, then held out her hands in a gesture of reluctant agreement.

'Which would you like?' said Issy, bending close to the little girl on the other side of the counter.

'Pink,' came the breathless voice. Issy put it on a plate and took it to her table ceremoniously while Des's coffee brewed.

By the time it was ready, he was marching the baby around the shop, constant movement apparently the only thing that kept him quiet.

'Don't worry about me,' he said to Issy's concerned look. 'I'll just take a bite every third circuit.'

After about the ninth rotation, the woman at the end of the sofa, who'd dipped her finger tentatively in the icing of her daughter's cupcake, eyed Des with sudden decisiveness.

'Excuse me,' she said. Des stopped in his tracks. Jamie immediately started up a yell like a plane taking off.

'Uh, yes?' he said, gulping a mouthful of coffee. 'Issy, that really is good,' he said out of the side of his mouth.

'Give me your baby,' said the woman.

Des glanced at Issy. The woman's face fell.

'I'm not bad lady. Give me your baby. I help him.'

A hideous un-PC silence hit the air until Des realised, with a sense of inevitability, that if he didn't hand over the baby he would look like he was accusing her of something shocking. Issy smiled encouragingly as he gave the screeching baby to the woman, whose little girl immediately scampered up on tiptoes to have a look.

Jamie, surprised to find himself in a stranger's arms, had momentarily fallen silent and was gazing at her with his great blue eyes. The woman gently kissed the top of his head.

'Maybe she's a witch,' hissed Des to Issy.

'Sssh!' Issy said. Jamie opened his mouth to prepare himself for another yell and calmly and confidently the woman flipped the baby over on to just one arm, until he was lying there on his tummy, his tiny arms and legs flopping towards the floor. He wriggled and squirmed there for a second, Des instinctively moving forwards—it looked like he would fall, balanced so precariously—and then the impossible happened. Jamie blinked his huge, glass-blue eyes once, twice, then somehow his tiny rosebud mouth found his thumb and he settled. Within seconds, and with all of them watching, his eyes grew heavy, heavier . . . and he was fast asleep.

Des shook his head.

'What . . . what . . . Have you just slipped him something?'

The woman fortunately didn't understand. 'He is very tired.' She looked at Des. 'You too are very tired,' she said, kindly.

Suddenly, and very uncharacteristically, Des thought he was about to burst into tears. 'I am . . . a *little* tired,' he said suddenly, slumping down next to her on the sofa.

'What did you do?' asked Issy, amazed. It had been like magic.

'Um . . .' said the woman, clearly searching for the English words. 'Hmm. Let me see. When little babies have sore tummies . . . then they like to lie like the tiger in the tree. It helps their tummies.'

And sure enough, Jamie did look like a sleepy cat drooping happily over a branch. Expertly, the woman transferred him to his pram on his tummy.

'Uh,' said Des, anxious to show that he did, at least, know the first thing about parenting, 'you're not meant to put them on their stomachs.'

The woman fixed him with a strict look. 'Babies with sore tummies sleep better on tummies. You watch him. He not die.'

The woman took the blanket and tucked him in tight so he could barely move. Des, used to watching Jamie wrestle and squirm in his sleep like he was fighting an invisible enemy, could only stare.

'I think I'll have another cup of coffee,' he said in a disbelieving tone.

Issy smiled at the memory. Of course in the end it had netted her about four quid, but Des and the woman, whose name turned out to be Mira, had talked and got along rather well, and for a while at least there was a little hum of conversation in the café; the sound she'd been longing to hear. Then the ironmonger from next door had come up and studied the menu in the window for ages—agonisingly long—before heading off again. Issy had called a hello but he hadn't answered.

She was starting to hate the slow beat of the clock. Two teenage girls had come in at lunchtime and carefully counted out enough for one chocolate and ginger cake between them and two glasses of water, but they'd gone by the time the door dinged at half past three. It was Helena.

'That bad, huh?' said Helena.

Issy was amazed to find herself slightly irritated. She was never normally irritated by Helena, they'd been friends for so long. But for her to turn up now, just as she was feeling her most unsuccessful, seemed almost cruel.

'Would you like an unsold cupcake?' said Issy, slightly more sharply than she'd intended.

'Yes,' said Helena, and took out her wallet.

'Put your wallet away,' said Issy. 'I have to throw them out at the end of the day anyway, for health and safety.'

Helena raised her eyebrows. 'I won't hear of it. I shouldn't be eating these anyway. Although I did go up another cup size, so there's a bonus.'

'A cupcake size!' said Issy. 'Ha-ha. I am, at least, still hilarious.'.

'Why don't you close up early, we'll go home and watch a film?'

'That is tempting,' said Issy regretfully. 'But I can't. We're open till four thirty today. And I have to cash up and go through my weekly accounts.'

'Well, that's not going to take long, is it?'

'Helena?'

'Too harsh?'

'Yes.'

'I'll buy the wine.'

'Fine.' Just then the bell dinged again.

Austin looked around the shop warily. He knew they were just starting out, but nonetheless it would have been nice to see a few people here, and Issy maybe moving her butt a bit to get things done rather than sitting up at the counter mooning with her girlfriend.

Darny was at jungle gym, and Austin had had one of those realisations he had with wearying predictability, when he got the horrible feeling he'd forgotten something important and had to struggle to remember what it was. Then he realised that he'd lost his copy of the shop rental agreement and if he didn't get it for the files Janet was going to have his guts for garters.

'Uh, hi there,' he said.

Issy jumped up guiltily. It would be nice if people involved with her business would come along when there were lots of people in. She wished that Helena wasn't there, it didn't look very professional. Especially with Helena nudging her and raising her eyebrows like Groucho Marx.

'Hello!' she said. 'Would you like a cake for Darny?'

'Giving away cakes?' said Austin with a twinkle in his eye. 'I'm sure that's not in the business plan.'

'You can't have read it right,' said Issy, suddenly feeling flustered. It was that grin of his. It was distractingly un-bank-like.

'That's right, I didn't,' agreed Austin. 'And now I'm on the hunt for a copy of the rental agreement. How's it going?'

'Well, this is our soft launch,' said Issy. 'You know, obviously, it's going to take a while to build up.'

'I have full confidence in the business plan,' he said swiftly.

'The one you haven't read,' said Issy.

Austin would have smiled more if he had actually read it, but he had totally followed his gut as he always did when lending. It usually worked in his favour. 'You know, I know someone who does a marketing workshop,' he said, and wrote the details down for Issy. She pored over them carefully and asked some questions; it felt like he was genuinely taking an interest. Well, protecting his investment, obviously, she realised.

'Thanks,' said Issy to Austin. It was odd to hear him talk so much sense when he was wearing his stripy jumper inside out. 'Your jumper's inside out.'

Austin glanced at it. 'Oh, yes, I know. Darny decided that all clothes should have their labels sticking out, that's how you know you're wearing the right clothes. And I couldn't seem to convince him logically otherwise, so I decided to just, you know, play along till he figures it out.'

'And how's he going to figure it out if you've got it all wrong?' asked Issy, smiling.

'That is a very good point,' said Austin, and he pulled off the sweater. Inadvertently he pulled up some of his forest-green shirt with it, exposing a trim tummy. Issy caught herself staring at it, then realised Helena was staring at her, muted mirth in her eyes. She felt her cheeks flushing a deep, horrifying red.

'I don't know,' said Austin, who hadn't stopped talking. 'I was just trying to get him to jungle gym on time. I assume the other kids will call him horrible names and make him cry till he eventually falls into line.'

He pulled his jumper back on properly and looked for Issy, but she'd disappeared downstairs.

'Uh, I'll get those papers you need!' she shouted up the stairwell. Helena gave him a knowing smile.

'Stay for coffee,' she said.

Issy threw cold water on her face from the catering sink downstairs. This was ridiculous. She had to pull herself together; she wasn't twelve.

'Here.' She reappeared, only mildly flushed. 'A cupcake for Darny. I insist. It's . . . what would your marketing people call it? A sample.'

'Giving samples to people who get a pound a week pocket money probably wouldn't pass a cost/benefit analysis,' said Austin, 'but thank you.' He took the cake and found his fingers holding on to it just a second too long, as if reluctant to give up the traces of her touch.

The Sunday train was absolutely packed with weekend travellers. Issy found a quiet corner seat with her book and half gazed at her tired-looking reflection in the window, thinking back over her visit to Grampa Joe.

'Well, you didn't half perk him up with that party,' Keavie had said when she arrived. 'He's been tired since though . . . distracted.'

'It's starting again, isn't it?' Issy had said, stricken. 'It's taking hold.'

Keavie touched Issy briefly on the arm.

'You know, this is why he's here, you know that,' she said.

Issy nodded. 'It's just . . . he's seemed so well.'

'He has his moments,' said Keavie. 'He's had a good few days actually, you might be lucky. And he always likes it when you visit.'

Issy rearranged her face by an effort of will and marched into the room.

'Hello, Gramps!' she said loudly. Joe half opened his eyes.

'Catherine!' he said. 'Margaret! Carmen! Issy!'

'Issy,' said Issy gratefully, wondering briefly who Carmen was. She gave him a hug, felt the whiskery skin that seemed to droop off his bones even more every time she came. 'How are you doing, Gramps?'

Joe leaned forward as far as he could towards Issy. The effort made his chest rattle. 'Sometimes,' he said, slowly. 'Sometimes I don't always get things right these days, my Issy.'

'I know, Grampa,' said Issy, clasping his hand.

He seemed to lose his train of thought and stared out of the window. Then he came back to himself. 'I . . . I was thinking, Issy, but sometimes I get things wrong, sometimes I just dream things . . .'

'Go on.'

'Have you . . . has my little Issy got a bakery?'

He said bakery like he might have said Kingdom of Gold.

'Yes, Grampa! You've seen it, remember? You came to a party there.'

The old man clasped her hand hard.

'And is it doing well? Is it making a living?'

'Hmm,' said Issy. 'Well, it's early days. I'm finding it . . . I'm finding it all a little tricky, to be honest.'

'That's because you're a businesswoman now, Issy. It's all on your shoulders . . . Do you have children?'

'No, Gramps. Not yet,' said Issy, a little sadly.

'So you only have to provide for yourself. Well, that's good.'

'Hmm,' said Issy. 'But I still have to get people through the door.'

'Well, that's easy,' said Joe. 'People just have to smell a bakery and they're there.'

'That's the problem,' mused Issy. 'They can't smell us. We're too far away, tucked away.'

'That is a problem,' said Joe. 'Well, are you taking your products to the people? Getting out on the street? Showing people what you have?'

'Not really,' said Issy. 'Mostly I'm busy in the kitchen. It would feel a bit . . . desperate, don't you think, to shove food at people in the street? I'm sure I wouldn't take anything people offered me in the street.'

Joe's face grew perturbed.

'Have you learned nothing from me?' he said. 'When I started it were 1938. Right before the war. There were real poor folks then, Issy, and if a woman had a babbie at home she could barely feed, or someone was a bit short or there were just too many mouths to feed—those Flahertys, I remember, they had a babbie a year and Patrick never could hold down a job. Well then, you'd slip them a bit extra. A loaf that didn't turn out true or a few buns a couple of days old. And word would get around. And sure, some folks turn up to see if they'll be getting something for nothing. But some folks just turn up because you do right by them. And I tell you, every single Flaherty child—and there were gone thirteen of them—every single Flaherty child, and their children when they all grew up and got jobs, and then their children came along and went to college and everything, and every single one of them got their bread from Randall's for their whole lives. I could have run that bakery off of Flahertys alone. And that's how it is in business. Some'll rob you blind, some'll kick you when you're down, but you spread some good feeling and some warmth about and people like that. Aye.'

Joe sat back, looking tired out.

'Gramps,' said Issy, leaning over and kissing him square on the nose. 'You're brilliant.'

The old man looked up with watery eyes. 'What is it now? Who are you? Is that you, Marian?'

'No, Gramps. It's me. It's Isabel.'

'Isabel? My wee lass Isabel?'

He peered closer.

'What are you doing these days, my sweet?'

'*One, two, free!*' Louis, hands carefully washed, was allowed to put the mini cupcakes into their special tin. There were considerably more than three, but that was as far as his counting went. Issy was in a whip of excitement that morning, making up free samples for everywhere she could think of.

'We're changing our whole strategy,' she said to Pearl.

'So instead of throwing our cupcakes away at the end of the day we're throwing them at people instead?' Pearl had said, but didn't want to rain on Issy's parade; a big surge of positivity couldn't be a bad thing this early in the game. Issy had called up Zac and he'd drawn her up a pretty flyer and she'd made copies at the all-night Liverpool Street Kall Kwik when she couldn't sleep with excitement at 5 a.m.

> *Meet me at the Cupcake Café!*
> *Busy day? Stressful time?*
> *Need five minutes of peace, quiet, and*
> *some heavenly cake and coffee?*
> *Then come on in and soothe your soul at*
> *4 Pear Tree Court, off Albion Road.*
> *Free cupcake and relaxation with every*
> *cup of coffee and this flyer.*

Then the menu was printed underneath.

'Now, make sure you hand these out to all the mums and teachers at the nursery,' said Issy.

'Uh, yeah,' said Pearl. The nursery hadn't turned out at all like she'd expected. Although it was nominally a government-run scheme for young disadvantaged children it wasn't, as she'd imagined, full of mothers like herself, struggling to get by and make a living, maybe on their own too. There were lots of yummy mummies, affluent women who all seemed to know each other and discussed interior decorators and hiring children's party entertainers at full volume across the room.

And Pearl couldn't help but notice that when the party invitations came round, or the play-dates, Louis—who played beautifully with whoever was there; who shared his toys and cuddled the playleader; Louis at whom the other women directed pleasant but non-specific smiles and truisms of 'Isn't he adorable?'—was never invited. Her gorgeous, beautiful, delightful son.

And Pearl knew it wasn't, as her younger self would have once loudly asserted, because of the colour of his skin. There were Chinese and Indian children; mixed race, African and every shade in between. No, it was her, Pearl knew. Her clothes, her weight, her style, her voice. Rubbing off on Louis, her perfect boy. And now she had to go and hand out Issy's sodding leaflets and her sodding free samples to all those immaculate women, just so she could confirm every single thing those women already thought about her. She stomped out rather crossly.

Issy had rather the easier task; she strolled down to her old bus-stop, a large tin tucked under her arm, the drizzle not dampening her buoyant mood. Off to the bus-stop. It felt almost like the old days.

Sure enough, the line-up of familiar faces was still there. And Linda, whose face was wreathed in smiles when she saw her.

'Hello, dear! Have you got a job?'

'Well,' said Issy, smiling, 'I have done something. I've opened a little café . . . just up there!'

Linda turned round, and Issy enjoyed her astonishment.

'Oh, how *lovely*,' Linda said. 'Do you do bacon sandwiches?'

'Nooo,' said Issy. 'We do coffee and cake.'

'Like your hobby?' said Linda.

Issy bit her lip. She didn't like her baking being referred to as a 'hobby', especially not now. 'Well, they do say follow your passion,' she said, smiling through gritted teeth. 'Here! Have a cake. And a flyer.'

'I will,' said Linda. 'Oh, Issy, I'm so pleased for you!'

Issy headed up the line, and as the bus arrived even the young man who never took his iPod out grabbed a cake and made a cheers at her. She popped her head inside the bus and offered a cake to the driver but he fiercely shook his head and Issy withdrew, slightly flattened.

Hobby my bum, she said crossly to herself. She returned slowly to the shop, just in time to see two schoolkids charging out, each clutching two cakes in grubby paws.

'Get out of it!' she screamed, relieved that she had locked the till.

The man from the ironmonger's walked past, looking at her strangely.

'Hello!' said Issy. He stopped.

'Hello,' he said. He had a slight accent Issy couldn't place.

'We're the new shop,' said Issy. 'Would you like a cake?'

He was dressed fastidiously: suit, a narrow tie, a topcoat, a scarf and even a homburg. The effect was very old-fashioned. She'd have expected him to be in brown overalls, if anything. He bowed his head over her cake tin and selected the most perfect of the cappuccino cakes.

'I'm Issy,' she offered when he'd made his choice.

'Delighted,' said the man, and headed on back towards his shop, which, as always, had the shutters tightly closed. Peculiar.

'I am undaunted,' vowed Issy, even as Pearl returned from dropping off Louis, uncharacteristically bowed. She still had more than half the cakes in the tin. 'Joshua isn't allowed sugar,' she reported, 'and Tabitha has food intolerances. And Olly's mother wanted to know that the flour was fair trade.'

'Everything's fair trade,' said Issy, exasperated.

'I told her that, but she said she was going to say no just to be on the safe side,' said Pearl dully.

'Never mind,' said Issy. 'We soldier on!'

The following morning Issy headed up to Stoke Newington High Street, aiming to leave flyers and free samples in every shop. This wasn't as easy as it sounded. Every little shop already had every spare centimetre of space taken up with flyers for yoga classes, baby gyms and massage, circus school, jazz concerts, tango lessons, home delivery organic vegetables, knitting circles, library events, local theatre shows and nature walks. The world seemed papered in flyers, thought Issy, and Zac's beautiful, elegant designs appeared suddenly limp and colourless going up against neon oranges and bright yellows. The people in the little shops seemed uninterested, although they accepted the cakes of course.

About a third of the way down the street an angry-looking woman in a tie-dye T-shirt with messy hair came storming up to her with a bumptious look on her face. 'What are you doing?' she demanded peremptorily.

'I'm handing out samples for my new café,' said Issy bravely, proffering the tin. 'Would you like one?'

The woman made a face. 'Full of refined sugar and trans-fats, designed to turn us into obese TV slaves? Not bloody likely.'

Issy had encountered lack of interest, but this was the first open hostility she'd faced over the café, she realised. 'OK, never mind,' she said.

'But you can't just go handing stuff out,' said the woman. 'There's other cafés on this street! We've been here a lot longer than you, so you just have to butt out of our way.'

Issy turned round, and at the doors of several coffee houses and tea shops people were standing and watching, their eyes hostile.

'And we're a co-operative,' said the woman. 'We all work together in partnership. Everything is wholesome and everything is fair trade. We're not poisoning children. And that's what the community wants around here. So you can just back off.'

Issy felt herself shaking with upset and rage. 'I think there's room for everyone,' she managed, her voice shaking.

'Well, there's not,' said the woman. 'We were here first. We're helping communities in Africa, you're not doing anyone the least bit of good. Nobody wants you. So just piss off, OK?'

Someone in a doorway muttered, 'Hear, hear,' loud enough so that Issy caught it. She stumbled off, half blinded with tears, conscious of the eyes of the other café owners on her back. Hardly knowing where she was going, just that she couldn't turn back through that crowd—feeling she could never ever walk that street again—she headed to the main road where she could lose herself in the mass of humanity, of all colours and types, where no one would notice a crying woman in a vintage floral dress.

Austin was fighting his way to the pound shop to see if they had something good for Darny to wear to a fancy-dress party—there seemed no point in buying anything pricey as Darny rarely came home without huge rents in filthy clothing. As he'd nearly made it across the road he saw Isabel Randall standing by the *Wait* sign but not crossing.

'Hello,' he said. Issy looked up at him, blinking back tears.

She couldn't help it, she was glad to see a friendly face. But she didn't trust herself to speak, in case she suddenly broke down.

'Hello,' Austin said again, worried she hadn't recognised him. Issy swallowed hard and reminded herself that crying in front of her bank manager was possibly the worst look imaginable.

'Hello,' she managed finally.

'Are you all right?' he said. Issy wished he didn't sound so kind. He was going to set her off again. Austin could see quite a lot of restraining going on. He put a hand on her shoulder. 'Would you like to get a coffee?'

He cursed the words as soon as they were out of his mouth. To Issy's credit she managed not to actually burst into tears, but one lone drop did trickle slowly and obviously all the way down her cheek.

'No, no, no, of course you wouldn't . . . of course not. Um.'

For want of anywhere better to go, they ended up in a horrible pub, full of morning drinkers. Issy ordered a green tea and Austin looked around nervously then ordered a Fanta.

'I'm sorry,' said Issy several times. But then, somehow—and she was sure she would regret this—she ended up telling him the whole thing. He was just so easy to talk to. Austin winced.

'And now I'm telling you,' concluded Issy, worried she was going to start crying again, 'you're going to think I'm totally too wimpy for business and you're going to think I'll fail, and you know, it might fail. If they all gang up on me . . . it'll be like the mafia, Austin! I'll have to pay protection money, and they'll come round and put a horse's head in my oven!'

'I think they're all vegetarians,' said Austin. He leaned forward. Issy was conscious, suddenly, of how long his eyelashes were. Having his face so close to hers suddenly felt strange and intimate.

'Look, I know those guys up there. They came to us on a campaign to make us do more ethical banking and we pointed out to them that banking isn't terribly ethical and that we couldn't absolutely promise that some of our investments weren't in the defence industry, seeing as it is, you know,

Britain's biggest industry. They screamed and called us all fascists and stormed out, and then called us back later and asked for a loan. And there were about sixteen of them too. Their business plan included the four-hour weekly meeting they have to make the co-operative fair. Apparently it frequently ends up in physical violence.'

Issy smiled weakly. Of course Austin was only trying to cheer her up—he would do this for anybody—but nonetheless it was definitely helping.

'And don't you worry a bit about "café solidarity". They all hate each other's guts on that street. Honestly, if one of the cafés burned down they'd be absolutely delighted. So don't think they're all going to gang up against you, they can't even manage to gang up to clean their own toilet, as I noticed when I had to take Darny in there one day in an emergency. Does dreadful things to the digestion, too much vegan food.'

Issy laughed.

'That's better.'

Issy really did feel better.

Suddenly and fiercely as he opened the door for her, Austin was shocked to find how much he wanted to . . . no, he mustn't think that way. Really, he just so wanted Issy to succeed. That was it. She was a nice person with a nice café, and he really wanted things to start going right for her. And the wash of inexplicable tenderness that had come over him, looking at that lone tear roll down her pink cheek—that was just simple fellow feeling. Of course it was.

For her part, Issy looked up into his handsome, kind face and found herself slightly wishing that they could stay in the world's grottiest, smelliest pub for a little longer.

'Don't be too nice, Issy. Not in business. Just assume everyone around you is as much of an arse as that woman was—and you know, if you are going to survive, Issy, you'll just have to toughen up.'

And Austin, even as he was saying the words, wondered if he meant them. Obviously Issy should toughen up—toughen up and fight for this business. But he wondered if she wasn't a better, sweeter person the way she was.

'I will,' said Issy, with a worried look on her face.

'Good,' said Austin, shaking her small hand gravely. She smiled, and squeezed his hand back. Suddenly, neither of them wanted to be the first to take their hand away.

Fortunately Issy's phone rang—it was the shop number—so she could, slightly flustered, move away first.

'Um,' she said. 'But is it OK if I go the other way back to the café? Just this once? I don't want them to start throwing things at me.'

'You don't,' said Austin. 'Their flapjacks are rock solid.'

Chapter Seven

Brandy and Horlicks Get-Well Cake

A good strong healing cake will make you feel better, like the time you were coming home from a terrible day at school and it was getting dark and you were cold in your blazer and you came round the end of your road and saw the light on in your house and Marian was still there and she gave you a cuddle and something to eat and everything was much better. This cake tastes like that. It should not be too heavy, so it works well for invalids. Please send me a batch, Issy dear, so I can get out of this place.

8 oz butter, softened
4 oz caster sugar
5 eggs
½ tin sweetened condensed milk
8 oz Horlicks
8 oz plain flour
½ tsp vanilla extract
2 tbsp cognac

Grease the small square tin and line the base and sides with baking paper. Allow the baking paper to extend over the top by about an inch.

Beat the butter and sugar until pale and fluffy. Beat in the eggs, one by one, until well combined. Beat in the condensed milk until well mixed. Stir in Horlicks. Fold in flour. Finally stir in vanilla and cognac.

Pour the batter into the prepared tin (the batter will fill the tin to almost 90 per cent, but the cake will not rise too much, so don't worry, darling). Cover the top loosely with a piece of aluminium foil.

Steam over high heat for 30 minutes. Fill up with more hot water if the steamer is low on water after 30 minutes. Turn heat down to medium and steam for another 60 minutes, or until cooked (may steam for up to four hours in total if desired—this, according to wisdom, allows the cake to be kept for up to a month). Remember to replenish steamer with hot water whenever it is drying up.

MRS PRESCOTT was having strong words with Issy that week on cash flow. It was mid-April, and the weak evening sun was filtering through the basement blinds. Issy was dead tired, and couldn't even remember where they kept the steamer. Her feet hurt from standing up all day serving a total of sixteen customers, and she'd let Pearl go early when she got a phone call from the nursery saying Louis was upset.

'It's those horrible kids,' she'd said. 'They're calling him names.'

Issy was shocked. She had noticed that Louis was lingering longer and longer over his morning muffin, sitting on the counter singing sad little songs to himself. He didn't fuss or throw tantrums, but his normal ebullience seemed to seep away the closer it got to nursery time.

'What kind of names?' Issy asked, surprised by how furious she was.

Pearl's voice started to choke. 'Fatty bum-bum.'

Issy bit her lip. 'Oh.'

'What?' said Pearl defensively. 'There's nothing wrong with him! He's perfect! He's a gorgeous, plump baby.'

'He'll be fine,' said Issy. 'He's just settling in. Nursery's a new world.'

But she'd let Pearl take the afternoon off anyway. It didn't matter that they didn't have many customers, or that many of their tables and chairs hardly got used; every day Pearl scrubbed out the toilets, made the tables shine and washed down the arms and legs of the chairs. The place gleamed like a new pin.

'The thing is,' said Mrs Prescott, 'you have to watch your stock levels. Look what's going out in ingredients. I know it's not really my place to comment on how you run your business, but you're making too much stock and as far as I can tell just throwing it away. Or giving it away.'

Issy looked down at her hands and mumbled, 'I know. The thing is, my grandfather . . . my grandfather says if you do, kind of, good turns, and send things out in the world, then it will come back to you.'

'Yes, well, it's very difficult to account for good deeds,' sniffed Mrs Prescott. 'It's quite hard to pay a mortgage from good deeds as well.'

Issy was still looking at her hands. 'My grandfather was successful.'

'These are harder times, maybe,' said Mrs Prescott. 'People's lives are faster, their memories are shorter, do you think?'

Issy shrugged. 'I don't know. I just want to run a good place, a nice place, that's all.'

Mrs Prescott raised her eyebrows and didn't say any more. She made a mental note to start looking for another client.

Pearl had got home that night upset enough before she saw him, sitting casually on her step as if he'd merely forgotten his key. She felt, suddenly, Louis's little paw start to tremble in her hand with excitement. She knew that half of him wanted to run up to the man in glee, but he knew already that this would not please his mother.

Pearl swallowed hard. He was, she thought, still such a handsome man. Louis got his sweet smile from her, but the rest of his beautiful face came from his dad.

'Hey there,' said Ben, as if he hadn't been completely off radar for the last five months and missed Christmas.

Pearl gave him one of her looks. Louis was clutching tight to her hand.

'Hey, little man!' said Ben. 'Look how big you're getting!'

'He's big-boned,' said Pearl reflexively.

'He's gorgeous,' said Ben. 'Come say hi to your dad, Lou.'

What could Pearl do except invite him in for a cup of tea? Her mother was on the sofa, watching the early-evening soaps. When she caught sight of Benjamin she simply raised her eyebrows and didn't bother to greet him. Ben had said, 'Hello, Mrs McGregor,' in a slightly over-the-top fashion, but didn't look too surprised when he didn't receive a reply. Instead, he knelt down next to Louis, who was still struck completely dumb, and reached into his pocket.

Pearl switched on the kettle in the little strip of kitchen in the corner of the room, watching the pair closely. She had a speech prepared for Mr Benjamin Hunter for the next time she saw him. She had thought it over in her head and she had a lot to say—as did her friends—about his messing about, sending her not a penny for Louis, even when he was working. And he had a good job too. She was going to give him a proper lecture about his responsibilities, to her, and to his boy, and tell him to grow the hell up, or stop bothering Louis.

Then she caught sight of Louis's eyes, wide open in amazement and adoration, as his dad brought out of his pocket a bouncy ball.

'Watch this,' said Ben, and he bounced it hard off the cheap linoleum. The ball bounced up, hit the low ceiling, came whooshing back down again and did this twice more. Louis erupted in a screaming giggle.

'*Do again, Daddy! Do again!*'

Ben duly obliged, and within five minutes the ball was bouncing all over the tiny flat and Louis and Ben were rolling and tumbling after it, getting in the way of Pearl's mother's programmes and killing themselves laughing. Finally, they sat up, panting. Pearl was frying sausages.

'Do you have enough of those for a hungry man?' said Ben. He tickled Louis's tummy. 'Do you want your daddy to stay for tea, young man?'

'*Yes! Yes!*' hollered Louis. Pearl's brow darkened.

'Louis, go and sit with your grandma. Ben, I want a word. Outside.'

Ben followed her out, lighting a cigarette as he went. Great, thought Pearl. Another brilliant role model for Louis.

They stood by the wall of the alleyway, Pearl avoiding the eyes of neighbours coming to and fro who could clearly see them both there.

'You're looking well,' said Ben.

'*Stop it,*' said Pearl. 'Stop it. You can't . . . you can't just walk in here after five months and pretend nothing has happened. You *can't*, Ben.'

She had lots more to say, but, strong as she was, Pearl could feel the words choking in her throat. Ben, however, let her finish—that wasn't like him. Normally he was defensive, full of excuses.

Pearl pulled herself together, with some effort.

'It's not even about me,' she said. 'I'm over it, Ben. I'm doing just fine. But for him . . . can't you see how awful it is? Seeing you and getting all excited, then not seeing you again for ages? He doesn't understand, Ben. He thinks it's his fault that you leave, that he's not good enough.'

She paused, then spoke quietly. 'He is good enough, Ben. He's wonderful. You're missing it all.'

Ben sighed. 'You know, I just . . . didn't want to be tied down.'

'Well, you should have thought of that before.'

'Well, so should you,' said Ben, with some justification, Pearl knew. He was just so handsome, so nice . . . She'd let herself be carried away. She couldn't blame him for everything. On the other hand, that didn't mean he could just zip in and out whenever he wanted.

'I mean, I figure some of me is better than nothing, right?'

'I'm not sure,' said Pearl. 'Some of you on regular days . . . when he knows you're coming . . . yes, that would be a wonderful thing for him.'

Ben scowled. 'Well, I can't always plan ahead that far.'

Why not? thought Pearl mutinously. She had to.

Ben finished his cigarette and crushed it out on the big wheelie bin.

'So can I come back in or not?'

Pearl weighed up the alternatives in her head. To deny Louis the chance to spend some precious quality time with his father . . . versus teaching Ben a lesson he would probably ignore anyway. She sighed.

'OK,' she said.

Ben headed in the door. Brushing past her, he brusquely handed her an envelope. There was cash inside. Pearl stayed outside a second or two longer in amazement, clutching the envelope and listening to Louis doing tiger-roaring inside, till the sausages started to burn.

Pearl and Issy felt the *crumping* sound as well as heard it; it was extremely loud and startling in the quiet Saturday morning air. A large, twisted metal noise, punctuated with shattering glass, then sudden screams, and car alarms, and horns beeping and tooting furiously.

Along with their two customers, they charged outside to the entrance to Pear Tree Court.

'Oh no,' said Issy, stopping dead in her tracks.

Pearl was grateful Louis was home with her mother and felt her hand fly to her mouth.

Strewn right across the road, the bulk of the number 73—the huge, elongated, unloved bendy bus—lay smashed and on its side. It blocked the road completely; the smell of wrecked machinery was horrifying; smoke rose from the undercarriage, a mass of exposed metal and piping.

A cab with its roof bashed in had come to a stop, skewed at a crazy angle across a reservation. Behind it could just be glimpsed a dirty white Ford Escort that had ploughed straight into the back of it. And most ominously of all, several metres in front of the top-right corner, was a twisted, bent bicycle.

Issy felt sick, her heart pounding in her chest. She rummaged in the pocket of her apron for her mobile phone and glanced, light-headed, at Pearl, who had already found hers and was prodding 999 into the handset.

People were already running from shops, from the bus-stops, from houses, to help. Issy picked up her phone again.

'Helena,' she gasped into it. She knew her flatmate had a day off—a precious day off—but she was two streets away.

'Hmm?' said Helena, obviously still half asleep. But within two seconds she was wide awake and pulling on her clothes.

At one end of the bus, people were hammering on the window; it didn't seem to be breaking. With the smoke seeping out of the pipework, Issy wondered—everyone wondered—if the engine was going to explode. In the middle of the bus, a tall man was desperately trying to open the doors from the inside, above his head. One of the men from the coffee shop was already clambering up the side of the bus—what had been the roof, but was now the side—and other people were anxiously shouting guidance to him. From inside the bus Issy could hear screaming; the driver looked unconscious.

There was a scream from a woman halfway down the road. A young man—obviously a cycle courier, in skintight lycra, now ripped, with a huge walkie-talkie still on his hip—was lying in the gutter, his arm at a very strange angle. Issy looked over her shoulder and was relieved to see Helena tearing down the road at full pelt.

'Over here!' she shouted, then ushered Helena through. 'She's a nurse! She's a nurse!' Helena ran to the boy as the sirens grew louder.

'I'm a medical student,' volunteered a young man standing watching on the kerb.

'Come with me then,' Helena said grimly.

Issy glanced around. Suddenly, she noticed a very calm, quiet figure. While everyone else was either stock still in shock or tearing about like a wild thing, the figure was approaching steadily from Pear Tree Court. It was the strange man from the ironmonger's. He was carrying an enormous metal box. It must have weighed a ton, but he hoisted it effortlessly.

Her eyes followed him as he headed towards the bus, knelt down by the windscreen away from the driver's side, opened his box and selected a heavy mallet. Indicating to the panicking passengers inside to stay well back, he hit the glass sharply three or four times until it shattered. He then carefully selected a pair of pliers and lifted out the large, dangerous shards from the black rubber rim of the window frame. Then and only then did he beckon the people inside to come forward; first a screaming baby, which he handed to the person nearest to him—Issy.

Two seconds later the baby's mother was out, her hands outstretched, the buggy twisted and discarded behind her.

'Here you are,' Issy said. The mother could barely articulate her distress.

'I thought she was . . . I thought we were . . .'

The baby, back in the familiar scent of her mother's arms, hiccuped and snuggled her damp face into the crook of her mother's neck, peering round to gaze at Issy with huge dark eyes.

'It's OK,' said Issy, patting the mother on the shoulder. 'It's OK.'

And as she could see other people clambering out behind her—some clutching their heads, some with rips in their clothing, all sharing a similar expression of shock and bemusement, Issy thought that it just might not be too bad . . . Nobody seemed to be horribly injured. Except for the cyclist—she glanced back, but all she could see was Helena bent low over him, gesticulating at the medical student.

The bus driver was still lying contorted across the huge steering wheel.

'Everyone, get away from the bus!' the ironmonger said loudly, in a tone that brooked no argument. The bystanders and rubberneckers were hanging about the pavement, watching; no one seemed to know what to do for the confused commuters with their cuts and bruises.

'Perhaps,' said the ironmonger to Issy, 'you might be able to make these people a hot drink. And I've heard sugar can be good for shock.'

'Of course!' said Issy, stunned that she hadn't thought of it herself.

By the time they started feeding tea and cake to the victims, five minutes later, the ambulances and fire engines had arrived; the police were ushering everyone away from the bus and had cordoned off the road. Everyone was absolutely delighted by the hot tea and buns Issy and Pearl had rounded up, and the bus driver, already beginning to stir, had been loaded into the ambulance.

Helena and the medical student, whose name was Ashok, had stabilised the cycle courier and been congratulated by the ambulance crew. The survivors of the crash were already sharing stories of where they'd been on their way to, and hadn't everyone always been sure that these bendy buses were going to cause trouble one day; the joy and luck that no one, it appeared, had been too seriously injured or killed made people quite voluble and everyone rounded on Issy to express their thanks. One or two people pointed out that they lived just round the corner and they hadn't even known she was there.

The photographer from the local paper turned up, and as well as taking pictures of the shattered bus from every angle (the ironmonger had disappeared as smoothly as he'd arrived; Issy hadn't even noticed him go), he also took a shot of her smiling with all the passengers. When the *Stoke Newington Gazette* came out the following week the headline to part of their crash coverage was LOCAL CAKES BEST MEDICINE and after that, things started to change quite a lot.

'**W**here's my little man Chunks?' asked Issy as Pearl turned up—a little late, but frankly she was so grateful to Pearl that she was going to overlook the small things. 'I miss him.'

Pearl smiled tightly and rushed in to grab the Hoover and mop so she could run round before they opened up.

'He just loves being with his grandma,' she said, realising as she did so what an idyllic cake-baking, duck-feeding picture that presented, rather than the cheerless, fuggy little flat. 'Anyway, let me just get round here quickly, the morning rush will be on soon.'

They smiled at each other, but it was true that since the accident there had been a steady stream of people—the ambulancemen, the bystanders, the mother with the lovely baby girl, and Ashok, who had popped in to ask for Helena's phone number, which made Issy's eyebrows rise so much he'd apologised instantly. Issy had taken his and passed it on, fully expecting Helena to drop it in the hospital incinerator.

The long bendy buses had been replaced with the original double-deckers, which held far fewer passengers. As a result a lot of people couldn't get on during rush hour and found themselves popping in for a coffee to pass the time; Issy had started serving croissants. Short of growing another pair of hands, she sadly admitted to herself, she had to buy them in; she'd sourced the most wonderful boulanger who delivered a mixed box of pains au chocolat, croissants and croissants aux amandes at 7 a.m. sharp every day; there was never a single one left by nine.

Then came the morning coffee; Mira, with little Elise, had managed to find herself some new friends among other mums, and they came often and chattered loudly in Romanian on the grey sofa, which was beginning to take on the soft, well-used sheen Issy had hoped for it. Some of the yummy mummies had started to make their way down from the nursery; if they recognised Pearl, she would smile briefly then busy herself (now not difficult) fetching organic lemonades and juices.

Lunchtime was a rush, then the afternoon was a little calmer, with office girls and women organising children's parties coming in to buy boxes of half a dozen or even a dozen cakes; Issy was considering putting a sign up to invite personalising and special orders. In between there were endless lattes, teas, raspberry specials, vanilla-iced blueberry cakes; signing for suppliers, invoices, post; cleaning up, wiping up spills, smiling at children and waving to regulars. By four, Issy and Pearl would be ready to lie down on one of the huge sacks of flour in the storeroom.

The Cupcake Café was afloat; it had launched, it was sailing, tipping slightly from side to side—but it was afloat; it felt to Issy as much a part of her as her left hand. It never went away; she sat poring over the books with Mrs Prescott late at night; she dreamed in buttercream and icing, thought in kilos and deliveries and sugar roses. Friends called and she begged off; Helena snorted and said it was like she was in the first grip of a romance.

And although she was tired—exhausted—from working all out six days a week; although she desperately wanted to go out and have a few drinks without thinking how much she would suffer for it the next day; although she would have liked to just sit and watch some TV without wondering about stock levels and expiry dates and disposable catering gloves, she shook her head in complete disbelief whenever she heard people mention the word 'holiday'. She was happier, she realised, deep down, than she'd been in years; happier every day, when she earned the rent money, then the utilities, then Pearl's salary, then, finally, finally, something of her own, from something she was turning over with her own two hands, made to cherish and make people feel good.

At 2 p.m. a large group of mothers entered, tentatively at first, many with huge three-wheeled buggies. The shop was so small, Issy would have liked to ask them to leave the buggies outside, but frankly she was a little frightened of these Stoke Newington women, who had perfectly highlighted hair and wore very tight jeans with high heels all the time. Issy sometimes thought it must be a little exhausting, having to look identical to all your friends. But she was delighted with their business.

She smiled a warm hello, but they glanced past her and their gazes alighted on Pearl, who looked semi-pleased to see them.

'Um, hi,' said Pearl to one of the mums, who glanced around.

'Now where's your *darling* little Louis?' she said. 'He's usually here somewhere! I'd think a cake shop was a perfect environment for him.'

Issy glanced up. She recognised that voice. Sure enough, with a slight stab of nervousness she saw that it belonged to Caroline, the woman who had wanted to turn the café into a wholefood centre.

'Hello, Caroline,' said Pearl stoically. She sweetened her voice considerably to talk to the serious-eyed blonde girl and small boy still in the buggy at the bottom of the table.

'Hello, Hermia! Achilles, hello!'

Issy sidled up to say hello, although Caroline seemed to be ignoring her quite competently.

'And you know Kate, don't you?'

'Well, this is just charming!' said Kate, looking around approvingly. 'We're doing up the big house across the road. Something like this is just what we need. Keep the house prices going in the right direction, you know what I mean. *Haw!*'

She had two girls who were obviously twins, sitting holding hands on the same stool. One had a short bob and was wearing red dungarees and one had long blonde curls and was wearing a pink skirt with a puffed-out underskirt.

'Aren't your girls lovely!' exclaimed Issy, moving forward. 'And hello, Caroline, too.'

Caroline nodded regally to her. 'I'm amazed this place appears to be taking off,' she sniffed. 'Might as well see what all the fuss is about.'

'Might as well!' said Issy cheerfully, bending down to the little ones. 'Hello, twins!'

Kate sniffed. 'They may be twins, but they are individuals too. This is Seraphina.' Kate indicated the little girl with the long blonde curls. 'And this one here,' she pointed to the other one, 'is Jane.'

Seraphina smiled prettily. Jane scowled and hid her face in Seraphina's shoulder. Seraphina patted her hand in a maternal fashion.

'Well, welcome,' said Issy. 'We don't normally do table service, but as I'm here, what would you like?'

'Well,' said Kate, after deliberating over the menu for some time. Seraphina and Jane who must have been four, walked up to the cake cabinet, rose on their tiptoes and pressed their noses to the glass.

'You two! Snot off the glass, sweethearts,' said Pearl, firmly but kindly, and the girls withdrew giggling, but stayed mere centimetres away where they could examine the icing carefully. Hermia looked at her mother.

'Please may I—' she risked.

'No,' said Caroline. 'Sit nicely please.'

Hermia looked longingly at her friends.

'I shall have a mint tea,' said Kate finally. 'Do you do salad?'

Issy couldn't bring herself to meet Pearl's eyes.

'No. No, at the moment we don't do salad,' she said. 'Cakes mostly.'

'What about, you know, organic flapjacks?'

'We have fruit cake,' said Issy.

'Can we have a cake, Mummy? *Pleeease!*' begged Jane from the counter. 'Oh, darlings . . . '

Kate looked on the brink of giving up. 'What do you think, Caroline?'

Caroline's face didn't move but Issy still got the sense she was disappointed. She glanced at Hermia, who was gazing at her friends, one tear dripping slowly down her face. Achilles sorted it for her.

'*Mummy! Cake! Now! Mummy! Cake! Cake! Mummy!*' He went red-faced while wrestling with the buggy straps. '*Now!*'

'Now darling,' Caroline said, 'you know we don't really like cake.'

'*Cake! Cake!*'

'Fine,' said Caroline, desperate to stop her son screaming. 'Two cakes. I don't care which ones. Hermia, little bites please. You don't want to blow up like—' Caroline immediately stopped.

'Yes!' shouted the twins by the counter.

'I want pink! I want pink!' they both yelled simultaneously, in voices so similar Issy wondered how you really did tell them apart.

Later, Caroline came over to chat.

'This is actually quite quaint,' she said. 'You know, I love to bake too . . . obviously, much healthier than this, and mostly we eat raw, of course. In fact, you know,' she peered down the stairwell, 'I think my oven is probably bigger than yours! My main oven of course, I have a steam oven and a convection oven too. But no microwave. Terrible things.'

Issy smiled politely. Pearl let out a snort.

'I am dreadfully busy with everything now . . . I've taken on a lot of charity work, my husband's in the City, you know . . . but maybe one day I could bring you one of my recipes! Yes, I create recipes . . . Well, it's hard when you have a creative side, isn't it? After children?'

She looked at Issy as she said this, and Issy tried to look polite to a customer, even an idiot, and even an idiot who was clearly implying that Issy looked old and dumpy enough to have loads of children. Caroline of course weighed about the same as a fourteen-year-old.

'Well, I'm sure that would be fascinating,' said Pearl, before Issy's mouth drooped open any further. 'Uh, Caroline, is that your son taking off his nappy and putting it in your Hermès bag?'

Caroline turned round with a squeal.

By 4.30 that Friday afternoon, after their busiest week ever, they were exhausted. Issy locked the door and turned the sign to *Closed*. Then they went downstairs to the cellar and Issy took from the catering fridge their now ritualistic end-of-the week bottle of white wine. Saturday was a quiet day—although it too was picking up, especially around lunchtime—so they could indulge a little on a Friday without suffering too badly.

As had also become a habit (and would be severely frowned upon by health and safety, Issy knew, if they ever found out), after counting up the day's takings they would slump down on the big flour sacks in the cellar, using them like gigantic bean bags.

Issy poured Pearl a large glass.

'That,' she said, 'was our best week so far.'

Pearl wearily raised her glass. 'I'll say so.'

'Compared, obviously, to not very much,' said Issy. 'But . . .'

'Oh,' said Pearl, 'I forgot to say. I ran into your fancy bloke at the bank.' Pearl did the banking.

Issy's interest was piqued. 'Oh, yes? Austin? Uh, I mean, really? Who?'

Pearl gave her a very Pearlish look. Issy sighed.

'OK. How is he?'

'Why are you asking?' said Pearl.

Issy felt herself colour and buried her face in her glass. 'Just politeness,' she squeaked.

Pearl sniffed and waited.

'Well?' said Issy after a minute.

'Ha!' said Pearl. 'I knew it. If it really was politeness, you wouldn't be that bothered.'

'That is not true,' said Issy. 'It's an entirely professional . . . relationship.'

'So it's a relationship?' teased Pearl.

'Pearl! What did he say? Did he ask about me?'

Pearl relented. 'He was looking quite smart. He'd had a haircut.'

'Oh, I liked his hair,' said Issy.

'I wonder who he got his hair cut for?' mused Pearl. 'Maybe it was you.'

Issy pretended not to be pleased with that remark, but men like Austin always had girlfriends. She sighed. She just had to come to terms with it now; she was a career girl for the moment. Shame though. She found herself imagining, just for one second, gently stroking the back of his neck, where a wisp of hair had been left behind . . .

'*And*,' said Pearl loudly, noticing Issy had vanished into a reverie, '*and* he said he had a message for you.'

'A what?' said Issy, sitting bolt upright on her sack. 'What was it?'

Pearl tried to get it exactly right. 'It was . . . "Tell her, 'You showed 'em'.'"

'You showed them? I showed them what? . . . Oh,' said Issy as she realised he meant the other café owners of Stoke Newington. 'Oh,' she said, going pink. He had thought about her! OK, maybe only from the point of view of his business investment, but still . . .

'Oh, that's nice,' she said.

Pearl was looking at her.

'Private joke,' said Issy.

'Oh, is it?' said Pearl. 'Well, on the plus side, I suppose you're keeping him sweet.'

Issy glanced at Pearl. 'What about you?' she said. 'How's your love life?'

Pearl grimaced. 'Is it that obvious?'

'You cleaned the same table four times,' said Issy.

'Well,' said Pearl, 'Louis's dad . . . he came round.'

'Oh,' said Issy. 'And is that good, bad, fine, terrible, or all of the above?'

'Or e) I don't know,' said Pearl. 'I think e) I don't know.'

'Oh,' said Issy. 'Is Louis pleased?'

'Ecstatic,' said Pearl grumpily. 'Can we change the subject?'

'Um. OK. Right. Well, here we are having wine, so I might as well go for it. I hate to ask a delicate question, but . . . are you losing weight?'

'Not on purpose, and,' said Pearl, 'don't tell the customers, but . . . I seem to have gone off sweet things. I'm sorry, Issy! I'm sorry! Don't sack me!'

Issy started to laugh. 'Oh, Pearl, I haven't eaten a cake in six weeks.'

They both made horrified faces, then burst into fits of laughter.

'What are we like?' said Pearl. 'Next time, can we open a chip shop?'

'Absolutely,' said Issy. 'Chips and crisps.'

'I am dreaming about this place,' said Pearl. 'Every second of every day. I'm not saying it's not great, Issy, honestly. But the hours . . . the hours are filling me up.'

'Me too,' said Issy. 'Me too. For me to admit I don't like eating cake any more . . . it's a complete denial of me. As a person.'

'This is bad,' said Pearl. 'Could be bad for quality control.'

'Hmm,' said Issy. 'Maybe we need a new member of staff.'

Pearl made a quiet fist of triumph underneath the sack.

Of all things, Issy hadn't expected finding someone else to help out the least bit difficult. Times were hard and people were desperate for jobs, weren't they? As soon as she'd put a sign up in the window, she figured she'd get the whole thing organised in ten seconds flat.

However, the stream of people who responded to the card—and later, the ad they took out in the *Stoke Newington Gazette* extolling the success of the café and thanking the supportive community—were all unsuitable.

'It's not that difficult,' Issy had explained to Helena, who was putting on make-up. 'It's that they can't even be arsed to pretend they love cakes.'

'You sound five thousand years old,' said Helena, smoothing some shimmery greeny-gold stuff on her eyelids that made her look goddess-like rather than tarty. Not that Ashok wouldn't treat her like a goddess anyway. Madly, it was Issy being so busy that had finally swayed her in his direction. She missed her best mate and having someone to go out with.

One day, Ashok, looking very dashing in a pink shirt under his white coat, had sidled up to her in A&E. He had said, 'Now I suppose you are very busy on Thursday evening. However, just in case you aren't, I took the liberty of reserving a table at Hex, so do let me know.'

Helena had stared after him down the corridor. Hex was the coolest new restaurant in London. It was meant to be nearly impossible to get a reservation. Although, of course, she couldn't go.

'You do look gorgeous,' said Issy, focusing on her friend for the first time. 'What are you doing anyway? Where are you going?'

'Out,' said Helena. 'It's a kind of place and it's not your house and not your shop. Things happen there that people talk about called current affairs and social life.'

Normally she'd have told Issy straight away what she was up to. But she was torn—partly because she felt it needed a longer conversation, but also because she didn't want to take the teasing she would get for going against all her principles to date an underpaid junior doctor. 'When you're back in the social world,' said Helena, 'you can find out.'

Issy raised her eyebrows. 'You're right, I have got boring. I just never think about anything other than baking cakes and the café.'

'What about that hot scruffy bloke from the bank with the horn-rimmed glasses?'

'What about him?'

'*Nothing*,' said Helena. 'It's just good to know you're not sitting around waiting for Graeme to come back.'

'No,' said Issy suddenly, 'no. I'm not. Hey, why don't I come with you?'

Helena started putting on mascara. 'Um, you can't.'

'Why not? Lena, have you got a *date*?'

Helena calmly went on layering her mascara.

'You have! Who is it? Tell me everything.'

'I would have done,' said Helena, 'if you'd stopped going on about the Cupcake Café for one second. As it is, I'm late.'

And she kissed Issy firmly on the cheek and swept out of the room.

The next morning the croissant rush was just about finished and Pearl was practising making up the new, candy-striped boxes they'd ordered. She wiped her brow. It was taking a bit of time to get the hang of folding them up. The doorbell went and she glanced up at the railway clock; just a few minutes' peace before the 11 a.m. sugar rush kicked off

Issy was downstairs, trying to make the world's first ginger beer cupcake. The scent of cinnamon, ginger and brown sugar filled the shop, and smelled absolutely intoxicating; people kept asking to try one and then, when told they weren't ready, camping by the stairs. One or two were striking up conversations with each other, which was nice, Pearl thought, but really right at the minute she needed everything cleared out of the way, so she could get to the coffee cups and stack the dishwasher. A delivery of eggs had just arrived fresh from the farm and she had to sign for that and put them away downstairs while still serving the ongoing queue, which she couldn't because she had no cups.

Suddenly the door banged open. Into the shop crashed someone she recognised immediately, and her heart dropped. It was Caroline, health-food Nazi of Louis's nursery, original bidder for the Cupcake Café.

Caroline marched straight to the front of the queue. As she got closer, Pearl noticed she wasn't her normal immaculate-looking self. She wasn't wearing make-up. And she had lost weight, taking her slender form into the realms of extreme thinness.

'Can I speak to your boss, please?' she barked.

'Hello, Caroline,' said Pearl, trying to give this incredibly rude woman the benefit of the doubt in case she just hadn't recognised her.

'Yes, hello, em . . .'

'Pearl.'

'Pearl. Can I speak to your boss?'

'Issy,' bellowed Pearl down the stairwell, with such force it made Issy jump. She came up the stairs to see Caroline propped against the wall, tapping her foot anxiously.

'Oh . . . oh, hello!' Issy wiped her hands warily. Caroline and Kate hadn't been back to the café since that first day; Issy had taken it rather personally. Still, local business was local business.

'You know,' said Caroline. 'Uh, you know when I didn't get the site?'

Pearl went back to serving the other customers.

'Yes,' said Issy. 'Have you . . . did you find anywhere else?'

'Um, well, obviously I weighed up lots of offers. Actually . . .' Caroline lowered her voice. 'No. Er, here's the thing. Ha, I know this will sound absolutely crazy and everything, but . . .' Suddenly, her face seemed to crumple. 'My bastard husband has finally left me for that stupid bint in the press office—and he's told me that I need to get a *job*!'

'**N**o way,' said Pearl afterwards. 'No no no no no.'

Issy bit her lip. Of course it had been an unorthodox approach. But Caroline was smart. She had a degree in marketing, and had worked for a prestigious market research outfit before giving it all up for the children, she'd sobbed bitterly. But once she'd stopped bawling, over about a pint of tea and some hazelnut tiffin, it transpired that she did in fact know loads of people in the area; she could turn the café into the place to get your baby-shower cakes, your birthday icing; she could work just the hours they were looking for, she lived round the corner . . .

'But she's *horrible*,' Pearl pointed out. 'She doesn't even need the job. It should go to someone who needs it.'

'She says she does need it,' said Issy. 'Apparently her husband told her if she wants to keep the house without a fight she needs to start working.'

'So she wants to swan about here being snobby to people,' said Pearl. '*And* she'll want to introduce wholemeal flour and raisins and wheatgrass juice and talk about BMIs and yap on and on all day.'

Issy was torn. 'I mean, it's not like we've seen loads of wonderful candidates,' she argued. 'And she'd be covering a lot of your time off, it's not like you'd have to see her that much.'

'This is a very small retail space,' Pearl said, darkly. And Issy sighed and put off making the decision for a while.

Things didn't ease off—which was fantastic, but also brought its own problems. Now it was phones constantly ringing, and lists, and Issy falling asleep during dinner, and Helena being out all the time, and she hadn't seen Janey since she'd had the baby, and Tom and Carla had moved into their new place in Whitstable and she hadn't even made it to their housewarming. And when she had five minutes she was still missing Graeme, or even just missing someone, anyone, to hold her hand occasionally and tell her that everything was going to be all right, but she didn't have time for that, didn't have time for anything.

She pushed her feelings back down inside herself and worked even harder, but the day Linda pushed her way through the door, she was very close to her wits' end.

It was a lovely Friday in late spring. They were doing a roaring trade in boxes of light, lemon-scented cupcakes with a velvet icing and a little semicircle of crystallised fruit on the top. And people were buying more cold drinks too, which took pressure off the coffee-making routine. Issy had stuck to prettier drinks rather than fizzy ones. They fitted better with the ethos of the shop. And also, Austin had pointed out, the profit margins were better.

Then, best of all, at 4 p.m., just as they were calming down, the door pinged open to reveal Keavie, pushing her grandfather in a wheelchair. Issy rushed up and flung her arms round his neck.

'Gramps!'

'I don't think,' the old man said, heavily, 'you quite know what you're doing with a meringue.'

'I totally do!' exclaimed Issy, affronted. 'Taste this.' She set in front of him one of her new miniature lemon meringue tarts. You could scoff the whole thing in two seconds, but the memory would stay with you all day.

'That meringue is too crunchy,' pronounced Grampa Joe.

'That's because you have no teeth!' said Issy, indignant.

'Bring me a bowl. And a whisk. And some eggs.'

Pearl made a hot chocolate for Keavie and they looked on as Joe and Issy gathered together the ingredients and Issy sat on a stool next to him.

'You've got the elbow action all wrong,' said Gramps.

'That's because . . .' Issy's voice tailed off.

'What?' said Gramps.

'That's because I use an electric whisk,' said Issy, blushing, and Pearl laughed out loud.

'Well, that proves it,' said Gramps. 'No wonder.'

'But I have to use an electric whisk! I have to make dozens of these things every day! What else can I do?'

Gramps just shook his head and carried on whisking. At that moment the ironmonger passed by the window, and Joe beckoned him in.

'Did you know my granddaughter uses an electric whisk on meringues? After everything I've taught her!'

'That's why I don't eat here,' said the ironmonger, then when he saw Issy's shocked face, he added, 'Apologies, madame. I don't eat here because, lovely though your shop is, it's a little out of my price range.'

'Well, have a cake on us,' said Issy. 'One without meringue.'

'Very good,' he said, through a mouthful of chocolate brownie cupcake.

'Imagine how good she'd be if she hand-whisked,' said Gramps.

'This is *industrial* catering, Gramps.'

Grampa Joe smiled. 'I'm just saying.' He handed over the bowl of perfectly crested egg whites and sugar, standing up stiff and glazed.

'Stick it on some greaseproof paper, give it forty-five minutes . . .'

'Yes, I know, Gramps.'

'OK, I just thought you might be putting it in the microwave.'

Pearl grinned. 'You're a hard taskmaster, Mr Randall,' she said, leaning down to his wheelchair.

'I know,' said Joe in a whisper. 'Why do you think she's so brilliant?'

Later, after they'd eaten Gramps's amazing meringues with freshly whipped cream and a spoonful of raspberry coulis over the top, Keavie had taken Gramps off to the van, and the cleaning up was finally done.

Issy could feel a solid bone-weariness deep down, but there would be wine tonight, and they didn't open till 10 a.m. on a Saturday, which felt like a huge lie-in, then early closing and the whole of Sunday off . . . she was enjoying this thought when suddenly the door burst open. At first Issy didn't recognise the woman who crashed into the room. Then she realised it was haberdashery Linda, normally so composed, whose life was never upset or the least bit disorganised.

'Hello!' Issy said, pleased to see her. 'What's up?'

Linda glanced around the shop and Issy realised with a slightly annoyed pang that this was the first time Linda had ever been in. She'd thought she might have been a bit more supportive, seeing as she was local and everything, and they'd stood together in rain and shine.

Issy's irritation was swept away in an instant, however, when Linda stopped and took a breath.

'Oh dear, it's lovely in here. I had no idea, I thought it was just a little sideline. I'm so sorry! If only I'd known.'

'Well, you're here now,' Issy said. 'Welcome! What would you like?'

Linda looked anxious. 'I have to . . . I have to . . . Can you help me?'

'What is it?'

'It's . . . it's Leanne's wedding—tomorrow. But her cake company . . . A friend said she would make her cake and then she got it all muddled up or something and anyway Leanne's paid hundreds of pounds but she doesn't have a wedding cake.'

Issy later realised what it must have cost Linda to utter these words about her perfect daughter. She looked close to breaking down. This was the wedding Linda had been talking about for over a year and a half.

'OK, OK, calm down, I'm sure we can help you,' she said. 'How many are we talking about? Seventy?'

'Um . . .' said Linda, 'four hundred. It's all going to fall apart. My only daughter's wedding! It's going to be a disaster!' And she burst into sobs.

By seven thirty, when they'd only got the second batch in, Issy already knew they weren't going to make it. Pearl was a saint, a hero and an absolute trooper and had stayed on without a second thought, but they couldn't use today's cakes. They had to start absolutely afresh, as well as designing some kind of structure to hold the cupcakes in the shape of a wedding cake.

'My arm hurts,' said Pearl, stirring in ingredients for the mixer.

Issy sighed. 'If only I knew someone who wants to . . .' She stopped short and looked at Pearl. 'Of course I could phone . . .'

Pearl read her mind instantly. 'Not her. Anyone but her.'

'There's nobody else,' said Issy. 'Nobody at all.'

Pearl sighed, then looked back at the bowl. 'I want to cry.'

'Me too,' said Issy. 'Or, phone someone who might be a bit of a time-and-motion specialist.'

Pearl hated to admit it but Issy had been right. The scrawny blonde had marched in in an immaculate professional chef's uniform—she'd bought it for a week's cooking in Tuscany, she informed them—and immediately organised them into a production line.

After a while, once they were in the swing of things, Pearl put on the radio and they found themselves, suddenly, dancing in a row, adding sugar and butter, baking and icing, tray after tray after tray and the pile in front of them steadily grew. Caroline improvised a cake stand out of old packaging and covered it beautifully with wedding paper they picked up from the newsagent.

The cupcakes they smothered in a pure creamy vanilla icing, seemingly whipped effortlessly by Issy to perfection, with silver balls marking out the initials for Leanne and Scott. This was the worst job. But still the cakes grew and balanced and turned into, indeed, a magnificent wedding cake dusted with pink sparkly icing sugar.

'Come on, chop chop,' shouted Caroline. 'Stir like you mean it.'

Pearl glanced at Issy. 'I think *she* thinks she works here already.'

'I think maybe she does,' said Issy quietly.

Caroline beamed and momentarily stopped production.

'Oh,' she said. 'Thank you. This is . . . this is the first good thing that's happened in a while.'

When they finally got to go home just after midnight, Pearl knew they couldn't have done it without her. 'Thanks,' she said, grudgingly.

'That's all right,' said Caroline. 'Are you catching a cab home?'

Pearl grimaced. 'Cabs don't go where I live.'

'Oh, really?' said Caroline. 'Are you out in the country? How lovely.'

Issy ushered Caroline out before she could get herself in more trouble, and asked her to start off by covering a good lunch hour for Pearl and herself, before increasing her hours, all going well, to make them all happy.

'Absolutely,' said Caroline. 'I'm going to order my book group to start meeting here. And my Stitch 'n' Bitch. And my Jamie at Home Tupperware party. And my Rotary Club.'

Issy hugged her. 'Have you been terribly lonely?'

'Dreadfully so.'

'I hope you start to feel better.'

'Thank you.' And Caroline accepted the bag of cakes Issy pressed on her.

'Don't give me that look,' said Issy to Pearl, even though Pearl was standing behind her. 'You are *mostly* right, I'll give you that. That's not the same thing as *always* right.'

Chapter Eight

ALWAYS THE CATERER, never the bride, thought Issy to herself, a tad ruefully after she and Pearl had inched across town in a cab, terrified their confection would wobble apart, but it held firm. They arranged it as the centrepiece of a huge table covered in pink stars and balloons. Linda and Leanne were delighted.

Arriving back at the café, Pearl whipped off her apron. 'I'm off to give my boy a cuddle and tell him he might be able to see his mother occasionally, now that the wicked Witch of the West has started work.'

'Stop it!' said Issy teasingly. 'She's going to be fine. Now, scoot.'

Pearl kissed her on the cheek. 'Go home and rest,' she said.

But Issy didn't much feel like getting some rest; it was a glorious after-noon and, having shut the shop for the first time ever on a Saturday, she was considering hopping on a bus at random and going for a wander, when she spotted a familiar figure at the bus-stop. He was bent over, fiddling with the laces of a small skinny boy with sticky-up auburn hair and a cross look on his face.

'But I *want* them like this,' the boy was saying.

'Well, you keep tripping over!' The man sounded exasperated.

Austin straightened up and was so surprised to see Issy there, he nearly stepped backwards into the road. 'Oh, hello,' he said.

'Hello.' Issy tried to make sure she didn't go red.

There was a pause. 'Who are you?' said the small boy, rudely.

'Hello. I'm Issy,' said Issy. 'And you must be Darny. You came to my café launch, but I didn't get to say hello.'

'Oh. Yeah. Are you going to be one of Austin's drippy girlfriends?'

'Darny!' said Austin in a warning tone.

'Are you going to come round at night and cook horrible suppers and use a silly voice and say, "Oh, so *tragic* for Darny to lose his mummy and daddy, let me look after you", kissy kissy kissy smooch smooch yawn stop telling me when to go to bed?'

Austin wanted the ground to open and swallow him up. Although Issy didn't look offended; rather, she looked like she was about to laugh.

'Is that what they do?' she asked. Darny nodded, mutinously. 'That *does* sound boring. No, I'm nothing like that. I work with your brother and I live up this road here, that's all.'

'Oh,' said Darny. 'I guess that's all right.'

'I guess so too.' She smiled at Austin.

'Where are you off to?' asked Austin.

'In fact I've been working all night, you'll be pleased to hear,' she said. 'Catering for a wedding at a nearby town hall. *And* I've taken on a new member of staff. She's great . . . slightly evil, but on the whole . . .'

'Oh, that's terrific,' said Austin, and his face broke into a large smile. He was genuinely, truly happy for her, Issy realised.

'No, where are you going *now*?' said Darny. 'That's what he asked you. Because we're going to the aquarium. Would you like to come?'

Austin raised his eyebrows. This was totally unprecedented. Darny made a point of disliking all grown-ups and being rude to them to forestall their mooning all over him. To invite someone somewhere was unheard of.

'Well,' said Issy, 'I was thinking of going home to bed.'

'While it's *light*?' said Darny. 'Is someone making you?'

'In fact, no,' said Issy.

'OK,' said Darny. 'Come with us.'

Issy glanced at Austin. 'Oh, I probably should . . .'

Austin knew it wasn't professional. She probably wouldn't even want to. But, he couldn't help it. He liked her. And that was that. 'Come,' he said. 'I'll buy you a frappucino.'

'Bribery,' said Issy, smiling. 'That's what'll get me to spend my Saturday looking at fish.'

And at that moment the bus arrived; all three of them got on it.

The aquarium was quiet—the first lovely sunny day of the year had prompted most people out of doors—and Darny was utterly transfixed by the tanks of fish. Austin and Issy talked; quietly, because the dark, warm underground environment seemed to encourage a quiet tone of voice; small revelations; and it was easier, somehow, to talk in the half-light, barely able to see one another except for the outline of Issy's curls backlit by jellyfish or the phosphorescence that shimmered and reflected in Austin's glasses.

Issy found the worries and cares of the café, which had lain on her relentlessly for months somehow get soothed away in the strange underwater tranquillity, as Austin made her laugh with stories about Darny at school or touched on, without a trace of self-pity, how hard it was to be a single parent who wasn't even a parent. And Issy found herself talking about how her mother had danced in and out of her life.

'Were your parents happy?' she asked.

Austin thought about it. 'Yes, I think they were. They were close, always physically close, holding hands, close to one another on the sofa.'

Without thinking, Issy glanced down at her own hand. It was silhouetted in front of a gently glowing tank of darting eels, not far from Austin's. How would it feel if she was to take his hand then and there? Would he pull away? She could almost feel her fingers tingle in anticipation.

'And of course, there was the fact of them being completely and utterly ancient and having another baby when all their friends were becoming grandparents. At the time I thought it was totally disgusting . . .'

Issy smiled. 'I bet you didn't really. I bet you loved him from the get go.'

Austin glanced over at Darny, his gaze following the shark around its tank, completely hypnotised. 'Of course I did,' mumbled Austin, and turned away slightly, his hand moving further from Issy's.

'I'm sorry,' she said. 'I didn't mean to be so personal.'

'It's not that,' said Austin, his voice a little muffled. 'It's just . . . I would have liked to know them, as a grown-up, not an overgrown teenager.'

And almost without realising he was doing it, Austin put out his hand to take hers, at first in a gentle squeeze, but then suddenly he didn't want to put it down.

'Ice cream!' came a very loud voice from below them. Immediately they dropped each other's hand.

Austin looked at Issy, trying to read her face, but it was impossible in the gloom. It was very awkward, all of a sudden. 'Um, ice cream?' he said.

'Yes, please!' she said.

The three of them sat by the river, watching the boats go by and the great wheel of the London Eye overhead, and were still enjoying each other's company, so much so in fact that Issy hardly noticed the time. When Darny finally came off the high climbing frame and grabbed Issy's hand as they left the park, she didn't mind a bit—was pleased in fact (Austin was stupefied)—and they decided as a special treat to take a cab back to Stoke Newington, whereupon Darny curled up in the back and fell asleep on Issy's shoulder. When Austin glanced over two minutes later, he saw Issy, too, fast asleep, her black curls tangled with Darny's spikes, her cheeks pink. He stared at her all the way home.

Issy couldn't believe she'd fallen asleep in the cab. OK, she'd had no rest the night before, but still. Had she dribbled? Had she snored? Oh, how horrific. Austin had just smiled politely and said goodbye . . . She thought again of the moment when he'd held her hand. She couldn't believe how much she'd wanted him to go on holding it. Putting her key in the door, Issy moaned. Helena would know what to do.

She caught sight of herself in the filigree mirror that hung in the tiny hallway, over the flower-sprigged retro wallpaper she was so proud of. She hadn't realised till then that she must have had that big white streak of wedding-cake flour in her hair all day.

'Helena?! Lena! I need you,' she bawled, stalking into the sitting room.

Then she stopped. There on the sofa, sure enough, was Helena. And beside her, someone she thought she recognised. They were in the exact positions of people who'd suddenly jumped apart.

'Oh!' she said.

'Hello!' said Helena. Issy looked at her carefully. Could she . . .? She couldn't possibly. Could she be blushing?

Ashok jumped up immediately.

'Hello, Isabel. How lovely to see you again,' he said politely, shaking her hand. 'I'm—'

'Ashok. Yes, I know,' she said. He was much more handsome than she'd remembered.

'So what is it you need to ask me?' said Helena.

'Um, not to worry,' said Issy. 'Who'd like some wine?'

'Your gramps called,' said Helena, when they were all ensconced in the sitting room. Ashok made for very easy company, Issy noted, pouring wine and adding comments when needed.

'He wanted to know if you got his cream of soda scone recipe.'

'Ah,' said Issy. She had got it. But the thing was, she'd got it four times, all copied out in the same wavering hand. She'd forgotten about that.

'And,' said Helena, 'he didn't recognise me on the phone. I don't have to tell you what that means.'

'No,' said Issy quietly. 'He seemed fine yesterday.'

'It can ebb and flow,' said Helena. 'You know that.'

'I'm sorry,' said Ashok. 'The same thing happened to my grandfather.' He offered her a little more wine, but Issy, overwhelmed with tiredness, bade good night to them both and stumbled off to bed.

'I'm calling the nursing home,' said Issy, after a long, luxurious lie-in the next morning.

'Good,' said Helena. 'What was it you wanted to ask me before?'

'Ooh,' said Issy. 'Well.' And she told her about her day with Austin. Helena's smile got wider and wider.

'Stop that,' said Issy. 'That's exactly the look Pearl gets every time his name comes up in conversation. You two are totally in cahoots.'

'He's an attractive man . . .' said Helena. 'And at least he's seen you at your dribbliest. It can only get better from now on in.'

'Shut up!'

Helena grinned. 'I reckon he's going to phone you.'

Issy felt her heart beat a bit faster. Just talking about him felt nice.

'Do you think?'

'Even if it's just to bill you for the dry-cleaning.'

Austin did phone. First thing Tuesday morning.

But it wasn't the kind of phone call he really wanted to make. The fact that he had to make it to Issy really made him think that, once and for all, and however sweet she might be and however interesting he found her and however pretty she looked, he couldn't mix business with pleasure, and that was that. And it didn't help that Darny kept mooning around the place, asking when he could see her again.

Well, it had to be done. He sighed, then picked up the phone.

'Hello,' he said.

'Hello!' came the warm tones immediately. She sounded really pleased to hear from him. 'Hello! Is that Austin? How nice to hear from you! How's Darny? Can you tell him I have been looking for fish cake-shapes to make fishy cakes but apparently nobody likes fishy cakes and I can't find any. Well, they like fishcakes, you know what I mean, but not . . . anyway, do you think dinosaurs would do and . . .' Issy was aware she was babbling.

'Um, fine, he's fine. Um, look, Issy . . .'

Her heart sank. That tone of voice was one she recognised. In that instant she knew that whatever she thought might have happened on Saturday was not really on the agenda; that he'd reconsidered, if he'd ever considered it in the first place. She was surprised just how acute her disappointment was: she'd thought she was still getting over a broken heart, but this felt much more painful than thoughts of her old boss.

'Yes?' she said, in a clipped way.

Austin felt cross with himself, stupid. Why couldn't he just say, look, would you like to meet for a drink? Somewhere nice. Somewhere they could have a glass of wine, and maybe a bit of a laugh . . . He felt like smacking himself on the head. Concentrate.

'Look,' he managed. He was going to keep this short and terse, make sure he didn't say anything inappropriate. 'I've had Mrs Prescott on the phone.'

'And?' Issy was ready for good news. Earnings were marching steadily upwards, and she fully expected Caroline to make a huge difference. She was already proving herself an icon of efficiency.

'She says there's a . . . she says she needs to send out an invoice and you won't let her.'

'Well, I've explained it totally to Mrs Prescott,' said Issy stiffly, thinking Mrs Prescott was proving to be maybe a little *too* efficient. 'I was doing a wedding favour to a friend.'

'She says there was an unaccounted-for amount of ingredients missing that would add up to about four hundred cakes . . .'

'She's good,' said Issy. 'Four hundred and ten, actually. In case some got squashed.'

'That's not funny, Issy. That's a week's profit for you.'

'But it was a wedding gift. To a friend.'

'Well, the invoice should still have gone through, even at a heavy discount. You have to charge for raw materials.'

'Not for a gift,' said Issy stubbornly. How dare he take her out and be all soft and mooshy on Saturday, then three days later phone her up and think he could give her a bollocking. He was just as bad as Graeme.

Austin was exasperated.

'Issy! You can't run a business this way. You just can't. Don't you understand? You can't just shut up the shop unannounced, and you can't go giving stock away like that.'

'But we're loads busier these days,' said Issy.

'Yes, but you've taken on more staff and you're paying overtime,' said Austin. 'It doesn't matter if you have a million people a day, if you don't take in more cash than you spend you're going to the wall, and that's the end of it. You didn't even open on Saturday.'

That was a step too far and they both knew it.

'You're right,' said Issy. 'Obviously on Saturday I made a mistake.'

'I didn't mean it like that,' said Austin.

'I think you did,' said Issy.

There was a pause. Then Issy said, 'You know, my grandfather ran three bakeries at one point. He was famous when I was growing up; everyone got their bread from him. And if they were sick or couldn't make the bill that week, he'd help them out, or if a hungry child or a sickly mum or an old soldier was passing by, he'd always have a cake for them. Everyone knew him. And he was a huge success. And that's what I want to do.'

'And I think that's wonderful,' said Austin. 'He sounds like a fine man.'

'He is,' said Issy fervently.

'And that's how businesses worked for hundreds of years—then the big boys came in and built huge shops and made everything loads cheaper and invented central distribution and however much everyone liked the little shops and knew the people, they all went to the big shops.'

Issy stayed silent. She knew that was true.

'So if you're going to offer personal service and a small shop with all the overheads involved in single-service marketing, you do, I'm afraid, have to fight a bit harder than your grandfather did.'

'Nobody fights harder than him,' said Issy defiantly.

'Well, that's good. I'm glad you've inherited his spirit. But, please, please, Issy, apply it to the modern age.'

'Thank you for the business advice,' said Issy.

'You're welcome,' said Austin.

And they hung up, both upset, both frustrated.

Telling herself she had been foolish to think that anything might have happened over the weekend, Issy took Austin's words to heart. She immersed herself in the business; paid her bills on time, kept on top of the paperwork; used Caroline's new hours to organise and streamline everything. She was even at risk of wringing a smile out of Mrs Prescott. She was in early to bake cupcakes—the standard favourites plus a constantly rotating menu of new recipes to keep the regulars coming back for more.

Caroline and Pearl were continuing to clash. Pearl was always left feeling like the junior partner. One day, when Pearl was alone in the shop, Kate marched in with the twins. Seraphina was wearing a pink ballet tutu, Jane was wearing blue dungarees.

'I'm here for the order.'

'What's that?' Pearl said, pleasantly.

'For the cakes with messages. Caroline said it was a brilliant concept and she'd get you right on it.'

'Did she?' said Pearl. Kate was saved from a classic Pearl snort by the two little girls suddenly falling over.

'Seraphina! Jane! What are you doing?'

The girls were all tangled up in each other's clothing and were rolling around the floor in hysterics.

'Get up,' shouted Kate. 'Or it'll be the naughty step for you, Seraphina, and the naughty corner for you, Jane.'

The two girls slowly disentangled themselves, heads hanging.

'Honestly,' said Kate, shaking her head at Pearl.

'They're adorable,' said Pearl, missing Louis. She couldn't believe how much you could miss someone you were going to see in a few hours.

'Humph,' said Kate. 'So, can you do it?'

'Do what?' said Pearl.

'I want letters piped on the cakes.'

'Oh,' said Pearl. It would be time-consuming but they'd be able to charge a premium, she supposed.

'Can we have cake, Mummy?' Seraphina asked sweetly. 'We'll share.'

'*We like to share*,' shouted Jane.

'No, darlings, this is all junk,' said Kate absent-mindedly. Pearl sighed. Kate took a quick phone call while Pearl stood there, cursing Caroline and all her friends, then Kate turned off her phone.

'All right,' she said briskly. 'I want lemon cupcakes, orange icing, and "H-A-P-P-Y-B-I-R-T-H-D-A-Y-E-V-A-N-G-E-L-I-N-A-4-T-O-D-A-Y".'

Pearl wrote it down. 'I think we can manage,' she said.

'Good,' said Kate. 'I hope Caroline was right about you.'

Pearl privately thought she was not.

'Goodbye, twins!' She waved.

'Bye bye!' called the twins in one voice.

'Actually it's Seraph—'

But Pearl had disappeared downstairs to give the good news to Issy.

Dashing in one morning to get the coffee machine warmed up before the morning rush, Pearl realised she hadn't opened yesterday's post. Plonking Louis on one of the high stools they'd recently got to line the mantelpiece and give people somewhere extra to sit, she passed him a pain au chocolat and opened up a letter from the nursery. Then she stared at it in disbelief.

The doorbell tinkled. Issy was meeting a sugar rep that morning and was going to be in a little later, so Caroline was opening up.

'*Buens deez, Caline!*' shouted Louis, who had been learning how to say hello in different languages at nursery.

'Good morning, Louis,' enunciated Caroline carefully, who thought Louis's diction was absolutely dreadful and that she was the only person who could save him from sounding lower class. 'Good morning, Pearl.'

Pearl didn't utter a peep. She was holding a letter in her hand, staring into the middle distance—and she was crying.

Caroline crossed the room instantly. 'What is it? What's the matter?'

'*Mamma?*' said Louis in alarm. He couldn't get down from the high stool on his own. '*Mamma? Booboo?*'

With some effort, Pearl pulled herself together. In an only slightly shaky voice she said, 'Oh no, darling. Mamma doesn't have a booboo.'

Caroline touched her lightly on the shoulder, but Pearl, hands trembling, could only give her the letter as she picked up Louis.

'Come here, baby,' she said, cradling his face into her wide shoulder so he couldn't see her eyes. 'There we go,' she crooned. 'Everything's fine.'

'*Me not go nursery,*' said Louis decisively. '*Me stay with Mamma.*'

Caroline glanced at the letter. It was formally marked North East London Strategic Health Authority and stated that the results of a medical showed that Louis fell in the Overweight to Obese category and an appointment had been made for Pearl to see a nutritionist counsellor.

Caroline put it down. 'This letter is absolutely disgusting,' she announced, her nose twitching. 'They're all horrible bossyboots nanny-state socialist interfering cruel bloody left-wing idiots.'

Pearl blinked at her. Caroline couldn't have said a better thing to cheer her up. 'But . . . it's their official letter.'

'And it's officially a total disgrace. How dare they? Look at your adorable boy. Well, yes, he is too plump, but you know that anyway. It's none of their business. Would you like me to rip it up for you?'

Pearl looked at Caroline with something close to amazement.

'But it's official!'

Caroline shrugged. 'So what? We pay taxes. The fewer nosy busybodies they employ to do this kind of thing, the better for everyone. Shall I?'

Shocked and feeling naughty, Pearl nodded. Normally, anything official she paid very close attention to. In her world, you did what those letters said or bad things happened. Seeing Caroline rip up the letter like it was nothing—something stupid to be ignored—worked a surprising change in her. She felt oddly liberated.

'Thank you,' she said to Caroline quietly, with a hesitant admiration.

'You know,' said Caroline, 'you don't *look* like you're the kind of person who would let anyone push you about.'

Pearl sat Louis back up on the high chair. Was he plump? He had round little baby cheeks and an adorable pot belly, and a high little round bottom and chunky kissable thighs and fat pudgy fingers. How could he be fat? He was perfect.

'You're gorgeous,' she said, looking at him. Louis nodded.

'*Louis is gojuss*,' he said, grinning merrily and showing all his teeth.

Caroline moved towards Louis who eyed her warily. Caroline prodded him in his fat tummy and he giggled and wriggled obligingly.

'You are gorgeous, Louis,' she said. 'But you shouldn't have that.'

'It's just a baby tummy,' protested Pearl strongly.

'No, it has rolls,' said Caroline, whose contemplation and understanding of human body fat in all its permutations bordered on the maniacal. 'That's not right. And I never see him without a cake in his paws.'

'Well, he's a growing boy,' said Pearl defensively. 'He's got to eat.'

'He does,' said Caroline thoughtfully. 'It all depends on what.'

A tap at the door alerted them to their first customers.

As they handled the morning rush, and Louis sat cheerfully greeting the regulars, who found it hard to pass him without tweaking his sticky cheeks or rubbing his soft shorn head, Pearl kept sneaking glances at him in the faded antique mirror that hung over the room. Sure enough, there was old Mrs Hanowitz, who liked a huge mug of hot chocolate and a proper *kaffeeklatsch*, scratching his roly tum as if he were a dog—then she popped the marshmallow from the top of her chocolate into his mouth. Issy didn't help matters by running in from her early meeting to get started on the baking, but not without going up to Louis for her morning cuddle and announcing loudly, 'Good morning, my little chub-chubs.' Pearl's brow furrowed. Was this what he was? Everyone's plump pet? He wasn't a pet. He was a person.

Caroline caught her looking. Pearl's distress had given her an idea . . .

'**W**ell, maybe she's right,' said Ben, lounging against the kitchen counter. 'I dunno. He looks all right to me.'

'And me,' said Pearl. Ben had 'popped in' on his way home, even though he was working in Stratford, which was right across the other side of town. Pearl pretended that he was just passing, Ben pretended he didn't really want to stay the night (although Pearl's cooking was worth it on its own). The little boy bumbled past them covered in a blanket.

'Hey, Louis,' said his dad.

'*I'm not Louis. I'm a turtle.*' Ben raised his eyebrows.

'Don't ask me,' said Pearl. 'He's been a turtle all day.'

Ben put down his cup of tea and raised his voice. 'Any turtles around here who would like to *go outside and play some football?*'

'*Yaaayyyy,*' said the turtle.

Pearl looked at her mother in amazement as Ben led his boy outside.

'Don't think it,' said her mother. 'He comes for a bit then he goes again. Don't let the boy get too fond.'

It might be too late for that, Pearl found herself thinking.

'I just wanted to try out something new,' said Caroline, trying to look suitably humble and helpful the next morning when she turned up with a Tupperware box. 'It's nothing really, I just tossed them together.'

'What the hell is brown rice syrup when it's at home?' said Pearl, glancing down the recipe. 'Safflower oil?'

'It's simple, wholesome fare,' said Caroline. In fact, it had taken her five hours slaving over her country kitchen table and much cursing to get the mixture right and make the cupcakes stick together. How did Issy make it look so damn easy, throwing ingredients together to produce cakes that tasted light as air and melted in the mouth? Well, of course she was using evil refined ingredients that would send her to an early grave. But as she'd mixed and reworked them, Caroline had had an image in her head—of her wholesome treats outselling the sugary rubbish and becoming famous; eclipsing the Cupcake Café with Caroline's Fresh Cooking; converting children to the benefits of a healthier, slenderer lifestyle . . . She wouldn't be the part-time member of staff then, no siree . . .

Pearl and Issy looked at one another, their hands close to their mouths.

'Well?' said Caroline. 'Give one to Louis.'

'*Yes, please!*'

Pearl put her hand down. 'Yes, in a minute.'

Issy fought an urgent desire to scrape the bits of raw carrot off her tongue. And what was that custardy aftertaste that hinted at broccoli?

'Here, little man.' Caroline took the box over to him.

'He's not hungry,' said Pearl desperately. 'I'm trying to cut down, you know.'

But Louis had already cheerfully stuck his fat little paw in the box.

'*Ta, Caline.*'

'Thank you,' said Caroline, unable to help herself. 'Don't say ta, say thank you.'

'I don't think he'll be saying either in a minute,' muttered Pearl to Issy, who was surreptitiously sipping coffee and rolling it round her mouth to try to remove the taste. Pearl had simply scoffed some of Issy's brand new batch of Victoria sponge cupcakes to change the taste and Issy didn't blame her for a second. Caroline fixed her eyes on Louis expectantly.

Louis bit into the cupcake-shaped object confidently enough, but as he started to chew, his face took on a confused, upset expression.

'There we go, darling,' she said encouragingly. 'Yummy, huh.'

Louis signalled his mother with his eyes desperately, then simply, as if it wasn't connected to him in any way, let the lower half of his jaw drop open so that the contents of his mouth started to fall out and crumble to the floor.

'Louis!' shrieked Pearl. 'Stop doing that immediately.'

'*Yucky, Mummy! Yucky!*' Louis began frantically shoving his hand over his tongue to scrape off any remaining pieces of the cake.

'*Yucky, Caline! Yuck!*' he cried accusingly, as Pearl gave him a drink of milk to calm him down and Issy fetched the dustpan and brush.

Caroline stood there with a pinkish blush at the top of her very high cheekbones. 'Well,' she said, when Louis was himself again, 'obviously his palate has been completely ruined by junk.'

'Hmm,' said Pearl crossly.

'*Caline,*' said Louis seriously. '*Bad cake, Caline.*'

'No, yummy cake, Louis,' said Caroline tightly.

Issy hastily got in the middle before it turned into a genuine argument between a forty-year-old and a two-year-old.

'It is,' she said, 'a brilliant idea, Caroline. Really great.'

Caroline eyed her beadily. 'Well, I still own copyright on the recipe.'

'Um, well . . .' said Issy. 'Yes . . . of course. We could call them Caroline's cupcakes, would that work?'

Caroline was reluctant to hand over the rest of the cakes (Issy didn't want her sneaking them to a customer; she trusted Caroline completely with money, stock and hours but didn't trust her one iota in terms of thinking she knew best when it came to their clients' tastes), but Issy insisted she needed them for an experiment, and, well, it was true that they hadn't stuck together as well as Caroline had hoped. Rennet wasn't quite as good for making delicious firm cakes as the all-natural cookbook had assured her it would be. Issy subtly got rid of them.

And there were two good effects immediately: Caroline was absolutely right about one thing. There was a market for 'healthy' cupcakes.

'Caroline's cupcakes', as amended by Issy, little apple sauce, raisin and cranberry muffins in tiny baking cases with fire engines or pink umbrellas on them, were an instant hit with mothers anxious to avoid their children getting stuck into icing once a day, and Issy faithfully added a kilo of carrots to their stock order every week, then took some home each night. Caroline genuinely believed they had gone into the recipe. Helena and Ashok, who appeared to have practically moved in, ate a lot of soup. But Issy never did find a use for the rennet.

The second good result was that Louis became entirely suspicious of every cupcake in the shop and refused to eat a second breakfast there. It did him no harm at all, and with Caroline working more hours and Louis skipping to the bus-stop with his mum every day, his second weigh-in went without a hitch. Which didn't matter to Pearl and Caroline, who cheerfully tore up the health authority's letter regardless.

Three weeks later, Pearl came in to find Caroline bent over the counter, stock still. 'What's up?'

Caroline couldn't answer. She was stiff as a board.

'What's the matter, sweetheart?'

'I'm . . . fine,' stuttered Caroline.

Pearl gently but firmly turned her round. 'What's happened?'

Caroline's usually immaculately made-up face was tear-stained and tragic, mascara pouring down.

'What is it?' asked Pearl.

Caroline choked and indicated her trouser zip. She was wearing a pair of very closely draped cigarette pants, clearly expensive. The zip, however, had burst and pulled off a button at the top to boot.

'Look!' she wailed. 'Look at this!'

Pearl squinted and examined it. 'You've bust the zip! Are you scoffing ginger cookies in secret when we're not looking?'

'No!' said Caroline. 'No, definitely not. It caught on a door.'

'If you say so,' said Pearl. 'So, what's the problem?'

'These are D&G Cruise 10,' said Caroline, a sentence which meant absolutely nothing to Pearl. 'I . . . I mean, they cost hundreds of pounds. And I won't . . . I won't be able to buy any more now. The Bastard says he's not paying for my lifestyle.' Her voice tailed away in sobs. 'I'm going to have to wear . . . high street.' Caroline's sobs grew louder.

Pearl couldn't see the problem. 'Let me take a look at it. It's only a busted zip. I can fix it for you.' Caroline blinked her wide blue eyes.

'Really? You'd do that for me?'

'What would you do otherwise?'

Caroline shrugged. 'I suppose . . . just buy another pair. In the old days. Of course, I'd give them to the charity shop.'

'Of course you would,' said Pearl, shaking her head. Hundreds of pounds for a pair of trousers, thrown out because of a zip.

The doorbell rang and Doti the postman came in. 'Hello, ladies,' he said politely. 'What's going on here?'

'Caroline is out of her trousers,' said Pearl, unable to help herself.

'Oh good,' said Doti.

'*Why* is that good?' spluttered Caroline.

'You need a bit of meat on your bones,' said Doti. 'Skinny women look . . . sad. You should eat some of these delicious cakes.'

'I do not look *sad*. Do Cheryl Cole or Jennifer Aniston look sad?'

'Yes,' said Pearl.

'I look in shape, that's all.'

'You look nice,' said Doti, then turned to Pearl. 'But you look beautiful.'

Pearl smiled and said thank you as Doti left, and Caroline's mouth fell open. 'What?' said Pearl, still pleased enough by Doti's compliment not to be too bothered by Caroline's unflattering amazement. 'You don't think he meant it?'

Caroline looked her up and down. 'No,' she said, in a humbler voice than Pearl had ever heard before. 'No. You are beautiful. It's my fault. I didn't even notice. I don't,' she added, 'always notice much.'

So Pearl took Caroline's trousers home and replaced the zip, and the button, and turned up a trailing hem and was slightly disappointed, actually, at the quality of the rest of the sewing on trousers that cost hundreds of pounds. Caroline was so genuinely grateful she didn't pick Louis up on his pronunciation for almost four full days, until he said 'innit' and she absolutely couldn't help herself.

Chapter Nine

Best Birthday Cake Ever
4 oz Breton soft butter, first churn
8 oz white caster sugar, sifted
4 large free-range eggs, beaten
6 oz self-raising flour
6 oz plain flour
1 cup milk
1 tsp vanilla essence

Icing
4 oz Breton soft butter, first churn
16 oz icing sugar
1 tsp vanilla essence
2 oz milk
2 tsp essence of roses

Grease three small cake pans. Cream the butter until as smooth as a child's cheek. Add sugar very gradually. No dumping like you normally do, Isabel. This has to be fluffy; properly fluffy. Add a grain at a time through the whisk.

Add the eggs slowly. Beat well at all times.

Mix the sifted flours and add a little milk and vanilla; then some flour, then some milk and vanilla and so on. Do not rush. This is your birthday cake for you, and you are very special. You deserve a little time.

Bake for 20 minutes at 350°F/gas mark 4.

For the icing, add half the icing sugar to the butter. Add milk, vanilla and essence of roses. Beat thoroughly, adding sugar till the icing reaches the desired consistency.

Ice layers and top of cake. Add candles. Not too many. Add friends. As many as you can. Blow candles out while making a happy wish. Do not tell anyone a) your wish, b) your recipe. Some things, like you, are special, my darling. Love, Gramps

THE SUN CAME THROUGH the shop window so strongly, Issy wondered if you could get a suntan through glass. It was, undoubtedly, the only way she'd get a suntan this year.

'It's burst into summer without me noticing,' she said. 'We ought to be outside, all our clients sitting about for ages. It's a shame we can't afford the tables and chairs.'

'Drunks as well as sugar addicts,' said Pearl. 'Hmm. Anyway, it wouldn't be right.' She indicated a table by the window occupied by four old men.

'Oh, yes!' giggled Issy. It had been the oddest thing. One day two old men had trudged in the door, quite late in the day. They had looked, frankly, a bit like drunken tramps. They already had a local tramp, Berlioz, who came by most days for a couple of bits and bobs to eat and a cup of tea when it was quiet but these chaps were something new.

One came shuffling up. 'Um, two coffees, please,' he asked in a croaky, cigarette-ruined voice.

'Of course,' Issy had said. 'Do you want anything with them?'

The man had dragged out a brand new ten-pound note and Austin's card had fallen out too.

'No,' he said. 'Oh, but we're to tell you Austin sent us.'

Issy squinted for a minute, then remembered. They were the all-day drinkers from the pub Austin had taken her to.

'Oh!' she said in surprise. She had been avoiding Austin completely; she was still embarrassed about having thought he was interested in her rather than just her business, and things were going so much better there was no reason for the bank to complain. She did think of him sometimes though, wondering how Darny was doing. She hadn't used the dinosaur moulds yet. And she wasn't sure about her new customers.

But from that day on, they came in three times a week, gradually joined by more furtive-looking characters. One day, cleaning up around them, Pearl had realised they were holding an informal AA-type meeting. Issy, shaking her head, wondered how Austin had managed to persuade them to do that.

'Longest day of the year,' said one of the old men.

'Is that the date?' said Issy suddenly. Once they'd got past the financial year-end deadline, she'd slightly lost track of the days; now, finally, the Cupcake Café seemed to be on a reasonably even keel and earning its keep. It looked like, mortgage money aside, there was a possibility that she could start drawing a salary from it. Which was kind of ironic, Issy thought, seeing as she'd been so all-focused on the shop that she hadn't actually done any shopping for herself in months. And anything she wore was covered in an apron all day, so it scarcely mattered. She sighed.

'What's up?' said Pearl, who was cutting out templates for the cappuccino chocolate. She didn't know why customers liked little flowers on top of their foam so much, but they did, and she was happy to oblige.

Issy shrugged. 'Oh, nothing. It's just . . . Well, you know. It's my birthday coming up. On Thursday in fact. It's just . . . it must have crept up on me. Normally I never forget my birthday.'

Issy called Helena.

'Uh, Lena. You know Thursday is my birthday?'

There was a pause. 'Oh, Issy, I'm on night shift Thursday and I've already swapped once, I can't do it again. I'm so sorry.'

'That's all right,' said Issy, feeling dejected.

'Want to do something on Sunday? Ashok's off too.'

'The weather might be gone by Sunday,' said Issy, conscious she sounded like she was moaning. Plus, what was she expecting? She'd been ignoring her friends for months while she got the shop up and running; she could hardly complain now that they wouldn't drop everything at a second's notice to celebrate her special day when she couldn't even remember to send cards for their first babies or house moves.

She was a little sharper than usual in saying no to Felipe when he came in politely, as he did once a week, to ask her if he could serenade her customers on the violin. Felipe never seemed remotely perturbed, merely spinning a few notes and moving on, tipping his black hat as he went.

The sun was still shining on Thursday morning, that was one good thing. Issy swallowed: she was suddenly wishing she'd never mentioned the birthday thing to anyone, just completely ignored it. It was embarrassing in front of Helena and Ashok, like they were her only friends; and a horrid reminder that time was ticking away. No. She wouldn't think like that.

Thirty-two was *nothing*. She was definitely in a better place than she'd been a year ago. At least the Cupcake Café made her happy. The phone rang. For a tiny, fluttery second, she found herself wondering if it was Graeme.

'Hello?' said an old voice, a little crackly down the line. 'Hello?'

Issy smiled to herself. 'Gramps!'

'Are you going to have a lovely day, darling?' came her grandfather's voice. It sounded weaker than of late; breathier, as if he was getting lighter and lighter; untethering himself.

Issy took a deep breath.

'Yes,' she lied, stoutly. 'I'm having a big party with all my friends in a lovely restaurant.' She tried not to let a wobble escape into her voice. Hearing a knock at the door, she knew instantly that it was the Parcelforce man, delivering her annual box of Californian wine from her mother.

'Gramps, someone's at the door,' she said. 'I have to go. But I'm going to get up to see you on Sunday.'

'Hello? Hello?' her grandfather said into the phone. He sounded like he'd been connected to a different line altogether. 'Hello? Can you hear me? Who am I speaking to?'

'It's Issy, Gramps.'

'Hmm. Issy. Yes. Good,' he said.

Issy felt a cold grip of fear on her heart. The door buzzed again, loudly 'I have to go. I love you.'

'Yes. Hmm. Right. Yes.'

Issy wrapped her ugly but comfy dressing gown round her and answered the door. She signed for the box and peered inside. Californian red again. Her mother must know that Issy only drank white and pink wine, mustn't she? That whenever they'd been out, she had never ever ordered red wine as it gave her a headache? Maybe it was her mother's way of encouraging her not to drink too much. Maybe it was her way of showing she cared.

At the shop, Louis cheered her up a little by giving her a huge cuddle and a card he'd made, covered in orange splodges.

'Thank you, darling,' she said, admiring the card and hanging it up in the café.

'Happy birthday, boss,' said Pearl. 'I would offer to bake you a cake . . .'

'I know, I know,' said Issy, strapping on her apron.

'So . . .' said Pearl. She turned round and reached into her bag and pulled out a Tupperware box. Opening it up, Issy squealed with delight and stuck her hand in front of her mouth. There was, tentatively hanging together, a little cake shape. But instead of sponge, it was made of interlocking crisps; a net of Nik Naks, piled up on top of a base of square crisps, crowned with a Hula Hoop tower, with a chipstick flag sticking out the top.

'I got some very odd looks on the bus,' said Pearl. 'It's held together with Marmite.'

Issy threw her arms round her. 'Thanks,' she said honestly, feeling her voice getting slightly choked up. 'For everything. I wouldn't . . . I don't know how I'd have managed without you.'

'Oh, you and Caroline would be expanding to Tokyo by now,' said Pearl, patting her on the back.

'What's that about me?' said Caroline, marching in. They turned to look at her. She wasn't due in till lunchtime; she *never* got her shifts wrong.

'Yes, yes, I know, I'm early. This is my birthday present for you. It's a morning off. Pearly Gates and I can hold the fort, can't we?'

Issy knew this was meant to be an affectionate name for Pearl, but she could feel her colleague bristle. 'Are you sure?'

'Of course,' said Pearl, 'we can hold the fort. Off you go!'

'But I won't know what to do with myself!' said Issy. 'Time to myself . . . I just don't . . .'

'Well, it finishes at two thirty when I have my reiki session,' said Caroline. 'So I'd get on with it if I were you.'

The sun was already warm on her back as Issy marched up the road, feeling oddly light and free. She should get a bus to Oxford Street and go shopping. Hmm, maybe she didn't have enough money to go shopping, she really needed to check with Austin. She had no idea what shape her personal finances were in. She felt incredibly uncomfortable having to ask him about it. But they had no personal relationship at all, so she shouldn't worry about it: she could ask him a professional query. He'd made it 100 per cent clear that was where he thought they should stand, and anyway, she didn't care. She cared a little bit about having to walk past all the other cafés on Stoke Newington High Street though. She hadn't forgotten what happened the last time. It had been horrible, but they hadn't come round to bother her since.

Well, she wasn't going to care about anything today. It was her birthday, and if she wanted to walk up past all the other cafés on the high street, then she would. Head in the air, hoping to render herself unrecognisable, she strode up the road, careful to avoid eye contact and feeling a bit nervous, but also defiant. Whether everyone else liked it or not, she was part of this community now and that was an end to it. She belonged.

At the pub opposite the bank, she sat down on one of their new outside tables. She asked for a coffee. At ten past nine he appeared, scurrying as usual, with his shirt coming out from his trousers—over, Issy couldn't help noticing, rather a nice bum. It must be the sunshine. She never normally noticed anyone else's bum, not compared to Graeme's gym-hardened buttocks of which she sometimes thought he was unpleasantly proud. Anyway, she wasn't looking at Austin's bum. She needed to ask him a professional question, that was all. It wasn't that she was desperate to see him, even if the blue shirt went beautifully with his eyes. Not at all.

'Austin!' she called tentatively, waving her newspaper. He turned round then, seeing her, looked at first very pleased, then anxious. Issy felt cross. He didn't have to look like she was some kind of scary stalker.

He crossed the road. Inside, he was annoyed with himself about how pleased he was to see her. It would be a business proposition, for sure.

'Don't look so frightened, it's just a business proposition,' said Issy. She'd meant it to sound light-hearted, but now she felt it had come out terribly weird-sounding.

'Hooray,' he said, sitting down. Issy felt disappointed. 'OK then. Can we have coffee and I'll call it a business meeting?'

Issy watched as Austin called Janet. 'Yes, I forgot to mention . . . really? I'm double-booked? Oh, please tell them I'm terribly sorry . . .'

Issy shook her head. 'How does Janet cope with you?'

'She makes a face like this,' said Austin, giving a stern scary look. 'I've told her the wind will change, but she won't listen.'

His coffee arrived. 'This place has got better,' he noted.

'Really?' said Issy, sipping the bitter dregs of the catering-jar 'beverage'. 'I'll take your word for it.' She was glad to feel that at least there wasn't any residual awkwardness. She didn't ask about Darny. Too personal. 'Now, I need to know . . . do I have any money?'

'Well, that depends,' said Austin, 'on what you want to do with it.'

'Actually,' said Issy, 'I was wondering . . . can I go shopping?'

Issy had moved her personal accounts to Austin's branch shortly after the shop opened; as she was funding so much of the café herself, it seemed to make sense to have everything under the same roof.

'For what?'

Issy felt a bit embarrassed suddenly. 'Well . . . it's my birthday.'

Austin looked half surprised, half guilty. 'Cheers! What a surprise!' he said. 'Oh no, hang on, that sounded a bit phoney. I knew that. It's on all your application forms,' he said, feeling himself getting a bit flustered. 'Um, I happened to be filing them away just recently. So. Kind of. I know. But I didn't want to make a big thing of it in case you were ignoring it. You know. Except you wouldn't of course, so: happy birthday.'

He smiled weakly and not entirely successfully.

'I should have ignored it,' admitted Issy. 'Honestly. It's a bit of a shit one. Well, apart from work. Work's been nice. But that means,' she said fervently, 'that I've based my entire life around my job rather than finding my work/life balance.'

'You should be so proud of yourself at this stage of your life,' said Austin. 'Look at you, businesswoman all afloat.'

'I know,' said Issy. Suddenly, she decided something. OK, so she'd been rebuffed before. Yet somehow her feet had taken her here . . . She could easily have rung Janet for the balance on her accounts. But she hadn't, had she? She was going to do it. 'Um,' she said, 'would you . . . and Darny, I suppose, or maybe you can get a baby sitter? Or maybe no, obviously no, it would be a stupid idea, forget I mentioned it.'

'What?' Austin needed to know what she was going to say.

Issy was now staring at the floor, looking tortured. 'I was going to ask if you fancied a drink tonight, but really that's daft, don't listen to me. I'm just being stupid because I should have told my friends—and I have loads of friends actually—'

'I'm glad to hear it,' interjected Austin.

'—well, anyway, it doesn't matter,' Issy ended miserably.

'OK,' said Austin. 'Actually, I'd have loved to. I have something on tonight though.'

'Oh,' said Issy, still not looking up.

They fell silent. Issy was too humiliated—what on earth was she thinking? Was she asking her banking adviser for a drink? After he'd already made it clear he wasn't interested? And now, as if to rub it in even more, he'd just *turned her down*. This was turning into the best birthday ever.

'Well, I'd better get on,' said Issy quietly.

'OK,' said Austin. Then they both awkwardly stood up at the same time and turned to cross the road.

'Uh, 'bye,' said Issy.

''Bye,' said Austin. Then in a clumsy gesture he raised his arms as if to kiss her on the cheek, and Issy leaned in, equally clumsily, before she thought that maybe that wasn't what Austin was doing at all and tried to lean back again. But it was too late and Austin leaned in to kiss her cheek, just as she dodged and accidentally got the side of her mouth by mistake.

Issy leaped back, pasting a broad fake smile on her face to cover her consternation, while Austin couldn't help his hand flying to his mouth.

'*Bye!*' said Issy brightly, feeling her face as hot as the sun—and, just momentarily, tantalisingly, the feel of his surprisingly soft lips against hers.

Austin was even more distracted than usual that morning.

Issy didn't go shopping in the end. Instead, she bought a cream cheese and smoked salmon bagel and a tiny bottle of champagne with a straw and a magazine, and went to sit in the park.

Lots of friends were sending remote regards via Facebook which, while she realised it wasn't exactly as good as everyone coming to celebrate her birthday, was better than nothing, and made her phone ping cheerily every time another one came through. After the bagel, she bought an ice cream too, and lay down and looked at the clouds for a bit and reflected that truly, from last year to this, she had come a long way, she really had. So she must stop being so grumpy and be more positive and . . . nope. It didn't help. Suddenly, in the midst of the bustling park and the noisy people, she felt terribly lonely.

'**C**heer up, love,' said one of the builders who was renovating the house belonging to Caroline's friend, Kate.

Issy turned to Pearl. 'Nine,' she said.

'Nine what?' asked the builder, who was already slurping the Smarties off his cinnamon cupcake. 'Mm, these are great.'

'Nine times someone has come in and said, "Cheer up, love."'

'And three "It might never happens",' added Pearl helpfully.

Issy glanced around the café. It was bustling nicely; she'd bought a bunch of lilies on her way back from the park to cheer herself up, and the scent was permeating through the room; with the windows thrown open and the door held wide (totally against fire regulations, Pearl had pointed out), the café felt fresh and summery, filled with the chink of china and the sounds of conviviality. Issy wasn't even that keen to close up at the end of the day; she didn't chivvy the hang-backers fiddling with their laptops, or bundle up the newspapers for recycling. She held back, straightening everything up for the following day. Pearl looked at her.

'I have to go get Louis now, OK?'

'OK.'

Pearl nodded. 'Bye then!'

And the bell dinged, and she was gone. It was still a beautiful afternoon outside, the shadows lengthening. Sod it, thought Issy, turning the sign to *Closed* and locking the door. This was ridiculous. She had done nothing but mope about all day. Well, that was going to stop. Almost without thinking, she propelled herself out of the shop and up to the high street again. A little boutique had opened up, run by a friend of Caroline's. The shop, just called 44, was packed tight with clothes, and smelled beautiful and expensive. Issy tried not to feel intimidated by the elegant blonde saleswoman with the perfect red lipstick and fifties sunglasses sitting behind the counter.

'Hello,' she said. 'I was looking for . . . well, a dress.'

'You've come to the right place,' said the woman, eyeing her up and down in a professional manner. 'Evening? Or just something kind of smart but not too over the top?'

'Yes. That.' Issy glanced about. 'And not *too* expensive.'

The woman raised an eyebrow. 'Well, you know, quality does show.'

Issy felt her face go a little pink again, but the woman bustled away through the back. 'Stay there!' she called, and Issy stayed rooted to the spot, gazing around at the beautiful chiffon cocktail dresses hung on the wall, looking as if they demanded to be drenched in perfume and taken out to dance; little bags with shiny patent bows; extraordinarily beautiful shoes. It was so lovely it reminded Issy how long it had been since she'd got dressed up for something, or someone.

The woman returned, bearing just one garment.

'Come on then.' She harried her into the tiny dressing room. 'Are you wearing a decent bra? Nope, thought not.'

'You're as bossy as Caroline,' said Issy.

'Caroline! That woman is a pushover. Now, bend down.'

Issy did. And when she straightened up, the soft mossy-green jersey of the dress rippled down her as the silk slip fitted her skin.

The dress skimmed her curves, gave her a tiny waist, and the full skirt swooshed out and swung every time she moved. The green brought out her eyes and contrasted wonderfully with her black hair; the boat neck showed off a hint of white shoulders and the elbow-length sleeves fitted perfectly. It was a dream of a dress.

'Oh,' said Issy, looking in the mirror, then doing a spin. 'It's lovely.'

'Yes, I thought it would work,' said the lady, peering over her specs.

Issy smiled. 'How much is it?'

The woman named a figure that was almost, but not quite, more than Issy would ever have dreamed of paying for a dress. But as Issy turned and twisted to catch sight of herself once again, she realised: this would be hers. Because it was lovely, yes, but because every penny it would take to pay for it wasn't a wage, or a credit card bill, or something random and untouchable. This was her money, earned by her, every penny.

'I'll take it,' said Issy.

She went back to the café then, conscious she'd dashed out without finishing up, but utterly thrilled that she had. Once she'd let herself in, she ran the coffee machine one more time, made herself a large foamy latte, covered it in chocolate powder, selected one of the few leftover cakes—a chilli chocolate—picked up the evening paper and collapsed onto the sofa, her head well down and her back to the window so no one would see her over the arm of the chair and think they were still open for business. She had nothing to do and no one to do it with, so she wasn't going to hurry to get anywhere. She would just sit for a few minutes, that was all . . .

When Issy woke up, the shadows had lengthened in the courtyard, the tree casting its shade right into the shop itself, and she blinked, not at all sure where she was. There was a noise that sounded vaguely familiar . . . yes, it was Felipe playing his violin. But why would he bother at this time of night, when everything was closed? So what was all that noise? She turned round, stretching out her arms sleepily and . . .

'*Surprise!*'

Outside, in the just fading daylight, she saw the little stumpy tree with fairy lights strung from branch to branch. But what surrounded it was even more surprising. Felipe, dressed in a rather dishevelled dinner jacket and bow tie, was playing 'Someday' and standing around him was . . . everyone.

Helena was there, with Ashok of course. Zac was there with his girl-friend, Noriko. Pearl and Louis, laughing their heads off, and Hermia and Achilles bounced excitedly next to Caroline. But more than that, all her old friends were there—Tobes and Trinida from college, all the way from Brighton. And Tom and Carla from Whitstable. And Janey, looking utterly exhausted, had managed to drag herself away from her new baby. Paul and John were there; Brian and Lana . . . Issy's heart flooded. She rushed out of the shop then realised she had locked it behind her, and had to fumble around to find the keys. Everyone laughed heartily and, when she finally let them in, launched into a rousing chorus of 'Happy Birthday to You' that brought instant tears to Issy's eyes, as did the thoughtful, lovely gifts, as did the hugs and kisses that greeted her.

'This is your last chance,' said Zac. 'Stop neglecting all your friends.'

'OK,' said Issy, nodding frantically. Everyone who hadn't been in the café before oohed and ahhed, and Helena unleashed the crates of champagne they'd hefted over from the house, after they'd realised she wasn't coming home. Pearl had figured it out first and rung Helena, and they'd crept into the square one by one, giggling. And now it was time to party! And she even had the perfect new dress.

Felipe played up a storm as the friends, clients and random people mingled and chatted. The evening was wonderfully warm, and the soft lighting of the Cupcake Café blended with the fairy lights of the tree and some candles Helena had brought putting a magical glow over the whole of Pear Tree Court. It had turned into an enchanted space, a private par-adise full of laughing friends, cheerful toasts, birthday cake and the sounds of companionship and gaiety spread up through the brick houses.

By the time Austin had finally settled Darny with the baby sitter and could consider leaving the house, Issy was pink in the face and entirely overexcited.

'*Austin!*' Issy yelled when she saw him, a glass of champagne or two to the wind. What the hell, she found herself thinking. So he didn't like her—it didn't matter. But he was here! Graeme wasn't here; no one had even mentioned him. It was her birthday. She was looking lovely in her green dress, and suddenly she felt absolutely wonderful; full of happiness and love and joy. This was the party her grandfather had wanted her to have and she wanted to share it with everyone.

She waltzed up to him. 'You *knew* about this!' she said accusingly. Austin thought how pretty she looked. 'You knew!'

'Well, of course I knew,' he said mildly, accepting with some surprise her arms thrown round him. He remembered back to their near-miss kiss that morning and smiled. 'Pearl told me. Well, I say told me, Pearl ordered me here. And when Pearl tells you to do something . . .'

Issy nodded fervently. 'Oh, yes. If you know what's good for you.'

Pearl, standing on the other side chatting to friends of Issy's glanced over. The lights gleamed off Issy's hair as she stretched up on tiptoes to hear what Austin was saying; he was so tall and messy-looking. Whatever it was, Issy had opened her mouth in laughter, grabbing Austin's arm as she did so. Pearl smiled to herself. She thought that one looked about right.

'*Ahem*,' said Helena, suddenly standing next to Issy.

'Yes?' she said. Then, 'Oh, Lena. I can't believe . . . I can't believe you did all this. I'm so, so, *so* . . . It was a lovely thing to do.'

'You need to mingle more,' said Helena to Issy. 'All these people have come a long way. *He* works across the road.'

Issy smiled apologetically at Austin. 'Oh, yes, I suppose . . .'

Issy hugged Helena. 'Thank you,' she said. 'Thank you, my dear friend. It's wonderful. It's just fantastic.' And she hurried off to chat to her long-travelling, long-suffering friends, while Austin chatted to Des the estate agent, which wasn't his ideal notion of where this party was headed, but still, the baby sitter hadn't rung yet and this was a personal record.

At 9.30, suddenly, there was a bolt of noise, the familiar rattle of a shop grille coming up with a noisy snap. It was the ironmonger's. He couldn't, Issy thought, still be here at this time of night. But he was. With solemnity and funereal speed, the ironmonger emerged from the shop, which was in pitch darkness, and glided towards Issy. She smiled a welcome to him and offered him a glass of fizz, which he refused.

'Happy birthday, my dear,' he said, and gave her a very small, wrapped parcel. Then he vanished out of the little close and into the dark night.

Everyone gathered round as Issy opened the parcel, which was wrapped in brown paper. Inside was a small cardboard box, which Issy opened with slightly shaky fingers. Then she drew out, to gasps of admiration, a tiny keyring; a fine filigree of metal, twisted exquisitely into the shape of the logo of the Cupcake Café, with, next to it, an exact representation of the pear tree they were currently underneath.

'Oh,' said Issy, suddenly feeling quite faint.

'Let me see! Let me see!' said Zac, anxious to hold a 3D representation of his design. It was absolutely lovely; pure craftsmanship and beautiful.

'That is far too lovely to be a keyring,' said Pearl straight away.

'I know,' Issy said. 'I think I'll hang it in the window.'

And although everyone else's gifts would be treasured, somehow Issy knew that the keyring was the most special gift of all. There was something about it being metal—this would last for many, many years. Which made her think that the café might, too.

There was one person missing. She knew if he'd been well enough, nothing would have kept him away. And in the midst of all her happiness, Issy felt a cold chill blow through her.

Even though the evening stayed warm, people started to drift away after that; Issy turned round at one point to realise that most people were gone, and there were only a scattering, slightly drunk now, dotted around the courtyard. Felipe was playing a winding-down kind of a song.

She looked up and realised that, one, she was in front of Austin, and two, she was very pissed. Very pissed and very happy, she realised. Was it because she was in front of Austin? Could that be the connection? She always seemed happier after she saw him. It was all very confusing.

Austin looked at Issy. She did look so pretty and so sweet, but she was obviously quite drunk, so it was definitely time for him to go home.

'Hey,' said Issy.

Issy, thought Austin to himself, had got under his skin. He couldn't deny it. It was her eager face; the slightly wounded look it took on if she thought anyone was in trouble; the optimism of her little pink-iced cakes, and the dogged man hours she had put into making the shop a success. He liked it. He had to be honest. He liked all of it. He liked her. And here she was, face rosy and tentative, gazing up at him. The fairy lights glowed in the tree, and the stars shone brightly overhead, and after her 'hey' neither of them spoke: it didn't seem to be in the least bit necessary. Slowly, almost without even thinking what he was doing, he took his hand and gently, with a feathery touch, ran it down the line of her jaw.

Issy shivered and he saw her green eyes widen. He brought his hand up now, and cupped her face with a firmer grasp, all the time staring into her eyes. The blood began to pump faster in Issy's veins. She leaned into Austin's warm hand, feeling its embrace on her skin, then looked at him with a message that was very clear: yes.

Graeme stepped out of the cab. His flight had been late getting in from Edinburgh, but he didn't care; he had no time to waste. It was entirely possible she was still hanging about her stupid shop, icing buns or whatever it was she did, and if she wasn't, he could just go straight to the flat. He slammed the cab door, not forgetting to ask for a blank receipt. He could see there were people outside the café, though it was hard to make out in the dim light. Issy must be among them. He walked out of the shadows and those who knew Graeme fell silent.

Issy, caught up in Austin's eyes, felt the change in the air around her. She turned her head, as Graeme, handsome as ever, beautifully dressed, stood underneath the street lights.

'Issy,' he said, quietly. Issy leapt back from Austin as if she'd been stung.

Austin took one look at Graeme and decided to leave.

Graeme had been doing a lot of thinking in Edinburgh. There was just something about that place. A lot of expensive real estate, but it was just so bloody quaint; full of alleyways, hidden squares and cobblestones. And everyone was completely mad for properties that looked cute. It was all about character nowadays. People wanted quaint old places.

That was when Graham had had his brilliant idea. He was incredibly impressed with himself. He had to get back to London right away, it was so brilliant. The Pear Tree Condominiums.

He knew condominium only meant flat, but it sounded American, and in his experience American was always better. Live/work spaces in a quaint old courtyard, only steps from Stoke Newington High Street, but lovely and peaceful and away from the road. And the clever bit—the *really* clever bit—was that they would look old, but in fact that would just be the frontage. They'd redo the whole thing. They'd tear out all those stupid little windows with the glass you couldn't see through, and the draughty old wooden doors, and replace them with proper PVC frames and metal doors with a fingerprint entry system (the City boys loved those), and security cameras perched above them—in fact, his heart had really started to beat fast at this bit. Maybe they could even put a gate across the alleyway, so it was like you had your own private compound. That would be ace! And they'd cut down the tree so you could park in the courtyard. It would all look cute but have the latest hi-tech gizmos.

The best thing was, he congratulated himself, he could cut Issy in on the deal. After all, it was only fair; she'd brought the area to his attention, which deserved a finder's fee. She could come back and work with him— but not taking the minutes now, she could be a proper agent if she wanted. That would be a huge leg-up for her. *And* he was going to . . . he couldn't believe he was going to do it. If anyone had said Graeme, you are going to turn into a house cat, he wouldn't have believed them.

But there were things, he had come to realise since they'd been apart, that were good about Issy: her cooking; her interest in him; the way she made everything feel slightly softer, slightly easier and gentler in his life when he was out fighting like a tiger all day. He liked it. He was prepared to make the biggest sacrifice, while also improving her life immeasurably *and* making a huge pile of money into the bargain. He had solved everything. He knew what he wanted. And of course she'd agree.

'Issy,' he said again, and she looked at him. She seemed slightly nervous, he realised. She must be expectant and excited; she must know something was up. He was going to blow her mind, right from the off.

'Iss . . . I've been an idiot. I was a total idiot to let you slip through my fingers. I've really missed you. Can we get back together?'

Issy's mind was a hive of confusion. Helena was shaking her head. Graeme stepped forward, noting quickly the cards and gifts piled up and coming to the obvious conclusion. Why, this was even better!

'Happy birthday, darling,' he said. 'Did you miss me?'

Issy stood frozen to the ground. She couldn't believe it. The very thing she'd dreamed of happening; wept over; wished for more than anything: Graeme, here, begging forgiveness, for another chance.

Graeme fumbled in his bag and pulled out his airport purchase.

'Uh, here,' he said.

Graeme! Bringing her a present! Still unable to speak, Issy drew the gift out of the plastic bag. It was a bottle of whisky.

'Finest malt,' said Graham.

Issy forced her face into a smile. 'I don't drink whisky,' she said.

'I know,' said Graeme. 'I thought you might like to put it into your cakes or something. For your very important, very successful business.'

Issy looked at him.

'I'm sorry,' he said again. 'I didn't take you seriously. I was wrong. Can I make it up to you?'

Issy stood, hugging herself. It was definitely getting colder. Graeme peered into the windows of the Cupcake Café, then glanced up at the empty properties around it. He did a full circuit of Pear Tree Court, tapping his fingers meditatively.

'You know,' he said. 'I always knew this place would come good.'

'You liar!' said Issy before she could stop herself. 'You thought I was going to starve to death.'

'Hmm. Reverse psychology,' said Graeme. 'That's what it was. Anyway, it's come good. Good for you.'

'Good for Issy!' said Helena loudly, and raised her glass, then the few remaining party people raised their glasses too, and it felt like the party was over after that, and Issy didn't know what to do. Helena was no help, setting off home with Ashok.

'We need to talk,' she said to Graeme, buying time.

'We do!' said Graeme cheerfully, hailing a cab to take them both to Notting Hill, and confidently slipping a breath mint into his mouth.

Chapter Ten

Issy SAT UP, hugging her knees, several days later, as Graeme got ready for an early morning squash match. 'What's with you, Iss?' he said, smiling. She still couldn't believe how handsome he looked. He winked at her staring. Ever since she'd come back with him that night he'd been like a different person: romantic, thoughtful, always asking her questions about the bakery and Pear Tree Court and how she liked it there.

But still, a bit of her was cross with herself. She wasn't at his beck and call. She didn't run back to him just because he happened to be around. Issy hated to think that all he had to do was wiggle his eyebrows and she would jump into bed.

But she had got so lonely she'd nearly made a complete fool of herself in front of her banking adviser, for goodness' sake. It was embarrassing. She went pink just thinking about it. And when she saw how happy Helena and Ashok were, or Zac and Noriko, or Paul and John or any of her friends, all coupled up at her party—well, why couldn't she have a bit of that? She wished they could see her now, all loved up and sweet.

'I'm fine,' she said. 'Just wish we didn't have to get up today.'

Graeme leaned over and kissed Issy on her lightly freckled nose. It all seemed to be going well. He was delighted she'd come back to him, if not that surprised. He was about to unleash the next stage in the campaign. By the time he came to getting her to give up the bakery, he was going to have a very grateful girlfriend. And a lot of money, and more prestige at the firm.

'I have a question for you,' he said.

Issy smiled cheerfully. 'Oh, yes?'

'Um . . . Well. Um.' Issy looked up. Graeme was being uncharacteristically reticent. He was not, as a rule, one of life's hemmers and hawers. He just thought a show of shyness might go down well.

'Well, I was thinking,' he continued. 'I mean, we seem to be getting on all right, don't we?'

'For the last five days, I suppose, yes,' said Issy.

'I was going to say, I really like having you here,' said Graeme.

'And I like being here,' said Issy, a curious sensation—a mixture of happiness and nerves—stealing over her.

'Well, I was going to say . . . Would you like to move in with me?'

Issy stared at Graeme in shock. Then she felt shocked that she was shocked. After all, it was absolutely everything she'd ever imagined. Everything she'd ever hoped for—living with the man of her dreams, in his lovely flat, sharing his life, cooking, hanging out, chilling on the weekend, planning their future—here it was. She blinked.

'*What* did you say?' This didn't feel right. She should be ecstatic, bouncing with happiness. Why was her heart not leaping and pounding with joy? She loved Graeme, of course she did. And when she looked at him, his face was so excited; nervous too. She could see, as she very rarely could, what he must have looked like as a little boy. Then she saw on his face again a slight puzzlement, as if he'd been expecting her (as indeed he was) to throw herself into his arms with sheer delight.

'Um, I said,' said Graeme, now stuttering slightly for real as he hadn't got the anticipated reaction. 'I said, would you like to come and live here? You could, I don't know, sell the flat or rent it out or whatever . . .'

Issy realised she hadn't even considered that. Her lovely flat! With its pink kitchen! OK, she didn't spend much time there nowadays, but still. All the happy times she'd had with Helena; all the cosy evenings; the baking experiments that succeeded or otherwise; the times she'd spent poring over her relationship with Graeme and every tiny sign he gave out— she felt another pang, realising that she'd missed doing exactly the same in return over Helena and Ashok, she'd been so immersed in the café— the pizza nights . . . all of those things. Gone for ever.

'. . . or we could have a trial period . . .'

Graeme hadn't been expecting this. He'd been expecting wild gratitude; excited plans; he'd anticipated having to tell her to slow down and not to think too much about marriage just yet; then being the joyful recipient of grateful sex, before explaining how he was also going to make her rich and release her from the shackles of her tiny shop. This look of consternation and air of distraction weren't at all what he had planned. He decided to play the hurt card.

'Sorry,' he said, making his eyes droopy and sad-looking. 'Sorry, but . . . I might be wrong but I thought this was getting quite serious.'

Issy couldn't bear to see him—her Graeme—looking sad. What was the matter with her? This was ridiculous. Here was Graeme, who she loved; who she'd dreamed of for so long. He was offering her everything on a plate and here she was, being stupid and churlish; who on earth did she think she was? Issy rushed to his side and clung to him.

'Sorry!' she said. 'Sorry! I was just—I was just so surprised I didn't know what to think!'

Wait till you hear what else I've got up my sleeve, thought Graeme, pleased his tactics had worked. He returned her embrace gladly.

'Can we . . . ? What about . . . ?' attempted Issy.

Graeme stilled her mouth with a kiss. 'I have to get to squash,' he said. 'Let's talk through the details tomorrow,' he added smoothly.

Issy went straight over to the flat after work. Helena was there on her own. 'So, how's the new life with the old man? Fun?'

Issy threw her arms round her. 'Thank you so much for the party,' she said. 'It was *amazing*. I can't thank you enough for doing it for me.'

'You can actually,' said Helena. 'After the first four hundred times you thanked me on the night.'

'OK, OK. But listen, guess what happened?'

Helena raised a well-plucked eyebrow. 'Go on then,' she said.

'Graeme's asked me to move in with him!'

Helena was surprised. She just didn't see Graeme as the warm, naturally hospitable type. But then she'd thought Ashok was a shy, retiring sort rather than the most amazing man ever, so what did she know.

Helena looked at her friend's face. Her tone was upbeat but . . . was it real? Was she genuinely over the moon? Three months ago she would have been in paroxysms of joy, but now she seemed . . . 'And you're happy?' she said, realising with a wince that she sounded a little sharper than she'd intended to.

'Um, shouldn't I be?' said Issy. 'I mean, you know . . . it's Graeme. Graeme. Who I've been mad about for ages and ages and ages and he's asked me to move in with him.'

'You know, you don't have to. If you don't feel like it. There's plenty of time.'

'But I do want to,' said Issy, sounding agitated, as if she was trying to convince herself. 'And there isn't plenty of time, Lena, don't pretend there is. I'm thirty-two. I mean, everyone's settling down. And I want that, Lena. A good man who loves me and wants to share my life and do all of that. I'm not a bad person to want that, am I?'

'Of course not,' said Helena. And it was true; that nice chap from the bank, well, he couldn't be trusted to put his underpants on the right way round, never mind look after Issy, could he? And he already had a child to look after. Graeme was an earner, he was good-looking, he had no other baggage hanging over his head—by anyone's standards he was a catch.

And Issy was right, Helena had seen it happen. Just because someone wasn't absolutely perfect for you, you threw them over and expected someone better to come round the corner, but they didn't always. She knew too many friends and colleagues feeling marooned and terrified at forty and wishing with all their hearts they hadn't thrown over Mr Nice but Not Quite Perfect when they were thirty-one. So he had taken a while to take Issy seriously—that didn't make him a bad guy, did it?

'It's great,' said Helena.

Issy felt slightly embarrassed and a little crestfallen. She'd rather expected Helena to dive in with her usual alacrity and say don't be ridiculous, of course she couldn't live with Graeme, she had to stay here and nothing would change and it would all be fine and there were a million fantastic guys and fantastic things waiting to happen, just round the corner. But Helena hadn't said that. Which meant that Issy was being a total idiot; of course this was the right thing to do. And she was excited deep down, of course she was. It was natural to feel a little nervous, that was all.

Helena smiled at her, hopefully. 'And, you know . . . well, just say no if this is all too sudden or anything like that, but, well . . .'

'Spit it out,' said Issy. It wasn't like Helena to be nervous about anything.

'Well,' said Helena, 'I know someone who might like to rent your room.'

Issy raised her eyebrows. 'Might he be a . . . *doctor* by any chance?'

Helena looked pink. 'He was looking for a flat but your place is so nice and—'

Issy held up her hands. 'You've been plotting this!!'

'I haven't, I swear.'

'And you think I would stand in the way of true love?' said Issy.

'Do you mean it?' said Helena. 'That's brilliant! I'll just phone him quickly! Ooh! Look at us!' she announced. 'The cohabitees!'

She kissed her erstwhile flatmate and rushed to the phone.

Issy couldn't help contrasting how unbelievably thrilled Helena was with her own doubts. Almost imperceptibly, it felt like something was moving between them and their friendship. Issy was delighted to see Helena so happy, she was. But the dynamic had definitely changed. They were both moving on, that was all, she told herself.

After Issy had packed up some of her stuff, they went out and pretended it was just like the old days, but as one bottle turned into two, Helena put her cards down on the table.

'Why?' she said. 'Why did you go back to him so fast?'

Issy looked up from where she'd been surreptitiously glancing at her phone—she'd texted to say she'd be a bit late, but hadn't heard from him.

'Well, because he's great, and he's available, and I really, really like him.'

'But he picks you up and drops you whenever he feels like it. And coming back into your life like this . . . . you don't know what he's up to.'

'Why does he have to be up to anything?' said Issy.

'Well, you know, with my Ashok . . .'

'Oh, yes, it's fine with your Ashok, your perfect Ashok, oh, look at my gorgeous handsome doctor who everybody loves and who adores me and I'm so in love. But then when it's Graeme you're all snooty.'

'I'm not *snooty*. I'm just saying he's put you through an awful lot of heartache and—'

'And I'm not good enough to have someone love me the way Ashok loves you, is that what you're saying? That it's so unlikely that any man would want me that he has to have some sort of ulterior motive?'

Helena wasn't used to seeing Issy so riled up.

'I didn't mean it like that.'

'Really? That's how it sounded. Or maybe you just think old Issy won't answer back, is that it? That I'm completely spineless?'

'No!'

'Well, you got one thing right. I'm not completely spineless.'

And she got up and walked out of the bar.

What's up, princess?' said Graeme, as Issy got home.

'Oh, girl stuff,' she said.

'Oh,' said Graeme, who didn't have the faintest idea what to do about girl stuff, and didn't really care either. 'Don't worry about it. Come to bed for some boy stuff.'

'OK,' said Issy, although she hated to think of her friend going back to her house and the two of them having fallen out. Graeme stroked her dark curly hair.

'Come on,' he said. 'Oh, and I thought . . . now we're shacking up and everything . . . want to come and meet my mum some time?'

And those were Issy's last thoughts before she fell asleep: he did love her. He did care for her. She lived with him, she was meeting his family. Helena was wrong about him.

Graeme lay awake a little longer. He had meant to tell her about the development tonight—he'd pitched it in the office and they'd gone mad for it. A keen landlord with an eye for a sound deal, apparently, and no problem tenants—the whole thing was going to be perfect.

Issy rolled out of bed with the sun the next morning, confusedly pulling clothes out of bags.

'What's the rush, babes?' said Graeme, sleepily.

Issy squinted at him. 'I'm going to work,' she said. 'Those cupcakes don't bake themselves.' She stifled a yawn.

'Why don't you skip work today?' said Graeme. 'You work too hard.'

Issy smiled. 'You of all people, saying that.'

'Yes, but wouldn't you like to slow down a bit? Work a bit less? Go back to a nice cosy office with sick pay and lunch breaks and office parties and someone else doing all the paperwork?'

'You know,' she said. 'I really don't think I would. I don't think I could go back to working for someone else. Not even you!'

Graeme looked at her in consternation. He would tell her later.

Pearl was actually humming coming in the doorway.

'What's with you?' said Caroline. 'You seem oddly cheerful.'

'Can't I be cheerful?' said Pearl, getting out her broom as Caroline polished the coffee machine. 'Are only middle-class people allowed to be cheerful?'

'Quite the opposite,' said Caroline, who had received a particularly nasty solicitor's letter in the post that morning.

'Quite the opposite to what?' said Issy, coming up the stairs to greet Pearl and grab a coffee, with her eyebrows covered in flour.

'Pearl thinks middle-class people are jolly.'

'Not any more I don't,' said Pearl, reaching out her finger to dip it in Issy's bowl.

'Stop that,' said Issy. 'If the health inspector saw you he'd have a fit.'

'I have my plastic gloves on,' said Pearl, showing her. 'Anyway, all chefs taste their own produce. Otherwise how would you know?'

Pearl tasted Issy's concoction. It was an orange and coconut cream sponge, soft, mellow and not too sweet.

'This tastes like a pina colada,' she said. 'It's wonderful. Amazing.'

Issy stared at her, then glanced at Caroline.

'Caroline's right,' she said. 'What's up with you? Yesterday you were miserable and today you're Rebecca from Sunnybrook Farm.'

'Can't I be happy once in a while?' said Pearl. 'Just because I don't live in your neighbourhood and have to take the bus?'

'That's not fair,' said Issy. 'I am a bus connoisseur.'

'And I'm going to have to move out of the neighbourhood,' said Caroline. She sounded so gloomy, the others looked at her in some amazement as she too dipped her finger in Issy's bowl.

'Fine,' said Issy, exasperated. 'I'll throw this lot out and make a new batch, shall I?'

Pearl and Caroline took this as an invitation to get stuck into the batter in earnest, and with a sigh Issy put down the bowl, pulled up a chair and joined them.

'What's up?' said Pearl.

'Oh, my evil bloody ex-husband,' said Caroline. 'He wants me to move out of the home. The home that, by the way, I renovated almost all by myself; furnished all eleven rooms including his study, managed the building of the all-glass back wall *and* oversaw the construction of a fifty-thousand-quid kitchen, which by the way is no picnic.'

'Although it comes with, obviously, an integrated picnic unit,' said Pearl, before realising from Caroline's face that this was no time for levity. 'Sorry,' she added, but Caroline had hardly heard her.

'I thought if I got a job, showed willing . . . But he says it means I obviously can work, so I can manage by myself. It's so unfair. I can't possibly keep my staff and the house and everything on what I earn here! This barely keeps me in pedicures.'

Issy and Pearl concentrated on the cake mix.

'Sorry, but it's true. So I don't know *what* I'm supposed to do.'

'He wouldn't force you to move out with your children, surely?' said Issy.

'Well, the letter says "steps may be taken",' said Caroline.

'But surely he can see you're trying?' said Issy. 'Doesn't that count for anything?'

'He doesn't want me to try,' hissed Caroline. 'He wants me to disappear. So he can keep getting it on with Annabel fucking Johnston-Smythe.'

'How does she even get that on her credit card?' wondered Pearl.

'Anyway, let's change the subject,' said Caroline testily. 'Why *are* you so happy, Pearl?'

Pearl looked embarrassed and said a lady never kissed and told, which made both of them squeal so much Pearl got quite cross and they realised there was a queue of punters at the door, unwilling to intrude.

'I have work to do,' said Pearl stiffly and got up to serve.

'You take it nice and easy,' said Issy, heading downstairs hastily as the first client of the day asked to try out the coconut and orange she had already chalked up on the specials board.

'Soon, soon,' she said to the customer.

'Don't you deliver?' said the woman. They looked at each other.

'We should do that,' said Pearl.

'I'll put it on the list,' said Issy.

She felt cheered by Pearl's good humour—the fact that she wouldn't admit to the identity of the chap made Issy wonder if it wasn't Louis's dad, but she would never dream of asking. She worried about Caroline's divorce, partly for her and partly for selfish reasons, because she didn't want to lose her. She was prickly and snobbish, but she also worked hard and had an ability to present the cakes in the most beguiling of styles; she'd also improved the room with tiny floating candles that emerged after dusk and cosy cushions in awkward corners that softened the place.

But, mixing a new batch of cakes, sprinkling the coconut with a light hand and switching the white sugar to brown to intensify the depth of flavour, she couldn't help thinking about Helena. They'd never fallen out. She'd go round. And take a gift.

Issy met Helena on the way.

'I was just coming over . . .' said Helena. 'I'm so, so, so—'

'No, I am,' said Issy.

'I'm happy for you, honestly,' said Helena. 'I just want you to be happy.'

'Me too,' said Issy. 'Please, let's not fight.'

'No,' said Helena. The two women embraced in the street.

'Here,' said Issy, handing over the piece of paper she'd been carrying about all day.

'What's that?' said Helena. Then, as she stared at it, she understood. 'The secret recipe! For my favourite doughnuts! No way!'

'Well,' said Issy. 'Now you have your heart's desire.'

Helena smiled. 'Come back,' she said. 'Come and have a cup of tea. It's still your flat.'

'I should get back,' said Issy. 'Got to see my man, you know.'

Helena nodded. She did know. Which didn't make it any less odd, as they hugged tightly once again and parted, for them to head off home, but going in different directions.

Helena had given her her mail too. And Issy's heart had sunk. More recipes; but they were ones she'd already had, or things that didn't make sense. She'd spoken to Keavie on the phone, who'd said yes, he had been on good form when she'd seen him, but overall things weren't good, and to pop in whenever she could, which she did the next day.

To her surprise, when she reached the nursing home, someone was already in the room; a short man with a hat on his knee, sitting on the chair next to the bed, chatting away. When he turned round she realised she knew his face but for a second she couldn't place him. Then she did: it was her neighbour, the ironmonger.

'What are you doing here?' she said, rushing over to kiss Gramps, so very pleased to see him.

'A darling girl!' said Gramps. 'I am mostly but not completely sure which one. This delightful man has been keeping me company.'

Issy eyed him shrewdly. 'Well, that's kind of you.'

'Not at all,' said the man. He put out his hand. 'Chester.'

'Issy. Thank you for the keyring,' she said, suddenly shy. The man smiled back, shy too.

'I met your grandfather through your shop. We've become good friends.'

'Gramps?' said Issy.

Her grandfather smiled weakly. 'I just asked him to keep an eye on you.'

'You asked him to spy?'

'You use an electric whisk! What next? Margarine?'

'Never,' said Issy vehemently.

'It's true,' said Chester. 'She has never had a margarine delivery.'

'Stop spying on me!'

'All right,' said Chester. There was that trace of a Middle European accent she couldn't place. 'I won't.'

'Or . . . well, if you must,' said Issy, who rather liked the idea of having someone looking out for her. It hadn't happened before. 'At least come in and try one of the cakes.'

The man nodded. 'Your grandfather warned me off eating your profits. He said you were too kind not to feed me for nothing and that I wasn't allowed to ask for anything.'

'It's still a business,' said Grampa Joe weakly from the bed.

Keavie popped her head in. 'Hi, Issy! How's the love life?'

'So you know everything too!' said Issy, stung.

'Give over! Anyway, he does your grandfather a power of good. Perks him right up.'

'Hmm,' said Issy.

'And I like it,' said the ironmonger. 'Selling spanners is a lonely road.'

'And we both know the shop trade,' said Gramps.

'All right, all right,' said Issy. She'd been used to being the only person her gramps would turn to for so long, she wasn't sure about him having a friend. Now, though, Gramps was looking around, confused.

'Where is this?' he said. 'Isabel? Isabel?'

'I'm here,' said Issy, as Chester made his goodbyes and left. She took Gramps's hand.

'No,' he was saying. 'Not you. Not Isabel. That's not who I meant. That's not who I meant at all.'

He grew more and more agitated, and his grip on Issy's hand grew stronger and stronger, till Keavie came in with a male nurse and they persuaded him to drink some medicine.

'That'll calm him down,' said Keavie, looking straight at Issy. 'You understand,' she went on, 'that calming him down, making him comfortable . . . that's all we can really . . .'

'You're saying he's not going to get any better,' said Issy miserably.

'I'd say his lucid moments are going to get fewer and further apart,' said Keavie. 'And you need to prepare yourself for that.'

They looked at the old man settled back into the pillows.

'He knows,' Keavie whispered. 'Even patients with dementia . . . Everyone is so fond of your grandfather here, you know. They really are.'

Issy squeezed her hand in gratitude.

Two Saturdays later, Des, the estate agent, popped his head round the door. Jamie was squawking his head off.

'Sorry,' he said to Issy, who was enjoying the 'The Guide' section of *The Guardian* before the Saturday shoppers' lunchtime rush arrived. Her Cupcake Café keyring was sparkling in the summer sunlight through the polished windows.

'Oh, that's all right,' said Issy, jumping up. 'I was just enjoying a quiet moment. Hang on, what can I get you?'

'I wondered if you'd seen Mira?' said Des.

Issy glanced at the sofa. 'Oh, she normally comes in around this time,' she said. 'She should be here any moment. They've got a proper flat now, and she's got a job.'

'That's brilliant!'

'I know. Aha!' said Issy as Mira and Elise arrived. 'Speak of the devil.'

Mira immediately took Jamie off Des and, as was his wont, he stopped howling to regard her with his large round eyes.

'Ems has kicked me out the house . . . for a bit,' added Des hastily. 'He's been right as rain, Mira, since he got over that colic. He's a great wee man. The thing is, the last couple of days have been just awful, just terrible.'

Mira raised her eyebrows.

'The doctor said it's nothing, just teething.'

'So you brought him to the baby-whisperer!' Issy said cheerfully, lining up a black coffee, a babycino for Elise and a large cappuccino with plenty of grated chocolate. Jamie, previously content, was now opening his mouth in preparation for a huge wail, as Mira poked her fingers in his soft gums.

Des looked sheepish. 'Uh, well, something like that.'

Mira gave him a stern look as Jamie screamed. 'Give me a knife.'

Issy and Des looked at each other. 'Knife. I need a knife.'

Des put up his hands. 'Honestly, we can't take much more of this at home. Ems is sleeping at her mum's as it is.'

Somewhat nervously, Issy handed Mira a serrated knife. Quick as a flash, Mira stuck Jamie down on his back on the sofa, pinned down his arms and made two little darts inside his mouth with the knife. Jamie screamed the place down.

'What . . . what have you *done?*' said Des, grabbing Jamie up from the sofa and cradling him in his arms. Mira shrugged. As Des glared at her he noticed that Jamie, once the initial shock and pain had passed, was gradually calming down. His great heaving gulps of air grew slower and slower, and his tense, infuriated little body started to relax. He nestled his head lovingly into his father's chest and, no doubt utterly exhausted from his painful, sleepless nights, his eyelids started to droop.

'Well,' said Des. 'Well.'

Issy shook her head. 'Mira, what did you do?'

Mira shrugged again. 'He has teeth coming. They are pushing through the gum. Very painful. Now I cut through the gum. Teeth through now. Not sore. Not rocket science.'

'I have never heard of that,' said Des softly, so as not to disturb his now snoozing baby.

'Nobody here has heard of anything,' said Mira.

She accepted the tea, and Elise, who had been sitting very quietly with a book, murmured a little thank you for the babycino. Des rushed to pay for them.

'This has saved my life,' he said. 'Actually, can I have mine in a take-away cup? I'm going to go straight home and attempt a nap.'

'Of course,' said Issy.

Des looked around. 'So . . . ahem . . . I hear rumours on the grapevine.'

'What's that then?' said Issy pleasantly, ringing up the sale.

'I heard something about you selling up . . . assumed you were off somewhere bigger.' Des looked round appraisingly. 'You've done a really good job with this and no mistake.'

Issy handed him his change.

'Well, you've heard totally wrong,' she said. 'We're not going anywhere.'

'Excellent,' said Des. 'I must have misheard. Sleep deprivation, you know. OK, well, thanks again.'

Suddenly there was a loud scraping noise outside. Issy rushed out; Des stayed inside in case Jamie woke up again. In the bright summer sunlight, the ironmonger was dragging two wrought-iron chairs past the tree. Next to that was a beautiful table. Issy stood and stared.

'That's amazing,' she said and rushed to help drag the furniture into position. There were two tables, each with three chairs, and all were freshly painted in cream. They were absolutely lovely. Two heavy chains were attached to the legs to stop them being stolen in the night.

'Your grandfather ordered the whole thing,' said Chester, putting up his hands as Issy gave him a hug. 'And paid for it, so don't worry about it. He reckoned you needed them.'

'I do,' said Issy, shaking her head. 'What a stroke of luck you turned out to be. You're our guardian locksmith.'

Chester smiled. 'You have to look out for each other in the big city,' he said. 'And I know he told me not to but . . .'

'Coffee and cake?'

'That would be lovely.'

Pearl came out with a tray all ready and sat down to admire the new view. 'Perfect,' she said.

Any day now, thought Issy. Any day now she was going to stop feeling like a guest in someone else's home. She would be able to stop tiptoeing everywhere, terrified of making a mess. She hadn't realised Graeme's commitment to minimalism was so . . . so absolute.

Yes, the flat was lovely, but it was more the habits: getting into the habit of taking off her shoes; never putting anything down, not even a coat, not even for a second. Of having no magazines lying around; of lining up the remote control; of trying to find a tiny space for a chest of drawers to take her clothes, as Graeme's were all hung up, still wreathed in their plastic wrappers from the dry-cleaner's. His bathroom cabinet was full of every sort of product imaginable, for skin, for hair; all of it immaculate.

The cleaner scuttled in twice a week and scrubbed down absolutely everything. Toast had become a happy memory—too many crumbs on the shiny glass surfaces of the kitchen—and they were eating a lot of easy-to-clear stir-fry, even though Issy chafed a little in a kitchen that bothered with a boiling water tap, a wok flame and a wine fridge, but not a proper oven to bake anything in. Would it ever really feel like home?

Graeme, on the other hand, was already feeling he could get used to this. As long as he gave her a bit of a sharp look whenever she left stuff on the floor—why were women always so messy? Apart from that, it was nice to have someone there at the end of the day—she finished so much earlier than he did. It was nice to have someone ask him how his day had been, to produce a home-cooked dinner rather than the ready meals he usually lived off; to pour him a glass of wine and listen to the litany of his day. It was really good actually; he was surprised he hadn't thought of it before. She'd asked him whether she could bring her books over and he'd had to say no; he didn't have bookshelves, it would spoil the layout of the sitting room, and he absolutely didn't want her kitsch cooking gear in here. But she didn't seem to mind that. All of that was fine.

However, there was something else playing on his mind. The London office were gung-ho for him to go full steam ahead on this Pear Tree Court idea now. They saw it as a move from just letting offices to actually selling lifestyles, and if it went well, he could see a seriously major future for himself in lifestyle development. It was big-time stuff.

But now it was becoming clear to him that actually, Issy really liked running this stupid little shop and being treated like a skivvy all the time. The more they sold and the harder she had to work, the happier she seemed to be. And the money was still total rubbish. Surely she'd see sense when he explained it . . .

Graeme scowled to himself; he wasn't 100 per cent sure this Issy situation would resolve itself quite as easily as he'd believed.

As the summer progressed, the shop showed no signs of slowing down; quite the opposite, in fact. Issy made a mental note for next year to think about stocking some proper homemade organic ice creams; they would have gone down a treat. Perhaps they could have a barrow outside for people wandering past. Maybe Felipe could staff it, and play his violin in quiet times. More forms, of course, for the council, to run an outdoor food concession, but she sent them in anyway. It was amazing, she thought, how the paperwork, which had once seemed so daunting, was now so easy to handle. She realised, with a start, that she was blushing less too. What a funny side effect of baking for a living.

Coming in from a quick break in the park (complete with ice cream), she could hear Pearl and Caroline squabbling. They'd seemed to be on pretty good terms recently; Pearl was mostly cheerful, and Caroline had taken to wearing tiny vest tops that on someone twenty years younger would have looked cute but on Caroline emphasised her jutting collarbones and Madonna-like arms. Issy was aware that the builders made rude comments about her and Pearl together, but ignored them. Pearl anyway was looking miles better; simply coming to a job every day instead of staying indoors had meant she'd dropped a couple of dress sizes and now, to Issy's eyes, looked very much the size she was born to be, perfectly in proportion in every way.

'We'll have his aunties round, and everyone will bring a bottle, and that will do,' Pearl was saying stubbornly.

'No, it *won't* do,' Caroline was saying. 'He needs a proper party like everybody else.'

Pearl bit her lip. Louis, eventually, due to his unstinting good nature, and the mothers' desire to look inclusive and non-prejudiced, had started to receive a party invitation or two, but Pearl had looked at them and worriedly turned them down. They all seemed to be held in really expensive places like the zoo or the Natural History Museum, and she just wasn't sure she could afford them yet. Now the shop was doing better, Issy had increased her wages (against Mrs Prescott's advice, she knew), but Pearl was using the money to pay off catalogues for stuff she really needed—a proper bed for Louis, new sheets and towels—not buying expensive gifts and going to expensive parties.

'It will be a proper party,' she said. On top of all that, she didn't like Caroline being right about anything. 'There'll be plenty of presents.'

'Why don't you have his friends round?' persisted Caroline in that annoyingly blinkered way of hers. 'Just invite ten or so.'

'What's this?' asked Issy cheerfully.

'We're planning Louis's birthday party,' said Caroline brightly.

Pearl shot her a look. 'Maybe.'

'Well, I'll ask him if he wants a proper party,' said Caroline.

Pearl looked at Issy with desperation in her face. Issy had an idea.

'I've been thinking about this for a while,' she said. 'You know how quiet we are on Saturdays? I was thinking about shutting then, but Mrs Prescott will kill us and then Austin will kill us too. So, one thing I thought we might do is have . . . cupcake-themed birthday parties. The idea is that the kids come and they have to bake and decorate their own cakes, and we have little aprons and mixing bowls for them, and we charge for the hire of the place. It could be quite a nice little money-spinner. And good for kids. No one learns to bake any more.'

'That is brilliant,' said Caroline. 'I shall tell my gals immediately and insist that they do it. And we can serve the grown-ups tea. Although,' she added thoughtfully, 'I personally have never got through one of those wretched children's parties without a strong drink or two.'

'So, Pearl,' said Issy, 'we could have Louis and his friends as a test case to see if it's going to work. Take some sweet photos of them all covered in flour, use them as publicity, that kind of thing.'

'So it will be just like every working day, except more so,' said Pearl.

'All children's birthdays are like that,' said Caroline. 'Hell on wheels!'

Graeme tried to feel as confident as he knew he looked. Nonetheless, although normally he felt like a tiger at meetings, aggressive and confident that he would be the top man, today he was nervous. It was getting ridiculous. He was Graeme Denton. He didn't get silly about a girl, ever. He still hadn't told Issy his plan, But every day Kalinga Deniki wanted to know his progress, were pushing for planning applications and the green light. They had already had preliminary surveyor's reports and now he was meeting with Mr Barstow, the landlord for most of Pear Tree Court.

Mr Barstow didn't bother with the formalities when he walked in. He extended his small plump hand and grunted. Graeme nodded and began his presentation, talking about how a bulk buyout of both occupied and vacant space would be a great thing for Barstow, at some bulk discount to KD. By the third graph, Mr Barstow's eyes were glazing over. He waved his hands at them.

'OK, OK. Write the figure down on a piece of paper.'

Graeme paused, and decided to do exactly that. Mr Barstow glanced at it contemptuously and shook his head. 'Nah. Anyway, got someone in number four. Running a little caff. Making not a bad fist of it either. She's bringing up the prices around the place.'

Graeme inwardly groaned. This was all he needed; Issy was actually making his job harder for him. 'She's coming to the end of her six-month contract though. We'll make it worth your while.'

Graeme felt a momentary twinge. He shouldn't know when Issy's contract was up, but he did of course. Mr Barstow raised his eyebrows. 'So you've talked to her about it then? Well, I suppose, if she's amenable . . .'

Graeme didn't change his expression, either to imply he'd spoken to her or not. It was none of Mr Barstow's business.

'Don't know how I'll get that ironmonger out though. He's been there longer than I have,' reflected the landlord. He rubbed one of his chins. 'Don't know how he turns a dime.'

Graeme didn't care either way. 'I'm sure we can make him an offer he can't refuse.'

Mr Barstow looked doubtful again.

'I think you'd better keep writing on that piece of paper, mate.'

Issy was looking forward to meeting her possible future mother-in-law. In her mind's eye she was a nice, slightly rounded, eager-to-please lady with Graeme's handsome dark hair and twinkling eyes, and they could share recipes and bond. Maybe she'd have liked a daughter in her life. At any rate, it was with some excitement that she'd dressed up in a pretty summery frock and taken along her lightest Victoria sponge as a gift.

Mrs Denton lived in an immaculate modern townhouse on a group of streets that looked exactly alike in Canary Wharf. The house was tiny with low ceilings, but had all mod cons—Graeme had found it for her.

'Hello,' said Issy warmly, looking past her at the pristine hallway. There were no pictures on the walls, apart from an enormous one of Graeme as a schoolboy, and no clutter of any kind anywhere. 'Ooh, I can see where your son gets his tidiness from!'

Graeme's mother smiled, seemingly lost in thought for a moment.

'I brought you some cake,' Issy went on cheerfully. 'Did Graeme tell you I was a baker?'

Carole felt rooted to the spot. She had been so excited—this was the first girl Graeme had brought home in four or five years. She'd been quite impatient for a while now for Graeme to get moving. She'd pictured maybe one of those delicate, pretty girls, very clever and so on, but utterly ready to give up her career and look after her boy, and desperate for some advice on Graeme's likes and dislikes, how to cook his favourite things.

That was what she was expecting, after Graeme had called and said that he was bringing 'Issy' to tea. So when she opened the door to see this diminutive, rounded, rosy-cheeked brunette—who had to be at least, what, thirty-four? Thirty-five? Could she even still *have* children? What on earth was Graeme thinking? Graeme was so handsome, everyone said so. And so smart, with his smart car and his smart suits and his smart flat. There was absolutely no way . . .

'Cake!' said Issy again. 'Um, I don't know if you like cake.'

Issy felt the familiar blush spreading across her cheeks and grew hot and cross with herself. She glanced hurriedly at Graeme, who normally ignored his silly mother, but even he could see that her behaviour could be construed as quite rude. He gave Issy's hand a quick squeeze.

'Issy's my girlfriend,' he said. 'Uh, Mum, can we come in?'

'Of course,' said Carole weakly, standing back. Without thinking Issy walked straight in, then froze as she realised that, behind her, Graeme had bent down and taken off his shoes. Of course he had.

'Ah,' said Issy, taking off her sandals and realising as she did so that she could do with a pedicure. She noticed Carole checking out her feet too.

'Shall I put this cake in your kitchen?' said Issy brightly. Carole gestured ahead. The kitchen was utterly spotless. Laid out on the side were three neat bowls with prewashed salad, a small pile of neatly trimmed white-bread ham sandwiches and a jug of lemonade.

Issy put the cake down. This could turn into a long afternoon.

'So do you work?' asked Issy politely when they sat at the obviously rarely used round table. It was a glorious day and Issy had looked longingly at the immaculately tended garden, but Carole had announced loudly that she was terrified of wasps and flying insects and never ever sat outside. So now they were all sitting indoors with the windows shut and the television on so that Graeme could watch the sport.

Carole looked surprised at the question. 'Well, presumably Graeme's told you about my charity work?' she said stiffly. 'And of course, the Rose Growers Association keeps me busy. Although I mostly do the admin for that. Insects, you see. They never seem very grateful.'

'The insects?'

'The rose growers.' Carole sniffed. 'I slave over the minutes for them.'

'I know what that's like,' said Issy sympathetically, but Carole didn't seem to hear her.

'Do they all still love you in the office, darling?' she cooed to Graeme. Graeme grunted and indicated that he was trying to watch the television. 'He's ever so popular there,' she said to Issy.

'I know,' said Issy. 'That's where we met.'

Carole raised her eyebrows. 'I thought he said you worked in a shop.'

'I run my own business,' said Issy. 'I'm a baker. I make cakes and so on.'

'I can't eat cakes,' said Carole. 'They interfere with my digestion.'

Issy thought with some regret of the lighter-than-air sponge sitting in the kitchen. They'd already eaten the ham sandwiches—it had taken two minutes—and she now felt trapped and unsatisfied, still sitting at the table, waiting for the tea to cool.

'So, er,' said Issy, desperate to get this conversation on track. Graeme was whooping a goal. She decided to stick to the safest possible ground.

'So, Graeme was totally the most popular at work. He's doing brilliantly there, I think, still. You must be very proud.'

Carole almost softened for a second before remembering that this chubby, ageing harpy sitting in front of her had had the temerity to show up with a cake, implying that she, Carole, didn't bake for her own son, and had swanned in here with her shoes on like she owned the place already.

'Yes, well, he always did go for the best, my son,' she said, larding the comment with as much double meaning as she could manage. Issy had been completely crestfallen.

'She hates me,' Issy had pointed out mournfully on the way home.

'She doesn't hate you,' said Graeme, grumpy because his team had lost again. In fact, Carole had taken him into the kitchen to tell him in no uncertain terms that she wasn't happy. Wasn't Issy terribly old? And just a baker? Graeme, unused to his mother questioning his judgment on anything, had tuned out. He didn't need Issy nipping his head about it too. 'She just thinks you're a bit old.'

'That's what she said?' said Issy quietly.

'Mm,' said Graeme.

'Do you think I'm a bit old?'

'For what?' This was a conversation he didn't want to be in.

Issy closed her eyes tightly. So close, she thought. So close; she could just ask him now. Was this her happy-ever-after? But what if she did ask and the answer was 'no'? And what if she did ask and the answer was 'yes'?

If both the answers were going to make her unhappy, well, what did that mean? What did that make her? Suddenly she saw the years stretching ahead . . . Graeme, marching forward with his career, using her, maybe, as a sounding board if he needed to vent, but otherwise as a general slave . . . ignoring her to watch TV, the way he did his mother. An easy, non-demanding doormat. Well, maybe she had been a bit like that. But she had changed. The café had changed her.

'Graeme . . .' she said, turning to him in the rain-flecked car.

What do you mean?' Graeme had said. He'd been more upset than Issy had expected, but of course she didn't know what this meant for him at work.

'I don't think . . . I don't think this is going to work out, do you?' said Issy, as calmly as she could. After swearing repeatedly, he had shut up like a clam and refused to speak to her any more. As soon as was legally possible, he had simply stopped the car and dropped her by the side of the road. It felt oddly fitting somehow, thought Issy, watching the sports car zip away. Allow him his petty little victory; she didn't even mind too much; and when a cab cruised past, its yellow light shining like a friendly beacon, she hailed it to take her home.

Helena shrieked when she came in, and demanded all the details of her disastrous visit to Graeme's mother.

'It just became obvious,' said Issy, 'that, regardless of *what* is out there . . . well, it was doing me no good. Although,' she said, with slightly wobbly bravado, 'I would have liked to have a baby.'

'You'll have a baby,' said Helena reassuringly.

'Thanks, Lena,' said Issy, and her friend took her in her arms and gave her a long, reassuring hug.

Chapter Eleven

LOUIS'S BIRTHDAY finally arrived.

'You are bouncing this morning,' observed Pearl, folding up Buzz Lightyear napkins.

'Of course I am,' said Issy. 'It's beautiful Louis's birthday, isn't it.'

'*It's my birfday*,' agreed Louis, who was sitting on the floor making his new Iggle Piggle and Tombliboo (gifts from Issy) kiss each other and bake imaginary cupcakes.

'And are you having a birthday party today?'

'*Yes. All my friends coming to Louis party.*'

Issy glanced at Pearl, who nodded. 'Well, they all said yes,' she said, looking faintly surprised.

'Why wouldn't they?' said Issy.

Pearl shrugged. She still felt forced into this. It was one thing asking the kids at nursery to Issy's safe, well-known cupcake shop, right next to their homes. It would have been a different story altogether if she'd invited them to *her* home. Being the first kid in the area to get exclusive access to a baking party was one thing. Doing it for Louis was quite another.

'Who else is coming?' asked Issy.

'My mum,' said Pearl. 'My pastor. A couple of people from the church.'

She didn't add that she'd hardly asked any of her friends. It wasn't that she was ashamed of where she worked, or that Louis was in with a group of new people. She just didn't want them to think that she was showing off, and she didn't want anyone to imagine she was getting above herself. Most of all, she didn't mention Ben. He knew where the party was. And he'd promised to be there.

'Well, it'll be fantastic,' said Issy, sorting out the raw ingredients into little bowls. She'd also invested in a dozen tiny aprons.

'*It's my birfday!*' announced Louis loudly, seeing as no one had mentioned it for at least three minutes.

'Well, is it there, little man?' said Doti, coming through the door. 'Just as well I have some cards for you then.' And he opened his bag and revealed half a dozen bright coloured envelopes. Some were addressed to him, others simply to 'the little boy at the Cupcake Café'. Pearl squinted.

Issy picked him up. 'Have you been telling everyone it's your birthday?' she asked him solemnly.

Louis nodded. Pearl and Issy exchanged slightly worried glances.

Pearl put her head next to Louis. '*Who* did you ask to your birthday, baby?' she asked gently.

'Well, me for one,' said Doti. 'Thought I'd come by when I've finished my rounds. I have quite the present for you, young man.'

'*Yay!*' said Louis, rushing up to the postie and throwing his little arms round his knees. '*I do like presents, Mr Postman.*'

'Well, that's good.'

Doti checked his bag. 'Oh, there's another couple here.'

Pearl rolled her eyes. 'He's invited half the town.'

Austin groaned. There was a *mountain* of work mail that he had thrown in his satchel the previous evening before he left the bank. He absolutely had to look at it. 'OK,' he said, opening the sitting-room door. 'You can watch that Japanese strobe-y thing you like on TV. I have work to do.'

'And we have a party this afternoon,' said Darny laconically. Austin looked at him suspiciously. Darny didn't get asked to many parties.

'Whose party?' asked Austin doubtfully.

'Louis's party,' said Darny.

'I'm not getting it,' said Austin. 'Who's Louis?'

'The boy in the café,' said Darny.

Austin squinted. 'What, little Louis? The baby?'

'You're very prejudiced,' said Darny. 'I would hate to only have friends from my own age range.'

'It's his birthday today? And he's invited you to his party?'

'Yes,' said Darny. 'When you went in with the bank bags.'

Austin had popped in the previous week. After Issy's party he had wanted to see her, even if just to make sure that things were all right between them and not too embarrassing. Also, even though it was tough to admit it to himself, he missed her. He liked spending time with her.

At any rate, when he'd gone to the shop after school one day, she wasn't there, just Pearl and that scary-looking woman. And sure enough, Darny and Louis had been on the floor together, playing.

'Hmm,' said Austin. Well, it was a beautiful July day, and he didn't really have a plan for them that afternoon. He sighed. 'I'm going to work in the front room, OK? Don't turn the music up too loud.'

Austin was worrying about whether he had time to get Louis a birthday present when he opened the first of the work mail he'd brought home in a rush. He had to stare at it for a couple of minutes before he got his head round it. It was a loan application for a property development initiative marked Kalinga Deniki . . . He looked at the address. Then he looked at it again. It couldn't be. It couldn't be right. Pear Tree Court. But not one number in it: the whole of it. 'A new paradigm in work/life style, conveniently situated in the heart of buzzing Stoke Newington,' it said.

Austin shook his head. It sounded horrible. Then he glanced at the name at the bottom of the paper and shut his eyes in dismay. It couldn't be. It couldn't. But there it was. Graeme Denton.

Austin lowered the paper in total shock. Surely not? Surely not Issy's Graeme. But, of course, it was. Graeme. Which meant, as he had clearly seen at the birthday party, Issy and Graeme. Together.

So they must have planned the whole thing. This must be their little scheme. Posh up the area with a little cupcake shop then cash in on it. It was, he had to admit, very clever. The cachet would certainly add value to the properties. Unbelievable. He was almost impressed. He glanced at the architect's plans enclosed with the applications. There it was; a great big gate across the entrance to Pear Tree Court. Making it a private road. Blocking off that lovely little courtyard and the tree from everyone else. Austin remembered it just a few weeks ago, with the fairy lights in the tree and Felipe playing his violin. It had seemed such a happy place. He wondered how they'd managed to persuade the ironmonger to move.

Well, people as ruthless as that . . . He supposed they'd stop at nothing.

He couldn't help remembering, though, how eager, how keen Issy had seemed about her business; how hard she'd worked, how convincing she'd been. He'd been completely taken in.

Austin realised he was pacing the room. This was stupid. Stupid. She was someone who'd needed a bank loan, and was well on the way to paying it back, and now they needed another and had good security and backing. It was a simple business proposition, and one that technically he'd support. Graeme's company was a respectable one, and raising money from a local bank rather than a City titan made good practical sense for everyone and would definitely impress the planners.

But he couldn't believe his instincts about Issy had been so far off base. It made him doubt himself completely. She wasn't what he'd thought at all, not a tiny bit of it. Amazing.

Outside it was a glorious day, and Issy and Louis had already had a long game of running round the tree. Pearl looked on. Issy had told her everything that had happened. She thought it was for the best. Graeme had seemed such a petulant man. And when children came along, you didn't want two infants to deal with.

She let her thoughts flicker briefly to Ben. But people could change. She was sure of it. Of course they did. Boys grew up. Became men. But still, in Issy's case, she thought it was probably for the best.

Pearl set her jaw. And even without Ben—she glanced over at Issy tickling Louis—sometimes you took your family where you could get it. She heaved a sigh. That nice, scruffy young man from the bank. There was a real man. There was a man who knew how to look after his family.

'OK!' said Issy, spotting the first 4x4 pulling up and a beautifully groomed young mother emerge, with a spotless child in a button-down shirt and chinos clutching a large gift. Louis dashed out to meet them.

'Jack! Ayo, Jack!'

'Hahyo, Louis!' hollered Jack.

Louis looked at the gift expectantly.

'Give the present to Louis,' said the mother briskly. Jack looked at the present. Louis looked at the present.

'Hand it over now, Jack,' said the mother, slightly tight-jawed. 'Remember that this is Louis's birthday.'

'*Mah bifday*,' chimed in Jack, burying his head in the present.

Jack's lip wobbled. Issy and Pearl dashed out.

'Hello, hello,' said Pearl. 'Thank you so much for coming.'

'Look what I've got for you,' said Issy, leaning down next to Jack and Louis with two tiny pinnies. 'Do you want to be a top chef and come and make cakes?'

'Going to eat cakes?' said Jack suspiciously.

'Yes, we're going to make our own cakes and then eat them,' said Issy.

Jack reluctantly allowed himself to be taken by the hand, as other children started to arrive behind him. But not just children: Kate's three builders, who'd brought their own children; Mira and Elise, of course; Des, the estate agent, and Jamie; and Zac, Helena and Ashok.

'Louis invited you?' said Issy, delighted to see them. Ashok and Helena were entwined in each other's arms.

'He certainly did,' said Helena. 'We bought him a doctor's kit. It's a real doctor's kit with all the sharp bits taken out.'

'I thought the NHS was underfunded,' said Issy, turning on the coffee machine. They'd pushed all the tables together so there was a long workbench, and as soon as everyone was here and Oliver had stopped crying in the corner and his mother stopped telling him off for crying in a corner, they were going to start.

Graeme had woken up at 5 a.m., sat bolt upright, then lain staring at the ceiling, feeling his heart race. What was he thinking? What had he done? This was an absolute disaster. How had he let Issy break up with him already? She could do whatever she liked once the deal was done.

He cancelled his squash game, thinking maybe he'd go for a run, get it out of his system . . . He returned to the flat, sweating—partly from his run, partly from sheer nerves. There was a message in his inbox. It was from the bank where they'd put in for a loan, asking him to go in for a meeting on Monday. They were going to say yes. Of course they were. Graeme was moving towards the shower when he saw something that made his blood run cold. The bottom of the email . . . Where did he know that name from?

Austin Tyler.

He shook his head. Fuck. It was that lanky friend of Issy's. The same guy. Obviously it was meant to be confidential but . . . he'd been at her birthday party, he'd seen him. If they were mates . . . If Austin had read the application, he would almost certainly tell Issy about it. He did her banking. It would be weird if he didn't ask her about it. And if she found out from someone other than him . . . Graeme's blood ran cold. She wouldn't like it. And the consequences for him, for them, for his job, if Issy didn't like it . . .

Graeme showered in double-quick time then threw on the first clothes he came to—very unlike him—and ran to the car.

'**O**K!' said Issy, once everyone finally had a coffee. There were people squeezed against the back walls. It was ridiculous in here. Even Louis's nursery minders had come, and Issy couldn't believe that after having the children all day for five days the staff would voluntarily come out on a Saturday, but here they were. It was nice when you thought about it. A really lovely nursery. The other mothers had spotted it too and were asking themselves why they hadn't thought to invite the nursery staff. It smacked of favouritism, they sniffed.

Pearl sniffed back in their general direction. Of course it was favouritism. Who wouldn't want her radiant Louis over Oliver, who had now wet his pants and the floor and whose mother was almost as close to hysteria as he was. She looked around. There was one person missing.

'OK,' said Issy, and everyone settled down. 'Now, first of all, has everyone washed their hands?'

'*Ye-es*,' chorused the little ones.

'Well, first we take the flour . . .'

'**A**ustin! I want to go to the party!'

'I said no.'

'I'm going on my own,' said Darny. 'You can't stop me. I'm ten.'

Darny sat down and started lacing up his shoes. Austin didn't know what to do if Darny insisted. Austin just didn't want to see Issy right now. He was cross; he felt let down and hoodwinked, even though he realised he had no right to feel that way. She'd never promised him anything. But she had taken a tiny corner of the area he'd grown up in, an area he loved, and she'd made it lovely; put flowers in the square, and a coloured canopy over the windows, and pretty little tables. It was a nice place to be, to go; to see other people enjoying some peace and quiet, or a good chat, over a slice of absolutely heavenly cherry pie. And now she was closing up shop; shutting it all off, for the sake of a few measly quid. He was totally not in the mood for a children's party. They weren't going.

He was jerked out of his reverie by a slamming door.

'**N**ow,' said Issy. 'This is the tricky part. Could the mummies help with the eggs, please?'

'*Nooo!*' said a dozen little voices simultaneously. The mothers swapped looks. Issy raised her eyebrows.

'Well, how about we get another mummy to help you? All the mummies move one child along.'

Sure enough, the toddlers were happy to be helped by someone who wasn't their mother. Issy took note of this and filed it away for future reference. A ray of sun beamed through the windows and lit up a happy tableau: the adults, chatting and making friends around the periphery of the shop, and in a row the little boys and girls, focusing intently on their wooden spoons and mixing bowls. At the top of the table, wearing a special chef's birthday hat, was Louis, banging happily and commenting on everyone else's work like the café authority which, Issy supposed, he probably was by now.

Deep inside, listening to the clink of cups and the chatter of conversation and the squeaks and snuffles of the children, she suddenly felt a sensation of great peace; of accomplishment; of something created with her bare hands out of nothing. I made this, she thought to herself. Suddenly, she felt almost teary with happiness; she wanted to hug Pearl, Helena, everyone who'd helped her make this a reality, given her the privilege of earning money by getting herself covered in flour for a three-year-old's birthday party.

'Very good mixing, everyone,' she said just as Darny burst into the shop, pink in the face, partly from running and partly from crossing the road without waiting for Austin, who was going to go absolutely nuts. Darny was counting on him not wanting to go nuts in front of all the people in here. He might save it for later, but being Austin, he might also forget all about it. It was a risk worth taking.

'Hello, Louis,' he announced cheerfully.

'*Dahnee!*' said Louis adoringly, and not pausing to wipe the cake mixture off himself, he threw himself on Darny.

'Happy birthday,' said Darny. 'I brought you my best bow and arrow.'
He solemnly handed it over.

'*Yay!*' said Louis. Pearl and Issy exchanged glances.

'I'll just put that somewhere safe,' said Pearl, deftly lifting it from Louis's fingers and sticking it on the fruit-tea shelf well out of reach.

'Hello, Darny,' said Issy, welcomingly. 'Do you want to bake?'

'Yeah, all right,' said Darny.

'OK then,' said Issy. 'Where's your brother?'

Darny stared at the ground.

'Um, he's coming . . .'

Just as Issy was about to question him further, the doorbell tinged. Austin entered, his face pink.

'*What did I say to you?*'

Theatrically, Darny turned round and indicated the room full of people. 'OK, outside,' said Austin, looking stressed.

'Oh, can't he stay?' said Issy. 'We're just doing some baking . . .'

Austin looked at her. It was almost impossible to believe. Here she was, in a flowery pinny, her cheeks pink, her eyes sparkling, with a bunch of rug rats, baking cupcakes. She didn't look anything like an evil property developer. He tore his gaze away.

'I told him he couldn't come,' Austin muttered, feeling disgruntled, with everyone's eyes upon him.

'*It's my birfday. I'm free!*' said Louis. Then he added, '*Dahnee give me bow an arrows.*'

Austin glanced at Darny. 'Did you give him that bow and arrow?' he asked in surprise.

Darny shrugged his shoulders. 'He's my friend, innit.'

'Don't say innit,' said Austin automatically. 'Well, well done. Good. That was good.'

'Does that mean he can stay?' said Caroline from behind the counter. 'Oh good. *Hello*, Austin darling, can I get you anything?'

Darny skipped off to the end of the long tables where Pearl was helping everyone spoon their cake mix into the cupcake baking cases.

'Now, we're going to go downstairs to put these in the oven, then you guys are going out to play around the tree,' she was explaining. 'When you've finished the games and come in again, the cakes will be ready.'

'*Yay!*' yelled the little ones.

'No, thanks,' said Austin, then reconsidered. 'Yes, get me a latte. Last chance of a decent cup of coffee for a while.'

Issy was surprised by how jolted she was when he said this.

'Why?' she said. 'Going somewhere?'

Austin stared at her. 'No,' he said. 'You are.'

'What do you mean?' said Issy. Why was Austin staring at her like that? It was a strange look, full of curiosity, but also something a little like contempt. She stared back at him. It was odd, she thought, how little she'd noticed him when they first met—beyond seeing how scruffy he was, but she'd rather got used to that. Whereas now, when he looked a little fierce, she noticed what she'd missed: he was gorgeous. Not man-in-a-razor-blade-advert gorgeous, like Graeme. Gorgeous in an open, honest, kind, smiling way, with a wide forehead, those shrewd grey eyes always narrowed as if thinking of a private joke; the wide, dimpled grin; the tousled, schoolboy hair. Funny how one didn't notice these things always, not at first. No wonder she *had* wanted to kiss him at her party.

'Unbelievable,' said Austin, turning round. 'Forget the coffee. Darny, I'll be back to pick you up in an hour. Meet me outside.'

Darny waved vaguely, as excited as the three-year-olds by the enormous oven Pearl was leading them down to see, with many dire warnings as to what would happen if they so much as wiggled a finger near it.

Issy was trying to figure out why Austin was so upset. Could it be because he'd seen her with Graeme? Her ego couldn't help being a little excited by the idea; that he did like her, that it wasn't just a drunken flirt at a birthday party. But if that was the case, what should she do?

As she was thinking this, the door was pushed open, almost into Austin's face. He had to jump back. Graeme didn't give him as much as a second glance as he stormed into the café.

Graeme looked around in consternation. Who were all these people? Normally there was nobody here on a Saturday afternoon. He looked at Issy, who looked horrified to see him. Austin found himself trapped between the door and a crocodile of tiny children in aprons, who were now being shepherded out into the sunshine by Pearl. Seeing Issy with children, reminded Graeme of his mission. Then he caught sight of Austin.

'You,' he said.

'Our meeting's not till Monday,' Austin said quietly.

'What meeting?' said Issy. 'What are you talking about?'

Austin turned to Issy. The entire room was watching what was happening intently. 'You know,' he said. 'The meeting on Monday. When you come to borrow money for the development.'

'What development? What the hell are you talking about?'

Austin stared at her for a long time. Issy felt panicky and confused.

'What's going on? Do I have to start throwing cakes at people to get some answers round here?'

Austin looked back at Graeme. This man was even more of an arsehole than he'd taken him for. Unbelievable. He shook his head.

'You haven't told her?'

'Told me *what*?'

There was silence in the café.

'Um,' said Graeme, 'can we go somewhere quiet and discuss it?'

'Discuss what?' said Issy. She found she was shaking. Graeme looked so strange—both men did. 'Tell me here. Tell me now. What is it?'

Graeme rubbed the back of his hair, nervously 'Uh, Issy. Actually, it's great news. For us. We've been granted planning permission to turn Pear Tree Court into apartments!'

'What do you mean, "us"?' said Issy. 'There is no "us".'

'Well, you, me, Kalinga Deniki, you know,' said Graeme. 'This whole space will be an amazing flagship development for Stoke Newington.'

'We don't want a flagship development,' said someone at the back. 'We want a café.'

Issy stepped closer to Graeme. 'You mean you were thinking of doing something that involves . . . closing the café? Without *telling* me?'

'But listen, sweetie,' said Graeme, leaning in close. He spoke quietly so the rest of the café couldn't hear, though Austin caught the gist of it. 'Listen. I thought you and I could do the deal together. We were so good together, we could be again. We can make a lot of money. Buy a bigger house of our own. And you won't have to get up at six in the morning any more, or spend all night doing paperwork, or haggling with suppliers, or getting yelled at by that accountancy woman. Huh?'

Issy looked up at him. 'But . . .' she said. 'But . . .'

'You've done such a great job here, it's going to give us real financial independence. Really set us up. Then you can work on something much easier, huh?'

Issy gazed at him, half disbelieving, half furious. Not with Graeme—he was a shark; this was what he did. With herself. For staying with him as long as she had; for letting this snake into her life; for stupidly believing that he could change; that the man she had met—sharp, selfish, attractive, not interested in commitment—would suddenly turn into the man she wanted him to be, just by her blindly wishing for it to be so. After all, how would that happen? She was such a total idiot.

'But you can't,' she said suddenly. 'I have a lease. I rent this place.'

Graeme looked regretful. 'Mr Barstow . . . he's more than happy to sell to us. We've already spoken. You're nearly at the end of your six months.'

'And you'd have to get planning—'

'That's already in process. The exterior may be listed, but overall it's not exactly an area of outstanding natural beauty.'

'It bloody is!' said Issy. Infuriatingly, she felt tears sparking in her eyes and a huge lump in her throat; outside the window, the children were laughing and playing around her beloved, stumpy, twisty, unbeautiful tree.

'Don't you see?' said Graeme, desperately. 'This is for us! I was doing it for us, darling! We could still work it out.'

Issy glared at him.

'But don't *you* see? I love getting up at six o'clock. I love doing the paperwork. I even love Mrs Prescott. And why? Because it's *mine*, that's why. Not yours, not somebody else's and *not* bloody Kalinga Deniki's.'

'It's not yours,' said Graeme softly. 'It's the bank's.'

At this Issy turned to Austin. He held out his hands towards her and was shocked to see the rage in her face.

'You *knew* about this?' she yelled. 'You knew and you never told me?'

'I thought you knew,' protested Austin, taken aback by her fury. 'I thought it was your little plan all along. To tart up this joint then flog it to some naff City boys.'

'You thought I would do that?' she said, all anger gone and pure sadness taking its place. '*You thought I would do that?*'

Now it was Austin's turn to feel awful. He should have trusted his instincts after all. He stepped towards her.

'Stay away from me!' Issy yelled. 'Stay away from me! Both of you! Go! Get out! Get out of here!'

Austin and Graeme shot each other a glance of mutual loathing, and Austin hung back to let the shorter man leave first.

'Hang on!' Issy shouted suddenly. 'How long . . . how long have I got?'

Graeme shrugged. Dumpy, blushing Issy. How dare she dump him. How dare she get in the way of his plans. He suddenly felt coldly furious that she would cross him like this.

'A month,' he said.

The café went silent, as the oven pinged. Louis's cakes were ready.

Pearl looked at the tears flooding down Issy's face and the crowd of concerned well-wishers around her as she ushered the children back in and decided it was time for the emergency white wine to be deployed, licence or no licence. Two of the mums sorted out the children's cakes, which they could decorate as soon as they cooled a little, with blue or pink icing, hundreds and thousands and tiny silver balls. There were also bowls set out of chopped fruit, sesame seeds, carrot sticks, hummus and twiglets. Caroline had managed this side of the catering 'as a gift to darling Louis'.

Pearl and Helena bundled Issy downstairs.

'Are you all right?' said Pearl, worriedly.

'That *snake!*' shouted Issy. 'I'll kill him! I'll sort him out. We'll establish a fighting fund. We'll start a leafleting campaign. I'll bury him. You'll help, won't you, Helena? You'll get on it with us?'

Issy turned to Helena, who was suddenly looking rather distracted having left Ashok behind upstairs. Issy explained everything again. She started to cry a little as she did so.

'I mean,' Issy protested, 'they can't do that. They can't just march in here, can they? Can he?'

Pearl shrugged. 'Well, it belongs to Mr Barstow.'

'You'll find another property,' said Helena.

'Not like this,' said Issy, looking round at the immaculate storeroom, the tiny view of the cobbles in the street; her beautiful, perfect oven. 'It won't be like this.'

'It might be better,' said Helena. 'You know you can do it. Maybe it's time to expand. They're queueing out of the doors here now.'

Issy stuck out her bottom lip. 'But I'm happy here. And it's the principle of the thing.'

Helena snorted. 'Well, it's not like you ever listened to me when I told you what a shit Graeme is.'

'I know,' said Issy. 'I know. Why do I never listen to you?'

'I do not know.'

'She doesn't listen to me either,' said Pearl.

'And I want to show him,' said Issy. 'I want to show him that you can't just buy and sell people when it suits you. You can't just tell people to up and leave. Oh,' she said, 'Lena. Are you sure you're all right with us all living together for a while longer? This could take a bit of unravelling.'

'Actually,' said Helena, looking uncharacteristically nervous, 'no, I think we really are going to have to move.'

'Why?'

Helena seemed nervous and excited and full of anticipation, and she glanced up the stairwell for Ashok. 'Well,' she began, 'it's been a bit quicker than we'd have planned, but . . .'

Issy stared at her, completely confused. Pearl was delighted and guessed immediately. 'A baby!'

Helena nodded, looking demure for the first time in her life. It was going to take some getting used to, she thought.

Issy summoned up every reserve of courage, every tiny brave part of her. She almost made it. Her lips almost made it into the smile she so wanted to give; that Helena so deserved. But at the very end, her strength deserted her. Her throat clogged up and her eyes stung.

'Con—' she stuttered. Then, suddenly, she was in floods of tears. She had nothing and Helena had everything. It felt so hard, so unfair.

'Oh, Issy . . . what? I'm so sorry, I thought you'd be pleased,' said Helena. 'Oh, darling. Sorry. We'll need to find a new place, of course, but you won't be on your own . . . It was an accident, but we're both delighted, but . . .'

'Oh, dear Lena,' said Issy, 'you know, I am absolutely thrilled for you.' And the girls hugged again.

''Course you are,' said Helena. 'You're going to be the best godmother ever. Teach it to bake.'

'You'll be able to deliver the baby yourselves!' said Issy. 'Oh, someone get me a tissue.'

A mum appeared at the top of the stairs.

'Um, shall we sing "Happy Birthday"?'

'My baby!' said Pearl. 'I'm coming, I'm coming.'

As Issy emerged from the cellar to join in a rousing chorus for Louis, she was surrounded by a sea of people, commiserating about the shop, offering support and threatening to write to planning, or host a sit-in, or boycott the estate agents. It was overwhelming.

'Thanks, everyone,' Pearl said finally, addressing the room. 'We will—well, we don't know what we can do but we will try everything, I promise, to keep the café open. And now, let's enjoy Louis's party!'

She turned up the music and watched the children dance around, sticky faces filled with happiness, Louis at the centre of it all. She didn't want this to go either. This wasn't just a job. This was their lives now.

It was utter torture for Issy to last until the final child had been sent home with a bouncing ball and an extra piece of cake in a bag; to politely wave goodbye to clients and friends and thank them for their concern; to collect the debris and clean up the mess. She scarcely knew how to endure it. But what had to come next was worse. Pearl saw her face.

'Must you go now?' she asked Issy. 'Darling, it isn't going to change if you pick your stuff up later.'

'No,' said Issy. She felt like she had a huge hole in her stomach, tangled up and cramped and filled with anxiety. 'No. If I leave it at Graeme's, I'll just have it in front of me to dread. I'll have to do it fast. Just get in. There's hardly anything there anyway. He was always a bit tight with cupboard space. Needed a lot of room for his hair gel.'

'That's the spirit,' said Pearl. They looked at Louis, who was happily exploring his presents on the floor.

'You know,' said Pearl, 'I wouldn't change a thing about my life, not a tiny little thing. But sometimes . . . well, I would say it is probably easier breaking up before. Rather than after. If you know what I mean.'

Issy nodded her head slowly.

'But Pearl . . . I'm thirty-two. Thirty-two. What if that was my last chance to have a baby? If I have to go and work somewhere else now . . . how will I ever meet anyone? If I'm stuck in someone's back kitchen, working for a chain . . . I can't build it up again, Pearl. I can't. This place took everything I have.'

''Course you can,' Pearl urged her. 'You've done all the hard stuff. Made all the mistakes. The next one will be a breeze. And thirty-two is nothing these days. Of course you'll meet someone. What about that handsome banking adviser? I reckon he'd be a far better fit for you.'

'Austin?' Issy's face tightened suddenly. 'That I can't believe. I can't believe he thought I was behind all this, that I'd sell out in five minutes. I thought he liked me.'

'He does like you,' said Pearl. 'There you go. Of course you'll meet someone. I know things seem a little bleak now . . .'

They looked at each other. Then they both started to laugh. Issy got a little hysterical, tears standing in her eyes. 'Yes,' she gasped when she could catch her breath. 'You could say a *little* bleak.'

'Oh, you know what I mean,' protested Pearl.

Louis wobbled up to them, wanting to know what all the laughter was about. Issy looked at him ruefully. 'Hello, pumpkin.'

Louis stretched his hands out to his mother.

'*Best birfday,*' he said proudly. '*Louis best birfday.*' Then he went a little quieter. '*Where's Daddy, Mummy?*'

Ben, in the end, hadn't shown. Pearl's face was completely impassive.

Graeme's flat had no windows facing the street, so Issy had no way of knowing whether he was in or not, short of ringing the intercom, and she had no intention of talking to him unless it was absolutely necessary. She swallowed hard, unwilling to get out of the taxi.

'All right, love?' asked the cabbie.

'Yes,' she said. Surely he'd have gone out. It was Saturday night after all. He'd be out with his mates, trying to pull someone new in a nightclub, probably. Laughing about how much money he was going to make with this new deal. She swallowed hard. He didn't give a shit about her. He never had. It had always been about the money for him, always. He'd strung her along like an idiot, and she'd fallen for it completely.

She was so convinced he would be out having a wonderful time, that Issy wasn't at all expecting to see Graeme when she entered the dimly lit hallway. He was sitting in his fake Le Corbusier armchair, in his dressing gown—Issy hadn't known he owned a dressing gown—glass in hand, staring out of the window at the minimalist courtyard garden nobody ever visited. He started when she entered, but didn't turn his head. Issy stood there. Her heart was thumping painfully.

'I'm here to get my stuff,' she announced loudly.

'Whatever,' said Graeme, not looking at her.

Issy packed up her bits and pieces into a small suitcase. There wasn't much. Graeme didn't move a muscle the entire time. Then she marched into the kitchen, which she'd stocked up with supplies. She took 250g of flour, five eggs, an entire tin of treacle and a small sachet of hundreds and thousands, and whipped them up with a wooden spoon.

Then she brought the whole lot into the living room and, with a practised flick of the wrist, poured it all over Graeme's head.

Her flat felt different. It was the sense not just of someone new living there that she'd had for a couple of weeks—Ashok was interesting, serious and entirely charming—but of a shifting dynamic. And she felt less comfortable striding into her pink kitchen and collapsing on the huge squishy settee—like a stranger in her own home. Which was ridiculous, she knew. But more than anything else it was the shame of her first, her only experiment in cohabitation ending so quickly and so badly.

Helena knew that pointing out Graeme had always been a wrong'un wasn't particularly useful, but being there probably was, so she did her best to do that instead, even if she tended to fall asleep every five minutes.

'What are you going to do?' she asked, ever practical. Issy sat, staring unseeingly at the television.

'Well, I'm going to open up on Monday morning . . . After that, I'm not so sure.'

'You've done it once,' said Helena. 'You can do it again.'

'I'm just so tired,' said Issy. 'So tired.'

Helena put her to bed, where Issy thought she wouldn't be able to get to sleep at all. In fact, she slept halfway through Sunday. The sun pricking through her curtains made her feel just a tiny bit more optimistic.

On Monday morning, she picked up an envelope off the mat. Yes, there it was. A notice to quit once her lease was up, from Mr Barstow. Tied with white cord to lampposts around the courtyard were plastic laminates with the outlines of the planning application. Issy could hardly bear to give them a second glance. She started off the day's baking on autopilot, going through the motions of normality in the hopes that it would quell her rising panic. It would be fine. She'd find something. She'd speak to Des, he'd know. In her confusion, she called him before realising it was still only just after seven in the morning. He answered immediately.

'I'm sorry,' said Des instantly. 'I'm sorry. Did you call to yell at me?'

'What about?' said Issy.

'About we might have to handle the apartment sales. Sorry. It wasn't my decision, it's just . . .'

Issy hadn't even thought about this, she was only calling to ask about vacant properties. But of course.

'. . . business,' she said dully.

'Yes,' said Des. 'I thought you knew.'

'No,' said Issy. 'I didn't.'

'I'm sorry,' said Des, sounding like he truly meant it. 'Are you looking for another property? Would you like me to ring round a few people? I'll ring everyone, OK? Try to find something just right for you. I really am sorry.'

Jamie started to wail down the phone.

'Jamie is sorry too.'

'It's OK,' said Issy. 'You can stop apologising now, it wasn't your fault. And, yes, if you see anything . . . yes, please.'

He was still apologising as Issy hung up the phone.

Pearl was looking gloomy. 'Cheer up,' said Caroline. 'Something will come along.'

'It's not that,' said Pearl. Ben hadn't returned for two days. He'd been out with his friends, having a good time, and he didn't see what the big deal was, Louis was going to have loads of birthdays and he'd bought him a present (in fact a huge racing-car track that wouldn't fit in the flat). Pearl had heard him out then closed the door in his face.

'I can't believe he would miss his kid's birthday,' she explained to Caroline, who harrumphed.

'That's nothing,' she said. 'My ex didn't make a single birthday, carol concert, school play, sports day . . . not a single one. "Working",' she sniffed. 'My bum.'

'Well, exactly,' said Pearl. 'That's why he's your ex.'

'That's not why he's my ex,' said Caroline. 'None of the dads here do that stuff. They're too busy working to pay for the big swanky houses. None of the kids knows what their dad looks like. I dumped him for sleeping with that gruesome tart. Showed he had absolutely the worst taste imaginable. Ha, if you dumped a man for neglecting his children . . .'

The door pinged. It was the builder, the one who'd brought his son to Louis's party.

'Cheer up, love,' he said, his traditional greeting.

Caroline gave him an appraising look, up and down, noting his nicely honed pecs, cheeky grin and clear lack of a wedding ring.

'You *do* cheer me up,' she said, and leaned right over the front counter, which would have exposed her cleavage, had she had any. 'Bit of cheering up once a day . . . I do like it.'

'Posh birds,' said the builder under his breath, then smiled happily. 'Give us a bit of froth, love.'

Pearl sighed.

'Has he embarrassingly slept with any of your friends?' asked Caroline, when the builder had left with a wink and a telephone number.

'Not yet,' admitted Pearl.

'Well, there you go,' said Caroline. 'I wouldn't give up on him right away.' She brandished a letter. 'You won't believe what I got this morning.'

'What?'

'From his lawyers. Apparently if I could have guaranteed my employment here, he'd have kept me in the house, local enough not to need a nanny to pick up the kids.' Caroline shook her head. 'But now I'm back to square one. No job, but I've proved I can work, so I have to. So I'll have to move. No wonder I need a bit of flirting in my life.' She sighed.

'Hmm,' growled Pearl, going back to her sheets of paper.

'What are you doing?' Issy asked her, coming up the stairs.

'I'm writing to the planning commission of course.'

'Oh,' said Issy.

'Don't you think that's a good idea?'

'Unlikely. Plus, I know Kalinga Deniki. They never move with this kind of thing unless they know they've already got it in the bag.'

'OK, well, do nothing then,' said Pearl, going back to writing.

Issy took her coffee cup and went out into the courtyard, regarding the shop critically. Since the warm weather had arrived, they'd done some upgrading. Now they had a striped awning, which looked fresh and pretty in the sunlight and matched Gramps's tables and chairs. In the sunshine, the shade of the awning looked incredibly inviting, the keyring glinted in the sun, and the plants Pearl had set either side of the door only added to the effect. She blinked away tears. She couldn't cry any more. But neither could she imagine creating her little oasis anywhere else; this was her corner of the world; her little kingdom.

Issy meandered up to the ironmonger's shop The metal grille was still closed, at 10 a.m. Issy screwed up her face and tried to peer through. What was in there? There were little holes in the grille, although the bright sunshine stopped her from seeing much. She kept focusing in. As her eyes adjusted, she started to make out shadowy shapes on the other side of the glass. Suddenly a pale shape moved.

Issy let out a yelp and jumped back from the grille. With a deafening noise, it began to open automatically. Someone must be inside—someone, presumably, whom she'd already seen. She swallowed hard.

After the grille was wound up fully, the door was opened from within, out towards her. The ironmonger was there. Wearing pyjamas. Issy was struck dumb. It took her a second to collect herself.

'You . . . you live here?' she said in amazement. Chester nodded his head in that formal way of his. He bade her enter.

For the first time, Issy went into the shop. And what she saw took her aback completely. At the front were pots and pans, mops and screwdrivers. But in the back of the shop was an exquisite Persian carpet, and laid out on it, a carved wooden Balinese double bed; a small bedside table piled high with books and a Tiffany lamp; a large mirrored armoire.

'Oh my,' she said, then again, 'You . . . you live here.'

Chester looked embarrassed. 'Um, yes. Yes, I do. Normally I have a little curtain to hang during the day . . . or I shut the shop whenever it looks like anyone is coming in to buy something. Coffee?'

Through the back Issy saw a small, immaculate galley kitchen. An expensive Gaggia coffee pot was bubbling away on top of the stove. It smelled wonderful.

'Um, yes,' said Issy, although she had already had far too much caffeine that morning. But this little Aladdin's cave felt completely unreal. The man directed her to a floral-upholstered armchair.

'Please, sit down. You've made my life very difficult, you know.'

Issy shook her head. 'But I've been passing by this alleyway for years, and this shop has always been here.'

'Oh, yes,' said the man. 'I've been here for twenty-nine years. Nobody's ever bothered me before. That's the beauty of London.'

As he spoke, Issy noticed his accent again.

'No one knows your business. I like it like that. Until you came of course. In and out, leaving me cakes, wanting to ask me things. And customers! You're the first person ever to bring people into the alley.'

'And now . . .'

'Now we have to go, yes.' The man looked at the notice to quit in his hand. 'Ah, it would have happened eventually. How's your gramps?'

'Actually, I was going to go and ask him.'

'Oh good, is he up to having a conversation?'

'Not really,' said Issy. 'But it makes me feel better. I know that's selfish.'

Chester shook his head. 'It's not, you know.'

'I'm so sorry,' said Issy. 'I brought the developers here. I didn't mean to, but I did.'

Chester shook his head. 'No, you didn't,' he said. 'Stoke Newington . . . you know, it used to be considered half a day's ride from London. A lovely village, nice and far out of town. And even when I arrived, it was always a bit raffish and run down, but you could do what you wanted here. Have things your own way. Be a bit different.'

He served up the coffee with cream in two exquisitely tiny china cups and saucers.

'But things get sanitised, gentrified. Especially places with character, like round here. There's not much of old London left really.'

Issy cast her eyes down.

'Don't be sad, girl. There's lots good about new London too. You'll go places, look at you.'

'I don't know where though.'

'Hmm, that makes two of us.'

'Hang on, are you squatting?' said Issy. 'Can't you just claim residency?'

'No,' said Chester. 'I think I have a lease . . . somewhere.'

They sat there sipping their coffee.

'There must be something I can do,' said Issy.

'Can't stop progress,' said Chester, setting down his coffee spoon with a light tinkle. 'Believe me, I should know.'

Austin was early for once. And smartly dressed. He ran his hands through his thick hair. He couldn't believe he was doing this. He could risk everything. And for what? Some girl who wouldn't look at him.

Janet was there, of course, bright and efficient as ever. Austin had made her aware of what was going on at Pear Tree Court.

'It's horrible,' she said, with unusual ferocity. 'It's horrible what that man wants to do.'

Austin looked at her.

'To that nice girl and that lovely shop and to turn it into more featureless rubbish for more stupid executives, it's horrible. That's all I want to say.'

Austin's mouth twitched. 'Thank you, Janet. That's helpful.'

'You should call Issy.'

'I'm not going to call her,' said Austin. Issy wouldn't touch him with a bargepole now and, he supposed with a sigh, she had good reason.

'You should.'

Austin reflected on it, drinking the coffee Janet had gone all the way down to the Cupcake Café to get for him. It was cold, but he fancied he could still smell the sweet essence of Issy clinging to it somewhere. He inhaled it deeply, and very briefly closed his eyes.

Janet knocked. 'He's here,' she said, then led Graeme in with an uncustomary frostiness of manner.

Graeme didn't notice. He just wanted to get this over and done with. Stupid local micro-financing, he hated local banking and piddling mortgage snarl-ups more than any other part of his business.

Well, he needed to rubber-stamp this money, call Mr Boekhoorn and get the hell out of it.

'Hey,' he said, scowling, as he shook Austin's hand.

'Hi,' said Austin.

'Shall we keep this short?' said Graeme. 'You hold the existing mortgages on the extant properties, and we need to combine them so you can give me a new rate on the amalgamated loan. Let's see what you can do, shall we?'

He scanned through the documents quickly. Austin sat back and took a big breath. Well, here went absolutely nothing. It would probably ruin his career if his bosses took a proper look at it. It shouldn't really matter to him one way or another whether his corner of the world got more and more corporate and homogeneous and white-bread. But it did. He liked Darny having lots of different friends, not just ones called Felix. He liked being able to buy cupcakes—or falafel, or hummous, or bagels—whenever he felt like it. He liked the mixture of hookah cafés and wooden toy emporiums and African hair-product shops that made up his neck of the woods. He didn't want to be taken over by the stuffed shirts, the quick bucks, the Graemes of this world.

And, more than anything, he couldn't get out of his head the image of

Issy's face, sparkling and flushed and joyous in the fairy lights. When he'd thought she was one of them, out for herself and anything she could get, it had upset him so much. Now he knew that she felt the same as him, that she believed in the same things he did . . . now he had finally realised that mixing business with pleasure was exactly what he wanted to do, he found it was all too late. However, there was one thing he could do for her. He leaned over his desk.

'I'm sorry, Mr Denton,' he said. 'We have a local community investment guidance programme' (they did, although no one from the bank ever read it) 'and I'm afraid your scheme goes against that. I'm afraid we won't be able to combine the mortgages.'

Graeme looked at him as if he couldn't believe what he'd just heard.

'But the planning authority is behind us,' he said sullenly. 'So it obviously is in the interests of the community.'

'The bank doesn't think so,' said Austin, mentally crossing his fingers and hoping the bank never got to hear of him turning down an absolutely sound investment. 'I'm sorry. We're going to continue to hold on to the mortgages as they stand.'

Graeme stared at him for a long time.

'What the hell is this?' he burst out suddenly. 'Are you just trying to screw with me? Got the hots for my girlfriend or something?'

Austin tried to look as if he'd never heard of such a thing.

'Not at all,' he said, as if offended. 'It's just bank policy, that's all. I'm sorry, you must understand. In the current financial climate . . .'

Graeme leaned over. 'Do. Not,' he enunciated very slowly, 'Tell. Me. About. The. Current. Financial. Climate.'

'Of course, sir,' said Austin. There was a silence. Austin didn't want to break it. Graeme lifted up his hands.

'So you're telling me I'm not going to get this loan here.'

'That's right, sir.'

'That I'd have to bring in another bank and pay them commission to take on and untangle all your stupid loans that have probably been packaged in with some bunch of junk and sold up some untraceable river somewhere?'

'Yup.'

Graeme stood up. 'This is bullshit. *Bullshit.*'

'Also, I've heard there's quite a lot of late opposition to the planning.

Enough that might even make the planning authority change its opinion.'

'They can't do that.'

'Planning officers can do whatever they like.'

Graeme was turning pink with fury.

'I'll get the money, you know. You'll see. Then you'll look the fricking idiot in front of your bosses.'

Austin reflected that he did already and was surprised to find he wasn't too fussed. Maybe it didn't always matter what your bosses thought, he figured. He wondered who had taught him that.

Graeme eyed Austin one more time before he left.

'She'd never go for you, you know,' he sneered. 'You're not her type.'

Well, neither are you, thought Austin mildly. But he felt a tugging sadness in his heart.

There was no time for that, however. He grabbed the phone and dialled the number he had in front of him on the desk. He sent his instructions through as soon as he was connected. A chorus of swearing reached him from the other end. Then a pause, and a sigh, and a barked command that he had fifteen minutes to stop arsing around and go back to spending time on serious businesses.

Then he had to make the other call. He used the bank phone to call Issy's mobile. She'd have to pick up now. Fingers crossed.

His heart racing, he tapped in the numbers . . . numbers he realised he'd actually memorised. What an idiot he was.

'Hello?' she said, her voice sounding unsure and nervous.

'Issy!' said Austin, his voice coming out rather strangulated. 'Um, don't hang up, please. Look, I know you're angry and stuff, but I think . . . I think I might be able to do something. For the café. But I think . . . argh. I don't have time for this. Listen. You have to go out onto the street right now.'

'But I can't,' said Issy, panic in her voice.

She had hardly recognised the old man on the bed; he was a wraith. Her beloved grandfather; so strong, his huge hands pushing and kneading and moulding great lumps of dough; so delicate when shaping a sugar rose, or intricate when cutting a long line of Battenburg. He had been, truly, mother and father to her; always there when she needed him; a safe haven.

Yet now, at her lowest ebb, when Issy felt her dreams about to slip through her fingers, he was powerless. As he lay on the bed while she told him her story, his eyes had widened, and Issy felt a terrifying clutch of guilt round her heart as he tried to sit up.

'No, Gramps, don't,' she'd insisted, in anguish. 'Please. Please don't. It's going to be fine.'

'You can do it, sweetheart,' her gramps was saying, but his breathing was ragged and laboured, his eyes rheumy and bloodshot, his face an awful grey.

'Please, Gramps.' Issy rang the bell for the nurse, holding on to her grandfather with all her might, trying to calm him down. Keavie came in, took one look at him and immediately called for back-up; two men came in with an oxygen cylinder and struggled to get a mask over his face.

'I'm so sorry, I'm so sorry,' Issy was saying, as they worked on without her. That was when her mobile rang, and Keavie ushered her outside while they fought to stabilise him.

Issy went back into the room after Austin had hung up, terror clawing at her, but Gramps had the mask on, his breathing much quietened.

'I'm so sorry,' said Issy in a rush. 'I'm so, so sorry.'

'Hush,' said Keavie. 'It wasn't you. He's been having these episodes.'

She held Issy's arm very tightly and pulled her round until they were face to face. 'You have to realise, Issy,' she said, speaking kindly but firmly. It was a voice Issy had heard Helena using when she had to pass on bad news. 'This is normal. This is part of the process.'

Issy stifled a sob, then went and held Gramps's hand. The colour had come back to his cheeks and he was able to take his mask off.

'Who was that on the phone? Was it your mother?'

'Uh no,' said Issy. 'It was . . . it was the bank. They think they know a way to save the café, but it had to be done right then and there, and I'm sure they missed it . . .'

Issy felt her grandfather's pressure on her hand grow extremely strong.

'You go!' he said, sternly. 'You go and save that café right now! Right now! I mean it, Isabel! You go and you fight for your business.'

'I'm not leaving you,' said Issy.

'You bloody are,' said Grampa Joe. 'Keavie, you tell her.'

And he let go of her hand and turned his face to the wall.

'*Go!*' said Keavie. '*Go!*'

Issy tore down the road to the station and, for once, just for once, the world and London Transport were on her side, and the stopping train that would let her out at Blackhorse Road was right there waiting for her. She flung herself on board and phoned Austin.

'I'm stalling it,' said Austin grimly, not wanting to let on how much danger he'd just put himself in. 'Be as quick as you can.'

'I'm doing that.'

'How's . . . how's your grampa?'

'Well, he's well enough to be cross with me,' said Issy.

'That's something,' said Austin.

'We're coming into the station.'

'Run like the wind! Whatever he offers you, take it! Whatever it is!'

Issy raced down Albion Road. Then, right in front of her, a huge black car drew to a halt. She glanced at it. Could this be what Austin meant? The tinted windows made it impossible to see in, but very slowly the back window came down. Issy bent over, squinting in the bright sunlight.

'You! The girl with the cakes! Give me a cake!' came a gruff voice. Issy automatically passed over the powdered honey blossom she had intended to give to her grandfather. Mr Barstow took it and for a few seconds all she could hear was contented chewing. Then he looked out at her.

'I hear the developers are having some trouble getting the money,' he said. 'Well, I can't be buggered with that. Give me my money. Here. Sign.'

He passed her over a contract. It was an increase in rent—but not an impossible one. And it was an increase in the lease, to eighteen months. Eighteen months! Her heart leapt. It wouldn't make it hers, but it would be enough time, surely, to get on more of a secure footing. And if they did well . . . perhaps, at the end of eighteen months, even she might be happy to look for bigger premises. Unless . . .

'Stay here,' she said, then dashed across the courtyard and pounded on the ironmonger's door. She dragged Chester over to the car.

'Him too,' she said, pushing him up front. 'I'll sign for him too. Or he can sign for me.'

Mr Barstow sighed and lit a cigarette.

'I can't stay here,' protested Chester. 'It's over for me.'

'No,' said Issy. 'Don't you see? I can take over the ironmonger's too. We need room to expand, look.' She gestured at the Cupcake Café, a queue spilling out into the warm courtyard full of hungry, laughing customers, all anxious to stock up on Issy's sweet treats in case they got taken away.

'I've already had four more bookings for children's parties. And I could accept more gift orders if I had more space. If I take on both . . .' She lowered her voice. 'I suspect I'd need a nightwatchman. Seeing as we haven't got a security gate. Someone who could keep an eye on the premises at night. Of course, it wouldn't pay very well . . .'

Chester scribbled on the paperwork excitedly. And ten seconds later, they were standing on the pavement, watching the sleek black car pull away into the thickening traffic, staring at each other in disbelief.

'*Eeek!*' screamed Issy suddenly, as she realised what had just happened. She ran into the café. 'Pearl! We're safe! We're safe!'

Pearl's eyes widened. 'What do you mean?'

Issy brandished the contracts. 'We've got an extension! Graeme didn't get his loan.'

Pearl stopped in her tracks, her mouth open in disbelief.

'You are joking?'

Issy shook her head. 'Eighteen months. We've got eighteen months.'

Pearl had worked so hard to keep from Issy how much this job had meant to her. How hard it would be to find something else; how loath she was to pull Louis out of that nursery where he was so happy—and even, she reluctantly admitted, popular. The worry and the expectation of disaster had built up in her for so long that she simply sat down on the stool behind the counter and burst into tears.

'And,' said Issy, 'we're going to expand! We're going to take on the ironmonger's! You're going to head up the other part of the Cupcake Café, where we make special gifts and do catering. Bit of a promotion.'

Pearl wiped her eyes with one of the candy-striped tea towels.

'I can't believe I've got so attached to a stupid job,' she said, shaking her head. Issy looked around at the slightly confused-looking customers. Caroline stepped forward.

'I knew you'd do it,' she said. 'And I can stay! I can stay!'

The three women hugged. Issy finally looked up.

'Sorry, everyone,' she said. 'We thought we were going to have to close. But I've just found out we don't.'

There were smiles of pleasure up and down the queue.

'So, I think this means . . . I've always wanted to say this . . . ,' said Issy, taking a deep breath, with Pearl and Caroline's arms round her—

'Cupcakes on the house!!'

It was almost worth it, Austin thought, for the admiration on Janet's face alone. Almost.

'I've seen him off for now,' he said. 'Won't last, of course. He'll just regroup and come back stronger. That's how cockroaches work.'

'You did a good thing,' said Janet. 'Give me the paperwork. I'll try to smooth it with the bosses. And now go and make five hundred really amazing investments to distract their attention.'

'Not now,' said Austin. 'I am full of adrenaline. I'm going to get Darny out from school for lunch and we are going to the park to do roaring.'

'I'll tell that to your twelve o'clock, shall I?' Janet said affectionately.

'Yes, please,' said Austin.

He had been surprised Issy hadn't rung him back, but then, well, not really. She was just out of a relationship and had had a narrow escape with her business, and was probably celebrating in the café or figuring things out or . . . well, she'd made it clear she wanted nothing to do with him. So. Well. Never mind. He bought sandwiches and crisps from the corner shop and popped his head into the school to pick up his brother.

Sometimes, he thought, all the aggro, all the yelling, the persuading, the restrictions to his social life and his sex life; the ongoing fug of his plans . . . sometimes, all of it was vindicated by the delighted face of a ten-year-old boy when he sees his big brother surprising him with lunch in the park. Darny's smile reached his ears.

'*Auussstttttiiinnnn!*'

'Come on then. Your big brother, by the way, is a total hero.'

'Are you a goodie?'

'Yes.'

It was a glorious day. Darny and Austin followed the stream through Clissold Park gates. Just as they reached them, however, Austin heard someone calling his name.

'Austin! Austin!'

He turned round. It was Issy, pink in the face, carrying a large box.

'You look very red,' said Austin.

Issy closed her eyes. This was such a stupid idea. And of course she was blushing again. She was probably covered in sweat too. This was really daft. She followed them into the park. Darny had come straight up to her and taken her hand. She squeezed it, needing the reassurance.

'I like it,' said Austin. 'Red suits you.'

He wanted to kick himself for saying something so stupid. They stared at one another for a bit. Nervous, Austin turned his attention to the box. 'Are those for me? Because you know I can't take—'

'Shut up,' said Issy. 'I just wanted to say thank you. Thank you. Thank you. I can't . . . anyway, they're not for you to eat, they're for Darny. And they didn't come out right anyway, they're a mess, and . . .'

Without even thinking about it, Austin took the box in his hands and hurled it with all his might. It flew from his long fingers straight into a copse of nearby trees. The pink of the ribbon streamed against the bright blue of the sky and the green of the trees, but the box did not burst.

'Darny,' said Austin, 'that was a huge box of cakes. Go and find it and they're all yours.'

Darny shot off like a bullet from a gun.

Issy looked after him in consternation. 'Those were my cakes! With a message on them!'

Austin took her hands suddenly, urgently, feeling that he didn't have much time. 'You can make more cakes. But, Issy, if you want to send me a message . . . please, please, just tell me what it is.'

Issy felt the warm, firm pressure of his hands on hers; found herself staring up into his strong, handsome face. And suddenly, suddenly, for almost the first time in her life, she felt the nerves desert her. She felt calm and at peace. She was conscious of nothing other than her absolute and present desire to be held by this man. She took one deep breath and closed her eyes, as Austin tilted her face up towards his, and she gave herself up entirely to his fierce and perfect kiss, in the middle of a busy park, in the middle of a busy day, in the middle of one of the busiest cities in the world.

'Me sick?' came an angry-sounding voice from somewhere far away. 'Why are you sick? Who's sick?'

Reluctantly, and both more than a little pink and sweaty, Austin and Issy jumped apart. Darny was standing there looking puzzled.

'That's what your cakes said.'

He held up the battered and bruised box, with the remnants of five cakes inside, one missing. He'd arranged the letters to spell M-E S-I-K.

'Is that the message you wanted me to get?' said Austin.

'Uh, not quite,' said Issy, feeling dizzy and light-headed.

'OK,' said Austin, smiling broadly. 'OK, Darny. We are going to have lunch, then five minutes of playing lions, and then Issy and I have some business to attend to, OK?'

'Are you coming for lunch?' asked Darny, before haring off to chase some pigeons. 'Cool!'

They stood and watched him go, smiling.

Issy looked at Austin, eyes wide.

'Come here,' he said urgently. 'I feel like I've waited ages for you.' He kissed her hard, then stared at her so intensely she felt like her heart might burst. 'Stay,' he said, fiercely. 'Please stay as sweet as you are.'

Chapter Twelve

Simnel Cake

6 oz butter

6 oz soft brown sugar

3 eggs, beaten

6 oz plain flour

pinch salt

1 tsp ground mixed spice (optional)

12 oz mixed raisins, currants and sultanas

2 oz chopped mixed peel

zest of 1 lemon

1–2 tbsp apricot jam

1 egg, beaten, for glazing

Buy almond paste from the supermarket. You can make it yourself, but we are not crazy people.

Knead the paste for one minute until it is smooth and pliable. Roll it out to make a circle 18cm in diameter.

Preheat oven to 140°C/gas mark 1. Grease and line an 18cm cake tin.

For the cake, cream the butter and sugar together until pale and fluffy. Gradually beat in the eggs until well incorporated and then sift in the flour, salt and mixed spice (if using) a little at a time. Finally, add the mixed dried fruit, peel and grated lemon zest and stir into the mixture.

Put half the mixture into the prepared cake tin. Smooth the top and cover with the circle of almond paste. Add the rest of the cake mixture and smooth the top, leaving a slight dip in the centre to allow for the cake to rise.

Bake in the preheated oven for 1¾ hours. Test by inserting a skewer in the middle—if it comes out clean, it is ready. Once baked, remove from the oven and set aside to cool on a wire rack. Top the cake with another thin layer of almond paste.

'HE'S TAKEN A TURN for the worse,' whispered the nurse.

'That's OK,' said Issy, even though it wasn't, dammit. It wasn't fair. Her grandfather had lived so long, was everything to her, and surely he deserved to see her happy.

Austin had wanted to come. The more she got to know him, Issy realised, the more she . . . well, she wasn't going to say the L-word just yet. But now she was sure, she wanted it to spill off her tongue, to shout it to the world. But not until it was time. And now she wasn't sure she had time.

'Gramps,' Issy whispered. 'Gramps! It's me! It's Isabel.'

Nothing.

'I've got cake!' She rustled the wrapper. For once, she'd made his favourite rather than hers; the hard, flat simnel cake his own mother had made for him, decades and decades ago when he was a small boy.

She hugged him, and talked to him, telling him all her wonderful news, but he didn't respond to her voice, or to her touch.

Keavie put her hand on Issy's arm. 'I don't think it will be long now.'

'I wanted . . . this will sound stupid, but I so wanted him to meet my new boyfriend,' said Issy. 'I think he'd have liked him.'

The nurse glanced at Grampa Joe. 'I'm sure he knows . . .'

Issy sat down, not knowing what to do. Suddenly the door creaked open. Issy looked up. There stood a woman both incredibly familiar and almost unknown. She had long grey hair and she wore a long cloak; Issy noticed wrinkles settling deeply into her face.

'Mum,' Issy said, so softly it was almost a sigh.

They sat together, the three of them, almost not talking at all, although her mother held her grandfather's hand and told him how much she had always loved him, and how sorry she was, and Issy said, honestly, that her mother had nothing to be sorry for, everything had worked out all right in the end, and both of them, mother and daughter, were sure they felt a press on their hands from Joe. Issy felt her throat go tight every time she had to wait agonisingly long for a breath.

'What is this?' her mother asked softly, picking up the bag with a plain-looking, flat-baked cake in it. She stuck her nose in it. 'Oh, Issy,' she said, 'my grandma used to bake this for me when I was little. It smelled exactly like this. Exactly! Your grandfather adored it. It was his favourite thing.'

Issy had known this already. She hadn't known her mother knew too.

'Oh my, this takes me back.'

Her mother was sobbing now, tears running down her lined face. She went forward and sat on the bed, then opened the bag. She put the entire bag over his nose, so that he could inhale the spicy scent. Issy had heard somewhere that when all other senses had gone, smell lingered; a direct line to the heart of consciousness; to emotion, to childhood and to memory. But how much of her gramps remained?

Both of the women heard him take a deep, rattly breath. Then, giving them a start, his eyes popped open. He breathed in again, smelling the cake; and once again, deeper, as if he were trying to inhale its essence. Then suddenly his eyes were focused on something Issy couldn't see.

'She's here,' he said, in a gentle, wondering tone. 'She's here!' And then he half smiled and closed his eyes again and they knew that he was gone.

The pale afternoon light was falling through the windows of the Cupcake Café—they'd put the awning away in the autumn when it had turned windy and cold—and spreading in soft pools over the tables and the cake stands piled high with baby cupcakes in pink and blue, and the wrapping paper, cards and baby gifts strewn all across the floor. Helena sat, a huge, imperious ship in full sail, her tight brown dress stretched unashamedly across her enormous bump, and her splendid bosom emerging over the top of it; Titian hair cascading down her shoulders. Ashok, dwarfed beside her, looked as though he was going to burst with pride. Issy thought her friend had never looked more beautiful.

Outside, Ben was running around with Louis. One didn't, Pearl reflected, get everything. But whenever his father was there, Louis glowed and blossomed and there was nothing she would ever do to upset that.

Helena patted her bump complacently. 'Darling baby, I do love you,' she said. 'But you can come out now. I can't get up.'

'You don't have to get up,' said Issy. 'What do you need?'

'A wee,' said Helena. 'Again.'

'Oh. OK. Maybe I can't help you with that.' Issy offered her arm anyway, which Helena took with gratitude.

Pearl crossed the courtyard with more cakes. They had outfitted the new building as a shop in no time, and now Pearl did a roaring trade—helped by Felipe the violinist, who turned out to be quite nifty in the kitchen when he wasn't practising in the forecourt. Even Marian had chipped in quite a lot before the call of the road had grown strong again.

Meanwhile Issy had employed two cheerful Antipodean girls who were doing wonderfully in the café with Caroline, and the entire enterprise seemed to be nearly running itself. Recently Issy had found herself wondering whether there might not be room for another café somewhere . . .

Pearl hadn't wanted to tell Issy and she certainly couldn't bear the 'I told you so' glances she was going to get from Caroline, but it would come out sooner or later, she supposed.

'Looks like we might be moving,' she said.

'Moving where?' said Issy, delighted.

Pearl shrugged. 'Well, now I'm manager, it looks like I can afford a place . . . and we thought . . . well, maybe Ben and I thought . . .'

'So it's official?' said Caroline gleefully.

'It is what it is,' said Pearl heavily. 'It is what it is.'

'But what?' said Issy. 'What are you doing?'

Caroline guessed immediately. 'You're moving up here.' Then, 'No . . . no,' she said, putting her hand to her forehead in the manner of a soothsayer. 'You're moving to Dynevor Road. Or thereabouts.'

Pearl looked utterly exasperated. 'Well,' she said. 'Well . . .'

'What's in Dynevor Road?' asked Issy, getting desperate.

'*Only* William Patten, *the* best school in Stoke Newington,' said Caroline. 'The mothers fight tooth and nail to get their children in there.'

'But that's great,' said Issy. 'It's not betraying your roots to put your kid in a good school.'

'No,' said Pearl, looking unconvinced. 'The problem is with Louis, you know, I think he might be gifted and need, like, special help, and that's just not always available in other schools.'

Caroline threw an arm round her shoulders. 'Listen to you,' she said, beaming with pride. 'You sound like a Stoke Newington mother already.'

Helena gathered everyone round.

'I can't wait for Austin,' she announced. 'He's always late. And thank you for all my gorgeous presents, we're completely delighted, and thank you so much for letting us hold the baby shower here, Issy.'

Issy waved a tea towel modestly.

'We have something for you. It's taken for ever as Zac has been *so* overwhelmed with work.'

'Thanks to you,' said Zac. 'But we have a little gift for you.'

Issy stepped forward as Helena gave her a large flat parcel. Opening it up, she gasped. In the familiar pear-blossom livery of the Cupcake Café was a book that simply said *Recipes*. Inside were page after page compiled from the scraps of paper, the letters and typed notes, everything Gramps had ever sent her—typeset and printed guidelines to every cake in the Cupcake Café repertoire—with Zac's floral designs down the margins.

'So you can stop leaving them lying around the flat,' explained Helena helpfully, handing back the originals too.

'Oh,' said Issy. 'Oh. Gramps would have *loved* it. And I do too.'

The party continued late into the evening; Austin was late and they had a lovely baby carrier for Helena that they wanted to give her together, and she wanted to show him her beautiful book.

As the moon rose behind the houses, she finally caught sight of his tall, scruffy silhouette, and her heart jumped with love, as it always did.

'Aus!' she shouted, rushing outside. Darny shot out from behind him, yelled a hello to Issy then charged in to see Louis.

'Darling girl,' Austin said, holding her close and kissing her hair.

'Where were you? I need you to see something.'

'Ah, yes,' he said. 'I've had some news.'

He held up the carrier, which he'd clearly wrapped in the dark. 'Shall we hand over the gift first?'

'No,' said Issy, forgetting about her own present. 'News is news.'

The timer Austin had fixed to the fairy lights came on and the stumpy little tree glowed and became beautiful.

'It's the office,' said Austin. 'They've . . . well, apparently I've done quite well recently in one thing or another . . .'

It was true. It was as if his handling of Graeme and the snatching of the girl of his dreams had acted like a wake-up call to Austin. That, plus some subtle and not-so-subtle rearranging of his affairs by Issy, who preferred things neat and cosy at home and who had moved in in all but name, had given him a sudden huge appetite for new deals and new opportunities.

'Anyway, they wanted to know if I'd like to go, um, abroad. Away.'

'Away?' said Issy, a cold fear clutching her guts. 'Where?'

Austin shrugged. 'I don't know. They just said "overseas posting". Somewhere near a good school for Darny.' He looked at her expectantly.

Issy's pretty face was grave, her brow a little furrowed.

'Well, I suppose,' said Issy, finally, 'it could be time to expand the empire . . . internationally.'

Austin's heart leapt.

'You think?' he said, delightedly.

'Somewhere,' reflected Issy, 'where the bank managers are very receptive to bribes.'

They smiled at one another. Issy's eyes were shining.

'But, Austin. I mean, it is huge. Scary, and huge.'

'Would it help,' said Austin, 'if I told you that I love you?'

'Would you kiss me under the fairy lights while you say it?' whispered Issy. 'Then I think I'd follow you anywhere. Please let it not be Yemen.'

'I do love Stokey,' reflected Austin, later. 'Though you know what? Maybe home is just wherever you and Darny are.'

And he kissed her hard, beneath the glowing branches of the little, stunted pear tree, already dreaming of spring.

Jenny Colgan

Where did you grow up?

I grew up in Prestwick, on the west coast of Scotland. It's a small seaside town, with an airport stuck right next to it.

Can you tell us a little about yourself and your life now?

I live mostly in France, because my husband Andrew is a marine engineer and his work is based here. We have three children: Wallace, who is six, Michael-Francis, who is four, and Delphine, who is two (but thinks she is six).

Do you speak fluent French?

Oh *lordy*, learning a foreign language is difficult. Well, it is for me. I can get by, and the mothers at the school have been infinitely sweet and patient with me. I'm sure my accent is horrible. With the children, however, if you hadn't met Wallace before, you'd think he was local. I feel so lucky on their behalf that they get to grow up with a second language, because I know how horrible it is to learn one as an adult!

What is a typical day in the life of Jenny Colgan?

Well, when you work and have children, it's pretty regimented! The boys go to school at 8.30 and Delphie goes to *garderie* just afterwards, but only for the morning. A wonderful woman comes in four days a week and looks after the house and picks up the baby in the morning, while I go for a run along the beach. After that I work till

1.30, then I'm done for the day. I write 2,000 words a day. In the afternoon Delphine and I will get on the bicycle and go to see friends or run errands, then the boys get home at 4.30, ready for play. Wallace is just about to start *classes primaires*, so he'll be getting homework. If Andrew's about we can all eat together, ideally outside. Then the children get half an hour of telly if they've finished their supper, then it's early to bed. We go to bed early too. I like to read in the bath and have lights out by about 10.15. At the weekend we go to the beach, and barbecue and see friends.

Did you always want to be a writer?
Well, of course, but I didn't think anyone would ever pay me money to do it! I kind of put it up among my teenage dreams, like being a pop star or a ballerina.

Where do you write?
I write in a local café for two good reasons: one, they make a great *pain au chocolat*, and two, there is no internet connection to disturb me.

Do you plan your novels or do you just leap straight into your plots and characters?
I have a rough idea, but for me it is always about the characters. The people make a story. If you don't care about the characters, you don't care what they go through.

What was your starting point for *Meet Me at the Cupcake Café*?
When I had children I started cooking, because I was the fussiest child you can possibly imagine, and I hated being a picky eater, I was really ashamed of it. So I wanted to introduce them to lots of tastes as early as possible. Along the way I got interested in baking, too, and I loved making cupcakes. So from there really.

Have you got a 'signature' cupcake?
My signature cupcake is a coffee sponge with a maple syrup buttercream. Eating just one is frankly not possible.

Do you share Helena's mantra: 'Behave like you might meet John Cusack' at any moment?
Ha, no, I wish it was. You've just reminded me that I need my roots doing. I do love John Cusack though.

What are the three most important items in your handbag?
BlackBerry, Kindle, nappies.

What's the best piece of advice you've ever been given?
There are two: never ever think about what other people are thinking about you; they are far too busy worrying about themselves. I wish I'd known that as an adolescent. And the second one is, in my experience, it's not always the most talented who succeed, it's often the ones who work hardest.

What's your top tip for life?
Go! Go! Go!

It's sports day at Sidley House and on the playing field children are running races, watched by their proud parents. Suddenly smoke can be seen coming from the school building. Thick black smoke like a bonfire. The school is on fire. For Grace time stands still. Both her son and her daughter are inside. They are in danger. There is a fire and they are in there. She runs towards the flames . . .

1

I COULDN'T MOVE, not even a little finger or a flicker of an eye. I couldn't open my mouth to scream.

I struggled, as *hard as I could*, to move the huge, heavy hulk that my body had become but I was trapped under the hull of a vast ship wrecked on the ocean floor and moving was impossible.

My eyelids were welded shut. My eardrums broken. My vocal cords snapped off. Pitch-dark and silent and so heavy in there; a mile of black water above me.

Only one thing for it, I said to myself, thinking of you, and I slipped out of the wrecked ship of my body into the black ocean.

I swam upwards towards the daylight with all my strength.

Suddenly I was in a white room, brightly gleaming, smelling pungently of antiseptic. I heard voices and my name.

I saw the body part of 'I' was in a hospital bed. I watched a doctor holding my eyelids open and shining a light into my eyes; another was putting drips into my arm.

You won't be able to believe this. You're a man who dams rivers and climbs mountains; a man who *knows* the laws of nature and physics. 'Hogwash!' you've said when anyone talks about anything paranormal. You'll think it's impossible. But out-of-body experiences *do* happen. You read about it in the papers; hear people talking about it on Radio 4.

But if this was real, what should I do? Push my way through the doctors and elbow out the nurse who was shaving my head? 'Excuse me! Gangway! Sorry! My body, I think. I'm right here actually!'

Thinking ridiculous things because I was afraid.

Sick, goose bumps, shivering afraid.
And as I felt afraid I remembered.
Blistering heat and raging flames and suffocating smoke.
The school was on fire.

You were in your important BBC meeting this afternoon, so you won't have felt the strong, warm breeze—'A godsend for sports day,' parents were saying to each other.

The sun shone on the white lines painted on the grass; the whistles hanging round the teachers' necks glinted; the children's hair was shiny-bright. Touchingly too-big feet on small legs bounced on the grass as they did the 100-metre dash, the sack race, the obstacle course. You can't really see Sidley House in summertime, huge pollarded oaks hide the school from view, but I knew a Reception class was still in there and I thought it was a shame the youngest children couldn't be out enjoying the summer afternoon too.

Adam was wearing his 'I am 8!' badge from our card this morning. He came dashing up to me, his little face beaming, because he was off to get his cake from school right now! Rowena had to get the medals so was going with him; Rowena who was at Sidley House with Jenny all those moons ago.

As they left, I looked around to see if Jenny had arrived. I'd thought that after her A-level disaster she should immediately start revision for her retakes, but she still wanted to work at Sidley House to pay for her planned trip to Canada. I'd thought her being a temporary teaching assistant at seventeen was challenge enough—and now she was school nurse for the afternoon.

We'd gently crossed swords at breakfast.

'*It's just a little young to have that much responsibility.*'

'*It's a primary-school sports day, Mum, not a motorway crash.*'

But now her shift was almost over—with no accidents at all—and soon she'd be out to join us. I was sure she'd be itching to leave that small stuffy medical room stuck at the top of the school.

I'd noticed that she was wearing that short red frou-frou skirt with a skimpy top and I'd told her it didn't really look very professional, but when did Jenny ever listen to my advice on clothes?

'*Just count your lucky stars I'm not in bumsters.*'

'You mean the jeans that hang around boys' bottoms?'
'Yup.'
'I always want to go and give them a hitch up.'
She bursts out laughing.
And her long legs do look rather wonderful under the too-short, gauzy skirt. Despite myself I feel a little proud.

On the playing field, Maisie arrived, her blue eyes sparkling, her face one large smile. Some people dismiss her as a jolly-hockey-sticks Sloane in FUN shirts (long sleeves a different pattern to the rest), but most of us love her.

'Gracie,' she said, giving me a hug. 'I've come to give Rowena a lift home. She texted me a little while ago, said the tubes were up the spout. So Chauffeur-Mum to the fore!'

'She's getting the medals,' I told her. 'Adam's gone with her to get his cake. They should be back any minute.'

She smiled. 'What kind of cake this year?'

'An M&S chocolate tray-bake. Addie dug out a trench with a teaspoon and we replaced the Maltesers with soldiers. It's a World War One cake. Which is violent but fits with Key Stage 2, so I don't think anyone'll mind.'

She laughed. 'Fantastic.'

'Is she your __best__ friend, Mum?' Adam asked me recently.

'Probably, yes,' I said.

Maisie handed me a 'little something' for Adam, beautifully wrapped, which I knew would contain a spot-on present. She's brilliant at presents. It's one of the many things I love her for. Another is that she ran in the mothers' race every single year that Rowena was at Sidley House, and always came last by a mile but didn't give a hoot! Unlike virtually every other mum at Sidley House, she has never been inside a gym.

I know. I'm dawdling on that sunny playing field with Maisie. I'm sorry. But it's hard. What I'm getting to is just so bloody hard.

Maisie left to find Rowena in the school.

I checked my watch; it was almost three. Still no sign of Jenny or Adam.

The PE teacher blew his whistle for the last race—the relay—bellowing through his loudspeaker for teams to get in position. I worried that Addie would get into trouble for not being in his designated place.

I looked back towards the school, thinking surely I'd see them coming towards me any moment.

Smoke was coming from the school building. Thick black smoke like a bonfire. I remember the calm most of all. The absence of panic. But knowing it was accelerating towards me, like a juggernaut.

My children are in danger. It hit me in the chest, full on.

There is a fire and *they are in there*.

Then I was running at the velocity of a scream. Running so hard that I didn't have time to breathe. A scream that can't stop until I hold them both.

Darting across the road, I heard sirens blaring on the bridge. But the fire engines weren't moving. There were abandoned cars by the traffic lights blocking their path, and women were getting out of other cars just left in the middle of the road and running across the bridge towards the school, screaming as they ran, like me. I recognised one. They were the mothers of the Reception children coming to do their usual pick-up. One had left a toddler in her abandoned SUV and the toddler was hitting the window as he watched his mother in this ghastly mothers' race.

I was there first, before the other mothers, because they still had to cross the road and run down the drive.

The four-year-olds were lined up outside the school with their teacher, a neat little crocodile; Maisie was with the teacher. Behind them black smoke poured out of the school, staining the summer-blue sky.

And Adam was outside—*outside!*—by that bronze statue, sobbing against Rowena and she was holding him tightly. In that moment of relief, love flooded out from me not only onto my boy but onto the girl who was comforting him.

Then I was looking for Jenny. Bobbed blonde hair, slender. No one like Jenny outside.

From the bridge the sirens wailed. The four-year-olds were starting to cry as they saw their mothers, running full tilt towards them down the drive, tears streaming down their faces, arms outstretched, waiting for that moment to hold their child.

And I turned towards the burning building, black smoke billowing out of the classrooms on the second and third floors.

Jenny.

I ran up the main steps to the school and opened the door into the small vestibule and for a moment everything was normal. There was that framed photo on the wall of the first pupils at Sidley House, smiling their baby-teeth smiles. (Rowena exceptionally pretty then, Jenny our gawky little duckling.) There was the day's lunch menu, with pictures as well as words; fish pie and peas. It was like coming into school every morning.

I tried to open the door from the vestibule into the school itself. It was heavy, a fire door. My hands were shaking too hard to get a grip on the handle properly. And it was hot. I had my sleeves rolled up. I unrolled them and tugged them over my hands. Then I pulled the door open.

I screamed her name. Over and over. And each time I screamed, smoke came into my mouth, throat and lungs until I couldn't scream any more.

The sound of burning, hissing and spitting; a giant serpent of fire coiling through the building. Above me something collapsed. I heard the thud. Then a roar of rage as the fire discovered fresh oxygen.

The fire was above me.

Jenny was above me.

I could just see my way to the stairs. I started climbing them, the heat getting stronger, the smoke thicker.

I got to the first floor. The heat punched me full in the body and face. I couldn't see anything—blacker than hell.

I had to get to the third floor. To Jenny.

The smoke went into my lungs and I was breathing barbed wire. I dropped onto my hands and knees, remembering that this is where oxygen is found. By some small miracle I found I could breathe.

I crawled forwards, a blind person without a stick, fingers tapping in front of me, trying to find the next flight of stairs. I ought to have been crossing the reading area with the huge, brightly coloured rug. I felt the rug under my fingers, the nylon melting and crinkling in the heat, and my fingertips were burning. I was afraid my fingertips would soon be too burnt to feel. I was like the man in Adam's mythology book, holding onto Ariadne's thread to find his way out of the labyrinth, only my thread was a melting rug.

I reached the end of the rug and felt the texture change; then I felt the first step. I began to climb the stairs up to the second floor, on my hands and knees, keeping my face down to the oxygen.

I felt dizzy, poisoned by something in the smoke.

Another step.

It was a battle. Me against this living fire that wanted to kill my child.

Another step.

I knew I'd never get to the third floor; that it would kill me before I could reach her.

At the top of the stairs I felt her. She had managed to get down one flight. She was my little girl and I was here. Everything was going to be all right.

'Jenny?'

She didn't speak or move. I tried to pick her up as if she was still tiny, but she was too heavy. I dragged her down the stairs, trying to use my body to shield her from the heat and smoke.

I cried to you, silently, as if by telepathy I could summon you to help us. And as I dragged her down, step by step, trying to get away from burning heat and raging flames and smoke, I thought of love.

Maybe there was telepathy between us. At that moment you must have been in your meeting with the BBC commissioning editors about the follow-up to your 'Hostile Environments' series. You'd done hot, steamy jungles and blazing, arid deserts, and you want the next series to be in the frozen wilds of Antarctica. So maybe it was you who helped me envisage a silent, white acreage of love, cool and clear and quiet, as I dragged Jenny down the stairs.

But before I reached the bottom, something hit me, throwing me forwards, and everything went dark.

2

I TOLD YOU ALREADY what happened when I woke up—that I was trapped under the hull of a vast ship wrecked on the ocean floor.

That I slipped out of the wrecked ship of my body into the inky black ocean and swam upwards towards the daylight.

That I saw the body part of 'me' in a hospital bed.

That I felt afraid and, as I felt fear, I remembered.

Blistering heat and raging flames and suffocating smoke.

Jenny.

I ran from the room to find her. Do you think I should have tried to go back into my body? But what if I was trapped, uselessly, inside again, but this time couldn't get out? How would I find her then?

In the burning school, I had searched in darkness and smoke. Now I was in brightly lit white corridors, but the desperation to find her was the same. Panicking, I forgot about the me in the hospital bed and I went up to a doctor, asking where she was: *'Jennifer Covey. Seventeen years old. My daughter. She was in a fire.'* The doctor turned away. I went after him, shouting, 'Where's my daughter?' He still walked away.

I interrupted two nurses. 'Where's my daughter? *She was in a fire. Jenny Covey.'* They carried on talking to each other.

I started screaming, loud as I could, but everyone around me was deaf and blind.

Then I remembered that it was me who was mute and invisible.

I ran down a corridor, away from the ward where my body was, and into other wards, frantically searching.

I thought of you, what you would do, and made myself slow down.

You would start on the bottom floor, far left, like you do at home when something is lost, and then you'd work your way to the far right, then up to the next floor, methodically doing a sweep and finding the missing mobile phone/earring/number 8 Beast Quest book.

Thinking about the details of our lives calmed me a little.

So I went more slowly along the corridors, although desperate to run, trying to read signs rather than race past them. There were signs to lift banks, and oncology and outpatients and paediatrics—a mini-kingdom of wards and clinics and operating theatres and support services.

A sign to the mortuary tore into my vision, but I wouldn't go to the mortuary. Wouldn't *even consider it.*

I saw a sign to Accident & Emergency. Maybe she hadn't been transferred to a ward yet. I ran as fast as I could towards it.

I went in. A woman on a trolley was pushed past, bleeding. A doctor was running, his stethoscope flapping against his stomach; the doors to the ambulance bay swung open and a screeching siren filled the white corridor, panic bouncing off the walls. A place of urgency and tension and pain.

I looked into cubicle after cubicle, flimsy blue curtains dividing intense scenes from separate dramas. In one was Rowena, barely conscious. Maisie was sobbing next to her, but I only paused long enough to see that it wasn't Jenny and then I moved on.

At the end of the corridor was a room rather than a cubicle. I noticed doctors going in, and none coming out. I went in.

There was someone appallingly hurt on the bed in the middle of the room, surrounded by doctors.

I saw sandals on the person. The sandals with sparkly gems that I'd got her from Russell & Bromley as an absurdly early and out-of-season Christmas present. Lots of people have those sandals, lots and lots. It doesn't mean it's Jenny. It can't mean it's Jenny. Please.

Her blonde glinting hair was charred, her face swollen and horribly burnt. Two doctors were talking about percentage of BSA and I realised they were discussing the percentage of her body that was burnt. Twenty-five per cent.

'Jenny?' I shouted. But she didn't open her eyes. Was she unconscious? I hoped that she was, because her pain would be unbearable.

I left the room, just for a moment. A drowning person coming up for one gulp of air before going back into that depth of compassion as I looked at her. I stood in the corridor and closed my eyes.

'Mum?'

I'd know her voice anywhere.

I looked down at a girl crouched in the corridor, her arms round her knees. The girl I'd recognise among a thousand faces.

I put my arms round her.

'What are we, Mum?'

'I don't know, sweetheart.'

It may seem strange, but I didn't even really wonder. The fire had burnt away everything I once thought of as normal. Nothing made sense any more.

A trolley with Jenny's body on it was wheeled past us, surrounded by medical staff. They'd covered her up using a sheet like a tent so the fabric wouldn't touch her burns.

Beside me I felt her flinch.

'Did you see your body?' I asked. 'Before they covered it, I mean.' I'd tried to let out the words delicately but they fell with a clump on the floor, forming a boorish, brutal question.

'Yeah, I did. "Return of the living dead" kind of summarises it, doesn't it?'

'Jen, sweetheart—'

'This morning I was worried about blackheads on my nose. *Blackheads.* How ridiculous is that, Mum?'

I tried to comfort her, but she shook her head. She needed me to ignore her tears and believe the act she was putting on. The one where she is still funny, lively, buoyant Jenny.

A doctor was talking to a nurse as they passed us.

'The dad's on his way, poor bloke.'

We hurried to find you.

The large hospital atrium was crowded with press. Your TV fame from presenting the 'Hostile Environments' series had attracted them.

A smartly dressed man arrived and the people who'd been buzzing round with cameras and microphones moved towards him. I wondered if Jenny also felt vulnerable and exposed in this swarm of people, but if she did, she gave no sign of it. She's always shared your courage.

'Grace and Jennifer Covey were admitted at four fifteen this afternoon with serious injuries,' the suited man said. 'They are now being treated in our specialist units. Rowena White was also admitted suffering from minor burns and smoke inhalation. At this point we have no further information. I'd be grateful if you would now wait *outside* the hospital.'

'How did the fire start?' a journalist asked the suited man.

'That's a question for the police, not us. Now if you'll excuse me.'

They carried on shouting out their questions, but we were looking out of the glass wall of the atrium for you. It was Jenny who spotted you first.

'He's here.'

You were getting out of an unfamiliar car. The BBC must have driven you in one of theirs.

Sometimes looking at your face is like looking in the mirror—so familiar it's become a part of me. But there was a mask of anxiety covering your usual face, making it strange. I hadn't realised that you are nearly always smiling.

Jenny ran to you and put her arms round you, but you didn't know she was there and hurried on, half running up to the reception desk, your stride jerky with shock.

'My wife and daughter are here, Grace and Jenny Covey.'

For a moment the receptionist reacted, she must have seen you on the telly, and then she looked at you with sympathy. 'I'll bleep Dr Gawande, and he'll come to get you straight away.'

Your fingers drummed on the counter, your eyes flicking around; a cornered animal.

The journalists hadn't yet spotted you. Maybe that mask over your old face had foxed them. Then Tara, my ghastly colleague at the *Richmond Post*, made a beeline towards you. As she reached you she smiled. *Smiled.*

'Tara Connor. I know your wife.'

You ignored her, seeing a young doctor hastening towards you.

'Dr Gawande?' you said.

'Yes.'

'How are they?' Your quiet voice was screaming.

Other journalists had seen you now and were coming towards you.

'The consultants will be able to give you a fuller picture,' Dr Gawande said. 'Your wife has been taken off to have an MRI scan and will then return to our acute neurology ward. Your daughter has been taken to our burns unit.'

'I want to see them.'

'Of course. I'll take you to your daughter first. You can see your wife as soon as she's finished her MRI, which will be in about twenty minutes.'

As you left the foyer with the young doctor, journalists hung back a little, demonstrating unexpected compassion. But Tara brazenly followed.

'What do you think about Silas Hyman?' she asked you.

For one moment you turned to her, registering her question, and then you walked quickly on.

The young doctor accompanied you swiftly past outpatient clinics, which were deserted now, the lights off. But in one empty waiting room a television had been left on. You stopped for a moment.

On the screen, a BBC 'News 24' interviewer was standing in front of the gates to the school. Its pastel blue stuccoed façade was blackened and charred, its cream window frames burnt away to reveal the destruction inside. That gentle old building, so intricately associated with Adam's warm hand holding mine at the beginning of the day and his running, relieved little face at the end of the day, had been brutally maimed.

You looked so shocked, and I knew what you were thinking because I'd felt the same when the rug was melting in my hands—if fire can do this to bricks and plaster, what damage must it do to a living girl?

'How did we get out of there?' Jenny asked.

'I don't know.'

I caught fragments of what the TV reporter was saying. '. . . private school in London . . . cause at the moment unknown. Fortunately most children were at sports day . . . Emergency services were prevented from reaching the scene as desperate parents . . . One thing as yet to be explained is the arrival of press before the fire services . . .'

Then Mrs Healey came onto the screen, and the camera focused on her.

'An hour ago,' the reporter said, 'I spoke to Sally Healey, the head-mistress of Sidley House Preparatory School.'

You went on with the young doctor, but Jenny and I stayed for a little while longer watching Sally Healey. She was immaculate in pink linen shirt and cream trousers. I noticed her make-up was flawless; she must have retouched it.

'Were there any children in the school when the fire started?' the reporter asked her.

'Yes. But not one child at the school was hurt. I'd like to emphasise that.'

'I can't believe she put on make-up,' Jenny said.

'She's like one of those French MPs,' I said. 'You know, with the lip gloss next to the state papers? Make-up in the face of adversity.'

Jenny smiled; sweet, brave girl.

'There was a Reception class of twenty children in the school at the time of the fire,' Sally Healey continued. 'Their classroom is on the lower-ground floor.' She was using her assembly voice, commanding but approachable. 'All our children had rehearsed an evacuation in the event of fire. Our Reception class were evacuated in less than three minutes. Fortunately our other Reception class were at an end-of-term outing to the zoo.'

'Have you any idea yet how the fire started?' the reporter asked.

'No. Not yet. But I can reassure you that we had *every* fire precaution in place. Our heat detectors and smoke detectors are connected directly to the fire station and the alarm went immediately through. Two weeks ago some of the fire-fighters came to give a talk to our Year One children and let them look at their fire engine. We never dreamed, any of us, that . . .'

She trailed off. The lip gloss and assembly voice weren't working. Under that carefully put-together frontage she was starting to fall apart. I liked her for it. As the camera panned away from her and back to the blackened school it paused on the undamaged bronze statue of a child.

We caught up with you in the corridor that leads to the burns unit. I could see you tense, trying to ready yourself, but I knew nothing could prepare you for what you'd see inside. Next to me I felt Jenny draw back.

'I don't want to go in.'

'Of course. That's fine.'

You went through the swing doors into the burns unit with the doctor.

'You should be with Dad,' Jenny said.

'But I don't want to leave you on your own.'

'I don't need baby-sitting, really. Besides, I need you to keep me updated on my progress.'

'All right. But I won't be long. Don't go anywhere.' I couldn't bear to have to search for her again.

'OK,' she said. 'And I won't talk to strangers. Promise.'

I joined you as you were taken into a small office, grateful that they were doing this by degrees. A doctor held out his hand to you. I thought he looked almost indecently healthy, his brown skin glowing against the white walls of his office, his dark eyes shining.

'My name's Dr Sandhu. I am the consultant in charge of your daughter's care.' As he shook your hand his other hand patted your arm, and I knew he must be a parent too. 'Come in, please. Take a seat, take a seat . . .'

You didn't sit down, but stood, as you always do when you are tense.

'I'd like to start on the positives,' he said and you nodded in vehement agreement; the man was talking your kind of talk. '*However tough the environment*,' you say in the middle of some godforsaken place, '*you can always find strategies to survive.*'

You hadn't seen her yet, but I had, and I suspected that 'starting with the positives' was putting a few cushions at the bottom of the cliff before pushing us off it.

'Your daughter has achieved the hardest thing there is,' continued Dr Sandhu. 'Which is to come out of that fire alive. She must have huge strength of character and spirit.'

Your voice was proud. 'She does.'

'And that already puts her ahead of the game, as it were, because that fight in her is going to make all the difference now.'

I looked away from him to you. The smile lines round your eyes were still there, too deeply etched by past happiness to be rubbed out by what was happening now.

'I need to be frank with you about her condition. You won't be able to take in all the medical speak now, so I'll just tell you simply. Jennifer has sustained significant burns to her body and face. Because of the burns, stress is being placed on her internal organs. She has also suffered inhalation injuries. This means that inside her body her airways, including part of her lungs, are burnt and not functioning.'

She was hurt inside as well.

'I'm afraid I have to tell you that at the moment she has a less than fifty per cent chance of surviving.'

I screamed at Dr Sandhu: 'No!'

My scream didn't even ruffle the air.

I put my arms round you, needing to hold on to you. You half turned towards me as if you felt me.

'We are keeping her heavily sedated so that she won't feel any pain,' Dr Sandhu continued. 'And we are breathing for her with a ventilator. We have a highly specialist team who will be doing everything possible for her.'

'I want to see her now,' you said in a voice I didn't recognise.

I stood close against you as we looked at her.

We used to do that when she was small, after coming in from a party. We'd go to her room and stand and watch her as she slept—soft pink feet sticking out of her cotton nightie, silky hair across her stretched-out arms. We made her, we'd think. Together we created this amazing child.

I was glad, for your sake, that her face was covered in dressings now. Just her swollen eyelids and damaged mouth visible. Her burnt limbs were encased in some kind of plastic.

Then you made yourself stand tall and your voice was strong. 'Everything is going to be all right, Jen. I promise. You're *going to get better*.'

A pledge. Because as her father your job is to protect her; and when that's failed you make everything better.

Then Dr Sandhu explained about the intravenous lines, the monitors and the dressings and, although he didn't intend this, it quickly became clear that if she got better it would be because of him, not you.

But you don't take that lying down. You don't just hand over power over your daughter. So you asked questions. What did this tube do *exactly*? That one? Why use this? You were learning the lingo, the techniques. This was your daughter's world now, so it was yours and you would master it.

'How badly will she be scarred?' you asked.

Your optimism was glorious! I knew you didn't give a *monkey's arse* about how she looked compared to whether she lived. Your question was to show your belief that *she will live*; that the issue of scarring is a real one because one day she will face the outside world again.

You've always been the optimist, me the pessimist (*pragmatist*, I'd correct). But now your optimism was a life buoy and I was clinging to it.

Dr Sandhu replied, 'She has suffered second-degree partial-thickness burns. This type of burn can be either superficial, which means the blood supply is intact and the skin will heal, or deep, which inevitably means scarring. Unfortunately it takes several days before the burns reveal which type they are.'

A nurse came up. 'We're arranging a family room for you to stay in tonight. Your wife has been brought back to the acute neurology ward, which is just across the corridor.'

'Can I see my wife now?'

'I'll take you there.'

Jenny was waiting for me in the corridor. 'Well . . .?'

'You're going to be fine. A long haul ahead, but you're going to be fine.' I couldn't bear to tell her what Dr Sandhu had said. 'They don't yet know if they're the kind of burns that leave a scar.'

'They might not?' she asked, her voice hopeful.

'No.'

'I thought I was going to look like that permanently.' She sounded almost euphoric. Relief shone out of her face; made her luminous.

Looking at me, she didn't see you come out of the burns unit. You turned your face to the wall and then your hands slammed onto it, as if you could expel what you'd seen and heard. And I knew then how hard-won your hopefulness was; the bravery and effort it took.

We heard footsteps pounding down the corridor.

Your sister was hurtling towards you, her police officer's radio hissing at her side.

I instantly felt inadequate. If Pavlov's dog had had a sister-in-law like Sarah it would be a recognised emotional reflex. I know. Unfair. But it's not that surprising, is it? The most important woman in your life from the age of ten till you met me, a sister-in-law/mother-in-law rolled into one; little wonder I feel intimidated by her.

Her voice was breathless. 'I'm so sorry, Mikey.'

She put her arm round you, held you tightly.

For a little while she didn't say anything. I saw her face stiffen, hardening herself to tell you.

'It was arson.'

Someone had deliberately done this. My God. *Deliberately.*

'But why?' Jenny asked.

At four years old we'd nicknamed her the 'Why-Why Bird'.

But why doesn't the moon fall on top of us? But why am I a girl not a boy? But why does Mowgli eat ants? But why can't Grandpa get better?' (Answers: Gravity; Genes; They are tangy and nutritious. By the end of the day, worn out: *'It's just the way it is, sweetie.'*)

There was no answer to the why in this.

'Do you remember anything, Jen?' I asked.

'No. I remember Ivo texting at half past two. But that's it. I can't remember anything after that.'

Sarah touched you lightly on the arm and you flinched.

'Whoever did this, I'll kill them.'

I'd never seen you angry like that before. But I was glad of your rage: an emotion that met this information head-on and fought back.

'I need to see Grace. Then I want you to tell me everything you know.'

I hurried ahead to my ward, wanting to know before you did what state I was in, as if I could prepare you in some way.

There were tubes and monitors attached to my body now, but I was breathing without any equipment, and I thought that must be a good thing. I was unconscious, yes, but I really looked hardly injured apart from the neatly dressed wound on my head. Maybe it wasn't so bad.

'I'll be outside then,' Jenny said.

She's never given us privacy before; never seemed to even consider we might need it. It's Adam who dashes out of the kitchen when we have a hug and a kiss. *'Being mushy! Yuck!'* But Jenny's radar hasn't detected any embarrassing parental passion. Maybe like most teenagers, she thinks that's long gone, while they discover it and keep it all for themselves. So I was touched.

I waited for you; wanting to hear your footsteps, your voice.

Then you were running over the slippery linoleum towards my bed.

You put your strong arms round my body, holding me tightly against you, the softness of your linen important-meetings-shirt against my creased stiff hospital gown. You kissed me: one kiss on my mouth and then one on each closed eyelid. For a moment, I thought that like a princess in one of Jenny's old storybooks your three kisses would break the spell and I'd wake up.

But thirty-nine's probably a little too old to be a sleeping princess.

And maybe a bash on the head isn't as easy to reverse as a witch's curse.

Then I remembered—how could I have forgotten, even for three kisses—Jenny outside, waiting for me. I knew that I mustn't wake up, not yet, because I couldn't leave her on her own.

You understand that, don't you? Because if your job as a father is to protect your child, and mend her when she's broken, my job as a mother is to be there with her.

'My brave wife,' you said.

'I didn't get to her in time,' I said to you, my voice loud with guilt.

But you couldn't hear me.

We were silent—when have we ever been silent together?

'What happened?' you asked me, and your voice cracked a little. 'What the hell happened?'

I started with the strong, warm breeze at sports day.

Your eyes are closed now, as if you can join me if your eyes are shut too. I've told you everything I know.

Of course you couldn't hear me. But words are the spoken oxygen between us; the air a marriage breathes. We have spoken every day since we first met. Nineteen years of talking to each other.

A woman doctor is coming purposefully towards us. I'm reassured by her being in her fifties; by her air of tired professionalism. Beneath her sensible navy-blue skirt she's wearing high, spiky red shoes. I know, a silly thing to notice. You're looking at her name badge and rank; the important things. 'Dr Anna-Maria Bailstrom. Neurologist. Consultant.' Is it the Anna-Maria in her that wears the red shoes?

'I thought she would look worse,' you say to Dr Bailstrom. 'But she's hardly hurt, is she? And she's breathing for herself, isn't she?' The relief in your voice strings your words together.

'I'm afraid that her head injury is severe. A fire-fighter told us that a part of the ceiling had fallen on her.' There's tension in Dr Bailstrom's voice. 'She has unequal pupil reflexes and isn't responding to stimuli. The MRI, which we will repeat, indicates significant brain damage.'

'She'll be all right.' Your voice is fierce. Your fingers tense around mine. 'You're going to be *fine*, my darling.'

Of course I am! I can quote medieval poetry and tell you about Fra Angelico or Obama's health reforms and the heroes in Beast Quest books—and how many people can do all that? The thinking me isn't in the body me, but I'm right here, my darling, my mind undamaged.

'We have to warn you that there's a likelihood she may never regain consciousness.'

You turn away from her, your body language saying, 'Bollocks!' And I think you're right. I'm pretty sure that if I tried, I'd be able to get back into my body. And then—maybe not right away but soon—I'd wake up again. 'Regain consciousness', to put it into Dr Bailstrom language.

Dr Bailstrom is now leaving, precipitous on her red spiky heels on the slippery lino. She's probably letting you have some time for it to sink in.

'Jenny's been badly hurt, darling,' you say. And my fear is swept away in compassion for you. You tell me that she'll get better. You tell me that I'll get better too. We'll be 'right as rain', again. Is it really possible to be as brave as you are now—this resiliently hopeful?

You talk about the holiday we're going to take when this is 'all over'.

'Skye. And we'll camp. Adam'll love that. Making a fire and fishing for our supper. Jenny and I can climb the Cuillins. Addie can manage the smallest one now. You can take a whole stack of books and read by a loch. What do you think?'

I think it sounds like a paradise on earth that I never knew was there.

I think that while I have my head in the clouds, you climb a mountain to do it. I cling onto your hope; let myself be carried by it.

I see that Sarah has arrived on the far side of the ward, on her phone. Busy, efficient Sarah. The first time you introduced us I felt I was being interviewed for something I'd inadvertently done wrong. But what? The crime of loving you and plotting to take you away from her? Or not loving you *enough*? Or maybe—the one I picked—not being worthy of you; not being as interesting and beautiful and downright *remarkable* as I should be if I was going to claim her brother and become a part of your clan.

Even before this, I saw myself paddling round a duck pond in a rubber dinghy, while she steered her life on a fast, direct course to a clearly mapped destination. And now here I am, unable to speak or see or move, let alone help you or Jenny or Adam, head partially shaved, in a hideous hospital nightgown—and she's sailed in, competent and capable, at the helm.

A nurse is with her and I see they're debating the phone, with Sarah flashing her warrant card, but the nurse is clearly adamant and Sarah leaves again. You spot her as she leaves, but stay with me.

We return to that camping trip to Skye—to arching blue-grey skies and still blue-grey water and huge blue-grey mountains, their soft colours so alike that they are almost indistinguishable from one another; to Jenny and Adam and you and me, softly coloured, not separated from each other. A family.

We leave my ward and I see Jenny waiting for me in the corridor.

'So, what's happening to you?' she asks me, her voice anxious.

'They're doing scans and whatnot,' I say.

She hasn't been giving us romantic privacy, I realise, but medical privacy; like me staying out of the room now when I take her to the GP.

'And that's it?' she asks.

'So far, yes. Pretty much.'

She doesn't question me more closely—afraid, I think, to know any more.

'Aunt Sarah's in the family room,' she says. 'She's been talking to someone at the police station. It's funny, but I think she knows I'm here. I mean, she kept kind of glancing round at me, like she'd caught a glimpse.'

It'll be Sod's Law if the only person who has any real inkling of Jenny and me turns out to be your sister.

It must be late evening now and in the family room someone has brought a toothbrush and pyjamas for you and put them at one end of the bed.

Sarah closes the phone as she sees you.

'Adam's at a friend's house,' she says. 'Georgina's on her way and will pick him up. I thought it would be best if he was in his own bed tonight and he's particularly close to Grace's mum, isn't he?'

In all of this Sarah has found space and time to think about Adam. Has had the kindness to worry about him. I've never been grateful to her before.

But you can't take Adam on board, not with me and Jenny already weighing you down this heavily.

'Have you spoken to the police?' you ask her.

She nods. 'We're taking statements. They'll keep me fully informed. The fire investigation team are working at the scene of the fire.'

Her voice is police officer, but I see her reach out her hand and that you take it.

'They've said that the fire started in the Art room on the second floor. Because the building was old, it had ceiling, wall and roof voids—basically spaces connecting different rooms and parts of the school—which means that smoke and fire could travel extremely fast. Fire doors and other precautions couldn't stop its spread.'

'And the arson?' you ask, and I can hear the word cutting at your mouth.

'It is likely that an accelerant was used, probably white spirit, which causes a distinctive smoke recognised by a fire-fighter at the scene. As it's an Art room, you'd expect to have some white spirit, but they think it was a large quantity. The Art teacher says that she keeps the white spirit in a locked cupboard on the right-hand side of the Art room. We think the fire was started in the left-hand corner. A hydrocarbon vapour detector should give us more information tomorrow.'

'So there's no doubt?' you ask.

'I'm sorry, Mike.'

'What else?' you ask. A man who has to be in full possession of the facts.

'The fire investigation team have established that the windows on the top floors were all wide open,' Sarah says. 'Which is another signifier for arson because it creates a draught, drawing the fire more quickly up through the school; especially given the strong breeze today. The head teacher told us that the windows are never left wide open because of the danger of children falling out.'

'What else?' you ask again and she understands you need to know.

'We think that the Art room was deliberately chosen, not only because there was a chance that the arsonist could get away with it—the use of an accelerant being camouflaged as it were by Art supplies—but because it's the worst possible place for a fire. The Art teacher has inventoried what materials were kept. There were stacks of paper and craft materials, which meant the fire could take hold easily. There were also paints and glues, which were flammable. She'd brought in old wallpaper samples for a collage, which we think were coated in a highly toxic varnish.'

As she describes an inferno of poisonous fumes and choking smoke I think of children making collages of hot-air balloons and papier-mâché dinosaurs.

'There were also cans of spray mount in the room. When they are exposed to heat the pressure builds and they explode.' She pauses; sees how pale you are. 'Have you eaten anything yet?'

The question irritates you. 'No, but—'

'Let's talk more in the canteen. It's not far.'

It's not up for negotiation. When you were younger, did she bribe you to eat then too? A favourite TV programme if you finished your shepherd's pie?

'I'll tell them where you are, just in case,' she says, pre-empting any arguments.

She goes to tell the staff in my acute neurology ward where you will be; you go to tell the burns unit.

Once you've gone, Jenny turns to me. 'It's true, what Mrs Healey said about the windows. Ever since that fire-escape accident, they're paranoid about children falling and hurting themselves. Mrs Healey goes round herself, checking them all the time.'

She pauses a moment, and I see that she is awkward. Embarrassed even.

'You know when I went to your bed?' she says. 'Before Dad got there?'

'Yes.'

'You looked so . . .' She falters. But I know what she wants to ask. How come I am so undamaged compared with her?

'I wasn't in the building as long as you,' I say. 'And I wasn't so close to the fire. And I had more protection.'

I don't say that I was in a cotton shirt with sleeves I could pull down and thick denim jeans and socks with trainers, not a short, gauzy skirt and skimpy top and strappy sandals, but she guesses anyway.

'So I'm the ultimate fashion victim.'

'I'm not sure I can do gallows humour, Jen.'

'OK.'

'Positive and even silly,' I say. 'That's fine. That's great. But gallows—well, that's my line.'

'Point taken, Mum.'

We could almost be at our kitchen table.

We follow you into the absurdly named Palms Café, the Formica-topped tables reflecting the overhead strip lights.

Sarah joins you with a plate of food, which you ignore.

'Who *did this*?' you ask her.

'We don't know yet, but we will find out. I promise.'

'But someone must have seen who it was, surely?' you say.

She puts her hand on your arm.

'Do you know what they were doing to Jenny when I left her just now?' you ask. 'They were giving her an eye toilet, *an eye toilet*, for Christ's sake.'

I feel Jenny stiffen next to me. Sarah's eyes fill with tears. I've never seen her cry. She hasn't yet asked how Jenny is. I see her brace herself. I will her not to do it.

'Have they told you the chances of . . .?' she asks, her voice trailing off, unable to continue.

'She has a less than fifty per cent chance of surviving,' you say.

I see Sarah pale, and in the colour of her face I see how much she loves Jenny.

'Why didn't you tell me?' Sarah asks you.

'Because she *will* be all right,' you say to Sarah, almost angrily. 'She will get better.'

'There were only two members of staff, apart from Jenny, who weren't at sports day,' she tells you. 'We think it highly unlikely it was one of them. The school gate is permanently locked with a code. The secretary buzzes people in via an entry phone from her office. No parents or children are told the code; members of staff know it, but they were all out on the playing field. So we're probably looking at an outsider.'

'But how could they get in?' you ask.

'He or she could have slipped in earlier in the day,' Sarah replies. 'Possibly behind a legitimate person who was buzzed in. Perhaps not been noticed if parents thought they were a member of staff and vice versa. Schools are busy places, lots of people coming and going. Or the arsonist may have watched a member of staff key in the code and memorised it and come back while everyone was out at sports day.'

'Surely you can't just walk in, though?'

'Once someone is through the main gate there's no more security; the front door isn't locked and there's no CCTV or other security device. That's really all we've got so far, Mike. But the investigation is urgent; they're allocating as many people as they can to it. Detective Inspector Baker is running the case. I'll see if he'll have a meeting with you but he's not the most sympathetic of people.'

'I just want the police to find the person who did this. And then I will hurt him. Hurt him like he's hurt my family.'

3

'YOUR DEFINITION OF "FINE" is a more than fifty per cent chance of dying?' Jenny asks. 'I don't want to look at myself but I *do* want to know what's happening. I need the truth, OK? If I ask for it, it means I can take it.'

I nod and pause a moment, chastened.

'The scarring,' I say. 'What I told you about that, it was the truth.'

I see her relief.

'I will be all right,' she says. 'Like Dad said, I know I will. And so will you.'

I used to worry about her optimism, thinking she hid behind it instead of facing things. '*In a way it's a good thing, Mum*,' she'd said about flunking her A levels. *'Better to realise I'm not cut out for university now, than three years and a large overdraft too late.'*

'Of course we will get better,' I say to her.

Further along the corridor, we spot Tara. She's tracked you here. Jenny has also noticed her.

'Isn't she the one who thinks the *Richmond Post* is the *Washington Post?*' Jenny asks, remembering our joke.

'That's the one.'

She reaches you, and you look at her, perplexed.

'Michael . . .?' she says, using her purring voice.

Men are usually hoodwinked by Tara's girlish rosy face, slender body and pretty glossy hair, but not a man whose wife is unconscious and daughter critically ill. You shy away from her, trying to place her.

Sarah joins you. 'Do you know her?'

'No. She was asking me about Silas Hyman earlier.'

'I'm a friend of Grace's,' Tara calmly butts in.

'I doubt it,' you snap.

'Well, more a colleague. I work with Grace at the *Richmond Post.*'

'So a journalist,' Sarah says. 'Time to go.'

Tara's not going to budge. Sarah flashes her warrant card.

'Detective Sergeant McBride,' Tara reads, looking smug. 'So the police *are* involved. I presume that this teacher, Silas Hyman, is a line of enquiry you'll be taking?'

'Out. Now,' Sarah says in her uniform-and-truncheon voice.

Jenny and I watch as she virtually manhandles Tara towards the lifts.

'She's fantastic, isn't she?' Jenny says and I nod, not graciously.

'She was wrong though earlier,' Jenny says. 'Or at least Mrs Healey was when she told her about the code on the gate. You know, that people don't know it? Some of the parents do. I've seen them letting themselves in when Annette takes too long answering the buzzer. And a few of the children know it too.'

I don't know the code, but then I'm not pally with the in-the-know kind of mothers.

'So a parent could have come in,' I say.

'All the parents were at sports day.'

'Perhaps someone left.'

I try to think back to this afternoon. Did I see something and not realise?

The first thing I remember is cheering on Adam in the opening sprint, his face anxious and intent, his spindly legs going as fast as he could make them, desperate not to let down the Green Team. I was worrying about him coming last and you not being there and Jen's retakes; not seeing the huge truth that we were all alive and healthy and undamaged. Because if I had, I'd have been sprinting round that field, cheering till my voice was hoarse at how fantastic and miraculous our lives were. A blue-skies and green-grass and white-lines life; expansive and ordered and complete.

But I must focus. *Focus*.

I can remember a group of parents from Adam's class asking me if I'd go in for the mothers' race.

'Oh go on, Grace! You're always a sport!'

I look again at their smiling faces. Did one of them, shortly afterwards, leave for the school? Perhaps he or she had left a container of white spirit in the boot of their car. But surely their smiles were just too genuine to be hiding some wicked intention?

A little while later, and Adam hurried up to tell me he was going to get his cake *right now!* Rowena had to collect the medals so she was going with him. And as he left with her, I thought how grown-up she looked now in her linen trousers and crisp white blouse; that it hardly seemed a minute since she was a little elfin girl with Jenny. I'm sorry, not relevant at all. I have to look harder.

I turn away from Adam and Rowena, swinging my focus to the right then to the left, but memory can't be replayed that way and nothing comes into focus.

But I did check round the playing field, looking for Jenny. Maybe if I concentrate on that memory I will see something significant.

She'll be so bored, I was thinking as I scanned the playing field. Up in the sickroom on her own. Surely she'll leave her shift early.

A figure at the edge of the playing field, half obscured by azalea bushes. The figure is still and its stillness has attracted my attention.

But I only looked long enough to know it wasn't Jenny. Now I try to go closer, but I can't get any more detail. Just a shadowy figure on the edge of the field; the memory yields nothing more.

Back on the playing field, Maisie came to find Rowena and I told her she was at school. I remember watching Maisie as she left the playing field. And something snags at my memory. Something else I saw on the outskirts of the playing field that I noted at the time; that means something. But it is slipping from my grasp and the harder I try and pull at it, the more it frays away.

'**M**um?'

Jenny's worried voice brings me back to the brightly lit hospital corridor.

'I've been trying to remember,' she says. 'You know, if I saw someone or something, but when I try and think about the fire I can't . . .'

She breaks off, shaking. I hold her hand.

'It's OK when I think about being in the medical room,' she continues. 'Ivo and I were texting each other. I told you that, didn't I? The last one I sent was at two thirty. It was nine thirty in the morning in Barbados and he said he was just getting up. But then . . . it's like I can't think any more, I can only feel.' A judder of fear goes through her.

'You don't need to think back,' I say to her. 'Auntie Sarah's crew will find out what happened.'

I don't tell her about my shadowy figure half glimpsed on the edge of the playing field, because he doesn't amount to very much, does he?

'I was worried you'd be bored up there,' I say to her lightly. 'I should have known you and Ivo would be texting.'

Put together, they must have texted the equivalent of *War and Peace* by now. When I was her age, boys didn't say much to girls, let alone write, but mobiles have upped their game. Some must find it pressurising, but I think it appeals to Ivo to send love sonnets and romantic haikus through the airwaves.

Jenny's gone off to be with you, while I 'pop to my ward to get an update on how I'm doing'.

Maisie is sitting by my bed, holding my hand, talking to me, and I'm moved that she thinks I can hear too.

'And Jen-Jen's going to be all right,' she says. 'Of course she is.'

Jen-Jen; that name we used for her when she was little.

'She's going to be just fine. You'll see. And so are you. Look at you, Gracie. You don't look too bad at all. You're all going to be all right.'

I feel her comforting warmth. Maisie, my surprising kindred spirit. Our daughters, those chalk-and-cheese little girls, never became friends, but Maisie and I did. We'd meet on our own and share small details of our children's lives: Rowena's tears when she didn't make the netball team and Maisie offering Mr Cobin new team outfits or sex if he'd make Rowena wing attack—and having to explain the second offer was a joke! Rowena's horror when her big teeth came through and demanding the dentist give her small ones again; exchanged like a gift with my dentist story of Jenny refusing to eat or smile when she got a brace until we found a make that was bright blue.

And it was Maisie I turned to when I started my third miscarriage at Jenny's seventh birthday party, when you were away filming. She kept twenty children entertained while I went to hospital; had Jenny to stay that night.

Three years later, she waited for those twelve weeks with me till Adam was safe and likely to go to term. She understood how deeply precious Adam is to us, our hard-won baby.

And now she's sitting next to me, my old friend, crying. She cries all the time—'Stupidly soppy!' she'd say at carol services—but these are painful tears. She tightens her grip on my hand.

'It's my fault,' she says. 'I was inside, going to the loo, when the fire alarm went off. I didn't know Jenny was in the building. I just went looking for Rowena and Adam. But they were fine, outside in no time.'

At sports day I'd told her Adam and Rowena were at the school. If I'd said, 'And Jenny,' she'd have called for her too, made sure she was out before the fire took hold.

Two words.

Her voice is a whisper. 'Then I saw you running towards the school. And I knew how relieved you'd be when you saw that Addie was safe.'

I remember Maisie outside, comforting the Reception teacher, Rowena comforting Adam by the bronze statue of a child, as black smoke was swirled by the wind, dirtying the delphinium-blue sky.

'Then you shouted for Jenny and I realised she must be in there. And you ran inside.' She pauses, her face pale. 'But I didn't go to help you.' Her voice is staccato with guilt.

But how can she think I blame her? I'm just moved that she thought, even for one moment, of going into a burning building after me.

'I wasn't brave enough,' she continues. 'So I ran to the fire engines that were still on the bridge. I told them there were people inside. I thought if they knew they'd get there more quickly. And they did. As soon as I told them, one of the fire engines drove at a parked car and shoved it off the road onto the pavement. Then people parked behind them realised what was happening and got out of their cars, and the firemen were shouting that there were people in the school and then everyone was pushing the cars out of the way so they could get through.'

I want to ask her if Rowena's all right, because I remember seeing her in A&E and the suited man talking to the journalists and saying Rowena was in hospital too. But I hadn't paused to think about her since, anxiety for my own child selfishly pushing out space for anybody else.

Why is Rowena hurt when I saw her safely outside next to the statue with Adam?

Dr Bailstrom arrives on her precipitous red heels and Maisie has to go. I think she leaves reluctantly as if there's something more she wants to tell me.

It's late now and the pull of home is unbearably strong. Own bed. Own house. Own life back again to be lived as usual tomorrow.

You are on the phone to Adam. I hurry close to you, listening for his voice.

'I'm going to spend the night with Mum and Jenny here. But I'll see you as soon as I can, OK?'

I can just hear him breathing. Short, hurried breaths.

'OK, Ads?'

Still just breathing, terrified breathing.

'I need you to be a soldier right now, Addie, please?'

Still he doesn't speak. And I hear the gap between you, the one that used to make me sad and now frightens me.

'Good night then. Sleep tight, and send my love to Granny G.'

I have to hug him, *right this moment*; feel his warm little body and ruffle his soft hair and tell him how much I love him.

'I'm sure Granny G will bring him to see you tomorrow,' Jenny says to me, as if reading my thoughts. 'I'd probably scare him too much, but you look all right.'

You want to spend the night next to me and next to Jenny—splitting yourself in two, to keep watch over both of us.

A nurse tries to persuade you to go to the bed they've sorted out for you. She tells you that I am unconscious and therefore unaware of whether you're with me or not, and that Jenny's too deeply drugged to be aware of anything either. As the nurse says this, Jenny pulls a silly face at her and I laugh. There's really a lot of opportunity for bedroom-farce-style comedy here and I think Jenny will try to beat me to it.

The nurse promises you that if my condition or Jenny's 'worsens' they'll get you immediately.

She's telling you that neither of us will die without you.

Perhaps I jumped the gun a bit in the potential for comedy.

You still refuse to go to bed.

'It's late, Mike,' your sister says firmly. 'You're exhausted. And you need to function properly tomorrow for Jenny's sake. And for Grace's.'

That decides you—it's optimistic to go to bed, demonstrating your belief that we will still be alive in the morning.

Jenny and I stay with you as you sleep fitfully.

I think of Adam in his bunk bed.

'He has several lions among his soft toy menagerie,' I tell you. 'But his favourite is Aslan and he needs Aslan to get to sleep. If he's fallen off the bunk, you have to find him. Sometimes you have to pull the whole bed out because he falls down the side.'

'Mum?' Jenny says. 'Dad's *asleep*.'

As though when you're awake you can hear me. I am touched by this distinction.

'Anyway,' she continues. 'He must know about Aslan.'

'D'you think?'

'Of course.'

But I'm not sure you do. Anyway, you think it would be better if Adam grew out of soft toys, now he's eight. But he's only *just* eight.

'You'll be able to put Adam to bed yourself soon,' Jenny says.

I think of holding Adam's hand in mine as he drifts into sleep. All of that.

'Yes.' Because *of course* I'll be at home again. *I have to be.*

'Is it all right if I go for a walk?' she asks. 'I'm feeling a little stir-crazy.'

'Fine.'

Poor Jenny; an outdoorsy person like you, it's terrible for her to be cooped up in a hospital.

We're alone and I look at your sleeping face.

I remember watching you as you slept not long after we'd started going out together and I'd thought of that passage in *Middlemarch*—I know, not fair! I can quote to you now and there's not a thing you can do about it! Anyway it's when the poor heroine realises that in her elderly husband's head there are just dusty corridors and musty old attics. But in yours I imagined there to be mountains and rivers and prairies—wide-open spaces with wind and sky.

You hadn't yet said you loved me. But it was a given, wasn't it? A taken-as-read thing, as it has been for the last few years. In our early days you'd write 'I love you!' in the steamed-up mirror in the bathroom after you'd shaved, for me to find when I came in later. You'd phone me, just to tell me. I'd sit down at my computer and you'd have changed the screen saver so that 'I love you!' marched across it. You'd never done this to anyone before, and it was as if you needed to keep practising.

I know hearts don't really store emotion. But there must be some place in us that does. I think it's a jagged and anxiously spiky place until some-one loves you. And then, like pilgrims touching a rough stone with their fingertips, nineteen years of practising wears it smooth.

Someone has just passed the family room. I saw a glimpse in the glass panel in the door; a shadow fleetingly under it. I'd better just check.

A figure is hurrying along the burns unit corridor. For some reason, I think of that shadowy figure on the edge of the playing field.

He's going towards Jenny's side ward. He goes in, and through the half-open doorway I see his shape bending over her.

I scream, making no sound.

I can see a nurse walking towards Jenny's room. Her plimsolls squeak-ing on the linoleum alert the figure to her presence and he slips away.

The nurse is checking Jenny now.

Out in the corridor, the figure has disappeared. I didn't get close enough to see his face, just an outline in a long, dark blue coat. But the door to the burns unit is locked, so he must have been authorised to be in here. He must be a doctor, perhaps a nurse, probably going off shift, which is why he wasn't wearing a white coat or uniform, but an overcoat. Maybe he just wanted to check on Jenny before going home.

I see Jenny returning and I smile at her.

But I feel afraid. Because who wears an overcoat in the middle of July?

Garish artificial lights snapping on; doctors already alert and moving in packs; loud crashings of trolleys and nurses briskly whipping away breakfast trays and pulling out drugs charts. All this noisy, bright, morning busyness turns my glimpsed figure last night into a quiet nothing.

When I arrive at my ward, I see that Mum's already here and in an office with Dr Bailstrom. She's aged years in a day; hard lines of misery are scraped across her face.

'Grace chattered all the time when she was a little girl, such a bright button,' Mum says, her voice quicker than usual. 'I always knew that she'd grow up to be really bright, and she did. She got three As at A level and a scholarship to Cambridge to read English.'

'Mum, *please!*' I say to no avail. Presumably she wants them to know what kind of brain I had—'A topnotch one!' as Dad used to say—so they'll know what to aim for. The 'before' photo.

'She got pregnant before finals,' Mum continues. 'So she had to leave. She was a little disappointed, we all were, but she was happy too. About the baby. Jenny.'

I've never heard my life history potted before and it's a little alarming.

'That makes her sound like a brainbox, but she's not really like that at all,' Mum continues. 'She's a lovely girl. I know she's nearly forty now, but she's still a girl to me. And she'd do anything for anyone. *Too good for her own good*, that's what I used to say to her. But when my husband died, I don't know what I'd have done without her, juggling her whole life around for me.'

Mum never speaks in a rush. And hardly ever speaks more than two or three sentences at a time. Now she's haring along in paragraphs as if she's on a timer. And I wish there *was* a timer, because listening to this is terrible.

'I don't mean that she has to get better for me, though. You mustn't think that. I mean I love her more than you can possibly know but it's her children who really need her, and Mike. You think it's Mike who's the strong one, he looks it, but really it's Gracie. She's the heart of the family.'

She stops for a moment, and Dr Bailstrom pounces in.

'We'll do everything we possibly can. I can absolutely assure you of that. But sometimes, with a severe head injury, there's not a great deal that we can do. We'll let you know what we find out when we've done the next set of tests,' Dr Bailstrom says. 'We are having a specialists' meeting about your daughter later today.'

Adam is hunched by my bed.

Mum rushes over to him. 'Addie, poppet? I thought you were going to wait with the nurses for five minutes?'

He's lying with his face against mine, holding my hand, and he's crying. A desperate, terrible sound.

I put my arms round him and I tell him not to cry, I'm all right. But he can't hear me.

As he cries I stroke his soft, silky hair and I tell him over and over and over that it's all right, that I love him, not to cry. But he still can't hear me and I can't bear it a moment longer and I have to wake up for him.

I fight my way into my body, through layers of flesh and muscle and bone. And suddenly I'm here. Inside.

I struggle to move this heavy hulk of a body, but again I'm trapped under the hull of a ship wrecked on the ocean floor. Moving is impossible.

Adam is out there crying for me and I have to open my eyes for him. *Have to.* But my eyelids are locked shut and rusting over.

I've left Jenny on her own. Oh God. What if I can't get out again?

I hear the panic in my heartbeat.

But I can escape my body easily, just slipping out into the dark ocean and then struggling upwards towards the light.

Mum is putting her arm round Adam, magicking a smile onto her face for him, making her voice sound cheerful.

'We'll come back later, all right, my little man? We'll go home now, then when you've had a bit of a rest, we can come back.'

And by mothering my child she's mothering me.

She leads him away.

A few minutes later Jenny joins me.

'Have you tried getting back into your body?' I ask her.

She shakes her head. I'm an *idiot*. She can't even *look* at her body let alone try to get into it.

You're having a meeting with Sarah's boss in an office downstairs. We go to join you.

'Aunt Sarah's normal boss is on maternity leave,' Jenny says. 'Rosemary, remember, the really quirky one?'

I don't remember Rosemary-the-really-quirky-one. I've never heard of a Rosemary.

'Aunt Sarah loathes this guy, Baker. Thinks he's a fool,' Jenny continues. She's been fascinated by the flashing-lights-and-sirens side of Sarah's police life since she was six years old. And I get that. How can my part-time job writing an arts review page in the *Richmond Post* compete with being a detective sergeant in the Met? What film, book or exhibition is going to out-cool directing a helicopter during a drugs bust? But Sarah clearly tells Jenny the gossip too.

We reach the office at the same time as you and Sarah.

Why on earth are you holding a newspaper? I know that I have a go at you at the weekends for reading the papers rather than 'engaging with the family', and we've done the whole 'It's the caveman looking into the fire to have time to let the week settle' thing. But now? Here?

We follow you and Sarah in. The ceiling is too low, trapping the heat. There's no window. Not even a fan to shift the stale heavy air around.

Detective Inspector Baker introduces himself to you without getting up from his chair. His sweaty, doughy face is unreadable.

'I want to fill you in on a little of the background to our investigation,' he says, his voice as stodgy as his physique. 'Arson in schools is extremely common. Sixteen cases a week in the UK. But people getting hurt in arson attacks on schools is *not* common. Nor is it common for fires to be started during the daytime.'

You're getting irritated—*get to the point, man.*

'The arsonist may have thought that the school would be empty because it was sports day,' DI Baker continues. 'Or it may have been a *deliberate* attempt to hurt one of the occupants.' He leans forward, his sweaty polyester shirt sticking slightly to the back of his plastic chair. 'Do you know of anyone who may have wished to harm Jennifer?'

'Of course not,' you snap. 'She's seventeen, for God's sake.'

'That's ridiculous,' Jenny says to me, a shake in her voice. 'It was just a fluke I was in there, Mum. Pure *chance*, that's all.'

Your sister tightens her hand on yours.

'She was the victim of a hate-mail campaign, wasn't she?' DI Baker asks you, an edge now to his bland voice.

'But that stopped months ago. *It has nothing to do with the fire.*'

Beside me, Jenny has become rigid.

She never told us how she felt when she was called slut, tart, jailbait and worse. Or when dog mess and used condoms were posted through our letterbox addressed to her. Instead she turned to Ivo and her friends, excluding us.

'*She's seventeen now, darling, of course she turns to them.*'

You were so infuriatingly understanding, so 'I've-read the-manuals-on-teenagers' rational.

'*But we're her _parents_,*' I said. Because parents outrank everyone else.

'There's been nothing for five months,' you tell DI Baker. 'It's all over.'

DI Baker flicks through some notes in front of him.

I remember those awful things that were said to her. It was shocking. The ugly, vicious world had come crashing through our letterbox and into our daughter's life. And, this I think is key: *you hadn't kept it at bay*. You thought you hadn't done your job as her father and protected her.

You spent hours looking at the pieces of A4 lined paper, trying to trace the origin of the cut-out letters—which newspaper? Which magazine? Studying postmarks on the ones that had been posted. I'd understood after a little while that *you* wanted to be the person who caught him and made him stop.

Then, two weeks after—*two weeks*, Mike—the day the hand-delivered envelope with the used condom arrived, you told Sarah. As you'd predicted, she told us we must go to the police—and why the hell hadn't we done that to start with? We duly did but, as you'd also predicted, the police—apart from Sarah—didn't consider it as important as it was to you and me. And they didn't find out anything.

Poor Jen. So furious and mortified when the police interviewed her friends and boyfriend. The teenage paranoia that adults disapprove of their choices taken to an extreme. But you'd already interrogated most of them, grabbing them as Jenny tried to hurry them past us and up to her room. Those long-limbed, long-haired, silly girls seemed unlikely hate-mailers. But what about one of the boys who were friends with her?

And Ivo. I've always been suspicious of him. Maybe because he's so different to you, with his slight frame and fine features and his preference at seventeen for Auden over car engine manuals. I think he lacks substance. You disagree. You think he's 'a great lad'. Possibly because you don't want to be a possessive father? Because you don't want to alienate Jenny? But whatever our reasons, you support Jenny over Ivo, while I gybe.

I don't think he'd send her hate mail, though. He's her boyfriend, and she adores him, so why would he?

'When, exactly, was the last incident?' DI Baker asks you.

'February the 14th,' you reply. 'Months ago.'

Valentine's Day. A Wednesday. Adam worried about his times-tables challenge; Jenny late down to breakfast as usual. But we'd been up for an hour already, waiting for the sound of the letterbox. Just the click of metal shutting made me feel physically sick.

It was the letter with the C word across it. I can't say that word in connection with her. I just can't.

But the day after that letter there was nothing. Then a whole week went by with no hate mail. Then a fortnight. Until over four months had passed, so that yesterday I picked up the post hardly bothering to check.

'Could she have hidden something from you?' DI Baker asks.

'No, of course not,' you say, frustrated. 'The fire is nothing to do with the hate-mailer. Presumably you haven't seen this yet?'

You slap the newspaper you're holding in front of DI Baker. The *Richmond Post*. The headline shouts: ARSONIST SETS FIRE TO LOCAL PRIMARY SCHOOL! The by-line is Tara's.

DI Baker ignores your newspaper. 'Were there any other forms of hate mail that you didn't tell us about?' he continues. 'Texts on her mobile, for example, or postings on a social networking site?'

'I asked Jenny and there was nothing like that,' Sarah says. 'She would have told me, or her parents.'

But we hadn't just taken her word for it. We searched, you breaking every rule in the bringing-up-teenagers book, me being a normal mother.

'MySpace? Facebook?' DI Baker asks as if we don't know what 'social networking site' means, but you interrupt.

'The hate-mailer had nothing to do with it. Christ, how many more times?' You jab at the newspaper. 'It's this teacher, Silas Hyman, you should be investigating.'

'We haven't read the paper, Mike,' Sarah says. 'We'll read it if you'll give us a minute.'

She must be humouring you, I think. After all, what could Tara know about the fire that she—a policewoman and your sister—doesn't?

The picture of the burnt-out school dominates the front page, the oddly undamaged bronze statue of a child in the foreground. Under it is a picture of Jenny.

'It's from my Facebook page,' Jenny says, looking at her photo. 'The one

Ivo took at Easter, when we did that canoeing course. I can't believe she's done that. She must have gone onto my site and then just printed it off, or scanned it. Isn't that theft?'

I love her outrage. Out of all of this, to mind about her photo being used. But the contrast between our daughter in the burns unit and that outdoorsy, healthy, beautiful girl in the photo is cuttingly painful.

Maybe Jenny feels it too. She goes to the door. 'I'm going for a walk.'

'OK.'

'I wasn't asking permission!' she snaps. And then she leaves. Just the word 'hate-mailer' pushing those old buttons again.

After she's gone, Sarah opens the paper out to show a double-page spread, with a banner headline across both pages: JINXED SCHOOL. On the left-hand page is the sub-headline: FIRE STARTED DELIBERATELY, and another photograph of this POPULAR AND BEAUTIFUL girl.

Tara Connor has turned Jenny's torment into entertainment. 'Beautiful seventeen-year-old . . . fighting for her life . . . horribly burnt . . . severely mutilated.' Not news, but prurient news-as-porn.

Tara makes me out as a kind of superhero-mum racing into the flames. But a rather tardy superhero, arriving too late in the day to save the beautiful heroine. 'The police are continuing their urgent hunt for the person responsible for arson,' she finishes.

Directly opposite, on page 2, Tara's rehashed an article she'd written in March, adding a new intro:

> Only four months ago, the *Richmond Post* reported on Silas Hyman, 30, a teacher at Sidley House Preparatory School who was fired after a child was seriously injured. The seven-year-old boy broke both his legs after plunging from an outside metal fire escape onto the playground below in an alleged 'accident'.

Just as she had the first time, she doesn't say that Mr Hyman was nowhere near the playground at the time. And those quotation marks around the word 'accident'—saying that it wasn't. But who's going to sue her over quotation marks? Slippery as her patent leather Miu Miu bag.

Her bid for journalistic glory continues:

> Situated in a leafy London suburb, the exclusive £12,500-a-year school, founded thirteen years ago, is marketed as a nurturing environment where

'every child is celebrated and valued'. But even four months ago questions were being asked about its safety.

A mother of an eight-year-old girl told me: 'This is supposed to be a caring school, but this man clearly didn't look after the children. We are thinking about taking our daughter away.'

Another parent told me: 'I am very angry. An accident like this just shouldn't be allowed to happen. It's totally unacceptable.'

In March Tara had titled her article PLAYGROUND PLUNGE! but now she's changed it to TEACHER FIRED! So on the right-hand side of the newspaper is TEACHER FIRED and on the left-hand side is FIRE STARTED DELIBERATELY. And the connection crackles between them, an invisible circuit of blame—the fired teacher exacting his fiery revenge.

DI Baker's mobile goes and he answers it. The *Richmond Post* lies on the table, like a challenge thrown into the ring—your Silas Hyman contender for arsonist versus DI Baker's hate-mailer.

I know that you've never liked Mr Hyman. Before he was fired we'd had weeks of sniping over him. You thought I 'totally over-exaggerated' Mr Hyman's effect on Addie.

'"*Exaggerated*" doesn't need "totally" and "over" added to it,' I said frostily.

'*Not all of us did an English degree*,' you replied, stung.

'*Only half of one, remember?*'

Mr Hyman made us fight. And we don't normally fight.

'*Before Mr Hyman, Addie was miserable*,' I said. '*Don't you remember?*' He was picked on, couldn't do the work, had virtually no self-esteem. '*He's come through that because of Mr Hyman. He's sorted out who he sits next to, worked out the boys who are likely to become his friends, and they are now. They're asking him on playdates. He's got a sleepover this weekend. When's he ever had one of those? And he's got him confident in Maths and English.*'

'*He's just doing his job.*'

'*He calls Addie "Sir Covey". That's lovely, isn't it? A knight's name?*'

'*It'll probably make the other kids tease him.*'

'*No, he's got pet names for all of them.*'

Why didn't you appreciate him more?

I had wondered if your antagonism towards him—an attractive young teacher with a sparkle in his eyes—was because he had kissed me on the cheek when we went to parents' evening. 'Totally inappropriate!' you'd said, not realising that Mr Hyman is just very physical—tousling the children's hair as he passes them at their desks, a quick warm hug at going-home time. And, yes, we mothers did smile a little about him, but not in a serious way.

Until yesterday afternoon I'd have said suspecting him was completely ridiculous. But all my old certainties are burnt to the ground. Nothing is like yesterday any more. So I don't trust anyone. Not even Mr Hyman.

DI Baker stops his phone call and glances at the *Richmond Post*.

'One peculiar thing,' he says to Sarah, 'is how quickly the press were on the scene of the fire. Before the fire engines even. We'll need to know who told them, or how they found out.'

You are infuriated. 'It's not only the article,' you say, but DI Baker's radio interrupts. He answers it but you continue. 'I *saw him* acting violently at the school prize-giving a few weeks after he was fired.'

4

'DO YOU THINK I'll win a prize, Mum?' Adam said. 'For anything?'

It was the morning of the prize-giving. Adam, still seven then, was eating Coco Pops and watching *Tom and Jerry*.

Mr Hyman had been fired three and a half weeks before and already Adam hated going to school, so I was trying to compensate. You were away filming and I'd allowed myself to spoil him a little. My excitement about your homecoming was cloaked by anxiety for him.

'You should win a prize,' I said to him, fairly certain that he wouldn't. 'But if you don't, you mustn't be disappointed. Remember what Mrs Healey said at assembly? Everyone will get a prize in the end, even if it's not your turn this year.'

'That's such bollocks,' Jenny said, still in her dressing gown although we were meant to leave in ten minutes. 'I mean, think about the maths,' she continued. 'Number of children, number of prizes, number of prize-givings. It doesn't compute, does it?'

'And the same people always win them,' Adam said.

'I'm sure that's not—'

Adam interrupted me, hotly frustrated. 'It *is true*.'

'He's right,' Jenny said. 'I know they *say* every child is equally valued, blah blah blah, but it's rubbish.'

'Jen, you're not helping.'

'The school has to get pupils into schools like Westminster for boys or St Paul's Girls,' Jenny continued, pouring out cereal. 'Otherwise new parents aren't going to truck up with their four-year-olds next year. So it's the brightest kids that get the prizes, because it'll help them get into the top secondary schools.'

'Antony's already won it for Best in the Class,' Adam said, miserably. '*And* for Maths *and* for Leadership.'

'He's eight. Who's he meant to be leading, exactly?' Jenny asked with derision, making Adam smile. Thank you, Jen.

'It was Rowena White when I was at school,' Jenny continued. 'She cleaned up.'

Adam saw the clock and panicked. 'We're going to be late!' He raced to get his bookbag, his fear of being late temporarily outweighing his fear of school.

'I'll be super-quick,' Jenny said. 'I'll eat my Shreddies in the car.' She paused as she left the room. 'Oh, and you know all those silver cups and shields? They make the school seem older and more established than it really is. So the current parents are kept happy too.'

'I think you're being a little cynical,' I said.

'I've worked there, remember,' Jenny said. 'So I *know* to be cynical. It's a business. And prize-giving is a part of that.'

Eight minutes later, we were in the car. Adam is the only person Jenny will hurry for. We were going to arrive at school early, as we did every morning. I know you think we shouldn't *buy into his anxiety* but arriving five minutes earlier than necessary is just something you have to factor in when you're looking after him.

'How long till you're working at school again?' Adam asked Jenny as we neared Sidley House. He'd been so proud of her being a teaching assistant there last summer.

'After A levels,' Jenny replied. 'So just a couple more months.'

'That's really soon,' I said, panicked by the proximity of A levels. 'You must get that revision timetable sorted out this evening.'

'I'm going to Daphne's.'

'But Dad's coming home,' Adam said.

'He'll be at the prize-giving evening with you, won't he?' Jenny replied.

'S'pose so,' Adam agreed, not fully trusting that you'll turn up. That's not a criticism; he worries about anyone actually turning up.

'You should cancel,' I said to Jenny.

'Mum . . .' She was putting on mascara in the sun-visor mirror.

'Working hard now means you'll have so many more choices in the future.'

'I'd rather live my life now than revise for a future one, all right?'

No, I thought, it's not all right. And if only she could put the mental agility used in that rejoinder into her A-level work.

We walked the last bit, as we always do. Adam was gripping my hand.

'OK, Ads?'

Tears were starting, and he was trying not to let them out. But Adam stoically let go of my hand and went to the gate. He pressed the buzzer on the gate and the secretary let him in.

You'd been away filming since the day after Mr Hyman was fired, so you hadn't been there to see the consequences. For Adam it was almost like grief. Not only had he lost a teacher he adored, but the adult world had proved itself cruel and unjust and nothing like the stories he read. Beast Quest books and Harry Potter and Arthurian legends and Percy Jackson didn't end like this. He was prepared for unhappy endings, but not unjust ones. His teacher was sacked, for something he didn't do. And school was already mutating back into the hostile place it had been before Mr Hyman was his teacher.

At quarter to six, after a 'lightning-quick supper, Ads!' and a change into clean uniform, we arrived at the prize-giving with his shoes polished and his blazer brushed so he wouldn't get into trouble.

We were fifteen minutes early, partly because Adam is in the choir so had to get there in good time, but also because of his anxiety about being late, which had got so much worse in the last three weeks.

I spotted Maisie waving to me from near the front, even earlier than us.

Adam went to the side room to wait for the rest of choir and I joined her.

'Bagged you and Mike a good spot,' she said, budging up to make a space for me. 'Rowena was sorry not to be here, but it's just too close to their exams now, isn't it?'

So Rowena was revising, even though she'd been offered a conditional-but-virtually-guaranteed place at Oxford to read Science. While Jenny, who hadn't been offered a place by anyone, was at a friend's house. As small girls, Jenny used to gripe about Rowena being too competitive and needing to be 'the best' at everything. I'd wished she shared a little of those traits. I still did.

'Is Addie in the choir again this year?' Maisie asked. 'I do love hearing him sing.'

She's so tactfully sensitive, never asking, 'So do you think Adam will win a prize?' but instead celebrating his small contribution.

I saw Maisie smoothing her brown cotton dress over her tummy, trying to tug it flat, and tears starting in her eyes.

'Do you think I look like a bulimic hog in this?' she asked me quietly, almost furtively. It was such un-Maisie language that for a moment I didn't think I'd heard her properly.

'Of course not, my honey,' I said. 'You look gorgeous. Sex-on-a-stick lollipop-gorgeous.'

She giggled. 'Like a Shiny-Mum?'

The name we have for the mothers who wear shiny, slinky boots and expensive silky clothes and have shiny, salon-blow-dried hair.

'Shinier,' I said.

'You are the kindest woman in the world, Gracie.'

Then Donald arrived, holding the cup that he'd give out later.

'Just polishing up the silverware,' he said, his avuncular face beaming.

When Jenny first went to the school we were both left of centre, embarrassed our child went to a private school, and thinking 'Donald-and-his-cup' absurd and funny. But less hypocritical now, I find it touching that he still wants this link to the school.

I never got to know Donald well, Maisie and I usually meet in the day-time when he's at work and Rowena's at school, but I know from Maisie how much he adores his wife and daughter. I watched Donald take Maisie's hand, sit a little closer to her than he needed to, and felt jealous that you weren't there.

In the small, sweaty office, DI Baker has finally stopped his hissing radio conversation.

'The prize-giving was held in St Swithun's, a mile or so from the school,' you say. 'My flight was delayed so I arrived late, at about six fifteen. They didn't even have someone on the door. I just walked straight in. The school's policy on security was negligently bad.'

I saw you standing at the back with a group of fathers who'd also got there late. You caught my eye but the bustle of an airport and a busy important career was still hanging about you and your smile wasn't yet fully engaged with me.

Mrs Healey was about halfway through handing out the cups, interspersed with short musical performances. The school was meant to be '*Fostering Self-Confidence in* <u>*Every*</u> *Child*'—but I'd noticed that all the important cups were again going to the ablest children. Perhaps Jenny was right after all. I didn't like to think that we were part of a business model rather than a prize-giving that spring evening.

'At about six forty,' you say, 'Silas Hyman barged through the door. He shoved his way past the parents.'

The church door clanged behind him, silencing a wobbly solo clarinet. We all turned and stared as he pushed his way through the parents at the back. I saw that his suit was pressed, his shoes were polished, his face clean-shaven. But he was unsteady as he walked up the aisle and sweating profusely.

'He went up to the headmistress at the front,' you continue. 'And he *yelled* at her. Called her a "*bitch*". He said she'd made him a "*fucking scapegoat*".

'Then he said, and I remember it very clearly, "*You can't do this to some-one, you hear me?*" and he was jabbing with his hand, gesticulating around all the pews. "*All of you, at the back? Have you got this? You won't fucking well get away with it.*"'

He sounded desperate, I'd thought, on the edge of despair, choosing to rage instead of weep.

'Two fathers went and grabbed him,' you continue, 'and pulled him away from the headmistress.'

All you could hear was the scuffle as they tried to get him out of the church. Even the children—all 280 of them—were silent.

Then, in the silence, I heard a child's voice: 'Let go of him.'

Adam's voice.

I turned to see Adam—Adam of all people!—standing up, among the sea of seated pupils and teachers.

'Leave him alone!' His voice was louder now.

The whole church was quiet, all staring at Adam. He was terrified, I could see that, but he continued, looking all the time at Mr Hyman.

'It's not fair! He didn't do anything wrong. It's not fair to fire him. It wasn't Mr Hyman's fault.'

It was extraordinary. Heroic. A shy little boy, the boy who's afraid of getting into trouble if his homework isn't done, scared of being five minutes late, this boy was—literally—standing up for his beloved teacher. I'd always known he was good—not a goody-goody, but *good*—yet it still astounded me.

Then it was as if Adam connected to something in Mr Hyman. As if he made Mr Hyman aware for the first time of what he was doing. He shrugged off the two fathers and started walking towards the door. As he passed Adam he smiled at him tenderly, and it was a signal to sit down.

At the door Mr Hyman turned. 'I didn't hurt anyone.'

On the pew beside me I saw that Maisie's face was pale with an expression I'd never seen before.

'That man should never have been allowed near our children,' she said vehemently. And I saw that she loathed him, hated him even—gentle Maisie who's usually so quick to be kind.

'It was a clear threat,' you say to DI Baker. 'A violent one. You could see how much he hated the headmistress. All of us.'

'But at the time you didn't think it worrying enough to report it?' asks DI Baker, his tone blandly scornful.

'At the time I underestimated his capacity for violence. We all did. Otherwise this never would have happened. So you'll arrest him?'

'We already spoke to Mr Hyman, last night,' DI Baker retorts, sounding irritated.

'So you were suspicious enough to question him?' you ask.

'We would have spoken to anyone who may have had a grudge against the school straight away,' Sarah says. 'The headmistress or a governor would have given us the information that he'd been fired.'

'Mr Hyman didn't ask for a lawyer to be present. And he was happy to volunteer a sample of his DNA,' DI Baker says. 'In my experience, that is not the response of a guilty man.'

'But surely—'

DI Baker interrupts you. 'There is no reason to think Mr Hyman had anything to do with the fire. A scurrilous piece of journalism doesn't change that. And your account of his behaviour at prize-giving is interpretative rather than fact. However, I do appreciate your anxiety, Mr Covey. And, given what you are going through, and to put your mind at rest, I will get an update on our enquiry from one of my officers.'

He ostentatiously gets out his radio again, suggesting, without saying so, that you are putting him to unnecessary trouble.

'I'll be with my daughter,' you say, standing. 'You can "update" me there.'

I follow you along the corridor. As I look at your broad back, I long for you to hold me; and I remember how when I came out of the church, I scanned the group of parents, trying to find you. The father-crowd at the back had been first out of the church, but in the dusk I couldn't see you. The children weren't out yet.

I was worried Adam had got into trouble, and I wanted to tell him how *proud* I was of him; that what he did took great courage. All around me was the hiss of gossip as the incident turned into anecdote.

Donald and Maisie were a few feet away. I thought for a moment that they were arguing, but their voices were low and quiet, so I realised I must be mistaken. Besides, Maisie says they never argue. *'Sometimes I think we need a jolly good row, blow some cobwebs away, but Donald's just too good-natured.'*

Donald had a cigarette, dragging hard on it, making a fiery tip in the gloomy light. Maisie had never told me he smoked. He dropped the butt on the ground, stubbing it out with his shoe, grinding it down.

I saw Adam coming towards me. His face looked zoned out, trying to disconnect from the world around him. As he got closer, he passed Donald lighting another cigarette and flinched from the lighter's flame.

'Are you all right, Ads?' Maisie asked him.

He nodded and I put my arm round him. 'Let's find Dad.'

I finally saw you standing away from the main group of parents. You took my hand and your other arm gave Adam a hug. 'Hello, young cub.'

No mention of what he'd done. You saw that facial signal between parents over the head of their child when one isn't doing something right.

'You two go on home,' you said, ignoring my sign. 'I'll catch up with you later.'

We hadn't even kissed hello.

'I'll be home as soon as I can,' you said in a commanding way.

I was cooking a late supper when you arrived home. Adam had fallen asleep half an hour before.

You came up behind me and kissed me and I smelt beer on your breath. For a moment we met as a couple.

'Jenny not here?' you asked.

'Daphne's dad is driving her home now. He just called.'

You put your arms round me. 'Sorry that took a while, but I wanted to do some damage limitation. Been in that wine bar by the church, schmoozing the teachers. Mrs Healey especially.'

You didn't see my face.

'I asked her not to discipline him, but to let us handle it and she agreed.'

I turned and then we argued.

You thought Adam standing up for Mr Hyman wasn't from loyalty and courage, but because of 'some kind of brainwashing by *that man*.' You thought Silas Hyman had an 'unnatural hold' over Adam.

Then Jenny came into the kitchen, ending our row. We've never argued in front of the children, have we? They are our cease-fire treaty.

We've arrived at the burns unit and you're scrupulously washing your hands, following the diagrammed instructions. Sarah does the same. Then a nurse lets you in through the locked door.

As we reach Jenny's side ward I brace myself. You turn to Sarah.

'It's not the hate-mailer who did this to her.' Your voice is furious.

A nurse is taking the last of the dressings off Jenny's face.

Her face is blistered beyond recognition, far worse than in A&E. I quickly turn away. Because I can't bear to look at her. And because I'll have to tell Jenny what I've seen, rather than just glimpsed, because surely you can withhold your knowledge of something if you've only just glimpsed it?

But you don't look away.

The nurse sees your distress. 'Blistering the day afterwards is quite normal,' she says. 'It doesn't mean that her burns have got any worse.'

You lean towards Jenny, your face close to hers, and then you kiss the air above her as if it will float down on top of her.

And in that kiss I know why you're adamant that it *can't be the hate-mailer*. Because if it is, you haven't protected Jenny. You haven't stopped him from doing this. And that would mean it's your fault. You'd be responsible for her blistered face, her limbs wrapped up in God-knows-what, her decimated airways. For her possible death.

'It's not your fault,' I say, going to you, putting my arms round you. 'Really, my darling, whoever did this, *it's not your fault*.'

I understand now why you haven't just been suspicious of Mr Hyman but grabbed onto him, certain that it's him. Anyone but the hate-mailer.

And maybe you are right. I remember again Maisie saying, '*That man should never have been allowed near our children*.' Maisie, who always thinks the best of everyone and is kind to a fault. Maisie must have seen something bad in him too. Perhaps I've just been blind.

As we wait at Jenny's bedside for DI Baker, I think back to the rest of that prize-giving evening. I don't think there'll be anything useful but I need to escape from here back into the sanctuary of our old life.

Jenny was on the downstairs computer with Facebook open.

'Rowena's revising this evening,' I said as I passed her.

'I thought her place at Oxford was a cert,' Jenny replied, not hearing my subtext of criticism.

'She still wants to get the best A-level grades she can.'

'Well, bully for her, Mum,' she said. ''Night,' she called, as you went upstairs.

''Night, sweet prince,' you called back, as you have done since she was about five. Only now it's you who was going to bed before her.

I joined you in our room.

'It would be nice if she knew where that quotation came from. She's got her English A level in about seven weeks and she doesn't have a clue.'

'I thought her set text was *Othello*?'

'That's not the point. She should know her tragedies.'

You started laughing.

'I just want her to do well. So at least she has a shot at university.'

'Yes, I know,' you said affectionately. You kissed me. And the sum of our marriage was bigger than our differences.

Our argument about Adam was still there, as present as his warm, sleeping body in the bedroom next to ours; just as my anxiety about Jenny hovered somewhere in the house, as she played on her social networking site rather than open a book. But I was just so pleased you were home. You told me about your trip and I told you about small details while you'd been away.

A little later on, while you went to have a shower, I thought about Rowena. At Sidley House, she had been top of every subject, in almost every team, and now she was off to Oxford to read Science while our daughter would be lucky to pass a single A level.

My anxiety fanned outwards into jealousy. I knew from Maisie how much Donald adored his family. I was sure that if it had been Rowena bravely standing up in the church, Donald would have supported her and been *proud*.

I took off my make-up, which I'd put on so carefully earlier, and remembered Maisie's peculiar remark about her appearance, her 'bulimic hog' comment, and it burrowed away until it connected with other apparently innocuous incidents—the way she checked herself in our hall mirror on the way out, and then hurriedly looked away. 'God, what a crone,' she'd say. 'Beyond Botox!' The bruise on her cheek from a 'trip against the garden shed—that's the problem with two left feet!' The cracked wrist: 'Went dashing out on the icy pavement, in *court shoes*. My own silly fault. Just went flying, *what a twit!*' One by one none of these incidents had seemed worrying, but put together at my dressing-table mirror they became something sinister.

I'd hoped thinking back would be a little respite, but it hasn't worked out that way. Because that uncomfortable memory about Maisie is pulling at another—the memory I couldn't retrieve earlier.

It's Maisie leaving the playing field, but then stopping to check her face in her handbag mirror. A gesture that I've come unknowingly to associate with her. The gesture that made me realise how unconfident she is now compared with the flamboyant mothers'-race Maisie in her 'not giving a hoot!' days.

Such a small thing; not the important memory I'd hoped for. So I wonder why it won't leave me.

DI Baker arrives, and flinches when he sees Jenny. Is that why you wanted him to come here? To make him realise? If so, you were right.

'I hope you will be reassured to know,' he says in his bland, irritating voice, 'that Mr Hyman's alibi has been checked by one of my officers. He couldn't have been at the school at the time the fire started.'

A red flush of anger creeps down your neck.

'Who gave him the alibi?'

'It would be inappropriate for me to tell you that. I will assign a family liaison officer to keep you informed of any new information.'

'I don't want an FLO,' you say. 'I just want to know when you've arrested Hyman.'

DI Baker pauses a moment. 'We will be pursuing the hate-mail enquiry urgently. And treating the arson as the attempted murder of your daughter.'

Sarah puts her hand on your arm, but you shrug her off.

'I have a meeting to go to,' you say.

You murmur something to Jenny, too quietly for anyone but her to hear, then leave the room.

DI Baker turns to Sarah. 'I gather we interviewed her friends, but didn't do any forensic tests, except for the DNA test on the used condom?'

'Yes. But we didn't find a match.'

'No samples were taken from a boyfriend or friends?' DI Baker asks.

'No, we didn't have—'

'We'll do it now. What about the locations of the postmarks?'

'Random,' Sarah replies. 'But all within London. One of the letterboxes has a CCTV camera in the street. There's a chance the hate-mailer was filmed posting the letter, but at the time we didn't have the resources to—'

'I'll put someone onto it.'

I find Jenny in the corridor, back from her wanderings.

'I saw Tara,' Jenny says, choosing a neutral kind of subject. 'She was hanging around on the ground floor.'

'The lazy journalist's way to ambulance-chase,' I say. 'Wait for them to come to you.'

'Does Aunt Sarah think it's the hate-mailer?' she asks, ending our decoy conversation.

'I think she'll be considering everything. About the hate-mailer, was there anything you—'

'No, don't start. Please. It was bad enough you and Dad doing it at the time.'

'I just—'

'No one I know would do this to me,' she says, just as she did at the kitchen table during the hate-mailer days.

'I'm not suggesting for one minute that it's one of your friends. Really. I just want to know if there was anything you didn't tell us.'

She looks away from me and I can't read her expression.

'You got pretty fed up with us always wanting to know your movements,' I say.

'You *policed* me,' she corrects. 'Dad *tailed* me, for heaven's sake. I used to see him.'

'He just wanted to make sure you were safe. That's all.'

'I'm *seventeen*.'

Yes, only seventeen. And so pretty. And so unaware.

'Then Maria's party, you wouldn't let me go,' she continues. 'Because it didn't start till nine. Everyone else went but you grounded me because of something I didn't even do.'

She's right. It wasn't fair, was it? And our need to keep her safe just fuelled her desire to pull away from us.

'I went,' Jenny confides, 'to Maria's party. It was the night I was staying over at Audrey's after the squash tournament. She'd been invited too.'

Why has she felt the need to come clean about this? Did something happen at that party? I wait, but she doesn't say anything more.

'Was there *anything* you didn't tell us about the hate mail?' I ask her again. 'In case we "policed" you even more?'

She turns a little away from me.

'Sometimes, I'm back there, inside the school,' she says quietly. 'I can't get out. I can't see anything. I mean, it's not like a memory. Just pain. And fear.' She's shrinking into herself.

I put my arms round her. 'Hey, it's over. All over.'

There must be something she didn't tell us. Because asking her made her think deeply about the fire, made her *feel* it again, as if she connected the two. But she's trembling and I can't ask her again. Not yet.

I think that she will tell me though, in time. When I used to pick her up from school she'd tell me that school was 'fine, Mum'. But an anxiety was often slipped up a sleeve, fears hidden under a jumper. You had to wait patiently for a rumpled problem to be pulled out as you drove home; the fear revealed from under the jumper on the sofa at TV time.

She gestures towards the burns unit. 'So how am I?' she asks.

I've been preparing my answer. 'I didn't see you properly. But the nurse says you're doing everything they'd expect. It's still another few days until they'll know about the scarring.' That much is true at least.

'Is Dad there?' she asks.

'No, he's had to go to a doctors' meeting,' I say. It's the meeting with my doctors about me. They'll have the results of my brain scans now. 'Shall we go and see what Tara is doing?' I suggest. I don't want Jenny to hear what the doctors say to you. *I* don't want to hear. Not yet.

Tara is by the hospital shop, multitasking flicking her hair with reading a text on her mobile. She sets off down the corridor, a sashay to her stride. Jenny and I follow her.

Jenny smiles. 'Starsky and Hutch or Cagney and Lacey?'

But actually there is something a tiny bit thrilling about following someone.

In the cafeteria Tara meets a man at a table. Older than her, a little paunchy. I recognise him.

'Paul Prezzner,' I tell Jenny. 'He's a freelance journalist. Not a bad one actually. He mainly gets his stuff into the *Telegraph*.'

'She's got a *broadsheet* onto this now?'

Both of us worry that your fame will attract more 'press interest'.

I see him leer at Tara and feel relieved. So that's the reason he's here.

We go closer to eavesdrop.

'The fact it's a school is irrelevant,' Prezzner is saying. 'The point is that it's a business. A multi-million-pound business. And it's gone up in smoke. That's what you should be investigating. That's the angle.'

'The *angle* is that it's a *school*,' Tara says, taking a teaspoon of cappuccino froth into her mouth. 'OK, so no children got hurt, but a seventeen-year-old girl did. And that's what people want to read about, Paul. Human drama.'

'You're being naive.'

'I simply understand what readers want to know about. Even the ones who buy the *Telegraph*.'

He leans closer to her. 'So you're just supplying their need?'

She doesn't back away from him.

'It'll be about the money in the end, Tara, it always is.'

'Columbine? Texas High? Virginia Tech? No financial motive in any of those, was there?'

'They were gun attacks, not arson.'

'Same difference. It's violence in our schools.'

'*Our* schools? Your examples are all in America.'

'Dunblane?'

'A one-off. Fifteen years ago. This guy you're fingering, he's not a deranged student or ex-student but a teacher.'

'*Ex*-teacher. That's the point.'

'Well, you've got yourself a good story, I'll say that for you.'

He smiles at her. I can't take much more of this sickening flirtation.

'Let's go and find Dad,' I say.

We leave the cafeteria and I remember DI Baker asking how the press got to the school so quickly. Did Tara have something to do with it?

'**H**e's right,' Jenny says. 'About the school being a business. I already told you that, didn't I?'

'But even if it is a business,' I say, remembering the uncomfortable feeling at the prize-giving that we were part of a successful business model, 'I don't see why anyone would want to burn it down.'

'Some kind of insurance fraud?' she asks.

'I can't see why. The school is full. And they keep on putting up the fees. In business terms it must be doing well. There'd be no point.'

'Perhaps there's something we don't know about,' Jenny says, and I realise that she's grabbing onto this as you grabbed onto Silas Hyman. Anything or anyone but the hate-mailer; for this not to be an attack on her.

As we arrive at my acute neurology ward, I hear Dr Bailstrom's high heels clicking quickly across the linoleum. She turns to a senior nurse.

'The case meeting on Grace Covey?'

'Dr Rhodes's office. The whole crew.'

'Waiting long?'

'Fifteen minutes.'

She hurries towards an office as fast as her shoes will let her.

'Shall we wait for Dad here?' I ask Jenny.

She doesn't reply. I turn to look at her. Something is terribly wrong. Her eyes glitter and she's shimmering with light; too bright; too vividly colourful; heat pulsating out of her.

I am mute with terror. I cannot move.

'Find out what's happening to me,' Jenny says. Her voice is so quiet I can hardly hear it. Her face is iridescent now, so dazzling I can barely look at her.

You're leaving the meeting room and running full tilt down the corridor, doors swinging back behind you, people getting out of your way.

I'm running after you, trying to keep up.

You reach the burns unit. A nurse is expecting you and opens the door hurriedly. She says Jenny's heart has arrested. They're trying to restart it.

I catch up with you by her bed.

There are too many people, their actions speeded up, and machines are bleeping and flashing and in the middle of it all is Jenny. You can't reach her; the people round her bed block your path. I feel your frustrated anguish. But if she's to be saved it's these people who'll do it, not you.

And I start to scream. On the heart monitor is a flat line. A depiction of death. She can't be dead. *She can't.*

They're trying so hard to bring her back to us, speaking quickly to one another with words we don't understand, their actions deft and practised.

A spike on her heart monitor. Her heart is *beating!* She's alive.

Elation buoys me up and everyone around me so that for a moment we are all outside the normal, contained, pragmatic world.

Jenny arrives next to me, no longer too bright. 'Still here,' she says, and smiles at me. She can't see her body, screened by the doctors and nurses.

Dr Sandhu turns to you. His brown face looks exhausted. What must it be like to hold someone's life in your hands? How heavy Jenny's must be for him, weighted with our love for her.

'We'll be taking her to our intensive-care unit,' he tells you. 'I'm afraid we think her heart is likely to have suffered damage. Possibly very severe damage. We'll be running tests straight away.'

'You'll get through this,' you say to Jenny's unconscious body. 'You *will get better.*' As if you know that Jenny can hear you.

'I'm Miss Logan, Jennifer's consultant cardiologist,' says a young woman who was at the forefront of the resuscitation. 'Let's talk when we have her test results back. I have to warn you that—'

But you leave the room, refusing to hear the end of her sentence.

Sarah's waiting outside.

'She's alive,' you say.

Sarah hugs you. She's shaking.

'It was amazing, Mum,' Jenny says. 'It was as if all the light and colour and warmth and love in my body was leaving it and being put into me,' she says. 'It was beautiful. The feeling. And what I was. Beautiful.' She searches for the right words. 'And I think what was happening was that my soul was being born.'

I am stunned by her description. Not just by the content but by the way she describes it; our daughter who has previously never used more than one adjectival phrase in a sentence.

'But it's not going to happen again,' I say. 'Not till you're an old lady, OK?'

Dr Sandhu joins you and Sarah.

'One of our nurses has told us that a piece of equipment we're using to help Jenny, the endotracheal tube which connects to her ventilator, came loose last night. There's a chance that it was tampered with. She should have reported this last night but I'm afraid it hasn't been brought to light until this emergency.'

My anxiety for Jenny last night expands to terror.

'Was that why her heart stopped?' Sarah asks.

'There's no way to be sure,' Dr Sandhu replies. 'We were already concerned about organ failure.'

I saw him. The figure in the coat. *I saw him.*

'Someone did this to her?' you ask, incredulous.

'Pieces of equipment can be faulty,' Dr Sandhu says. 'It's rare, but it happens. And it's very hard to see how tampering could have occurred. We are one of the few units in the hospital with a low turnover of staff. The door to the unit is kept locked, with a code keypad. Only members of staff know the code and visitors have to be let in.'

Just like the school. Why hadn't I realised that before?

I see anxiety pinching at Sarah's face. 'Thank you,' she says quietly. 'One of my colleagues will need to talk to you.'

'Of course. In fact, we have already followed protocol and the clinical director has just spoken to the police. But I wanted to tell you myself.'

Next to me Jenny has gone rigid, her face afraid. 'You heard him, Mum. Equipment can be faulty.' She doesn't want to believe this.

'Yes,' I say, because how can I tell her what I saw last night? How can I frighten her more now?

You walk away down the corridor, and I go after you, away from Jenny.

'Someone's trying to kill her, Mike,' I say to you. But you can't hear me.

'I'll stay with Jenny,' you say to Sarah. 'Twenty-four seven. Make sure the bastard can't get to her.'

I love you.

An hour or so later and Jenny has gone for a wander round the hospital. I'm with you, next to Jenny's bed. The world of the intensive-care unit is so alien to anything in our previous life that having a policeman next to Jenny now is no more peculiar than the banks of monitors that surround her. You hover close to her, still wanting to protect her yourself.

'Mr Covey?' Miss Logan, the cardiologist, has come up to you. 'We have the results of Jennifer's tests back now. Shall we go into my office?'

I follow you into a doctor's office, the air dense with heat.

Dr Sandhu is waiting. He takes your hand in his and pats your arm and I try not to think that he's giving you sympathy in advance.

Nobody sits down.

And I *hate* this hot institutional room with its depressing carpet-tiles and plastic stacking chairs and drug-company calendar. I want to be in the kitchen with Adam and Jenny, just back from school, making Jenny tea and squash for Adam and listening to gripes about homework. For a moment I imagine myself there so clearly that I almost hear the thump of Jen's bag on the table and Adam asking if there are chocolate mini-rolls left. Surely there's a wormhole you can step into, taking you into a parallel universe where your old life, your real life, is going on the same if only you can find your way back to it.

It's Dr Sandhu who speaks first, taking responsibility for breaking the news. 'We've run extensive tests on Jenny and I'm afraid that, as we feared, her heart has suffered catastrophic damage.'

I look at Dr Sandhu's face and in his expression I see there's a moment when a doctor realises that the life he holds in his hands is too fragile for the medicine he knows.

'Her heart will only be able to function for a few weeks,' he says.

'How many weeks?' you ask, each syllable a physical strain, tongue forced against the palate of your mouth, sounds bitter as wormwood.

'It's impossible to be accurate,' he says, *hating* having to do this.

'How many?' you ask again.

'Our guess would be three weeks,' replies Miss Logan.

'This time in three weeks we'll be in Italy! Only three weeks till Christmas, Ads! Just three weeks to A levels, don't you realise how soon that is?'

When Jenny was born her life was measured first in hours, then days, then weeks. At about sixteen weeks it turned to months—four months, five months, eighteen months—until two, when you measure your child's age in half years. Then gradually the measurement of her life became whole years. Now they're measuring what's left of it in weeks again.

I won't let it happen.

'There must be something you can do,' you say, as always, even now, certain there must be a solution.

'Her only option is a transplant,' said Miss Logan. 'But I'm afraid it's highly unlikely that a donor whose tissue matches Jennifer's will be found in time.'

'Then I'll do it,' you say. 'I'll go to that place in Switzerland, Dignitas or whatever it's called. They let you die if you want to. There must be a way of doing it so that my heart can be donated to her.'

I look at their faces; I can't bear to look at yours. I see compassion rather than astonishment. You can't be the first parent to suggest this.

'I'm afraid there are many reasons why you can't do that,' Dr Sandhu says. 'Primarily legal ones.'

'I heard that your wife is still unconscious—' tough Miss Logan begins but you interrupt her.

'What the hell are you suggesting? That I donate *her* heart?'

I feel a leap of hope inside me. Can *I* do this? Is it possible?

'I just want to offer my sympathy,' Miss Logan says. 'It must be particularly hard for you with Jennifer. In any case, even if your wife is found to have extremely limited brain function, she is breathing for herself so—'

'She can also hear me,' you interrupt, vigorously. 'And she's thinking and she's feeling. She can't show it yet. But she will. Because she will get better. And Jenny will too. They'll both recover.'

And I admire you so much because you refuse to admit defeat for Jenny or for me. Inside your head now, on those wide-open prairies, I see a one-man stockade of hope, built by your strength of spirit.

Dr Sandhu and the young cardiologist say nothing. An honest, ghastly quietness in place of agreement or reassurance. You leave the mute room.

I want to bolt to your one-man stockade of hope, but I can't, Mike. I just can't get there. I can't move at all. Because I am surrounded by sharp spikes of information and a step in any direction will mean I am pierced through. So if I don't move, I can stop it from being true.

The spikes are coming towards me and they have a sound; the sound they've had since the words 'three weeks' were spoken—a *tick-tick-tick* over every thought, every action, every word until they are used up.

Jenny's heart has become a watch, beating or ticking into an ending of silence.

5

JENNY IS WAITING FOR ME as I come out of ICU.

'Well?' she asks.

'You're going to be all right,' I say. A brazen, barefaced lie. A deceit. A shawl woven of untruths in which a mother wraps her child.

She looks so relieved. 'But they can't be *totally* sure?' she asks.

'Not *totally*.' As close as I will get to the truth.

We see you going towards my ward. Sarah must be with Jenny.

You sit next to my comatose body and you tell me what the doctors have said. You tell me that she will get a transplant. She will be all right. *Of course she will!*

I press against you and I can *feel* your courageous hope for Jenny. I hold onto it as I hold onto you. For now, at least, I can believe in your hope for her and the ghastly ticking down of Jenny's life is paused.

Jenny is in the corridor.

'Shall we go to the garden?' she suggests. She must see my surprise because she smiles with a note of triumph. 'I found one.'

She takes me to a corridor with a glass wall. I look through the glass to see a courtyard garden. It's in the heart of the hospital, walls rising up on all four sides. It must have been designed to be seen from the many over-looking windows. Through the glass, the garden looks so pretty with its profusion of English flowers: tissue-paper pink roses and frilly white jas-mine and velvet peonies. There's a wrought-iron seat and a fountain; a stone birdbath.

I go outside with Jen.

Through the glass wall, which abuts one side of the garden, you can see through to rooms and corridors. We watch people walking along. And I know why she likes it now, because even though it's not outside *proper*, we are separate from the hospital.

We carry on watching people through the glass wall. Jen seems soothed by it and it is quite soporific, like watching tropical fish in a tank.

'That's Rowena's dad, isn't it?' Jenny asks. 'Why's he here?'

Among the melee of fish-people I spot Donald. 'Yes. Rowena's in the hospital,' I say. After Maisie's visit, I'd again forgotten about her.

'Why?'

'I don't know. I saw her with Adam outside the school and she looked fine then.'

'Maisie will be with her,' Jenny says. 'Shall we go and visit?'

It's sweet of her to think I'd like to be with my old friend.

We're near the burns unit now and are catching up with Donald. A nurse is with him. As we follow him, I'm glad that for a little while at least Jenny and I have a focus that is not on her injuries or mine.

Donald is wearing a dark suit, jacket still on despite the hotly humid day, and is carrying a briefcase. I can smell cigarettes on his clothes. I've never noticed that before, but my sense of smell has become so much more acute now, overpoweringly so.

We're now close enough to hear the nurse talking to him.

'. . . and when someone has been in an enclosed space in a fire, we have to monitor them extremely carefully in case there have been any inhala-tion injuries. It can take a little while before there are any symptoms.'

Donald's face looks severe, barely recognisable from the avuncular man I last saw at the prize-giving. It's probably these glaring strip lights par-titioning the corridor ceiling that make people's faces look harsher.

The nurse presses a keypad on the door to the burns unit and holds the door for him. 'Your daughter's bed is this way,' she says.

But surely he's been to see her before? He wouldn't have waited a day before coming. Maisie has told me how protective he is. *'He'd kill crocodiles for us with his bare hands! Good job there aren't that many crocs in Chiswick!'*

Jenny and I reach Rowena's side room a little before Donald and look through the glass panel in the door. Rowena has a drip in her arm and her hands are bandaged. But her face is undamaged. Next to her is Maisie.

I wait for Donald to arrive and take Rowena in his arms and for the three of them to be reunited.

Donald goes into the room, passing Jenny in the doorway. I notice she's very pale.

'Jen?'

She turns to me, as if snapping out of a reverie. 'I know it's mad but for a moment, well, it was like I was back in the school, really back there, and'—she pauses—'I heard the fire alarm going off. *I heard it*, Mum.'

I put my arm round her. 'Has it gone now?'

'Yeah.' She smiles at me. 'Maybe it's mad person's tinnitus.'

We look through the glass in the door to Rowena's room.

Donald is going towards Rowena. I think she looks panicked. But that can't be right, surely? His back is towards me; I can't see his face.

Maisie is pulling down her sleeves to cover large bruises on her arms. 'I told you he'd be here soon,' she says to Rowena in a too-bright, nervy voice.

Donald has reached Rowena. He grabs hold of her bandaged burnt hands; she gives a sharp scream of pain.

'Quite the little heroine, aren't you?' There's hatred in his voice. Ugly and raw and shocking.

Maisie tries to pull him away. 'You're hurting her, Donald, please. Stop.'

Still he holds Rowena's bandaged hands, and she's trying not to cry out. He lets go of Rowena's hands and turns to leave.

Rowena is crying. 'Daddy . . .'

'You disgust me,' he says.

Maisie puts her hand on him, trying to stop him from leaving.

'Your bruises,' he says to her. 'Have you shown anyone?'

Maisie drops her head. Her FUN sleeves cover her bruises now; the same long-sleeved shirt she'd been wearing at sports day, despite the heat.

'It was an accident,' Maisie says. 'Of course it was. And you can hardly see any more. Really.'

Donald leaves the room abruptly.

'He didn't mean it, sweetheart,' Maisie says to Rowena.

Rowena is silent.

I turn away from them, as if they're too naked for me to watch, the bones of the family exposed.

'I never knew,' Jenny says to me, shocked.

'No.'

But I think again about Maisie's 'bulimic hog' comment, her bruised cheek, her cracked wrist, her lack of self-confidence. I again see the sinister image I'd glimpsed as I looked into my dressing-table mirror the night of the prize-giving.

I didn't ask Maisie about Donald. Not just because in daylight it seemed an absurd suspicion, but because I thought it was a territory beyond our friendship. I didn't know how to step outside our customary domestic landscape in which we were both so comfortable.

Even if I'd managed not to see what was happening to Maisie, I should have seen what was happening to Rowena. Because when Donald grabbed hold of her burnt hands that surely wasn't the first time he'd hurt her. I remember her in Reception, that elfin beautiful child. Was it happening then?

'I thought she was a spoilt little princess,' I say to Jenny, remembering the hand-painted rocking chair, fairy-tale bed and princess party-dresses. I used to worry that when the little princess grew up her adult life could only be a disappointment to her. Never once guessing at this.

'She always had to be the best,' Jenny says. 'At everything. It used to freak me.'

I'd wished Jenny had a little more ambition, yes, but I'd found Rowena's need to excel repellent at times. It wasn't just the scholarship to St Paul's Girls, it was being two grades ahead of anyone else on the violin as well as captain of the swimming team and the lead in any play.

'She was trying to make him love her, wasn't she?' Jenny says.

'Yes,' I say.

And I'd condemned her for being overly competitive. Not once seeing an abused child trying to win her father's love. Was that why she worked so hard to get into Oxford? Was she still trying to make him love her?

And Maisie. Why didn't she leave Donald? For Rowena's sake if not her own. It must kill her to see Rowena being hurt. Why has she kept up this elaborate charade, protecting him?

Jenny waits outside ICU and I go in to join you.

You're sitting at Jenny's bedside. The other side of her is a uniformed policeman, who's pretending not to be there as you talk quietly to her.

Your gentleness and loyalty and love are such a contrast to Donald.

At Sidley House, I'd thought Maisie too soft on Rowena. Rowena talked back to her and her tongue could be sharp and she rarely did what Maisie gently asked of her. But how could Maisie discipline her for small instances of bad behaviour when Donald was abusing her? When his abuse was probably the reason for Rowena's 'bad behaviour' in the first place?

When I was safely pregnant with Adam, Maisie had confided in me that she was desperate for another baby. She'd been putting it off for 'various reasons' but she was nearly forty so it was 'now-or-never time!' Six months later, she told me that Rowena had 'absolutely forbidden!' her to have another baby. I'd thought it another instance of spoilt-princess-Rowena bullying tenderhearted Maisie to get her own way.

But I think now Rowena may have been trying to protect another child, not yet born.

The PC gets a hissing message on his radio. He tells you that Detective Inspector Baker wants a meeting with you and is waiting in the office on the ground floor.

Jenny and I go with you to your meeting with DI Baker.

As we reach the office, Jenny stops.

'Do you think it could be Donald who started the fire?' she asks. 'Maisie and Rowena were almost the only people in the school at the time. Maybe it was aimed at them.'

'He couldn't possibly have known that,' I counter.

And surely there's a world of difference between bruises and trying to burn someone alive.

But I remember that figure I saw yesterday afternoon on the periphery of the playing field: an innocent bystander, most probably, but just conceivably Donald.

We go into the office, which is oppressively hot and airless. Like the family rooms and the doctors' offices it has peeling institutional green paint and ugly carpet-tiles and a clock. Always a clock.

'I know you don't want to go far from your daughter and wife,' DI Baker says to you. 'Which is why we're having our meeting here.'

You nod your thanks, surprised by his thoughtfulness.

'A new witness came forward shortly after we met,' he continues.

Sarah barges into the room, uncharacteristically flustered. No, flustered is wrong. She's *angry* and she's been running. Her forehead is filmed with sweat.

'I've just come from the station,' she says to DI Baker. 'They told me—'

'No one should be telling you anything,' he says curtly. 'I've given you a week of compassionate leave, so take it.'

'It's a mistake,' she says to DI Baker. 'Or deliberate misinformation.'

'The witness is entirely credible.'

'So why wait till now to report it?' she asks.

'Because this person knows how much the Covey family are dealing with and didn't want to add to their distress. But with the press accusations felt it was their duty to come forward.'

Sarah is more emotional than I've ever seen her. 'Who is "this person"?'

He looks at her with silent rebuke, and then continues. 'They have asked for their identity not to be revealed, which is a request I granted. There will be no trial so no need for identification. Neither we nor the school will be pressing charges.'

You look stunned. But also, I think, relieved. As I am. This wasn't done maliciously. It can't have been, if there aren't going to be any charges. It isn't the hate-mailer or Silas Hyman or Donald. Thank God.

But why is Sarah so upset?

DI Baker pauses a moment, before he speaks to you.

'Your son was seen leaving the school Art room moments before the automatic smoke detector went off. He was holding matches. There is no doubt in our mind that it was Adam who started the fire.'

Adam? For God's sake, how can he say that?

'Is this some kind of sick joke?' you ask.

'Whoever told you that is lying,' Sarah says. 'I've known Adam all his life and he's the most gentle, kind child imaginable. There's not an iota of violence in him.'

DI Baker looks irritated. 'Sarah—'

'He likes reading,' Sarah continues. 'He plays with his knights and he has two guinea pigs. They are the parameters of Adam's world. He doesn't play truant, he doesn't graffiti, he doesn't get into trouble. Reading, knights, two guinea pigs. Have you got that?'

'You're saying that *a child* took white spirit into the Art room?' you say.

'I think the Art teacher may well have been mistaken about the quantity of white spirit kept in the Art room. I had a brief talk with her earlier and she admitted she's not one hundred per cent certain at all.'

I think of Miss Pearcy, sensitive, artistic Miss Pearcy, who'd be so easily intimidated by DI Baker.

'Of course she's not,' Sarah says. 'Are you "one hundred per cent certain" when you go on holiday that you didn't leave the oven on? When there's a crash are you "one hundred per cent certain" you checked your mirror before turning? It just means that this Art teacher has a conscience and the courage to admit to her fallibility.'

'I understand your loyalty to your nephew but—'

She interrupts, sparks flying off her words. 'You can't think *a child* had the knowledge of fires and the premeditation to open the windows at the top of the school?'

'It was a hot day,' DI Baker replies. 'A teacher could easily have opened the windows to let in the breeze, despite it being against the rules.'

You have been stunned into silence, but now you move towards DI Baker and I think you're going to hit him.

'Have you ever seen Adam?' you ask, then gesture to beneath DI Baker's breast pocket. 'He'd come up to about here on you. He's *eight*, for God's sake. A little boy.'

'I appreciate it's hard to believe an eight-year-old child could do this. But according to fire-brigade records, children were responsible for ninety-three per cent of all intentionally started school-time school fires. We think it was most likely a prank, a bit of fooling around that went wrong,' DI Baker says, as if this will appease you.

'But Adam *knows* lighting a fire is wrong,' Sarah says. 'He'd *think* about the terrible consequences that may happen. For a child that age he's extremely mature and thoughtful.'

I didn't realise how well Sarah knows Adam. I've always thought she was critical of him, seeing him as wet, not like her tall, athletic sons.

'And he knew Jenny was in the school,' Sarah continues, desperately trying to convince him. 'His own sister was in there, for God's sake.'

'Is there any animosity between the siblings?' DI Baker asks.

'What are you suggesting?' you ask and there's violence in your voice.

'I'm sure he didn't intend the fire to do the terrible damage—'

'He didn't do it.'

Yours and Sarah's voices overlap with the same certainty.

'What about the intruder?' you ask. 'The one who tampered with Jenny's oxygen. You think that was a little boy too, do you?'

'There is absolutely no evidence that there ever was an intruder,' DI Baker responds impassively. 'We have talked to the medical director and connections sometimes become faulty. It's not significant.'

'There *was* an intruder! I saw him!' I shout, but no one hears me.

'It was Hyman. Jenny must have seen Hyman at the school,' you say. 'Maybe his accomplice. Something that implicated him. That's why he came here, to—'

DI Baker interrupts you. 'It really isn't helpful to indulge in unsubstantiated theories.'

'Adam wouldn't do it,' Sarah says again, with controlled fury. 'Which means that someone else did. I think we should look at every possibility. You told us Silas Hyman voluntarily gave a sample of his DNA, but have we actually *got* any DNA evidence from the scene of the fire?'

Baker looks irritated. 'It's really not productive to—'

'I thought not. And now we won't be looking for it, will we? If it was Hyman behind this, he'd happily volunteer his DNA if he knew that within twenty-four hours his accomplice would nail a child for it, and the forensic search would stop. He could well have banked on nothing being found for the first twenty-four hours.'

DI Baker looks at her with doughy immovability. 'The truth is that we have a reliable witness who saw Adam Covey coming out of the Art room, where we know the fire was started, holding matches. But we are satisfied that he didn't intend the terrible consequences of his actions and that he's been punished enough as it is. So we'll just interview him and—'

'No,' you say vehemently.

They are not going to interview Adam. They can't do that to him.

'You can't accuse him of this,' Sarah says. 'He can't know people thought him capable of this.'

'He doesn't need to go to the police station. We can do it here, so that his father can be present. You too, if you want. But I do need to interview him. You know that, Sarah.'

'What I know is that a totally innocent child has been set up.'

'I have asked a constable to bring Adam and his grandmother to the hospital. They should be here in half an hour. I suggest we reconvene then.'

Baker leaves the room and I hurry after him.

'You don't know Adam,' I say to him. 'So you don't understand why he couldn't have done this. He's *good*, you see. Not in a goody-goody way but a moral way.'

'Mum, please, he can't hear you,' Jenny says.

'He likes reading Arthurian legends,' I continue. 'His favourite is "Sir Gawain and the Green Knight". And that's what he wants to be. Not a pop star or a footballer, but a knight like Sir Gawain; he's trying to find a modern equivalent. You might think that quaint or funny, but for him it's a moral code that he wants to live by.'

'Even if he could hear you,' Jenny says, 'I don't think he knows about Gawain.'

She's right, this man wouldn't have a clue.

'He also likes history programmes,' I continue. 'And asks not only why people are wicked and do wicked things, but why people allow themselves to be led by such people. He *thinks* about these things.'

How can you make someone understand a boy like Adam?

DI Baker seems to be hurrying now, speeding his pace. I keep up.

'You probably think that all mothers say these things about their sons, but they don't. Really. They boast about how fantastic their boy is at sport and doing outdoorsy things—not being good and kind like Adam. And if it would make him happy I'd swap his kindness for being in the football team in a blink and trade decency for popular. But he doesn't have the choice, because that's how he is. And I am so *proud* of him.'

'He's afraid of fire,' Jenny says to DI Baker, joining me. 'He won't even hold a sparkler,' she continues to his back.

And she's right. He *is* afraid of fire. I remember, again, him flinching from Donald's lighter.

DI Baker reaches the exit of the hospital and I yell at him: '*Don't do this to him! Please!*'

You're at Jenny's bedside. There's no longer a police officer as it's 'no longer deemed necessary'.

Sarah arrives. 'Ads is on his way,' she says.

'I can't leave Jenny on her own, now that Baker's taken away her protection.' Because in protecting Jenny you're showing your belief that the real criminal is still out there and a threat. 'Look after him,' you say to Sarah.

As she leaves, I go after her, desperate to tell her that I saw the attacker. Before Adam was accused, the police were on the case and I was sure they'd find him. But now the police have abandoned us and this piece of information is crucial.

In the goldfish-bowl atrium, Sarah's on her BlackBerry while Jenny and I wait for Addie.

The young PC who was previously guarding Jenny comes in through the main doors. Mum and Adam are just behind him.

Sarah gives Adam a kiss, and gently pushes his fringe out of his eyes. He looks thin and pale and bemused.

Sarah turns to Mum; her voice is quiet. 'Has he said anything yet?'

'Nothing. I've tried, but he still can't. Not a word since it happened.'

Addie didn't speak to you on the phone last night; nor when he came to my bedside. But can he really not speak *at all*?

'Does he know what this is about?' Sarah asks Mum.

'Yes. Can you stop it? Please?'

Sarah turns to the young PC. 'Give me five minutes.' Speaking as his boss, not a member of Adam's family.

We follow Sarah back into the oppressively hot office. DI Baker is sitting on a plastic chair that's too small for him.

'This interview is pointless,' Sarah says. 'Adam can't talk.'

'Or won't,' asks DI Baker.

'He is suffering post-traumatic stress. Sufferers can become mute—'

'He has a diagnosis for that?' interrupts DI Baker.

'Adam saw his mother running into the burning school, screaming for his sister. And he waited. Watching the burning building. Lots of parents tried to get him away, but he wouldn't leave. Then he saw fire-fighters bringing his mum and sister out, both of them unconscious. He thought they were dead. I think that qualifies as trauma, don't you? You can't put him through an interview. You just *can't*.'

'Where's your brother?'

'With Jenny. As there's no longer a police guard.'

DI Baker looks irritated. He knows the point you're making. 'Are they here?'

Sarah's hostile silence annoys him.

'If you are willing to cooperate in this you can stay with him, but if—'

She cuts off his threat. 'He's outside.'

'**S**it down, Adam,' DI Baker said. 'I need to ask you some questions, all right?'

Adam is silent.

'If you find it hard to speak, then you can nod.'

Adam is totally still.

'I'd like to talk to you about the fire.'

The word 'fire' makes Addie crumple into himself.

I put my arms round him but he can't feel my touch. Then Sarah pulls him onto her knee. Small for eight, he's still able to sit on knees. She clasps her hands in front of her, encircling him.

'Let's start with yesterday morning,' DI Baker says. 'It was your birthday, wasn't it?'

Maybe this is his attempt to put Adam at his ease.

'Sorry, Ads,' Sarah says. 'Useless aunt. I always forget, don't I?'

'I always open my presents at breakfast,' DI Baker says to Adam. 'Did you do that?'

I'd piled up his presents in the middle of the kitchen table, ours done up with a blue satin bow, to make it look extra present-like. Inside, a 'play-space enclosure' for his guinea pigs.

I'd got him a card with an 'I am 8!' badge so he could wear it to school, because it's important that everyone knows it's your birthday.

Adam came down the stairs hurriedly, two at a time. He did almost a comic-book double take when he saw the presents. 'All for me? *Really?*'

Calling up to Jenny and you that the birthday boy was here and knowing he liked being called that and thinking that next year he probably wouldn't.

Jenny came downstairs, far earlier than usual, and—amazingly—dressed already. She hugged Adam and gave him her present.

'Aren't teaching assistants meant to be smartly dressed?' I said. 'Professional looking?'

She was wearing her short, gauzy skirt and skimpy top. 'It'll be fine, Mum, really. Besides, my outfit goes with the shoes.' She stuck out her suntanned bare legs and the jewels in her sandals glinted in the morning summer sunshine.

'I just think you should be a little more . . .'

'Yeah, I know,' she said and teased me about bumsters.

Then you came into the kitchen, singing 'Happy Birthday' loudly. And Adam laughed.

His voice was quiet. 'I hate going to school on my birthday.'

'But your friends will be there,' you said. 'And it's sports day, isn't it? So not all work today.'

'I'd rather have work.'

A flash of annoyance on your face—or was it sadness—covered because it was his birthday. You turned to Jenny. 'Don't kill anyone, Nurse Jen.'

'Being school nurse is a serious thing, not something to joke about,' I said, snappish.

'It's just for the afternoon, Mum.'

'Children can be severely injured if they fall wrong. All sorts of unforeseen accidents can happen.'

'Then I'll dial 999 and call in the pros, OK? I'm not *totally* incompetent?' A rise at the end of her sentence, like all teenage girls.

I didn't argue with her any more. There was no point. I'd be there, with the alibi of cheering Adam on at sports day, to keep an eye on things.

'Run super-fast,' you said to Adam. 'And I'll see you tonight.' Turning to me: ''Bye. Have fun.'

I don't think we kissed goodbye. Not in a pointed way, but in a kiss-taken-as-read way. We thought we had a never-ending supply of kisses and had become careless with the ones we didn't use.

'**A**nd did your mum make you a cake?' DI Baker asks Adam.

But he doesn't reply. Can't reply.

'Right, let's move on then,' DI Baker says. 'I spoke to your form teacher, Miss Madden, and she told me that children are allowed to bring a cake in on their birthdays?'

I remember counting out eight blue candles and putting the cake tin into the jute bag with the square base, which is perfect for cake tins. And then—

'Oh God.'

'Mum?' Jenny asks but DI Baker is talking again.

'She told me that parents supply the candles and also the matches.'

A slight stress on 'matches'. Sarah reacts as if scalded.

I plead with her to stop this Sherman tank of an interview before it reaches its destination. But she can't hear me.

'Miss Madden told us that she keeps the cake, with the candles and matches, in a cupboard next to her desk. Usually she would get it out at the end of the day, just before the children go home. But if it's sports day, the birthday child can take it out to the playing field to have at the end?'

Adam is silent and still.

I remember how anxious he'd been that his birthday cake would be forgotten and he'd miss that once-a-year singing to him, all the children clustering around him.

'She told us that you went to get your cake from your classroom?'

I remember him dashing up to me, his face one big smile. He was going to get his cake right now!

'So you went to your classroom, which was empty?' DI Baker asks, not waiting for a reply any more. 'And then did you take the matches to the Art room?'

Adam is mute.

'Did you use your birthday cake matches to start a fire, Adam?'

The silence in the room is so loud that I think my eardrums will burst with the force of it.

'You just have to say yes or no, lad.'

But he's stock-still; frozen.

Adam's standing by the statue of the bronze child, watching me running into the burning school, smoke pouring out and I'm screaming for Jenny.

'We don't think you meant to hurt anyone, Adam,' DI Baker says.

But how can Addie speak with the noise of sirens and shouting and his own screams? How can he make himself heard above that din?

'How about if you just nod or shake your head?'

He doesn't hear Adam screaming. Just as he can't hear me as I yell at him to leave my child alone.

'Adam?'

Addie is staring at the school, waiting for me and Jenny. The smoke and the sirens and the waiting. A child turned to stone.

'I am giving you a caution, Adam,' DI Baker says to him. 'Which is a serious thing. If you ever do anything like this again we will not be so lenient. Do you understand?'

But Adam is watching us being carried out by fire-fighters. He sees Jenny's charred hair, her sandals. He thinks we are dead.

Sarah's arms are locked round Addie. 'That's the evidence? That he brought in matches? And that someone saw him?'

'Sarah—'

She interrupts, coldly furious. 'Someone's made him the perfect patsy.'

6

ADAM COMES OUT OF THE OFFICE, looking dazed.

In the corridor, he retches and then he runs, trying to find a loo, but he can't find one and he's sick on the floor. I hold him but he can't feel me.

Mum is coming down the corridor. As she sees Addie she magics that smile onto her face. 'Poor old you,' she says, giving him a hug.

Sarah has come out of the office now. She wipes his face with a tissue from her pocket, then bends down so that her face is level with his.

'I'm really sorry the policeman said those things to you. Someone has lied to him and we are going to find out who, I promise. Then I expect he'll want to apologise to you. I'm going to talk to him right now.'

Mum takes Adam's hand. 'Let's go and get some fresh air, shall we?'

She takes him towards the hospital exit and Jenny goes with them.

I go with Sarah back into that hot, vile office.

DI Baker is writing notes on a form; a done-and-dusted form, I imagine, naming Adam and a caution and a job finished. He's irritated to see her.

'I need to know who said they saw Adam,' she says.

'No. You don't. You're not a part of this investigation.'

'Whoever told you was lying.'

'I think I'm the best judge of that. Believe me, it gives me no pleasure to have to caution a child.'

'You said that on sports day the birthday child takes his or her cake, with matches, out to the playing field? I think the arsonist wanted to set fire to the school on sports day—maybe because the school would be virtually deserted. He chose the child who had a birthday that day, knowing that the child would go back to school to get their cake and matches and could be made a scapegoat.

'The school PTA make a calendar every year with a photo of the children who have birthdays that month,' Sarah continues.

Adam gave her one for Christmas.

'Yesterday's date has "Sports Day" written in large type and "Adam Covey is 8" in small type. It's on the wall of my kitchen. I saw it last week then forgot about it. Anyone with a calendar would know it was Adam's birthday on sports day, including the arsonist. He *planned* for the blame to fall on him.'

'Let's suppose, for one moment, that you're right,' DI Baker says. 'Why didn't Adam *deny it*? All he had to do was shake his head. But he didn't.'

'I think he could be suffering from amnesia. It is another recognised symptom of PTS. Memories of the trauma, and often a little while before or afterwards, are blanked out by the brain as a means of self-preservation.'

'Oh, come on. So he's conveniently wiped the whole thing?' he asks.

'No, the memory is there. But his self-defence mechanisms have blocked access to it. It explains why he doesn't respond to your questions,' Sarah continues. 'He can't. Because he doesn't remember. And he's an honest child, so he wouldn't deny something he can't remember.'

'The only time I've seen genuine amnesia is when someone is drugged or has had a bash on the head. This is claptrap and you know it.'

'Retrograde amnesia following a traumatic event is a recognised psychological condition.'

Being Sarah, she probably knows all this. But she must have brushed up on her knowledge to have the terms at her fingertips. That must be why she was on her BlackBerry as she waited for Adam to arrive. I used to get annoyed at the amount of time she spent on that thing.

But I don't think Adam is suffering from amnesia but the opposite. I think he hasn't forgotten the traumatic event but is locked into it and that's why he can't speak.

I have to find him.

Jenny is in the large goldfish-bowl atrium at the entrance to the hospital, looking through the glass wall.

'He's with Granny G and Aunt Sarah,' she says, and gestures to a municipal patch of grass a little distance away, where I can just see them.

'I tried to go with them,' she continues. 'But it hurts to be outside. Really hurts.'

I long to go to him, but Jenny has no one with her and I can feel her unhappiness.

'We all know that Adam didn't do it,' Jenny says. 'If his family believe in him then—'

'He'll have to grow up with this,' I say, interrupting her without meaning to. 'He'll be the boy who tried to kill his sister and mother. School. University. Wherever he goes, this terrible thing that's being said about him will go first.'

She's silent for a little while, watching Addie.

'There's something I didn't tell you,' she says. 'About the hate-mailer. He threw a can of red paint at me.'

My God. He was *following* her.

'Did you see who it was?' I ask, trying to sound calm.

'No. He threw it from behind. I don't remember anything useful at all. Nothing that will help Addie. I just remember this woman screaming. It was red gloss, the paint. She thought it was blood. It covered the back of my coat. And all down my hair. It was on May the 10th.'

That was just a few weeks ago. Just *a few weeks*. It hadn't stopped at all. *It had got worse.* Not just posting her vicious letters, but following her and throwing paint at her. Is he stalking her now? Attacking her for real?

'If I'd told the police, they might have stopped him. And Addie . . .' Guilt crumples her face; she looks more like ten right now than seventeen.

I put my hand on her, but she shakes me off.

'I tried to convince myself it wasn't the hate-mailer who set fire to the school. But now with Adam being accused, I can't . . .'

She's admitting this awful possibility out of love for Adam.

'Who else knows?' I ask.

'Just Ivo,' she replies. 'I made him promise me he wouldn't tell anyone.'
You'll think it's unfair of me to hate Ivo now, but he *should have told us*.
'When's he coming home?' I ask.
'Ten days. But he's bound to find out about this and come back sooner.'
As I nod, a man brushes past me. Mr Hyman.
I feel jolted by shock. What is he doing here?
He's in shorts and T-shirt, looking so suntanned in this white place. At
school he had to wear a formal jacket and trousers. He goes through a
door I hadn't noticed before. I follow him.
'Mum?'
'I want to know what he's up to.'
She comes with me.
The door leads onto steep concrete steps. We follow him down to a
basement car park. After the bright sunshine of the atrium, the basement
is oppressively dark. The heat smells of petrol fumes and exhausts.
Mr Hyman reaches an old yellow Fiat and sticks a ticket from a vending
machine on the windscreen. There are three children's seats crammed
into the car.
'What's he doing here?' I say.
'He has probably come to have it out with Tara,' Jenny says. 'She
deserves it.'
'But how would he know that she hangs around here?'
'I don't know,' Jenny says. 'Or he's just trying to get away from his wife.
He used to pretend to run the after-school scrapbook-making club so he
could get more time away from her. She's horrible to him. She told him he
was a loser. Said she was embarrassed by him. But she won't get divorced.
Says if he leaves her, he'll never see the kids.'
'He *told you* that?' I ask.
'So?'
You were sixteen last summer and he's thirty, I want to say, but don't.
'Perhaps he's come to see one of us,' Jenny continues. 'Bring flowers or
something. He's really kind, remember, Mum?'
A challenge to remember him as I used to think of him.
We follow him back up the basement steps, me staring at his back, as if
I can X-ray through his body to see the inner man. He's hot and sweating,
his T-shirt sticking to him, and I see how muscular he is.
Back in the goldfish-bowl atrium I spot Adam coming in with Mum

and Sarah. As I look at him, I lose sight of Mr Hyman. Mum has her arm round Adam.

'Mummy will still be having a few bits and bobs sorted out,' she says to him, reducing MRIs and CT scans to bits and bobs and I love her for it. 'So let's get a drink to settle your tummy and then we can see her later.' I so admire her strength as she tries to shelter him.

I go up to Sarah, desperate to talk to her. Because I have information that will surely exonerate Addie. I now know that the hate-mailer attacked Jenny with red paint. It didn't stop in February but in May, just a few weeks ago. And maybe he's attacking her now, trying to kill her. I know that a man sabotaged Jenny's ventilator—I saw him.

But I also think you're right to be suspicious of Silas Hyman because what the hell was a thirty-year-old man doing badmouthing his wife to a sixteen-year-old? And what's he doing here? Now?

And I've seen Donald being vicious to Rowena and I think he's probably been violent to Rowena and Maisie for years. Both of them were in the school at the time of the fire. But they won't tell anyone about him, not when they haven't done so in the past.

I feel like I've become the keeper of the keys and one of them, surely, will unlock the truth. It's my job now to find out everything I can. Then I will make sure that Adam is proved innocent.

You're at Jenny's bedside, staring at the monitors around her. You barely glance at Sarah as she arrives.

'Baker still thinks it's Adam. He didn't speak. He *can't speak*. There was nothing I could do, Mike. I'm so sorry.'

'Oh Christ. Poor Ads.' You stand up. 'How the hell can Baker believe Hyman's lies?'

'It can't have been Silas Hyman who said he saw Adam,' Sarah says. 'He'd have had no business being in the school in the first place.'

'So he got someone to lie for him.'

'Mike . . .'

'And who gave him an alibi?'

Sarah doesn't answer.

'You know, don't you?' You look at her and she finally meets your eye.

'It was his wife.'

'I'm going to see them.'

'I really don't think—'

'I don't give a monkey's arse what anyone thinks. Will you stay here?'

'I don't think you'll achieve much, Mike.'

You are silent.

'A friend brought your car from the BBC to the hospital car park,' she says. 'They've paid for an extended stay. Here.' She hands you a parking chit and takes your seat next to Jenny.

'There's been no change since this morning,' you say. 'Stable, they said. Let me know if there's anything, right away.'

Jenny is outside ICU. 'Where's Dad going?'

'Silas Hyman's house.'

'If I could remember more about that afternoon then maybe the police wouldn't blame Addie; you and Dad wouldn't blame Silas. But *I can't remember!*'

'It's not your fault, sweetheart.'.

I touch her on the shoulder but she shakes me off, as if angry with herself for needing comfort.

'There's something called retrograde amnesia.' I want her not to blame herself; to have a reason she can understand. 'It's when your brain blocks off access to a traumatic memory so you can't get it.' Although I'm pretty sure this doesn't apply to Adam, it might be true of Jen.

'So it's like a protective thing?' she asks. 'But the memory *is* still there?'

'I think so, yes. Is it OK if I go with Dad?' I ask her.

''Course. But won't it hurt you to go outside?'

'Oh, I'm a tough old bird,' I say to her.

I leave the hospital with you. My skin is scalded by the warm air and the gravel is shards of glass under my feet, as if the hospital building with its white walls and cool, slippery linoleum has been giving me protection and now it's ripped away.

I grip hold of your hand and, although you don't feel me, you give me comfort.

We reach our car and I see Adam's books stuffed into the pouch behind the driver's seat, a lipstick of Jenny's in the bit meant for a mug, a pair of my boots that need re-heeling on the back seat, like archaeological finds of a long-ago life.

We drive away from the hospital. The pain hits me like blows, so I must focus on something else. But what?

It's silent in the car. It's never silent in the car. Either we are chatting, or there's music playing (blaring if it's Jenny in charge). You involuntarily reach your left hand across towards the passenger seat to hold mine, as you always do when you drive. For a moment we are driving out to friends for dinner, with you praising Sat Navs because we can talk instead of map-read, our bottle of wine rolling around in the boot. Then you move your hand away.

You take our turning off the main road.

I think back to Jenny being attacked with red paint. I imagine a man going into a DIY superstore, a few days before, a huge place where no one will remember him walking along an aisle lined with paint tins, until he finds the oil-based polyurethane glosses. I imagine a girl on the check-out not finding it strange that he's bought red paint and white spirit. Because the only way of getting out gloss paint is with white spirit and, yes, there is a large quantity, but there's a queue building behind him now.

Did Jen go to a friend's house to wash her hair? Not knowing that gloss can be impossible to wash out. Did she then go to a hairdresser or did a friend or Ivo snip the evidence? Did she take her coat to a dry-cleaner's? Why didn't she come to me?

You're turning into a street, three away from ours. Mr Hyman's road. I didn't know you'd listened to me when I said we often passed Mr Hyman on the way to school.

You're pulling over, not bothering to park. You slam the driver's door.

From the car, I watch you as you ring doorbell after doorbell asking which number Silas Hyman lives at. The pain is getting worse the longer we are away from the hospital. I'd thought it was bodies that feel pain, but maybe skin and flesh and bones are protecting something exquisitely tender inside.

I join you as you press Mr Hyman's doorbell, keeping your thumb hard down on it.

His wife answers the door. I remember she's called Natalia. I met her at the school 'soiree' two years ago. She'd looked like something out of a Tolstoy novel then. But Natalia's striking beauty has become subtly coarsened since, something—anxiety? tiredness?—slackening the skin on her face, causing her green cat-eyes to lose their perfectly outlined shape.

'Where's your husband?' you ask.

Natalia looks at you; features stiffening, sensing threat. 'You are . . .?'

'Michael Covey. Jenny Covey's father.'

Adam whips off a plastic helmet with a flourish as he pretends to be a Roman gladiator as played by Russell Crowe.

'My name is Maximus Decimus . . .'

'Meridius,' prompts Jenny.

'Maximus Decimus Meridius. Commander of the armies of the north. General of the—'

'It's the next bit that's good.'

'OK. I am Maximus Decimus Meridius. Father to <u>a murdered son</u>, husband to <u>a murdered wife</u>. And I will have my vengeance, in this life or the next.'

'It gives me shivers,' Jenny says. 'Every time.'

Adam, holding his helmet, nods solemnly in agreement. You are trying desperately not to laugh and I daren't catch your eye.

Yes, I know your situation is nothing like Maximus Decimus Meridius', because your wife and child are still alive.

'**M**y husband isn't here,' Natalia says.

'Where is he?' you ask.

'A building site.'

He's lied to her. I feel a flash of anxiety for Jenny and Adam. But Sarah is with Jenny, Mum is with Adam. Neither of them would desert their posts.

'Where is the building site?' you ask.

'I don't know. It's different every day. Unskilled labourers don't have the luxury of regular work.' She sounds upset for him. 'I read about your wife and daughter.' I wait for her to offer sympathy but she doesn't.

Instead she turns her back on you, leaving the door open behind her, and walks away. I follow her into the hotly oppressive house. There are three small children, looking grubby and out of control, two of them fighting.

Their house is almost identical to ours, but a door blocks off the entrance to the first floor. It's a flat, not a house. I've never really thought of the financial discrepancy between the teachers and parents at Sidley House before.

She goes into the small kitchen. The school calendar is hanging on the wall, with three children's photos for July. On July 11 is 'Sports Day' in large type, 'Adam Covey is 8' in small type. The date is ringed in red.

Adam had been so pleased that Mr Hyman had sent him a birthday card.

Natalia picks up a copy of the *Richmond Post*. 'Is this why you're here?' she asks. 'Because of this load of crap? It's lies,' she says. 'All of it.'

'The alibi you gave him,' you say to her. 'What was it?'

'How about I tell you what I know,' she says. '*Then* I will answer your questions.'

You are wrong-footed, I can see that.

'Silas is the most gentle man you could meet,' she says, taking advantage of your hesitation. 'To be honest, it annoys me sometimes that he's so gentle. Our boys could do with a little discipline. But he won't. Doesn't even raise his voice to them. So the idea that he could set light to a school, well, it's just ridiculous.'

'At prize-giving?' you say. 'He was hardly "gentle" then.'

'He wanted to tell everyone it wasn't his fault,' Natalia replies. 'Can you blame him for wanting his chance to tell the truth? You didn't give him one before firing him, did you?'

I feel her hostility now, crouching behind her words.

'It's not surprising he had a few drinks first to find the courage. He's passionate. And he even gets a little drunk sometimes, but he'd never set fire to something, let alone risk hurting anyone.'

Her fingers are sweating, smudging the picture of Jenny.

'It doesn't tell you in here that he spent his free time doing teaching plans and researching new ways of inspiring his class, finding field trips and teaching resources, even what kind of music helped kids concentrate best. He still talks about them all. He still calls them "his" class. And here our kids are, not likely to see the inside of a private school unless they're lucky enough to teach in it, with our eldest starting in September at the local thirty-in-a-class failing primary. But I'm still really proud of him. For being the best bloody teacher that school could have.'

Aggression is pressing up against her words.

'His friends from Oxford are all having high-flying, highly paid careers in media and law,' she continues. 'While he is—was—just a primary school teacher. Not that he ever got any credit for that. You think it's any wonder he went and sounded off at your prize-giving?'

A child has come to join her. She holds the little boy's hand. 'That's where I met him,' she says. 'At Oxford. I was working as a secretary. I was so proud to be with him. I couldn't believe it when he chose *me*; married *me*; made those vows to *me*.'

Is that what this is about? For richer for poorer; to lie for and cover for?

'He's a good man,' she continues. 'Loving. And decent. There's not many you can say that about.'

Does she believe her version of her husband? Or is she, like Maisie, presenting an image to the outside world, no matter the cost to herself?

'It wasn't Silas's fault, what happened to that boy in the playground. It was—'

You interrupt; you've had enough. 'Where was he yesterday afternoon?' Your voice angry, loud; frightening the child.

'With me and the kids,' she says. 'All afternoon. There wasn't any work for him yesterday. So we went to the park for a picnic. He said we might as well make the most of him not being in work. And it was so hot indoors. Left here about eleven, got back around five.'

'A long time.' Your disbelief is clear.

'Nothing to come back for. And Silas likes playing with them outside, giving them rides on his back, playing footie, he's devoted to them.'

Jenny said he'd pretended to be running an after-school club so he could avoid coming home. This picture of a family man that Natalia is painting doesn't exist.

'Did he ask you to say this, or did you come up with it yourself?' you ask and I am relieved you're challenging her.

'Is it so hard for you to believe that a family like ours could have an afternoon out together?'

I think by 'like ours' she means a family in a flat, not a house, with no money and the dad working on a building site. And no, of course, it's not hard to believe a family like that could enjoy an afternoon in the park. But she's keeping something from you, I'm sure of it. She has been from the moment she opened the door to you.

'Did anyone see you in the park?' you ask. 'Anyone who'd remember?'

'It was packed. There was an ice-cream van, maybe that guy would remember.'

A hot July afternoon in a park, how many families with small children did he see yesterday? How likely is it he'd remember?

'Who did your husband get to lie for him?' you ask. 'To say they'd seen Adam?'

'Sir Covey?'

That pet name infuriates you but I think her surprise looks genuine.

'I've no idea what you're on about,' she says.

'Tell him I want to speak to him,' you say. You start to leave but she comes after you.

'Wait. I haven't finished! I told you, you need to hear the truth. The accident in the playground was Robert Fleming's fault, nothing to do with Silas.'

You hurry on, not listening. You open the car door.

'Children can be little bastards,' she says, catching up with you. 'Evil.' She holds the car door so that you can't close it. 'You made Mrs Healey fire Silas for not supervising the playground properly, didn't you? You got the *Richmond Post* to print that crap about him, to make sure he was pushed out.'

'I have to get back to my daughter.' You yank the car door out of her grasp, slam it shut and drive away.

Maybe she should seem more like a victim to me. After all, in return for her loyalty Silas lies to her and badmouths her to teenagers. But her spikiness and aggression means she can't be pigeonholed so neatly. Is her rage because she genuinely thinks that Silas has been wronged? Or is it the anguish of a woman who knows she made a terrible mistake in the man she married?

The pain has gone. It stopped the moment I stepped into the hospital, as if this white-walled building offers me its own skin.

My mother is sitting next to Jenny. I know she won't have left Addie on his own; a nurse must be with him. Amid the shiny, hard equipment she looks so gentle in her cotton skirt and Liberty-print blouse. Her hand hovers over Jenny, as yours often does, unable to touch her.

You go up to Sarah, who's standing a little distance away.

'Hyman wasn't there,' you say to her. 'And his wife would do whatever the bastard asked.'

Then Mum sees you. 'Is there any more news on Gracie?' she asks.

'Not yet,' you reply. 'I was meant to have a meeting with her doctors earlier, but I got called away.' You don't say you were called away because

Jenny's heart stopped. You haven't told Mum about the three weeks. 'They've said they might not have time now,' you continue. 'Apparently there's been some awful coach crash, so it's all hands to the pumps.'

And for one moment this hospital isn't all about us. There are others too, God knows how many; all that anguish and anxiety compressed into this one building. I wonder if it leaks out of the windows and roof.

Trying to think this to avoid ugly, awful thoughts.

But I suspect you're thinking them too.

Will any of the coach casualties die? Will any of them be a match for Jenny? How strange that selfless love can make you morally ugly.

'I'm sure they'll have the meeting as soon as they can,' you say.

She nods. 'Adam's in the relatives' room,' she tells you.

'I'll go and see him in a minute. I'd just like a little time with Jen first.'

I go to the relatives' room. A fan whirrs the heated air. Addie is huddled close to Mr Hyman, who has his arm round him, reading him a story.

I go cold.

Jenny is on the other side of the room. 'He saw Granny G and Adam in the café,' she says calmly. 'He offered to look after Adam, so that Granny G could be with me.'

Mum would never suspect anything. She's heard me and Addie praise Mr Hyman countless times.

Over the whirr of the fan, I listen to him reading. At his feet is a bunch of flowers.

'He told his wife he was going to work on a building site,' I tell Jenny.

'Poor bloke. Is that all the work he can get?'

'He lied to his wife, Jen.'

'Probably to get away from her.'

She looks at me, and I see exasperation in her expression.

'You can't still think it's Silas. There is *no way* that he is anything to do with the hate mail. Quite apart from the fact that he's just not that kind of person, why would he?'

I also think it's very unlikely that Silas Hyman is the hate-mailer turned stalker. Even if he had a reason, which he doesn't, I can't imagine an Oxford-educated, highly articulate man cutting out words from a newspaper or a magazine and sticking them onto A4. He's far too subtle and intelligent for that.

But the fire might be nothing at all to do with the hate-mailer. It could be, as you are so certain, simply revenge by Silas Hyman.

'He tried talking to Addie,' Jenny says. 'But Addie couldn't say anything back. That's when he started reading him the Percy Jackson story. Perfect choice, isn't it?'

'Yes.'

You missed most of Addie's Percy Jackson phase, but he's a schoolboy who can vanquish evil monsters against impossible odds. Mr Hyman knows that Adam loves Arthurian legends but knights would be too adult for him to relate to them now. They wouldn't offer him any fantasy escape from what is happening. This is a better choice.

I'm disturbed by how well he knows Addie.

Mr Hyman. Silas. Two names. Two men.

I watch Silas's face, so close to Adam's. I remember again Maisie's words at the prize-giving: *'That man should never have been allowed near our children.'* And I want him to get away from my children. *Get away!*

Then Mum comes in. She's again, somehow, forced colour into her cheeks and energy into her voice, that magic smile appearing on her face.

'Have you had a good story, Addie?' She turns to Silas Hyman. 'Thank you for giving me time with my granddaughter.'

'Of course. It was great to be with Addie.' He gets up. 'I'd better be going now.'

Silas picks up the bunch of flowers and leaves the room. I follow him. The flowers are yellow roses—mean buds that will never open, plastic-wrapped and scentless. He must have got them from the hospital shop.

He presses the button on the door of the ICU ward. A pretty blonde nurse comes to answer it. I see her notice his attractiveness. Or maybe it's just his vigorous health, which stands out in this place.

The nurse opens the door and explains that flowers aren't allowed because they are an infection risk. There's a flirtatious tone to her voice.

'For you then,' he says, smiling at her. She takes the flowers and lets him into ICU.

A smile and flowers. That simple.

I follow him.

To be fair to the pretty nurse, she's accompanying him all the time, making him wait while she puts the flowers in the nurses' station. But are all nurses so cautious?

He follows her towards the section that has Jenny's bed. Through the glass wall I see you sitting next to her, Sarah a little distance away.

'That's Jennifer Covey, there,' the pretty nurse says.

Silas Hyman looks pale, his forehead sweaty; stricken by what he sees. I think I hear him whisper, 'Oh God.'

He turns away and shakes his head at the nurse. He isn't going closer.

Or is he pretending this is the first time he's seen her since the fire? A brilliant performance so that nobody will suspect him of being the person who tampered with her oxygen tube?

Through the glass wall, you see him turning away. You hurry out after him. You catch up with him in the corridor.

'What the hell are you doing here?'

'I saw Adam and his grandmother earlier and—'

'Your wife said you were at a building site.'

For a moment he is speechless; caught out.

'A load of crap, wasn't it? Like your alibi. Lying bastard!' Yelling now.

Adam and my mother come out through the open door of the relatives' room, but you don't see them, rage-focused on Silas Hyman.

'Who lied for you about my son?'

'What do you mean?'

My mother tries to be appeasing. 'Someone said they saw Addie starting the fire,' she tells him.

'But that's ridiculous,' Mr Hyman says. 'For goodness' sake, of all people to accuse.' He turns to Adam. 'I know you wouldn't do that, Sir Covey.'

He bends towards Adam, perhaps to stroke his hair or give him a hug.

'Keep away from him!' you roar, moving towards him, going to hit him.

And then Adam is standing between you and he's pushing you away from Silas Hyman; protective of him, furious with you.

I see the terrible hurt on your face. It's the first time you've seen Adam since the fire.

Silas turns and walks away.

Mum takes Adam's hand in hers. 'Come on, sweetheart, time to go home.' She leads him away.

'Go after him!' I say to you. 'You've got to tell him you know he didn't start the fire.' Silas Hyman said that straight away.

But you turn away. You think that he must know you think he's innocent. I hope to God that he does.

You return to Jenny's bedside.

'Can you stay here?' you ask Sarah.

Something in your voice sounds a warning. 'Why?'

'Hyman told his wife he was on a building site,' you say. 'But all the time the bastard was *right here*. I need to find out who Hyman got to lie about Adam,' you say. 'I need to do that for him.'

But what Addie needs from you is to be with him. It makes me so sad you don't know this.

'Finding out who this witness is—and the arsonist—should be *my* job,' Sarah says. 'I'm a police officer; it's what I do.'

'I thought Baker had made you take compassionate leave?'

'He has.' She pauses a moment. 'OK, we know there were only two members of staff, apart from Jenny, who weren't at sports day—a Reception teacher and a secretary. We need to speak to them, especially the secretary because it's her job to buzz people in and out of the school.'

'I'll go now,' you say, standing up. 'He's my son.'

She puts a hand on your arm. 'Exactly. And what if she recognises you? Do you think that'll help if she is involved in this?'

You are silenced and frustrated by her logic.

'The most useful thing for you to do is to stay here and guard Jenny,' she continues. 'I will share everything with you, update you on everything. You think the arsonist is Silas Hyman, with an accomplice who lied about Adam, and we'll come back to him, but we also have to look at the hate-mailer.'

She waits for you to argue. Like me, she heard your categorical denial of the hate-mailer being responsible to DI Baker. But you don't contradict her. For Addie's sake you want the truth so will keep an open mind.

'Because hate mail is a crime under the Malicious Communications Act,' Sarah goes on, 'it can be fully investigated by the police.'

'They didn't get far last time,' you say.

'DI Baker's asked for a much wider investigation. There'll be more welly than last time: looking at CCTV footage; wider DNA testing. The works.'

'And Hyman?'

'With the arson investigation closed, there's no reason for the police to investigate him further.'

'But you will?'

She hesitates a moment. 'Every interview I do now is illegal,' she says.

'So we have to weigh up very carefully what we want to achieve because I'll be treading on thin ice and it *will* give way; it's just a question of how much I can find out before it does. I need to be well informed before I talk to him. I need to read the witness statements and interviews taken straight after the fire. We need to be armed with as much information as possible before going after any suspects.'

I'm stunned by how many rules Sarah will be breaking.

7

'GRACE, MY DARLING,' you say as I reach you, as if you know I am there.

You could run a florist's shop from my bedside table. Only one vaseful is ugly—odourless, last-minute shop-bought roses. *To Mrs Covey, with all best wishes, from Mr Hyman.*

But you don't see the flowers, looking only at me.

'There's still no news on Jenny's heart,' you say. 'But they'll find one for her. I know they will.'

Thinking panicky loud thoughts, I try to drown out the ticking that has started again—faint but audible; a ghastly unstoppable rhythm.

'Sarah said she'd told you about Addie,' you say.

'*You have the right to know, Grace. You must hate the police for this. But I promise you we'll get it put right.*' She was so awkward with me, not realising how much I like her now. You were worried that telling me this, *on top of Jenny,* would sap the remaining life force I have. But Sarah understands that for a mother, when your children are threatened, your life force isn't sapped but galvanised.

You hold my hand. 'Ads doesn't want me near him,' you say.

'That's *not true.* And you need to go to him right now and tell him you know he didn't do this and be with him. Sarah can stay with Jen for a bit. The detective stuff can wait for a little while, surely.'

But you can't hear me, nor can you guess what I am saying to you.

'We always do this, don't we, Gracie?' you say. 'Talk about Addie or Jen. But I'd like to talk about you and me, just for a few minutes.'

I'm touched. And yes, I'd really like to do that too.

'Remember our first date?' you ask.

Not so much a change of subject as a rewind of twenty years to a safe past. Leaving this white-walled London hospital far behind for a teashop in Cambridge. Pouring with rain outside; inside, fuggy with talk and damp anoraks. Chintzy curtains and china cups.

We talked about attraction. You, a scientist, were all pheromones and biological imperatives, while I was all coy mistresses and eyebeams threading on a double string. You thought Marvell was a comic.

'You quoted something about a man spending a century admiring each bosom and I got the hint.'

In that prim little teashop you told me that you were desperate to be away from the confines of university and 'out there doing stuff'.

I'd done a year of an English degree and my friends were all black-clothed, earnest arts students with a thesaurus for a vocabulary. I didn't know anyone who used the word 'stuff'. I liked it. And I liked it that you weren't pale with cheekbones studying Kant, but were muscular and robust and wanted to be mountaineering and white-water rafting and bivouacking the world rather than reading and philosophising about it.

'I liked the climbing-a-volcano thing,' I say. 'Mad, but kind of mad in an attractive way.'

'I wanted to impress you. You were so beautiful.'

'Thanks so much.'

'Sorry. *Are* so beautiful.' As if you'd heard me.

'You had two Chelsea buns,' you say. You *remember* that? 'And I liked it that you ate so much.'

I didn't want you to guess that I was nervous so I ate to prove that I was cool about this.

'It rained.' Lashing against the ditzy little windowpanes, and the sound was wonderful. 'I'd brought an umbrella.'

You asked if you could walk me home.

'I knew we'd have to get close.'

I spotted your bike and you looked annoyed that I noticed it.

'That bloody bike. Should have locked it round the corner.'

You walked me back to Newnham in the rain, pushing your bicycle on the road with one hand, but staying on the pavement next to me with your other hand holding the umbrella.

'I couldn't touch you at all.'

We should be talking about our children now. And we will, in a few moments. They are with us all the time. But there is a glimmer of happiness here in the time before them, and we want to hold it a little longer. So I carry on walking next to you through the cold Fen rain, your stride so much longer than mine, wondering what will happen when we reach Newnham.

But of course I know what happened.

The memory pulls me towards you until I reach you here and now in this room; somehow closer than before. This close to you, I can *feel* your brave optimism for Jenny go into me. And as you hold me tightly, I too believe that Jenny will get better.

The curtains are pulled back abruptly and Dr Bailstrom is there.

'Can you come for the meeting now?' she asks you.

'I'll be back a little later, my darling,' you say to me, telling Dr Bailstrom that I can hear and understand.

I've never seen you look slight before. But in here, outnumbered by doctors, you look hollowed out. Dr Bailstrom doesn't fully look at you as she speaks.

'We have run a series of tests, Mr Covey. Many of them are repeats of the ones we did yesterday. I'm afraid you're going to have to start preparing yourself for Grace never regaining consciousness.'

'No, you're wrong,' you say.

Of course she's *wrong*! The thinking, feeling part of me will rejoin my body and *I will wake up*.

'I know it's a lot to take in,' Dr Bailstrom continues. 'But she shows only the basic responses of gagging and breathing. And we don't think there will be any improvement.'

You shake your head, refusing to allow the information entry.

'What my colleague is saying,' interjects an older doctor, 'is that the damage to your wife's brain means that she can't speak or see or hear. Nor can she think or feel. And she won't get better. She won't wake up.' He's obviously from the sock-it-to-them-straight school of medicine.

'What about those new scans?' you say. 'People who'd been written off as cabbages were told to imagine playing tennis for yes, and the brain scan then picked it up.'

I'd heard it on Radio 4 and told you about it. I'd liked the idea of imagining playing tennis for yes. A smash, I'd imagined, or an ace serve. Such a positive and vigorous yes.

'We will try all the tests there are,' the sock-it-to-them doctor says. 'But I need to be honest with you. The bottom line is that she isn't going to get better. All our scans show massive and irreparable trauma to her brain.'

'You just don't get it, do you?' I say. 'The mother thing. My son needs me. It's not just proving that he's innocent. In the mornings, I help him design an imaginary shield to put over his heart so it won't hurt so much if people are mean to him. And some evenings he'll only be able to get to sleep if he holds my hand.'

'But all of that could be bullshit, right?' says a voice in the doorway. I turn to see Sarah come into the room. Behind her is my mother. Both of them have clearly heard the doctors.

'Dr Sandhu is with Jenny,' Sarah says to you. 'Sarah Covey. Mike's sister,' she announces. 'This is Grace's mother, Georgina Jestopheson. There have been patients who have woken up from comas after years, haven't there? With cognitive function?'

The doctor is unabashed. 'Yes, there are occasionally stories in the press about such cases, but on scrutiny you'll see they are different medically.'

'And what about stem-cell therapy?' you ask. 'Growing new neurons or what-have-you?'

The doctor turns from Sarah to you. 'There's no proof that any of these therapies will work. They've been used mainly on patients suffering from degenerative disease, such as Parkinson's and Alzheimer's, rather than on massive trauma. She's breathing for herself and we are feeding her through a tube. So this state can go on indefinitely. But I'm not sure that it qualifies as *living*. And although now it seems a relief that she's not going to die, it can have problems for the family.'

'Are you talking about a court order for withdrawing food and fluid?' Sarah asks, and I think if a tiger was reincarnated as a police officer she would look like Sarah.

'Of course not,' Dr Bailstrom says. 'It's early days and would be premature to—'

'But that's where you're headed?' Sarah interrupts, prowling around her.

'In time, there may be a conversation about whether it's in Grace's best interests—'

'She knows about books, paintings, all sorts of stuff,' you say, interrupting. 'She doesn't see how clever she is but she's the brightest person I've ever met. All those thoughts she has and feelings and knowledge, all that kindness and warmth and funniness. It can't just *go*.'

'Mr Covey, we will continue to do tests,' Dr Bailstrom says to you. 'But there really is no chance that your wife will ever regain consciousness.'

'You said that she could live for years,' you say to her. 'So one day there'll be a cure. And we'll just have to wait, for as long as it takes.'

A little while later Mum arrives at my bedside. Unlike you and Sarah, she didn't argue with the doctors, and I'd seen each medical fact—*supposed* medical fact—hitting her face like flying glass.

'A nurse is with Addie,' she says. 'I can't leave him long. But I had to talk to you on my own.' She pauses. 'Someone's going to have to tell him that you're not going to wake up.'

'Mum, you can't do that!'

'I just want what's best for him,' Mum says quietly.

'How can this be best for Ads? Jesus!'

It's been years since we argued. Of all times and places we shouldn't start now, here.

'I know that you can hear me, Gracie, angel. Wherever you are.'

'I'm right here, Mum. And soon their tests will pick it up. I'm going to be Roger Federer, smashing the ball at 100 miles an hour for a "YES, I CAN UNDERSTAND YOU!" And once they know that I can still think, they'll try to find a way of getting me well again.'

'I'd better get back to Addie.'

She pulls the curtain aside. Jenny is waiting and has clearly overheard. She looks so anxious.

'Granny G is wrong,' I say to her. 'And so are the doctors. I can think, talk and feel, can't I? Their scans aren't sophisticated enough, that's all. So one day, hopefully soon, I'll give them a great big surprise.'

But she's still anxious, her head bent down and her narrow shoulders hunched together. 'You were so brave. Going into the school for me.'

'It's really nice of you, but it was just instinct. Something any mother would do for their child.'

We are interrupted by Sarah arriving, with a ramrod-straight woman with steel-grey hair in her late sixties, who I know but can't quite place.

'Mrs Fisher,' Jenny says, surprised. The old secretary at Sidley House.

She's brought me a fat bunch of sweet peas. The scent is glorious.

Sarah looks along my vases of flowers, then deftly bins Silas Hyman's ugly yellow roses. She smiles at Mrs Fisher. 'I think in the race for space here, yours win.'

'I didn't think I'd actually see her,' Mrs Fisher says to Sarah. 'I just wanted to bring her flowers. We used to talk about gardening sometimes.'

'Would you mind having a chat with me?' Sarah asks. 'I'm a police officer and Grace's sister-in-law.'

'Of course,' Mrs Fisher replies. 'But I don't think I'll be of any help.'

Sarah escorts her into the relatives' room.

'You said you were the secretary at Sidley House?'

'For almost thirteen years. I had to leave in April. Apparently I was too old to do the job. The head teacher told me that if I looked at my contract I'd see that there was "a policy of non-voluntary retirement for all support staff at sixty". I'm sixty-seven. She'd waited seven years before enforcing the clause.'

'Can you tell me what your duties were at the school?'

'Certainly. I did all the basic secretarial ones, such as answer the phone and type up letters. I was also responsible for the registers. I was the first point of contact for potential new families, sending out prospectuses and organising invitations to open days; then getting the paperwork ready for all the new children. I was also the school nurse. That was the part of my job I enjoyed most actually, really just putting on ice packs and sometimes using an EpiPen. I'd tuck the child under a blanket on my sofa and then wait with them for Mum or a nanny to arrive.'

'And were you too old for the job?'

'No. I was still good at it. Everyone knew it, including Sally Healey.'

'So do you know why she got rid of you?'

'You don't mince your words. No. I've no idea.'

Sarah took out a notebook, one with little owls on it, and wrote something down. 'Can I have your details?' she asks. 'Your full name is Mrs . . .?'

'Elizabeth Fisher. And it's Ms. My husband left me six months ago.'

Sarah looks sympathetic but I feel cold. Mrs Healey sent all the parents a letter saying Mrs Fisher's husband was terminally ill and that was the reason she'd had to leave the school. I'd organised a card and Maisie had traipsed off to some snazzy flower place in Richmond for a bouquet for her. Why did Mrs Healey lie?

'Can you write down your address?'

As Elizabeth writes down her details, Sarah asks her, 'Do you know Silas Hyman?'

'Yes. He was a teacher at Sidley House. He was fired a month before me.'

'Why he was fired?'

'In a nutshell? An eight-year-old boy called Robert Fleming wanted him out.'

'And the longer version?'

'Robert Fleming loathed Silas because he was the first teacher to stand up to him. Silas called Fleming's parents in, during the first week he had Robert in his class, and used the word "wicked" about their son. Not suffering from some attention deficit disorder or a problem with socialisation. Wicked.

'In March, when Silas was on playground duty, Fleming told him that an eleven-year-old boy had locked himself in the toilets with a five-year-old little girl, and she was screaming. Fleming said he couldn't find any other teacher. So Silas went to the little girl's aid. For all his faults, he's very kind like that.

'When he'd got Silas out of the playground, Fleming forced a boy called Daniel up the fire escape and then managed to get him over the edge. God knows what he must have said to the little chap. Then Fleming pushed him. He broke both his legs. It was lucky it wasn't his neck. I looked after him until the ambulance arrived. Poor little mite was in terrible pain.'

I'd had only Adam's version of events, and adult rumours, distorted as time went by. It became a terrible accident, not deliberate, and the blame was targeted on Mr Hyman for not supervising the playground. Because who wants to believe an eight-year-old child can be that malevolent?

But we already knew that he was from Adam, who lived in physical fear of him. We knew this wasn't like regular teasing and bullying. He pulled Adam's tie round his neck, leaving a red welt for a week afterwards, saying he'd kill him if he didn't 'kiss his butt'. He wound a skipping rope round Adam, tying him up, while he drew swastikas on his body. Jenny called him psycho-child and you agreed.

It was after the swastika incident that you got a guarantee from Mrs Healey that Robert Fleming wouldn't be coming back to Sidley House in September.

'Mrs Healey knew that a playground accident like that should never have happened in a primary school,' Mrs Fisher continues. 'She needed someone to blame, so she blamed Silas Hyman. I don't think she wanted to fire him for it. She could recognise a gifted teacher, as a business asset if nothing else. But then there was that article in the *Richmond Post* and the phone didn't stop ringing with parents wanting action. So she had no choice, as she saw it. Parents have a great deal of power in a private school.

'The really appalling thing is if that wicked boy *had* been blamed and hauled over the coals, there might have been a fighting chance of stopping him before it was too late. If he can plan and execute *at eight* breaking a boy's legs, what will he do at eighteen?'

'Do you know who told the press?'

'No. I don't.'

'Does Silas Hyman have any enemies?'

'None that I know of.'

'You said earlier, "for all his faults". What do you mean by that?'

'I shouldn't have said it. I just mean that he was arrogant. Male teachers in a primary school are a rare species. He was a cockerel in the hen-house.' She pauses and I can see she's fighting off tears. 'How are they,' she asks, 'Jenny and Mrs Covey?'

'Both of them are critically injured.'

Elizabeth Fisher's ramrod-straight posture bends a little and she turns her face from Sarah, as if embarrassed by her emotion.

'Adam's a lovely little boy,' she continues. 'A credit to Mrs Covey. I wish I'd told her that, but I didn't.'

Sarah looks moved by her, and Elizabeth Fisher has the encouragement she needs to continue.

'Some of them hardly bother to say hello to their mothers at the end of the day, and the mothers are too busy gossiping to really focus on their child. But Adam runs out there like a plane coming in to land, with his arms out to Mrs Covey, and she looks like there's no one else in the entire place but him. I used to watch them out of my office window.'

She hasn't got anyone to talk to about us, I realise, with her husband gone. And she can hardly contact anyone at school after the embarrassing flowers-for-a-dying-husband.

'Have you any idea who might have set fire to the school?' Sarah asks.

'No. But if I were you, I'd look for someone like Robert Fleming as an adult—because no one intervened early enough.'

As Jenny and I return to my ward, I remember that meeting you had with Mrs Healey about Robert Fleming. I'd been annoyed she'd listened to you when she hadn't listened to me all those times I'd gone into school and complained. I'd thought it was because you're a man and I was just another mum with spare PE socks in my handbag. You said it was because of your celebrity status: 'I can kick up a smellier stink.'

Maisie is arriving next to my bed. She sits down and takes my hand. I now know that the confident, exuberant, 'not-giving-a-hoot!' Maisie doesn't exist, but her kindness and warmth are genuine.

'You're looking lots better,' she says to me, smiling at me as if I can see her as well as hear her. 'Roses in your cheeks! And you don't even use blusher, do you? Not like me. I have to slap on the stuff, but you look that way naturally.'

When she came to see me last time, I was sure she was going to tell me something but was interrupted. Maybe she'll confide in me now about Donald. I hope so. One of the things about all this I find so hard is that she didn't, or couldn't, turn to me.

She's fumbling in the pocket of her cardigan. She takes out Jenny's mobile, with the little charm on it that Adam gave her for Christmas.

'Tilly, the Reception teacher, gave it to me,' Maisie says.

Jen is staring at her phone in silence. Inside are texts of parties and travel plans and everyday chat with her friends; a teenage life in eight cen-timetres of plastic.

'Tilly found it on the gravel outside the school,' Maisie continues. 'Gave it to me as I got in the ambulance with Rowena. Wanted to make sure I gave it to Jenny. Then I just forgot about it. I'm sorry.'

'How could she just *forget*?' Jenny asks.

'There was a lot going on,' I say, marvelling at my understatement.

Maisie finds a space between the vases of flowers for the phone. 'Found it in the pocket of my cardi and wanted her to have it back. You know girls and their mobiles.'

'But Ivo and I were texting each other while I was up in the medical room. And then it was the fire and I was still inside. So how come she found this *outside*?' asks Jenny.

'I don't know, sweetheart.'

'Maybe the arsonist stole it from me and then dropped it by mistake.'

'But why would he steal it? Maybe you went outside for some reason,' I say. 'And then returned.'

'But why would I do that?'

I have no idea. We're both silent.

Maisie chatters on as if we're in her kitchen together. Until today I'd thought Maisie's babbling way of speaking was from a surfeit of things to say, a friendly warm outpouring, but maybe it's more of a nervous habit, a flow of chat to swirl over underlying jagged unhappiness.

Like the baggy, soft cardigan now covering her bruises.

'They wouldn't let Jenny have her phone in the intensive-care unit,' she continues. 'In case it interfered with the machinery. So I'll leave it next to you and tell Mike it's here.' Maisie turns slightly away from me. 'There's something I have to tell you, Gracie. I don't want you to hate me for it. Please. Donald came to visit Rowena earlier.'

Finally, she'll confide in me. And I want her to. Maybe it will unburden her a little.

'He's so proud of her.'

'Oh, for God's sake,' Jenny says. But I try to understand. Perhaps Maisie needs to keep that film of a happy family playing, because the reality— Donald hurting her already injured child—is just too hard.

'You know I'd do anything for Rowena,' she says quietly. 'Don't you, Gracie?'

'Except leave your husband so that he can't hurt her any more,' Jenny snaps.

'It's not that simple, Jen.'

'Oh, I think it is.'

'I didn't finish telling you what happened,' Maisie continues. 'So you don't know why he's so proud.'

'This is absurd,' Jenny says. I beckon her to be quiet so we can hear.

'I told you that when you ran into the building, *I ran away*, to the bridge, and we all pushed cars out of the way. While I was there, Rowena went into the school. She'd seen you run in too. Heard you screaming for

Jenny. She found a towel in the PE shed and she soaked it in water. She put it over her face. Then she went into the school to help you.'

Dear God. Rowena going into a burning building. For Jenny. For me.

'They think she must have been overcome by fumes. She was unconscious when the firemen got to her. She's not badly hurt, but they were worried she might have some kind of internal damage; they're still keeping a lookout for that.'

I never guessed she had that kind of courage. Instinct and love made me run into that building and then pushed and shoved me onwards. I needed Jenny in my arms more than I needed to save myself. But Rowena went in without instinct. With just her courage pushing her on.

Rowena was comforting Adam as I ran into the building, not pausing to even speak to him. Was it Adam's misery that prompted her?

'I didn't realise she was even missing,' Maisie says. 'When the fire engines got to the school there were so many people and I thought she was there, among the crowd.'

'I think she was trying to make her father proud, again,' Jenny says.

'And then a fireman brought her out and she was unconscious,' Maisie continues. 'When I told Donald—'

She breaks off, distressed. Then, with effort and emotion, continues, 'You shouldn't condemn someone, should you? If you love them, if they're your family, you have to try to see the good. I mean, that's what love is in some ways, isn't it? Believing in someone's goodness.'

Maisie holds my hand more tightly.

'It's funny, in one afternoon you know what you're made of. And you also discover what your child's made of. And you can feel such *shame* and such *pride* at the same time.'

But it's her father, not her mother, who Rowena wants to be proud of her. It was for him she went into the burning school. And it was in vain.

I remember the ugly hatred in Donald's voice. '*Quite the little heroine, aren't you?*' Her cry of pain as he grabbed hold of her burnt hands.

Sarah arrives, looking as briskly efficient as ever, and I am grateful for her competence. Maisie is sitting silently next to me, as if spent.

'Hello, Grace, me again,' Sarah says. 'It's like Piccadilly Circus in here this evening.'

'You think she can hear too?' Maisie says.

'Absolutely. I'm Sarah. Grace's sister-in-law.'

'Maisie White. A friend.'

'So are you Rowena White's mother?' Sarah asks, a savvy police officer instantly recognising names.

'Yes.'

'There's a canteen open somewhere. Would you like to get a cup of tea with me? Or at least something that passes for tea?'

She isn't giving Maisie much option.

I hope to God she'll get Maisie to tell her about the domestic abuse so Sarah will add Donald to her list of suspects.

As they leave, Sarah spots Jenny's mobile phone.

'It's Jen's,' Maisie says. 'A teacher found it outside the school.'

Sarah picks up the phone and puts it in her pocket.

'I'll be in the garden,' Jenny says, her frustration and upset clear.

I follow Sarah and Maisie to the cafeteria. The Palms Café is empty and the strip lights turned off, but the door's open and the hot-drinks machine is working. Sarah gets styrofoam cups of something masquerading as tea and they sit together at a Formica table. The only light now is from the corridor, making this room shadowy and strange.

'I'm trying to find out a little more about what happened,' Sarah says.

'Grace told me that you're a policewoman. I mean, I already told the police.'

'Right now, I'm just Grace's sister-in-law and Jenny's aunt. Would you mind telling me what you remember about yesterday afternoon?'

'Of course. I'd come to pick Rowena up from school. She's a teaching assistant. I was chuffed when she asked me to give her a lift home. I hadn't seen much of her lately. You know what teenage girls are like.' She trails off. 'Sorry, this isn't important, sorry.'

Sarah smiles at her, encouraging her to continue.

'I thought she'd be out on the playing field helping with sports day. But Gracie told me she'd gone into the school with Addie, to get his cake—' She breaks off, putting her knuckle into her mouth to bite away a sob. 'I just can't think about it properly, about Addie, with his mum so . . .'

'That's all right. Take your time.'

'I'd just gone into the school to find her when I heard a loud noise, like an air-raid siren. It took me a few moments to realise what it was. I hurried out, worried about Rowena. Then I saw her coming out of the secretary's office. I saw Adam was safely outside by the statue. But I didn't know about Jenny.'

'Which floor is the secretary's office?' Sarah asks.

'The upper ground. Just next to the main door. I told Rowena to look after Addie and I went to help the Reception children. I went down to the lower-ground floor where their classroom is. It wasn't so smoky down there and they have their own exit with a ramp leading back up to the area outside the school. Tilly—Miss Rogers—was getting all the children out. I helped her calm them down. I know them all, you see. I read with them once a week.'

'Did you see anyone other than Rowena and Adam and the Reception teacher?'

'No. Well, not in the school. But about five minutes later the new secretary came outside. There was a lot of smoke by then but she was smiling, like she was enjoying it, or at least she was not at all upset, and she had lipstick on. Sorry. Silly.'

'It was five minutes after the alarm that she came out? You're sure?'

'No, I can't be totally sure. But we'd got the children out and lined up, counted them at least five times. She brought Tilly the register to officially check they were all accounted for, but we knew they were.'

Sarah hasn't drunk her tea, concentrating every ounce of attention on Maisie, while not letting her feel it. 'And then?'

'A few minutes later, the fire got worse. There was a huge bang, and flames, and smoke was pouring out of the windows. I saw Gracie running towards the school, screaming. She was so relieved when she saw Adam, but then she was yelling for Jenny, over and over, and I realised that Jenny must be inside. And Gracie ran in.'

I see the pressure of tears building behind Maisie's face.

Sarah is looking at her intently now. 'Did you know that Adam has been accused of starting the fire?' she asks.

Maisie is astonished. Is that why Sarah told her—in order to gauge her response? She must clearly see now that Maisie's astonishment is genuine.

'Oh God, that poor family.' Tears break free and stream down her face. 'Sorry, selfish. I've no right to cry, have I, not when Gracie and Jenny . . .'

Sarah picks up Maisie's cup. 'I'll get you another?'

'Thank you.'

This small act of kindness seems to relax Maisie a little.

'What do you know about Silas Hyman?' Sarah asks as she goes to the drinks machine.

'He's dangerous,' Maisie says immediately. 'Violent. But you'd never guess that. I mean, he's a sham. And he gets people to love him. Young people. Exploits their feelings for him.'

I am taken aback by her vehemence, and how sure she is about him. How does she know?

'In what way is he a sham?' Sarah asks.

'I thought he was *kind*, really caring,' Maisie says. 'Wonderful, actually. When I read with the children, I take one at a time up to the first floor and we sit on the rug together. Mr Hyman taught in the other classroom on that floor. You'd hear his class laughing. And there was music too. He was always playing them something. I worked it out in the end. It was Mozart for Maths and jazz for getting changed for Sport because it speeded them up. And he had special names for them all. His whole focus in the school seemed to be the children, inspiring them and making them happy. He had me fooled.'

Sarah joins her with two new cups of tea. 'When did you realise you'd been fooled?' she asks.

Maisie takes the tea and fusses with a packet of sugar before she answers. 'At the school prize-giving. We give a prize, you see, every year. For Science. Rowena's going to read Science at Oxford. Sorry. I mean, that's why we were there. He barged in, looking so *angry*, and then he swore at the headmistress. Threatened all of us. But no one else took it seriously. They just found him embarrassing.'

'But you took him seriously?' Sarah asks.

At the prize-giving Donald was sitting pressed up next to her. Maisie knows first-hand that threats of violence can translate into the real thing.

'Yes. I phoned Sally Healey, the headmistress, later that evening and told her she should get the police to make sure he wasn't allowed near the school again. A restraining order, I think it's called? I'm not sure.'

'Did she?'

Maisie shook her head and I saw the upset on her face.

'You said he gets young people to love him,' Sarah continues. 'And exploits their feelings?'

'Grace told me that Addie adored him,' Maisie says. 'But I didn't realise how much till the prize-giving, when Addie stood up and defended Silas Hyman. Told everyone that he shouldn't have been fired.'

'That was brave,' Sarah says.

'It's wrong to make someone adore you,' Maisie says, emotion shaking her voice, 'when they're young and can't properly think for themselves. That's exploitation. And you can make them do what you want.'

Her anger is both startling and touching. I know what she's suggesting and so does Sarah. But no one could have made Addie light a fire.

I don't blame Maisie for thinking Adam easily manipulated. He's always been shy with adults, even Maisie. And after the prize-giving he'd looked so cowed, flinching from Donald's lighter.

'I should get back to my daughter,' Maisie says. 'I told her I wouldn't be long.'

'Of course,' Sarah says, standing up. 'One of my colleagues told me of her bravery at the scene. I'd like to speak to her, if that would be all right? Just to get it all straight for myself.'

'She's upset at the moment,' Maisie says, looking fearful. 'I mean, after everything that's happened. So would you mind waiting?'

Is she afraid Rowena will tell Sarah about Donald?

'Not at all,' Sarah replies. 'I'll pop by tomorrow. See if she's feeling up to talking to me then.'

Maisie leaves and Sarah writes up notes in the owl-covered notebook.

'So get her to give a new statement right now,' you say vehemently.

Sarah has joined you at Jenny's bedside.

'Tell Baker that someone else knew that he was violent,' you continue. 'Christ, if Maisie thinks that about him, other people will too.'

'At the moment there's no point,' Sarah says patiently. 'Not unless and until his alibi is broken. And I also need to pursue other avenues at the same time.'

She makes you go for a sleep, while she takes your place.

And I return to the garden where Jenny is waiting.

In the cool of the evening it's different out here. Someone has watered the flowers and filled the birdbath. If you look straight up, past the perpendicular walls on all sides, studded with glass windows, you can see the shot-silk dark blue sky that you get late on a summer's evening.

We don't feel pain out here and I think it's because although we're outside, the garden is in the middle of the hospital and those perpendicular walls that rise up all around us offer us protection.

My senses are much more receptive now—I can smell the subtlest, smallest thing, as if lacking a body has left my senses exposed. Now the air feels softly weighted with the heavy summer perfumes of jasmine and roses and honeysuckle. And there's another, sweeter perfume, igniting emotions I shouldn't be feeling—nervousness and excitement.

It's the smell of night stocks and I am in a Cambridge garden on a warm summer evening, my mind filled with paintings and books and ideas. I'm with you. And the stocks are releasing their fragrance like confetti over my love for you and my anxiety about exams and my excitement for the future.

Memories are usually like a DVD playing, not connected to the room you're in while you remember.

But I'm actually *there*, Mike. My feelings pungently real.

Love punches me in the solar plexus.

Then it's over and I'm back in this boxed piece of summer.

There's something significant about what's just happened, something I can use to help my children. But the thought is slipping away and I have to grab it by its coattails before it's gone.

It was Jenny hearing the fire alarm going off at the school. '*It was like I was back in the school, really back there.*'

I turn to her. 'When we saw Donald White with Maisie and Rowena, do you remember smelling something?'

Because I remember now the smell of Donald's cigarettes.

'Perhaps. Yes,' Jenny replies.

'Do you think that's why you heard the fire alarm?' I ask.

'My mad person's tinnitus? It's possible, I suppose. I didn't really analyse it.'

I hear a child screaming. Adam. I jerk my head round. He isn't here.

'No! She's not dead. She's *not*!' Too small a voice for such huge words.

I run to him.

He's hunched over my bed, silent. He'd never cried out his grief but I'd heard him. Mum's arms are round him.

'I'm here!' I say to him. '*Right here*. No one knows that yet but they will.

And I'll wake up, my sweetie! Of course I will! I'm giving you a kiss and you can't feel it, but I'm here. Kissing you now.'

I force myself into my body but my vocal cords are still snapped and useless and my eyelids still welded shut. I try with all my might to touch him, but my arms are beams of impossible weight. There is nothing I can do to reach him.

Mum's face is white as she tries to comfort Adam. Maybe I should feel angry with her. But it's tearing her apart and I know the courage it took.

Addie pulls away from her and runs. She goes after him and grabs him. He goes limp and she puts her arms round him, like a body cushion against excruciating pain.

His face looks so pale, bruised shadows under his eyes. He's withdrawn even further into himself as if his whole body is now mute.

I will wake up. One day *I will wake up.*

As soon as I see your face, I know that no heart has been found for her. I go close to you and you tell me that there's time! It's still going to be all right! Not to be defeatist! She will get better. *Of course she will.* You don't need to speak for me to hear your burly tough optimism. Because although we no longer have a solar plexus love, we have the married kind, which means that your voice—you—are inside my mind.

Sarah arrives, her clothes crumpled. She was doing shifts at Jenny's bedside with you last night.

'I got through to Ivo,' she says. 'He's trying to get a standby flight.'

You just nod.

You *knew* about this, Mike? You must have done for Sarah to have his number. And you thought this was *OK?* My voice clearly isn't in your head, because this is a *terrible* idea. Or perhaps my voice is in your head and you just ignored me. Yes, I'm cross. Of course I'm bloody cross.

Has Sarah told him what Jenny looks like now?

Can anyone describe Jenny's face and body now?

Last Saturday they went to Chiswick House together. *'What did you do?'* I'd asked her that evening, thinking they'd gone to the café, or had a picnic. When she didn't answer, I'd imagined all sorts of canoodling. Finally, a little embarrassed, she'd told me—they'd just looked at one another; spent the long sunny hours staring at each other's faces.

Maybe if you'd known how they spent their afternoon, you'd have known it wasn't a good idea. Because what will he think when he looks at her now? And how can she bear his rejection?

I'm sorry. You think she's unconscious and will be totally unaware of him. You've no idea how badly she may be hurt by this.

Crossness and apologies. As in our old life together, our children pull us apart as frequently as they unite us.

In the corridor Jenny is beaming. 'He's going to get a standby flight. Aunt Sarah phoned him.'

'Did she . . .' How can I ask this?

'No. She didn't tell him what I look like now, if that's what you're worried about? But it won't matter. That sounds stupid. Of course it will matter. What I mean is, it won't change anything.'

What can I say? That only tough-as-old-boots married love could withstand this, not their fragile five-months-old romance; that 'love is not love which alters when it alteration finds' doesn't apply to teenage boys.

'I thought you'd be pleased,' Jenny says, a little baffled. 'I mean, I know you don't like him much.' A very short pause, just space enough for me to argue, but I don't and she continues, 'He'll tell the police about the red paint now, won't he?'

'Yes. Of course.'

Sarah walks past us on the phone. 'This takes precedence,' Sarah says, then pauses. 'No, *you* take some time off work. [Pause.] I don't have time for this right now.'

She must be talking to Roger. You try to like him out of loyalty to your sister, but I annually resent his sneering face at the Christmas table when he actually tries to win pulling the crackers. Competitive about his own children, dismissive of ours; frankly, I loathe him, and perhaps that's one reason I used to dislike Sarah, for being a unit with him.

She hasn't mentioned her own family to you, putting us absolutely centre stage. I'm only just discovering that how someone behaves in everyday life gives no clue how they'll be when it counts.

'She and Uncle Roger don't get along any more,' Jenny says to me as if reading my thoughts. So Sarah has talked to Jenny about her marriage. My God, who isn't talking to Jenny about their marriage?

Sarah abruptly ends the conversation, saying she has to go.

Jenny and I go with her.

A nurse answers the door of the burns unit, surprised to see Sarah.

'Jenny's been taken to ICU, didn't anyone—?'

'Yes, actually it's Rowena White I want to see. She's been friends with Jenny since primary school, and you know how people become friends of the family too.' She stumbles as she speaks; telling half-truths has never been Sarah before.

The nurse lets her in and we follow her to Rowena's side room. A woman is wheeled past on a trolley.

'I can't do this right now, Mum,' Jenny says and I curse myself for bringing her into the burns unit. 'I'll be back in a little while, OK?'

She leaves.

In Rowena's room, a nurse is taking the dressings off Rowena's hands. 'Some of the blisters have burst . . .?' she says to Rowena, surprised.

'Yes, I know. I told the other nurse about it yesterday.'

The nurse looks through Rowena's notes. 'So you did. You said you . . . slipped . . .? But there's damage to the top of your hands as well as the palms?' the nurse says.

Rowena is silent and doesn't meet her eye.

'It may mean you'll have to stay here longer. We have to be so careful about infection. You know about all that, don't you? I think I already read you my riot act?'

'Yes, you did. Thank you.'

'I'll be back to see you in a bit.'

As the nurse leaves, Sarah comes in.

'Hello, Rowena. I'm Sarah, Jenny's aunt. I'm also a police officer. Is your mother not here?'

'She's gone to get me a few things from home.'

'How are you feeling?' Sarah asks.

'Fine. Getting much better now.' Rowena seems at ease with Sarah.

'It was incredibly brave. What you did.'

Rowena looks embarrassed. 'You saw it in the paper?'

Rowena's rescue effort was hidden in the middle pages of the *Richmond Post*. I'm not sure if you read that far. It was in the mode of 'Very Small Earthquake Not Many Killed'—'Plain Girl Runs To Help But Doesn't Rescue Anyone And Is Slightly Hurt'. Tara wouldn't let anything detract from the main story of beautiful Jenny.

'I saw it, yes,' Sarah says.

'It wasn't brave though. I mean, I didn't have time to be brave. Wasn't thinking really.'

'Well, I disagree,' Sarah says. She sits down next to her.

'Mum told me about Adam,' Rowena says. 'It's just so terrible. I mean, he's such a lovely boy. He was only a baby really when I was at Sidley House with Jenny. But I got to know him last summer, when I was doing work experience there. I was his classroom assistant and he was just so . . . well, good. And thoughtful. Really polite. It's just wrong what they're saying about him. Awful.

'And *anyone* could have got in,' Rowena continues earnestly. 'Annette, the school secretary, is pretty lax about security. Presses the buzzer to let people in without looking at the monitor on her desk.'

'Can you tell me what you remember from Wednesday?' Sarah asks. 'Start from when you went to the school with Adam?'

'OK. He wanted to get his birthday cake. I knew he'd be embarrassed if his mum went with him. I mean, it's not cool in front of his friends, is it, to go with your mum? So I asked him if he'd like me to go with him. I had to get the medals anyway. We went into the school together, and I went straight to the secretary's office and Adam went to get his cake.'

'Which floor is Adam's classroom on?' Sarah asks.

'The second. But it's the other side of the hallway from the Art room. That's where they said the fire started, isn't it? I mean, it's on the second floor too, but not close.'

She seems young and not terribly convincing as she tries to help Adam.

'So you were in the office, while Adam went to his classroom?' Sarah prompts.

'Yes. Annette was in there and she chatted to me about something silly. Then the alarm went off. I went out of the office, calling for Adam. And then I heard Mum calling for me.'

'So you were with Annette in the office when the alarm went off?'

'Yes.'

Sarah must be crossing people off her list of suspects. The office is two floors beneath the Art room. Neither Rowena nor Annette could have started the fire.

'I saw Adam running out of the school,' Rowena continues. 'Mum told me to go outside with Addie and then she went to help with the Reception children.'

'Do you remember if Adam was holding anything?'

'No. I'm sure he wasn't. I'd have noticed. Do you want me to tell some-one that? Is it important?'

Sarah shakes her head. Presumably because DI Baker would say that Adam could easily have discarded the matches by then.

'Did you see anyone else?' Sarah asks.

'I'm not sure. I might have done. It was only a glimpse. I'm sorry, that's not helpful at all, but I can't remember any more. I'm not sure if I just imagined it.'

'If you do remember—'

'Yes, of course. I'll tell the police. Straight away.'

'OK,' Sarah says. 'So you went outside to join Adam. What happened then?'

'He was panicking, looking for Jenny. He said that she wasn't out at sports day. When I saw Annette come out, I asked her if she'd brought the office register. You know, the book where you sign in and out? But she hadn't. She said it was OK because there was no one else in the building. I asked her if she was sure and she said that she was. The fire was really bad by then. There'd been this big bang, and loads more smoke and flames.' She looks upset. 'I never even thought that Jenny might still be in there.'

'Then Adam saw his mother running into the building shouting for Jenny,' Rowena continues. 'He tried to go after her. I had to stop him. It was awful.'

'And that's when you went in?'

Rowena nods.

'Before you went in, do you remember how long it was until Annette came out to join you?'

'She wasn't there straight away. I suppose if I had to guess, it would be a few minutes.'

'Your mum said Annette had lipstick on.'

'I don't remember that. Is it important?'

'It's a little odd to put on lipstick in the circumstances, don't you think?'

I think Sarah's confiding in Rowena to win her trust a little so that Rowena will confide more in return. Maybe she's sensed Rowena is keep-ing something from her.

'I don't know if it's odd,' Rowena says stiffly. 'And I didn't notice. I'm not much good at things like make-up, actually.'

She's so awkward and I feel for her.

'You said you were Adam's classroom assistant last summer,' Sarah says. 'Does that mean you were assisting Silas Hyman?'

'No. Addie was still in Year Two then. Mr Hyman teaches Year Three.'

'Did you get to know him?'

Rowena shakes her head. 'He wouldn't have talked to someone like me. Wouldn't have noticed me.'

'But you noticed him?'

'Well, he's very good-looking, isn't he?'

'What did you think of him?'

Rowena hesitates a moment. 'I thought he could be violent.'

'What made you think that?'

I think it's the years of violence by her father, which makes her more perceptive to viciousness.

'I used to watch him sometimes,' Rowena says. 'He never noticed me.'

'You saw through him?'

'I don't think it's like that, like he's hiding the real person inside. More like he's two different people.'

'One good, one bad?'

'I know it sounds strange, but if you read about it, I mean literature going way back when, it's something that's been happening for centuries. You know morality tales in the Middle Ages, the good angel and the devil? And the Jacobean plays with fighting for someone's soul. It's not the person's *fault* the devil is there. You have to help that person get rid of him.'

Was she talking about Silas Hyman or her father? She wasn't doing English for A level so must have scoured books looking for something to make sense of it all.

'You said to me that you weren't really thinking,' Sarah says. 'When you went into the school.'

'That's right.'

'You were thinking enough to get a towel and soak it in water.'

'I should have taken three, shouldn't I? And I didn't do any good. Didn't help.' She starts to cry. 'Sorry. Being a twit.'

The same word that Maisie uses about herself; a self-denigrating, middle-aged word.

'Don't say that, please don't,' I say to her. 'It's not a word that any teenager should use. You went into a burning building, for God's sake.'

'Mum?'

I see Jenny has come in.

'She did. And don't tell me it was all about Donald, and some wish to make her father proud.'

'OK . . .'

'You listen to me, Rowena! Whatever made you do it you're extraordinary. And I will not let your father's abuse blind me—or anyone else—to your bravery.'

'Blimey, Mum, you socked it to her. In a good way, I mean.'

'Shame she can't hear me.'

Sarah is looking through her notes. 'If I could just go back to the secretary for a moment? Are you sure that she said everyone was out?'

'Yes. Definitely. Later, I mean after Jenny had been brought out, she said that Jenny had signed herself out. Said she remembered her doing it.'

'It would explain why your phone was outside,' I say to Jen.

'Maybe,' she says, her voice unusually quiet. I see that she looks pale and tense, her fingers knotting together. 'I can't remember, Mum. It just doesn't make sense. Why would I sign myself out, and then go in again? But why would Annette lie?'

SARAH FINDS THE NURSE who was with Rowena earlier.

'The injuries to Rowena White's hands, do you think they were an accident?' she asks. 'I mean, the more recent damage?'

So she's guessed.

'You're Jenny's aunt, right?'

'Yes. I'm also a police officer.'

'Have you got ID?'

Sarah digs in her bag for her warrant card and shows it—Detective Sergeant McBride. 'My married name,' she says.

'OK. I don't think the injuries were accidental. At least, I can't see how she could have got them if she tripped. The blisters on the tops of her hands have been damaged too.'

I remember Donald brutally gripping hold of her bandaged hands. Rowena's sharp scream of pain.

'Do you know when the injuries happened?'

'No. But the blisters were undamaged at four thirty yesterday. I changed her dressings myself. But then I went off shift at five.'

'Do you know who was on after you?'

'Belinda Edwards. I'll find her for you.'

Ten minutes later, Sarah is with Belinda.

'It was after her father visited,' she says. 'I spoke to her when I arrived on my shift and she was fine, cheerful even. Her father came to see her shortly afterwards. He wasn't with her long. When he'd gone, I went in to give her her drugs. She and her mother were distressed. Rowena was trying not to show how much pain she was in, but it had clearly increased. I took the dressings off her hands and saw that the blisters had burst on both hands.'

'She told you she tripped . . .?' Sarah asks.

'Yes, and that she put her hands out to save herself. But that wouldn't explain the damage on the tops of her hands too.'

'Do you have Rowena's past medical record?'

'We're not computerised yet, so I'll have to chase up the records.'

'And can you get Maisie White's, her mother's?'

Belinda's eyes meet Sarah's and an unspoken accord passes between them. 'I'll chase them up for you in the same way,' she says.

Sarah is going to go to the police station.

'We need to know everything,' I say to Jenny. 'Can you stay here in case Donald comes back? We need to watch him too.'

She looks at me. 'How long d'you think it takes, from Barbados?'

'About nine hours,' I say.

She smiles a shy, happy smile and I hate Ivo for making her smile like that and for what will happen when he gets here.

I leave the hospital with Sarah.

In the car Sarah talks to Roger on her hands-free, finishing their earlier argument. He accuses her of forgetting it was 'your son's' deadline for his coursework this week. She tells him that you need her more. He says she should start allocating her time 'more carefully'. She tells him there's a call waiting and hangs up.

She parks and we go inside the police station and down a corridor with paint-peeling walls and concrete floors. A young woman police officer comes down the corridor. She hugs Sarah and asks her about Jenny and me. Then an older male officer takes her hand as he passes her and says how sorry he is and asks if there's anything he can do.

We go into a main office area, which reeks of deodorant and sweat, fans overhead whirring noisily and ineffectually against the heat. And everyone in here comes up to ask after Jenny and me, to offer sympathy. I realise she is loved and valued here.

She goes into a side office and an attractive man in his thirties, with caramel-coloured skin, virtually runs across the small space and puts his arms round her and holds her tightly. He's not wearing a uniform so must be CID.

'Hi, Mohsin,' she says, as he hugs her.

'Poor baby.'

Baby? Sarah? Behind them, a woman in her twenties is pretending to look at a computer monitor. A sharply cut auburn bob frames her angular face. She's the only person who hasn't offered sympathy.

'Penny?' Sarah says, and the severe-featured young woman turns to her. 'Where are we on the hate-mail investigation?'

'I'm going over the original statements now. Tony and Pete are trying to locate footage from the CCTV camera which records the postbox where the third letter was posted.'

'I think the hate mail could well be linked to the arson attack,' Sarah says.

Penny and Mohsin say nothing.

'All right,' Sarah says, tightlipped. 'Maybe it is just an extraordinary coincidence that Jenny was sent hate mail and then her place of work was set on fire and she was the only member of staff to be badly injured.'

'But the campaign against her had stopped, right?' Penny asks. I hope to God that Ivo will tell them about the paint attack just a few weeks ago.

'We need a connection, honey,' Mohsin says.

'Her oxygen may have been tampered with,' Sarah says.

Penny's eyes flick to hers. 'May?'

'It's being downplayed,' Sarah continues. 'By the hospital and by Baker.

But I think that someone tried to make sure they finished the job.'

'Downplayed?' Penny asks and I see the irritation on Sarah's face. 'Baker's not incompetent.' She turns back to her computer screen.

'Who was this witness who supposedly saw my nephew?' Sarah asks, going closer to her.

'Detective Inspector Baker has made it absolutely clear that the witness's anonymity must be respected.'

Sarah turns to Mohsin. 'It's not in the file?'

'No,' responds Penny. 'DI Baker thought you might come asking for it.'

'So he's hidden it?'

'He's just respecting the witness's right to privacy and anonymity.'

'And this way he doesn't have to spend any time or money but gets a great clear-up rate. It would be a big-budget number to do a full-scale arson and attempted murder investigation. The witness gave him a gift-wrapped package.'

Mohsin tries to put his arm round her, but she moves away from him.

Penny is going to the door. 'I'll tell you what Tony and Pete find out,' she says.

'Has anyone investigated Silas Hyman's alibi?' Sarah asks.

'Take that compassionate leave,' Penny says sharply as she leaves.

Sarah is alone with Mohsin. 'Jesus,' she says. 'Does she always have to speak like there's a cork up her bum?'

He laughs and I'm frankly a little shocked. Sarah doesn't talk that way. And I've never seen her be so physical with someone before. But I can't believe she's having an affair; not *Sarah*, of all people, surely?

'Do you know who the witness is?' she asks him.

'No, I don't. It was Penny who took the statement. You might not like her, but she *is* good. If the witness was dodgy in any way she would have been onto it. She's a sniffer-dog Rottweiler-mix, that woman.'

'Can you get her to tell you who it was?'

'I can't believe you asked me that.'

'Mohsin . . .'

'Well, you know how the *files* sit around on that stack of trays after they've been typed up,' he says. 'And people seem to find better things to do than put them where they're meant to be? It's woefully insecure, that area. I'm sure that the anonymous witness statement isn't left so open to abuse like that. But other transcripts . . .'

'Yeah, thanks.' She lightly kisses his caramel-coloured cheek.

'So how's that husband of yours?' he asks.

She pauses. 'You think that when it really *matters*, someone'll be more than they are the rest of the time. Better, somehow.'

'So are you still going to wait till Mark's eighteen?'

'Neither of us wants the boys to go through a divorce. Not until they're grown-up. I told you that.' She goes to the door. 'Can I ask you a favour?'

He nods.

'There's a printer's called Prescoes, which printed the school calendar for Sidley House some time before Christmas. They had their name printed on the back, but no contact number. Could you get hold of them and find out how many they printed?'

'No problem. Be careful, won't you? Call me if you need to. Any time.'

'Yup. Thanks.'

So Sarah has a best mate I never knew about, who she can speak to in a language she never uses to anyone else. I'm glad for her.

I go with her to a room where there are files of paperwork. She takes a file and tucks it under her jacket, hiding it. Her hands are shaking.

She goes into a photocopier room and starts to make copies. The door suddenly opens behind her. She starts. An older man comes in. From the pips on his shoulder he's clearly senior to her. I feel dread for her.

'Sarah? What on earth are you doing here? Haven't we given you compassionate leave?'

'Yes.'

'So stop whatever work you're doing and get off home. Or to the hospital. You may think that it's better to bury yourself in work, but frankly it's probably not a wise thing to do.'

'No. Thank you.'

'I'm sorry. About your niece and sister-in-law.'

'Yes.'

'And your nephew. We all are.'

He leaves. She hurriedly stuffs the photocopies into her handbag, not folding them first, scrunching them, then takes the file back.

Annette Jenks's name and occupation—secretary—is on the cover sheet, with her contact details. Annette was with Rowena when the alarm went off; she couldn't have started it. But she was in charge of who came in.

'This is illegal, right?' Jen asks.

I nod.

We are in the Palms Café, now brightly lit. Sarah takes a piece of paper out of her bag and tries to smooth out the crumples. As she reads the transcript, a woman in a cleaner's uniform comes up. 'You eating?'

Sarah goes to buy a sandwich as rent for her table, taking the statement with her, and we wait.

'Did you get to know Annette Jenks?' I ask Jenny.

You've never met Annette so you don't have an image in your head of an overly made-up twenty-two-year-old with talon-nails who looks as if she's about to go clubbing at eight twenty in the morning.

'I try to avoid her,' Jen continues. 'But she often collars me. Always has some big drama-queen number going on. You know, has a friend of a friend who's been *murdered* or has married a Mormon with seven wives already. And there's always some starring role for her.'

I smile but feel uneasy.

'Do you think she and Silas could be in a relationship?' I ask. 'She's very, well, alluring.' Her on-display cleavage was something of a standing joke among us buttoned-up mothers. 'And you said yourself that he was unhappy in his marriage.'

She gives me one of her withering looks. 'Even if he was having an affair, I expect he'd want at least a scattering of brain cells. Anyway he'd left before she started working there.'

Sarah returns with her sandwich. She turns over the cover page. At the top is a key: PP stands for Detective Sergeant Penny Pierson. AJ stands for Annette Jenks. The time of the statement is 6.00 p.m. on Wednesday. We read the document with Sarah.

PP: Can you outline for me your duties at the school?

AJ: Yes, I'm the secretary, so I sort out the mail, take phone calls, that kind of thing. I also get the registers and send out the letters for Mrs Healey. And I buzz people in through the gate.

PP: Anything else?

[AJ shakes head.]

Elizabeth Fisher had had so many more responsibilities than Annette Jenks. And she had been the school nurse as well as the secretary. Why didn't Annette have that role too?

PP: I'd like to ask you about who you let in earlier today.

AJ: You think it was deliberate? I mean, like arson? It's a bit weird, isn't it? To suddenly get a fire, like, out of nowhere? I mean, yeah, it's hot. But it's not hot like Australia, is it? I mean, we don't get bush fires, stuff like that.

'I told you,' Jenny says. 'I bet she loved this, being interviewed by the police.' The drama queen finally gets her stage.

PP: During sports day, who did you let in?

AJ: There were a couple of children who needed to use the toilets and Mrs Banks, the Year Two teacher, was with them. There were a couple more teachers who'd forgotten something or other. Then there was Adam Covey and Rowena White, and then her mum. She's always very polite, Mrs White, waves a thankyou at the camera so I see it on the screen. Hardly anyone does that.

PP: Anybody else?

AJ: No.

PP: You said you have a screen. Do you always look at it before pushing the buzzer?

AJ: Yeah, not much point having it if I don't, is there?

PP: But it must be tempting when you're busy just to push the button and let them in.

AJ: 'Course I look at the bloody screen. Sorry. It's stress. I mean it's just so tragic, isn't it? What's happened.

'That's bollocks,' Jen says. 'I've *seen* her press the buzzer and not look at the screen. She's done it while she's talked to me, for Christ's sakes.'

It's what Rowena had said too, in a milder way.

PP: What about earlier in the day?

AJ: You mean like somebody came and hid?

PP: Could you please answer the question?

AJ: No, just the usual. People who are a part of the school. One or two suppliers, bringing things in. A caterer and a cleaning guy.

PP: Where were you when the fire alarm sounded?

AJ: In the office. As per usual.

PP: On your own?

AJ: No. Rowena White was with me. She'd come into the office to get the medals for sports day. I was telling her about a friend of mine's problems when the alarm went off. Christ, it made a din.

PP: You said that as part of your job, you keep the registers. Can you explain how that works?

AJ: Well, yeah, at eight forty and again after lunch the teachers tick off all the kids in their class against the class register. Any kid who isn't there is marked as absent. Anyone leaving before the end of the school day has to sign themselves out in that too.

PP: Anyone being who?

AJ: Kids, mainly, leaving early because they've got to get to the dentist's or whatever. But adults too, sometimes, like parent readers.

PP: And teachers?

AJ: Yeah, but hardly ever. I mean, they get in before me and leave later. But teaching assistants, well, they're different. I mean, it's like me. An eight-thirty-to-five deal and any excuse to leave early. So they sign themselves out.

PP: What did you do after the fire alarm went off?

AJ: I went outside.

She hasn't told Penny that she waited for five minutes before going outside. Nor what she was doing in that time.

AJ: I gave Tilly Rogers, the Reception teacher, the register for her class. Then I saw a boy getting hysterical. By that statue. Rowena was trying to calm him down. She asked me if I'd seen Jenny. I said not to worry, that I knew she wasn't inside. Because she'd signed herself out in the register.

PP: What time was that?

AJ: Around three, I suppose. I didn't check the time.

PP: Why didn't you bring the register out?

AJ: I didn't think it mattered. I just thought the Reception-class one mattered.

PP: Surely the whole point of that register is to know who's in the building in case of fire?

AJ: Look, I'm new, OK? Only been here a term. They had a fire practice a few weeks back but I was off sick. Even if I had brought the register out it wouldn't have made no difference, right? It would have said Jenny was out of the building.

I glance at Jen, enough to know that she still can't remember and that it's tearing her up. Because why on earth would Jenny go in again?

PP: When did you realise that Jennifer Covey was still in the building?

AJ: I saw her mother running in, yelling for her. And then that daft cow went in too.

PP: Do you mean Rowena White?

AJ: Yeah. There were fire engines coming up the road by then. She should have left it up to them, not made their job even harder for them. They ended up having to rescue her too. Not sure what she was trying to prove.

I hear Annette Jenks's jealousy. When it came down to it, the drama queen failed to do anything remotely deserving of attention.

[Detective Sergeant Baker asks PP out of the room. After three minutes PP returns.]

PP: Do you know Silas Hyman?

AJ: I've no idea who Silas Hyman is. What kind of a name is Silas?

PP: He was a teacher at the school, who left in April.

AJ: I wouldn't know him then. Only started working there in May.

PP: Nobody gossiped about him?

AJ: No.

PP: A teacher who'd been fired only a few weeks before and there was no gossip?

[AJ shakes head.]

PP: I must say that I find it hard to believe.

My respect for the harsh-faced PP goes up a notch.

Sarah gets another statement out of her bag.

Her mobile rings and she starts, as if someone has seen her. I go closer and hear Mohsin's voice at the other end.

'Prescoes, that printing company, they printed three hundred copies of the Sidley House calendar. Does that help at all?'

'Three hundred people knew that it was Adam's birthday on Wednesday. And also that it was sports day so the school would be virtually empty. What about the witness?'

'Sorry, honey, Penny won't budge on that, and no one else is talking to me either. They probably don't trust me. God knows why.'

She thanks him and hangs up. Then she smoothes out the next statement. The key this time is SH for Sally Healey. The interviewer is AB—Detective Inspector Baker. The time it started was 5.55 p.m.

I remember Sally Healey on telly the evening of the fire—her pink linen shirt and cream trousers and assembly voice and immaculate make-up. And how the carefully assembled frontage had started to fall apart.

AB: Can you tell me who you knew to be in the building at the time of the fire?

SH: Yes. There was one Reception class. All their names are in the register I gave you. There was also Annette Jenks, the school secretary; Tilly Rogers, a Reception teacher; and, of course, Jennifer Covey, who's a temporary classroom assistant.

AB: Was every other member of staff out of the building?

SH: Yes, at sports day. We needed all of them. We are ambitious in the number of activities and it would be chaotic unless there were enough staff to run things smoothly.

AB: Did you see any staff return to the building?

SH: Yes, Rowena White. Or, at least, I didn't see her but I was told she'd gone to get the medals.

AB: Anyone else?

SH: No.

AB: I know one of my officers asked you about this at the scene of the fire, but if you'd bear with me, I need to go over the same territory again. How easy is it for people to get into the school?

SH: We have one entrance to the school, which is a locked gate. It has a numerical keypad. Only members of staff know the code. Everyone else needs to be buzzed in from the office. We have had a monitor installed and our school secretary has to watch exactly who she is letting in.

AB: So you think your school is secure?

SH: Absolutely. Security for the children is our top priority.

'Mrs Healey must know what Annette's like, surely?'

'Yes. And she knows that parents and some children know the code. Gets really annoyed about it.'

If she is lying about the security on the gate, what else might she be lying about?

AB: Do you know of anyone who has a grudge against the school?

SH: No, of course not.

AB: I have to tell you that it looks as if the fire was arson. So can you please think if there is anyone who may have a grudge against the school? Perhaps—

SH: No one would do this.

AB: Have any members of staff left the school recently? Say, in the last six months to a year?

SH: But that's nothing to do with the fire.

AB: Please answer the question.

SH: Yes. Two. Elizabeth Fisher, our former school secretary. And Silas Hyman, a Year Three teacher.

AB: What were the circumstances?

SH: Elizabeth Fisher was getting too old to be able to do the job. So sadly I had to let her go. There were no hard feelings. Though I know she misses the children.

AB: I'll need her contact details, if that's possible?

SH: Yes. I have her number and address in my palmtop.

AB: You also said Silas Hyman, a Year Three teacher?

SH: Yes. Circumstances there were more unfortunate. There was an accident in the playground when he was on duty. I had to ask him to leave. As I said, health and safety is our top priority.

AB: You actually said security was your top priority.

SH: It all lumps in together, in the end, doesn't it? Keeping the children safe from harm.

AB: Are Silas Hyman's details also in your palmtop?

SH: Yes. I haven't updated it.

AB: Can you write them down for me?

[SH writes down Silas Hyman's details.]

AB: If you could please excuse me one moment.

[AB leaves the room and returns six minutes later.]

Baker must have gone to tell Penny about Silas Hyman. Presumably he also sent someone to find him—he told you the police had spoken to Silas Hyman that evening.

AB: Can you tell me about the fire regulations at the school?

SH: We have appropriate fire-fighting equipment—extinguishers both foam and water, as well as fire blankets and sand buckets on every floor and in the kitchen. Staff are trained in the use of appropriate equipment. We have signed exits in every classroom and the Art room, dining room and kitchen. We also routinely practise evacuating the building. We have certified smoke detectors and heat detectors, which are linked directly to the fire station. We have quarterly, yearly and three-yearly maintenance and testing by a qualified engineer as required by BS 5839.

'It sounds like she's memorised it all,' Jen says. I agree, but why?

AB: You have all those facts to hand?

SH: I am the head teacher. As I just told you, safety is my number-one concern. I delegated myself as the fire-safety manager. So, yes, I have the facts to hand.

AB: Fire-fighters reported that windows at the top of the school were wide open. Can you comment on that?

SH: No. That's not possible. We have window locks to prevent them being opened more than ten centimetres.

AB: Where are the keys to the window locks kept?

SH: In the teacher's desk.

AB: You said your staff were trained to put out fires? But the staff were all out at sports day? Apart from the three you told me about?

[SH nods.]

AB: Why was Jennifer Covey inside the school and not at sports day too?

SH: She was in charge of the medical room. For minor injuries.

AB: Where is the medical room?

SH: On the third floor. We used to use the secretary's office. Elizabeth was a qualified nurse. But the new secretary isn't medically trained so there was no point keeping it there.

AB: How long had you known that Jennifer Covey would be the nurse this afternoon?

Right at the beginning he'd suspected the fire was aimed at her. I suppose he'd have put her name in the computer and the hate-mail case would have come up instantly.

SH: I announced it at the Thursday staff meeting last week.

AB: Who was at the Thursday staff meeting when you announced
      the change?
SH: The senior management team. Then they disseminate the
      information to all the other members of staff.
[SH is silent.]
AB: Mrs Healey?
SH: Jenny, is she going to die?
[SH cries.]

Sarah takes the final photocopy out of her bag. I'd hoped it would be a transcript of Silas Hyman's interview but it's Tilly Rogers's, that archetype of a Reception teacher—pink cheeks and long fair hair and smiling face with white, pearly teeth. A healthy, clean-living, nice girl, who will do this job for a few years before marrying and having a family of her own. Children in her class love her, fathers feel wistful, mothers maternal.

I can't imagine she has anything to do with the fire.

Tilly's interview started at 6.30. It was AB, Inspector Baker, who interviewed her.

I skim-read it, just getting the basics. She was with her class doing circle time when the alarm went off. Maisie White helped evacuate the children. She didn't mention a delay before Annette brought her the register, maybe because she didn't notice. It's two pages before I see a question that seems relevant.

AB: Is there anything else you think may be relevant?
TR: Rowena White. I don't know if it's relevant but it was
      extraordinary.
AB: Go on.
TR: I was outside the school with the children but most of their
      mothers had got there by then, so I was able to look around. I saw
      Rowena running into the PE shed and coming out with a towel. A
      big, blue swimming one. The children leave them in there some-
      times. There were two bottles of water on the gravel at the side of
      the school, and she poured water on the towel. Then I saw her
      going into the school. As she got to the door, I saw her putting the
      towel over her face. It was just so brave.

Sarah leaves to find you. Jenny and I wait a moment, both quiet with disappointment. No magic sentence to free Adam from guilt.

9

A LITTLE WHILE LATER, we join you and Sarah in the corridor of ICU. You're looking through the glass at Jenny, holding Annette Jenks's transcript.

'But how the hell can Jen have signed herself out?' you say as you read it. 'I don't understand.'

'I'm not convinced yet that she did,' Sarah says. 'It could be that Annette Jenks just wanted to stop people from blaming her.'

'So there's nothing useful from it.'

'I wouldn't say that. She says she was with Rowena White in the office when the alarm went off and Rowena told me the same thing earlier. The office is on the upper-ground level; the Art room on the second floor. So neither of them could have started the fire.'

'Could she have let Hyman in?'

'She claims not to know him, but I find it strange that she didn't hear any gossip about him at all. She strikes me as a gossipy kind of girl. And we know from both Maisie and Rowena White that she waited a few minutes before coming outside. In here she makes no mention of that. We have to find out what she was doing.'

As I expected, Sarah is bang on the button.

You read through Sally Healey's transcript.

'It's like she's memorised the fire manual,' you say to Sarah.

'I agree. And Baker picked up on it too. I think Sally Healey was worried about the real possibility of a fire. Almost as if she *knew* it was going to happen and was trying to minimise the consequences. No fire regulations would have stood a chance against an accelerant and open windows and an old building.'

'Maybe she knew that?'

'I can't see why she'd burn down her own school. But something's not right. She said there were no hard feelings when Elizabeth Fisher, the old secretary, left. But on Elizabeth's side there clearly are.'

I feel sick as I reread the head teacher's statement. Because this time her telling Baker that the medical room is *on the third floor*, right at the top of the building, leaps out at me. So too does her *announcement* that Jenny would be nurse, and that the information would be *disseminated* to *all* the other members of staff.

Everyone at the school knew Jenny would be up on the top floor, on her own, in a virtually deserted building.

'You'll talk to Silas Hyman?' you ask.

'Yes. And I've already set up a meeting with the head teacher. And while I'm doing that, you can go home and see Addie.'

You are silent.

'ICU is heavily staffed, Mike. If you're still worried, I could get Mohsin to sit with her.'

You are still silent and she doesn't understand.

'Addie's only got you right now, Mike. He needs you to be with him.'

You shake your head.

Her grey-blue eyes look deeply into your matching ones, as if searching for an answer there. Because you are a loving father; not a man who would ignore his eight-year-old child, especially not now.

You look away from Sarah as you speak. 'They told me Jenny has three weeks to live unless she gets a heart transplant. A day less now. I can't leave her.'

'Oh God, Mike . . .'

I am looking at Jenny's face. She leaves the room and I hurry after her. 'Jen, please . . .'

In the corridor, she stops and turns to me. 'You should have told me.' Her face is white and her voice shaking. 'I had a right to know. I'm not a child any more.'

I want to tell her that I was trying to protect her. 'Jen—'

'Can't you get it, Mum? Please? I'm an adult now. I have my own life. You can't run my life for me. What's left of it.'

I see her at six in a pink-and-orange flowery swimming costume, diving underwater before popping up with a beaming wave, *our little fish!* And I am watching her, my eye beams a rope round her, because I will jump in and rescue her the moment she's in difficulty. And then she's twelve years old, self-conscious in a modest navy sports swimsuit, checking everything's in place as she swims; and then a metallic silver bikini over a perfect teenage body that makes everyone stare at her, and she feels their gazes like sunshine on her skin, enjoying her beauty.

But she's still the little girl in the pink-and-orange flowery swimming costume to me, and I still have my invisible rope round her waist.

'You can have my heart,' I say.

She looks at me a moment and smiles and I see in her smile that I'm forgiven. 'Oh, for heaven's sake,' she says.

'If no one else's turns up.'

'"Turns up"?' She's teasing me. 'It's really kind,' she says. 'That's a huge understatement. But there are a few snags in the plan. You're *alive*, for a start. And even if Dad and Aunt Sarah let them, which they won't, they're not going to stop giving you food and water for ages.'

'Then I'll just have to find a way of doing it myself.'

'How, exactly?'

All these smiles! I was wrong earlier. She hasn't taken in the reality of how desperate the situation is at all. I used to wish that she took life 'a little more seriously'.

'Walking out of an A-level paper isn't funny.'

'It's not that I'm laughing at.'

'So what is it?'

'No one ever tells you when you're doing all that coursework and revision and timed essays and study skills that it's an option.'

'But it isn't an option.'

'It is, because I just took it.'

And she found it funny, as if she'd been released from prison rather than had slammed the door shut on her future.

I had despaired of this trait she has of hiding behind humour rather than facing the truth. Now, I'm glad.

Sarah walks on towards the exit of the hospital.

'You go with Aunt Sarah,' Jenny says. 'I'll wait here, in case Donald White comes back.'

'I'll stay with you.'

'But you said we need to know everything, in case we're the ones who have to put it all together.'

She *wants* me to go with Sarah.

She wants to be on her own.

I used to hate that—the closed bedroom door, the little walk away from me when she was on her mobile. I still hate that. I don't want her to want to be on her own.

'We have to let her make her own mistakes,' you said, a few weeks ago. 'Spread her wings. It's natural for her to do that.'

'Bubonic plague is "natural",' I snapped. 'Doesn't mean it's good for you.'

You put your arm round me. 'You have to let go, Gracie.'

But I can't let go of my rope round her. Not yet. I'll keep on holding it until she can safely swim out of her depth, without drowning.

I walk with Sarah along the gravel path to the car park but the stones are no longer needle-sharp and the harsh midday sun doesn't scald me yet, as if I'm building up some kind of protective covering for myself.

Sarah stays bang on the speed limits, sticking to one small law as she drives to break larger ones.

'Jenny didn't come to you about the red paint, did she?' an inner voice says, rapping me harshly over the knuckles with a hard-edged fact. 'She didn't need you then.'

It was May 10. We thought the hate mail had stopped.

Jenny came back that evening, later than she'd said, her long hair cut into a bob. She'd seemed anxious and I thought it was about her new haircut. I tried to reassure her that it suited her.

Even for Jen, she spent an absurdly long time on the phone and although I didn't hear what she was saying (her door was closed), her tone sounded fraught.

If she'd come to me, I'd have got the paint out of her hair somehow and she wouldn't have had to have it cut. I'd have taken her coat to that expensive dry-cleaner's in Richmond. I'd have reported the attack to the police and maybe she wouldn't be in hospital now.

Snared in thoughts about Jenny, I'm shocked to see we're driving up to the school. I'm afraid of seeing the site of the fire; nauseous with anxiety.

Sarah turns off along the road towards the playing field and parks next to it. There are three Portakabins on the field now. They make it look so different from sports day and I'm relieved. I don't want to remember.

Sarah knocks on a Portakabin door and Mrs Healey answers it. Her foundationed face is flushed, her linen skirt creased and covered in dust.

'Detective Sergeant McBride,' Sarah says, holding out her hand—disguising by default that she is related to us.

We go into the stifling Portakabin. Stale particles of Mrs Healey's perfume, Chanel No.19, float like scum in the hotly humid air.

'On Monday we are getting ten more Portakabins plus toilet facilities,' Mrs Healey says, her voice quick with uncharacteristic nervous energy. 'The council have given us a temporary emergency licence. The children will need to bring packed lunches but I'm sure parents will understand that. Fortunately we use cloud computing so we've got a back-up of everything—contact details, lesson planning, children's reports.'

'That's very organised.' Sarah sounds politely interested, but I wonder if there's a tougher reason for her observation.

'Every family will have a letter tomorrow outlining what's happening.'

A printer whirrs, spitting out letters. On the floor is a pile of addressed envelopes.

'Will this take long? I have a huge amount to do, and I have already spoken to the police.'

'We can talk and you can carry on, if you like,' Sarah says. I remember washing up with her once and her saying that she wished she could do the washing-up with a suspect—he'd be far more likely to talk and tell the truth while occupied with a task.

'You were told Adam Covey was accused of starting the fire?' Sarah says.

'Yes. My decision not to press charges, or take it any further, has the full backing of the governors. From what I understand it was a prank that went wrong and poor Adam has been punished more than enough already. He must feel desperately guilty.'

'Do you know him well?'

'No. I'd recognise him, of course. But head teachers are more like chief executives than teachers nowadays so, sadly, I don't get to know very many of my pupils.'

When Jenny was at Sidley House, Mrs Healey taught each class once a week herself to keep in touch. But Adam barely saw her.

'You don't think it odd that an eight-year-old could commit arson?' Sarah asks.

'Apparently it happens relatively frequently. From my time as a teacher, with children this age, I am not surprised. It's horrifying what children are capable of.'

'Adam isn't that kind of child,' Sarah says.

'He didn't do it?' asks Mrs Healey.

'You seem concerned.'

'All right, yes. I am. I need this to be sorted out. So that we can all move on. For his sake though, I'm glad, of course. So is that why you're here?'

'I have some questions. I'm sorry if you have to go over old ground.'

Mrs Healey nods an acknowledgment. She's folding the letters now and putting them into the envelopes.

'Where were you when the fire started?' Sarah asks.

'I was at sports day, running the sack race for our Year Two children. As soon as I knew what was happening, I made sure that the children I was in charge of were delegated to a form teacher, then made my way as quickly as I could to the school. By the time I arrived, all the Reception children had been safely evacuated.'

'And Jennifer Covey?'

'She hadn't followed our procedure. Our school secretary, Annette Jenks, told me she had signed herself out of the school but not signed herself back in. There was no way anyone could have known she was still in the building.'

'Why didn't you tell us that Silas Hyman had threatened revenge on the school at the prize-giving?'

Mrs Healey looks thrown by this abrupt change of subject. Or is it Silas Hyman's name?

'Because he didn't mean it.'

'A school burns down, two people are left critically injured and a man has threatened revenge but—'

'I *know* that he didn't mean it.'

'Have you any evidence for that?'

She's silent.

'Did a parent phone you after the prize-giving and ask you to get a restraining order or injunction against him to make sure he couldn't come near the school again?'

'You mean, Maisie White? Yes.'

'So why didn't you do as she asked?'

'Because her husband phoned me an hour later and said his wife was overwrought and that there was no need to contact the police. Like me, and the rest of the staff and parents, he knew Silas Hyman was all hot air and bluster, that he didn't mean any of it.'

Why had Donald countermanded Maisie? Why would he protect Silas?

'So you weren't worried, *at all*?'

'Yes. I was. But not about Silas doing something violent. I'd spent *months* building up a good reputation for Sidley House after the playground fiasco and I thought that in five minutes of drunken idiocy he could have destroyed it. But apart from Mrs White, nobody took him seriously. He'd made an idiotic spectacle of himself, that was all.'

'Can you tell me about that "playground fiasco"?'

'A child was seriously injured when he fell from the fire escape. He broke both his legs. Silas Hyman was meant to be supervising the playground but he wasn't.'

'So you fired him?'

'I didn't have any alternative.'

'Did you fire him before or after the article about the incident in the *Richmond Post*?'

'Clearly the article increased the pressure from parents. I had to fire him three days later. Without the article he could have stayed in post till the end of that term.'

'Do you have a system of warnings?'

'I'd already given him one warning when he called a child "wicked". Naturally, the parents complained. His language and attitude towards the child were unacceptable.'

I think of Robert Fleming's callous cruelty.

'Do you know how the *Richmond Post* found out about the playground incident?'

'I really don't know who told the press.'

'What effect did this playground accident have on the school?'

'It was very hard for a while. I don't deny that. Parents put their children into our care and one of them was badly injured. I understood their anger and upset. I could completely understand why a few parents wanted to withdraw their children. I spoke to all the parents, class by class at special meetings. If parents were still anxious I met with them individually. And we weathered the storm; not a single parent took their child away. On sports day there were two hundred and seventy-nine children in school. There is just one place free in a Year Three class because a family relocated to Canada at the end of last term.'

I know she's telling the truth. At sports day every class each had twenty children, the maximum Sidley House allows.

'What is your own opinion of Silas Hyman?' Sarah asks.

'A brilliant teacher. Gifted. The best I've come across in my career. But too unorthodox for a private school.'

'Was he having a relationship with anyone at the school?'

She hesitates. 'Not that I know of.' A careful answer.

'Was there any gossip?'

'I don't listen to gossip. I try to discourage it by example.'

'Can you tell me what the code was on the gate on Wednesday?'

'Seven-seven-two-three,' she replies. I think she looks wary. 'I told another officer that already.'

'I wanted to confirm it for myself,' Sarah says coolly, and for the moment Mrs Healey is pacified. But that ice Sarah told you about seems perilously thin.

'Why did you get rid of Elizabeth Fisher?'

Sally Healey looks startled and tries to hide it. Her normally powder-dry face is sweating profusely now, the sweat glistening.

'She was too old to do the job. I already told the police that. We have a policy of retirement at sixty for all support staff.'

Mrs Healey is kneeling on the floor, but has stopped putting the letters into envelopes.

'Yet you waited seven years to enforce it,' Sarah says.

'I was being kind. But the school is not a charity.'

'Is Annette Jenks an improvement?' Sarah asks, seemingly without irony.

'The governors and I made an error of judgment when we hired Annette Jenks.'

Elizabeth Fisher did her job well. So why did Mrs Healey really get rid of her?

'I noticed how meticulous all your fire precautions were,' Sarah says, again abruptly switching tack. Maybe it's deliberate, to unsettle the other person into spilling out more than they want. 'So you fulfilled all the legal requirements?'

'*More* than the legal requirements.' Mrs Healey wipes her sweaty face with her hand. 'But with old buildings it's impossible to prevent a fire spreading. And how can anyone plan for an individual's act of destruction? When that person starts the fire in the worst possible place in the school with virtually no staff on hand to contain it?'

'When did this start?' Sarah asks, unmoved. 'This "more than" fulfilling of the legal requirements?'

'We had a governors' meeting at the end of May. We agreed to examine and update our fire safety and I took charge of implementation.'

'This meeting was after the prize-giving?'

'Yes. But it's not connected. Like all schools, we regularly look at ways to update and improve our safety systems.'

'Just six weeks later there's a catastrophic fire. It looks as if you expected it?'

'We *planned* for it. Yes. We plan for what to do with the children if London comes under a terrorist attack; we plan for a madman coming in with a gun. We have to. But it doesn't mean that we thought something would actually happen.'

'There's one thing I find a little surprising,' Sarah says. 'Why do you let children bring *matches* into the school?'

'It's just on a birthday. And the matches are handed over directly to the class teacher. Unfortunately, human errors do occur. Adam's teacher should have made sure the matches were safely stored.'

'Presumably, the building is insured?' Sarah asks. 'And the insurance company will want to know that all the fire precautions have been met before they'll pay out?'

'I have already spoken to the insurers about the matches and fortunately it doesn't invalidate our claim. It was one member of staff's error of judgment, a human error. All our systems were in place.'

'Do the governors have a financial stake in the school?'

'Yes, they own it.'

'So the governors are also the shareholders?'

'Yes.'

'Do you have any shares?'

'I was given a shareholding when I took the job of head teacher. But my shareholding is relatively small. Only five per cent.'

'In a business worth, presumably, several million, that is a sizable amount.'

'What are you insinuating? My God, people were *hurt*. Terribly hurt.'

'But even so, you must be relieved that the insurance money can't be contested because of your impeccable fire precautions.'

'Yes, I am relieved, but only inasmuch as I can continue to run a school of excellence. A school that nurtures and educates children to the highest possible standard.' She sounds impassioned and I remember her as the ardent educationalist she'd been when Jenny joined the school. 'What was burnt down was a *building*, not a *school*. I will find alternative accommodation and be ready to start in September for our new academic year. The teachers, the children, the ethos, the parents are what make a school and we will simply relocate and pick up from where we left off.'

'Can I have the names of the governors?'

I see suspicion hardening Sally Healey's face. 'I already gave them to the police.'

It wasn't in her transcript. Perhaps it had been during a phone call, someone tying up a few loose ends. The ice thins beneath Sarah but she affects not to notice.

'Of course. I'll confer with my colleagues,' Sarah says.

'And I've already been asked all about the shareholders as governors.'

'Yes,' Sarah says, going to the door. 'Thank you for your time.'

Sally Healey watches her as she walks away, the ice creaking under her.

On the edge of the playing field, next to Sarah's Polo, Mrs Healey's black sports car gleams. The woman I'd met all those years ago when Jenny started at Sidley House bicycled to school. '*Can't mess up the planet for the children, can we?*' she'd said with a bicycle clip round her trousers.

With only sixty children then, the school had been such a nurturing place. When Adam joined, nine years later, I hadn't wanted to see the change. But Jenny had seen the school as a business. And you'd annually fumed about the ever-increasing fees.

As I see the ugly, boastful sports car, I know my image of the school is as outdated as Sally Healey with a bicycle clip.

'**S**o are you going to tell me what happened, then?' Jenny asks as we follow Sarah to ICU. 'No, don't tell me. You've discovered it was *Mrs Healey* having the affair with Silas?' She sees my expression. 'It was a joke.'

I outline our meeting with Mrs Healey. 'The thing I find strangest is Donald phoning Mrs Healey the night of the prize-giving, and countermanding Maisie. Why would he protect Silas Hyman like that?'

'Maybe because he didn't find Silas threatening. Just like you didn't. Not until this happened and blame started being thrown around the place.'

I find her innocent certainty about Silas Hyman, a man more than a decade older than her, another reason to still see her as not yet an adult.

'Maybe Mrs Healey wasn't *worried* there was going to be a fire,' Jenny continues. 'But *planned* to start it herself and wanted to make sure the fire precautions were in place so the insurance paid out. She knew they wouldn't make any difference, because the building was old.'

'But Mrs Healey was at sports day,' I say. 'People would have noticed if she'd left.'

'Nearly all the teachers are on short-term contracts, which she can choose not to renew. And they're dependent on a reference from her to get another job. She could have blackmailed someone into it. She'd choose sports day because there'd be virtually no staff to try and put it out.'

I agree with her about sports day being a deliberate choice of date. It also meant there was hardly anyone there beforehand to see the arsonist.

'But what good would it do her?' I say, gently. 'Why would she want to burn down a successful business? There won't be any financial benefit. She'll just use the insurance money to rebuild.'

We still haven't spoken about the three weeks, less a day, left to her. My grip on your optimism isn't strong enough to confront the ticking clock. And I think Jenny is deliberately turning her back on it too. But the fact is there, huge and monstrous.

As we arrive at ICU, you see Sarah. And you run. I see the urgency in your body with *big news* to tell her. A heart must have been found! The monstrous fact smashed to pieces.

Then I see your face.

'Mike?' Sarah asks.

'He was here. Watching her through the glass. I saw him watching her.'

'Who was it?' Sarah asks.

'I don't know. He had a hood up, and there was a trolley in the way so I couldn't see his face,' you say.

'How did you know he was dangerous?'

'He was still. No one just stands there, watching. Everybody's moving. He was waiting for her to be alone. He wants to kill her.'

'Did you see anything else?' Sarah asks.

'He turned away, when he saw me looking, and I just saw the coat, that's all. A blue coat with a hood.'

'I'll be in the garden,' Jen says. I see that she's afraid.

'OK.'

She leaves, turning her back on this.

'It could have been Hyman,' you're saying to Sarah. 'If Jen saw him at the school, or something that incriminated him.'

'Or the hate-mailer has become more dangerous than we realised,' Sarah says. 'I'll phone the station.'

She leaves ICU to make the call and again I wish to God I could tell her about the paint attack.

I hug you, resting my face against your shirt, feeling your heart beating. I feel so close to you now, my darling. And we are totally united against the threat to our daughter.

Sarah rejoins us.

'Can you stay with Jen?' you ask. 'Till the police get here? I need to be with Addie, just for a bit, and—'

She puts a hand on your shoulder. 'There's nobody coming. I'm sorry.' The police were hardly going to find someone *standing still* cause for alarm. 'I'll go and see Silas Hyman, find out where he's been this morning,' she says. 'And I'll talk to the *Richmond Post*, and see who told them about the fire.'

'But first, I need to see Addie and—'

Sarah interrupts you. 'If someone is trying to kill Jenny, we need to find out who it is *as soon as possible*. And that will help Addie too. Because I don't want him to spend another day being accused of this.'

You nod, and stay by Jenny's bed. But I know that you again feel the pain of being torn in half.

I go to Jenny in the garden. The sun is directly overhead.

Jen is sitting with her arms round her knees.

'I'm going with Aunt Sarah,' I say.

She turns to me. 'You know when you asked me if a scent could have made me hear the fire alarm at school. Do you think a smell could make me remember more?'

'It might do,' I say.

'It's *before* the fire that I need to remember,' she says. 'When the person was lighting it. I have to do something to help Addie. You go with Aunt Sarah and I'll go on a scratch-and sniff tour of the hospital,' she continues.

Natalia Hyman opens the door, looking hot and flushed and furious.

'Yes?' Her voice is aggressive, ambient rage surrounding her.

'Detective Sergeant McBride,' Sarah says. 'Can I come in?'

'Like I get a choice?' Natalia says, but there's fear on her face.

Sarah doesn't answer her question, but follows her into the flat.

'Is your husband home?'

'No.'

It's sweltering in the flat. A grimy toddler is screaming, his nappy sagging heavily. Natalia ignores him, going into a bathroom. Sarah follows.

'Do you know where he is?' Sarah asks her.

'A building site. Been there since first thing this morning.'

Two little boys are in the bath fighting, one of them swishing the water over the edge of the bath onto the chipped tiled floor.

'Do you know which building site?' Sarah asks.

'Maybe the same as yesterday's. A big development in Paddington. But he didn't know if they'd want him again. Get out of the bath, Jason. *Now!*'

'Early for bathtime?' Sarah says. I think she means to be friendly but it comes out as a criticism.

Natalia glares. 'I'll be too knackered to do it later.'

The youngest one is still screaming, more desperately, his nappy almost at his knees with the weight of urine. Natalia sees Sarah looking at him.

'You know how much they cost? Nappies? Do you know that?'

'Do you know when he'll be home?' Sarah asks.

'No clue. He was out till past ten yesterday.'

Natalia grabs one of the boys and pinions him in a towel. No wonder her exotic beauty is fading so fast. Three boys under four in a small flat.

'Does Silas know Donald White?'

She wants to know why Donald phoned Mrs Healey the night of the prize-giving, countermanding Maisie's request for a restraining order.

'Who?' Natalia says and looks genuinely blank; or maybe she's a proficient actress.

'Would it be all right if I wait for Silas in the sitting room?'

'Suit yourself.'

In the hallway Sarah passes the open doorway to the kitchen and goes in. She's noticed the school calendar hanging on the wall: July 11— Adam's birthday and sports day—ringed in red like a curse.

She goes into the sitting room and quietly rummages through a pile of papers in an untidy heap on a table. I don't know what will happen to Sarah if she's found out, but she continues, quickly and methodically with that quiet courage of hers that I've only just discovered.

Natalia comes into the room behind Sarah, and Sarah starts.

Two of the little boys, trailing water, run into the room; one is screaming, the other hitting him, their commotion not filling the silence between the adults.

Sarah goes towards the front door.

'You're not waiting for Silas, then?' Natalia asks.

'No.'

I think Sarah has been jolted by something. Perhaps it's just hit her how many laws she's breaking by coming to their house and going through their things.

Natalia yells at the children to shut up. Then she blocks the door to Sarah. She looks hostile and sweaty and plain.

'I didn't used to be this way,' she says, as if seeing herself through Sarah's eyes.

No, I think, you were exotically beautiful and poised not that long ago, when Silas was still in work and you only had one child.

'You didn't used to be this way?' Sarah asks, *fury* in her voice. 'Jenny didn't used to be this way either,' she continues. 'And Grace used to be able to talk. Smile. Look after her children. Count yourself lucky your children are healthy and you can be a mother to them.'

Natalia stands aside as if Sarah's blast of words have shoved her, and Sarah leaves.

We arrive at the offices of the *Richmond Post*.

It's been an age since I was here, preferring to send in my monthly page by email. As we go in, I'm embarrassed that Sarah will discover that I'm not loved here as she is at her police station. Frankly, I'm probably no more valued than the out-of-date yucca plant in the corner of what passes for reception.

Sarah must have phoned ahead because Tara arrives almost immediately, pink cheeks glowing.

'I spoke to one of your colleagues,' Sarah says curtly. 'Geoff Bagshot.'

'Yes, I recognised the name, Detective Sergeant McBride,' she says. 'You chucked me out of the hospital. Geoff's left it for me to handle.'

I see Sarah stiffen at Tara's 'handling' of her.

'There's an office we can use this way,' Tara says.

'When I met you, you said you were friends with Grace?' Sarah says.

'I was trying to gain access to her ward, so I stretched the truth a little. Clearly I don't have much in common with a thirty-nine-year-old mother of two.'

'Nor she with you. Clearly.'

Thank you, Sarah.

Tara escorts her into Geoff's office. It looks like the set for a film about journalists—old mugs with the dregs of cold coffee in them and illegal ashtrays brimming with butts.

'What time did you arrive at Sidley House School on the day of the fire?' Sarah asks, wasting no time on preliminaries.

'Three fifteen p.m. I already told your buddy.'

'That was extremely fast?'

'What is this? Interviews in duplicate?' She's enjoying herself.

'You arrive barely fifteen minutes after a fire started and I need to know who told you.'

'I can't reveal my source.'

'Your tip-off was hardly from Deep Throat. And this,' she says, gesturing around the crummy office, 'isn't exactly the *Washington Post*.'

'Can we do a deal?' Tara asks. 'I'll tell you in return for information that you will only give to my paper. You can't think the kid did it any more or you wouldn't still be investigating.'

Sarah says nothing, which Tara takes as an affirmative. She glows with satisfaction. 'So are you going to investigate Silas Hyman properly this time?' she says.

Again, Sarah says nothing.

'I need something back if I'm going to play ball here,' Tara continues.

'Adam Covey isn't responsible for the fire,' Sarah says. 'And in a few minutes we'll discuss Silas Hyman.'

Tara almost purrs with self-satisfaction. 'It was Annette Jenks,' she says. 'The secretary at the school, who phoned us. At a minute or so past three. She had to shout above the sound of the fire alarm.'

'Why did she call your paper?'

'I've been thinking about that. We did an article a few weeks back when the school raised money for a charity. She'd have our number from that.'

'Did she phone any other papers?'

'I don't know. But she did phone a TV station. Their reporters and cameramen arrived about half an hour after us. She wanted us to take her picture. I think our photographer took a few to keep her quiet. But once the TV mob arrived she was all over them.'

I remember Maisie talking to Sarah. '. . . *she was smiling, like she was enjoying it, or at least she was not at all upset, and she had lipstick on.*' The idea of someone getting a kick out of this is horrible. But is it anything more than that?

'Going back to Silas Hyman,' Sarah says. 'You published a story about him a few months ago. After the incident in the playground. How did you find out about that?'

'An anonymous text message was sent to the land line here. It was read out by one of those weird electronic voices. Couldn't trace it. It was from a payphone. But it wasn't Annette Jenks, if that's what you're thinking, because she wasn't working at Sidley House then. It was still that old cow of a secretary. Took me ten minutes before she'd let me speak to the head to confirm the story.'

'So you published your article. You had quotes from outraged parents. Did you tell parents about the incident, or did they come to you?'

Tara tosses her silky hair. 'I really don't remember.'

'I am sure you do.'

'All right, I phoned around a few families; got a couple of quotes in response to what I told them. So what do the police have on him then?'

'Nothing.'

Tara looks at Sarah, coldly furious. 'You said you'd do a trade,' she says, petulantly. Her parents really should have made her play Monopoly and lose once in a while.

'No,' Sarah says coolly. 'That's what you inferred.'

In the car, Sarah phones Mohsin on hands-free. 'Hi, Mohsin.'

'Hey, baby, you hanging in there?'

'Has Penny got anything on the hate-mailer?'

'No, not yet.'

'Until she does, I'm going to work on the assumption that Jenny saw either the arsonist or someone connected to the arsonist, which is why he wants to kill her now. You did hear about the attacker?'

'Yes.'

'It was the secretary, Annette Jenks, who tipped off the *Richmond Post* about the fire,' Sarah says. 'But there was another tip-off, four months ago, about Silas Hyman not supervising the playground. Someone wanted him out of the school. Silas Hyman has the school calendar with Adam's birthday ringed. And his wife, she's lying. Or hiding something.'

'You went to his house?' Mohsin sounds horrified.

'No one else is doing anything, are they?' she snaps.

'What'll happen if someone finds out, darling, and—'

Sarah interrupts, her tone weary now. 'I know. Actually from a getting-into-hot-water angle, it's a lot worse. His wife was bathing their kids and I just didn't clock it. I'm a mother, an aunt; bathing children is just so normal and . . .'

So that's what rattled her. She'd been pretending to be on police business when children were naked.

'I left once I realised,' Sarah continues. 'But it made me so angry that I was in this position. And then I felt so angry about everything. And then this bloody woman was feeling sorry for herself!'

'Do you think she'll report you?'

'If she finds out I didn't have authorisation to go there, probably yes.'

'Well, I'm kind of impressed, actually,' Mohsin says. 'I always knew you had a subversive streak but never had you down as an out-and-out rebel.'

'Thanks. Anyway, I need the names of the investors in Sidley House.'

'Penny told me that fraud was ruled out almost straight away,' Mohsin says. 'They're comfortably in the black, according to the bank.'

'Yes, and they're starting the school up again in September. But I need to check all of it. I also need to know if we've got anything on a man called Donald White. I'm pretty sure he's abusive to his daughter, possibly his wife.'

'OK. I'll do what I can,' he says. 'I'm doing an extra shift tonight. So I'll meet you for breakfast tomorrow morning. Is that hospital café still going?'

Back at the hospital I follow Sarah towards ICU. Jenny is leaning against a wall in the corridor.

'I tried the scratch-and-sniff memory thing,' she says. 'But it's no good. A school doesn't smell like a hospital. At least Sidley House didn't.'

It's what I'd been banking on. Sidley House smelt of polish and hoovered carpets and cut flowers, not disinfectant, antiseptic and lino.

A little ahead of us, the last point before ICU where mobiles are allowed, Sarah is scrolling through her texts and emails. We look over her shoulder. There's a text from Ivo. He will be here in the morning. I look at Jen, expecting to see her beamy-happy, but her face is tight with anxiety.

'Jen—' I begin, but she cuts me off.

'I was about to go in,' she says, pointing at a door behind her. It's the entrance to the hospital chapel.

We go in together. Wooden pews and a carpet, threadbare but a carpet nonetheless. Even lilies, like the ones Mrs Healey always has in the waiting area outside her office; their smell pungent in the room.

The combination of scents transports me momentarily into Sidley House; as if the gateway to a memory has a keypad and the right sensory code is punched in. Looking at Jenny, I know that she feels it too.

'I was near Mrs Healey's office,' she says. 'And the lilies smelt really strong.' She pauses a moment and I wait. She's going further into the memory. 'I'm feeling happy. And I'm going down the stairs.'

Behind us, the door closes. An elderly woman has come in. It's broken the sensory thread to the past.

'You were going *down* the stairs?' I ask. 'Are you sure?'

'Yeah. I must have already got to the upper-ground floor because that's where Mrs Healey has those lilies.'

Maybe Annette Jenks was telling the truth about Jenny signing out.

Jenny closes her eyes again. She's back at school.

She screams.

'Jenny—?'

She's running out of the chapel.

At the back, the elderly woman has lit a candle, the smoke no more than a charcoal line in the air. But enough.

I catch up with her. 'I'm sorry, I should never have—'

'I'm fine now, Mum. I wasn't actually back in the fire, just close.'

I put my arm round her and she's shaking.

Out in the garden, the shadows are lengthening into soothing darkness.

'It was a good idea,' I say. 'To think of the chapel.'

'That wasn't why I was there,' she says. 'I was hoping to suck up to God. A last-minute dot com search for a place in heaven.'

Anxieties hidden in sleeves and fears stuffed up jumpers, but my God, Mike, I didn't expect this.

'I'm not that scared actually,' she says. 'I mean, this whole thing, whatever we are now, does make it likely there's some kind of an afterlife, doesn't it? It *proves* that the physical world isn't all there is.'

I've imagined talking to her about so many things: drugs, abortion, STDs. Some of these we have actually discussed and I had all my research to hand. But I've never imagined this conversation. I thought we were so liberal, bringing up our children without God. I just didn't think it through; never thought what it would be like facing death with no knowledge of a heaven or a God to go to.

'Do Christians believe that you go to purgatory if you're not baptised?' Jenny asks.

'You won't go to purgatory,' I snap, furious.

She's not going to drown. I won't let her.

My certainty startles me. And there's fear in it; the nervous, jittery-as-hell kind. But anything else is simply unthinkable.

'You're going to live,' I say to Jenny. 'You don't need to think about any of this.' I have my rope round her.

10

DR SANDHU TELLS YOU Jenny is getting weaker; slowly deteriorating, as they'd predicted.

'Can she still have a transplant?' you ask.

'Yes. She's still strong enough for that. But we don't know how much longer that will be the case.'

Jenny is waiting for me outside ICU. She doesn't ask if a heart has been found. Like me, she can now read an expression at ten paces and interpret a silence.

'Aunt Sarah's gone to meet Belinda, that nurse,' Jenny says. 'And she got a text from someone to meet in the cafeteria in half an hour. She looked really pleased. Do you think it could be her man?'

I was jealous of Jen's closeness to Sarah, but now it's the other way round. Jen and I don't talk about this kind of thing at all. Even the language is a minefield. For example, 'sexy' is old-fashioned and shows I don't have a clue, but 'hot' is embarrassing for someone as old as me (*a thirty-nine-year-old mother of two*).

But I have to break off this little cul-de-sac of a conversation because we've caught up with Sarah who's striding briskly down the corridor.

'She had a cracked wrist, last winter,' Belinda says. 'She said she slipped over on an icy doorstep.'

'Any reason for the doctors looking after her to be suspicious?'

'No. A and E gets filled with broken arms and legs when it's icy. Then at the beginning of March this year there's this.'

I read, with Sarah, the notes about Maisie being admitted unconscious to hospital with two broken ribs and a fractured skull. She'd said she'd fallen down the stairs. After being discharged from hospital she had failed to keep any of her outpatient appointments.

There's nothing else in Maisie's records. She hadn't shown any doctors her bruised cheek, nor the bruises on her arms the day of the fire, hidden under her long FUN sleeves.

Belinda gets out Rowena's notes. 'She had a significant burn to her leg last year. She said she dropped an iron on it and the burn mark suggested an iron.'

Was Rowena's scar the reason she was wearing long trousers on sports day? I'd thought she was just being more sensibly dressed than Jenny.

'I'd like you to tell me if Donald White comes to visit again,' Sarah says. 'I don't want him to have unsupervised access.'

Sarah joins Mohsin in the cafeteria. His caramel-coloured face is tired; shadows under his eyes. Their heads are bent close together; old confidants. We join them.

'We've got nothing on him,' Mohsin says. 'One speeding ticket, issued last year, sum total.'

'What about the investors at Sidley House?'

'There are a couple of venture capitalists who invested in a number of similar projects; legit business people. Another investor, the largest one, is the Whitehall Park Road Trust Company.'

'Do you know who that's owned by?'

He shakes his head. 'It could be one case of domestic violence. Another of malicious mail. And another of arson. All three completely separate.'

'There's a connection. I'm sure there is.'

Mohsin takes her hand, gives it a squeeze.

'I should get back to Mike,' Sarah says.

Almost before they've gone the cleaner sprays the table.

I see that Jenny's very still.

The cleaning fluid is still pungent on the Formica table.

'I went into the school kitchen,' she says. Her eyes are closed. 'They'd cleaned it all up. And it was steamy because the dishwashers had been running.'

In here there's steam from newly washed cups and saucers being placed on a rack by the coffee machine.

'I got two big bottles of water out of the kitchen,' Jenny continues. 'It was my job to bring out extra water at the end of sports day in case they didn't have enough. The plastic handles are too narrow and they dig into my hands. I take them up those steps, you know, the exit by the kitchen?'

Then she stops and shakes her head.

'That's it. I was going out of the school, definitely *out*. But I don't know what happened then.'

I don't know what to say.

'Maybe that's when I lost my phone,' she says. 'When I bent to put the water down. It was in that little pocket at the top of my red skirt.'

'Yes.'

'You should go and see what Aunt Sarah's up to,' she says. 'I'll stay here if that's OK. It's the only place that's halfway normal.'

I leave Jenny in the cafeteria and go to ICU.

Ivo is standing in the corridor. Just seeing his narrow back view and trendy haircut brings vivid memories of Jenny, a whole dimension of her that has been left behind since the fire—the exuberant, energetic teenager with *joie de vivre*; walking on air as she fell in love, so trusting of Ivo to catch her.

He hasn't gone to her bedside but neither has he run away.

I go closer. His face is white as he looks at her through the glass wall; I feel overwhelming pity for him. Sarah is with him.

'I spoke to her on Wednesday,' he says. 'And she sounded just like usual. Happy. And then we texted each other. The last one, from me, she must have got at just after three, her time.'

'It was arson,' Sarah says. 'We don't know if someone deliberately targeted Jenny. Possibly it's connected to the malicious mail. Do you know anything?'

'No. She hadn't got any idea who it was.' His voice is quiet and shaken.

I see you leaving Jenny's bedside and coming out into the corridor, but they haven't seen you yet.

'Someone threw red paint at her,' Ivo says.

Sarah jumps on this. 'When was this, Ivo? Did she see who it was?'

'No. It was from behind. About eight weeks ago.'

'Do you know where it happened?'

'In Hammersmith shopping arcade, just by Primark. She thought he must have run into a shop or a side exit to the street straight afterwards. I should have made her go to the police,' Ivo says. 'She said her parents would be so upset if they found out. She didn't want to worry them.'

'I'd like you to give a statement at the police station to a colleague of mine. I'll get a car to pick you up and drop you back again.'

Ivo nods.

Sarah gives him Jenny's mobile. 'Can you look through this, see if there are any contacts you don't recognise? Or messages that seem strange to you? I've looked, but I can't see anything odd.'

He takes it, fingers tightening round it. 'Now?' Ivo asks. 'While I wait?'

'Yes.'

Sarah sees you. 'There was red paint, Mike—'

'I heard.' Your whole body seems caved in and your face gaunt.

'Why don't you go and see Adam?' Sarah says. 'I can stay with Jenny.'

Ivo interrupts. 'I'm not sure if it means anything, but the last text I sent her on Wednesday afternoon has been deleted.'

'She could have done that,' Sarah suggests.

'It was a poem. She wouldn't have deleted it.'

'Jenny's phone was found on the gravel outside the school,' Sarah says. 'Anyone could have tampered with it. We couldn't get prints because it's been handled by the Reception teacher and Maisie.'

'But why would someone want to delete my message?' Ivo asks.

'I don't know,' Sarah says.

'Should I wait here for the ride to the police station, or down in the foyer bit?' Ivo asks.

He still hasn't gone to Jenny's bedside. I think he's relieved by the opportunity to be away from her.

I find Jenny in the goldfish-bowl atrium, people swarming past her.

'Ivo's here,' I say. 'He's in ICU with Dad and Aunt Sarah.'

'I don't want to see him,' she says, her voice quiet.

Yesterday she was excited about him coming. Perhaps she's realised that their relationship is based on physical beauty. She's so vulnerable.

I don't tell her that he stared at her through the glass and was tortured by what he saw.

'He's told Aunt Sarah about the red paint,' I say instead. 'He also said that he sent you a text at three, but it's deleted.'

'But I never delete his texts.'

'Maybe someone did that after you dropped your phone. He's going to the police station to give a statement.'

'So he'll come through here?' Her voice is panicked. She turns and hurries away from the atrium.

I go after her. 'How many people know your mobile number, Jen?'

'Loads.'

'I don't mean friends, I mean, well, people at the school, for example?'

'Everyone. It was written up on a notice board in the staffroom. Teachers were meant to call me if they needed anything from the sickroom during sports day.' She hurries on, fleeing from the possibility of seeing Ivo.

But I stand still a moment, feeling frustration as a physical force. Sarah needs to know that Jenny was outside the school, but then went back in. Something or someone must have persuaded her. Could it have been a text? And could the person who sent it have deleted it, and deleted Ivo's too in their haste?

The only time you've been with Addie since the fire, he pushed you away from Silas Hyman. But now, alone together, it will surely be different. I'm desperate to see you and Addie together.

In Addie's bedroom, Mum is drawing the curtains. He's in bed.

'You're exhausted, poppet,' she's saying. 'And I'll sit with you.'

I long to go to him, but I know he won't feel me and I don't think I can bear that now; so instead I watch Mum.

She sits down next to him in the darkened room. She takes his hand and I see his face relax a little.

I hear the front door closing and your footsteps in the hall. I almost hear you yell 'I'm home!' up the stairs and Adam yelling, 'Daddy!' 'A Railway Children moment every day,' you said once. But then you'd had to go away more frequently and got home later. Your Railway Children moments with Addie had become few and far between.

Adam sits upright, his whole body tensed.

Mum goes downstairs to find you. Away from Addie, her face looks terrified. 'Has anything happened?' she asks.

'All the same.'

'Addie's in bed, but he's awake.'

She looks so sad, so vulnerable without her mask for Addie in place.

Your footsteps sound heavy on the stairs, weighted down.

You knock on Addie's door. He doesn't answer.

'Ads?' you say. 'Open the door, please.'

Silence.

The other side of the closed door, Adam is curled up on top of his bed, as if unable to move as well as speak.

For God's sake, Mike, just go in there right now and tell him you know he didn't start the fire.

But you say nothing. You think he already knows.

Outside the ICU, Sarah is on her mobile to Mohsin.

'Hi, me. I've got five minutes while Jenny's having some tests done.'

'Her boyfriend's giving a statement to Davies, right now,' Mohsin says. 'Jesus, honey, why didn't they tell anyone?'

'They didn't want to worry us. What's happening with the hate-mail investigation?'

'It's turned into stalking and assault, so the enquiry's upped several gears. Penny's going to widen the DNA search and she's got people sweating blood over the CCTV footage. She'll get stills of mugshots, from which she's hoping to get an ID.'

'Is anyone connecting it to the arson attack?'

'Not yet.'

'You?' She tenses as she waits for his reply.

'I think that someone tracking Jenny and then physically assaulting her means it's far more likely the fire was aimed at her. I believe it's more than possible that the witness, whoever they are, was lying.'

'You must have been right about Donald White,' she says. 'It must be a separate thing.' She pauses. 'Has Ivo told you about his missing text?'

'Lord Byron? Thank God there wasn't texting when I was a teenager.'

'If he really sent his poem at just after three, the fire had already taken hold. She wouldn't have been deleting poems. Can we get the techno guys to check it out?'

'Sure. Though I don't know what we're checking for.'

You come to my bed and pull the curtains round.

'He doesn't want to see me.'

'Of course he does. He loves you. And he needs you. And—'

'I don't blame him. I've been a bloody useless father. No wonder he turned to Silas Hyman. I was never there, was I?'

'That's not true. You were earning the money so—'

'But even when I was with him I got it wrong. He's never wanted me in a crisis. Always you. And now . . .'

'I've just been there. You just need to be with him. Talk to him.'

But you can't hear me. Your insecurity about Adam blocks out what I am telling you as much as my lack of a voice.

And your loss of confidence with Addie is my fault. I was always telling you off and pointing out what you should be doing with Adam, never letting you just do it your way. So many small things—what kind of birthday present; what to write in his homework diary if he hadn't finished so that he wouldn't get into trouble. 'Let him get into trouble,' you'd said and I'd thought you cruel. But maybe if he had got into trouble, he'd have realised it wasn't so awful. And perhaps I *should* have risked being late to school with him, as you wanted. He might have seen that the world didn't collapse, and then maybe he'd have stopped worrying.

And I'm sorry that I said you didn't stand up for him at the prize-giving. Because a few months later, you made sure Robert Fleming wouldn't come back the next academic year. And it was nothing to do with you being a man or your celebrity status. Mrs Healey realised that she was no match for you when you were protecting your son.

You didn't want Adam to find out about your meeting, worried he might feel guilty for Robert being made to leave. But I think you should tell him now, so he knows that you're there for him when it counts.

You are still silent.

'You *can do this*, Mike.'

Dr Bailstrom pulls the curtains back. 'It's important to observe your wife at all times,' she says curtly.

'To prove that you're right and there's damn all to observe?' you snap back at her as you leave for Jenny's bedside.

I leave with Sarah, and as I get to the atrium I catch a glimpse of Jen outside, screened by a knot of smokers. I hurry out.

She sees me. 'I need to know the reason I went back into the school. For Addie. There's gravel by the kitchen exit. And I thought the sound of it—the feel—would help. But it hasn't done any good.'

A smoker strikes a match, cupping it in his hands to light his cigarette. The smoke from a match is flimsy, unable to push open a memory door.

Then Sarah walks past us on her way to the car park. The sound of her footsteps crunching gravel joins the faint smoke trail from the match.

'The fire alarm was going off,' Jenny says. She pauses as the memory comes into focus. 'I thought it was a mistake,' she continues. 'Or a practice and Annette wouldn't have a clue what to do. I thought it would be mean to leave her on her own, so I put the water bottles down on the gravel and I went back in. Then I smelt smoke. And I knew it wasn't a practice.' She stops, frustrated. 'That's it. That's where I get to.' She's upset. 'I'd thought I went in because I saw something, you know. A person doing something. But it was just to make sure Annette was OK.'

But why wasn't she able to leave again? Annette had time to phone the *Richmond Post* and a television station and put on lipstick and still get out.

If there really is a deleted text, then maybe it wasn't to get her into the school but *to keep her there*. Maybe it was the reason she was at the top of the school. She was *two floors above* Annette's office when I found her.

'Go inside, sweetheart,' I urge her, and she does. She hasn't said anything about Ivo, and I don't press her on it.

I catch up with Sarah by her car.

Twenty minutes later Sarah parks on a fast busy road in Hammersmith, her car half straddling the meagre pavement. I follow her to a small terraced house, the bricks stained black by exhaust fumes.

Sarah rings the doorbell. A moment later Elizabeth Fisher calls through the door, without opening it. 'If you're from any religion or an energy company I'm already sorted out on both fronts.'

'It's Sarah Covey. Grace's sister-in-law. Can I come in?'

Elizabeth looks pleased to see Sarah. She leads her hospitably into her tiny sitting room. Outside the traffic thunders past, shivering the walls.

'I heard the parents at Sidley House sent you flowers when you left?' Sarah says.

'Delphiniums and some freesia bulbs, with a lovely letter. Mrs White and Mrs Covey organised it.'

'They thought your husband was dying.'

Elizabeth turns away and she looks ashamed. 'Somehow they got the wrong end of the stick.'

'Didn't you put them straight?'

'How could I? After those beautiful flowers and their kind letter, how could I say that my husband had left me and that I'd been fired for being too old?'

'I have a query I want you to help me with,' Sarah says. 'You mentioned your job involving new admissions—sending out prospectuses and sorting out the forms?'

'Yes. It was quite an onerous task.'

'Your successor doesn't have admissions as part of her job description.'

'No, well, I suppose the new girl wouldn't have to do admissions, or at least—' She breaks off. She looks suddenly older and frailer.

'After the accident in the playground,' Sarah says, 'were there fewer new admissions?'

Elizabeth nods. 'The admissions didn't fall off straight away. It was after the *Richmond Post* article about the accident. Before that I'd get two to three phone calls a week from prospective parents. Why choose Sidley House when there are two other private schools in the area with good results and no children almost being killed in the playground?'

'How many new children were coming to Sidley House in September?'

'At the time I was booted out, we were down to six in the two Reception classes for the next academic year.'

When Adam went to Sidley House, both Reception classes were full with another fifteen children on a waiting list if a place became vacant.

'Who knew about this?' Sarah asks.

'Sally Healey. And the governors, I imagine. She didn't want to worry the other staff; she said she'd be able to sort it all out.' Elizabeth's posture is hunched now.

'Thank you. You've been very helpful.'

She tries to regain her composure. 'She didn't want anyone to find out. That's why she fired me, isn't it?'

I get in the car with Sarah. Almost immediately the in-car phone rings.

'Sarah?' Mohsin's voice sounds different. And he almost never calls her Sarah, always 'darling' or 'baby'.

'I was about to call you,' she says and she's buzzing. 'I just saw the old secretary. The one Annette Jenks replaced.'

'You mustn't—'

'I know. Shouldn't have done that. But—'

'Sarah, please. Listen to me. Baker's had Sally Healey checking up on you. He's talking about disciplinary procedures.'

'Right. Well. You'd better not be caught fraternising with the enemy then.' She hangs up. The phone rings again but she doesn't answer it.

After three days of intense heat, the grass is parched; the azalea flowers, once blooming up to chest-height, lie desiccated on the ground.

Sally Healey's Portakabin door is open.

Sarah knocks on the door. Sally Healey is visibly startled to see her.

'I know that you made a complaint about me. And I understand that. It's fair enough. But I'm here now as Jenny's aunt and Grace's sister-in-law.'

Sally Healey looks shocked. 'I didn't know.'

'If you want me to leave, just say so.'

Sally Healey says nothing and barely moves. The hot humid air seems to weigh us all down in the small space.

'Shall we walk and talk?' Sarah says.

Sally Healey joins Sarah outside. There's a faint breeze. They start walking round the large playing field and I follow.

'You told me that your school was full on sports day,' Sarah says. 'And how hard you'd worked to achieve that.'

'Yes, and we will start again, as I said, in September.'

'But there are only a handful of new children joining Reception, isn't that right?'

'I can get new children to join. I'm going to offer bursaries and scholarship schemes. Target families who wouldn't normally go to private schools.' But as she speaks her voice is limp, wrung out by the energy needed for such optimism.

'Do the other investors share your confidence?' Sarah asks.

Sally Healey is silent.

'I imagine,' continues Sarah, 'they only saw the school facing financial ruin. Which would become apparent to everyone in September. Presumably the rest of the school would start to fall apart too. No one wants their child in a school that's going down the tubes. Was it you who decided to get rid of the member of staff in charge of admissions? To keep things quiet?'

Sally Healey's stride has become jerky. She doesn't reply.

'Was it you who made up the story of Elizabeth Fisher's husband dying? You must have known her husband had left her, for your ploy to work. And you used that information against her. You made sure she'd be too embarrassed to contact parents and tell them about the fall in admissions.'

'We just couldn't afford any more negativity. I'm not proud of what I did. But it was necessary.'

'You then replaced her with an unintelligent young secretary who could be relied on not to notice that no new families were signing up.'

'That's not how it was.'

'I think that's exactly how it was.'

We've reached the edge of the playing field now. Through the branches of the horse chestnuts, lining the driveway, you can just glimpse the black cadaver of a school.

'And this?' Sarah says. She turns to Mrs Healey, her eyes blazing. '*Whose idea was this?*'

'I had nothing to do with it,' Sally Healey says. 'Nothing! I spent years building up a school to be proud of.'

'So was it an investor who wanted a fire?'

'Nobody wanted a fire. *Nobody!*'

'Wasn't that why you wanted those fire precautions in place, so that the insurance would pay out?'

'No!'

'And no one gives a damn about Jenny and Grace. Just *money*.'

Mrs Healey is staring at her school. 'I heard that some of the children have already been given places in other schools,' she says, her voice very quiet now. 'And who's going to give me a job? When I allowed my school to burn down, when one of my teaching assistants is so badly hurt?'

'A colleague of mine will interview you formally,' Sarah says, curtly.

Tears mix with the sweat on Mrs Healey's cheeks. 'We were never going to come back from this, were we? Whatever I did.'

On her car phone Sarah tells Mohsin about the ticking financial time bomb at Sidley House. I remember the *Telegraph* journalist talking to Tara. *'The point is that it's a business. A multi-million-pound business. And it's gone up in smoke. That's what you should be investigating.'* Jenny had thought so too.

'We'll get people onto it straight away,' Mohsin says.

'Thanks.'

'I leave you alone for an hour,' he says, his voice affectionate, 'and you create a whole new line of enquiry. New suspect. New motive.'

Adam is *so close* now to being cleared. And surely that will help him; surely that will mean he can talk again.

'Baker's getting Davies to contact you about the disciplinary meeting,' Mohsin says. 'He wants you to come in at three today. But this may make him drop it.'

'I doubt that, somehow. The thing is, though, I've just got too much to worry about to really notice that I'm worrying about that too.'

We arrive back at the hospital, but I can't see Jenny. I follow Sarah to ICU.

You and Ivo are standing next to each other in the corridor. You're looking at Jenny through the glass, but Ivo isn't. Have you noticed that?

No, that isn't a criticism of him, because none of us can bear to look at her; but we are her parents, so we have no choice.

'I'm pretty sure it was fraud, Mike,' Sarah says to you.

'Do you know who?'

'Not yet. We're checking it all out, making sure the paper trail's there.'

She doesn't tell you about her disciplinary meeting with Baker; that the ice has given way beneath her now.

'Does it matter?' Ivo says. 'Who did this or why?'

No one's yet told him that Adam's been accused, that he's the reason it matters.

Ivo turns away and leaves. The doors of ICU bang shut behind him.

Where is Jenny?

I go after him, calling out, 'No. Don't go. Please. She doesn't mean it, saying she doesn't want to see you. She's just trying to protect herself, but it won't last. She wants to see you desperately, I know. And she needs you to be at her side.'

He walks quickly along the ground-floor corridor towards the exit, not hearing me.

I yell at him, *'Don't do this to her!'*

He gets to the glass wall that abuts the garden. He stops. In the garden, Jenny is sitting on the wrought-iron seat. He looks at her through the glass, totally still now. People swarming past him. *How does he know she's there?*

Ivo's emotion seems to shatter the glass between them. Not a hormonal tide, as I'd once patronisingly assumed, but something finer and lighter and purer—love that is young. I was wrong about him. Horribly so.

He looks for the door and finds it. He goes towards Jenny.

But she hurriedly leaves.

'Jenny . . .?' I say, not understanding.

'I don't want to see him! I told you that!' She walks quickly away from the garden.

Ivo looks around, as if searching for her. Then he leaves too, confused.

I don't understand her, Mike. I don't know her and I thought I did.

Ivo waits by the garden, hoping she'll return. And I wait too. But there's no sign of her.

I'm not sure how long we've been here, waiting by the garden, but I've just spotted Mohsin hurrying along an upper walkway.

When I catch up with him, he's meeting Sarah.

'I tried to get you on your mobile, but it's switched off,' he says. 'The head teacher is giving a statement backing up what you said and Davies has been looking more closely at the investors. The Whitehall Park Road Trust Company put two million pounds into Sidley House School thirteen years ago. It's owned by Donald White.'

The fraud has a face now.

'It fits with what you suspect,' Mohsin continues. 'If he's capable of

domestic violence then I think he'd be capable of arson. Baker's "reassess-
ing" the witness report against Adam. He now thinks—we all do—that
this was fraud. And that Adam played no part in the arson attack.'

Relief feels like a cool wind; a balm. And I see that Sarah feels it too.

'Donald White could have attacked Jenny that first night,' Sarah says.
'When her oxygen was tampered with. His daughter was in the burns unit
too. If he'd been discovered no one would have questioned him being
there.'

'Baker's brought him in for questioning,' Mohsin says. 'I'm going to talk
to Rowena and Maisie White now. See if they can shed any light on what
Dad's been up to.'

Sarah kisses Mohsin lightly on the cheek. 'I'll tell Mike.'

I go with Mohsin into the burns unit and towards Rowena's room.

Maisie is with her, unpacking some toiletries from a floral washbag.

'. . . and I've brought your nice Clinique soap as well as—' She sees
Mohsin and stops talking. I think she seems afraid.

'Maisie White?' He holds out his hand and she takes it. 'I'm Detective
Sergeant Farouk.' He turns to Rowena. 'And you're Rowena White?'

'Yes.'

'I'd like to ask both of you a few questions.'

Maisie steps towards Rowena. 'She's not really in a state to—'

'That's why I've come to talk to you here, rather than ask you to come to
the police station.'

Rowena rests her bandaged hand on her mother's. 'I'm fine. Really.'

'I gather that Mr White was an investor in Sidley House School?'
Mohsin asks.

'Yes,' Maisie says, her voice oddly terse.

'Why didn't he use his name?'

'We wanted to keep it private,' Maisie says. She looks anxious. 'I mean,
we didn't want anyone thinking Rowena was getting special treatment or
anything when she was at the school. And I didn't want friends to watch
what they said about the school. Using a trust name made it feel not so
much to do with us. And that's what it felt like. I mean, we all sort of
forgot about it.'

'Forgot about a two-million-pound investment?' Mohsin asks.

'Mum didn't mean it like that,' Rowena explains. 'It was more that we dissociated the school with the financial investment Daddy had made.'

Maisie is blushing and I think she feels 'a twit'. And I feel sorry for her.

'But it must have generated an income?' Mohsin asks.

'It's been our only source of income actually,' Rowena says. 'Dad's other businesses didn't weather the recession very well.'

'Did you know that you were about to lose all of that money and the income it generated?'

'Yes,' Rowena says immediately. 'We discussed it as a family,' she continues. She's trying to be the adult; mature.

'We'll be all right,' Maisie says. 'I mean, we're going to have to sell the house. Get somewhere smaller or rent. But in the great scheme of things, well, money isn't everything, is it? That's not what happiness is about, is it? And Rowena's finished at school now, so there are no more school fees. That would have been the only really hard thing to change, if she'd had to leave her school.'

'And how does your husband feel about this?'

'He's disappointed,' Maisie says, quietly. 'He wanted to give Rowena everything. In her second year at Oxford she has to live out of college and Donald had planned to buy her a little flat of her own. And it would be an investment, too, we thought. But clearly that's not possible.'

But I think there might be a more sinister reason for Donald wanting to buy Rowena a flat. Did he want to continue controlling her?

'I don't mind not having the flat,' Rowena says. 'Really. Not a bit.'

'And she'll have to get a student loan and a job while she's at university,' Maisie says. 'That's hard. I mean, when you're studying as well. I don't mind for me. I mean, I've always rather wanted a job, actually.'

'Mummy, the police officer doesn't want to hear all of this.'

'I have to tell you that your husband has been brought in to Chiswick Police Station for questioning.'

'I don't understand.'

Rowena is pale. 'The fire, Mummy. They must think it's fraud.'

'But that's just ridiculous!' Maisie says. 'He once joked that he'd burn the place down, but it was just a *joke*. You don't joke about something like that if you're actually going to do it, do you?'

'I'd like to talk to you in private later, Mrs White, but for now I want to ask Rowena a few questions.'

Very gently, Mohsin probes Rowena about Donald. But each avenue of questioning is blocked off by Rowena's loyalty. No, he's never lost his temper. No! He'd *never* hurt her in any way at all. He's a devoted father.

'You've got it all wrong!' she finally bursts out. 'Daddy didn't do anything. He wouldn't hurt anyone. You've got it *all wrong.*'

As Rowena cries, Maisie puts her arms protectively round her.

She and Maisie have both covered for him over the years, and surely they're covering for him now. Jenny thought Rowena ran into the burning building to make Donald proud, but was it to protect him, by trying to limit the harm he'd done?

Mohsin, clearly frustrated, winds up his interview. Maisie is going to the police station, despite Mohsin telling her she won't be allowed to see Donald. I don't understand her loyalty to him. Not with Rowena being hurt too.

But the hows and whys don't matter. Adam is cleared.

You are at my bedside, silent. I expected not a smile on your face but a relaxation in your body now that Adam is exonerated. But your body looks unnaturally stiff, like a marionette. Where's the man in the Cambridge teashop who was going to climb and abseil and white-water raft through life?

You tell me about the insurance fraud; that Adam won't be blamed any more. For a moment there's an energy in your voice, but that's as much relief as you have. Because no heart has been found for Jenny and I am still in a coma.

Then you tell me that a heart *will* be found for Jen, and that I *will* wake up. And that man is right here by my bedside. Not a marionette but a climber. How absurd I was to think you could relax at all now. Every fibre of your strength is needed to carry us both up that mountain of hope.

I return with you to ICU for yours and Sarah's changing of the guard at Jenny's bedside. Despite Donald being in custody, you've refused to stop guarding her.

Like me, I think that each time you leave her ward and then return you allow yourself to hope that a heart has been found for her. And that somehow not being there will make it more likely; a watched-pot-never-boils on a life-and-death scale.

Nothing has changed.

Jenny is outside ICU.

'No heart?' she says. 'Sounds like a bid in bridge.'

'Jen . . .'

'Yeah. Gallows. Sorry. Aunt Sarah's phoning Addie and Granny G.' Her face crumples. 'He's in the clear, Mum.' Her relief is expressed in tears. Her love for Addie is one copper-bottomed fact about her that never changes.

'About Ivo, Jen—'

She pulls sharply away from me. 'Lay off the interrogation. Please.'

She walks quickly away.

In the car park Mohsin is waiting to drive Sarah to the police station.

'It's really not good form to be late for your own disciplinary meeting,' he says, teasing her. But she doesn't smile.

'Addie still isn't talking,' she says.

But surely now everyone knows he's innocent, he'll be feeling a little better? Surely he can now at least turn away from the burning building?

'I just spoke to Georgina,' Sarah says. 'I thought that when he knew he was cleared it would change things for him, but . . .'

'Give him a little more time,' Mohsin says. 'Maybe it hasn't really sunk in yet.' Both Sarah and I hold on to his words.

Sarah goes into DI Baker's office, closing the door behind her. There's no need for me to shadow her any more, now that we know the arsonist, but I want to be with her when she's hauled over the coals.

DI Baker glances up as she comes in. 'Take a seat.' His voice is curt.

He gestures to a plastic chair but Sarah remains standing.

'Ends do not justify means, Detective Sergeant. I understand the emotional strain you must be under but there are no excuses. All police investigate cases *by the book*. And rightly. Fortunately,' he continues, his voice icy, 'the person who made the complaint against you withdrew it just over an hour ago.'

Perhaps Mrs Healey thought the police would go easier on her if she'd been kind to a fellow police officer.

'However, that doesn't detract from the *seriousness* of your misconduct—' Baker goes on, but a knock on the door interrupts him. The sharp-featured Penny Pierson comes into the room.

'What is it?' Baker snaps.

'Silas Hyman gave a sample of DNA when we questioned him about the fire. His DNA didn't match anything at the site of the fire but it matches the semen in the condom sent to Jennifer.'

11

'WE ARE NOW CERTAIN that Silas Hyman is Jennifer Covey's hate-mailer,' Penny continues. 'We think it must be Silas Hyman who also attacked Jennifer Covey with red paint. We therefore need to seriously consider whether he also tampered with her oxygen. It could have been an escalation of his previous assault.'

I was totally wrong when I thought Silas Hyman too intelligent, too subtle a personality, to cut out letters and stick them onto A4, let alone to post a used condom and dog mess through the letterbox.

And I remember him flirting with the pretty nurse. A smile and flowers, that was all it took to get through the door of a supposedly secure ward.

'You need to send someone to guard Jenny straight away,' Sarah says.

Baker looks at her. 'I will decide in due course what steps should be taken against you.' He turns to Penny. 'You will arrest Silas Hyman in relation to the malicious mail and question him about the assault against Jennifer Covey with paint.'

'And the guard?' Penny asks, winning my respect, but Baker is clearly infuriated by two women confronting him.

'The intensive-care unit has a very high ratio of medical staff to patients; Donald White is in custody for the arson attack. And Silas Hyman will shortly be arrested and put in custody.'

Sarah phones to tell you about Silas Hyman. I don't hear your response. She joins Penny in the police-station car park.

'I checked with Sally Healey,' Penny says. 'Jenny Covey was a teaching assistant with Silas Hyman last summer. That's when they must have got to know each other.'

I remember he confided in Jenny about his failing marriage last summer. I'd thought it was shabby of him but nothing more.

Sarah gets in the car next to Penny—an unspoken agreement that Sarah should be there when Silas Hyman is arrested.

'You still think that Donald White is the arsonist?' Sarah asks Penny as they drive.

'Yes. After your one-woman investigation,' Penny says with a faint smile, 'we are working on the assumption that it was fraud.'

'So we're still working on two separate cases. Let's see how Mohsin is doing,' Sarah says. She phones him.

'White's keeping quiet,' Mohsin says, 'waiting for his expensive lawyer. But his wife is kicking up a fuss. She says that he was in Scotland the afternoon of the fire.'

'She'd say anything he wanted her to,' Sarah says.

'Yeah. And the technical guys have been looking at Jenny's mobile. They think that two messages were wiped. They're trying to retrieve them but aren't sure it's going to be possible.'

She thanks him and hangs up.

'Why did Silas Hyman volunteer his DNA, do you think?' Sarah asks Penny. 'He must have known we'd trace it.'

'Maybe he didn't know that we cross-reference cases. Or he just assumed that the hate-mail investigation was over. But without the DNA we wouldn't have got him. The CCTV footage didn't have anything.'

We drive in silence, the police radio hissing. Sarah's face is tense.

'Can you tell me who the witness is who saw Adam?' she asks.

'Not yet. I'm sorry. I will once it's authorised.'

I wonder if anyone will ever inspire enough love in Penny for her to break the rules, let alone risk her career as Sarah has for Adam.

At Silas Hyman's house, another police car draws up behind us. A young uniformed officer, the archetype of a fresh-faced bobby, gets out and enthusiastically half jogs up to Silas Hyman's door and rings the bell. Penny follows more slowly.

Natalia appears furious and tired. She's looking at the two police cars outside her house. 'What is this?'

Penny is walking slowly towards them, staring at Natalia.

Natalia holds Penny's eye as she gets close to her.

'It was you,' Penny says to Natalia. 'Not your husband. You.'

Natalia steps away from her. 'What are you going on about?'

'I've got you on CCTV,' Penny said. 'Posting one of your nasty letters.'

'Posting a letter is a crime, is it?' But she's backing into the house.

Penny puts a hand on her shoulder, preventing her from retreating any further. 'I'm arresting you under the Malicious Communications Act. You do not have to say anything, but it may harm your defence if you do not mention, when questioned, something which you later rely on in court. Anything you do say may be given in evidence.'

Their house is only three streets from us. Easy to hand-deliver and get home again. Other times she'd posted her disgust from places all over London—was it to muddy the geography of where she really lived? I think about the red paint down Jenny's long fair hair. A woman's touch. And who'd notice a harassed mother with children in a shopping arcade? She'd have blended in and disappeared.

But how could Natalia have got into a locked ward? And did her hatred really extend to murder?

'**S**o why did you do it?' Penny asks.

In the back of Penny's car, Sarah next to her, Natalia is silent, picking at a thread in her seat belt, and I think she's itching to talk.

I remember Sarah telling a rapt dinner table that the best time 'to get info out of a suspect' is when you first arrest them, before they've reached the police station; before they've had time to think or take stock.

'You love him, do you?' Sarah asks, a note of sarcasm cutting through her words.

'He's a little shit. Weak. Useless. Fucked up my life.'

'So why bother with the hate mail then?' asks Penny.

'Because the little shit belongs to me, right?' Natalia snaps.

Not loyalty but possessiveness. I remember Jenny saying, '*She told him he was a loser. Said she was embarrassed by him. But she won't get divorced.*' Silas Hyman was telling her the truth.

'The head teacher told me I should keep my husband on a tighter leash,' Natalia continues. 'Like he was a dog. She'd got his measure. I asked what she meant. She said flirting with teaching assistants wasn't acceptable. Flirting, not fucking. She's very refined, Mrs Healey. But clever. She delegated him to me to deal with.'

'But you punished Jennifer Covey, not your husband?' Penny says.

'The stupid bitch made me a fool.'

I lift my hands to cover my face as if her words are spit.

'I saw them, her all long legs and short skirt and long blonde hair, a tart. He was flirting his pants off at her.'

'And the red paint?' Penny asks.

'The tart had to get her hair cut.'

'Why send the condom? When you knew it would be traceable?'

'I never thought . . .' Natalia begins, picking at the thread again. 'I wanted her to know that we were still having sex. That he was still making love to me.'

'**F**or Christ's sake, his wife made a mistake.'

'I know that, Mike,' Sarah says patiently. 'I just wanted to tell you.'

'It's *ridiculous*. The man's *thirty years old* and *married*, for God's sake!'

Jenny is listening to you and Sarah, in the corridor of ICU. She turns to me, bemused. 'His wife thought I was having an *affair* with him?'

I nod. Then summon up my courage. 'Were you?'

'No. He flirted with me, he flirts with everyone, but nothing more.'

And I believe her; of course I do.

She smiles at me. 'But thank you for asking.' She means it.

I don't ask her about Ivo, who I saw sitting in the corridor by the garden.

'Dr Sandhu's here,' Jenny says.

I turn to see him, with Jenny's cardiologist, the young Miss Logan.

'We'll be taking Jennifer for an MRI and CAT scan later today,' Miss Logan says. 'To check that she's still a candidate for transplant.'

'You think it's likely then,' you say, grabbing at her words.

'The time frame is extremely narrow. We are simply following protocol.'

'Remember we talked about the two kinds of burns?' Dr Sandhu says. 'We now know that Jenny's burns are superficial second-degree partial-thickness burns, which means that the blood supply is intact and her skin will heal. There will be no scarring.' But he sounds defeated rather than pleased.

'That's fantastic!' you say, refusing to be defeated too.

They go into the ward. Jenny stays in the corridor with me.

'Dead but not scarred,' Jenny says. 'Well, that's comforting.'

'Jen . . .'

'Yeah, well, sometimes only gallows humour cuts it.'

'You're not going to—'

'So you keep saying.'

'Because it's the truth. You're going to live.'

'So why didn't Dr Sandhu or Miss Logan say so? I need a walk.'

Sarah is waiting in the cafeteria, fingers tapping. She has her owl note-book out and has been reading through it. I sense increased energy in her exhausted face. She stops tapping as she sees Mohsin and Penny arrive.

'Natalia Hyman's been charged,' Penny says. 'She's admitted to all the incidents of hate mail and the paint attack.' Her features are softened with satisfaction at a job well done. 'Silas Hyman had nothing to do with his wife's hate-mail campaign. He didn't even know it was happening.'

'And the tampering with Jenny's oxygen?' Sarah asks.

'Natalia swears blind it wasn't her,' Penny says. 'And I believe her. I really don't think she's the saboteur.'

'And Donald White?' Sarah asks Mohsin.

'His alibi checks out,' Mohsin replies. 'He was on a BMI flight at three on Wednesday, halfway between Gatwick and Aberdeen. He must have had an accomplice.'

'Or the arsonist was Silas Hyman,' Sarah says.

Mohsin and Penny are taken aback.

I want her to stop, right now. I don't have the emotional capacity or the mental energy for this. We have it *sorted out*. Donald White burnt the school down to get the insurance money. Possibly Jenny saw something that incriminated him, which is why he may be the person who tried to kill her. That's it.

'But we've found out about the fraud,' Mohsin says to Sarah.

'We've found a motive, yes,' Sarah says. 'But I now think the arsonist could equally well be Silas Hyman.'

'Taking revenge on the school?' Mohsin asks.

'Yes.'

'But what about his wife giving him an alibi?' Mohsin asks. 'She clearly loathes him, so she'd hardly lie for him, would she?'

'If he gets sent down, she'll be a single mother with three children and no income,' Sarah says. 'It's in her own interests to lie for him. In any case, I think she still has feelings for him, in her own weird way.'

I agree, because sitting next to Natalia in the car, I glimpsed something fragile and wounded.

'OK,' Penny says to Sarah, a note of derision in her voice. 'Let's say he did want to torch the place. Even if he knew the gate code, how would he have walked through the school up to the second floor, unnoticed?'

'I've thought about that,' Sarah responds calmly. 'Although most of the staff were at sports day, there were still three members of staff in the building and it would have been risky. So he had an accomplice. Someone who made sure the coast was clear for him. What if it was Rowena White who was helping him? What if she kept lookout? Possibly made sure the secretary was distracted while he got in?'

'And why on earth would she do that?' Penny asks.

'Because I think that Silas Hyman was having an affair with someone at the school. A teaching assistant. But it wasn't Jenny. It was Rowena.'

I am startled. Rowena?

'But Natalia was *clear* it was Jenny,' Penny says. 'She *saw them* together.'

'Saw her husband flirting with Jen, yes,' Sarah says. 'But he flirted with every female at the school. Elizabeth Fisher called him a cockerel in the henhouse. I think he flirted with Rowena too. That it went further.

'Sally Healey just said it was a teaching assistant,' Sarah goes on. 'Natalia drew her own conclusions from that. And if you put the two girls side by side it's easy to see why you'd pick Jenny.'

'OK, but why ugly, dumpy Rowena when he has Natalia at home?'

'Because Natalia is the kind of woman who shoves shit through letter-boxes?' hazards Mohsin.

'And Rowena's extremely intelligent,' Sarah says. 'Maybe he's attracted to that. Or maybe he knew he could seduce her because she's vulnerable. Or she's seventeen and that's beauty enough. I don't know his reason.'

'Because there isn't one,' Penny says.

'There's more,' Sarah said, rummaging in her bag. 'I've got my notes here from when I spoke to Maisie White.'

Penny watches her, alarmed. 'Does DI Baker know about this?'

You arrive, interrupting.

'Is Jenny on her own?' Sarah asks, her anxiety clear. Because if it's Silas Hyman, as she thinks, he's out there somewhere and a threat.

'Ivo's with her,' you say. 'And a load of doctors. About Rowena White. After we spoke I remembered something. When I talked to Silas Hyman's wife, she accused me of getting her husband sacked. I thought she meant me as a parent, but I think she meant me *personally*. She thought *I'd* got him fired because he was having an affair with my daughter.'

Sarah nods and Penny is silent.

When you leave, there's a pause before anyone speaks again.

'I think Mike's right,' Sarah says. 'And it would explain the escalation of violence. She just got the wrong girl.'

'You said you spoke to Maisie White . . .?' Mohsin asks.

'Yes.' She opens her owl notebook. 'She told me, "It's wrong to make someone adore you, when they're young and can't properly think for themselves." I thought she was talking about Adam. But I think now that she was referring to her teenage daughter. She said that Silas Hyman got young people to love him because no one realised he was a sham. She said that he "exploits their feelings for him".'

Penny is now, like Mohsin, listening intently.

'I asked her when she'd changed her mind about Hyman. From my notes she didn't answer immediately. She then said it was at the prize-giving,' continues Sarah. 'But I think it was before then—when she found out about Silas and her daughter.'

I remember Maisie saying at the prize-giving, *'That man should never have been allowed near our children.'*

Silas Hyman was at the school the previous summer when Rowena was a sixteen-year-old teaching assistant. Why didn't I realise she meant Rowena? And why hadn't Maisie told me—and later Sarah—the truth? I think it's probably because she thinks it's a slur on her daughter.

And she's used to keeping secrets.

'When I spoke to Rowena the next day,' Sarah says, 'she told me that Silas was violent.'

'You have your notes on that interview too?' Mohsin asks.

She nods and gives him the notebook. 'The good angel and the devil thing, that's interesting,' Mohsin says as he reads.

'If she helped him with the arson attack,' Penny says, 'it would explain why she ran back in. Maybe she hadn't realised that people would get hurt.'

'Let's talk to her,' Mohsin says, getting up.

'I'll call the station,' Penny says. 'Get them to find Silas Hyman urgently.'

I follow Mohsin and Sarah to the burns unit and I look through the glass wall at Rowena. No one with an undamaged face can ever look even plain to me now, but I do understand Penny's harsh honesty about her.

Yet she was beautiful as a little girl. Like a fairy child, with her enormous eyes and elfin face and silky honey-blonde hair. But at six her tiny white perfect teeth had been replaced by uneven gappy ones. Her eyes seemed to shrink as her face grew and her shiny fair hair turned dull matt brown. I felt for her. It must have been so hard to have been so gloriously pretty and then to lose that.

Jenny did the opposite: our gawky duckling grew into a beautiful teenager, while Rowena suffered the adolescent blight of acne. Growing up must have been fraught for Rowena, even without her father's abuse. I doubt she's had many romantic bids from boys her own age. Did all of this make her vulnerable to a man like Silas Hyman?

Sarah and Mohsin go into her room.

'Hello, Rowena,' Mohsin says. 'I'd like to ask you a few more questions.'

Rowena nods, but she's looking at Sarah.

'As you're under eighteen,' Mohsin says, 'you should have an adult with you to—'

'Can Jenny's aunt stay with me?'

'Yes, if that's what you'd like.'

Mohsin looks at Sarah and some kind of communication passes between them.

Sarah sits in the chair next to Rowena's bed. 'Last time we spoke,' she says, 'you said that Silas Hyman was very good-looking? You said you used to watch him . . .?'

Rowena looks so acutely self-conscious that I feel uncomfortable too.

'Did you find him attractive?' Sarah asks, kindly.

Rowena is silent.

'Rowena?'

'I had a crush on him from the moment I saw him. I knew he'd never look at someone like me. The handsome ones never do.'

'You also told me you thought he could be violent.'

It's as if Sarah has slapped her. 'I shouldn't have said that,' she says. 'It was stupid. I really don't see him that way at all. I mean, I just guessed that he could be. I mean, anyone has the capacity for it, don't they?'

'Was he ever violent to you?' Mohsin asks.

'No! He never touched me. I mean, not in a bad way.'

'But he did touch you,' Sarah says.

Rowena nods.

'Were you having a relationship with Silas?' Mohsin asks.

Rowena looks at Sarah, seemingly torn.

'I'm a police officer asking you a question,' Mohsin continues. 'And you have to tell me the truth. Doesn't matter what promises you've made.'

'Yes,' Rowena says.

'But you said he didn't look at you?' Sarah asks gently.

'He didn't. I mean, not to start with. It was Jenny he wanted. He was besotted with her; flirted with her all the time. She didn't flirt back, got a little irritated I think. But I was always there. And finally he noticed me.'

'How did that make you feel?' Sarah asks.

'Unbelievably lucky.' For a moment she looks happy and proud.

'Has Silas been to visit you here?' Mohsin asks.

'No. It's over between us. A while ago, actually. But even if we were still together, well, he wouldn't want Mum to see him with me.'

'Your mum doesn't like him?' Sarah asks.

'No. She wanted me to break it off.'

'Was it your parents who told the *Richmond Post* about Silas, after the playground accident?' Mohsin asks.

'It was just Mum. Daddy said it wasn't fair to try to get someone the sack for personal reasons. But Mummy hates Silas.'

Good for Maisie. She might not have left Donald but she stood up for her daughter with Silas. Though I'm not sure if she knew that her phone call would lead to the bankruptcy of her family.

'You must have missed him, after you broke it off?' Sarah asks.

Rowena nods, upset.

'Did he try to get in touch with you again?'

She nods, tears spilling now.

'Did he ever ask you to do something for him? Something that you knew was wrong?'

'No, of course not. I mean, Silas wouldn't do something like that to me. He's always been kind to me.'

She's a terrible liar.

A nurse comes in. 'I need to change her dressings.'

Mohsin stands up. 'We'll see you a little later, Rowena, OK?'

Mohsin and Sarah leave.

'Do you think Silas Hyman asked her to start the fire?' Mohsin asks.

'I don't know. It's possible, but I think it's more likely that she enabled him to do it. She's clearly vulnerable to him and I think he'd exploit that.'

Penny is hurrying down the corridor towards them.

'Donald White has been released without charge,' she says. She sees Sarah's expression. 'He has an alibi and a good lawyer. There was nothing we could do to legitimately keep him any longer.'

'Do you know where he's gone?' Sarah asks.

'No.'

'And Silas Hyman?'

'We're looking at the building sites. Nothing yet.'

I follow Sarah along a glassed-in walkway towards ICU. As I look down to the parched, too-hot garden beneath, I can see Jenny's blonde head and, beside her, Ivo. From above I watch him move closer towards her. She bends her body towards his.

You are in the corridor of ICU with Sarah, keeping watch on Jenny through the glass.

'But there must be some way they can find him?' you say, incredulous.

'We don't even know if he's actually working on a building site, or if that's a line he spun his wife. We'll keep looking for him. And Donald White,' Sarah says. 'Have you spoken to Ads?'

Emotion tenses your face. You shake your head. 'I'll go and see him as soon as you've found them both.'

Sarah nods. 'Maybe when the arsonist is locked up it'll be different for Addie,' she says.

Will he speak then? Surely he will.

Ivo walks past you and into Jenny's ward. But only I see that Jenny is with him. They go up to her bed.

This is the first time she has seen herself since right after the fire. Her face looks swollen and blistered. Even though she knows she won't be scarred, I dread what she must feel as she sees her burnt face.

Her tears are falling onto Ivo's face and he wipes them away as his own. I know it's not her appearance that distresses him. It's what she must have suffered.

I think she was afraid of his rejection before and she was protecting herself. And now she doesn't have to. It's his love that gives her the strength to look at herself.

You tell Sarah and Ivo that you need to see me. Sarah wants to catch up with the police, but there's now Ivo as a member of the guard rota at her bedside. And I trust him, as you do.

'Ivo's with Jenny, darling,' you say to me. 'I think that's what she wants. You think she's too young for something to be so serious, but . . .'

'She's nearly grown up now,' I finish off. 'And I ought to see that.'

She's become an adult; a young adult, yes, but still an adult with spaces that are hers alone.

'I know she'll always be little Jen too, to us,' you say. 'But we have to kind of disguise that. For her sake.'

'I don't think any parent really ever lets go,' I say to you.

Again a watched-pot hope as we return to Jenny's bedside together.

She isn't here.

A nurse sees your panic and tells you she's just been taken to the MRI suite and her boyfriend and a doctor from ICU have gone with her. You hurry out.

I try to still my panic. I slow my pace to a walk while you race on.

I pass the chapel door and hear a low, animal keening sound. I go in.

She's kneeling at the front of the church. Her crying is the sound of despair.

Every nerve in me jangles into a run to her. I put my arms round her.

'I didn't want to be with him, Mum.'

'But he loves you. I saw that.'

'I know he loves me. I've always known that.' She turns to me and I can hardly bear to look at the anguish on her face. 'I knew that if I saw him I'd want to live too much.'

'Jenny-wren—'

'I don't want to die,' she shouts; and her shout echoes around the chapel until it's a sonic boom of emotion. '*I don't want to die!*'

Her face is starting to shimmer. She's getting too bright to look at.

This can't happen. Please.

And I'm running to the MRI suite, down corridors, through swing doors.

She needs a heart. Right now. The surgeons need to be taking her old damaged one out and putting in one that will keep her alive.

I race to the lifts and get in as the doors close.

But Miss Logan said that she had to be stable first. Not dying. Not this.

Doctors surround her and their machinery makes inhuman noises and you are there and I think of the River Styx and Jenny being rowed towards the underworld. But the doctors are trying to reach her, throwing ropes with grappling hooks over the side of the boat, and they're pulling it, pulling her, back to the land of the living.

You are staring at the monitor.

It has a trace!

'Her physical condition has drastically deteriorated,' Miss Logan tells you and Sarah at Jenny's bedside. 'We can keep her stable for two, maybe three, days.'

'And then . . . ?' you ask.

'We've run out of options. I have to tell you that the chance of finding a donor heart in the time frame left to her is non-existent.'

I feel your exhaustion. The boulder of love you've been carrying up that mountain has slipped all the way down to the bottom. You have to start that Sisyphean task all over again.

Mohsin arrives.

'I'm sorry, but I thought you ought to know straight away. It was deliberate. Just now, while she was in the MRI suite, someone disconnected her respirator. Baker's sending proper protection now.'

Penny is in the small institutional office where Baker once accused Adam. With her is an ashen-faced doctor. Ivo is waiting outside.

'And you're *sure* you were next to her, *all the time*?' Penny asks.

'Yes, like I said. Right next to her.'

Sarah and Mohsin come in, but Penny gestures at him to carry on.

'Someone must have walked past and quickly tugged out the endotracheal tube. It must have been quickly because I didn't see. I mean, I didn't take my eye off her for long. I was just looking at her chart and checking the details for her scan . . . Then I heard the alarm go off, the device that alerts us to a cardiac failure. And I was dealing with that. It was only when other people came to help that I saw the tube to the respirator had been disconnected.'

'Thank you,' Penny says. 'Could you wait in the corridor and a colleague will come to take a full statement.'

When he's left the room, Penny turns to Sarah and Mohsin.

'The MRI suite has four scanning rooms and a waiting room, with changing rooms and lockers. It has a secure door, but it's far busier than ICU. There's administrative staff as well as medical personnel—not only doctors and nurses, but also porters bringing patients into the suite, and outpatients. I've got Connor interviewing the reception staff, and I'm hoping her boyfriend might have something.'

She calls Ivo in and he walks in determinedly tall.

'She's not going to die,' he says.

He reminds me of you. Not the denial in the face of the facts, that bullish optimism, but the strength it takes to walk upright. So she's gone for a man like her father after all.

All these revelations; all so quickly.

'Can you tell me what you saw?' Penny asks.

'Nothing. They wouldn't let me in with her. Other patients had partners with them, I saw them going in, but I wasn't allowed to.' He is furious with himself. 'I told her father I'd look after her.'

'Did you wait for her?' Penny asks.

'Yes. Outside the MRI bit. In the corridor.'

'Did you see anyone?'

'Just what you'd expect. Doctors, nurses. Porters. And patients, some in normal clothes so I suppose they're not staying in the hospital.'

Ivo leaves to return to Jenny. Penny answers her phone.

'She was already dying for crying out loud,' Sarah says to Mohsin. 'Why shorten her life any more?'

'Maybe whoever did this doesn't know she's dying,' Mohsin says. 'When you've spoken about it, it's been about her needing a transplant. Maybe that's what he has heard too. Perhaps he was worried about her getting a transplant.'

'I was here, all the time, and I didn't stop it.' Sarah breaks down.

Mohsin holds her. 'Darling . . .'

'How can I help Mike?' Sarah says. She pulls away from Mohsin, furiously blows her nose. 'We need to find the bastard. Mike's daughter is dying and his wife is dead in all but name and he won't care at all about justice now—what difference will it make? But it's all I can do for him.'

Penny gets off the phone. 'Baker wants us to wait for him before talking to Rowena. Fifteen minutes. This time, we'll get the truth out of her.'

You're at my bedside. You're silent, but I am used to that now, as if you can tell when I'm actually with you.

Ivo is with Jenny and I'm glad you're demonstrating your trust in him by letting him guard her again.

I reach you and put my arms round you.

You tell me the doctors have said she will only live another two days.

'Just *two days*, Gracie.'

And as you tell me the truth of it hits you. That open green prairie of your mind, with its stockade of hope, is flooded with terror for her.

You hold my hand and I feel you shaking and I can't help you.

A nurse and a porter arrive to take me for a scan. The one where you need to pretend to hit a ball for 'yes', to light up a part of your brain for their monitors.

'Hit it for yes, Gracie,' you say. 'Hard as you can. Please.'

Rowena and Maisie are waiting in an office, with a young police officer I don't recognise. Sarah is with Mohsin and Penny just outside.

'Baker's on a call. He won't be long,' Mohsin says. 'I'm still not sure about allowing Maisie White to be present at this.'

'We'll be able to watch her reaction too,' Penny replies. 'And questioning Rowena might tip Mum finally into telling us the truth.'

'Has Maisie White told us yet where her husband is?' Sarah asks.

'Claims she has no idea,' Penny says. 'The stupid bitch is lying again for him.'

Baker arrives and they go in, while Sarah waits outside.

Rowena looks frail in her nightdress and dressing gown, her damaged hands still bandaged. Maisie fusses around her, sorting out her drip stand.

Mohsin formally introduces everyone in the room while the young police officer records it.

'Your father has an alibi for the time of the fire,' Mohsin says, his voice matter-of-fact; but I see him studying Rowena's face intently. Penny is watching Maisie.

'Yes,' Rowena says, barely reacting. 'Daddy was in Scotland on Wednesday.'

'Did your father ask you to light the fire, Rowena?' Mohsin asks, still matter-of-fact.

'Of course he didn't,' Maisie says, her voice too high. A vein is flickering in her temple.

'What about Silas Hyman?' Mohsin says to Rowena, his voice sterner.

'No, I told you before,' Rowena says, distressed. 'He didn't ask me to do anything.'

'An hour ago someone tried to kill Jennifer Covey,' Baker says. 'We don't have the time or patience for you to protect the man who did it.'

I hear a sharp intake of breath. Maisie has gone white.

Rowena is silent, struggling. She turns to her mother. 'I think it's best if you left.'

'We can find another competent adult to be with Rowena,' Baker says.

'Is that what you'd like?' Mohsin asks Rowena.

She nods.

Maisie leaves the room. I don't see her face.

'If you just give me a little while,' Penny says to Rowena. 'We need to find someone—'

'I have to tell you the truth now. Because of Jenny. I have to. It wasn't Dad. It wasn't anything to do with him. It was Mummy,' Rowena says.

Maisie?

I see her loving face and feel her encompassing hugs. I think of her that day at the sports field, handing me a 'little something' for Adam, beautifully wrapped, a spot-on present inside. She'd known it was his birthday. Of course she had! She'd known him since he was born. And 300 other people knew it was his birthday. The spool of our friendship stretches back through the years and won't unravel.

'Mummy's afraid of being poor,' Rowena continues. 'She's always had lots of money. My grandparents were rich and she's never had to work.'

But Maisie said it wouldn't matter to her being poor and she didn't mind working. *I've always rather wanted a job, actually.*

'She went into Sidley House to read,' Rowena continues, 'so that she could keep a check on what was happening after I'd left. Sally Healey didn't tell anyone that there were no new admissions. But Mum found out from Elizabeth Fisher.'

She didn't go in to spy! She went in to read because she loves being around young children.

'Did she ever leave your room?' Mohsin asks.

'Well, yes, she goes and gets things to eat. She goes out to use the phone, too.'

'An hour or so ago, when we left you with your mother,' Mohsin says, 'did she leave your room again then?'

Rowena's voice is so quiet that I have to strain to hear it. 'Yes. Almost right away.'

There is no way, *no way*, that Maisie tried to kill Jenny. Everyone's got this *wrong*.

'Thank you, Rowena. We'll need to interview you again, formally.'

Outside the office, Baker turns to the young policeman.

'Chase up that social worker. I'm not going to give a defence lawyer any rope on this one.'

'Maisie White must have seen Jenny being taken out of ICU and followed her,' Mohsin says. 'Got lucky with the MRI suite. Security's not as tight.'

Sarah nods. 'When Jenny's ventilator was tampered with, it was in the burns unit. Maisie was staying in Rowena's room just down the corridor. No one would have questioned her being there.'

'So you think it was Maisie, not Natalia Hyman?' Mohsin asks.

I'd only seen a back view—but it couldn't have been Maisie.

'Yes. Jenny must have seen her at the school,' Sarah says.

'And she had Jenny's mobile,' Mohsin says. 'If there was anything incriminating on it, she'd have had plenty of time to delete it.'

As they speak it's as if a painting-by-numbers portrait is being filled in, one colour at a time.

But I won't look at their vicious portrait of my friend.

Because Maisie's known Jenny since she was four. She's heard me talk about her and Adam, all the time. She knows how much I love them.

She's my friend and I *trust her*.

I can't add this to what has happened, so I turn away from their picture.

'What about the domestic abuse?' Mohsin asks.

'God knows what's been going on in that family,' Sarah says.

'Find Maisie White,' DI Baker says to Penny. 'And arrest her for the arson attack and attempted murder of Jennifer Covey.'

I follow Sarah back into the stifling office.

'OK, Rowena, we're waiting for a social worker. In the meantime—'

'Will Mummy be taken away?' Rowena asks.

'I'm sorry, yes.'

Rowena says nothing, staring at the floor. Sarah waits.

'You don't have to say anything. This isn't an interview. Just a chat. If you'd like it.'

I don't think Sarah is seizing an opportunity. I think she's just being kind to Rowena. Or perhaps she just needs to know now, unable to wait.

'Mummy feels terrible. Really guilty. It's been awful for her,' Rowena says. 'She needed to tell someone.' She starts to weep. 'She'll hate me now.'

Sarah sits down next to her.

'This is awful, but I was glad that she confided in me,' Rowena continues. 'She doesn't do that. Never has. Everyone thinks we're close, but we're not. I'm her "little disappointment".'

But Maisie *adores* her. Surely to God, if there is one thing about Maisie that I am absolutely convinced of, it's that she loves Rowena.

'When I was little I was pretty, you see,' Rowena continues. 'She was proud of me then. But as I got older, well, I stopped being pretty. And she stopped loving me. I wasn't the kind of daughter she wanted any more.'

Argue with her, I urge Sarah. Tell her that mothers *don't do that*. They don't stop loving their children.

Sarah says nothing.

'It's hard, you know,' Rowena says. 'Not being pretty. I mean, at school the popular girls are the ones with the pretty faces and long hair. Not the clever girls with bad skin. Not me. A cliché really, isn't it, for a clever girl to be ugly? And then you go home and it's the same.'

'You're going to Oxford, aren't you?' Sarah asks.

'To read Natural Sciences. She doesn't tell people that bit. Pretends I'm off to May balls and parties and handsome undergraduates, not a Science lab. I thought she'd be pleased about Silas,' Rowena says, and I hear grief in her voice. 'I mean, he's handsome, isn't he? I thought it was like proving to her that I could be like a pretty girl too.'

'But he's *married* for crying out loud,' I say to her. 'And he's thirty. Of course your mother didn't want him to be your boyfriend; she wanted something better for you.'

'She went to see him,' Rowena continues. 'He'd sent me a Valentine's Day card. She went to his house. Told him he had to stop our relationship.'

The hate mail from Natalia stopped the day after Valentine's Day. Maisie's talk with Silas worked.

'I loved him,' Rowena says quietly. 'I thought he'd fight for me. But he didn't. Then Mum got him fired. She phoned the newspaper, not thinking what would happen to the school, just wanting to punish him.'

A nurse knocks and comes in. It's Belinda.

'There's a ward round and the doctors need to take a look at her.'

Sarah stands up. 'Of course.'

It's cooler up here in my ward, the open windows and white linoleum at least visually lowering the temperature. A porter is wheeling a trolley, with my comatose body on it, towards the bed. My scan must be finished.

You are waiting.

Dr Bailstrom's shoes click across the linoleum towards you.

She tells you that their scan shows I have no cognitive function. No brain activity beyond the basics of swallowing, gagging and breathing.

I wasn't out on a grassy tennis court, warm under my toes, thwacking a ball over the net. I was with Sarah as she spoke to Rowena. No wonder they think I'm not there.

You ask to be alone with me.

You take my hand in yours. You lay your head down next to me, so that our faces are close, my hair falling across your cheek. United by almost twenty years of loving each other and seventeen years of loving our child.

The essence of our marriage is distilled in this moment.

I move away from you. It will help you, my darling, if you think I'm not here. It will make this easier. And I want to make this easier for you.

I leave the room.

Outside the office on the ground floor, everyone is gathering for another interview with Rowena. The social worker is already in there.

'There's something you should know,' Penny says, not meeting Sarah's eye. 'You probably should have been told before.'

'Yes?'

'Maisie White was the witness who said she saw Adam coming out of the Art room, holding matches.'

I have never known her.

12

'SHE SEEMED GENUINELY DISTRESSED by what had happened to Jenny and Grace,' Penny tells Sarah. 'And was reluctant to tell me it was Adam. I thought I was having to force it out of her.'

'If I'd known—' Sarah begins.

'Yes. I'm sorry. Since you found out about the fraud we've been working under the assumption that she was protecting her husband. In retrospect she was playing us. I'm sorry.'

'I told Maisie that a witness had seen Adam,' Sarah says. 'And she was surprised. I thought it meant she had no idea.'

'A good actress?' suggests Penny.

Sarah thinks a moment then shakes her head. 'It's because I'm a police officer. She thought I would *already know* it was her who was the witness. She'd have assumed I'd been told. It was my ignorance that surprised her.'

There are so many people in here, making Rowena seem smaller. She is staring at the shiny carpet-tiles, not looking up.

'Why did your mother say she saw Adam coming out of the Art room?' Penny asks.

'She wanted a child to be blamed,' Rowena says. 'So that no one would suspect fraud. It was just chance that it was Adam's birthday that day.'

'So who actually started the fire?'

Rowena is silent.

'Was it you?' Mohsin asks. 'Did your mother ask you to do that?'

She doesn't reply.

'You said that you need to tell the truth?' Mohsin reminds her.

'She made Adam do it.'

But no one could make Adam do that. He's too good, too thoughtful.

'She told Adam that Mr Hyman had left him a birthday present in the Art room,' Rowena continues. 'She told him it was a volcano. They'd done that in Year Three—you know, with the vinegar and the baking soda, making an eruption? She told Adam he needed to light it. She said he could use the matches from his cake, which she'd fetched for him.

'She told him Mr Hyman had brought the volcano present to the school himself, even though he'd get into terrible trouble if he was found there. That Mr Hyman was waiting to say happy birthday to him. That he'd be back any minute. And that he'd be really disappointed if Addie wasn't playing with the birthday surprise.'

'What was in this volcano?' Penny asks.

'She said it was white spirit and another accelerant. She'd also put cans of spray mount round it. She told me Adam must have been chicken and thrown the match from a distance; otherwise it would have blown up in his face.'

'Did she intend to kill him?'

'No. Of course not. She *can't* have.' But her voice shakes, no scaffolding of conviction to sustain it.

'Is there anything else?'

Rowena nods, her face cloaked in misery and shame. 'She came up to Addie, when his mother had run in to find Jenny. She said, "You weren't meant to actually do it, for goodness' sake, Addie!" She told him it was a knight's test, and he'd failed it. That it was all his fault.'

And Adam believed her. Because Adam believes in quests and tests of courage and honour. Because in his eight-year-old imagination he was Sir Gawain. But instead of the giant nicking the side of your neck, your mother and sister are trapped in a burning building in front of you while you're told that you are to blame.

I have to run to him now and tell him it isn't his fault. *It isn't!* But my vocal cords no longer make sounds.

And Adam, too, is mute. Adam's guilt silenced him.

'That's why I went in,' Rowena says quietly. 'After what she'd said to Addie.' She pauses a moment, upset. 'I'd really like to see him, tell him it wasn't his fault at all. I mean, he probably won't want to see me, but I'd really like to.' Her voice peters out for a moment.

'It was partly my fault,' she continues. 'I told Mummy about the volcano experiment. I was in Adam's class as a teaching assistant, last summer term. And I thought it was so sweet the way he wanted to be like a knight—and I told her.'

But I'd already told Maisie that, countless times.

Rowena is miserably silent. I want one of them to tell her it wasn't her fault either, but they are police officers in that room, with a job.

'Do you know why your mother wanted to harm Jenny?' Penny asks.

'She didn't mean to. It wasn't till Grace ran in, shouting for her, that I knew she was in there. And Mum was the same, I'm sure. She wouldn't have hurt Grace or Jenny. I know she wouldn't. It was a terrible mistake.'

She's shaking violently now. Mohsin looks at her with concern.

'I don't think she's up to any more,' he says to Penny.

'Do you think your father knew what your mother intended?' Penny asks.

'No.' She pauses a moment. 'But he blames me for not stopping her in time. I mean, I was there. I should have stopped her.'

Penny escorts Rowena out of the room and back to the burns unit.

I go to my ward. The curtains are drawn round my bed.

Inside, you're lying with me, pressing yourself against me, sobbing so hard that your body judders the bed. Crying because you know I'm not there. I long to go to you but it will make it harder; so much harder.

Then Sarah comes in and puts her arms round you and I'm so grateful to her.

She tells you about Maisie, but you hardly listen. Then she tells you that Adam was tricked into lighting the fire; that he was told it was his fault.

For the first time you turn from me. 'Oh Christ, poor Ads.'

'You'll go to see him?' Sarah asks.

You nod. 'As soon as I've seen Grace's doctors.'

You've asked for the meeting with my doctors to be at my bedside, as if you need to see my comatose body right here in front of you to do this.

You've asked Dr Sandhu to be here too and it's his kind face I look at. I can't bear to look at yours.

You tell them that you know now that I won't wake up. That I am not 'in there' any more.

You tell them that Dad had Kahler's disease and that Jenny and I were tested to see if we were suitable donors for bone marrow. You tell them that Jenny and I are a tissue match.

You ask them to donate my heart.

I love you.

But Dr Bailstrom tells you I am breathing unaided. It will be at least a year, probably longer, before they'll even *contemplate* getting a court order to withdraw food and fluid.

You faced my living-death out of love for Jenny and you think nothing has come of it. Now you're left with the brutal fact.

Dr Sandhu suggests a 'Do Not Resuscitate' document. I imagine that it's pretty standard procedure in these circumstances. But, as Dr Bailstrom points out, there is no reason why I should collapse and need resuscitating. My body, ironically, is healthy.

I think Dr Sandhu is trying to give you a little kindness, a little hope. Because if my body does collapse, instead of being resuscitated it would be kept oxygenated until my organs could be transplanted.

In Dr Sandhu's office you sign the DNR form. Jenny comes in and watches.

'You can't do this, Mum.'

'Of course I can and you—'

'I've changed my mind.'

'It's too late to change your mind, sweetie. I am never going to wake up again, Jen, but you can get better. So logically—'

'Logically what? If you go ahead with this, I refuse to get back into my body. Ever.'

'Jenny, you want to live. You—'

'But not by killing you.'

'Jen—'

'I refuse!' She means it.

Yet she longs overwhelmingly to live.

You're going home to see Adam and I go with you. As we walk down the corridor, you lean a little towards me, as if you know I'm with you. Maybe now you no longer think I'm in my body you can sense me with you in other places.

As we pass the garden, the shadows lengthening into evening, Jenny is joining Ivo. Before, I'd marvelled at him knowing where she was, amazed at the connection between them. But looking at them now, I just want her to be in his world, the real world—*for him to be able to physically touch her.*

In our car, I fantasise, just for a minute or so, that we're back in our old life and we're going out to dinner with a bottle of wine in the boot. I wish, absurdly, that it could be me driving. '*That's a decent Burgundy in the boot, Gracie! So go gently on the bends!*'

I even fantasise a row. Let's make this a bit more realistic.

'You were heavy on the indicator there,' you say.

'Heavy on an indicator? How can you be *heavy* on an *indicator?*'

I'm quite enjoying this, a mixture of teasing and arguing and flirting.

'The stick, you need to be . . .'

I either laugh at you for being ridiculous in a mock row, or start a real row about you patronising me. We nearly always opt for the mock version. So I laugh at you and you hear what I am not saying.

The little fantasy shatters as I see our house.

The curtains are drawn in Adam's room. It's seven thirty now. Bedtime.

You turn to me, as if you've caught a glimpse of my face. Am I a ghost to you now? Haunting you?

You go into our house and I follow you.

In the kitchen my mother, bracing herself, says she told Adam after that first big meeting with my doctors that I wasn't going to wake up; that I was dead.

But you are grateful. I think that, like me, you see Mum's courage. The only one of us to take the body blow of what the doctors said first time.

You tell her about your failed attempt to donate my heart.

She says she hopes by some miracle it can happen.

'I couldn't bear it, for her to live when her child is dead. To suffer that.'

You put your arm round her. 'And you, Georgina?'

'Oh, you don't need to worry about me. I'm a tough old bird. I won't fall apart.'

You go up the stairs to Adam's bedroom door.

'It's Dad.'

The door remains closed.

'Addie . . .?'

You wait. Silence the other side.

Perhaps you're right to wait for Addie to come to you; showing him you respect him. I'd have just barged in there, but that's not the only way to do this.

'I know you think you're to blame, my lovely boy,' you say. 'But you're not.'

You've never called him 'my lovely boy' before. A whole phrase of mine you've adopted and I'm glowing about that.

'Let me in, please?'

The door is still shut between you.

'OK, here's how it is,' you say. 'I love you. Whatever you think you did I love you. Nothing—absolutely nothing—can ever change that.'

'It *is* my fault, Daddy.' The first words he's spoken since the fire. Words so huge they've been smothering speech.

'Addie, no—'

'It didn't really look like a volcano. Just a bucket, with some orange tissue paper on the top and something inside it. She said I was supposed to light it. But really it was a test. I wasn't meant to do it.'

'Addie—'

'I don't like matches. They scare me. And I *know* I'm not meant to use them. You and Mum and Jenny are always telling me that. So I knew it was wrong.'

'Please, listen to me—'

'Mr Hyman said Sir Covey would pass the test with flying colours. Sir Covey is me. He thought I was like a knight. But I'm not.'

'Mr Hyman was never there, Addie. He cares about you and he'd never, ever ask you to do something like that. She made it all up. The police have arrested her. Everyone knows it wasn't your fault.'

'But it is. I *shouldn't have done it*, Dad! Whatever she said to me. Sirens and the green giant's beautiful wife tempted people, but the good people didn't do what they said. The strong knights didn't do it. But I did.'

'They were grown men, Addie, and you're eight. And a very brave eight-year-old.'

Silence the other side of the door.

'What about the time you stood up for Mr Hyman? That was really brave. Not many adults would have the courage to do that. I should have told you that before. I'm sorry I didn't. Because I am really proud of you.'

'It's not just that,' he says. 'I didn't go and help them, Daddy.'

His voice, so full of shame, punches a hole in both of us.

'Thank God,' you say.

Addie opens the door and the barrier between you is gone.

'I couldn't bear it if I'd lost you too.'

You put your arms round him and something floods through his body, relaxing his taut limbs and frightened face.

'Mum's never going to wake up. Granny G told me. She's dead.'

'Yes,' you say.

He starts to cry and you hold him as tightly as you can.

Silence expands between you, a blown soap bubble around the emotion it contains, then breaks.

'You have me,' you say. Your arms round Adam aren't trying to hug him now, but clinging onto him. 'And I have you.'

Five hours have gone past and it's nearly midnight now.

I've been back to the hospital with Mum and I need to tell you what happened.

The goldfish-bowl atrium was almost deserted, just a few straggling patients; a single doctor hurrying. Lights from cars flashed through the glass of the window from the darkness outside.

I thought about Mr Hyman and how afraid I'd been of him when he came to the hospital. '*Get away from my children!*' He's deeply flawed, yes, but not guilty of any sin. A fallible man but blameless of any crime. Addie was right to trust him. And I'm so glad you told Addie that Mr Hyman cares about him.

Mum went to Jen's bedside. In the corridor, I saw Jen waiting for me.

'I need to know,' she said. 'Why I went back to the school, and why I went up to the top again, and my mobile phone thing. I need to know all of it.'

We had the big picture then, the huge facts, but not the details.

'The police will find out when they question Maisie tomorrow,' I said.

'But I might not have that long,' she said. 'I told you, Mum, I'm not going through with your plan. And I'm *not going to change my mind*.'

I didn't argue with her, because as well as courage, our daughter has inherited your infuriating stubbornness. '*Independence of mind!*' you'd correct. '*Strength of character!*' I also knew that she had plenty of time, because that's what I would give her. I would win that argument.

'I need to remember it all, Mum,' she said. 'Because if I don't, it's like a part of my life didn't happen. The part of it that changed everything.'

We went towards Rowena's room, because Jen had had her 'mad

person's tinnitus' memory there. At the time, we'd thought it was the smell of Donald, not Maisie, that had prompted it. I wondered which of the scents in the room had prompted that memory—perhaps Maisie wore perfume that I hadn't consciously noticed before.

When we reached Rowena's room, Maisie's cardigan was still draped over a chair. She must have left it behind when she was arrested. Jenny closed her eyes.

I waited with Jenny for a few minutes. I braced myself to face the stranger that my friend had become.

'I'm taking water out of the kitchen,' Jenny said. 'I get outside. The fire alarm is making a hell of a din. I think Annette won't know what to do. So I put the water down and go back in. Bloody hell, it really is a fire.'

She broke off. We'd got to this point before. Jenny took my hand.

'I was afraid to do this alone,' she said. 'I mean, go any further.'

She closed her eyes again. 'The smoke isn't that bad,' she said. 'You can smell it, but no worse really than when there's something in the oven that's caught. I'm not frightened, just working out what I should do. I think that actually Annette won't be worried at all, she'll be loving this. Finally she has her drama.'

I saw Jenny struggling as she reached the final doors in the memory corridor.

'And then I see Maisie,' she said.

Her body had gone rigid.

Maisie, in her long-sleeved FUN shirt, is crying. 'I saw Adam coming out of the Art room,' she says. 'Oh God, what have you done, Ro?'

Rowena, in her sensible linen trousers, is facing her, blazing with anger. 'You saw Adam, and you blame *me*?'

'No, of course not. I'm sorry I—'

Rowena slaps Maisie's face, brutally hard.

'You sent me a text,' Maisie says. 'I thought you'd—'

'Forgiven you?'

'I just wanted what was best—'

'You take away my lover and then you bankrupt us. Stunning, Mummy.'

Maisie rallies for a moment. 'He was too old for you. He was exploiting you and—'

'He's a pathetic piece of shit. Spineless. And you are an interfering bitch.' Shouting at her, whipping her with words.

'I should go and help,' Maisie says. Then she turns to Rowena, finding courage. 'Did you make Addie do it, Ro?'

'You decide, Mummy.' She wipes the tears off Maisie's face. 'You need to wash your face.'

Maisie leaves to help with the Reception children. She hasn't seen Jenny.

But Rowena sees her.

She sees Jenny and knows she's heard everything.

Jenny remembered that at that moment the fire didn't seem important. She knew there was virtually no one in the school and everyone could easily get out. All she could think about was Rowena hitting her mother.

'Adam's gone to look for you,' Rowena said to her. 'Up in the medical room.'

And everything changed.

The school was on fire and *Adam was at the top of the school.*

Jen ran to find him.

And Addie? Where was he, really? I need to rewind a little now so he can feature in this ghastly film too.

I watch him leave sports day with Rowena, who's suggested she takes him to get his cake. So carefully planned.

They reach the edge of the playing field. By the chest-height jewel-coloured azalea bushes I think they pause a minute, while Rowena tells Addie about the birthday present Mr Hyman has left for him. And Addie is really pleased.

That still figure I saw on the edge of the playing field was Rowena, with Adam next to her; but he was too small to be seen above the azaleas.

They walk on towards the school.

Rowena goes with Addie up to his classroom to get his cake. She takes the matches out of Miss Madden's cupboard. She tells him that Mr Hyman's present is in the Art room. It's a different kind of volcano. He has to light it. He can use his birthday-cake matches.

But Adam doesn't want to, surprising Rowena, because she underestimated him; so she tells him Mr Hyman brought the volcano present to the school *himself*, even though he'll get into terrible trouble if he's found there. She tells him Mr Hyman will be coming up to the Art room soon and will be so disappointed if Addie isn't playing with his present. So Addie reluctantly agrees.

Rowena leaves and goes down the stairs to the office.

Addie goes to the Art room. He trusts Mr Hyman, loves him even. But he's afraid of matches and he's never lit one before, isn't sure how to do it.

Rowena has time to listen to Annette's chatter, hardening her alibi.

Adam gets a match to light. He stands well back and throws it at the volcano.

And the bucket, full of accelerant, pauses a second as the flame catches, and then it explodes, flames leaping out. Addie is terrified and runs.

I know, darling, I want to have been with him then too. Made it all right for him too.

Maisie is coming out of the ladies' toilets, the alarm sounding, and she sees him as he runs from the Art room.

Adam dashes down the stairs, past the secretary's office, and out of the main exit.

And the two films collide now because Maisie sees Rowena. 'Oh God, what have you done, Ro?' Jenny sees Rowena hit Maisie. So Rowena tells her that Adam is looking for her up in the medical room.

A single sentence and our family is destroyed. Because Jenny goes up to the third floor, looking for Addie.

She smells smoke, but it's not too bad, not yet; maybe she hears flames, but nothing yet to see. She doesn't know that the fire is travelling through the wall cavities and ceiling spaces and through vents.

Outside, on the gravel next to the statue, Rowena has her arm round Adam. And I think it's now that Rowena texts Jenny. I think she tells Jenny that Adam is still in the school, to keep her in there.

By the side of the school, near the discarded water bottles, Jenny's mobile bleeps with a message. But no one hears.

Because the fire explodes. Flames ricochet along walls; heat tunnels along corridors and through ceiling cavities, punching through into rooms and blowing out the windows and the school is drowning in choking smoke.

On the playing field I see the thick black smoke and start running.

Next to the bronze child Rowena tells Addie that it's all his fault.

Jenny had opened that fire door into her memory, and it was terrifying. She was shaking violently. 'I'm in the fire. Addie must be here too. And it's everywhere, the fire, burning, and . . .'

I put my arms round her and told her that she was safe now. I helped her to come back to me.

Rowena was still sleeping. We left her room; neither of us could bear to be near her now.

'Addie was outside all the time, wasn't he?' Jenny said. 'I mean, that's what Annette's statement said, and Rowena's.'

'Yes.'

They'd both been outside; for a minute, maybe two, both had been safe. But Jenny had gone back in.

'She planned to kill Addie,' Jenny said. 'Must have done.'

I remembered Rowena describing the white spirit and accelerant in the 'volcano', and the cans of spray mount stacked up behind. Brilliant at Science, Rowena would know which chemicals explode and burn.

'It was meant to blow up in his face,' Jenny said. 'She must have been terrified when he was OK—then thought it was bloody Christmas when he couldn't speak.'

'Yes.'

'She only had one injury, the burn from an iron. It *was* an accident, just like she said. I don't think her dad ever hurt her before,' Jenny continued. 'Just that one time. Because he knew what she'd done to us.'

I remembered that scene in Rowena's room, Donald grabbing her hands. *He knew.* 'You disgust me,' he'd said.

'He realised she'd only gone into the fire to look good,' Jenny said. 'She probably just went as far as the vestibule. Then lay down knowing the firemen were coming. She wanted to make sure no one suspected her.'

'*Quite the little heroine, aren't you?*' Donald said. His fury was shocking.

I remembered another time; Maisie's voice; the sadness in it. '*You shouldn't condemn someone, should you? If you love them, if they're your family, you have to try to see the good. I mean, that's what love is in some ways, isn't it? Believing in someone's goodness.*' It was her daughter, not her husband, she'd been protecting all this time.

Had Rowena planned, from the start, to blame her mother? '*She texted me a little while ago, said the tubes were up the spout.*' I don't suppose there was anything wrong with the tubes.

'You need to get better, Jen,' I said. 'And then you can tell everyone what you heard and saw.'

She half smiled at me. 'Good try, Mum. But Addie will tell everyone it was Rowena who made him do it.'

'Yes, and Dad will believe him, and so will Auntie Sarah, but no one else will. Maisie will have given a full confession by now.'

'*You know I'd do anything for Rowena,*' she'd said. '*Don't you, Gracie?*'

'The police are not going to believe an eight-year-old against adults,' I said. 'Maybe they might have listened to Addie at the start. Not now though, when it's taken him so long.'

'But they *might*,' she insisted.

'Oh God.'

'Mum?'

Thoughts were circling round something so horrible that I couldn't bear to look at it; but they were getting inexorably closer. '*I'd really like to see him, tell him it wasn't his fault,*' Rowena had said.

Jen shook her head as I told her, as if that would stop it being true. But she knew that it was.

'You need to get better,' I said to her. 'To make sure Adam is safe.'

I hated blackmailing her like that. But it was the only way. The life of your child trumps everything.

'You can do that,' she said.

'I can't because—'

Mum—'

'Let me finish. Please. OK. There won't be any miracles. I believe in a lot of things now that I didn't before. Ghosts, angels. I think they're all real now. But I don't believe I'll get better. I have no cognitive function, Jen. I'll never recover from that. I can't protect him,' I said. 'But you can. You can live and give him an adult's voice.'

'Angels, Mum?' Jenny asked, trying to smile. 'You think that's what we are now?'

'Possibly. Maybe angels aren't really good or special, just ordinary, like us.'

Then her voice was quiet and ashamed. 'I want to live so much.'

'I know.'

'I will never love anyone the way you love me.'

'You stayed looking for Addie in the fire. You didn't get the text, but you stayed anyway.'

We arrived home. Mum went to bed, exhausted, and I was the only one awake. It was almost the witching hour, the house silent, everyone asleep. The last time I'd been up on my own like this was when Adam was a young baby.

I went to Jenny's bedroom. I'd left her with Ivo in the garden, promising I'd see her again in the morning. No goodbyes yet.

'What's it like to have a teenage daughter?' a mum at school, whose eldest child is the same age as Adam, asked me once.

'There are always boys in the house. Huge great boys with huge trainers in the hallway,' I said, because I always trip over them. 'You're always out of food because the same boys are always hungry. The girls eat nothing and then you worry about anorexia, and even if your daughter eats fine you worry about bulimia. The main thing,' I continued, warming to my theme, 'is sex. It's everywhere.'

'You mean they . . . in your house?' She sounded horrified.

'No, not exactly,' I said, wondering how to explain that sex comes into the house and takes it over, wafting through the corridors and loafing on the stairs, hormones funnelling out of the windows.

The scent of it lingered there, in Jenny's room. Not sex or hormones, I realised, but great quantities of life still to be lived.

I sat at her desk and saw that there were virtually no books, but a whole shelf of Ordnance Survey maps for hiking and climbing. As far as I could tell, her desk had mainly been used to paint her nails. I could see little smudges of shiny red on it.

Did I tell you that a few weeks before her A levels she said she'd rather 'live my life now, than revise for a future one'? So different to me at that age, desperate to get to university, swotting the whole way through sixth form.

I thought university would be wonderful for her too. I thought she'd do the full three years and love every moment of it. It wasn't that I wanted her to live out the unlived part of my life, but that I thought what made me happy would make her happy too.

And I was cross with you when you didn't try to stop her from going climbing in the Cairngorms instead of doing revision, or when she swapped a French exchange visit for canoeing in Wales with Ivo. I was so sure that she was not thinking of the future—not realising that she was living a life-choice right there in front of me. An outdoorsy girl, like you, my darling, who prefers canoeing and climbing to Dryden and Chaucer.

I should have looked at her life from her perspective; climbed up a mountain with her and seen the surrounding landscape of other ways to achieve fulfilment and happiness.

I'm lying next to you in Adam's room. You are on the top bunk, Adam on the bottom, Aslan tucked in next to him. From up here, I can see a new perspective on his so-familiar room. I can see that the top of his globe lampshade needs dusting. 'A tidy house is a sign of a wasted life,' Maisie once told me, kindly, knowing my antipathy to housework, and that's good, because from up here mine's clearly been profitably spent.

I'm actually really proud of my mothering now, of both Jenny and Adam, if I had any hand in the making of the people they've become. And I have no regrets about my choices, even the default ones. Other people can write the great book, paint the wonderful painting, because I don't need a work of art to speak for me after I've gone; my family will do that.

I go down to Addie's bunk.

I've always known how much you love him. But until the fire, I didn't know how much he was loved by Jenny and Mum and Sarah too. Between you, there's enough love to inflate a lifeboat for him.

I walk into his dreams and I tell him how special he is.

'The most special boy in the whole world,' I say.

'The galaxy?'

'The universe.'

Another oven-hot day; the sky a sadistic cloudless blue.

I return to my ward. The windows are open but there's no breeze, heat from outside seeping in. Nurses are sweating, wisps of hair sticking to their foreheads.

No sign of Dr Bailstrom's clicking red heels and I'm grateful that I won't be distracted by fashion in what should surely be a serious, high-minded moment.

I fight my way back into my body, through layers of flesh and muscle and bone, until I am inside.

I am trapped, as I knew I would be, under the hull of a vast ship wrecked on the ocean floor. My eyelids welded shut; my eardrums broken; my vocal cords snapped off. Pitch-dark and silent and so heavy in here; a mile of black water above me.

All I can do is breathe.

I remember that the Latin word for breath and spirit is the same.

I hold my breath.

When Jenny faced her death in that chapel and looked for a heaven, I faced mine too. Properly. Fully. I told you then that I wouldn't let her die.

I knew that my child staying alive trumps everything. Adam's grief. And yours. My fear. Everything.

I must not breathe.

But I still hoped it would be someone else. Somebody else's mother and daughter and wife. Someone else's life.

My hope was desperate and ugly and futile. Because it was never really going to be someone else. And maybe that's fair. We keep our child but lose me. A balance.

I must not breathe.

I think of Adam up there on the surface in his inflatable lifeboat made out of other people's breath.

I think of Jenny reaching the shore of adulthood.

I think that the fear of my children drowning showed me how I could do this.

So little air in my lungs now.

Will you read Addie 'The Little Mermaid'? It's in his *Stories for Six-year-olds* on the bottom shelf of his bookcase. He'll say he hasn't read those stories for years, Dad, and in any case it's too girlie, but you'll insist. You'll put your arm round him, and he'll turn the pages for you.

You'll read to him about the pain the little mermaid felt when she left the water, walking on knives, because she loved her prince so. Because I want him to know that the hardest thing in this world is leaving him.

I slip out of the wrecked ship of my body into the mile-deep dark ocean.

You told me once that the last of the senses to go is hearing. But you're wrong. The last of the senses to go is love.

I am floating up to the surface, and with no effort I am slipping out of my body.

An alarm is going off, shuddering the air, and a doctor is running towards me. A trolley loaded with equipment is being speeded across the lino, a frightened nurse at the helm.

My heart has stopped.

I hear clicking red heels.

Dr Bailstrom says there's a DNR order. They talk of transplant. They will keep my body functioning until my heart can be given to Jenny.

I watch their machinery as my inert body has oxygen artificially pumped through it. You are ushered hurriedly into a room to sign a consent form.

I shouldn't really be here, surely, hanging around like this, still talking to you? A guest still at the table when the hosts are washing up in the kitchen. Shouldn't I be going to the next place now?

It must be when my heart is taken out and the machinery switched off that I will finally leave.

I go to ICU where Jenny is being prepared for the transplant. She's watching herself, Sarah bending over her body. I was jealous of Sarah's closeness to Jenny once, but I'm outrageously grateful now.

Jenny sees me and I take her hand.

'So much for becoming independent from me,' I say. 'I'll always be with you now. Beating away.'

'Mum, please! That's macabre!'

'Seriously,' I say, 'it's just a pump.'

'*Your* pump.'

'You have far more use for it.'

We don't know what to say. Neither of us has talked about whether she'll remember this.

'You'll get better,' Sarah says to Jenny, filling the silence. 'And you'll do a great job looking after Adam. But other people are going to look after him too. So be a girl, Jen, not a woman too early.'

'You're bloody marvellous,' I say to Sarah who, of course, can't hear.

I tell Jenny it's time to get back into her body now.

She hugs me and I want to hang onto her, but I make myself pull back.

'Ivo and Dad and Aunt Sarah and Adam are waiting for you,' I say, and she goes back into her body.

Surely there should be a dramatic storm; the pent-up compressed heat of the last four days released into thunderous drenching rain? But through the window of the ward the sky remains relentlessly blue, a heat haze fuzzing the edges.

I see you coming towards Jenny's bed.

You look at me. And in that moment you see me.

This is what love looks like after nineteen years, an uncountable number of words later.

I go to you and kiss your face.

I watch you go with Jenny as she is wheeled towards the operating theatre. I think about the angels of Fra Angelico, with their shining, jewel-coloured robes, long wings down their backs; Giotto's hovering above earth like larks; Chagal's blue angel with her sad, pale face. I picture Raphael's angels and Michelangelo's and the angels of Hieronymus Bosch.

I think that beneath each angel—just out of sight of the painting—are their children they were forced to leave behind.

But the heavenly afterlife isn't where I am, not yet.

I am sitting on the bottom step of our stairs packing Adam's bag with his uniform, which he'll need to change into after sports. I am knotting his tie so that all he has to do is slip it on and pull the skinny part because he still hasn't got the hang of tying his tie and I hope you know to do this for him.

And I'm in the sitting room, searching for a Lego piece down the back of the sofa, and you come up to me and hug me, 'Beautiful wife,' you say, and upstairs I hear Jenny on the phone to Ivo and Adam is reading on the rug and I am suffocated with need for you all.

They are taking my heart out.

All the light and colour and warmth in my body is leaving it now and coming into me—into whatever I am.

My soul is being born.

And Jenny is right, it *is beautiful*, but I rage against this birth of light. I want to see my grandchildren or just touch you once more and call to Jenny, 'Nearly supper, OK?', or to Adam, 'I'm coming!'.

Just a little more life.

But then the anger leaves and I am left without fear or regrets.

I am a sliver-thin light, diamond-sharp, that can slip through gaps in the world that we know. I will come into your dreams and speak soft words when you think of me.

There is no happy ever after—but there is an afterwards.

This isn't our ending.

Rosamund Lupton

Did you always want to be a writer?

Yes, ever since I could hold a pencil. I began writing stories when I was five.

What prompted you to start your first novel, *Sister*?

I'd had an idea for a novel about two sisters simmering away for years. When my youngest child started school ful time I decided to try to write it. It was far harder than I'd imagined, but I kept going.

Did you go on writing courses?

No, but I am an avid reader and I think that's a great way to prepare for writing your own book.

How did you juggle being a mother and writing to a deadline once you had a publishing deal for *Sister*?

I had three months to rewrite about half the book and was completely panicked! My friends stepped in to help look after my children, and so did my parents. I was very touched by how kind and generous people were with their time.

Were you amazed by the phenomenal success of *Sister*?

Yes, completely astonished! When we first saw my name next to Stieg Larsson's in the best-seller lists, my husband and I just laughed. I kept thinking that there must have been a mistake. I still find the statistics for its sales a little unbelievable.

What's the best thing that's happened to you since?

I think it's the emails that I receive from readers. I had one yesterday from a nurse in Australia who'd read my book during a long night-shift. It makes me feel connected to the world in a different way.

After *Sister* was published, were you worried that you would be unable to write a second novel? Or had you already written *Afterwards*?

I was worried about writing a second novel but once I had the idea for *Afterwards*, I was excited about writing it. Fortunately, I'd almost completed the first draft when *Sister* was published.

Do you have a writing regime?

I write from the minute I drop my children at school to the time I go to pick them up. I sometimes work when they've gone to sleep. It means that the house is usually in a fair degree of chaos, and food shopping is done on the internet at midnight.

How did the idea for *Afterwards* develop?

I had the idea of a mother and daughter chatting together as spirits while they watched what was going on. I haven't a clue where it came from, but I knew I wanted to write about it. The other part of the idea came from a walk to school to collect my children. A fire engine went past, siren blaring, and it wasn't till it had passed the school that my heart stopped beating too fast.

Did you find it difficult to portray Grace and Jenny communicating as spirits?

I didn't find it hard because I just wrote them as if they were 'real' people, talking to each other. Hopefully readers feel that they are three-dimensional characters.

Who is your favourite character?

It's probably Sarah, who developed in unexpected ways as I wrote her and I found myself liking her more and more.

And who was the most difficult to encapsulate?

I think it was Grace herself, even though she's the narrator. I wanted her to be more than just how she's portrayed in the book, as if she had had a life before the novel began as well as afterwards.

Discovering the identity of the arsonist is the mystery element of your novel. Do you think you will always write emotional mysteries?

I like to think that my writing will change and evolve over time, rather than being confined to one style.

What do you enjoy doing in your free time? Do you have any?

Being with my family and friends, gardening, going to art galleries, films, cafés—a hundred things! It's important for me to have time away from my writing, so that when I return to it I am newly inspired and passionate.

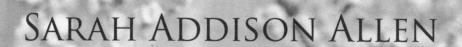

SARAH ADDISON ALLEN

THE PEACH KEEPER

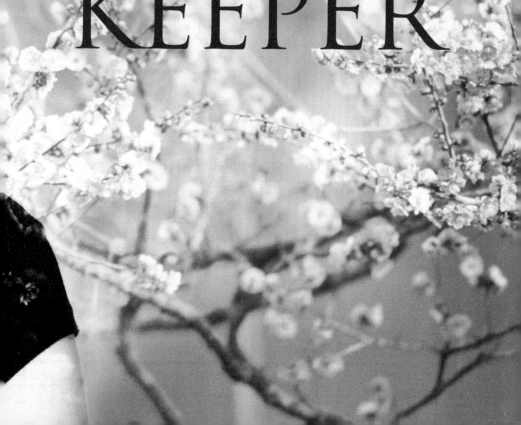

On August 12, 1936, a group of ladies in Walls of Water, North Carolina, formed a society that became the most important social club in the area.

Now, seventy-five years later, the current members are holding a gala dinner to celebrate this anniversary and hope that the two remaining founder members, Agatha Osgood and Georgie Jackson, will be happy to attend.

But Agatha and Georgie are far from happy—for the scent of peaches is in the air and untold trouble lies ahead.

CHAPTER ONE

HIDING PLACES

THE DAY PAXTON OSGOOD took the box of heavy-stock, foil-lined envelopes to the post office, the ones she'd had a professional calligrapher address, it began to rain so hard the air turned as white as bleached cotton. By nightfall, rivers had crested at flood stage, and for the first time since 1936, the mail couldn't be delivered. When things began to dry out, when basements were pumped free of water and branches were cleared from yards and streets, the invitations were finally delivered, but to all the wrong houses. Neighbours laughed over fences, handing the misdelivered pieces of mail to their rightful owners with comments about the crazy weather and their careless postman. The next day, an unusual number of people showed up at the doctor's office with infected paper cuts, because the envelopes had sealed, cementlike, from the moisture. Later, the single-card invitations themselves seemed to hide and pop back up at random. Mrs Jameson's invitation disappeared for two days, then reappeared in a bird's nest outside. Harper Rowley's invitation was found in the church bell tower.

If anyone had been paying attention to the signs, they would have realised that air turns white when things are about to change, that paper cuts mean there's more to what's written than meets the eye, and that birds are out to protect you from things you don't see.

But no one was paying attention. Least of all Willa Jackson.

The envelope sat untouched on the back counter of Willa's store for over a week. She picked it up curiously when it had been delivered with the other mail, but then she'd dropped it like it had burned her as soon as she'd recognised what it was. Even now, when she walked by it, she would throw a suspicious glance its way.

'Open it already.' Rachel Edney finally said with exasperation that morning. Willa turned to Rachel, who was standing behind the coffee bar across the store. She had short dark hair and, in her capris and sport tank top, looked as though she was ready to go climb a large rock. No matter how many times Willa told her she didn't have to dress in the clothes the store sold—Willa herself rarely deviated from jeans and boots—Rachel was convinced she had to represent.

'I'm not going. No need to open it,' Willa said, deciding on the mundane task of folding the new stock of organic T-shirts, hoping it would help her ignore the strange feeling that came over her every time she thought of that invitation. It felt like a balloon of expectation expanding in the centre of her body. She used to feel this way when she was younger, right before she did something stupid. But she thought she was past all of that. She'd padded her life with so much calm that she didn't think anything could penetrate it. Some things, apparently, still could.

Rachel made a tsking sound. 'You're such an elitist.'

That made Willa laugh. 'OK, explain to me why not opening an invitation to a gala thrown by the richest women in town makes *me* elitist.'

'You look at everything they do with disdain.'

'I do *not*.'

'Well, it's either that or you're repressing a secret desire to be one of them,' Rachel said as she put on a green apron with *Au Naturel Sporting Goods and Café* embroidered in yellow script.

Rachel was eight years younger than Willa, but Willa had never written off Rachel's opinions as those of just another twenty-two-year-old who thought she knew everything. Rachel had lived a vagabond life and she knew a lot about human nature. The only reason she had settled in Walls of Water, for now, was because she'd fallen in love with a man here. Love, she always said, changes the game.

But Willa didn't want to get into how she felt about the rich families in town. Rachel had never spent more than a few months in any one place. Willa had lived here her whole life. She understood the social dynamics of Walls of Water; she just didn't know how to explain them to people who didn't. So Willa asked the one question she knew would distract Rachel. 'What's on the menu today?'

'Ah. Excellent stuff, if I do say so myself. Trail mix with chocolate-covered coffee beans, oatmeal cookies with coffee icing, and espresso brownies.' She gestured like a game-show hostess to the snacks in the glass case under the counter.

Almost a year ago, Willa had let Rachel take over the previously closed coffee bar in the store and gave her the go-ahead to put snacks that had coffee as an ingredient on the menu. It had turned out to be a great idea. Walking into the shop in the mornings was actually a pleasure now. Being met by the scent of chocolate mingling with brewing coffee had a dark, secretive feel to it, as if Willa had finally found the perfect place to curl up and hide.

Willa's store, which specialised in organic sportswear, was on National Street, the road leading to Cataract National Forest, known for its beautiful waterfalls in North Carolina's Blue Ridge Mountains. All the shops catering to hikers and campers were located here, in one busy stretch. And it was here that Willa had found her niche. Truthfully, she didn't care much for the outdoorsy stuff that sustained the town, but she was much more comfortable with the shop owners and people new to town than she was with the people she knew in her youth. If she had to be here, this was where she belonged, not with the glittery townies.

The stores were housed in old buildings that had been built more than a century ago, when Walls of Water was just a tiny logging town. The ceilings were pierced tin, and the floors were nail-worn and lemony. With the slightest pressure, they creaked and popped like an old woman's bones, which was how Willa knew Rachel had approached her.

She turned and saw Rachel extending the envelope. 'Open it.'

Willa took it reluctantly. Just to get Rachel off her back, she tore it open. The moment she did, the bell above the door rang and they both looked up to see who it was. But no one was there.

Rachel rubbed her bare arms, which were goose pimply. 'I just got a chill.'

'My grandmother would say that meant a ghost passed by you.'

Rachel shook her head sagely. 'Superstitions are man's way of trying to control things he has no control over.'

Willa snorted. 'Thank you, Margaret Mead.'

'Go on.' Rachel nudged her. 'Read it.'

Willa took out the invitation and read:

On August 12, 1936, a group of ladies in Walls of Water, North Carolina, formed a society that has become the most important social club in the area, one that organises fund-raisers, sponsors cultural events, and gives out scholarships.

It is with great pride that the current members of the Women's Society Club invite you to a commemoration of the 75th anniversary of the formation of this organisation.

Come help us celebrate 75 years of sparkling good deeds. The party will be the first event held in the newly restored Blue Ridge Madam, on August 12 at 7 p.m.

RSVP with the enclosed card to Paxton Osgood, President.

'See?' Rachel said from over Willa's shoulder. 'That's not so bad.'

'I can't believe Paxton's holding it in the Blue Ridge Madam.'

'Oh, come on. I'd give anything to see the inside of that place and so would you.'

'I'm not going.'

'You're crazy to pass this up. Your grandmother—'

'Helped found the club, I know,' Willa finished as she set the invitation aside. 'She did, I didn't. It has nothing to do with me.'

Rachel threw her hands in the air. 'I give up. Want coffee?'

'Yes. With soy milk and two sugars.' Just this past week, Rachel had become convinced that how people took their coffee gave a secret insight into their characters. Were people who took their coffee black unyielding? Did people who liked milk and no sugar have mother issues? She had a notebook behind the counter in which she wrote her findings. Willa decided to keep her on her toes by making up a different request every day.

Rachel walked to the coffee bar to write in her notebook. 'Hmm, interesting,' she said seriously, as if she'd figured Willa out.

'You don't believe in ghosts, but you do believe that how I take my coffee says something about my personality.'

'That's superstition. This is *science*.'

Willa shook her head and went back to folding shirts, trying to ignore the invitation, now sitting on the table. But it kept catching her eye, fluttering slightly as if caught in a breeze.

She flopped a shirt over it and tried to forget about it.

When they closed up shop that evening, Rachel headed off to meet her boyfriend for an evening hike, which was so annoyingly healthy that Willa made up for it by taking a brownie out of the snack case and eating it in three big bites. Then she got in her bright yellow Jeep Wrangler to go home to do laundry. Wednesday nights were laundry nights. Sometimes she even looked forward to it.

Yes, her life was monotonous, but it kept her out of trouble. She was thirty. This, her father would say, was called being an adult.

But instead of heading straight home, Willa turned onto Jackson Hill, her private daily detour. It was a steep mountain slope, but it was the only way to get to the antebellum mansion at the top, known locally as the Blue Ridge Madam. Ever since renovation had started over a year ago, Willa had made these treks to watch the progress.

The place had been abandoned years ago by the last in a series of shady developers. It had fallen into disrepair and was disintegrating when the Osgood family stepped in and bought it. Now almost fully restored, and soon to be a bed-and-breakfast with a banquet hall, the white Doric columns were back, spanning the length of the house. It looked like something out of the old South, a plantation manor where women in hoop skirts fanned themselves and men in suits talked about crop prices.

The Madam had been built in the 1800s by Willa's great-great-grandfather, the founder of the now-defunct Jackson Logging Company. It had been a wedding gift to his wife—a beautiful woman from a prominent family in Atlanta. She'd loved the house but hated Walls of Water, so she'd persuaded her friends from Atlanta to come for visits, to build homes, to treat this place as a playful paradise.

And so a rich society had formed in this tiny North Carolina town surrounded by waterfalls, a town once populated by rough logging men. These well-to-do families were incongruous and stubborn. Not welcome at all. But when the government bought the surrounding mountain forest and turned it into a national park and the logging industry dried up, these families helped the town survive.

The irony was that the Jacksons, once the finest family in town, lost their money when the logging stopped. When they couldn't pay the taxes, they moved out of the Madam. Most of the Jacksons left town. But one stayed, a teenager named Georgie Jackson—Willa's grandmother. She was seventeen, unmarried, and pregnant. She became, of all things, a maid to the Osgood family, who were once great friends to the Jacksons.

Willa pulled to the side of the road just before the driveway up to the Madam. The crew had left for the day. She got out of her Wrangler and climbed onto the hood, leaning back against the windshield. It was late July, the hottest part of summer. She put on her sunglasses against the setting sun and stared up at the house.

The only thing left to the renovation was the landscaping, which apparently had just got under way that day. That excited Willa. New things to study. She could see that there were wooden stakes and string markers making a patchwork of squares across the front yard. Most of the activity, however, seemed centred round the only tree on the flat top of the hill where the house sat.

The tree was right at the precipice of the left slope. Its leaves grew in long, thin bunches, its limbs were stretched wide. An excavator was parked next to the tree. Plastic strings were tied round the branches.

They were going to take it down?

She wondered why. It seemed perfectly healthy.

Well, whatever they did, it was guaranteed to be for the better. The Osgoods were known for their good taste. The Blue Ridge Madam was going to be a showplace again.

As much as Willa didn't want to admit it, Rachel was right. She would love to see what the inside looked like. She just didn't think she had any right to. The house hadn't been in her family since the 1930s. Even getting this close felt like trespassing . . . which, if she was honest with herself, was one of the reasons she did it. In her youth, she'd pulled every prank known to man and had been so good at it no one had known it was her until the very end. She'd been a legend her class had called the Walls of Water High School Joker. But this place was different. It'd had a mysterious push-pull effect on her, and still did. Every teenager who had ever broken into the house had come away with stories of mysterious footsteps and slamming doors and a dark fedora that floated through the air, as if worn by an invisible man. Maybe that was what had kept her from getting too close. Ghosts scared her, thanks to her grandmother.

Willa sat up and reached into the back pocket of her jeans. She brought out the invitation and read it again. It said to RSVP with the enclosed card, so Willa looked in the envelope for the card and brought it out.

She was surprised to find a Post-it attached to it that read:

Willa,

Your grandmother and my grandmother are the only two surviving members of the original club, and I'd like to plan something special for them at the party. Call me and let's try to work something out.

Pax

Her handwriting was pretty, of course. Willa remembered that from high school. She had once taken a note that Paxton had accidentally dropped in the hallway and kept it for months—a strange list of characteristics Paxton wanted her future husband to have. She'd read it over and over, studying Paxton's sloping *y*'s and jaunty *x*'s. She'd studied it so much she found she could replicate it. And once she'd had that skill, it had been impossible not to use it, which had resulted in a very embarrassing encounter between uppity Paxton Osgood and Robbie Roberts, the school's own redneck lothario, who'd thought Paxton had sent him a love letter.

The Walls of Water High School Joker had struck again.

'Beautiful, isn't it?'

Willa jumped at the voice, her heart giving a sudden kick in her chest. She dropped the invitation on the wind and it flew to the owner of the voice, standing a few feet from her Wrangler.

He had on dark trousers with a blue paisley tie sticking out of one pocket. His white dress shirt was translucent with sweat, and his dark hair was sticking to his forehead and neck. Mirrored sunglasses hid his eyes. The invitation hit him flat against his chest. He smiled slightly, tiredly, as he peeled it off. This was a sign, she thought. Though of what, she had no idea. It was just what her grandmother would say when something unexpected happened, usually accompanied by instructions to knock three times and turn in a circle, or put chestnuts and pennies on the windowsill.

He took off his sunglasses and looked up at her. A strange expression came over his face, and he said, 'It's *you.*'

She stared at him until she understood. Oh God. To be caught here was one thing; to be caught here by one of them was something else entirely. Mortified, Willa darted inside the Jeep. It was a sign, all right. A sign that meant run away as fast as she could.

'Wait,' she heard him say as she started the engine.

But she didn't wait. She kicked the Jeep in gear and raced away.

CHAPTER TWO

WHISPERS

PAXTON OSGOOD HAD STAYED late to finish some paperwork at the outreach centre, so it was dusk when she left. She drove home, following the flickering lights of lampposts as they popped on, like drowsy fireflies leading her way. She parked in front of her parents' house and got out of her car thinking that if she timed this right, she'd be able to have a quick swim before changing and heading back out to the Women's Society Club meeting that evening.

This plan was carefully hinged on not facing her parents. She'd spent weeks tinkering with her schedule just so she wouldn't have to stop and tell them about her day the moment she came in. This impatience, this avoidance was a new development and she wasn't sure what to do about it. Until recently, she'd never minded living with her parents. She loved Walls of Water. She loved being a part of its history. It struck a deep, resonant chord in her. She *belonged* here. And since her twin brother Colin's job took him all over the country, and sometimes overseas, Paxton felt it was only fair that their parents have at least one child nearby.

But last year, as age thirty loomed, Paxton had finally made the decision to move out, not to another state, not even across town, but to a town house that her friend Kirsty Lemon was trying to sell, a mere 6.3 miles from Hickory Cottage. But her parents had been so upset at the thought of her leaving, of breaking up their happy little dysfunctional unit, that she'd been forced to back out. She did, however, move out of the main house and into the pool house, a small step but a necessary one.

The pool house gave her some privacy, but unfortunately there was no way to get to it without walking through the main house, so her parents always knew when she was coming and going.

She walked up the steps to her parents' sprawling home, called Hickory Cottage because of the hickory trees on the estate. In the autumn, the back yard became a mass of lollipop-yellow leaves.

She opened the front door silently, then clicked it shut behind her. She would just tiptoe to the kitchen and out through the French doors without them ever knowing. She turned, and promptly fell over a suitcase. She landed on her hands on the marble floor of the hall.

'What on earth was that?' Paxton heard her mother say; then there was a rush of footsteps coming from the den.

Paxton sat up and saw that the contents of her tote bag had spilled out. All her lists were scattered around, which made her panic. Her lists were private. She picked them up and stuffed them back into her bag, just as three people appeared in the hall.

'Paxton! Are you all right?' her mother asked as Paxton stood, brushing herself off. 'Colin, do something about these suitcases, for heaven's sake.'

'I was going to take them to the pool house, but that was before I discovered Paxton had moved out there,' Colin said.

At the sound of her brother's voice, Paxton spun to face him. She instantly ran into his arms. 'You weren't supposed to be here until Friday!' she said, squeezing him tightly, breathing in that calm, easy-going air he always carried around him. She thought she might cry she was so happy to see him. Then she was so mad she thought about hitting him. Dealing with her parents would be so much easier if he would stop wandering around and come home for good.

'Things wrapped up sooner than I thought on my last project,' he said, pulling back and looking at her. 'You look great, Pax. Move out and get married already.'

'No, don't tell her to get married!' their mother, Sophia, said. 'Do you know who she's seeing right now? Sebastian Rogers.'

'I'm not seeing him, Mama. We're just friends.'

'Sebastian Rogers,' Colin repeated. 'Didn't we go to school with him? The effeminate kid in the purple trench coat?'

'Yes, that's him,' their mother said.

Paxton felt her jaw tighten. 'He doesn't wear a purple trench coat any more. He's a dentist.'

Colin hesitated a few beats before changing the subject. 'I guess I'll put my suitcases upstairs, then.'

Sophia grabbed her husband's arm. 'Donald, our babies are both here! Isn't this wonderful? Get some champagne.'

He turned with a nod and left the hall.

Over the years, Paxton's father had slowly let his wife take over all the decisions. Most of his time was spent at the golf course. As much as Paxton understood her mother's drive, and how much easier it was to do things yourself, she wondered why her mother didn't resent her husband's absence. Wasn't that the point to being married? That you had a trusted partner to help with decisions?

'I can only stay for one drink,' Paxton said. 'I'm sorry, Colin. I have a club meeting.'

'Don't worry. We'll catch up later. I need to go out, too.'

Sophia reached over and brushed some of the unruly hair off her son's forehead. 'Your first night here, and you're going out?'

Colin grinned at her. 'And you can no longer give me a curfew. Drives you crazy, doesn't it?'

'Oh, you,' she said as she walked toward the kitchen, motioning for them to follow her with a flick of her perfectly manicured hand.

As soon as she was out of earshot, Paxton sighed and said, 'Thank God you're here. Will you please move back already?'

'I'm not through sowing my wild oats.' He shrugged his lanky shoulders. All her family was tall, but at six foot five, Colin was the tallest. In high school, his friends called him Stick Man. His hair was darker than hers— which was a blond she kept meticulously highlighted—but they shared the same dark Osgood eyes.

'You wear a suit to work,' she said. 'That's not wild oats.'

He shrugged again.

'Are you OK?' she asked.

'I've been up for two days straight. I need sleep. So what's up with you and this Sebastian character?'

Paxton looked away and adjusted her tote bag on her shoulder. 'We're just friends. Mama doesn't approve.'

'Does she ever? The Blue Ridge Madam looks fantastic, by the way. Better even than the photos you emailed me. I went up there this afternoon. I need to make a few landscaping changes, now that I've seen it in person, but it looks like everything is on track.'

'Are you sure it will be done before the gala next month?'

He reached out and squeezed her hand. 'I promise.'

'Champagne!' their father called as he stomped up the basement steps. Colin and Paxton sighed, then went to join their parents.

That night's Women's Society Club meeting was being held at Kirsty Lemon's house, Lemon Tree Cottage, which was decked out in all things lemon. Paper lanterns following the walkway had die-cut images of lemon wedges. The topiaries at the door had fake lemons on them. The door itself was covered in yellow paper. Over the years, these meetings had become less about the actual charities they supported and more about trying to one-up each other in presentation.

Paxton knocked on the door, and Kirsty opened it. With her short brown hair and tiny hands, Kirsty made everyone around her seem larger than they really were. Paxton was five ten and had at least eight inches and fifty pounds on Kirsty. She hated how she towered over her, but she never let it show, never stooped or wore flats around her. That would be shifting the balance of power. 'Hi, Pax. Come in. You're a little late.'

'Sorry. Colin came home early. We were catching up,' Paxton said as she followed Kirsty to the living room. 'How are you?'

Kirsty rambled on about her perfect husband and her lovably unruly boys and her fabulous part-time job as a real-estate agent.

The twenty-four members sat in folding chairs, in straight rows across the living room. Some had snack plates in their laps, full of scoops of lemon-chicken salad and lemon and broccoli mini-quiches from the buffet table. There was a table at the back where three teenage girls whispered among themselves. They were called the Springs. These were the daughters of committee members being moulded to take their mothers' places. This was a young woman's club. After a certain age, it was understood that your daughter took your place. As a rule, rich Southern women did not like to be surpassed in either need or beauty. The exception was with their daughters. Daughters of the South were to their mothers what tributaries were to the rivers they flowed into: their source of strength.

Paxton smiled at the girls as she walked over and gave them small bags of chocolate. As president, she always gave the girls gifts at meetings. They all hugged her and she squeezed them back. She'd assumed she'd be married and have kids by this age, that she would be grooming her own daughter for this, as her friends were doing. She wanted it so much she would dream about it sometimes. But she'd never felt anything for the men she'd dated, nothing beyond her own desperation. And her desire to marry would *never* be strong enough to allow her to marry a man she didn't love.

She skipped the food and went to the front of the room. A strange breeze slithered by her, which sounded like whispers of secrets. She shook it off distractedly.

She took out her notebooks at the podium. 'Everyone come to order. We have a lot to discuss. RSVPs for the gala are pouring in. Moira has a request that the Madam open to overnight guests early, so attendees from out of town can stay there the evening of the gala. But first, the reading of minutes from the last meeting. Stacey?'

Stacey Herbst stood and flipped through her notebook. She had recently started dying her hair red, and though everyone told her they missed her brown hair, the truth was, she looked better as a redhead. But she would probably go back to brown soon. What people thought meant too much to her.

Stacey opened her mouth to read the minutes, but, amazingly, what came out was, 'I steal lipstick every time I go to the drugstore. I can't help myself. I drop a tube in my bag and walk out. I love that none of you know, that it's a secret I keep from you.'

She slapped her hand over her mouth.

Paxton's brows rose. But before she could say anything, Honor Redford blurted out, 'Ever since my husband lost his job, I've been afraid I won't be able to afford the club dues, and none of you will like me any more.'

Moira Kinley turned to the woman sitting next to her and said, 'You know why I like going places in public with you? Because I'm prettier and you make me feel better about myself.'

'I had that new addition built just because I knew it would make you jealous.'

'I really did have a boob job.'

Now everyone was talking at once, and each thing they said was more outrageous than the last. Paxton thought at first that they were playing a joke on her. But everyone looked panicked, their eyes like horses running scared. It was as if everything they were secretly thinking had been given a voice, and they were powerless to stop it.

'Order,' Paxton said. 'Everyone come to order.' This had no effect. The din escalated. Paxton stepped up onto her chair, clapped loudly, and yelled, 'Come to order! What is the matter with you?'

The noise dissipated as everyone looked up at her. She stepped down. She could feel it now, an uneasiness creeping along her skin. She had to stop herself from blurting out that she was in love with someone she shouldn't be, something she'd never admitted to anyone. She was aching to say it. It felt like she would choke on it if she didn't get it out. She swallowed and managed to say instead, 'Kirsty, I think something might be wrong with your air conditioner. I think we're being affected by fumes.'

'At least I have my own house,' Kirsty murmured as she got up and crossed the room to the thermostat. 'At least I don't live in my parents' pool house.'

'Excuse me?' Paxton said.

'Wh . . . I . . .' Kirsty stammered. 'I didn't mean to say that.'

Paxton rallied everyone and got them to open the windows and take deep breaths. As the July heat crawled into the room, she called the meeting to order and the list of things needing to be addressed was checked off. But Paxton could tell some women weren't listening. It was close to ten o'clock when the meeting finally ended. Everyone kissed each other's cheeks and rushed off to their houses to make sure everything was all right, that homes hadn't burned down, that husbands hadn't left, that their best dresses still fitted.

Paxton sat in her car in Kirsty's driveway, watching cars peel out, thinking to herself, *What in the hell just happened here?*

Instead of going home, Paxton drove to Sebastian Rogers' house. His lights were still on, so she pulled into his driveway.

When Sebastian moved back to Walls of Water to take over old Dr Kostovo's dental practice last year, he'd also bought Dr Kostovo's house, because Dr K was retiring to Nevada. It was a dark stone house with a stone turret, called Shade Tree Cottage. Sebastian told Paxton that he liked the drama of the place, that he liked to pretend he was living in an episode of *Dark Shadows*.

She knocked on his door. Moments later, Sebastian opened it. 'Hello, beautiful,' he said. 'I didn't expect to see you tonight.'

'I just wanted to say hi,' she said as she walked in. The words sounded lame even to her, like there necessarily had to be an excuse, even though she knew he didn't mind her stopping by.

She walked to the living room and sat on the couch. Judging by the outside, one would expect swords and coats of arms on the walls inside, but Sebastian had instead made it light and comfortable. He had moved back not long after she'd decided against buying the town house, and she'd enjoyed watching this place turn into his own. She took off her shoes and tucked her feet under her as Sebastian sat beside her. He was wearing jogging pants and a T-shirt. His feet were bare, his toenails neatly trimmed.

Sebastian was a beautiful man. Everyone presumed he was gay, but no one knew for sure. He neither confirmed nor denied it, not in high school and not now. Paxton, though, had seen the proof. In high school he'd been thin and fair, wore eyeliner and long coats, and carried a satchel when everyone else had L.L.Bean backpacks. He'd been hard to miss. That's why he'd caught her eye in the Asheville Mall their senior year. Asheville was about an hour outside of Walls of Water, and Paxton and her friends went there nearly every Saturday. Sebastian had been in the food court with a half-dozen other flamboyant teenage boys, boys not from Walls of Water. She and her friends had been walking by when she'd spotted him. Suddenly, one of the boys leaned over and kissed Sebastian on the mouth. During the kiss, Sebastian had opened his eyes and seen her, and his eyes followed her as she'd walked away. She couldn't remember ever seeing something as bold and seductive.

Thinking back to that kiss, it seemed so unlike him now. He was very controlled these days, almost asexual in the sharply tailored suits he wore, complete with silk ties so smooth they caught light.

'How was your day?' he asked, propping his elbow on the back of the couch, so close he almost touched her.

'OK, I guess.' She reached over and lifted his half-empty wineglass from the coffee table and took a sip. 'The bright spot was that Colin got here earlier than expected. The landscaping at the Madam is going to be done on time for sure now. But the club meeting tonight was so *odd*.'

'How so?'

She paused, thinking about it. 'Whenever I would get too nosy as a child, my grandmother would say, "When you learn someone else's secret, your own secrets aren't safe. Dig up one, release them all." That's what the meeting was like. Everyone was admitting things, secret things. And once they started, it was as though they couldn't stop.'

He smiled. 'Isn't that what the meetings are all about? Gossip?'

'Not like this,' she said. 'Trust me.'

'Then do tell,' he said, raising his eyebrows. 'What secrets have the society ladies been keeping? What's *your* secret?'

Paxton tried to laugh. 'I don't have secrets.'

He kept his eyebrows raised.

She *had* to admit something now. But not what she'd almost admitted at the meeting. 'I dread telling my grandmother about the gala. I promised my mother I'd do it tomorrow morning, but I don't want to. I feel terrible. Nana Osgood helped found the club. It was wrong to keep this from her for so long. She's just so . . .'

Sebastian nodded. He knew. 'Do you want me to go with you?'

'No. She treats you horribly.' Ever since she and Sebastian had started spending their Sundays together—something she looked forward to all week—he'd been coming with her to visit her grandmother on Sunday evenings. She wasn't going to make him come with her on a weekday, too. That was too much to ask.

'She treats everyone horribly, darling.' He reached over and took the wineglass from her and set it down, then took her hand in his. 'Let go of that tight-fisted control. You don't have to do everything yourself. I'll go with you. You know I'd do anything for you.'

She put his hand to her warm cheek and closed her eyes. His skin was cool and soft. Then she realised what she was doing and her eyes flew open. She let go of his hand and stood, fumbling with her shoes. 'I should go,' she said. 'Thanks for letting me vent.'

He watched her thoughtfully as he stood. The moment they'd met again when he'd moved back, just by chance after her book club meeting at Hartley's Tea Room last year, Paxton had felt a shock of electricity. She hadn't recognised him at first; she'd only known that he was beautiful, and she'd wondered what he was doing in Walls of Water. She'd unlocked her car door, staring at him as he'd walked to his car. He'd turned to see her, smiled, and said, 'Hello, Paxton.' He'd had to remind her that they had gone to school together. They'd ended up back in Hartley's Tea Room, talking for hours. By the time they'd parted ways that afternoon, she'd been done for. No matter how many times she told herself that nothing good could become of this, she couldn't help her feelings for him.

'Good night, lovely,' he said. He reached out and petted her hair almost apologetically. And that's when it hit her. *He knew.*

Appalled, she turned to the door. How long had he known? Had she done something to make him suspect? What an awful night this had turned out to be. It felt like the universe was playing tricks.

'Pax? What's wrong?' he asked, following her.

'Nothing. I'm fine. I'll see you tomorrow morning,' she tried to say brightly as she walked outside into a cloak of humid darkness.

She could have sworn she heard the whisper of someone's laughter.

CHAPTER THREE

CODE OF OUTCASTS

WILLA HEARD A KNOCK at her door as she was taking the last load out of the dryer that evening. She set the clothes on her kitchen table and walked through the narrow, rectangular house to the front door.

Willa had inherited this, her childhood home, when her father had passed away seven years ago. A house was nothing to sneeze at, especially considering she had finally paid off the credit card debt she'd acquired in college. Walls of Water had a high per capita of wealthy residents, and when she was younger, she hated not being one of them. It had been a heady feeling to have easy access to cash in college, to run fast and loose with it. Her father had died before he'd found out how deep in debt she'd become.

She was now the debt-free owner of a business and a home, all thanks to her father, who had left her the house and made her the beneficiary of his life-insurance policy. Being an adult was important to him. She owed him this. This was her penance for causing him so much grief, for her inability to tap down her restless energy when she was younger and live the quiet life he wanted.

She opened the door and the man on her doorstep said, 'We meet again.'

When she opened her mouth, all that came out was breath filled with dissolved words.

'You ran away so fast earlier today that you forgot this.' He held out the invitation.

She took it quickly and, inexplicably, hid it behind her back.

He put his hands in his pockets. The light beside her door made him squint, causing small lines to crinkle around his eyes. He stared at her a moment before he said, 'I took the blame for your pranks in high school. The least you can do is invite me in.'

That snapped her out of it. 'You didn't take the blame; you took the *credit*,' she said.

He smiled. 'So you do remember me.'

Of course she remembered him. It was what made being caught on Jackson Hill all the more embarrassing. Everyone in school knew who Colin was. He was an Osgood. He'd hung out with boys who wore polo shirts and played golf. He'd seemed destined to come back after college and take his father's place as King of the Links, but for some reason he stayed away.

Willa hadn't intentionally framed him for her pranks in high school. She'd snuck out one night and put a quote by poet Ogden Nash on the school marquee. *Candy is dandy but liquor is quicker.* She'd heard Colin say it and thought it was funny. What she didn't know was that Colin had just turned in an essay on Ogden Nash, so she had inadvertently pointed the finger at him. No one could prove it was Colin, and his parents made certain Colin was never held accountable, but every prank Willa had pulled up until then, and every one after, had been credited to him. He earned the respect of being the Walls of Water High School Joker, hero of students, bane of teachers' existence. It was only when Willa was caught three weeks before graduation that everyone realised it was her.

'Are you going to let me in or not? The suspense is killing me.'

She sighed as she stepped back. When he entered, she closed the door behind him, then turned to see Colin walking around, absently running his hand over the back of her super-soft couch. It was that kind of couch. You just had to *touch* it. After seven years, it was the first new thing she'd bought for the house, and it had been delivered just days ago. It was expensive and impractical, and she felt suitably guilty, but she was ridiculously in love with it.

'No one told me you'd moved back,' Colin said. 'How long have you been here?'

'Since my dad died.'

Colin's shoulders dropped. 'I was sorry to hear about what happened.' Her father had been killed trying to help someone change a tyre on the interstate during what would have been Willa's senior year in college, if she hadn't flunked out. Another thing her father hadn't known about. 'He was a great teacher. I had him for chemistry. He had a dinner for his students here at his house once.'

'Yes, I remember.' She'd hated those dinners, having kids come to her house to see how she lived. There was nothing wrong with the house; it was just old and small, nothing like the mansions half the kids lived in.

'I've thought a lot about you over the years, what you were doing, what mischief you were getting yourself into.' He paused. 'I had no idea you'd been here the whole time.'

She just stared at him, wondering why it mattered.

He looked around, then sat on the couch with a weary sigh. He ran his fingers through his hair. His hands were large. He was a big man, with a big presence. 'What are you doing these days, Willa?'

'I own a sporting goods store on National Street.' There. That sounded responsible, didn't it? Normal and practical.

'What do you do for fun?'

She gave him a funny look. 'Laundry,' she answered, deadpan.

'Married?' he asked. 'Kids?'

'No.'

'So no progeny to teach how to decorate the teachers' cars with peanut butter, or put scandalous quotes on the school marquee, or switch the items in the lockers of the entire graduating class?' He laughed. 'That was a classic. It had to have taken all night.'

It was as if it was a fond memory to him. But she'd purposely not revisited her pranks in years. And she hadn't given Colin a second thought. Now, suddenly, she was remembering the look on his face when she'd been escorted out of the school by police after pulling the fire alarm. The whole school was out on the lawn. *It was her*, they'd whispered. *Willa Jackson was the Walls of Water High School Joker!* Colin Osgood had looked completely poleaxed. Though whether it was because it was her, or because he couldn't take credit for her pranks any more, she didn't know.

They stared at each other from across the room. 'So, are you going?' He nodded to the invitation still in her hand. 'To the gala?'

She looked down at the invitation, as if surprised to find it there. 'No. It doesn't have anything to do with me.'

'So you only go to parties that have something to do with you? Your birthday party, for example.' After a short silence, he frowned and said, 'That sounded funnier in my head. Sorry. Everything seems funny when you've been up for forty-eight hours.'

'Why have you been up for forty-eight hours?'

'Couldn't sleep on the flight from Japan. And I've been trying to stay awake all day so I could go to bed at a regular hour.'

She looked towards the window, then turned and met his eyes. They were dark and unnerving and very, very tired. 'Are you OK to drive home? Let me get you some coffee.'

'If you insist. But the old Willa would have found some way to take advantage of this situation.'

'You have no idea who the old Willa was,' Willa said.

'Neither do you, obviously.'

Without another word, she turned and went to the kitchen. She just wanted to give Colin caffeine and have him be on his way.

'Do you go up to the Blue Ridge Madam often?' Colin called.

'No,' she answered. Of course he'd get around to that.

'So you weren't planning a prank for, say, the big gala?'

'Oh, for God's sake,' Willa mumbled.

Leaning against the kitchen counter, she watched the percolator gurgle, then poured coffee into a cup and took it to the living room.

He was sitting on her grey couch, his head against the cushions.

'Oh, no,' she said, panicking as she set the cup down on the end table. 'No, no, no. Colin, wake up.'

He didn't stir.

She reached over and touched his shoulder. 'Colin, I have your coffee. Wake up and drink.' She shook his shoulder. 'Colin!'

His eyes opened and he looked at her, a little unfocused. 'What happened to you? You were the bravest person I knew,' he murmured. Then he closed his eyes again.

'Colin?' She watched for a flutter of eyelashes. 'Colin?'

Nothing.

She stood there for a moment, stunned. She caught a whiff of something sweet. She inhaled, then nearly choked when it landed on her tongue with a bitter taste. It was so strong she made a face.

That, her grandmother had described to her once after making a bad lemon cream pie, was exactly what regret tasted like.

The thick morning mist in Walls of Water, common because of the nearby waterfalls, was beginning to disappear with the rising heat as Willa got in her Wrangler the next morning and drove to the nursing home. Thankfully, Colin had got up and left sometime in the night, taking his disappointment that she wasn't still secretly pulling pranks, that she wasn't still eighteen, with him.

She wished he'd never come to see her. She was doing the right thing being here. She'd grown up. The whole point of being here was so she *didn't* disappoint people any more.

'Hi, Grandmother Georgie,' Willa said brightly, when she got to the nursing home and walked into her room. Her grandmother was sitting by the window in her wheelchair, the morning sun on her white hair making her seem almost translucent. She'd been a beautiful woman in her day, with wide eyes and high cheekbones.

Her grandmother had been showing the first signs of dementia when Willa left for college. That's when Willa's father had moved her in with him, into Willa's old bedroom. Two years later, she'd had a stroke, and he'd been forced to move her to the nursing home. After her father died, Willa took his place coming to visit her, because she knew that was what he would have wanted. He'd adored his mother, and pleasing her had been his life's ambition.

Willa thought her grandmother was sweet, but she'd been one of those people with invisible thorns, preventing others from getting too close. Georgie Jackson had been a watchful person, not at all frivolous, which Willa had found extraordinary, considering how rich the Jacksons had once been. But after her family had lost their money, Georgie had worked as a maid for various wealthy families in town until she was well into her seventies.

She'd always been quiet, like Willa's father. Willa's mother had been the loud one in the family, and Willa could still remember her laugh, a sweet staccato sound like embers popping. She'd died when Willa was six. That had marked the phase when Willa used to like to play dead. She used to pose herself on the couch, or drape herself awkwardly across the car hood.

Once, her grandmother had caught her having an imaginary conversation with her mother and had immediately opened all the windows and burned sage. *Ghosts are horrible things,* she'd said. *You don't talk to them. You keep them away.* It had hurt Willa, and it had taken a long time to forgive her grandmother for denying her a link to her mother, for making her scared of it, no matter how silly.

Those superstitions were gone from her grandmother's memory now. Her grandmother didn't even recognise Willa any more, but Willa knew she liked the melody of voices, even though she no longer understood the words. So Willa came several times a week and talked about what was on the news, what was selling in her shop, what improvements she was making to her dad's house. She told her grandmother about the new couch, but not about Colin.

She hesitated before she finally brought the invitation from her back pocket. 'There's a party at the Blue Ridge Madam next month. The Women's Society Club is celebrating the formation of the club. Paxton Osgood wants to honour you at the party, which I guess is nice. But you never talked about it. I don't know if it meant anything to you. If I thought it did, I would go. I just don't know.'

Willa looked down at the invitation and did the math for the first time. Her grandmother had been only seventeen when she'd helped form the club. That had been the year her family had lost the Blue Ridge Madam, the year she'd given birth to Willa's father.

Willa had never been proud of being a Jackson when she was younger. But the older she got, the more she appreciated how hard her family had worked to support themselves, how no one but her ever cast their eyes down in shame at what they had lost. Willa accepted that her grandmother could no longer tell her things she wanted to know about her family, that she'd missed all the opportunities to ask her when she was clear-minded, or to ask her father while he was alive. But times like this she felt it acutely, all the things she wished she could go back and change, how she should have made them proud of her instead of constantly worrying them.

Willa looked up from the invitation and was surprised to find that Georgie had turned her head, and her light grey eyes, the same shade as Willa's, were looking directly at her, as if she'd recognised something familiar in what Willa had said.

Willa leaned forward. 'What is it, Grandmother Georgie? The Blue Ridge Madam? The Women's Society Club?'

Georgie tried to get her mouth to move, to form words.

It took a few tries before Willa recognised one word. *Peach.*

'Peach? You want peaches?'

Her grandmother's face went slack, as if she'd forgotten.

'OK, Grandmother Georgie,' she said as she stood and kissed her head. 'I'll make sure you have some peaches.'

She wrapped a shawl round her grandmother's shoulders and promised that she'd be back to see her soon. With one last look, she turned and left the room, stopping at the nurses' station to ask if her grandmother could have peaches with her next meal.

She put on her sunglasses and walked outside into the razor-sharp sunshine, crossing the wide brick patio towards the parking lot. The sun was already glinting off car windshields, which was why she didn't see that someone was approaching her until she was only a few steps away.

It was Paxton Osgood, wearing a cute pink dress and gorgeous shoes. Beside her was a man with blond hair and fair skin in a tailored suit, one of those people you couldn't quite figure out what side of masculine or feminine they fell on.

Not knowing what Colin had told his sister about last night, or what hard feelings Paxton still harboured for that time Willa had faked a love letter from Paxton to Robbie Roberts, Willa wasn't sure what to expect from her by way of greeting. She definitely wasn't expecting Paxton to smile and say, 'Willa! Hello! I'm glad I ran into you. Did you get my note about doing something special for our grandmothers at the gala?'

Willa found herself self-consciously patting at her wild, wavy hair because Paxton's hair was in her trademark chignon. She was always so polished. 'My grandmother isn't well enough to attend,' Willa said. 'She doesn't even remember me, much less the club.'

'Yes, I know. I'm sorry,' Paxton said kindly. 'I was thinking of honouring her through you. That you could accept a gift for her.'

'I . . . I have a previous engagement that evening,' Willa said.

'Oh,' Paxton said, surprised. There was an awkward pause.

Sebastian cleared his throat. 'Hello, Willa. Nice to see you again. It's been a while.'

'Sebastian. I heard you'd taken over Dr Kostovo's practice.' Sebastian Rogers reinforced Willa's belief that reinvention was not just a nice theory. It really did happen. Back in high school, Willa was quiet. She had the power to be invisible. But someone who looked like Sebastian never could be. He had endured constant taunts. And yet, here he was, a dentist in a suit that probably cost a year's worth of her Jeep payments. 'The last time I saw you, you had on eyeliner and a purple trench coat.'

'The last time I saw you, you were being arrested for pulling the fire alarm.'

'Touché. Come by Au Naturel on National Street sometime. You can have coffee on the house.'

'Perhaps I will,' he said, lifting one eyebrow.

Willa realised Paxton was looking at her curiously. She looked from Paxton to Sebastian, then back again.

'Well, I've got to go,' Willa finally said.

'Goodbye, Willa,' Sebastian said as she walked away.

Paxton watched Sebastian out of the corner of her eye. He was carrying a bouquet of hydrangeas as they walked down the corridor to her grandmother's room. 'I don't remember you and Willa being particularly close in high school. Were you?'

'No,' he said simply.

'She seemed happier to see you than me.'

'The code of outcasts,' he said with a smile. 'You wouldn't understand.' Before Paxton could ask, they had reached her grandmother's door. Sebastian put his arm round her waist and gave her a comforting squeeze. Then they walked in together, and Paxton cautiously approached her grandmother's bed. She'd been afraid of this woman all her life. She would look at her grandmother and feel absolute terror that she was going to turn into her one day. 'Nana Osgood?' she said gently. 'It's me, Paxton. Are you awake?'

Without opening her eyes, Agatha said, 'The fact that you had to ask should have given you a clue.'

'I'm here with Sebastian this morning.'

She finally opened her eyes. 'Oh, the fancy man.'

Paxton sighed but Sebastian smiled and winked at her. 'I brought you some hydrangeas, Agatha,' he said.

'Why are you bringing flowers to a blind woman? I can't see them. Give me my teeth.'

'Where are they?' Paxton asked.

'On the table where they always are,' Agatha said as she sat up. 'Why are you here? This isn't your day to come to see me.'

'I have something wonderful to tell you about the Blue Ridge Madam,' Paxton said, looking to the bedside table for her grandmother's teeth.

'There's nothing wonderful about the Blue Ridge Madam. Stay away from it. It's haunted. Give me my teeth.'

Paxton started to panic. 'Your teeth aren't here.'

'Of course they are.' Agatha threw her covers off as she stood. She patted the tabletop. 'Where are they? Someone stole my teeth!'

'I'll just put these in some water,' Sebastian said as he took a Waterford crystal vase from the cupboard and went into the en suite bathroom. Seconds later, he leaned out and said, 'Darling?'

Paxton was on her knees looking under her grandmother's bed. She looked up to find him trying to suppress a laugh. She loved that he was willing to go through this with her, that she didn't have to hide how horrible Agatha was. If he could live with her secret, then she could live with him knowing. Everything would be OK.

'I believe I've located Agatha's teeth,' he said.

After Paxton left, Agatha Osgood sat in her chair, her fingers pinching at her cardigan, which she could only assume matched her dress. Macular degeneration had all but taken her eyesight.

She'd thought her family consulted her on things. That was the impression they gave when they visited. But she realised now just how coddled she was. This place lulled residents into thinking that this was all there was to the world. It shrank everything down. It was startling to her that there was still a world outside these walls, one that went on turning even when she wasn't in it.

She couldn't believe her family had bought the Blue Ridge Madam. All those years of carefully constructing rumours of ghosts, of making everyone afraid of the Madam, of watching it crumble, waiting for the time when it would finally collapse and everything that had happened there would disappear, had been for naught.

If that wasn't bad enough, Paxton was planning a big gala celebrating the formation of the Women's Society Club there. Agatha had tried everything she could to get Paxton to cancel it. She'd said hateful things she didn't mean and made threats she couldn't keep, but nothing was going to stop it. Paxton was in control of the club now and Agatha felt her lack of power acutely.

Those girls had no idea what they were celebrating, what it took to bring Agatha and her friends together seventy-five years ago. The Women's Society Club had been about supporting each other, about banding together to protect each other because no one else would. But it had turned into a means by which rich ladies could congratulate themselves by giving money to the poor. And Agatha had let it happen. All her life, it seemed, was making up for things she let happen.

She knew it wasn't a coincidence that the club was celebrating in the Madam. There was no such thing as coincidence. It was fate. The reason they'd started the club in the first place had to do with the Madam. It was just a matter of time now before it was all going to come to light. Secrets never stay buried, no matter how hard you try. That's what Georgie had always been afraid of.

Agatha got up and walked out of her room, counting steps to the nurses' station. She could hear the morning nurse's voice as she approached. She was young. Too young. She sounded as though she should still be playing hopscotch with her friends.

'Hello, Mrs Osgood,' the nurse said in a tone that tried but fell short of pleasant. Agatha wasn't sure when it had happened, but sometime in the past ten years, she'd discovered that it made her feel better to make other people as miserable as she was. It was the help who'd hidden her teeth in the bathroom this morning, where the fancy man had found them. She was sure of it. 'What can I do for you?'

'If I need your help, I'll ask for it,' Agatha snapped as she walked by. Her papery fingertips trailed along the walls as she counted the doors to Georgie Jackson's room. When Georgie's son Ham had come to her and asked for help in getting Georgie a place here in the home, Agatha had given him the money without hesitation. All she'd ever wanted was to help Georgie, to make up for the time when Georgie had needed her the most and Agatha had turned her back on her . . . the one time that had changed everything. Agatha kept tabs on how Georgie was being treated, but she rarely visited her. Georgie wouldn't have liked it. She would have said, *You have your side; I have mine. That's the way it is now.*

When she reached the room, all Agatha could make out was a dark form. She mourned for a lot of things she'd lost, but this was the loss she felt the most—the loss of friendship. She missed her eyesight. She missed her husband. But those girls she grew up with were such an important part of her life. They were gone, all except for Georgie, who was suspended in life by only a thin thread.

She walked over to Georgie and sat beside her. 'It's finally happening,' Agatha whispered.

Georgie turned to her and said, 'Peach.'

Agatha found Georgie's hand, then held it in her own. 'Yes,' Agatha said. 'It's still there.' But the question was, for how long?

CHAPTER FOUR

WISH LISTS

COLIN SAT IN THE CORNER café of Au Naturel Sporting Goods, nursing his cappuccino and staring out of the store window. Because this road led directly to Cataract National Forest, there was a lot of traffic. This side of town had a completely different feel to it, hectic and touristy. It had been a long time since he'd been here, but nothing much had changed, like the fact that locals rarely came to National Street. The brick buildings were old, but the shops they housed were hip and new.

As much as he didn't like acknowledging it, he was still connected to this place. He'd seen a lot of the world in his work. Urban landscaping wasn't about homogenising cities, but drawing from their heritage. Learning about new cultures, travelling to new places, not staying in one place too long—it was exactly what he wanted to be doing. But then he would come home, usually only when forced by guilt from his mother, or, in this instance, a request for help from his sister, who never asked for help, and he would feel his feet growing heavy, as if he was sinking back into the root system of this place. And he didn't want to be that Colin any more, the one planted here, the one pruned to exactly the size and shape everyone expected him to be.

He heard the bell over the door ring and he turned.

Willa Jackson had just walked in. She was wearing jeans and a black sleeveless top. Her honey-brown hair was wavy in a way that was all curl and no volume. It'd been longer in high school, and she'd worn it in a messy braid. That was how he remembered it the last time her saw her, walking out of the school.

Now her hair ended just below her ears and she parted it on the side, catching the hair at one temple with a sparkly clip. He liked it because it suited the image of what he thought she'd become. He didn't realise he'd got it so wrong. *Surely* he couldn't have got it so wrong. Because if he was wrong about Willa, his inspiration, then maybe he was wrong about his own decisions, too.

Willa walked over to his table. 'I see you made it home alive.'

'Yes. And I want to apologise for last night. I haven't been that tired in a long time.' He rubbed his eyes with one hand. He felt like a ghost of his former self, like someone could reach for him and get only air. 'I could probably sleep for days more.'

'Then what are you doing here?'

'Pit stop on my way out.' He held up his cup of cappuccino.

'Leaving so soon?' The thought seemed to brighten her mood.

'No. I'll be here for a month. I'm just on my way to Asheville for the afternoon.' He gestured to the chair on the other side of the table. She stared at him, and her lovely light grey eyes narrowed slightly before she pulled it out and sat. 'So, you own this store.'

'Yes,' she said. 'As I mentioned last night. And undoubtedly how you found me this morning.'

He looked around. Willa seemed to have found something that set her store apart, specialising in organic wear and environmentally friendly equipment, with a café that made the place smell like roasting coffee beans. 'You must do a lot of hiking and camping.'

'No. The last time I was in Cataract was during a field trip in third grade. I got poison ivy.'

'Then you must love coffee.'

'No more than usual.' Willa nodded to a girl who stood at the counter. 'That's my friend Rachel's territory.'

'Then why do you own a sporting goods store and café?'

She shrugged. 'A few years ago I met someone who wanted to sell this place, and I needed something to do.'

'And this is what you chose.'

'Yes.'

He leaned forward and put his elbows on the table. Why did this bother him so much? When he'd recognised her yesterday on Jackson Hill, sitting on top of her Jeep, he'd felt a surge of happiness, like seeing a mentor. It was Willa Jackson, perpetrator of epic pranks. The care and detail and time that went into them was amazing—like her last one, pulling the fire alarm and then, when all the students were outside, unrolling a giant banner from the school roof, on which was written WILLA JACKSON IS THE WALLS OF WATER HIGH SCHOOL JOKER. 'I watched you that day the police took you from the school, and you didn't look embarrassed. You looked relieved. As if, finally, you could stop pretending. I thought you were going to leave here and never look back.'

She gave him an exasperated look. He didn't blame her. He should just shut up. This was none of his business.

But there was one more thing he needed to say. 'You're the reason I decided to follow my own path instead of coming back here and doing what everyone wanted me to do,' he said, which made her brows rise. 'No one thought you were capable of all that mayhem, and you showed them not to underestimate you. If you could be brave, then I thought I could be, too. I owe that to you. To the Joker.'

She shook her head. 'That bravery, as you call it, resulted in a class-two misdemeanour when I pulled that fire alarm. I was charged, nearly expelled, and wasn't allowed to go to graduation. And my dad was fired because of me, because I took his keys and his computer passwords to pull my pranks. Don't glamorise it, Colin. I'm glad you found your path. But I found my path, too, even if it wasn't what you expected.'

She thought her dad had been fired? Colin knew for a fact that he'd quit. Colin had been there when it had happened. Why wouldn't her father have told her?

Willa took advantage of his silence and stood. 'I have to get to work,' she said. 'Thanks for returning the invitation last night.'

'Still not going?' he asked as he, too, stood.

'No. And before you ask again, I'm not planning some prank.'

'Too bad. That group could use some shaking up.'

She walked past him. 'I'm not the girl to do it.'

He watched her walk away. She carried with her a fresh scent like lemons. 'Do you want to go out sometime?' he found himself calling after her, because he knew he would regret it if he didn't.

She stopped abruptly, then turned and walked back to him. 'I don't think that's a good idea,' she said in a low voice.

'I asked if you wanted to, not if it was a good idea.'

'You think they're two different things?'

'With you, Willa, I think they are *definitely* two different things.'

'You're going to be here one month. It's ridiculous to think you can make me see the error of my ways in that short period of time.' She had good instincts. She knew exactly what he was trying to do.

'Is that a challenge?'

'*No.*'

He walked to the door with a smile. 'I'll be seeing you, Willa.'

'Not if I see you first, Colin.'

Oh, yes, that was definitely a challenge.

Ha, the old Willa was somewhere in there, after all.

'**W**here were you last night? Mama had a hissy fit,' Paxton said when Colin got home that evening. She was coming in from work at the outreach centre, where she oversaw the Osgood family charity. They happened to meet in the driveway, a synchronicity they'd always had, a twin thing he sometimes missed.

'Sorry,' he said as they walked inside. 'I didn't mean to worry everyone. I fell asleep on someone's couch.'

'Someone? How very unspecific,' Paxton said as they walked to the kitchen. The housekeeper, Nola, was making dinner. Nola had been a fixture at Hickory Cottage for years. She was a stickler for manners and respect, and Paxton and Colin had always given it to her. In return, she'd given them secret snacks. Colin stopped to forage around in the refrigerator. Nola tsked at him and gave him one of the rolls she'd just made; then she shooed them both out.

Colin followed Paxton to the patio, where she stopped and turned to him. 'Out with it. Whose couch did you fall asleep on?'

He took a bite of the roll and smiled at her, which used to result in a smile back. Not now.

When he'd set eyes on his sister in the hall yesterday, it had been the first time in almost a year, when she'd flown up to spend a week with him in New York to celebrate their thirtieth birthday. She'd been so excited by the prospect of moving out of Hickory Cottage. But those plans had fallen through—and the difference between when he'd last seen Paxton and now was astounding. Unhappiness radiated from her like heat. She'd stayed too long in this house, shouldering absolutely everything it meant to be an Osgood. It was partly his fault. He'd left her to deal with this. He'd wanted to establish something that was his alone, to prove he could exist beyond Walls of Water. To Paxton, *nothing* existed outside Walls of Water.

'Come on,' she said. 'Tell me. Please?'

He finally shrugged and said, 'It was Willa Jackson's couch.'

Paxton looked surprised. 'I had no idea you were friends with Willa.'

'I'm not,' he said, finishing the roll in another two bites. 'When I was out yesterday, I saw her drop something, but I couldn't catch up with her, so I thought I'd just drop it by her house. I had no idea how tired I really was. I think I embarrassed her.'

That made Paxton laugh. She didn't do that often enough.

'So tell me about Willa,' he said, crossing his arms.

Paxton adjusted that ever-present tote bag on her shoulder. 'What do you want to know?'

'She seems to have a very quiet life.'

'Yes.' Paxton tilted her head. 'Why are you surprised? Her family has always been quiet.'

'But Willa was the Walls of Water High School Joker,' he said.

'Yes?'

Paxton didn't get it. Neither did he, exactly. 'I thought she would be more . . . outgoing.'

'She grew up, Colin. We all did.'

He scratched the side of his face. 'Why doesn't she want to go to the gala? Her grandmother helped found the Women's Society Club.'

'I don't know. When I sent her the invitation, I wrote a personal note about wanting to include her grandmother. But she blew me off.'

'She didn't want to have anything to do with the restoration?'

Paxton looked confused by the question. 'I didn't ask her.'

'You didn't ask if she had old photos or old papers? If she wanted to see what was going on inside as it was being restored?'

'There were enough photos on record to go by. Colin, honestly, this restoration was about contractors and designers and scouring art auctions and estate sales for period pieces. What could Willa have contributed?'

He shrugged as he looked out over the patio, to the pool, the pool house and the mountain landscape beyond. The rolling mountains looked like kids playing under a big green blanket. He had to admit, there was nowhere in the world like this place. Part of his heart was still here, somewhere. He wished he knew where. 'I guess it just would have been a nice thing to do.'

'I did the best I could,' she snapped. 'Where were you when all this was happening? You coordinated everything with the landscaping by phone and email. You wouldn't even do *that* in person.'

'I didn't know you wanted me here for the duration.' He paused, frowning at her reaction. 'No one asked you to take on this project alone, Pax.' He'd been surprised by Paxton's call last year, asking him to do the landscaping, but he couldn't say no. She'd wanted a large tree on the property, and, after a lot of networking, Colin had found one being threatened by development nearby. But transplanting a tree that heavy and old had to be planned down to the smallest detail. All year he'd been in touch weekly with the arborists they'd hired. And he'd taken off a month to oversee everything up until the grand opening of the Madam, which he'd considered a great sacrifice, because he hadn't been home for that long in over a decade.

Paxton threw her hands in the air. 'The Blue Ridge Madam is part of our town history. I did a good thing, even if I didn't ask Willa Jackson to help.'

'Calm down, Pax. What's wrong?'

She closed her eyes and sighed. 'Nothing's wrong. I just can't ever seem to do enough.'

'Enough for who? Mom and Dad? You have to get over that. You're never going to be happy until you live your own life.'

'Family is important, but that's not something you'd understand.' She turned to leave. 'Cover for me at dinner, will you? Tell Mama and Daddy I had to finish some work at the outreach centre.'

'Is that where you're really going?' he asked.

'No.'

Paxton drove to Sebastian's house and pulled in front. His car wasn't there. She remembered that he kept late hours on Thursdays at his office, which was the reason he'd had time to go with her to visit her grandmother that morning. Now she had to see him *twice* in order to get through the day? She wondered how she'd survived before he came to town. Basically, she'd kept her stress to herself, trying to work it out through her endless series of private lists.

She buzzed down the windows in her car and cut the engine. She felt better just sitting here, looking at Shade Tree Cottage. Reaching over to her tote bag, she brought out a small notebook. Most of her lists were about control, about breaking down her life into manageable pieces. But some of the lists were simply wishes. There was nothing more satisfying than putting what you wanted onto paper. It made it one step closer to being real.

She flipped to a clean sheet of paper and started a list about Sebastian. She had a lot of lists about him. Sebastian's Favourite Things. If Sebastian and I Went on Vacation Together, Where Would We Go? Today she started: Reasons Why Sebastian Makes Me Feel Better.

He doesn't care that I'm as tall as he is.

He holds my hand.

He's all clean lines and perfect manners.

'Do you do this often when I'm not here? Sit outside my house and work on your lists?'

Paxton gave a start and turned to see Sebastian, his hands on top of her car as he leaned down to look in her window. The sun highlighted his clear skin and turned his blue eyes crystalline. She hadn't heard him approach, but she could see now that his car was parked behind hers in the driveway.

She tucked her notebook away. 'No, I was just waiting for you.'

He opened the car door and helped her out. 'It's too hot to sit in your car.' He put his cool hand to her bare neck, which made her want to shiver. It was a base reaction from a place deep within her, a well full of sharp longings. She couldn't fill that well, couldn't stopper it, but for the sake of their friendship, she did everything she could not to show it.

She smiled. 'You never sweat. Are you actually human?'

'I enjoy air conditioning too much to ever be long without it. Come in.' They walked to his door, where he unlocked it and gestured for her to enter first. 'Have you had dinner yet?' he asked.

'No.'

'Join me, then. I'll grill salmon. I'm glad I came home first.'

'First?'

'Sometimes I go to that diner on the highway.'

'The Happy Daze Diner?' she asked, disbelieving. The place seemed so unlike him. It was a hole-in-the-wall greasy spoon.

He smiled at her reaction. 'Believe it or not, I have fond memories of the place. My great-aunt used to take me there when I was a kid.' He loosened his tie. 'So, how was your day?'

'The same. Until I got home this evening.' Paxton hesitated. 'I think my brother is interested in Willa Jackson.'

He raised a single brow. 'You don't approve?' His tie hissed as he pulled it off. It was a seductive sound. It made her skin prickle.

'No, it's not that. I'd love her for ever if she made him stay.'

'Then what's the problem?' he asked.

She hesitated, still bothered by it. 'He seems to think I should have invited her to participate in the restoration of the Blue Ridge Madam. Do you think I should have?'

He shrugged. 'It would have been a nice thing to do.'

'That's what Colin said. I didn't mean to slight her.'

'I know you didn't. You like being in control. It never occurs to you to ask for help.' He smiled and put a hand to her cheek. 'But some things are worth asking for, darling.'

'Easy for you to say,' she said miserably.

'No, actually, it's not,' he responded. 'I'm going to change. You haven't been upstairs since I redecorated my bedroom, have you?'

'No.'

'Come on, then.'

She knew where the rooms were—the guest room, the exercise room, his master suite. He'd mentioned having his bedroom painted, but she wasn't prepared for the major overhaul. The grey walls had a metallic sheen, and the furniture was all black lacquer. He'd spent time when he moved back decorating the downstairs and ridding the house of its medieval decor. She'd loved watching the transformation, watching it become more like Sebastian. This, though, wasn't anything like what she thought it would be. Dark, moody, masculine.

She started to leave so he could change, but he told her to stay and disappeared into his dressing room.

'Why did you choose a house this big, when there's only you?' she called as she walked around his bedroom. His bed was king-sized. There was room for someone else there; he just seemed to have no interest in issuing any invitations.

'Every life needs a little space. It leaves room for good things to enter it.'

'Wow, Sebastian. Profound.'

She heard him laugh as she walked by his bed, trailing her fingers along the silken black cover. She stopped to look at a painting over his chest of drawers. It was dark, obviously old, like something that should be in a folk art museum. It was of a red bowl filled with ripe red berries. A yellow and black bird was perched on the edge of the bowl, looking out angrily, as if daring someone to take a berry. The tip of his beak was red from berry juice, or maybe blood. It was a little disturbing.

'That belonged to my great-aunt,' Sebastian said. She could feel his chest brush the back of her arm as he stopped behind her. 'She loved it. It hung in her living room, next to her woodstove. It's all I have by way of family heirlooms. I had it packed away.'

'Why didn't you bring it out before now?' she asked.

'I wasn't sure I was going to stay in Walls of Water. I didn't know if things would work out.' He paused. 'But they did.'

Her scalp tightened, like in a barely avoided collision. She hadn't known she'd almost lost him. What was so wrong with this place that people wanted to leave? What was wrong with home and history and family? Her back still to him, she said, 'You've mentioned your great-aunt twice tonight. You've never talked about her before.'

'She was the only person in my family I knew loved me without reservation. But she passed away when I was ten.'

Sebastian didn't talk much about his family, but she knew his father was verbally abusive. They had lived in a trailer park west of town. She guessed she'd answered her own question. Maybe there were some things you had to get away from. She could understand it from Sebastian. She still didn't understand it from her brother. To change the subject, she smiled, turned round, and said, 'Dinner?'

She didn't realise how close he was. 'Unless there's something else you want to do up here,' he said.

She wouldn't touch that. She couldn't. 'Are you implying I need to use your workout room?' she joked.

He lowered his eyes and turned away. 'Never, darling. I love you just the way you are.'

CHAPTER FIVE

UNEARTHED

IT WAS HARD TO BELIEVE on a day like today, when Willa and Rachel were so busy that their lunch consisted of doughnuts and iced coffee from the café, but business on National Street fell off sharply in the winter. Rachel had lasted over a year, but Willa was afraid she was going to lose her in the coming winter. Rachel and her coffee were the only things she looked forward to now that the restoration of the Madam was complete and she didn't have an excuse to drive up Jackson Hill every day.

'Willa, look,' Rachel said at around four o'clock that afternoon, when they finally had a quiet moment. Willa turned to see Rachel looking out the window. 'Tall, dark and rich is heading this way.'

Colin Osgood was walking by the window, heading for the door.

'Oh. Tell him I'm not here,' she said, and turned to the storeroom behind the counter.

'What is the matter with you?' Rachel called after her.

She disappeared, closing the door behind her, just as she heard the store bell ring.

What was the matter with her? That was a good question. The winters were tough on Willa, too, because she knew she couldn't leave. That was the difference between Willa and Rachel. Her grandmother was here. Her father's house was here. Her history was here. Sometimes she would lean against the front counter, chin in hand, and stare at the snow, craving something different, which made her feel that nervous pull in her stomach, like how she would feel when weeks would go by in school after she'd promised herself not to do anything stupid again. The feeling would just get worse and worse, until she found herself hanging a rope of leotards out the dance tower window at two in the morning, so everyone coming to school would think that a group of dancers had got stuck up there and had had to tie their clothes together and climb out naked.

That's why she wanted to stay away from Colin Osgood. No one had ever said that she'd inspired them before, that they'd admired her. It went against everything she'd been told, everything anyone who had ever suffered through high school wanted to believe, that if you tried hard enough, you could actually get away from who you used to be. But, not for the first time, she found herself wondering, what if who she was then was her truer self?

She heard voices out in the store. The timbre of Colin's low voice, Rachel's laughter.

Suddenly, the knob to the storeroom turned. She instinctively pushed against it. But he had the strength and momentum. She gave up and stepped out of the way, letting the door fling open.

Colin caught the door before it hit the wall, then looked at her strangely. It had been a long day, and she'd taken a bandana and used it to push her hair away from her face. Completing the ensemble were jeans, platform sneakers, and a coffee-stained T-shirt that read *Go Au Naturel! Au Naturel Sporting Goods and Café*. 'Why were you leaning against the door?' he asked.

'I told you you wouldn't see me if I saw you first.'

'I didn't think that meant you would literally hide from me.'

He was wearing khakis and loafers. His sunglasses were tucked into the collar of his light blue T-shirt. He looked so put-together and in control. It was the particular power of all Osgoods, she supposed.

'What do you want, Colin?'

'I want you to come up to the Madam with me,' he said. 'There's something I want to show you.'

'I can't. I'm working,' she said. To prove her point, she picked up a box of paper cups and inched past him through the doorway.

'It won't take long,' he said, following her. 'We found something on the property today. Maybe you can help us figure out who it belonged to.'

'I doubt it. I don't know anything about that house,' she said. And it was true. Her grandmother had never talked about her life there. Willa handed the cups to Rachel, who was giving her a very juvenile you're-talking-to-a-boy look. She turned round and found Colin closer than she'd expected. 'What did you find?'

He leaned forward and smiled down on her. 'Come and find out,' he said seductively. He smelled intriguing, sharp and fresh.

It was too much to resist. She'd been wanting to see it for over a year, and now she had the perfect excuse, one that didn't involve evening dresses, small talk, or Paxton Osgood. It did, however, involve Colin Osgood, and some definite sexual tension. But he would be leaving in a month, so it wasn't as if she would have to hide from him for ever. 'Rachel, hold down the fort,' she said.

'Take your time,' Rachel said with a knowing smile.

Colin opened the door and said, 'I'll drive.' He pointed to the black Mercedes in front of them. He clicked the key fob he was holding and the lights flashed and the doors unlocked.

He stepped off the kerb and opened the car door for her. She sighed and got in, almost swallowed by the huge leather seats. Colin got behind the wheel, put on his sunglasses, and backed out. He manouevred the car through the traffic on National Street, one hand on the steering wheel, the other on his knee.

After several minutes of silence, she turned to him and said, 'Why are you going to be here a whole month?'

'I took some time off to help Paxton. And to attend the gala.'

'Where do you live now?'

'New York is my home base. But I travel a lot.'

Just then they turned the corner to the steep driveway up to the Madam, and she stopped trying to make small talk. She'd never been beyond this point. She turned her attention away from Colin and watched the house as it got closer. *This is going to be something significant,* she thought. *No ghosts. This is going to feel like coming home.*

When he stopped the car in front of the house, she couldn't wait to get out. Something was off, though. The wind blew in a sharp gust past her, sounding like voices in her ears. She turned in the direction of the wind and whispers. At the edge of the plateau, there was an excavator and a few men in hard hats were standing around.

'The tree is gone,' she said, realising what was missing.

Colin walked to her side of the car. 'The peach tree, yes.'

'It was a peach tree?' That surprised her. 'I didn't realise peach trees could grow at this elevation.'

'They can grow; they just can't bear fruit. The springs are too cold here. Kills the buds.' He leaned against the car beside her.

'Then why plant a peach tree here?'

He shrugged. 'Your guess is as good as mine. Paxton said it wasn't in any of the old photos of the place, so it had to have come up after your family moved out. Since it's not historical, and not fruit-bearing, she decided it could go.'

'How did you know it was a peach tree if it's never borne fruit?'

'I'm a landscape architect,' he said.

It was all starting to make sense. 'Ah. You're doing the landscaping. That's why you're here.'

'Yes. I drew up the plans, then contracted the work out before I arrived. My biggest contribution was finding a one-hundred-and-fifty-year-old live oak that was threatened by development, and the developer didn't want to get into it with the environmentalists, so he agreed to split the cost with us to transplant it here. The highway is going to close on Tuesday to move it.' He turned and smiled. 'You should come and watch.'

'Come and watch you plant a tree? Gee, you know how to show a girl a good time.'

That made him laugh. 'It's a lot more than that. Trust me. How can you own a sporting goods store and not like nature?'

Before she could answer, one of the men at the dig site suddenly yelled, 'Hey, Stick Man!'

Colin turned his head but otherwise didn't move. She could feel a ripple of tension go through him. He stared at the man who had called to him, until it became clear he wasn't going to yell back.

The man sighed and walked over to the car. Willa recognised him as Dave Jeffries. They'd all gone to high school together. He'd been on the football team and was still thick in the chest. 'What's up, Dave?' Colin asked as soon as Dave stopped in front of him.

'Just after you left, we dug up something else.' He held up a heavy, rusted, cast-iron frying pan, still crusted with dirt.

Colin studied it. 'A frying pan? This just gets more interesting.'

Dave smiled when he saw Willa. 'Willa Jackson,' he said, pushing his hard hat back. 'I never see you around. Remember that time you programmed the period bell to ring every five minutes? That was great. We kept filing out into the hallway every five minutes, and the teachers kept trying to get us back into the classrooms.' He gave her an assessing look, then wagged his finger between her and Colin. 'You and Stick Man aren't together, are you? Because you could give ol' Dave a try if you're lonely.'

'Tempting offer, Dave,' Willa said. 'But no thanks.'

Dave laughed and punched Colin on the arm with what seemed like entirely too much force. 'Good luck,' he said to Colin.

As soon as he walked away, Willa turned to Colin and said, 'Stick Man?'

'That's what they called me in high school. Thanks to Dave.'

'Because you're so tall?'

'That's what everyone thought.'

She waited, then said, 'You're not going to tell me?'

He sighed. 'Dave called me Stick Man because he said I acted like I had a stick up my ass.'

Willa was so surprised that she laughed without meaning to. She put her hand to her mouth and said, 'Sorry.'

'To be fair, it was true. I was a little rigid. It was how the men I knew acted, so I thought I was supposed to act that way, too. Dave made fun of guys like me, guys who had no concept of fun. It felt great our senior year when everyone imagined I was the Joker. They looked at me and thought, "Wow, I didn't know he had that in him."'

'I remember that feeling,' she said. Then, before they could get into another discussion about bravery, or her apparent lack of it now, she asked, 'So, what did you want to show me here?'

He took off his sunglasses and hooked them on the collar of his shirt; then he motioned her to follow him up the steps to the front portico of the house. The place was huge. It overwhelmed her. She'd spent so much time watching this place from a distance that it felt surreal to be actually climbing the steps, to touch the columns.

'While digging up the stump of the peach tree today, we found some buried treasure. A suitcase and a fedora. And a frying pan,' he added, giving the rusty thing a spin in his hand. 'When they showed me the fedora, it gave me chills, because every kid who has broken into the Madam for the past forty years has claimed to see a floating fedora in the house. My grandmother Agatha used to scare us by telling us stories of the ghost who lived here.'

'Did you ever see it?' she asked.

'I kept my eyes closed the one time I broke in here with my friends,' he said. 'What about you? Did you ever see it?'

'I never broke in,' she said.

'Are you kidding me? All the stunts you pulled, and you never once broke into the Madam? Why not?'

'My grandmother told me those stories, too.'

'*You're* afraid of ghosts?' he asked.

'I just think things that are laid to rest should stay there,' she said, realising she sounded a lot like her grandmother. She stepped over to the suitcase on the edge of the portico. It was made of black leather, covered in dirt, but still surprisingly intact. The contents had been removed and were lined beside it, next to the fedora.

She crouched down and looked through everything, mostly men's clothing. But there was also a disintegrating newspaper and an open scrapbook. She carefully lifted the pages of the scrapbook. It was bulging with clippings, its pages yellow and brittle. Whoever this belonged to liked to follow what movie stars were doing in the 1930s. There were photos, too, very old, of people in an orchard.

'Do these trees look like the peach tree here?' she asked. Colin looked over her shoulder. He was closer than he needed to be.

'Yes, they do. Interesting clue.'

As she looked through the rest of the book, she found a high school diploma from Upton Orphan School for Boys in Upton, Texas, made out to someone named Tucker Devlin.

'Does any of this seem familiar?' Colin asked.

'Not really, just . . .' She stopped when she reached the last page. There was a single photo of a handsome man in a light suit, wearing a fedora, maybe the same fedora buried with the suitcase. He was beautiful. He looked like he could get anything he wanted.

'What?' Colin asked.

'I don't know. There's something familiar about him.' Willa closed the scrapbook, not able to figure it out.

'That Asheville newspaper in the suitcase dates this back to August 1936, the year your family moved out,' Colin said.

'That was the month and year the Women's Society Club formed, according to the invitations your sister sent,' Willa added as she stood. 'I don't know anything about this. Sorry. Some of my grandmother's things are stored in my attic. Maybe there's a clue to this Tucker Devlin person. I could look.'

'That would be great.' He smiled. 'Would you like to see the inside of the house?'

It took everything she had not to say, *Yes, please!*

He went to the huge eight-panel door with the handblown bull's-eye glass on either side of it. A brass plaque to the left read *The Historic Blue Ridge Madam Inn*. The door clicked open easily.

Her hands were shaking as she stepped inside to a cool blast from the past. She saw the grand staircase hugging the wall in a long curving slope. At the top of the staircase was a portrait of a woman with dark hair and grey eyes, wearing a stunning dark blue gown.

It was overwhelming to think her grandmother had lived here like this. It was a hard thing to reconcile, the grandmother she knew and the one who had once flitted through these opulent rooms. She wanted so desperately to feel connected to this place, to feel . . . something. But as she looked around, she couldn't feel a thing.

The hall had been turned into a lobby, and there was a dark cherry check-in desk to the side. A woman in jeans and a T-shirt was on the phone. When she saw Colin, she gave him a wave.

Colin waved back as he took Willa through an archway and into the dining room. Dozens of round tables filled the space, awash in light from the ceiling-high windows. He led her out of the dining room, directly across the lobby to the opposite archway. 'This was the original library,' Colin said. 'Now it's a sitting room.' It, like most of the downstairs, was covered in old dark panelling.

The woman who'd been on the phone entered at that moment. 'Sorry about that, Colin. I'm still trying to find a laundry service. Paxton threw me a curve ball when she asked if the Madam might be ready for overnight guests the night of the gala.'

Colin made the introductions. 'Willa, this is Maria, the manager. Maria, you're looking at a direct Blue Ridge Madam descendant. This is Willa Jackson. Her ancestors built this place.'

'This is an honour,' Maria said. 'Welcome, Willa.'

'Thank you,' Willa said. She was beginning to feel uncomfortable and heat was creeping up her neck. She didn't belong here.

'Maria can back me up,' Colin said. 'You've seen the fedora, haven't you?'

Maria laughed. 'I'm sure it was my imagination. Once you hear a place might be haunted, every creak becomes a ghost.'

'I'm going to show Willa around upstairs,' Colin said. 'Are the guest rooms still unlocked?'

'Yes,' Maria said. 'Enjoy.'

They walked back into the hall. 'Beyond the check-in desk is the banquet hall. That's where the Women's Society Club will be holding the gala,' Colin said as he and Willa walked up the stairs. Once they reached the top, Colin stopped at the portrait of the lady in blue. 'That's your great-great-grandmother, Rebecca Jackson. The painting was found wrapped in blankets in a closet.'

Willa stared at her. So this was her grandmother's grandmother. Did Grandmother Georgie know her? She had no idea. 'I have her eyes,' she found herself saying.

'I know.'

'This is the first time I've ever seen her.'

Colin shook his head. 'Paxton should have let you in on all of this. I don't know why she didn't.'

'I wouldn't have been much help,' Willa said.

'The guest rooms are this way.'

She stopped him. 'No. I've seen enough.'

'What's wrong?'

'Nothing. It's a gorgeous place. Thanks for the tour, but I really have to get back. Sorry I couldn't be more help with the buried treasure.'

She started to turn. And that's when the earth moved.

She paused, then met Colin's eyes. He looked as confused as she was. 'Did you feel that?' she asked.

'Yes,' he said seriously. 'And I don't like it.'

He took off down the staircase. She followed him outside, only to feel that the shaking was more pronounced out in the open. The ground was rumbling, making the large outdoor chandelier sway.

Colin looked over to where they were digging up the roots of the peach tree, which had created a fairly significant hole. 'It feels like they hit a gas line. But there aren't any gas lines here.'

The rumbling seemed to be getting louder, vibrating the air around them in waves that made Willa's eardrums pound.

'Whatever it is, it's going to blow,' Colin said as he ran to the edge of the portico, waving his arms, trying to get the attention of the men at the dig site. 'Get back!' he yelled.

The men looked at him and didn't hesitate. They ran with full force away from the hole.

Colin turned as the rumbling escalated. He grabbed Willa and flattened her against the side of the house. She was sure something was going to explode. She squeezed her eyes shut and buried her face in Colin's chest. But just as it reached its crescendo, the rumbling stopped abruptly and everything became eerily quiet, with the exception of the chandelier slowly creaking as it swayed.

Colin pulled back, and he and Willa looked at each other for one long, heated moment. Then they turned toward the excavator. A cluster of black and yellow birds had settled on the machinery and were looking into the hole. One of the men approached cautiously. When he looked in, the expression on his face registered complete shock.

'What is it?' Colin called.

He tipped his hard hat back. 'You want to see this for yourself.'

'Are you OK?' Colin asked, turning back to Willa. He cupped the side of her head with one palm.

Willa nodded. Colin stepped back, then jumped off the portico and walked toward the hole. Willa followed.

Colin got there first and looked in. 'I think we just found the owner of the suitcase,' he said.

Willa looked in the hole. It took a moment to realise that what she thought was a large stone, wasn't a stone at all.

It was a human skull.

CHAPTER SIX

THE FAIRY TALE

PAXTON BROKE THROUGH the surface of the water and swam laps until her arms burned. When she couldn't push herself any more, she floated for a while. She wanted to stay like this for ever, the water shutting out all sounds, disconnected from everything.

She finally stood and pushed her wet hair out of her face and took a deep breath. She told herself that she could fix this. She could fix anything if she just put her mind to it.

She turned in the water to see Sebastian sitting on one of the lounge chairs. He'd taken off his suit jacket and had tossed it onto the lounge chair next to him.

'Sebastian. What are you doing here?' He'd never been to her house before. She got out, grabbed the towel at the edge of the pool, and dried off while walking towards him. She felt self-conscious because he'd never seen her in a bathing suit before. Not that it mattered to him.

He stood, picked up his suit jacket, and tossed it over his shoulder. 'I heard about the skeleton at the Blue Ridge Madam. I wanted to see if you were all right. You didn't answer your phone.'

'It's fine. Everything will be fine,' she said, which is what she'd been saying all afternoon. If she said it enough, maybe it would even become true. She wrapped her towel tightly around her, holding it together at her chest with her hand. She looked back at the main house, wondering what her mother thought of Sebastian being here. 'I can't believe you braved my parents just to see if I was all right. I hope they were nice to you.'

He didn't answer directly. 'I'm used to the looks. Don't worry about me. I can survive just about anything.'

For some reason, that struck a nerve. 'You don't think I can?'

He stared at her without a word. She'd never really been on her own. She was still living with her parents. She understood why he might think that.

'Let's go in,' she said, leading him to the pool house. 'How long have you been here?'

'A while. You have a nice backstroke.'

Paxton opened the door and he followed her in. She quickly grabbed some notes she'd been making from the coffee table and stuffed them in her tote bag.

'Would you like something to drink? All I have is whiskey.'

'No, thank you,' he said as he looked around. Her mother had had the place redecorated as a crazy dysfunctional thank-you to Paxton for not moving out. The place was meant to feel like a beach house. The colours were white and sand and gold, all the furniture square and soft. They weren't choices Paxton would have made. Nothing in this place bore her signature. Whenever she dreamed of being in a home, it was never here. Sometimes it was the town house she'd almost bought last year. Sometimes it was someplace she'd never seen before. But she always knew it was hers.

'So, you're fine,' Sebastian said as he sat down on her couch. He wasn't interested in the details of the skeleton they'd found at the Madam. He was worried about *her*.

'Yes,' she said, trying to laugh. 'Of course.'

He didn't look as though he believed her. Sometimes she didn't think it was fair that he knew her this well.

'Well, actually,' she said, 'I feel like hyperventilating. But I can't. It's all built up here, and I can't let it out.' She patted her chest. 'Colin is going crazy, trying to form a back-up plan because that one-hundred-and-fifty-year-old oak tree is scheduled to be delivered on Tuesday, and it will have to be planted right away or we'll lose it. But we don't know if the police will clear the scene and let us plant it yet. And do you want to know why I turned off my phone?' She didn't wait for him to answer. 'Because Women's Society Club members keep calling, worried about holding the gala at the Madam. Some of the members wanted to have it at the country club, anyway, but they were outvoted. They seem so eager to believe this is going to make the restoration fail. The manager at the Madam says people have called, worried about their reservations, when it doesn't even officially open for guests until *September*.' She stopped and took a breath.

Sebastian stood and walked over to her. He took her by her arms, looked calmly into her eyes, and said, 'You can't control everything, Pax. I keep trying to tell you this. You have this remarkable *resistance* against letting some things just happen. If you take a step back, you'll see that when this blows over, no one will question having the gala at the Madam.'

'But this is supposed to be perfect.'

'Nothing is ever perfect. No matter how much you'd like for it to appear that way.'

She shook her head. She knew that. She just didn't know how to live any other way. She'd been this way her entire life. She didn't know how to stop it, as much as she wanted to.

'Just let it go, darling,' he said, drawing his arms round her, not caring that she was wet. This, *this,* was why she loved him so much. 'Whatever it takes, just let it go.' With her hand still clutching the towel, she couldn't hug him back and stay covered, but she realised she liked that she could fold herself into him this way. She put her head on his shoulder and could feel his breath on her neck.

Her heart picked up speed, and she was sure he could hear it.

As the seconds passed by, she could almost feel the rope winding around them as the force of her desperation and desire pulled her closer to him. She slowly let the towel drop and lifted her arms around him, grazing her chest with his. She raised her head from his shoulder and put her cheek to his, nuzzling him slightly.

She was overwhelmed. That's the only reason she could think to justify her actions, her *weakness*. She turned her head slowly and her lips found his. Her hands went to his hair and she opened her lips. He wasn't unwilling. After a moment of surprise, he began to kiss her back. Her heart *sang*. Before she knew it, she was walking him to the couch and pushing him to sit. She straddled him, trying to kiss past his barriers, to get him into that seductive place when their eyes had met all those years ago when he was kissing someone else. If she just tried hard enough, she could make this happen. She could make him love her the way she loved him.

'Paxton . . .' Sebastian finally said in between her kisses. 'Think this through. Is this really a good idea?'

She opened her eyes and slowly leaned back. They were both breathing heavily. His colour was high, and it made him even more beautiful, that rose-red flush along his cheeks.

What was she doing? He'd told her to let it go, but she was sure he hadn't meant this way. And yet, he was going to *let* her. Oh God. How pitiful could she get?

She pulled away and wrapped the towel round herself again.

He leaned forward and put his elbows on his knees, clasping his hands in front of him, his breath still quick from their encounter. He was staring at the floor, seeming to collect his thoughts.

He finally stood. 'I think I should go,' he said.

She tried to smile as she nodded that she understood.

Without another word, he left.

She wanted to move out but didn't want to disappoint her parents. She wanted help with all she had to do but was too proud to ask. The Blue Ridge Madam project was supposed to cement their family's reputation, but there was a skeleton casting a pall over the project now. The Women's Society Club's seventy-fifth anniversary gala was supposed to be the crowning achievement of her presidency, but it was being threatened with a last-minute change of venue. And she'd wanted so badly for Sebastian to be something he wasn't that, just now, in a matter of minutes, she may very well have ruined the best thing that had ever happened to her.

How could someone with a life this full feel this empty?

She went to the cabinet and took out the vile bottle of whiskey and poured a glass. With a grimace, she forced it down.

Trying to stay awake after a very long day, Willa let the humid night air blow on her as she drove home from Rachel's party. She usually said no to Rachel's regular Friday-night barbecue. Friday night was vacuuming night. Sometimes jogging night, if she felt like it. Wild and crazy stuff. But the sight of the skull at the Blue Ridge Madam made her want to be around people tonight. Colin had taken her back to her store after the discovery of the skeleton, and she hadn't heard from him since.

She'd left the store with Rachel and had gone straight to Rachel's house. That had been seven hours ago. She'd stayed too late. Too late for her, anyway. Rachel wasn't your typical twenty-two-year-old, except when she got around other twenty-two-year-olds, and that was when Willa realised how much difference eight years can make in a life. She didn't exactly miss being that age—she'd been a college dropout and drank too much and partied too hard—but she did miss that sense of living in the moment, of living only to *feel*.

Heading back down the long road leading into Walls of Water, Willa passed a convenience store called Gas Me Up, a place that sold cheap beer and didn't always ask for ID. The parking lot had a few cars in it, and, as Willa yawned, she assumed her eyes were playing tricks on her when she thought she recognised one of them.

She slowed down to make sure.

Yes, that was definitely Paxton Osgood's white BMW roadster.

And that was definitely Paxton coming out of the store.

What was *she* doing there? She didn't think Paxton knew what this side of midnight looked like, much less this side of town.

Willa pulled over to the side of the road. She saw their old classmate Robbie Roberts come out of the store behind Paxton.

He'd grown up to be handsome in a fading kind of way. He was cocky and could be charming. But he got drunk too often, worked only long enough to get fired and collect unemployment, and was reputedly thrown out of the house by his wife on a weekly basis. Robbie was trouble, but soft trouble. A lover not a fighter.

But his two friends, the men hanging around outside the store, were definitely hard trouble.

Of all the things Willa thought she knew about Paxton Osgood, she'd been most certain that Paxton could handle herself in any situation. She had an air about her that made people pay attention. And it didn't hurt that, in heels, she was probably six feet tall.

But, as Willa watched, she realised Paxton was out of her element. It was one in the morning at a convenience store on a side of town that didn't often see the likes of her, in her red sundress and heels. She was standing outside the doors now, stopped there by the men, her arms heavy with bags that looked like they contained wine and potato crisps. Cheap wine and crisps? Not her usual fare. Her hair, normally in a chignon, was only half up. She seemed uneasy on her feet.

She was *drunk*.

Willa would have thought it was funny, would have enjoyed watching the spectacle of someone who had made a lifetime commitment to perfection fall flat on her face . . . if it weren't for the men surrounding her.

There was a universal understanding among women. They all knew the fear of being outnumbered, of being helpless. It throbbed in their chests when they thought about the time they left a store and someone followed them. The knock on their car window as they were sitting alone at a red light. Having too much to drink and losing the ability to say no. Smiling at strange men coming onto them, not wanting to hurt their feelings, not wanting to make a scene. Women knew these things, even if they had never happened to them personally. It was a part of their collective unconscious.

Willa couldn't just sit there. She had to do something. She jerked her Jeep into gear and crossed the road to the convenience store parking lot, thinking that nothing about this day had been normal. And she would never admit, not even to herself, that she kind of liked it.

She stopped in front of the group, her lights on high beam. She saw Paxton jerk her arm away from one of the men trying to touch her, then try to walk forward, only to be blocked by the other man.

Willa reached into her bag for her pepper spray and opened the door. 'Hi, Paxton,' she said. Her heart was racing, and she could feel the adrenaline surge. 'What are you doing here?'

The men turned. Paxton's head jerked up, and Willa saw her fear.

'Look, a mini one. We got enough for a real party now,' the man holding Paxton's arm said. He had *abuse* written all over him.

'Why don't you let go of her?' Willa said. Her hand was clenching the can of pepper spray. She was hyperaware of everything around her, every small sound, every change in the air.

Robbie sniggered. He'd always been the boy to hang out with the rough bunch, not really one of them, but close enough. And, like most people, he'd figured close enough was better than not fitting in at all. 'Come on, Willa, how often do we get a drunk prom queen around here? She sent me a love letter in high school. She denied it and made everyone laugh at me, but she sent it. Admit it, Paxton.'

'Robbie, for God's sake, *I* sent you that letter,' Willa said. '*I* was the Joker. That's the kind of stupid thing I did back then. She didn't have anything to do with it.'

He gave her a confused look.

Willa left them and marched to the convenience store door and called inside, 'Call 911.'

The counter assistant looked up from his magazine, then looked back down, ignoring her.

'That's my brother,' the second man said. 'He ain't calling no one.'

Willa slowly backed up. She knew she could run to her Jeep and call 911 and wait with her doors locked. But that would leave Paxton to fend for herself.

'Paxton, set down your bags,' Willa finally said. 'Let's take a ride in my Jeep, OK?'

She made a gesture with her hand and Paxton's eyes went to the pepper spray. Paxton dropped her bags. The wine bottles smashed.

'She ain't going nowhere,' the man holding her arm said. 'Except maybe behind the building for a little fun.'

Willa lifted the can and aimed. She got the first man in the face. The second man moved, and she had to chase him to the door before she got him. Once she did, she lunged over and grabbed Paxton's arm, dropping her spray in the process.

They were almost to the Jeep when Robbie stepped in front of them. The first man was coughing and rubbing his eyes, making it worse, making his anger rise. He yelled at Robbie to grab them. The second man had run into the store to get the assistant who was now coming towards the doors.

'Was the letter really a Joker prank?' asked Robbie.

'*Yes*,' Willa said.

'Oh. Sorry, Paxton.'

Paxton was holding on to Willa now with a force that was going to leave marks.

Robbie dropped to his knees and covered his face, screaming as if he, too, had been maced. Willa had no idea what he was doing until he took a break in his theatrics to say, 'Go, dammit.'

And that's exactly what they did.

Willa jumped behind the wheel and Paxton fell into the passenger seat. Willa was trembling so much she had trouble putting the Jeep in reverse. After she had set up particularly big pranks at school, which had sometimes taken all night, she had crawled back into bed and shaken like this. It hadn't felt bad, more like a thaw.

When Willa finally got in gear, Paxton nearly fell out from the speed with which Willa backed out of the parking lot. She had to grab a handful of Paxton's dress to keep her inside. Once they were on the road, Willa kept checking her rearview mirror, relaxing only when a couple of miles had passed and she realised they weren't being followed. Neither of them said anything for a long time.

Finally, Paxton asked, 'Do you have any tissues?'

Willa turned to look at her. Tears were streaming down Paxton's cheeks, and her nose was running. 'I have some paper napkins in the glove compartment.'

Paxton fumbled around until she found the napkins. 'I'm not crying,' she said. 'I got hit by some of the pepper spray.'

'Oh,' Willa said. 'Sorry. I thought my aim was better.'

Paxton snorted, which made Willa smile.

'Where are we going?' Paxton asked, blowing her nose as they reached the town proper.

'To your house.'

That had an immediate reaction. 'No, don't take me home!' Paxton said loudly. 'Let me out right now.' She started fumbling with the door handle.

Willa had to pull over, afraid Paxton was going to leap out of the Jeep while it was still moving. Now that the adrenaline rush was over, she could see what a problem she had. She had a drunk Paxton Osgood in her car and no idea what to do with her. 'Where do you want me to take you, then?' she asked. They were in front of a Tudor-style house in Paxton's neighbourhood. A dog barked somewhere inside. 'Kirsty Lemon's?'

Paxton leaned back against the seat. 'God, no. She'd love this.'

'I thought you two were friends?'

'Whatever that means,' Paxton said, which surprised Willa. Society ladies always seemed so hand in glove, giving looks to each other only they could interpret, sharing secrets.

'Sebastian's?'

Paxton seemed to think about that. She finally said softly, 'No.'

That left only one place. Great. Willa put the Jeep in gear. 'What were you doing at the Gas Me Up, anyway?' she said as she drove.

'It was the only place I could get alcohol at this time of night and no one would see me,' Paxton said as she rubbed her eyes. 'God, that spray was strong, and I only got a little bit of it. I hope they feel it for days.'

'No one in their right mind goes there after dark.'

'Well, I didn't know that,' Paxton said defensively. 'It's the first time I've been there.'

'Why tonight?'

'Because my life is crap and I needed alcohol.'

Paxton Osgood's life was crap. Right. 'You didn't have any alcohol in your house?'

'I drank it all,' she said.

'In a house the size of Hickory Cottage?'

'I drank all the liquor in *my* house. The pool house. And there was no way I could go to my parents' house for more. My mother would've given me hell. She always gives me hell. You know who else gives me hell? The Women's Society Club. One skeleton found at the Madam and suddenly they think the whole project is a wash out. As if they don't have tons of skeletons in their closets. If you only knew.' Paxton turned in her seat and Willa could feel her staring at her. 'And you gave me hell, too. In high school.'

'Only once,' Willa pointed out.

'I can't believe it was you who wrote that note to Robbie Roberts.'

'I'm sorry.' Willa pulled to the kerb and cut the engine. 'I really am.'

'I remember when I saw that note. You copied my handwriting so well I thought I *had* written it. You could've gone into forgery.'

Willa climbed out. 'That would have made my dad very proud.'

Paxton looked around, finally realising that they'd come to a stop. 'Where are we?'

'This is my house. Come on.'

'You're going to let me stay at your house?'

'The Ritz is too far to drive.'

Paxton wasn't steady on her feet, so Willa held her elbow and led her up the steps. She unlocked the door and led Paxton to the couch; then she left the room and returned with a pillow and a blanket.

Paxton took off her shoes and propped the pillow up on the couch. 'This is a great couch.'

'I'm thinking of calling it the Osgood Memorial Couch. Your brother slept on it, too.' Willa left again, this time to the kitchen, where she wet a cloth with cold water. She brought it out and handed it to Paxton.

'My brother likes you, you know,' Paxton said, lying back and putting the cool cloth over her swollen eyes. 'Make him stay.'

Willa flipped out the blanket and covered Paxton. 'I'm not involved with your brother.'

'You will be. You know why? Because that's what's supposed to happen. That's the fairy tale. You meet, you fall in love, you kiss, and neither of you is revolted by it. Then you get married and have kids and live happily ever after.'

'The not-being-revolted part is a nice touch,' Willa said.

'It comes from experience. I'm in love with Sebastian Rogers. But he's not in love with me.'

Willa probably should have been surprised, but she wasn't. She locked the door, turned out the light, and stood there a moment. 'Your life isn't as glamorous as I thought it was,' she said into the darkness.

'What tipped you off? The drunk run to the Gas Me Up, or admitting that I'm in love with a man who might be gay?'

'It's a tie,' Willa said, which made Paxton laugh. She was too used to people judging her, Willa realised.

Then something Willa never thought would happen suddenly did.

She actually felt sorry for Paxton Osgood.

This was enough revelation for one night. Exhausted, Willa left the living room and headed upstairs to her bedroom.

'Thank you, Willa,' Paxton called after her.

'You're welcome, Paxton.'

CHAPTER SEVEN

RELATIVITY

PAXTON SLOWLY OPENED HER EYES, which took effort. Her lashes seemed glued together. She sat up on her elbows, a small movement that actually felt like being slammed against a wall. She groaned but powered through it and sat all the way up.

She looked around. She was in a small house filled with dated furniture, except for the soft grey couch she was lying on. She was facing a picture window, and there was a yellow and black bird sitting on the sill, staring inside. A shrill ringing sound suddenly made her jump, and, startled by her movements, the bird flew off.

She put her hands to her head. Good God, what was that noise?

She heard footsteps and turned to see Willa Jackson stumble into the room wearing cotton shorts and a tank top, both twisted from sleep. Her short hair was like a cloud round her face.

'I thought I turned off your phone last night when it wouldn't stop ringing,' Willa said, lunging for Paxton's cellphone on the end table. She flipped it open and said, 'Hello?' She paused. 'Oh.' She handed the phone to Paxton. 'It's for you.'

Paxton took it, trying not to make any sudden movements for fear her head might fall off. Willa frowned and left the room.

'Hello?' Paxton said into the phone.

'I'm in the pool house. Where are you?' It was Colin.

She looked around. 'I think I'm at Willa Jackson's house.'

'That would explain her answering your phone. What are you doing there?' Colin asked.

It was all coming back to her. What a *fool* she'd made of herself.

'Have you been there all night?'

'I think so,' she said.

Colin paused, and she could tell what conclusions he was coming to. 'Are you drunk? There's a whiskey bottle in your living room.'

'No, not any more. And get out of my house.'

He laughed. 'What happened?'

'Like I'm going to tell you.'

'OK, all right. Listen, the reason I called is because I don't seem to have much authority when it comes to the Blue Ridge Madam. People want to talk to *you*, not me. Meet me at the police station. I need some answers about clearing the scene in order to move that tree.'

'Right,' she said, trying to rally. 'Give me an hour.'

She hung up, then sat there, her head cradled in her hands. She didn't know how much time had passed before Willa came back and said, 'Are you all right?'

She looked up at her. She was holding a cup of coffee and a packet of ibuprofen. She handed both to Paxton. 'You saved me last night,' Paxton said. She'd never forget the glare of the lights of the Jeep as it came to a stop, then the sight of Willa getting out and coming to her rescue. She'd never been so glad to see anyone in her entire life.

Willa shrugged. 'You were out of your element.'

'I can't believe you did that for me. Why?'

Willa looked like she thought it was an odd question. 'When someone needs help, you help. Right? I thought that was a tenet of the Women's Society Club . . . your sparkling good deeds,' she said, quoting what Paxton had put on the invitations to the gala.

Paxton wasn't sure what bothered her more, that Willa saw her as a charity case or that she could never imagine any of her friends in the club coming to her rescue like that. The Women's Society Club was about helping people in the most distant way possible, about giving money and then dressing up and celebrating it. The Osgood family charity that Paxton ran did real work and didn't ask to be congratulated. So why on earth did she still continue with the club? History, she supposed. Legacy. That was important to her.

She swallowed a couple of tablets with the coffee, then set the coffee and pills on the table in front of her and felt the contents churn in her stomach. 'Thank you. For everything. I've got to go. Where's my tote bag?' She suddenly panicked. 'Where is my *car*?'

There was a knock at the door. 'I don't know where your tote bag is, but your car is still at the Gas Me Up. Don't worry, I've taken care of it,' Willa said as she went to the door and opened it.

It was, of all people, Sebastian. He took one look at Willa in her little sleep outfit and said, 'My God, there's a woman under those jeans and T-shirts, after all.'

Willa rolled her eyes but smiled.

The morning light was hitting his pale hair, making him seem angelic. He should have been a welcome sight, but he was the last person Paxton wanted to see right now. She stood to turn away but immediately regretted the move. Her head felt tight, which made her slightly nauseated. 'What is he doing here?' she asked Willa.

Willa closed the door behind Sebastian, and the light left him, making him human again. 'He kept calling your cellphone last night. I had to get up and answer it. He was worried about you. I told him you were fine and sleeping over here.'

Sebastian walked up to Paxton and pushed some of her loose hair out of her eyes. He managed to bring everything that had happened between them last night back to her with just one look. All she wanted. All he couldn't give. 'She forgot to mention that a substantial amount of alcohol was obviously involved,' he said. 'Darling, if your eyes were any more red, you'd have X-ray vision.'

Paxton stepped back, avoiding his eyes. 'It's the pepper spray.'

'The *what*?'

Paxton looked to Willa, who shook her head. She hadn't told him. 'Nothing.'

Sebastian gave her an assessing look. 'I told Willa I'd come and get you and take you to your car, but I'm not sure you're able to drive.'

'I'm fine,' she said. 'I just need to use the bathroom first.'

'It's through the kitchen.' Willa pointed. Paxton stumbled through the pretty yellow kitchen and found the bathroom. She closed the door and put her hands on the basin, taking deep breaths so she wouldn't get sick. She couldn't believe Sebastian had seen her like this, pitiful and hung over, obviously drowning herself in her sorrows, like she couldn't handle his rejection.

Why had Willa let him come over? She remembered telling Willa she was in love with him, the *one* thing she'd sworn she'd never say out loud. She should have known. Secrets always find a way out.

She splashed her face with cold water and looked down at her red dress and heels. All this to go to a convenience store for wine. What had she been thinking? That was the point. She hadn't been thinking. She pinned her hair back and sighed. It wasn't much help. She decided to get this over with and walked back to the living room.

Sebastian and Willa were talking easily. They both went quiet when she entered the room. Then Sebastian turned. 'Shall we?'

'Thanks again, Willa,' Paxton said as she walked to the door.

'Sure,' Willa said. 'Anytime.'

Once they were outside, Sebastian opened the door to his Audi and Paxton slid in. He got behind the wheel and pulled out of the neighbourhood in silence. 'Do you want to talk about what happened last night?' he finally asked.

'No.'

'I know you don't want to talk about what happened between us,' he said quietly. 'I was referring to you and Willa.'

'It's just between us girls,' Paxton said, staring out the side window. She smiled weakly. 'Well, I guess you are one of the girls.'

'I'm not a girl, Paxton,' he said, and the coolness in his voice made her turn to him.

'I didn't mean to imply you were. Not literally. I just meant—'

'Where is your car?' he interrupted her by asking.

'The Gas Me Up on State Boulevard.'

'What were you doing there?'

She turned back to the window. 'It doesn't matter.'

Sebastian pulled into the lot of the Gas Me Up and parked beside her BMW, which was, mercifully, intact. 'My mother is going to hate seeing me like this,' said Paxton. 'This would be a lot easier if I didn't have to go home and change.'

'Bring some clothes to keep in my house. If you need them, they'll be there.' She turned to him, surprised by the intimacy of the offer, especially after last night. 'Why didn't you call me, Pax?' he asked, and she realised, incredibly, that he was hurt. 'If you didn't want to go home, you could have stayed with me.'

'Willa offered to drop me off at your house, but I was drunk. And we both know that me out of control isn't a pretty sight.'

'I always think you're beautiful.'

She couldn't handle this. Not now. She opened the door. 'I'll see you soon. Thank you for the ride.'

He reached out and took her hand, not letting her get out. 'I want to help you, Pax.'

'I know you do. That's why I'm not asking again.'

For reasons Willa didn't understand, and her grandmother probably would have said were signs, Osgoods were crawling out of the woodwork and into her perfectly normal life. Thankfully, Willa figured she wasn't going to see much of either Colin or Paxton any more, what with the brouhaha going on up at the Madam.

Over the weekend, a news crew from Asheville had come to do a story on the skeleton found at the Blue Ridge Madam, then reported that the unconfirmed cause of death could possibly have been homicide, because someone had noticed trauma to the skull. The news crew had also been given the name Tucker Devlin from an unnamed someone who had obviously seen the scrapbook and high school diploma, and they had found a man by the same name who had a record in Asheville for swindling several people out of their money in January 1936. He'd been a travelling salesman.

A travelling salesman? A possible murder? That had tongues wagging, and Willa was as curious as the next person, in a distant kind of way. She had finally accepted that what went on at the Madam didn't have anything to do with her, and never would.

Or so she thought until the police came to see her on Sunday.

'Did you see that man?' Rachel called from the coffee bar after their last customer left on Sunday afternoon. Willa had just cashed out the store register and looked up to see Rachel writing in her coffee notebook. 'He'd been hiking for a week and he's going home today. You know what he ordered? Iced mocha latte. That's a drink for people who are ready for comfort. I'm telling you, it's a science.'

Rachel's super-short hair was in spikes, and she was wearing one of the waterproof tops the store sold, along with a tiny plaid skirt. The ensemble was so off-kilter, so Rachel, that it made Willa smile.

'What?' Rachel asked when she saw Willa staring at her.

Willa shook her head, thinking how glad she was Rachel had walked into her store a year and a half ago. 'Nothing.'

'Quick, tell me what kind of coffee you want right now.'

'I don't want any coffee right now,' Willa said.

'But if you did, what would it be?'

'I don't know. Something sweet. Chocolate and caramel.'

'Ha!' Rachel said. 'That means you were just thinking of something that makes you happy.'

'Well, you've got me there. I was.'

The bell over the door rang. They turned to see who it was, but no one was there. 'That's the second time that's happened,' Rachel said. 'When are you going to fix that bell? It freaks me out.'

'I thought you said you didn't believe in ghosts,' Willa teased as she zipped the deposit bag and went to put it in the safe.

The bell rang again. 'Willa?' Rachel called. 'Someone's here to see you.'

Willa felt a catch in her chest, because for some reason she thought it was Colin. She didn't have time to process why exactly that would make her happy, because when she turned to the man at the door, she saw that it wasn't Colin. It was Woody Olsen, a detective from the Walls of Water police department.

Willa's father had taught Woody in high school, and Woody had always respected him. Woody had been the one who had called Willa in Nashville and told her about her father being hit and killed on the interstate. She'd been so young and directionless and full of grief at the time that Woody had helped her arrange everything. Yet even now, she still stiffened upon sight of him, because she would forever associate him with being the bearer of bad news. It wasn't fair, but she couldn't help it. What bad news was he bringing now?

'Hi, Willa,' Woody said. 'I need to ask you a few questions about your grandmother. Do you have a few minutes?'

'My grandmother?'

'Nothing's wrong. I promise.' He smiled and gestured slowly to the café. 'Let's have a seat,' he said.

Willa walked over to the café and sat. Woody took the chair opposite her. He was skinny but had a large belly. His tie sat on his stomach like a pet. 'What's this all about, Woody?' she asked.

'Your grandmother isn't able to communicate any more, so as her only living relative, our questions have to come to you. That's all.'

'But why do you have questions about her?'

Woody took a notepad from his interior jacket pocket. 'When did your grandmother's family move out of the Blue Ridge Madam?'

'Nineteen thirty-six. Why?'

'Did she ever mention anyone being buried at the Madam?'

This was about the skeleton. 'Oh. That. No. She never talked about her time at the Madam. Sorry.'

Woody looked at the pages of his notepad, not meeting her eyes. 'I understand she was pregnant when her family lost the house.'

Willa hesitated. 'Yes.'

'Did she ever say who the father was?'

'No. She was a teenager and unmarried, which was obviously scandalous at the time. She didn't like talking about it.'

'Did your father know?'

'He might have. He always said it was private. I didn't ask a lot of questions back then. I should have.' She bent her head, trying to meet Woody's eyes. 'This is ridiculous, Woody. The man buried up there isn't the father of Georgie's child. There's no connection.'

He finally looked up. 'Colin Osgood told me you had a look at the things buried with the skeleton.'

'Yes,' she said, 'before we knew there was a skeleton buried there. He asked me to look to see if I recognised anything.'

'So you looked at the scrapbook.'

She stared at him blankly. 'Yes.'

'You didn't recognise anything?'

'No. Did you?'

Woody put the notepad back in his jacket. 'Thanks for your time, Willa. That's all.'

He got up to leave, and a terrible thought occurred to Willa. 'Woody, you don't think my grandmother had anything to do with that skeleton being buried up there, do you?'

He hesitated. 'Whatever happened, it happened a long time ago. I doubt we'll ever know the whole story.'

'That didn't answer my question.'

'If anything else comes up, I'll let you know. Don't worry. It probably won't.' He offered a small smile as he opened the door.

Willa turned to Rachel, who had heard the whole thing.

'I need to . . .' Willa said as she stood. She couldn't seem to finish the sentence. She didn't know exactly what she needed to do.

Rachel nodded. 'Go,' she said.

Willa went directly to the nursing home, something she rarely did this late in the day, because her grandmother had a tendency to get restless at sundown. But her protective instincts took her there.

Georgie had already had her dinner and had been sedated, so Willa sat by her bed and tried to get her mind round what was going on. Willa knew that there was nothing in the items found in the grave that tied her grandmother to this Tucker Devlin person. She had no idea why Woody thought there was.

The newspaper found in the suitcase was dated August 1936. She wished she knew when exactly her grandmother moved out. If it was before then, there would be nothing to worry about.

The whole thing was preposterous. Her grandmother had always been a decent person. A beautiful bird of a woman who had known a lot of hardship but who had an incredible work ethic and had made a life for her and her beloved son. She would never have hurt anyone.

Willa stood and kissed her grandmother, wishing that there was some magical way to snap her fingers and bring her grandmother back from whatever faraway place she had floated off to.

She went to the nurses' station and asked them to contact her if anyone came to see her grandmother. She didn't mention the police specifically, but it was who she was thinking of.

As she was talking to the nurse, she saw someone round the corner beyond the station. It was Paxton Osgood, obviously there to visit her own grandmother. She looked better than the last time Willa had seen her. That is to say, she was back to looking perfect.

If Willa called out hello, she was fairly certain Paxton would act as if Friday night had never happened. So Willa was just going to turn round and leave. But then something occurred to her.

Agatha. Of course.

Willa had never had much contact with Agatha Osgood, but she'd spent enough time at the nursing home to have heard how stubborn and mean she could be. But Agatha and Georgie had been good friends as girls. Once Georgie had given birth to her son, Agatha had helped to raise him for a few years while Georgie worked for the Osgood family. They'd all lived together at Hickory Cottage until Ham was six years old. That's when Agatha got married. Willa's father once said his mother didn't feel right living there after that. The two women soon grew apart, not for any reason except Georgie hadn't thought of herself as one of their group any more.

Willa followed Paxton down the hallway and watched her disappear into a room. Willa reached the room and looked inside. Agatha's quarters were like a fine Southern lady's parlour. There were oil portraits on the wall, a matching suite of furniture, a small refrigerator. It looked like, at any moment, a maid in a white uniform was going to enter and serve strawberry tea and petits fours.

Paxton was standing with her back to her. Willa cleared her throat and said from the doorway, 'Paxton?'

Paxton turned, and after a moment of surprise, she actually looked relieved. 'Look, Nana,' Paxton said. 'You have company.'

Agatha was sitting on a love seat in front of her window, her body in a permanent stoop that reminded Willa of a seashell. But her movements were surprisingly quick, her head swinging round in the direction of Willa's voice in the doorway. 'Who is it? Who is there?' she asked.

'It's Willa Jackson, Mrs Osgood,' Willa said.

Agatha tried to stand. 'Is something wrong with Georgie?'

'No, ma'am,' Willa rushed to say. 'She's asleep right now.'

Agatha sat back. 'Then what do you want?' she demanded.

Both Agatha and Paxton were staring at her. Willa was struck by how much alike those stares were. Paxton certainly favoured her grandmother. 'I was wondering if I could talk to you about my grandmother? I could come back later if this is a bad time.'

'Of course it's not a bad time,' Paxton said, waving Willa to enter. 'Wouldn't that be nice, Nana? To talk about the old days?'

'Stop being stupid, Paxton. It doesn't become you,' Agatha said, then turned to Willa. 'What do you want to know?'

Willa walked in a few steps. 'It's hard to say. You were friends.'

'We *are* friends,' Agatha snapped. 'She's still here. I'm still here. And as long as we are, we'll always be friends.'

'You knew her the year her family moved out of the Madam?' Willa asked.

'Yes, of course I did. She moved in with me after that.'

'Do you remember anyone dying at the Madam that year, then being buried under the peach tree? The police were asking me about Grandmother Georgie, insinuating she might have had something to do with the man buried there. But that's preposterous. You knew her then.

She would never have done anything like that.' She caught Paxton's frantic hand motion a little too late. Uh-oh. This was obviously something they were trying to keep from Agatha.

The change in Agatha was remarkable. She gave a physical start, and her eyes grew wide. 'What? What is this about? Paxton?'

'It's OK, Nana,' Paxton said. 'We took down the peach tree at the Madam, and there was a skeleton buried there. Everything's fine now. We're bringing in a big tree to replace it.'

'The moment you told me you'd bought the Madam, I knew this was coming. You found him,' Agatha said. 'You found Tucker Devlin.'

Willa and Paxton exchanged glances.

'How did you know his name?' Paxton asked carefully.

'Anyone who met him would never forget his name.'

Despite the fact that she knew Paxton was upset with her for bringing this up, Willa found herself taking another step forward. 'You knew him?'

'He called himself a travelling salesman. He was really a con man. But even that didn't do him justice. He was . . . *magic*.' Agatha whispered that last word. Without realising it, Paxton and Willa moved in closer to each other. 'I'll never forget the day we first saw him. Georgie and I were sitting in the grass up at the Madam, making crowns out of clover flowers. The wind was high that day, and I remember our dresses were flapping around our legs. I kept losing my sight when my hair crossed my eyes, so Georgie laughed and made me turn so she could braid my hair, and that's when we saw him walking up the hill with his dusty suitcase. We had heard of him, of course. He'd been in town for a while, selling ladies cosmetics. But he was onto bigger and better things that day. He reached the door of the Madam and paused; then he turned to us. He saw me holding my dress so it wouldn't fly up, and he smiled—smiled like God looking down on His children. He whistled a few strange notes and the wind *stopped*. Just like that.' Agatha paused. 'The man could whistle and make the wind stop.'

When Willa's and Paxton's arms touched, they jerked apart and put some space between them.

'Don't worry, Willa. Your grandmother didn't kill him,' Agatha said. 'And I know that for sure.'

Willa smiled. 'Well, it's a relief to hear someone say that.'

'Because *I* killed him,' Agatha finished.

CHAPTER EIGHT

PARTY GIRLS

PAXTON TOOK SWIFT and immediate action. 'I think you've upset her enough,' she said, ushering Willa to the door with the skill of a hostess herding her last guests out. 'Now she's talking nonsense.'

'I haven't talked nonsense a day in my life!' Agatha barked.

Once in the hallway, Paxton said, 'She doesn't know what she's talking about. Don't come back here and upset her. I mean it.'

Paxton went back into the room and closed the door. Willa was tempted to get angry, but she'd seen something in Paxton that tempered the emotion. Paxton wanted to protect her grandmother. Just as Willa did.

So Willa left the nursing home with even more questions than she'd started with. There had been a surprising vehemence in her voice when Agatha had declared that her friendship to Georgie still existed. How far would that friendship go? Far enough to lie? Or far enough to tell the truth?

One thing she knew for sure: Willa was on her own when it came to finding answers now.

When she got home, she changed clothes and climbed the stairs to the only other place she knew to look for clues. The attic.

It had been a long time since she'd come up here. She broke through the spiders' webs to see large white boxes piled to the rafters. She began unearthing them, bringing them downstairs one at a time until they filled half the living room.

She picked a box at random. Her father had packed her grandmother's boxes and it must have been hard for him. He always respected his mother's privacy. She sat down, opened the box and began taking things out. Everything was wrapped in newspaper. A crystal candy dish. A Bible. A photo album. That had possibilities.

After she unwrapped it, she set the album on her lap and opened it. She remembered looking through it as a child. It contained photos of her father. Willa found herself smiling as she flipped through the pages. There was Ham as a baby, swallowed up in a large white christening gown. There he was as a chubby little boy in front of what looked like Hickory Cottage. School pictures. Graduation. Then came a series of photos of him in his carefree twenties. Willa had always loved these photos, watching her father's charm as it grew around him. If she hadn't known the path his life had taken, the one where he'd ended up a widowed, sedate chemistry teacher, she would have assumed from these photos that he was destined to become a charismatic movie star or politician.

But he'd wanted a small life. He'd wanted the life his mother had wanted him to have, because her opinion meant that much to him.

She turned the page and her smile faded. There was her father aged about thirty. His hair was long. His hands were in his pockets, and he looked at the camera in a way that almost made the photo tremor with the force of his personality. He looked like the world was a ripe peach and he was ready to bite it. It startled her and reminded her of something she couldn't quite put her finger on.

She thought of a conversation she'd had with one of her father's fellow teachers at his funeral. She'd told Willa that Ham had been something of a ladies' man before he'd married Willa's mother. She'd insisted that when Ham had come back from college, there had been something about him. Ham's mother had been very strict with him as a boy and he'd been quite shy. But he'd been transformed by adulthood. Female teachers had clustered around him and would bring him sweets. Occasionally, he would invite one of them on a date, and it would leave the recipient of his attention unable to leave footprints for days, as if they weren't quite touching the ground. Ham's female students were all so in love with him that sometimes they would cry over their Bunsen burners in his classroom and leave locks of their hair in his desk drawers.

Now, looking at this photo, Willa could finally understand what the teacher had been talking about. Grandmother Georgie had obviously snapped it; it was taken outside her apartment building. She, too, had seemed startled by what she was seeing. The photo was a little blurry, like the camera had moved just before she'd clicked.

Willa looked through the rest of the photos but found herself coming back to this one. She was supposed to be looking for clues, anything that proved her grandmother didn't have anything to do with the skeleton on the hill. Her father's photos weren't going to help her. She should put the album away and go on to the next box.

But she continued to come back to this one photo. Why did it seem so familiar, like she'd seen it recently?

Finally, she took it out of the album and set it on the coffee table.

She went through the rest of the boxes, and as she'd suspected, there was nothing from her grandmother's time at the Madam. She was going to have to figure out some other way to get information.

Willa turned off the lights, then went to the kitchen to get something to drink before going to bed. When she opened the refrigerator, light sliced through the dark kitchen, telescoping to the kitchen table at the far end of the room. She stood in front of the open door and drank some juice out of the bottle. When she finished, she put the bottle back and turned.

That's when she noticed it.

Leaving the refrigerator door open for light, she walked to the kitchen table. She had a few overripe peaches in a bowl. The fruit was starting to fill the air with the sweet premonition of decay.

Her scalp suddenly tightened and she backed away.

Propped against the bowl was the photo of her father, the photo she'd taken out of the album and placed on the coffee table in the living room.

And she hadn't moved it here.

Willa never thought she'd ever do this, never once thought she'd put any stock in the superstitions her grandmother had taken so seriously, but she'd been scared enough after finding her father's photo in the kitchen last night to put a penny on her windowsill and leave the window ajar, because her grandmother once said that ghosts often forget they're ghosts and will go after money, but if they get close enough to an open window, the night air will suck them out.

It didn't help her nerves when, that morning, a black and yellow bird managed to get in through the crack in her bedroom window, and it took an hour and a broom to get it to fly back out.

It was Rachel's day off, so when Willa got to the store, she unlocked the door and turned on the lights; then she ground some beans and started the coffee maker. Rachel had left Willa a box of coffee coconut bars, which she knew were her favourite. On the box was a note: *Made these especially for you. Call me if you need me.*

Willa had walked in feeling moody and distracted, but this made her smile. Rachel's magic was a cure for all ills. It helped Willa focus, to see reason—of course she must have moved that photo herself; she just didn't remember—and she decided on another plan of action.

The first lull in customers she had, Willa called her friend Fran at the library. Fran was a hiker and a frequent visitor to Willa's shop.

'Hi, Fran, it's Willa.'

'Willa! This is a surprise. What can I do for you?'

'How do I find out what went on in this town during 1936? What kind of archives do you have?'

'Police and reporters came in here asking the same thing when the skeleton turned up at the Madam,' Fran said. 'There wasn't a town newspaper back then. Why do you want to know?'

'I've been going through my grandmother's things, and there's not as much there about her life as I had hoped. Nineteen thirty-six was a big year for her. Her family lost the Madam. She gave birth to my father.'

Willa heard the tick of computer keys. 'We do have the *Walls of Water Society Newsletter.* That's what I showed the police.'

'What is that?'

'A weekly single-page gossip column, basically. It circulated in the 1930s and 40s.' Fran laughed. 'You should read these things. They're priceless. They document the lives of the society ladies.'

'Do you think I could take a look?' Willa asked.

'Of course. I'll be happy to set you up.'

A couple of tourists walked in, and Willa smiled and waved at them. 'How late are you open today?' she asked Fran.

'I'm about to go home.' Fran paused. 'I'll tell you what, call me at home when you get off work and I'll meet you here.'

'You're the best, Fran. Thanks.'

Fran was waiting for her that evening when Willa got to the library. She gave Willa the microfiche films she needed, then told her to lock the door when she left. When the door shut behind Fran, Willa stood there for a moment. It was a curious sensation, being in a library alone. She walked to the microfiche readers in the back of the room. She sat down, and the click and burr of the machine became a calming rhythm as she went through the films.

She started in January 1936 and worked her way through. The *Walls of Water Society Newsletter* was obviously the labour of love of a rich, childless woman named Jojo McPeat. It was full of gossip from social events, usually with one or two photos included.

Jojo made long-running commentaries on what women wore, and she loved to quote anonymous naysayers. What Willa found interesting were the small references to the town itself hidden in the text. Jojo quoted Olin Jackson, Georgie's father, promising that since the Jacksons gave this town an economy once, they would do it again, although he didn't say exactly how. Jojo questioned this statement by asking how a man who let his daughter dress in last year's clothes was going to save the town.

Willa leaned in to get a closer look at the grainy black-and-white photos of her grandmother, her breath catching at the unexpected gift of getting to see her grandmother like this. She was a stunningly beautiful young woman. She looked vivacious and innocent, and she was always surrounded by her girlfriends. Agatha Osgood, herself a handsome young woman in a more reserved and angular way, was regularly at her side.

Through these photos of Georgie, Willa found herself transported. She could hear the laughter, taste the perfume in the air, smell the tobacco. The girls seemed so carefree and happy. Their futures were sparkles in the air, waiting to be caught like fireflies.

And then Tucker Devlin arrived.

Jojo first mentioned him in February 1936 as a salesman of ladies' cosmetics, from whom Mrs Margaret Treble had bought a tonic and swore it made her skin feel like silk. Mrs Treble had invited Tucker Devlin to a ladies lunch to sell his wares, and everyone seemed to fall under his spell. Jojo quoted Tucker Devlin as saying, 'I come from a long line of peach tree farmers, born and raised in Upton, Texas, and proud of it. I love making women feel good about themselves, but this is just a job. What I know, what I'm best at, is peaches. Peach juice swims in my veins. When I bleed, it's sweet. Honeybees fly right to me.'

The first photo of him was in front of a table where he had displayed his pots and potions. He was obviously giving the ladies his spiel. Willa squinted at the photo. That was definitely the same man wearing the fedora in the photo found buried at the Madam. Her skin prickled with a sense of déjà vu, but she shook it off.

From that point on, not a single newsletter passed without mention of

Tucker Devlin. And there was a gradual progression in the photos. They started out with Tucker posing with older ladies, but then he started to favour the younger women. There were numerous photos of him with Georgie and Agatha. People seemed drawn to him. Over time, the women in the photographs began to get desperate, hungry looks on their faces. If it was a group shot, there was always one girl looking at another girl with narrowed, jealous eyes.

Several newsletters later, Jojo mentioned in passing that Tucker Devlin was living at the Blue Ridge Madam, which startled Willa.

He had *lived* there?

It took a while to piece together through the newsletters what had happened. Apparently Olin Jackson got wind of Tucker Devlin's former profession, or maybe Tucker Devlin himself approached Olin Jackson. Either way, a plan was hatched to turn Jackson Hill into a peach orchard. Jobs would be generated. The Jacksons would save the town again. Olin had invited Tucker to live with them while they created this new empire.

Willa couldn't help but wonder why anyone would plan a peach orchard at this elevation. If Tucker Devlin was who he said he was, he would have known that peaches wouldn't grow here. He would have known it was a venture that was bound to fail.

And yet he had convinced everyone that it was possible.

He was a con man, just like Agatha said.

But why kill him just for that?

Throughout the summer, Tucker appeared in the newsletter, and his favourite escorts at parties were always the same young ladies, with one notable exception. Georgie seemed to have disappeared. There were mentions of her feeling under the weather, but after May of that year, there wasn't another photo of her to be found.

Then, in August, Tucker Devlin disappeared as well. There was no explanation. There was no mention of what had happened with plans for the orchard. Later, Willa found a short note that the Jackson family had left the Blue Ridge Madam, as the result of a court order. The government had seized the house for failure to pay taxes. That was October 1936, two months after the body had been buried, if the Asheville newspaper buried with the body was anything to go by.

That meant Georgie and her family had indeed still been living in the Madam at the time of his death.

That wasn't what Willa had been hoping to find. And if the police had looked at these like Fran had said, then they knew this, too.

Willa printed out the 1936 newsletters, then gathered the papers, turned out the lights, and locked the door behind her. She felt like she was the last to leave a party. As she walked across the parking lot to her Jeep, she thought she saw a few silver party streamers float into the night sky. But she blinked and they were gone.

CHAPTER NINE

ROOT SYSTEMS

IT WAS HARD TO IGNORE the Mercedes parked in front of her house. Willa pulled behind it and got out, and found Colin sitting on the creaky swing on her porch. Moonlight was filtering through the trees, which made the air look like milk glass. Her grandmother used to say something about how the air around you will turn white when things are about to change. It gave her pause as she watched Colin glide slowly, one hand over the back of the swing. He was one of those men for whom fatigue went to their eyes in a sleepy, sexy way. He was exhausted, by the looks of him.

So of course he was on her front porch? Surely he didn't want to sleep on her couch again. What was it about her couch and the Osgoods?

'I like this neighbourhood,' Colin said when she reached the front porch. He'd watched her, silent, as she walked here. Maybe he'd felt it, too, that curious charge in the air. 'It's old and quiet.'

Willa stopped, keys in hand. 'What are you doing here?'

He stood. 'The police cleared the scene at the Madam for the tree planting tomorrow. I wanted to make sure you were coming.'

'What's the big deal about planting this tree?'

He shook his head as he walked over to her. 'I'm going to bring out your inner nature girl if it kills me.'

She unlocked the door. 'You certainly have strong opinions about how I should live my life.'

'I can be very persuasive,' he said from behind her, close enough to her ear that she realised he was only inches away.

'Well, cross nature girl off your list. It's already been tried,' she said, opening the door and walking in. She flipped on the light.

'Tried? By whom?' he asked as he followed her in.

She set her bag and the printouts from the library on the coffee table. 'My friend Rachel. She came through here while hiking the Appalachian Trail. She's tried to get me to understand. I just don't.'

'We'll see,' he said, as if there were some sort of compromise to be had. He looked at all the boxes in the room. 'Are you moving?'

'No. These are my grandmother's things I brought down from the attic.' She walked towards the kitchen. 'I haven't eaten since lunch. I'm going to fix a sandwich. Do you want one?'

'No, thank you,' he said as he joined her. 'I've already eaten. Dinner together is still mandatory at Hickory Cottage. I don't know how Paxton stands it.'

'Dinner together with your family doesn't sound so bad to me.'

'Maybe it isn't. It's residual resentment.' His voice sounded weary. He pulled out a chair at the kitchen table and sat. He saw the photo propped against the peach bowl and lifted it. She'd left it there because she was almost afraid to touch it, almost waiting to see if it would move again. 'This is a nice photo of your dad.'

'Yes,' she agreed. She opened the refrigerator door.

He watched as she brought out bread, turkey, bean sprouts and cream cheese. 'I'm sorry I haven't been in touch since Friday.'

Willa set the sandwich stuff on the counter, then reached to an open shelf to retrieve a plate. 'There's nothing to be sorry about.'

'It was a shock, seeing that skull. Are you all right?'

'Yes. Of course.' She brought out a knife and smeared some cream cheese on two slices of wheat bread. Without looking at him, she added, 'Woody Olsen came to see me on Sunday about it.'

'He did? Why would he do that?'

He sounded surprised. She looked over her shoulder at him. He didn't know about Woody suspecting her grandmother. That probably meant Paxton hadn't told him about Agatha claiming responsibility for the skeleton, either. She suddenly had hope that she and Paxton were on the same page about this—say nothing until they knew more. 'He wanted to know if my grandmother ever talked about anyone being buried on the hill. She didn't.'

'Is that why you brought down the boxes?'

'Yes,' she said, then changed the subject as she went back to constructing her sandwich. 'You look tired. Rough weekend?'

That made him laugh. 'Not nearly as rough as Paxton's. What exactly happened that night she slept over here?'

'She didn't tell you that, either?'

'Either?' he said. 'What other thing didn't she tell me?'

'Nothing.'

Colin hesitated before he asked, 'I know you and Pax aren't exactly friends, but you didn't get her drunk on purpose, did you? Like a prank?'

He thought it was *her* fault? 'I didn't even . . .' She paused, not knowing how to explain and not give Paxton away. She finally said, 'No, it wasn't a prank. And now I'm confused. I thought your belief in my latent wild nature was what you liked best about me.'

'I like a lot of things about you.'

She finished making her sandwich, flustered now. 'You shouldn't come to see me when you're so tired. I think you say things you probably wouldn't otherwise.'

She heard the scrape of the chair legs as he got up. 'Did it occur to you that's why I come to see you when I'm tired?' he asked as he approached her. He reached out and pushed some hair behind her ears. The gesture was tender, but it hit her with unexpected force. 'Come to the tree planting tomorrow,' he said.

She finally looked up at him. Bad idea. There were those tired, dark, sexy eyes, looking at her and seeing someone she didn't think she was any more. 'Why?'

He smiled. 'It's all part of my seduction.'

She let that penetrate, thinking how he'd pressed against her that day the ground shook at the Madam. 'This is a seduction?'

Slowly, he leaned into her and touched his lips to hers. She could feel herself sigh, swept up in his current. His hands cupped her cheeks as he deepened the kiss. She loved the rush, how it made her heart race in a way that wasn't fear or anxiety—which was how she used to achieve this feeling—but simple, raw pleasure.

She was now leaning back against the counter, her hands in his hair, trying to bring him closer, wanting more of this. She shifted slightly, and the knife she'd just used suddenly clanged to the floor.

They broke apart at the sound.

For a moment, they just looked each other in the eye. Colin's hands were still on her face. His thumbs brushed along her cheekbones once before he stepped back. 'Yes, this is a seduction.'

'Maybe I don't want to be seduced.' They both knew she was lying, but he had the good grace not to call her on it.

'Then what do you want, Willa?' When she didn't answer, he smiled and said, 'I'll look for you tomorrow.' Then he left.

Just days ago she'd had the answer down pat. She would have said that what she wanted was to put the past behind her and live a nice, quiet life. Now she wasn't so sure.

How exactly do you seduce a person with a tree planting? That, ultimately, was what made her go. She left Rachel to man the store, and she drove to Jackson Hill, only to have to park at the base of it and walk up, because the road had been blocked off to traffic.

Lining the hill all the way to the Madam were onlookers, photographers, and even a television crew, waiting for the tree to arrive.

How many people was he planning to seduce today? This was obviously a bigger deal than she'd thought.

When she reached the top of the hill, she stopped and looked up at the house. She tried to imagine her grandmother living here at seventeen, when this charming con man moved in and promised to save them all. Had Georgie fallen in love with him? *Had* he got her pregnant? No, of course not. Her mind simply wouldn't go there. But what if Agatha had fallen in love with him? What if she and Georgie had become rivals? Maybe that's why she killed him.

The mound of dirt where the peach tree had been was still clearly visible. It suddenly occurred to her that her grandmother had to have known what happened. The newsletters said she'd disappeared from society that summer. That meant she'd been here, watching everything. *She knew what Agatha did.* And she never said a thing.

Surveying the house, her eyes landed on Paxton. Willa couldn't look at Paxton now and not see a little bit of Agatha, not wonder what had happened between their grandmothers that summer.

The beeping of machinery drew her attention to the gigantic hole in the side yard of the Madam, and the scores of men and equipment surrounding it. She found Colin, pacing around the yard on his cellphone. He hung up and went to the precipice of the hill.

Willa followed his stare. He was looking out over the highway. Sure enough, the tractor-trailer soon appeared, slowly coming down the highway, which had been closed to traffic. There were police cars as an escort, their blue lights on. It was a resplendent sight. There was a majesty to this old tree standing proudly on the back of a modified flatbed.

It took forty-five minutes while the truck heaved its way up Jackson Hill, groaning with the monumental weight of its load. It was even more regal up close, this oak that had lived for more than a century. Nearly forty feet tall, with a branch span that had to be eighty feet, it evoked cheers and applause from people lining the hill.

Watching the actual planting was breathtaking. As the machinery lowered the gigantic root ball covered in burlap and wire, the men grabbed ropes tethered to the limbs. They yelled and the tree groaned and seemed to writhe against its restraints. The men moved in sync, running one way, then the next. And, finally, it was in.

It was one of the most glorious things she'd ever seen.

She was certain Colin had no idea she was there. He'd never once looked up from the site. When it was over, his colour was high, his clothes were wet with sweat and he was out of breath.

That's when he finally looked round and found Willa in the crowd. He slowly smiled and, *bam,* there it was, that lust she'd felt last night. It was heavy and elemental, connected to everything around them for one electric moment. How did he know the effect this would have on her, when she didn't even know herself?

It was too much, this feeling that she didn't know her own nature, her own root system, any more. She turned round and left.

For the rest of the day, Willa felt on edge. When she got back to work, she would give a start every time the bell over the door rang. When she got home, she kept expecting a knock on the door. She got in the shower because her skin felt hot, as though she'd been exposed to something that day that had had a lingering effect on her. She couldn't get rid of it.

The phone rang just as she got out of the shower. She ran to her bedroom to answer it. 'Hello?'

'I think that went well today,' Colin said in a low voice.

This was what she'd been expecting all day. 'Yes,' she said, swallowing, 'I think you accomplished what you set out to do.'

'Take Saturday off and spend it with me.'

Maybe the beauty of his being here for only a month was that she could get this itch he'd caused out of her system quickly. Then he'd leave, and she could go back to normal. That was her justification for finally giving in and saying, 'Yes.'

At dinner that night, Paxton's father clicked around on his smartphone, which had replaced the newspaper he used to bring to the table, and her mother chatted happily about what good news coverage the tree planting had had and how it would make up for all the negative publicity the skeleton had caused.

Colin cleared his throat. 'I'd like to make an announcement,' he said. 'I don't want anyone setting me up with a date for the gala. I know you may be tempted to. But don't.'

'But, Colin, I was thinking about Penelope Mayfield,' Sophia said.

'Ha!' Colin said, pointing a finger at their mother. 'I knew you were planning something. No. I refuse.'

'Oh, Colin,' Sophia said indulgently. Colin looked at Paxton and winked.

After dinner, Colin retreated quickly to the patio, something he had taken to doing all week. Tonight, Paxton followed him.

'I don't get it,' she said as she took a seat next to him.

'Get what?' Colin asked, his head back against the cushions.

'Mama adores you. Daddy isn't trying to make you play golf any more. And still you can't wait to get away.'

'It takes a lot of energy to keep up that deflector shield.'

'If you moved back, you wouldn't have to eat dinner with them every night. I do because I live with them. You'd have your own place. You don't have to live in New York for work. This could be your home base.'

'I don't know if I'm ready for that yet.'

'Ready for what? To be here for your family? Gee, Colin, it must be nice to be you.' She had no idea why she was picking a fight. He didn't deserve it. He wasn't even the real reason she was upset.

'I'm here now, aren't I? You asked me, I'm here.'

'For a month.'

He took a deep breath. 'I'm tired, Pax. I don't want to fight.'

Her brother never slept well. That, at least, was something they had in common. 'I don't, either. I'm sorry.'

The crickets made up for their lack of conversation. Paxton finally said, 'It's Willa Jackson you're taking to the gala, isn't it?'

'I'm working on it,' he said with a smile. He turned to look at her. 'What about you? Who are you going with?'

Before last week, before the kiss, she would have said Sebastian. Now she wasn't so sure. It was Tuesday, and she still hadn't heard from him, even after leaving him an apologetic message today. She didn't like being apart from him. It left a hole in her life she didn't know how to fill. But how could she look him in the eye after what happened, after knowing he could never give her what she'd wanted so much?

'I think I might go alone,' Paxton said. 'There will be too much to do for me to pay attention to a date, anyway.' She paused. 'Willa was at the tree planting today. Did you see her?'

'Yes, I saw her,' he said. 'I invited her to come.'

Paxton gnawed at her bottom lip. 'So you two . . . talk?'

'Yes. Why?'

'I guess she told you all about what happened Friday night.'

'No, actually,' he said. 'I asked. She wouldn't tell me.'

That surprised her. 'She didn't tell you anything?'

He lifted his head. 'I'm getting the same impression from you that I got from her. Is there more than one secret? What's going on?'

'Nothing.'

Colin sighed. 'That's what she said.'

Late that night, Sebastian sat in the back booth of the quiet, sagging Happy Daze Diner on the highway and nursed a cup of coffee, just like he used to do when he was a teenager.

His father had been an alcoholic, so Sebastian spent every hour he could away from him. He would sit at this diner, the one his great-aunt took him to when he was a boy, the only place she could afford, and nurse a cup of coffee and read library books until he was too tired to stay awake. Then he would go home and sleep on the porch so he wouldn't have to face his father's verbal abuse. He called Sebastian a fag, particularly when he was drinking.

'Hey, baby,' Lois said, coming to a stop at his booth in the back. 'I thought you might like some pie.'

Sebastian smiled at her. Lois had been a waitress here since he was little. She was a wiry old woman, with painted-on lips and a crooked blond wig. She wore a blue polyester dress and a frilly white apron. The place had few customers, and most were over the age of seventy. No one bothered him here, which was why this had always been a safe haven.

'I'm not hungry, Lois. But thank you.'

'Eat it,' she said, sliding the plate on the table. 'You're still too skinny. Can't hide it with those fancy suits, either.'

She walked away, her orthopaedic shoes squeaking on the cracked linoleum floors. Pie, to Lois, was love. And Sebastian appreciated it. The moment he'd walked back in a few months ago, he and Lois had found their old routine. She still tried to feed him. He still refused. She still let him stay as late as he wanted.

He pushed the pie to the side, then looked at his cellphone.

He picked it up and listened to Paxton's message again.

'Hi, Sebastian. It's me. I haven't seen you in days.' She paused. 'I just wanted to say I'm sorry. For everything. For Friday night. For not calling you when I got drunk and needed help. You're off the hook if you don't want to go to the luncheon and recital on Saturday. I know you don't like classical music and were only going for me, anyway. Just call and let me know you're OK. Bye.'

He set the phone back down next to his coffee.

Paxton Osgood was the last thing he'd expected to happen to him when he came back to Walls of Water. It had taken a lot of courage to come back here, but he'd been convinced that Dr Kostovo's retirement was a sign. Those who remembered him still looked at him oddly, but he'd slid into place so easily. No one said he didn't belong. Yet it felt nothing like he'd thought it would. He'd been prepared to face what he'd left behind armed with bitterness, only to find there weren't any battles left to fight, only his memories of a confused little boy who was too skinny and too pretty for his father to love him, who was made fun of by the other kids, and who was misunderstood by everyone. So no, no battles. Only ghosts.

And Paxton.

He'd couched his sexuality a long time ago. It only got in the way, the dissonance between what he was and how he was perceived. He didn't think the issue would come up when he first met Paxton. They'd hit it off, and Paxton became his friend, which wasn't much of a surprise. Women often wanted to be his friend. What was surprising was how Paxton had latched onto him as if she'd been wandering the desert and he was her oasis. And, he had to admit, it felt good to be her confidant. She was the town's golden girl, and *he* was the one she chose to confide in. But the longer they knew each other, the more comfortable she became in expressing affection, and he began to realise she was feeling more than friendship. His own feelings confused him, but they always confused him. He didn't know how to address what was happening between them, and since she avoided the subject, he'd assumed this was temporary, and they carried on like normal. Until that night at her house.

He took a deep breath. She'd been on edge. Tired. She'd immediately regretted it. That should have been it, right? But if she regretted it, and he wanted to move on from it, why were they dancing around each other now? Did she think she couldn't keep her hands off him?

Or was it the other way round?

He'd never expected to face this. He thought coming back here would put to bed a lot of issues. And it had. But it had also opened up new ones he'd convinced himself he'd never have to face again.

CHAPTER TEN

THE MAGIC MAN

LATE FRIDAY AFTERNOON, Paxton couldn't take it any more. She had to go and see Willa. Why was she keeping quiet? Was she planning on using all she knew against Paxton at a later date? The drunken altercation at the Gas Me Up, her confession about Sebastian, and, most of all, Nana Osgood's confession . . . the potential for public embarrassment was huge and that was the last thing she needed right now—more scandal surrounding the Madam.

Paxton drove into Willa's neighbourhood and parked behind her Jeep.

She straightened her shoulders and marched to the door and knocked. When Willa opened the door, the contrast between them couldn't have been more obvious. Willa was in casual jeans and a high-waisted shirt that looked like it was made out of large bandana squares. Paxton was in a beige sheath dress and tailored jacket that she sprayed throughout the day with a wrinkle releaser.

'Paxton,' Willa said, surprised. 'Come in.'

'I was worried you wouldn't be here,' Paxton said.

'I'm always here on Friday night. Friday night is vacuuming night. The fun never ends at Casa Jackson.'

Paxton adjusted the tote bag on her shoulder. 'Then what were you doing out last Friday?'

'I was at a barbecue I hadn't intended to go to.'

Luckily for me. Paxton took a deep breath. 'Listen, Colin told me he asked you about what happened last Friday and you refused to tell him. He also doesn't seem to know about Nana Osgood's confession.' She hesitated. 'I thought you'd tell him.'

Willa frowned. 'Why would I do that? When Colin didn't seem to be aware that the police had asked me about my grandmother, I figured we were on the same page. How do we know what really happened, anyway?'

'You're right; we don't know,' Paxton said, relieved. She looked around at the boxes in the living room. Her eyes fell on a beautiful grey dress draped over one box. The fabric was beaded and looked as though it was covered in twinkling stars. She stepped over and touched it. 'This is gorgeous. Is it vintage?' It had to be. It had the cinched waist and wide skirt of something from the early 1950s.

Willa nodded. 'It's from 1954. It still has its tags. It was in the original box with a card attached. It was a Christmas gift from your grandmother to mine. She kept it all this time but never wore it.'

'They really were good friends, weren't they?' Paxton said.

'At one time, yes, I believe they were.'

Paxton gestured to the other boxes. 'What is all this?'

'My grandmother's things. I've been going through them.'

'Looking for answers?' Paxton surmised. Of course she was. Georgie Jackson wouldn't hurt a fly. And Willa was out to prove it. That was a big difference between them. Paxton wasn't sure what Nana Osgood was capable of. And she didn't want to know.

'I'm not out to incriminate Agatha, if that's what you're thinking. I just want to know what happened. Nothing was the same for my grandmother after that year. And I think Tucker Devlin might have had a hand in it.' She walked over to the coffee table and riffled through some papers. 'I found this at the library.' She handed Paxton a printout of an old society newsletter and tapped a grainy photo of a man in a suit, standing between two teenagers. 'That's Tucker Devlin. He's with Georgie and Agatha.'

Startled, Paxton looked closer. Sure enough, there were her grandmother's sharp cheekbones, her large dark eyes. She looked so *happy*. Paxton couldn't remember ever seeing her grandmother happy. What had happened? Where did this girl go?

'There's something that's been bothering me,' Willa said. 'Do you think it's just a coincidence that the Women's Society Club was formed around the time he was killed?'

'How could the two possibly be connected?'

'I don't know. All I know is, according to these newsletters, our grandmothers were devoted friends; then Tucker Devlin arrived and suddenly they were competitors for his affection. He disappeared in August, when they became tight again and formed the club.'

Paxton rubbed her forehead. Why did that have to make so much sense? 'Please don't let that theory get out. I only have a tenuous hold on the club as it is.'

'I thought we just went over this. I'm not going to tell anyone,' Willa said. 'Would you like something to drink?'

'Yes,' Paxton said. 'Thank you.'

When Willa left the room, Paxton went to the couch and sat on it. She set the newsletter printout down with the other papers on the coffee table, then noticed a photo album with a single photo sitting on top of it. She picked it up and studied it. He looked so magnetic in this photo. Why would her grandmother kill him?

Willa came back with two bottles of Snapple and handed one to Paxton. 'Tucker Devlin certainly was handsome,' Paxton said. 'If our grandmothers fell for him, I can see why.'

Willa looked confused. 'That's not Tucker Devlin. That's an old photo of my father I found in the album.'

Paxton looked at it again. 'It is? It looks just like Tucker Devlin.'

Willa set her bottle down, took the photo from Paxton and looked at it.

Then she lifted the newsletter printout. She compared the two, a look of comprehension coming over her face as she sat beside Paxton. 'Oh, God, I was trying *so hard* not to believe it.'

Seconds later, it hit Paxton, too. Georgie Jackson had been pregnant when her family lost the Madam; everyone knew that. But no one knew who the father was. Until now.

That was it. The thing that turned everything around. Tucker Devlin might be Willa's grandfather.

'I think we need to talk to Nana Osgood,' Paxton said.

Agatha was sitting on the love seat in her room as the sun set that evening. She could feel the way the warmth moved across her face. There was a hint of peaches in the air.

She didn't want to eat in the dining hall, so she requested that her food be brought to her room. She liked eating her food alone. Her one last pleasure. She didn't care much for mingling with the people here. She was far too old to make friends now. She found herself living more and more in the past these days, especially since hearing about the Madam and the discovery of Tucker Devlin's remains.

'Nana Osgood?' It was Paxton's voice in the doorway.

'Paxton, what are you doing here? What did you bring me?'

'Willa Jackson,' Paxton said as she walked into the room.

'Hello, Mrs Osgood,' Willa said. Willa had been a sneaky child. Not a mean one. Not a deceitful one. But sneaky nonetheless. Agatha had always seen it. Georgie had, too, but, as with Ham, she'd been convinced that she could trample down any wild hair that reminded her of Tucker Devlin and make her family as quiet and normal as possible. It hadn't always been to their advantage. Ham could have gone on to great things if his mother hadn't instilled in him such a sense of his own smallness. But Georgie had felt she was only balancing out the magical stormy nature Ham and Willa had inherited from Tucker.

'The two of you here together can only mean one thing,' Agatha said. 'You want to know what happened.'

'Willa found something called the *Walls of Water Society Newsletter*. We've pieced some things together.'

'The *Society Newsletter*. I'd forgotten about that.' Agatha laughed. 'Jojo McPeat was the nosiest person ever created.'

'Mrs Osgood, was Tucker Devlin my father's father?' Willa asked her suddenly.

That hit Agatha in the place her heart used to be. 'Figured that out, did you?'

'What happened?' Paxton asked, taking a seat beside Agatha. Willa lingered in the doorway. 'Did you really kill him?'

'Yes. I did,' Agatha said. For all the things she couldn't give Georgie, she could at least give her this.

'Why?'

'Because we're connected, as women. If there's trouble, we all know it. But most of the time we're just too scared or selfish or insecure to help. But if we don't help each other, who will?'

'So you killed him *for* Georgie?' Paxton asked.

'We were once as close as shirt buttons, Georgie and I. I didn't think anything would change that. Until Tucker Devlin. You have to understand what it was like back then. It was the Depression, and the new national forest meant no more logging. Those of us who had managed to keep our money were trying to help those who had lost theirs. When he arrived, it was like we came alive again. Days were brighter. Food was sweeter. He promised us each the thing we wanted most. And we believed him.

'He knew the best way to get what he wanted was to break down what made us strong. Our friendships were what made us strong. He changed all that. That's why we were so jealous when Tucker moved into the Blue Ridge Madam with his big plans to save the town by turning Jackson Hill into a peach orchard. Georgie was the prettiest of our group, and now she had him under her roof.'

Agatha turned her head. She could hear the food trolley coming down the hall. It was the only sense of anticipation she had left.

'Nana?' Paxton said.

Where was she? 'Oh. Well, Georgie tried to tell us what was happening. She said Tucker slept in the attic and paced a lot, and he affected the whole house. Mice fled, but birds were always trying to get in. She would say things like *He's got a mean temper*, and *He won't leave me alone*. But we hated her for it, because we wanted him for ourselves. Georgie started avoiding us. She didn't go to parties any more. We thought she was saying we were no longer good enough for her. But she did it because she was scared and ashamed. When we turned our backs on her, she had no one left.'

'What was she scared and ashamed of?' Willa asked.

'There was no love story going on up there,' Agatha said. 'Tucker raped her. That was one of the reasons he wanted to move there in the first place. To get to her.'

Silence from the girls. The food trolley was getting nearer.

'When she finally got up enough nerve to tell me she was pregnant, I was so angry with myself. She was my best friend and she had tried to tell me what was happening, but I'd let my jealousy get in the way. I could have stopped it, could have stopped it all.'

'So you killed him because of what he did,' Paxton said.

'No. I killed him because he wouldn't stop doing it. He was terrorising her. I hit him over the head with a frying pan.'

'The frying pan that was buried with him,' Willa surmised.

'Yes.'

'Did no one know?' Paxton asked. 'Did you bury him under the peach tree by yourself?'

'Georgie knew. We buried him together. And there wasn't a peach tree there at the time. It came up later.' There was a knock at the door. 'He always did say he had peach juice in this veins.'

'Here's your dinner, Mrs Osgood,' the food-service girl said.

'Go now,' Agatha said. 'I want to eat.'

'But—' Paxton said.

'If you want to know more, come back. The story has been around for seventy-five years. It's not going anywhere.'

Every year, the Women's Society Club sponsored one international performing group for an American tour, and in return they received a special, private back-yard concert. It was always the highlight of the summer social season—except for this one. This season, the gala was all anyone was talking about, much to the consternation of Moira Kinley, whose year it was to host the concert.

It was barely a week until the gala, and Moira knew what she was up against. But she was smart. And she was Southern. So she scheduled the concert as a luncheon instead of a night-time affair, and managed to procure Claire Waverley as the caterer. *Everyone* wanted Claire Waverley, from nearby Bascom, to cater their affairs. Her food was something you remembered fondly for years. It could affect you in magical ways.

'Introduce yourself to Claire Waverley,' Paxton's mother said to her as she followed Paxton to the front door.

'I will,' Paxton said, checking her watch. She had hoped she'd have time to call Willa to see how she was this morning. Last night had been intense. But now she'd run out of time.

'Make a good impression,' Sophia said.

'I will.'

'Give her this.' Sophia handed her a small box.

Paxton looked at it curiously. 'What is it?'

'It's a gift for the caterer, a gold pin in the shape of a flower, because she works with edible flowers. I wrote her a nice note, too.'

It wasn't a gift, it was a bribe, but Paxton didn't point that out. 'You really want her to cater your anniversary party, don't you?'

'It's only eight months away!' Sophia said worriedly.

Paxton had reached the door by this time. 'Goodbye, Mama.'

'Yes, good-bye,' Colin said, appearing from out of nowhere and slipping out of the door ahead of them.

'Colin! Where are you going?' Sophia called.

'To commune with nature,' he called back.

Paxton walked out and caught up with Colin at the Mercedes. 'That was too easy for you,' she said. 'It took me ten minutes just to get to the door.'

'The trick is to not make eye contact. They don't charge if you don't make eye contact.'

She smiled in spite of herself. 'You're in a good mood.'

'Yes, I am.' He looked at her thoughtfully. 'But you're not. When was the last time you were in a good mood, Pax? Nothing is going to get better until you get the hell out of this house. Find what makes you happy. Obviously it isn't here.'

No, it wasn't here. She just wasn't sure where it was. 'Are you really going to commune with nature?'

'Actually, I have a date with Willa. I have to go.' He nodded in the direction behind her. 'Don't keep your date waiting, either.'

'I don't have a date. Thanks for pointing that out.'

'Tell him that,' he said as he got in the car.

Paxton turned to see that Sebastian had parked his car in front of hers in the round brick driveway. He was leaning against the car, hands in his pockets, as he watched her approach.

'I told you you didn't have to come,' she said, stopping in front of him.

'And I told you I'd do anything for you.' He opened the passenger side door for her. 'Shall we?'

She couldn't deny the relief she felt. She hadn't been looking forward to showing up alone. 'Thank you, Sebastian.'

They didn't talk much on the drive. They didn't mention what they'd been doing this past week that prevented them from seeing each other or returning calls. She wondered if anything between them would ever be the same. And the sad answer was probably not, because she still couldn't be near him and not feel that pull, that desire, that *something* that definitely wasn't friendship.

They pulled in front of Moira Kinley's house, and a valet for the event took Sebastian's car. They walked up the steps, and as they reached the door, he finally asked, 'Who is the gift for? Moira?'

'No. It's a bribe for the caterer. My mother wants her for her anniversary party. At some point I'm going to have to give it to her.'

When they walked inside, the maid directed them to the back of the house where they found the club members and guests mingling outside on the large lawn. Paxton noticed that there were quite a few women bearing gifts. Paxton's mother wasn't the only one who wanted Claire Waverley's culinary talents for her next party.

Moira was the first to greet them. 'Welcome!' she said. She pointed to the gift Paxton was holding. 'Let me guess, for Claire Waverley?'

Paxton shrugged. 'My mother insisted.'

'I'll tell you what I told everyone else. The kitchen is off-limits. No one allowed. I don't want Claire distracted. Sorry! But grab some wine and hors d'oeuvres and enjoy!'

As soon as she flitted off, Sebastian leaned in and said, 'These women should come with danger signs.'

As they walked under the canopy and tried to find their table, they were stopped by a handsome waiter in his twenties, his eyes all over Sebastian in a blatantly sexual way. He offered Sebastian some wine. Sebastian thanked him and took glasses for himself and Paxton, handed a glass to Paxton, then led her away with his arm tightly round her waist, obviously uncomfortable.

For the next half-hour, they mingled, ending up in a group that included Stacey Herbst and Honor Redford. Paxton was getting tired of holding the gift from her mother. She thought she was conspicuous with it, since everyone else had given up hope and had either stuffed their gifts in their bags or put them on their tables, so Paxton excused herself to put her gift at her table as well.

She wasn't gone long. As she made her way back, she had to admire Sebastian. He managed to make everyone else here look like they were dressed for manual labour. His suit was smoky grey, his shirt was starched white, and his tie was like water.

She wasn't the only one watching. The cute young waiter came back with a tray of appetisers. He offered the tray to Sebastian, who shook his head and turned away, taking a sip of his wine. The waiter seemed to offer the tray to the rest as an afterthought.

Paxton approached the group in time to hear one of the women say to Sebastian, 'He's cute. I think he's interested in you.'

'Darling,' Sebastian said to Paxton, 'before we were interrupted, we were talking about you and the Blue Ridge Madam. The pall of the skeleton seems to have lifted.' Just as he'd said it would.

'Yes,' Paxton said brightly. 'In your eye, Tucker Devlin.' She lifted her glass as if in a toast, but the glass tipped and sloshed onto Sebastian's jacket. It was the oddest feeling. She could have sworn someone pushed the glass. 'Oh, Sebastian, I'm sorry.'

'That's all right. It's too hot for a jacket, anyway.'

The waiter was hurrying over, but Sebastian held up his hand and shook his head, stopping him with irritation. He handed Paxton his glass and took off his jacket and shook it.

'My great-aunt used to talk about him,' Sebastian said, draping his jacket over his arm and taking his glass back from Paxton. 'Tucker Devlin. She said he held the town hostage with magic. You know that painting in my bedroom, the one that belonged to her with the bird perched on the bowl of berries?' he asked Paxton. That caused some subtly exchanged glances. They all knew now that she'd been in his bedroom. Paxton wondered if he'd said it on purpose. 'She told me Tucker Devlin came to visit her once, because he liked to court all the girls, and as he stood there talking to her, he reached into the painting and brought out a handful of berries and ate them right in front of her. His hand was bleeding, as if the bird had pecked it. I thought that was the strangest story.'

'My grandmother used to talk about a magic man, too,' Honor said.

'A salesman who travelled through here when she was a young woman. She said he stole hearts and warned, "If a man has so much heat he burns your skin, he's the devil. Run away."'

This set off a slew of stories that grandmothers had passed down to their granddaughters about the magic man, most of them warnings. Nana Osgood hadn't been exaggerating about just how forceful Tucker Devlin's personality had been.

A ripple of exclamations rolled through the gathering, and Paxton looked up to see a black and yellow bird flying around, causing people to duck. It flew in circles for a few minutes, and when it was gone, everyone had forgotten what they were talking about.

Finally, Moira asked that everyone take their seats. She gave a short speech, then introduced the group they had sponsored that year, a quartet of Ukrainian violinists. Lunch was then served, beautiful food garnished with edible roses and tasting of lavender and mint and lust. The quartet played ravishing melodies that were strange and exotic. There was a curious sense of longing in the air and everyone felt it. People began to think of old loves and missed opportunities. Finally, plates were cleared for dessert and everyone stretched at their tables, as if waking up.

Paxton turned to Sebastian, staring into his glass of wine. 'If dessert is ready, that means the caterer is leaving soon. I'm not going to get the opportunity to give my mother's gift to Claire Waverley.'

Suddenly Sebastian was gone. Paxton saw him talking to the young waiter who had been flirting with him earlier. Paxton looked away, a small ache in her chest.

Moments later, Sebastian leaned in from behind her and said, 'I've found a way to get you into the kitchen. Come with me.'

Paxton grabbed her bag and the gift and followed Sebastian. The cute young waiter was waiting for them. 'Follow me,' he said.

Paxton looked to Sebastian. He'd done this just for her. 'Go on,' he said. 'I'll wait for you in the living room.'

The waiter got her past the kitchen door. Paxton was so surprised and touched by Sebastian's act that, as soon as she walked into the kitchen, her agenda changed in a flash. She didn't have time to think it through. She was just going to do it. She put the gift on a shelf by the door and walked forward. She had one opportunity, and she was going to take it. Maybe she could still make this happen.

Two women were standing next to a stainless-steel prep table that was littered with flowers. Paxton felt a little leery as she approached them. Claire Waverley was a beautiful, mysterious caterer whom it was rumoured could make your love life better, your senses stronger, all with the food she created.

'Claire Waverley?'

'Yes?' Claire said, turning round. She was in her forties, with beautifully cut hair and a quiet intensity.

'My name is Paxton Osgood.'

'Hello,' Claire said. She put her arm round the young woman beside her. 'This is my niece, Bay.'

'I'm sorry to bother you,' Paxton said.

'You're not. Our work is done. Dessert is ready.' She gestured to the large trays of custard cups, ready for the waiters to pick up. 'Cups of lemon creme layered with hazelnut shortbread crumbles, pansies, lavender and lemon verbena.'

'That sounds wonderful.'

Claire said, 'You have a question.'

She was used to this, Paxton realised. She was used to lovesick people wanting something from her—a cure, a potion, a promise. She knew what Paxton was going to ask before she said it.

'Can you really make people feel differently with the food you cook, with the drinks you prepare?'

'I can change moods. What I can't do is change people. There is no magic for that. Who are you looking to change?'

The words brought her up short. She didn't want Sebastian to change. And being in love wasn't something that was wrong. She wouldn't change that. She realised this was her last-ditch effort to make things go her way. *Find what makes you happy*, her brother had said. This didn't bring her happiness, so why was she pursuing it? It was time to finally give up. 'No one, I guess,' Paxton said.

Claire gave her a small, understanding smile. 'It's for the best. The harder we fight, the worse it gets. I speak from experience.'

Paxton walked out of the kitchen, a little numb. But that was OK. She actually preferred it. She walked into Moira's living room to find Sebastian.

He was sitting on a leather couch, staring out of the window. He turned when she approached. He looked surprised. 'You didn't give her the gift.'

Paxton looked at the box in her hands. 'No. I think I'd like to go home.'

He uncrossed his legs and stood. He grabbed his jacket from the back of the couch and walked towards her silently. Once outside, Sebastian gave the valet his ticket. Paxton saw the Ukrainian performers climbing into a large van. Without another thought, she went over to them, handed them her mother's gift and said, 'Thank you. It was beautiful.'

They smiled, not understanding these strange American women.

The valet had delivered Sebastian's Audi by the time she walked back. Sebastian helped her in, then got behind the wheel.

Before he could start the engine, she said, 'I almost asked Claire Waverley for a love potion.'

He sat back and looked at her. 'Almost?'

'I don't want you to be something you aren't. You're wonderful just as you are. My feelings are inconvenient, but they're not wrong. I don't think I would change them, even if I could.'

With a sigh, he leaned over and put his forehead to hers, then closed his eyes. After a moment, he pulled back slightly and looked at her. His eyes travelled all over her face and then slowly he leaned into her again, watching her mouth. This had to be all her doing, somehow. She was creating this because she wanted it so much. 'Don't do this,' she whispered when his lips got close enough that she could smell the tang of wine from his last sip. 'Don't pity me.'

His eyes darted to hers, confused. 'What makes you think I'm pitying you?'

'I know it's not something you want to talk about, your sexuality. But I saw you, remember? Back in high school, our senior year. You were with a group of boys in the Asheville Mall. One of them leaned over and kissed you, and you looked right at me.' He leaned back in his seat, startled. 'I will never ask you to be something you're not. I know you can't feel for me what I feel for you.'

He shook his head. 'I'd forgotten about that,' he said.

There was an uncomfortable pause before he started the car and pulled out. He drove to an intersection and came to a halt, and Paxton recognised the car that had stopped to their left. It was Colin, with Willa in the seat next to him. Colin honked and waved at her.

If she didn't love her brother so much, she'd probably resent him. He'd obviously had a much better day than she did.

CHAPTER ELEVEN

STRANGE SEDUCTIONS

RACHEL WAS A PRACTICAL PERSON. She did not believe in ghosts or superstitions or bells that could ring on their own. But she did believe in love. She believed that it could change the course of your life.

And she was living proof.

She'd never lived in one place for more than a year when growing up. And she'd been all set to follow that same pattern into adulthood. A year and a half ago, she'd hiked through Walls of Water, broke and tired. She'd decided to stop and get a job long enough to stock up on some cash, and then leave again. She'd found work at a sporting goods store because you can't spend your childhood living in campsites without knowing a little about what you need to survive. Willa, the store's owner, had seemed relieved. Rachel liked Willa. She was nice and funny, but so full of unexpressed emotion that Rachel had tried everything she could to pop her balloon just to let some of that pressure out. Nothing ever worked, which was strange. Rachel wasn't usually wrong about people.

Even after finding work, Rachel had had to camp illegally in Cataract National Forest, because she couldn't afford to rent a place. That's where she'd been discovered one night by a park ranger named Spencer. He'd agreed to let her stay until morning if she'd promise to pack up and leave at first light. She'd been so grateful that she'd kissed him right there. He'd been embarrassed about it. He'd blushed as he walked away. But when he came back the next morning, he'd seemed relieved to find her there. And that's how it happened.

Rachel fell in love, and it changed everything.

She'd lived here longer than she'd lived any other place. Spencer was here and she knew she couldn't be anywhere he wasn't. So she got used to this curious place and its funny superstitions. She got Willa to let her open the coffee bar in the store. And to her surprise, she was good at it. Coffee, she'd discovered, was tied to all sorts of memories. Sunday mornings, friendly get-togethers, a favourite grandfather long since gone. Coffee *meant* something to people.

Coffee was a lot like love that way.

And, because Rachel believed in love, she believed in coffee, too.

But that was all. She still didn't believe in bells ringing on their own, even though the one in the store kept doing it.

She looked up when it rang again that Saturday, expecting to see no one there, but to her surprise, it was Willa.

'What are you doing here?' Rachel asked. 'It's your day off.'

'I'm going out with Colin Osgood today, and he's meeting me here,' Willa said, walking up to Rachel at the coffee bar. 'If you start making kissy noises, I will strip you of your coffee privileges.'

Rachel pretended to think seriously about it, then asked, 'Can I make a joke?'

'No.'

'Does this mean you and Colin are—'

Willa stopped her before she could finish. 'No.'

Just then, Colin walked in. He looked from Rachel to Willa, probably wondering why they were staring at him. He looked down as if to make sure he'd actually put on clothes that morning. He was wearing shorts, hiking boots and a long-sleeved T-shirt.

Rachel saw Willa's eyes narrow. 'You're dressed like . . . no.' She put one hand up. 'Absolutely not.'

'Guess what?' Colin said, grinning. 'We're going hiking.'

'I don't want to,' Willa said. 'I'm not dressed for hiking.'

'Are we, or are we not, standing in a sporting goods store?'

Willa crossed her arms over her chest. 'I'm not going.'

'Come on. Trust me,' Colin said.

'I'll get a pair of hiking boots while you change into shorts and a T-shirt,' Rachel said. 'I'll even let you wear my cowboy hat.'

'She'll even let you wear her hat,' Colin said, looking Willa in the eye and raising his brows, like this was the clincher.

In a matter of minutes, Willa was all suited up. 'Let's get this over with,' she said. 'But I told you, this has been tried before.'

'She went hiking with me once, saw a snake about ten steps into the trail and then ran back to the car,' Rachel said.

Willa shivered. 'I don't like snakes.'

'Most snakes are nice,' Colin said.

'Oh, great,' Willa said as she walked to the door. 'You like snakes.'

Colin followed her out. 'There's nothing to be afraid of. In fact, I could show you one you might like.'

'I don't want to see your snake, thank you very much. Anyway, I said I didn't like them, not that I was afraid of them.'

'Is that a challenge?' he asked.

'What is with you and challenges? *No.*'

'Get a room already,' Rachel said as they left.

'I heard that,' Willa called as the door closed behind them.

Yes, Rachel believed in love. And she knew it when she saw it.

They drove through the entrance of Cataract National Forest, along winding roads with savagely beautiful vistas. When Colin parked in the gravel lot at one of the trailheads, Willa looked around and said, 'Where are we going, exactly?'

'To Tinpenny Falls.'

All things considered, that was a relief. Tinpenny Falls was a popular attraction and the trail was probably not a treacherous one.

'Is this the first time you've been here?'

'No, don't worry.' He reached over and put his hand on her knee. His skin was warm against her leg and it made her breath catch. 'I know where we're going. When I come home for visits, I always hike. It helps me cope.'

'Cope with what?'

'With being here.'

This was certainly a strange seduction. She'd been so caught up in his challenges to how she lived her life that she'd never actually questioned what his real motivation might be. Until now.

Colin got out and shrugged on a backpack. He headed down the trail, and she followed him reluctantly into the leafy green beyond. He was a natural tour guide, pointing out interesting flora, but she didn't pretend to be fascinated. She mostly looked for snakes. She wasn't a nature girl, though for some reason he wanted her to be. He wanted her to be a lot of things. He'd told her that she had inspired him to leave, to follow his own path, and she was slowly beginning to understand that her life here, the fact that she came back and stayed, challenged how he'd chosen to live his own life. He didn't think he belonged here, so she was making him face some uncomfortable facts. People adapt. People change. You *can* grow where you're planted.

And Colin didn't like it one bit.

So where did the seduction fit in? Was it only a means to an end, part of his trying to influence her to change to fit his expectations so he could go back to thinking he'd made the right decisions in his life?

She didn't think so, but she couldn't be sure.

They finally reached the top of Tinpenny Falls, and were met by a magnificent sight. The river leading to the precipice was calm and surprisingly shallow. But when the water met the edge of the rock, it roared over and dropped more than 100 feet into a pool littered with large, flat rocks.

This was the area's most famous waterfall, named after Jonathan Tinpenny. As the story went, almost two centuries ago, Mr Tinpenny rode on horseback through the green mountains of North Carolina in search of the waterfalls where the waters were apparently healing and there were claims of curative miracles. When he found the falls, he dismounted, lost his footing and fell over, but miraculously he'd survived.

Colin led her across a natural bridge of flat rocks to the other side of the falls. 'What made you decide to become a landscape architect?' Willa asked when he reached back and took her hand in his.

He shrugged. 'There's a grove of hickory trees on my parents' estate, long rows of trees with their branches stretching into each other, constantly having to be cut back. I remember going out there as a boy and lying under them and staring up at the canopy. There was an uneasy symmetry to them. Their chaos was given structure by the landscapers, but that structure was always threatened by their own wild nature. I decided landscaping was like lion-taming,' he said. 'But I didn't decide to go into landscape architecture until after I graduated from college. My undergraduate degree is in finance, which is what my dad wanted. But after college, I went on a tour of Europe with my girlfriend at the time, and the castle gardens there reawakened my desire to lion-tame.' He paused. 'And then there was you.'

'Yes,' she said, knowing where this was going. 'And then there was me.'

'I was pretty miserable in college, and I remember thinking to myself, "Willa Jackson is probably doing exactly what she wants to do with her life right now." You went out with such a bang.'

'This may come as a surprise to you, Colin, but I wasn't any more happy when I left than when I was here. I was wild and irresponsible and flunked out of college. I was working as a gas station attendant when my dad died. I don't know what would have happened if I hadn't come back.'

'You never got the chance to find out,' he pointed out.

'No. Coming back and facing everything was exactly what I needed to do. And if I ever leave here again, I can do it with confidence. I won't be running from it.'

That made him stop and turn to her. 'Is that what you think I did?'

'I don't know,' she answered honestly. 'But here's some advice you don't want to hear: spend more time here and maybe people will see you as you are now, and not as Stick Man.'

'You sound like my sister,' he said.

'Don't give Paxton a hard time,' Willa surprised herself by saying. 'She's got a lot on her plate.'

'So now you're bosom buddies?' he said, smiling as he took her hand again. 'We're almost there.'

He led her off the trail to a small tributary of the river they'd just crossed. It trickled down a large flat rock and into a forest pool.

Colin took off his backpack and threw it to the bank below. Then he sat down and unlaced his boots. 'You know, the reason they say Jonathan Tinpenny survived is not because he fell off the falls, but because he actually slid down this rock instead.'

She suddenly understood what he was going to do. 'Did you see those signs? They said no sliding down the rock.'

'No, I didn't see them,' he said, walking out onto the glistening rock. He sat down and scooted to the edge. 'Come on. I dare you.'

'You think that's all it's going to take. A dare?'

'Until you tell me what you want, I'm going to make it up as I go along.' He propelled himself forward and slid down the wet rock.

'Colin!' she yelled after him.

He splashed into the water, shaking his head, flinging water out of his hair. He looked up at her. 'Come on! The water feels great.'

'We're going to get arrested!'

He floated on his back. 'That didn't used to stop you.'

Staring down at him, her fingers twitching with the thought of what a rush it would be to slide down this rock, she realised that, yes, there *was* a little bit of the Joker left in her. Enough to satisfy this need to feel her heart pound with adrenaline, but not enough to ruin the life she'd made for herself. And that made her feel better, not quite so afraid of herself any more. And not so afraid of Colin, either. So she was going to take her boots off and slide into the pool below and enjoy every moment, and definitely come up laughing.

And that's exactly what she did.

Colin and Willa lifted themselves onto the bank to dry themselves in the sun. They stretched out side by side in comfortable silence. The rock was warm underneath Willa, the gentle sound of the water was lulling, and the forest smelled like moss and pine. She wasn't much of a nature girl, but she could get used to this.

'There's something I've been meaning to ask you,' Colin said.

Willa turned her head. He'd taken off his T-shirt and his bare chest was tanned and taut. His eyes were closed, so she felt free to study him. She'd never spent time with someone so tall. There was so much of him. He overwhelmed her a little. 'Yes?'

'What makes you think your father got fired?'

That surprised her. 'Because he never went back to teaching.'

'I was there the day he left,' Colin said. 'And he wasn't fired. He quit.'

Willa sat up and turned to him. 'What?'

Colin opened his eyes, then lifted one arm to block out the sun. 'When you pulled the fire alarm and then let that banner fall announcing you were the Joker, my parents demanded an apology from the principal because I'd been his suspect since you put that Ogden Nash quote on the marquee. Your father was called in to apologise as well. By that time, everyone had figured out the reason you'd been so successful as the Joker was because you had your dad's keys and passwords. The principal said to your father, "I know it's not your fault you have a sneaky daughter." And your father just lost it. He said that when everyone thought it was me, no one took action, because of who my family was. He said he was proud of your acts of rebellion, that he'd wished he'd had the courage to do it himself when he was your age, and that he'd known what you were doing all along. He was tired of living such a cautious life, and for once he was throwing caution to the wind. And he quit.'

Willa was flabbergasted. 'That doesn't sound like my father.'

'I know,' Colin agreed. 'But that's what happened.'

'He knew?'

'Apparently so. I got the impression that he was even proud. I thought you should know.'

'That makes absolutely no sense.'

Colin shrugged and closed his eyes again, and it didn't take long to tell that he'd gone to sleep. She sat there, her arms wrapped round her knees, thinking about her father knowing about her pranks all along, about him saying he was finally throwing caution to the wind. What did that mean? She'd always assumed he was happy with his life.

She and Paxton planned to meet at the nursing home tomorrow to talk to Agatha again. Maybe Willa could ask Agatha about her father and Grandmother Georgie's relationship. If it was like everything else she'd learned lately, there was more going on than she'd thought.

She didn't know how long she sat there, lost in thought, before she turned to see Colin staring at her, one arm propped under his head. She smiled and brushed some of his hair off his forehead.

Their eyes met. As if by mutual consent, Colin leaned forward and she met him halfway, their lips touching gently. It wasn't long before gentle turned hungry and insistent. She leaned back and he went with her. He made her chest feel like it was going to explode. To feel this way without actually breaking the law was amazing. She felt his hand push at her shirt, and she arched against him. 'You're so beautiful,' he said as her shirt passed over her head, landing somewhere behind them. 'I think I've always been looking for you. I can't believe you've been here all along.'

She opened her eyes and focused on the top of the rock. Someone could come along at any moment. 'Colin, someone might see.'

He lifted his head. 'And tell me that doesn't excite you on some level,' he said as he put his lips to hers.

She pulled at his hair until he lifted his head again and looked down at her. He was breathing heavily. 'It excites me who I am now, Colin,' she said, because, for some reason, it was important for her to tell him. 'This isn't me being someone I used to be.'

He looked confused.

She suddenly felt sad. This wasn't going to be what she wanted it to be. How could it? 'You're not going to stay, are you?' she said.

He hesitated a moment before he said, 'No.'

'So your plan is to seduce me and then leave.'

His eyes bore into hers. 'Why don't you come with me?'

'I can't leave now. My grandmother is here.'

'Look me in the eye and tell me you're happy, Willa.'

'Why don't you do the same?'

He lifted himself off of her. 'Of course I'm happy.'

She found her shirt and put it on. 'Right. That's why you sleep so well.'

He used both hands to scrub his face, as if finally waking up. He sighed and watched the water for a moment. 'We should go,' he said, reaching over and handing her her boots.

They followed Tinpenny Trail back to the parking lot. It was mid afternoon by the time they climbed into Colin's car, and Willa left her window down to let the warm summer wind blow on her as Colin drove.

'Are you hungry?' he asked.

'Starving,' she admitted.

'Let's get something to eat. Let's not end the day on such an uncomfortable note.'

'Have you been to the Depot Restaurant on National Street?'

He smiled. 'Sounds perfect.'

Once out of Cataract, the first intersection they came to was a four-way stop. To their right was a blue Audi.

'That's Sebastian's car,' Colin said, giving them a honk and a wave. 'He and Paxton must be heading home from the luncheon.'

'Do you want to ask them to join us?' Willa asked.

Colin got out and jogged over to Sebastian's car at the intersection. He said something to them. When he jogged back and got back in, he said, 'Good call. They look like they could use a drink.'

From what Willa knew of Paxton and Sebastian's relationship, she wasn't surprised. 'Yes, I bet they could.'

They drove to National Street and parked at the old train depot, now a restaurant and visitor centre. The restaurant was full of hikers, their backpacks propped against their chairs. Willa, Colin, Paxton and Sebastian walked in and went to the bar. Paxton and her brother sat beside each other, Willa and Sebastian on either side of them. Willa enjoyed watching the siblings interact. She knew they were twins, but they were so unalike that she didn't really get their similarities until she saw them together—their dark eyes, their kind smiles, the way they sat with perfect posture.

After they had placed their orders, Colin, Sebastian and Paxton all commented on how nice the place was. They'd never been there before. That made Willa laugh. 'You're such *townies*.'

'And you're not?' Paxton asked with a smile.

'I've stretched my boundaries.'

When their drink orders came, Colin turned to Sebastian and asked, 'How long have you been back in Walls of Water?'

'Just a year,' Sebastian said. 'What about you? Any plans to move back?'

Colin avoided looking at Willa and Paxton as he said, 'No.'

'I don't get it,' Paxton said, taking a sip of her margarita. 'What's wrong with Walls of Water? It's home. Our history is here. Why would you want to be anywhere else? This place defines us.'

'You hit the nail on the head, Pax,' Colin said. Paxton and Willa both turned to him with similar expressions of exasperation.

'You don't like that this place defines you?' Paxton asked.

Colin shrugged. 'I'm not Stick Man any more.'

'And yet you still want to believe I'm the Joker,' Willa said.

'The Joker was stepping out of your shell. You proved that there was more to you than people thought. It was a good thing.' He toasted her with his glass.

'It wasn't all about proving I was more than what people thought of me. Being the Joker was a manifestation of a lot of unresolved family problems.'

Sebastian snorted and everyone turned to him. 'You two had it easy. Try being the Freak sometime.'

'You're the only one who hasn't changed, Pax,' Colin said, 'because you had yourself figured out long before any of us.'

That seemed to hurt Paxton. 'I guess I'm just the princess of the group, aren't I?'

'I meant that as a compliment.'

'No, you didn't,' Paxton said. 'You want to know the real difference between me and all of you? I don't love any of you any less for not being exactly who I want you to be.'

'No, you reserve that criticism for yourself,' Sebastian said softly.

'Did this conversation suddenly get too serious?' Willa said.

They tried to laugh it off, and soon Willa's and Colin's sandwiches arrived. As they ate, Paxton told them all about the magical food at the luncheon and Sebastian told funny stories about the society ladies.

When Paxton noticed Colin's empty plate, she said, 'Can I ride back with you to Hickory Cottage?'

Colin wiped his mouth with his napkin. 'I need to take Willa back to her Jeep first.'

'It's just up the street at my store,' Willa said, setting her sandwich down. 'I can walk.'

Paxton stood and Colin followed suit.

'Thanks for the hike,' Willa said.

'Sure. Anytime.' Colin met her eyes for a moment longer than necessary, then left.

Sebastian moved down to sit beside her. He nodded to her sandwich. 'Finish. I'll drive you to your Jeep.'

'That's OK. I'll walk.'

'Then I'll walk with you,' he said.

Willa stared at her sandwich. She wasn't hungry any more. 'Let's go, then,' she said as she slid off the stool. 'I'm done.'

It was early evening when they walked outside, the sky the colour of pink lemonade. Her grandmother used to tell her that a pink sky meant someone had just fallen in love, a rare moment of whimsy from a woman who had been scared of everything. National Street was still busy as they walked down the sidewalk together.

'How long have you and Paxton been . . . close?' Willa asked.

'Since I came back to town.'

Did he know Paxton was in love with him? Was that something Willa should tell him? She had no idea why she was even considering getting involved. She guessed she didn't like the thought of Paxton being hurt by someone who hadn't figured himself out yet.

'You and Paxton seem to be getting to know each other pretty well,' Sebastian commented after a stretch of silence.

'"Understand" is probably a better word. Our grandmothers had a connection a long time ago. We're sorting through the details.'

They reached Willa's store. The lights were off inside and Rachel had already left. 'Thanks for the walk. This is my Jeep,' she said.

'You know, Colin was right about one thing,' Sebastian said. 'By being the Joker, you did prove there was more to you than people thought. You can't say that you didn't intend for it to happen. You made certain we all knew it was you, with that banner.'

Willa smiled sheepishly. 'I thought I was never coming back to Walls of Water after college. I wanted the legend to have a name.'

'You inspired me a little.'

'I did?'

'Back then, I needed to break free of some things, too. I needed to stop being what everyone thought I was. But there will always be a little bit of the Freak in me. It's part of who I am.'

She'd always thought of Sebastian as the master of reinvention. But she now realised that he hadn't reinvented himself at all. He'd *become* himself. 'How did you come to terms with it?'

'It's surprising how little say we have in who we are. Once you accept that, the rest is easy.' He leaned in to kiss her cheek. 'Good night, lovely.'

'Good night,' she said as she watched him walk away.

Willa had already showered and was ready for bed when there was a knock at the door. When she opened it, her favourite insomniac was there, looking absolutely miserable.

'I'm sorry,' Colin said. 'I'm sorry I implied that your life is anything less than what it needs to be. I made this all about me.'

'Yeah, I figured that out.' She stepped back and let him enter.

'I don't know why this place affects me like it does, like I can't be myself here. Maybe I think if I do come back, I won't be as good an Osgood as the rest of my family. That's always been a big fear of mine. But I don't want society parties and days spent on the golf course.' He ran both hands through his hair.

Willa folded her arms. 'Has anyone actually made you do anything you didn't want to since you've been coming back for visits?'

He frowned. 'Well, no.'

'So you're just creating conflict that isn't there.' She laughed. 'Guess what, Colin? There's still some of Stick Man in you.'

He went to her couch and sank down onto it. 'I'm embarrassed. And so damn tired. Why can I never sleep?'

'Maybe you're afraid to relax and let some things just happen.'

'You're right. Falling for you just happened.' He chuckled and leaned his head back. 'And that's the best thing that's come out of coming home.'

Willa's arms fell to her sides with surprise. 'I keep telling you, stop dropping by when you're tired. You say things you shouldn't.'

He looked at her seriously. 'Why shouldn't I say that?'

'Because I'm not entirely sure you know who I am,' she answered honestly. How could he, when she had only recently begun to figure it out?

'On the contrary. I've been paying very close attention.'

She shrugged. 'Tell me that in the morning, and I might believe you.'

'OK.' He rubbed his hands on the couch. 'Can I sleep on your couch again? That was the only good night's sleep I've had since I've been here.'

'OK,' she sighed. 'Let me get you a pillow.'

'No, no pillow,' he said as he made room for her. 'Just you.'

All sorts of things flew through her mind, the most surprising of which was the instantaneous *Yes!* she heard. But she'd been denying those impulses for too long to follow them. 'Colin . . .'

'I just want you to lie here with me until I fall asleep, OK?'

She reached over and turned off the lights, then walked over to him. He was so tall that she fitted easily into his side. He put his arm round her and she rested her head on his chest. This felt right.

What an impossible situation.

'I'm not sure I can live here,' he said into the darkness, as if reading her thoughts. She could hear his voice deep in his chest.

'I'm not sure I can leave,' she responded.

They were quiet for a while.

'I think I might try to live here, though,' he whispered.

'I think I might try to leave,' she whispered back.

'But still no chance of turning you into a nature girl?'

She laughed and snuggled in deeper. 'Go to sleep, Colin.'

And, finally, he did.

The next morning, Willa was standing on a chair in her closet, reaching back for a shoe box full of high school mementoes, when Colin said from behind her, 'What are you doing?'

'That's funny, I was just wishing that a tall man would suddenly appear and help me,' she said as she jumped off the chair. 'Will you get that box off the shelf up there for me?'

He showed off by doing it easily.

'What is that?' Colin asked as he handed it to her.

'Just something I want to return to Paxton when I meet her today,' she said as she set the box on her dresser.

'So this is your room,' he said, looking around at her cast-iron bed and hand-painted furniture.

'Yes, this is my room.'

He had a serious case of bed head, his shirt was untucked, and his feet were bare, which for some reason she found endearing. He turned to her and said, 'I slept.' Then he walked up and put his arms around her. 'You know what this means?' He bent down and said into her ear, 'We're going to have to do it again.'

She laughed. 'OK, just not on the couch again. I'm too used to my bed.'

He looked over his shoulder. 'It's a nice bed.'

She took his hand and led him over to it. 'It's very comfortable,' she said as she sat on it. 'And it fits two.'

Colin leaned over, making her lie back. Still standing, but with his hands on either side of her, he looked down and said, 'Willa?'

'Yes?'

'It's morning.'

'I know.'

'And I'm still in love with you.'

CHAPTER TWELVE

LOST AND FOUND

JUST AFTER LUNCH that Sunday, Paxton met Willa in the parking lot of the nursing home and they walked to Nana Osgood's room. Willa was pensive but cheery, almost like she was cautiously optimistic about something. Paxton wondered if it had anything to do with her brother not coming home last night. She really wanted to ask Willa but figured that was the kind of thing you shared only with friends.

'How are you with all that Nana Osgood told us on Friday?' Paxton said. 'I couldn't ask you yesterday, not with Sebastian and Colin there.'

'I'm OK. How are you?'

'A little worried about what more she has in store for us today.'

Paxton had brought a box of chocolates. Once she gave the chocolates to Nana Osgood, she settled beside her on the love seat. Willa sat in the chair opposite them.

Agatha stroked the box of chocolates on her lap. 'If the police go after Georgie,' she said, 'I want you to tell them what I told you.'

'I don't think they're going to,' Willa said. 'I haven't heard anything from Woody Olsen.'

'I don't care what you think,' Agatha said. 'If it comes down to it, promise me you'll tell them!'

'It's all right, Nana. We promise.'

'OK, then.' She petted the chocolate box some more.

'The gala is this Friday,' Paxton said. 'I still want you to come.'

Agatha pshawed. 'You silly girls.'

'Willa and I noticed the date of the formation of the Women's Society Club is around the same time Tucker Devlin disappeared seventy-five years ago. Is that just a coincidence?'

'No, it's not a coincidence. The night we buried him, I told Georgie I'd always be there for her. She was afraid. She was pregnant. And I was going to help her. The next day I got four friends together and told them Georgie needed us. I didn't give them the details, but the town seemed to know Tucker was gone. Everything felt differently, like we were waking up. The six of us formed the Women's Society Club to help Georgie. We promised we would never turn our backs on each other again. We decided to become a society of women, a club to make sure women were protected. The club was something important back then. Not like it is today.'

'What happened to make it change so much?' Paxton asked. She'd been having mixed feelings about the club lately, and finding this out just made her more confused about her role in it.

'Life happened,' Agatha said. 'Georgie left the club about ten years later, when the rest of us started having our own children. That's when we began to use the club as a way to compare notes. Who had the best cook. Whose husband made more money. Georgie's life was so different that I don't think she felt like she belonged any more. But I kept my promise. I was always there if she needed me. She just stopped asking. I was close enough to Ham, though, that he would come to me when she wouldn't.'

'Grandmother Georgie was very strict with my father,' Willa said. Paxton turned to her. She didn't understand the context, but Willa was obviously going somewhere with this.

'She was terrified he was going to turn out just like Tucker. She was terrified of everything. She was terrified that Tucker's body was going to be found.' Agatha shook her head. 'All her superstitions were because she wanted his ghost to stay buried.'

'Did my dad know who his father was?'

'Georgie told him he was a travelling salesman. He might have deduced more, but what Ham knew for sure was that living a small life was what his mother wanted for him. And he did that for her. It was a shame he died just as he was finally coming into his own.'

Willa leaned forward. 'What do you mean?'

'He was going to sell his house and travel.'

'He never told me that!'

'I don't think he told you a lot of things.'

Willa asked, 'Did he quit his job at the school because of me?'

'Yes. He was impressed by you. I can't imagine why.' Agatha made a face. 'All those pranks. And when he found out you'd dropped out of college, he just thought you were finding yourself.'

'He knew I dropped out?' Willa's brow rose.

'Of course he knew.'

'How do *you* know?' Paxton asked, amazed that her grandmother had been harbouring not only her own secrets, but Willa's father's as well. What else was in that hard head of hers?

'Ham and I had a very long conversation when the time came for him to move his mother into a nursing home. He was going to travel. I promised I'd watch over Georgie.'

'Why did you never tell me the club had lost its way?' Paxton asked. 'Maybe I could have done something.'

'Paxton, I think you've tried to make the club more about the deed than the social aspect, and I give you credit for that, but I also believe it's more because you don't have friends than because of a higher calling.' Paxton reared back at that. 'Friendship started that club, and if you ever want to see it back to what it was, you have to understand what it means to be a friend.'

'Will you come to the gala?' Paxton asked again. 'I think it's important that you be there.'

'Maybe. Keep bringing me chocolate like this and . . . maybe. Leave me to eat in peace,' she said, opening the box.

Paxton and Willa stood, each lost in her own thoughts as they walked down the corridor. 'Do you want to have some coffee?' Willa asked, pointing over her shoulder to the dining room.

Paxton smiled. 'Yes. That would be nice.'

They got their cups and filled them, then walked to a table near a window. 'Why do you think we never became friends?' Paxton asked. 'You never liked me, did you?'

'It's not that,' Willa said. 'I guess it was jealousy in high school. I hated not having what you had. I resented my family because of it.' Willa shrugged. 'You set an impossible standard. Your clothes are perfect. Your hair is perfect. You juggle a work schedule that would take three normal people to manage it. Not all of us can do that.'

Paxton looked into her cup. 'It's only because everyone seems happier than I am. They have their own homes, husbands, children, businesses. I sometimes think there's something wrong with me.'

'There's nothing wrong with you,' Willa said. 'Why did *you* never make friends with *me*?'

'Oh, that's simple.' Paxton smiled as she looked up. 'You scared me.' That made Willa laugh. 'Seriously. You were so quiet and intense. Like you could see right through people. If I had known you were the Joker, maybe it would have been easier to get to know you. I would have at least known you had a sense of humour. Then, when you came back, you took up with the National Street set and didn't want anything to do with the people you grew up with.'

'It's not that,' Willa said. 'After my dad died, I made a promise to myself to be happy with what I had. Being around people I grew up with brought back all those insecurities, so I just avoided it.'

'There's no avoiding me now,' Paxton said. 'You know my secrets. You maced people for me. You've got me for life.'

Willa laughed and tried to wave that off. 'Any of your friends would have done the same thing.'

'No,' Paxton said. 'They wouldn't.'

'Oh, I almost forgot,' Willa said, reaching into the back pocket of her jeans. 'I need to return this to you.' She handed Paxton a folded piece of notebook paper.

'What is it?'

'It's a note you dropped one day at school. I picked it up and read it. After that, I was just too embarrassed to return it to you.'

Paxton took it and opened it. She laughed in surprise. 'My list of qualities in the man I wanted to marry.'

'I'm sorry,' Willa said sheepishly.

'This is how you forged that note to Robbie Roberts!'

'Yes. I'm really, really sorry.'

Paxton put the note in her tote bag. 'That's OK; it's just a list.'

'It's an impressive list,' Willa said.

'I knew what I wanted back then.' Paxton smiled and decided to ask Willa what she was dying to know. 'My brother didn't come home last night. I don't suppose you know anything about that?'

Willa looked away. 'He might have slept on my couch.' She turned back to her. 'And I might have slept there with him.'

'I knew it!'

They laughed, and Paxton suddenly felt like she was on such a good footing with Willa. She never thought she was good at making friends. But maybe she was just trying to be friends with the wrong people.

They ended up talking long after their coffee had gone cold.

On Monday, Paxton worked through lunch in order to give herself the afternoon off. There were a million details to attend to before the gala on Friday night, but some things were more important.

She drove into the lot of Harris & Associates real-estate agents and parked her car. When she walked in, she saw Kirsty Lemon.

'Paxton,' Kirsty said, surprised. 'What are you doing here?'

'The town house on Teal Street is still on the market. I want to buy it.'

Kirsty looked cautious. 'Are you sure this time?'

'Yes.'

Kirsty sighed and grabbed her keys. 'Well, let's go and look at it.'

The town house was in a community called Waterview. The homes were redbrick colonial and beautiful. The town house Paxton had loved from the moment Kirsty showed it to her last year was in a cul-de-sac. Wisteria vines grew round the door, and Paxton remembered thinking how wonderful it would be to walk in and out in the springtime, when the wisteria would be in full bloom.

Kirsty unlocked the security box. Inside were cathedral ceilings and hardwood floors. Upstairs were three bedrooms. That had been a point of contention with her mother when Paxton wanted to move out last year. She had insisted Paxton didn't need so much room.

She thought about what Sebastian said about every life needing space, and how that leaves room for good things to enter it. She wished she had thought of that to say to her mother at the time.

Paxton walked around the open living space. She thought how nice it would be to have friends over for dinner. 'It's as beautiful as I remembered,' Paxton said.

Kirsty was standing by the front door. 'I was counting on the commission from the sale of this place last year. When you decided not to buy it at the last minute, I was so upset with you.'

Startled, Paxton turned to her. 'Why didn't you say anything? We used to tell each other everything. When did that change?'

'I don't know.' Kirsty walked forward. 'When you're a teenager, your friends are your life. When you grow up, friendships seem to get pushed further and further back.'

'You're important to me, Kirsty,' Paxton said. 'You always have been. For some reason I just stopped saying it, showing it.'

'Wow, Pax, this is a side of you I haven't seen in a while. What brought this on?'

'With the gala coming up, I've been thinking about our grandmothers, about how their friendships lasted their whole lives. I always thought it would be like that for us.'

Kirsty looked a little sad. 'Me too.'

And that was it. The acknowledgment that things had changed.

'OK. I want this place,' Paxton said. 'I'm making an offer.'

'P'axton, come here,' her mother called from the living room as soon as Paxton got in. Her mother and father were sitting on the couch, watching the evening news.

'Your dress was delivered today,' Sophia said, indicating the large white box on the corner chair. 'Be sure to try it on in case there are any last-minute alterations. I think you, your daddy and I should all go together, particularly since you don't have a date.'

Paxton walked over to the box and opened it, still feeling a little of that thrill she used to have at the thought of party dresses, the fantasy of it all. She smiled when she saw the shimmering pink material, the sparkling jewels at the neckline.

'I have to be there early, so I'm driving myself.' She put the lid back on the box. 'Mama, when did you move out of your parents' house?'

Sophia turned away from the television. 'After college. I moved in with a few of my girlfriends. I was with them for about two years before I started dating your daddy.' She frowned. 'Why do you ask?'

Paxton picked up the dress box and walked over to her mother. 'Because I'm moving out.'

Sophia waved that away with a flick of her wrist. 'Oh, Paxton, we went over this last year. You're better off here. You don't need a place of your own when Hickory Cottage has so much room.'

'I've put it off too long. You moved out right after college. All my friends did, too. I need to do this.' She took a deep breath. 'I put in an offer on a town house this afternoon.'

'Paxton! You didn't!' Sophia said.

'Yes, I did. You can come and see me any time you want. And I'll visit you here. But I'm decorating how I want to decorate. And I'm not giving you a set of keys. I'm thirty years old, Mama.'

'Donald!' Sophia said. 'Say something.'

'She's leaving, Sophia. Maybe it's time to try to work on just being you and me for a while.'

As Paxton left, Sophia was looking at her husband as if he'd just come back from a very, very long trip—and she wasn't sure whether she was glad to see him or not.

When Paxton got to the pool house, she picked up the phone and called Willa. She wasn't even sure why.

'Hello?'

Paxton hesitated a moment. 'Hi, it's Paxton.'

'It's your sister,' Willa said.

'Colin is there?'

'Yes. Do you want to talk to him?' Willa was in a good mood.

'No, I want to talk to you. I'll call back when you're not busy.'

'Don't be silly.' Paxton heard the squeak of a screen door, then the pop as it closed. 'Now I'm outside,' Willa said.

'I noticed you still haven't RSVP'd for the gala. Will you come? Please? I'd just like you to be there. And if Colin hasn't asked you yet, be prepared—he's about to. I think I've managed to convince Nana Osgood to come. After all she told us, I think she's coming to see what a mockery this generation has made of the club.'

'What's wrong, Pax?' Willa asked. It was the first time she'd used the shortened version of her name. 'You sound melancholy.'

'Not melancholy. Conflicted, I guess. I decided to buy a house today. I'm going to move out of Hickory Cottage.'

'That's great! Do you need help moving?'

'I don't have much to move. I don't even have a bed.' She paused. 'I'm going to take some measurements. Do you want to come see the place?'

'I'd love to,' Willa said immediately.

'Don't tell Colin. I'll tell him when he gets here. I'm a little scared, Willa,' she said softly, like she was afraid to even say it.

Willa sat down. 'Happiness is a risk. If you're not a little scared, then you're not doing it right.'

Paxton was silent, letting that sink in.

'Are you going to the gala with Sebastian?' Willa finally asked.

'He hasn't mentioned it. I think I'll be going alone. I'll be OK.'

'I'm here if you need me,' Willa said.

That, ultimately, was why she had called. She needed to hear that. 'Thanks, Willa.'

CHAPTER THIRTEEN

SHEDDING THE ARMOUR

'DR ROGERS WILL SEE YOU NOW,' the receptionist said to Willa.

It had been a long shot and Willa had waited almost an hour, but now she was finally going to talk to Sebastian. 'Thank you,' she said, trying not to look into rooms where the whirring and swishing noises were coming from. It made her queasy. She entered Sebastian's office, but he wasn't there.

She took a seat in front of his desk and looked around. There was only one photograph on his desk, a photo of him and Paxton, one where they'd held the camera in front of them and grinned as they snapped the shot.

Sebastian entered and smiled at her. He didn't have on his suit jacket, and his shirtsleeves were rolled up. He was so strangely beautiful. He had hidden it behind a lot of make-up in high school, but he seemed to have come to terms with it now.

'You've done a nice job with the office,' Willa said. 'It doesn't look anything like I remember Dr Kostovo's office.'

He walked behind the desk and sat. 'You mean it doesn't look like a medieval torture chamber any more.'

'Yes,' she said, shuddering. 'Who does that? In a dentist's office? As if half the patients aren't scared enough already.'

'You should have seen his house when I first moved in,' Sebastian said. 'He left behind a suit of armour. It's in my basement.'

Willa laughed. 'You should give it to Paxton as a housewarming gift. Can you imagine the look on her face?'

His brow knitted. 'Housewarming gift?'

'She bought a town house.' Willa paused, suddenly questioning her being there. In a fit of indignation, she had decided that if Sebastian didn't know how much grief he was causing Paxton, then someone had to tell him. But maybe this wasn't such a good idea after all. 'I take it she didn't tell you.'

'No. Is that why you came to see me?'

'Not exactly.'

He nodded in understanding. 'To answer the first question I know you want to ask: Yes, I know Paxton is in love with me. To answer the second question: No, I don't want to hurt her. I've been doing everything in my power not to.'

'Then try something else,' Willa said as she stood. 'It's not working.' She reached over and took a notepad and pen from his desktop. She wrote something down and handed it to him.

'What is this?'

'Her new address. She'll be there between four and five today.'

He nodded as he stood, putting the note in his pocket.

Willa opened his office door and walked out, and Sebastian followed. He escorted her to the front desk, putting his hand on her back, low and firm. That's when she finally understood. Just like that. *I needed to stop being what everyone thought I was.* That's what he'd said outside her store on Saturday.

Startled, she turned to look at him, and he winked.

Oh, Paxton, she thought. *You have no idea what's in store for you.* She walked out into the sunshine, smiling.

Happiness meant taking risks. No one had ever told Paxton that before. It was like a secret the world had been keeping from her. The fact that all the changes she'd made in the past few days scared her to death had to be a good sign.

At four o'clock, she let herself into the town house with the keys Kirsty Lemon had given her. Willa had called her earlier, telling her she couldn't make it after all. So Paxton decided to use this time to do what she did best. Make lists.

She was going from room to room taking measurements when the doorbell rang. She walked to the door, thinking maybe Willa was able to break away from work after all. She opened the door, and the one person she wasn't expecting was the very person who stood there. He'd loosened his tie, and his hair looked like he'd run his hands through it one too many times. 'Sebastian,' she said, thunderstruck. 'How did you know I was here?'

'Willa told me,' he said. 'Why didn't you?'

Willa told him? She stepped back numbly and let him enter. 'It happened pretty quickly.'

'This is a big step for you.' He looked around, his hands in his pockets. He seemed so shut off it made her heart ache. 'I have a question,' he said. 'One I can't stop asking myself. Why did you kiss me when you'd seen me kiss another man all those years ago? Is there some twisted side to you I don't know about, Pax? Did it turn you on?'

'No,' she said, appalled. 'It wasn't like that at all.' He stared at her and she shook her head. 'God, Sebastian, people fall in love all the time. And it's not always with the right people. And it's not always reciprocated. I fell in love with you. I couldn't help it. But I was prepared to deal with it in silence until it went away. That night at the pool house, I was out of control and I hated the feeling, and then you came by because you were worried about me when no one else was. If you cared that much about me, I thought maybe I could turn it into something more. It was careless and selfish and I'm sorry.'

'Sit down,' he said. 'I have something to tell you.'

'I don't have any chairs.'

He walked over to her and took her arm. He led her to the stairs. 'Sit down and listen to me,' he said in a tone she wasn't familiar with. He was *nervous.*

She sat slowly and set her notebook next to her on the step.

He stood in front of her. 'I didn't belong anywhere when I was growing up,' he said. 'Not at home, not at school. As a teenager, I spent a lot of time at that diner on the highway, mostly as a way to keep from going home and facing my father. One Saturday night, when I was sixteen, I was sitting there in the back booth when a group of teenage boys came in, asking for directions back to Asheville. They'd got lost. They were loud, flamboyant, happy, not like anyone I'd ever met before. One of them spotted me, and it was like he'd spotted a lost member of his tribe. He came back to me and started flirting. His friends joined him, and we all had coffee and laughed. A door suddenly opened for me, this door of *acceptance.* Hours later, they said they had to go. But they said if I could find a way to Asheville, they hung out at Pack Square every afternoon and if I wanted to join them, I could. Then that boy who had first come over to me, Alex, ran his hand over my hair and said, "Who knew something this beautiful grew way out in the backwoods?"' Sebastian shook his head. 'I think humans are basically pack animals. And I finally found a pack. I'd never had one before.'

'Are these the boys I saw you with at the mall?' Paxton asked.

'Yes. And the boy you saw kiss me was Alex. It was a confusing time for me. Those were my friends. They saved me. And on some level, I loved them. I loved Alex. But the reason I became one of them is that I needed to belong somewhere and they took me in. I didn't become one of them because I was one of them.' He gave her a look she knew was significant, but she didn't understand.

'What does that mean?'

'It means I'm not gay, Pax,' he said.

She felt his words burn into her skin.

'When I entered college, I started seeing a counsellor, who helped me work through some issues. The best, most accepting people I've ever known were gay. But it was a fallback position for me, and it wasn't who I was inside. I dated women in college. But none of them understood me—they saw me as a platonic friend or thought they were converting me. It got to the point where I was simply tired of defending myself. How people choose to live their lives, and who they fall in love with, should never *have* to be defended. I made the decision about five years ago to not address my sexuality any more. That decision made life much easier. Until I met you.'

She stood. 'What kind of game are you playing with me?'

She tried to walk past him, but he grabbed her by the arms and made her face him. 'I'm not playing a game,' he said in short, measured words, words that dropped like falling off a cliff.

'Then why are you telling me this?'

He let his hands drop. She swayed a little. 'Because I love you in a way that's deep and raw and terrifying. And I don't know what to do. I've never felt anything like what I felt when you kissed me.'

He was scared. She could see it now. 'Then why did you stop?'

He ran his hands through his hair. 'Because I was still clinging to my conviction that sex only gets in the way of good relationships.'

She swallowed. 'And now?'

'I didn't think there was a single person in the world who could know everything about me and love me anyway. Until I met you. I love you, Paxton, and I have every intention of being with you for ever, if you'll have me.'

She reached for him and kissed him. Her arms wrapped round him, holding on for dear life. He backed her against the wall. She pushed at his jacket until it was off, then reached for his tie. Their hands were everywhere, getting in the way. Paxton lost her balance when the toe of her bare foot got caught in the cuff of his trousers, and she went down, taking him with her.

Sebastian rolled over, pinning her to the floor. She reached, trying to pull his lips down to hers again, but he resisted.

'I need you to say it,' he said, breathless.

She looked up at him, confused. 'Say what?'

'That you'll have me.'

She suddenly thought about that list she'd made in high school. 'You're everything I've ever wanted, Sebastian.'

He kissed her again, and she worked at the buttons on his shirt. 'Are we going to do this here?' he asked against her lips. 'We can go back to my place.'

'No. Here. Now.' She felt his smile. 'At least you don't love me for my furniture. But don't you dare bring over that suit of armour.'

He lifted his head again. 'Willa told you?'

Her hands went to his hair. 'Some things she tells me; some things she leaves out.' Like telling her Sebastian was coming over.

He lifted a brow. 'You compare notes? I better make this good.'

She hesitated. 'It already is,' she whispered.

An hour later, Paxton woke up to her cellphone ringing. She reached over Sebastian and fumbled around until she found it.

She felt Sebastian put a hand on her back and lightly stroke it.

She looked at the screen. It was Maria, the manager at the Madam. She'd had an appointment with her an hour ago about last-minute details with the gala. She groaned as she put the phone down and turned to Sebastian. 'I have to go.'

'OK.' He winced as he scooted back to lean against the wall.

'Are you all right?' Paxton got up and started picking her clothes up off the floor.

'My back. Can I buy you a bed as a housewarming gift?'

She smiled as she dressed. 'You have very good taste in beds.' She walked over to him and went to her knees beside him. 'This is real, isn't it? It really happened?'

He put his hand to her hair. 'Regrets?'

She took a deep breath. All she smelled was cut grass from the open living-room window. 'None,' she said. 'What about you?'

'Not a single one. Well, maybe the lack of bed. Love me, love my creature comforts.'

She took his hand in hers. 'I do love you, Sebastian. And I'm scared out of my mind.'

'That makes two of us, darling.'

'Willa said happiness means taking risks. And if you're not a little scared, you're not doing it right.'

That made him laugh. 'If that's the case, we have nothing to worry about,' he said, leaning forward to kiss her.

On Wednesday morning, Willa got to her store before Rachel, so she began taking the chairs off the café tables by the window. She had just started the coffee when the bell above the door rang and Paxton entered.

'Hi,' Willa said, surprised. 'What are you doing here?'

Paxton shrugged. 'I was taking a different way to work this morning and saw your light.'

'Would you like some coffee?'

'Yes, that would be great. Extra cream, no sugar,' Paxton said.

Willa flipped through Rachel's coffee notebook on the bar and said, 'According to my barista, Rachel, your coffee order means you want comfort but you're afraid to ask for it.'

Paxton laughed. 'That is uncomfortably accurate.' There was a short silence before she said, 'Actually, I stopped by to thank you.'

'For what?' Willa asked as she poured the coffee into two cups.

'For going to Sebastian yesterday, telling him to come and see me.'

Willa picked up the two coffee cups and walked to a café table. 'So things worked out?'

They pulled out chairs and sat. 'I stayed at his place last night.'

That made Willa grin ear to ear. '*That's* why you were taking a different way to work this morning.'

Paxton hid her smile behind her cup of coffee. 'Guilty. I take it Colin stayed with you?'

'I left him asleep. I didn't have the heart to wake him up.' Willa leaned back in her seat. 'So what's on your agenda today?'

'I'll be at the Madam all day. Last-minute details for the gala. Plus, I have to write my speech.' Paxton gave her a worried look. 'You're still coming, aren't you?'

'Yes. I'm going to wear that vintage beaded dress your grandmother gave Georgie.'

Paxton gasped. 'Oh, Willa, that's *perfect.*'

The bell over the door rang and they both turned in their seats.

Woody Olsen had just entered.

As always, it took Willa a moment to recover when she saw him, to see past all the potential bad news he could bring.

Paxton said, 'Good morning, Detective Olsen.'

Willa finally found her voice.

'Woody, what are you doing here?'

'I'm on my way to work. I saw your light and wanted to put your mind at ease. We can't determine the cause of death of that skeleton found at the Madam. There was trauma to the skull, but it also appeared that he'd suffered a fall. I don't think we'll ever know what happened.'

Willa stood and walked over to Woody. 'I've been thinking about when you were in here last. You asked me if I recognised anything in that suitcase buried with the skeleton. You were talking about the photo in the scrapbook, weren't you? The photo of Tucker Devlin that looks so much like my dad.'

Except for his eyes darting once to Paxton, who was still at the table, Woody gave nothing away in his expression. 'I was the only one who made the connection. And I didn't say a thing.'

'Thanks, Woody.'

He nodded. 'Your dad was wonderful. Best teacher I ever had.'

The bell over the door rang again. Woody automatically stepped out of the way to let whoever it was enter. But no one was there.

'Don't pay any attention to that,' Willa said. 'It's been doing it a lot. I think it's broken.'

'You know that old superstition, don't you, the one that says when you hear a bell ring, good fortune is pouring down? It means you should cup your hands out and catch it.'

Willa automatically held her hands out. 'Like this?'

'Exactly,' he said as he turned to leave.

Willa smiled and walked back to Paxton. 'I think what he was really trying to tell me was that my grandmother was in the clear. So now we know Agatha won't be dragged into this, either.'

'But I don't get it,' Paxton said. 'If Tucker Devlin died from a fall, why did Nana Osgood say she killed him?'

Willa wrapped her hands around her coffee cup. 'I have a feeling our grandmothers never wanted anyone to know the whole story.'

'But what could be worse than what Nana Osgood told us?'

Willa raised her brows. 'Do you really want to know?'

'No,' Paxton said, shaking her head. 'It's time for things to be laid to rest.'

When Paxton drove to the Madam before the gala on Friday night, the sky was twilight blue. Spotlights were aimed at the old oak tree. As she approached, she could see the leaves shaking slightly in the tree, partly from the sprinkler system to keep it hydrated while it took root, but also from the dozens of birds that had flown here en masse and had taken up in the tree. They'd been the bane of Colin's existence all week.

She parked and walked up the front steps. The restoration was complete, and it was beautiful. This house stood as a testimony to life, to friendship, to good things coming out of bad situations.

Once Paxton was inside, she did a walk-through. The lighting cast a warm yellow glow off the dark panelling. The banquet hall was decorated with streamers and floral arrangements on every table. Every place setting had a small book documenting the charities the club had supported over the years. At the dais in front of the room was a podium and a large screen, on which flashed photographs of club members throughout the years.

Later, when she was in the kitchen checking to see if everything was on schedule, she heard voices in the lobby. The first guests were arriving. Soon there were people mingling everywhere. Waiters were carrying trays of champagne and hors d'oeuvres. Paxton greeted everyone, including her mother and father.

Her father was impressed, but her mother admitted nothing. She still wasn't happy about Paxton moving out and was even less happy when Paxton started referring to Sebastian as her boyfriend. But Paxton loved her mother and accepted her as she was.

Nana Osgood had arrived with the nurse Paxton had hired to attend to her that night. Paxton wondered what Nana Osgood thought about being here, after all these years.

A few minor emergencies took Paxton away until the food was ready to be served. She was about to tell Maria to cue everyone to be seated when she stopped and looked around.

It was a dreamlike setting of princess gowns and black ties. It was magical. But she was ready for it to be over, because the gala had been planned around everything that the Women's Society Club shouldn't be. And she'd fallen right into the trap.

With some relief, she saw that Willa and Colin had finally arrived. Willa looked beautiful in that vintage dress. Colin stood close to her. Paxton recognised the subtle shift that was happening in him. He seemed centred, almost calm. He'd even asked her if there were any town houses near hers up for sale. He'd like to have a home base for when he came back for visits.

It made her heart soar. Sebastian, Willa, now Colin. Sebastian had been right. If you make room in your life, good things will enter.

Paxton caught the manager's eye and nodded, and the signal was given that everyone should now enter the banquet hall. She went to the ladies' room and checked her make-up, then stared at herself, telling herself that she really could go through with this.

Sebastian had waited for her at the back of the banquet hall once everyone had been seated. She hadn't seen him in two days. They'd called each other, but it wasn't the same. She wanted to touch him, to have him near. But gala preparations had kept her at the Madam until the early hours of the morning for the past few days. Last night she'd even slept here.

'You look lovely, darling,' Sebastian said when she entered.

'I'm so glad you're here.' She took his hands and squeezed them. He had to feel that she was trembling.

'Everything is perfect. You even managed to get your grandmother to come.' He leaned in and added, 'I've missed you.'

She let that wash over her. 'I've missed you, too.'

'I know you haven't had time to order furniture for your house,' he said. 'So I had a bed delivered there today.'

That made her laugh. 'Then I can't wait to go home,' she said.

'I can't wait to take you there. I have good memories already.' He led her to the dais and whispered, 'Good luck. You'll do great.' There was applause as she walked to the podium, then Paxton watched as Sebastian took a seat with Willa, Colin, and Nana Osgood.

Her insides were shaking, and she thought for a moment that she couldn't go through with this. But then she thought of her grandmother and Georgie, how everything about this house and the club had to do with honouring them, and she knew it was the right decision. She cleared her throat and said, 'Welcome, everyone, to the Walls of Water Women's Society Club seventy-fifth anniversary gala.'

More applause.

'I wrote a speech months ago. Those who know me aren't surprised. I'm such a planner.' Some people laughed. 'The speech was about what good work we've done and how proud we should be of ourselves.' She paused. 'But I tore it up this week, because I realised we've got it all wrong.'

There was a change in the air.

'This club was formed to help each other. It wasn't formed to set us apart from others or to compete with one another. It was formed because seventy-five years ago, two best friends in the darkest moments of their lives said, "If we don't help each other, who will?" I don't know when it happened, but the Women's Society Club lost its focus. It's not what it was, and I can't bring it back. That's why I'm stepping down as president and removing my name from the roster.' The room started to rumble. 'I have not always been the best friend to any of you,' she continued. 'But I promise, from this night forward, I will be there for you if you need me, anytime, anyplace. That's the true nature of the club. It was never meant to be an institution. It was a pinky promise among teenagers who were afraid, and knowing that they could count on each other made them feel better. Our grandmothers knew they would be friends their entire lives. How many of us can say that? How can we know the true meaning of charity if we don't even know how to help those closest to us?' Paxton stepped back. 'That's all I wanted to say.'

She rubbed her forehead, squinting against the spotlight. The room was silent. Suddenly everyone turned towards a small sound coming from a table in front.

Agatha was chuckling, the sound rusty, like a piece of machinery that hadn't been used in years. 'That's my girl,' she said.

There wasn't much celebrating to be done after that. Dinner was served, then awards were given out, but the ceremony had a hurried and awkward feel to it and most were eager to leave. Paxton didn't care. It was the right thing to do and she felt much better now.

Most people avoided Paxton as they left. She was sure everyone wanted to talk to each other about it first, to come to some consensus about how they all felt about it. Those who decided to stick with her would be her true friends. The others would just be scenery.

At the end of the evening, Paxton and Willa walked Agatha out to the nurse's car.

'I'm proud of you, Paxton,' Agatha said as Willa and Paxton helped her down the front steps. 'What you did tonight took guts.'

'Thank you, Nana. Mama may never speak to me again.'

'Her loss.' Before Agatha got in the nurse's car, she said, 'You and Willa,

I think you might have finally made him go away. Real friendship was the only thing he was afraid of.'

'Him?' Willa asked.

'Tucker. He's been around these past few weeks. Haven't you noticed? I've felt him. There's been a strange sweet scent in the air. And the birds have been acting strangely.'

Willa and Paxton moved in closer to each other as Agatha got in the car, and the nurse reached over and buckled her seat belt. 'What really happened here, Nana? Did you really . . .'

'Yes, I did,' Agatha said. 'Don't forget.'

Paxton and Willa watched the car drive off. As they turned to walk back up the steps, the scent of peaches permeated the air for a moment, thick and cloying, before it faded into the night, then disappeared. The oak tree began to shake as dozens of birds took flight, their dark wings showing flashes of yellow like fireworks.

'Coincidence?' Willa asked, wrapping her arm in Paxton's.

'There's no such thing,' Paxton answered, holding on tight as they watched the birds fly away.

CHAPTER FOURTEEN

THE PEACH KEEPERS
1936

THE FIRST TIME IT HAPPENED, Georgie woke up, suddenly freezing. She didn't know why. It was so hot that summer she had to sleep on top of her bedsheets. But that night she woke up shivering. The world was changing, she thought. It had been changing for months. Now that Tucker, with his charming smile and magical ways, had moved into the Madam with them, Georgie felt the changes even more. There was hope in the air, hope that their financial problems would soon be over with this peach orchard they were planning. And her father, who ignored her on good days, and who blamed her for her mother's death in childbirth on bad ones, even seemed happy to see her at dinner now. He was happy to see her because Tucker was happy to see her. Tucker changed people that way. And because of that she ignored the way Tucker would brush up against her in the corridors, how he was always around when she got out of the bath. Agatha had told her she was being silly, anyway, and that she had no idea how lucky she was. Tucker had changed Agatha, too. She'd once been able to tell Agatha anything; now Agatha burned with something hot every time she saw Georgie, and Georgie didn't know why. Georgie had felt very alone lately, up here on Jackson Hill. Her friends had stopped coming to see her. And at parties, they ignored her. So Georgie spent most of her time in her room now, dreaming of the day when all these changes would be over and they could go back to being normal again.

There was the smell of smoke and peaches around her that night as she sat up, shivering in her bed. She was used to that, the peach smell, anyway. Tucker carried it on his skin. That's why he said birds bothered him, because they liked the way he smelled. But she always thought the birds swooping down on him seemed angry, not enamoured.

She looked around her dark room, and that's when she saw a small orange light by the door. The lit end of a cigarette. *Someone was standing by her closed door.* Her heart leaped in her chest.

Tucker walked out of the shadow. He put the cigarette to his lips and took a puff brightening his face and making it glow. He dropped the cigarette to the floor and stepped on it, and everything was dark again.

When he came to her, she didn't understand what was happening. When he finally left, she stayed in her bed the rest of the night, too afraid to get up. She heard him come back down from his attic bedroom in the morning, pause by her door, then walk away. When the house was quiet, she finally got up and washed, but then she propped a chair against the doorknob and wouldn't let anyone in until her father demanded she join them for dinner. A week, two weeks, passed, and Tucker made no move towards her again, and she thought that was it. She had actually begun to recover.

But then he came back.

It went on all summer. No matter how many times she reached out for help, no one listened to her. He made them not listen. She couldn't see an end to it. It was going to go on like this for ever unless she stopped it. But she wasn't that brave. She'd never been that brave.

Until the day she finally accepted that she was pregnant.

That day, she took the cook's frying pan to her room with her. And when night fell, she stood behind her door and waited.

After she hit him, an odd thud that sounded like something being dropped in the next room, she stood there, as if waiting for everything to go back to the way it was. She began to tremble. Nothing was different. She was still pregnant. And she had just hurt Tucker, maybe even killed him. No one would understand. Except . . .

'Show him to me,' Agatha said after Georgie had run to her house, tripping and falling along the way so that when she got to Hickory Cottage, she was covered in dirt and scratches. She'd sneaked past Agatha's parents' room, woken Agatha up, and begged her to help. She trusted Agatha more than anyone. And what had happened this summer couldn't have erased a lifetime of friendship. It didn't just go away like that. At least, she prayed it didn't.

Agatha was strangely quiet as Georgie led her back up to the Madam. Tucker was right where she had left him. The frying pan was sitting on his chest, like a weight keeping him from floating away. Agatha knelt by him, put one of her hands on his head, then jerked back as if she'd been burned. She stood and said, 'We have to do this quick. He's not all gone. We have to dig a hole close by. We can't carry him far. Hurry, Georgie, let's get started.'

They dug in the yard for hours. She would never forget how quiet it was. It felt like they were the only people in the world, two young women about to bury the symbol of their helplessness.

The half-moon had fled halfway across the night sky by the time Agatha said the hole was big enough.

They went back into the Madam. They dragged him to the window in Georgie's room and pushed him out. Then they took him by his arms and legs and dragged him across the back yard, leaving a trail of black like lightning had scorched the earth. After they were done, they stood there as the sun rose. They were dirty and shaky and mostly numb.

Agatha turned to Georgie and embraced her. Agatha was crying.

'Oh, Agatha,' Georgie said. 'I'm so sorry.'

'No!' Agatha said. 'You have nothing to be sorry about. This is my fault. What kind of friend lets this happen? I'm so very sorry.'

'What am I going to do?' Georgie asked. 'Tell me what to do.'

'We'll get through this. Don't worry. No matter what happens, I'm here for you. I'll never let you down again.'

'What if they find out it was me?'

Agatha took her hand. 'As long as I'm alive, Georgie, no one will ever know it was you. I promise.'

And seventy-five years later, Agatha had kept that promise.

Willa and Paxton walked up the steps to the portico. What a strange and lovely evening this had turned out to be. Imagine, Willa thought, a few weeks ago she'd had no intention of attending this gala. She'd also had no intention of falling in love, or finding a new best friend, or unearthing a lot of crazy family secrets.

Colin and Sebastian were waiting for them. Willa went to Colin, and he wrapped her in his arms and held her against his chest. Paxton stopped in front of Sebastian. He put a hand round her waist, pulled her to him and kissed her.

The four of them went back to the banquet hall and took a seat at a table. They stayed all night, talking and laughing.

This was the first time Willa had seen Paxton and Sebastian act like a couple, confidently and unabashedly. They made so much sense together. Every look, every touch, was a reassurance, almost electric, like they were shocking each other with every contact.

As for her and Colin, they were acting like they were having fun, but they were far more serious than either one was prepared to admit. They talked about what they wanted to do. Was Colin really ready to move back? Was Willa ready to leave? They decided that Willa would come with Colin to New York for a few weeks; then he would come back with her to Walls of Water for another few weeks, and then stretch it out longer and longer until they both knew what was right. They wanted to be where the other was, and it didn't matter where.

When daylight came, Paxton and Willa were still awake, but Colin and Sebastian had their heads on their table.

Paxton stood up. 'I'm going to see about getting some breakfast brought out. I'm hungry. Are you?'

'Starving. Should I wake them?' Willa asked.

'Not yet.' Paxton turned, then stopped. 'Willa, I'm glad you came tonight. I'm glad all this happened. I'm glad I have you.'

'I maced people for you,' Willa said. 'You've got me for life.'

When Paxton left, Willa sighed and closed her eyes. She hadn't felt this content in a long time.

If the future was hers to take, then she tried to imagine what it was going to be like.

She imagined that, from that day on, whenever she and Paxton would meet unexpectedly on the sidewalk, or in a store, they would laugh, like sharing a secret only they knew. Grandmother Georgie would still be here, because it was impossible to think of a future without her. Willa knew that one day she would be gone, but for now, in this future she was creating, Georgie was hanging on. Agatha would continue to look after her, and they would all make sure Agatha had all the chocolates she wanted. Willa and Colin would divide their time between New York and Walls of Water for a few years, leaving Rachel to manage the store and further her coffee studies. Rachel would probably publish a book about it one day. Willa and Colin would come home for good when Willa got pregnant. *Pregnant.* It was a far-off thought, but it still gave her a crazy feeling in her stomach, like planning the biggest and best adventure. Sebastian and Paxton, on the other hand, would probably get married right away and have three children in quick succession. Throughout marriages and children, Willa and Paxton would still call each other almost every night, sometimes just to say good night. Sometimes Willa would know it was Paxton without her ever having to say a word. She would be in bed, Colin asleep beside her, and the phone would ring, and she would pick it up and say, 'Good night, Paxton. I'm here if you need me.'

That, they knew, was true friendship. And they knew, if you're lucky enough to find it, you hold on to it.

Hold on and never let it go.

Willa opened her eyes and saw that Colin had woken up. His hair was tousled and his eyes were still droopy with sleep. He smiled at her, rubbing his hands along her legs, and said, 'I just had the best dream.'

She smiled back and said, 'Me too.'

Sarah Addison Allen

Forty Things about Sarah

I once spent an entire afternoon out shopping with an English accent, trying to convince people I was from England.

I have a recurring dream that I left something in my childhood home. I sneak back to get it, terrified the new owners will catch me.

I hate when people don't smile back.

I always think sweet potato casserole is going to taste better than it actually does.

I have to stop and think before I can tell left from right.

Favourite flower—gladiolus.

I wrote my first novel when I was sixteen, just to prove I could. It's so horrible it will never see the light of day.

I'm a classic emotional overeater.

I always think food is going to make everything better. It never does.

I love the colour orange but, for some reason, when asked, I always say my favourite colour is green.

Every time it snows, I still feel a tight happiness in my stomach and think, 'No school today!'

I met my best friend when we were both eight years old.

I once worked for an antique appraiser. Spent a lot of time in old homes. Probably why old homes are so prominent in my books.

I get bored brushing my teeth. I walk around brushing, watch TV, check email, anything but stand in front of the sink.

I frequently forget what day it is.

I eat the pie filling but not the crust.

It took twelve years of writing as close to full time as I could manage to finally make a living from it.

And every day for twelve years my dad asked me when I was going to get a real job.

I'm easily overwhelmed by email. Actually, I'm easily overwhelmed by just about everything.

I've always thought my sister Sydney got the better name.

I don't drink coffee but, mysteriously, I have dozens of latte bowls.

I never set my alarm clock to a regular :00 or :30. It's always some odd hour/minute combo like 6:16 or 7:37.

My signature perfume is Giardini di Montecatini VI, which hasn't been produced in years, so I hoard it when I find it on eBay.

I have accidentally maced myself.

My house is named Charlotte's Rose.

The Vicar of Dibley is my DVD equivalent of comfort food.

I was half asleep and fifteen, but I'm pretty sure I've seen a ghost.

I have telephonia: The uncontrollable fear that I'm calling people at a bad time.

For some odd reason, all my scars are on the left side of my body.

I am an excellent daydreamer.

I've always wanted to put a pink streak in my hair.

This isn't very Southern of me, but I hate when people just drop by.

I am, essentially, a big ol' introvert.

I can twist my tongue into the shape of a three-leaf clover. Isn't your life somehow richer for knowing this about me?

I love to pack. I hate to travel.

I feel contractually obligated to eat the whole cupcake, when all I really like is the frosting.

My childhood imaginary friends were named Tonka and Tinka, twin girls with dark bowl cuts. Tinka was nice. Tonka broke my crayons.

I am crazy superstitious.

I changed my name to Rose when I was a little girl.

When people ask me what I would do if I wasn't a writer, I have no answer.

Taken from 'Miscellaneous Things about Sarah' at
www.sarahaddisonallen.com

601-063 UP0000-1